# THE COLLECTED STORIES OF SAADAT HASAN MANTO

# THE COLLECTED STORIES OF SAADAT HASAN MANTO

Volume I
Bombay and Poona

Translated by NASREEN REHMAN

ALEPH

ALEPH BOOK COMPANY
An independent publishing firm
promoted by *Rupa Publications India*

First published in India in 2022
by Aleph Book Company
7/16 Ansari Road, Daryaganj
New Delhi 110 002

This edition copyright © Aleph Book Company 2022

English translation copyright © Nasreen Rehman 2022

All stories first published between 1 January 1955 and
31 December 2005 copyright © The Estate of Saadat
Hasan Manto

Cover photo © The Manto Family Archive

All rights reserved.

This is a work of fiction. Names, characters,
places, and incidents are either the product of the
author's imagination or are used fictitiously and any
resemblance to any actual persons, living or dead,
events or locales is entirely coincidental.

No part of this publication may be reproduced,
transmitted, or stored in a retrieval system, in any
form or by any means, without permission in writing
from Aleph Book Company.

ISBN: 978-93-90652-77-8

1 3 5 7 9 10 8 6 4 2

Printed at Thomson Press India Ltd., Faridabad

This book is sold subject to the condition that it
shall not, by way of trade or otherwise, be lent,
resold, hired out, or otherwise circulated without the
publisher's prior consent in any form of binding or
cover other than that in which it is published.

*In memory of Asma*
*for our children*
*Munizae, Mariam, Sulema, Nasheed, Jillani*
*and grandchildren*
*Natasha, Leah Tara, Lulu, Isaac, and Zaviyar*

# Contents

| | |
|---|---:|
| *Translator's Note* | ix |
| *Introduction* | 1 |
| 1. Women | 57 |
| 2. Suited Booted | 62 |
| 3. Miss Mala | 68 |
| 4. The Actress's Eye | 73 |
| 5. My Name Is Radha | 79 |
| 6. Scissors from Meerut | 93 |
| 7. Cause for Concern | 102 |
| 8. Uncouth | 111 |
| 9. The Psychoanalyst | 119 |
| 10. Empty Bottles and Empty Boxes | 123 |
| 11. Sahai | 130 |
| 12. Toto | 136 |
| 13. Ram Khelawan | 142 |
| 14. Shanti | 149 |
| 15. Babu Gopinath | 157 |
| 16. Dr Sherodkar | 171 |
| 17. Burmese Girl | 175 |
| 18. Fobha Bai | 184 |
| 19. Old Fogey | 192 |
| 20. Miss Tinwallah | 197 |
| 21. Peeran | 204 |
| 22. Janki | 210 |
| 23. Mrs D'Silva | 226 |
| 24. Sickness | 233 |
| 25. Nawab Salimullah Khan | 237 |
| 26. Miss Faria | 243 |

| | |
|---|---|
| 27. Loser | 253 |
| 28. The Urinal | 257 |
| 29. Siraj | 259 |
| 30. Majeed's Past | 268 |
| 31. Mrs D'Costa | 274 |
| 32. Khushya | 281 |
| 33. Ten Rupees | 287 |
| 34. Mammad Bhai | 298 |
| 35. Sharda | 310 |
| 36. Scent | 328 |
| 37. Green Sandals | 333 |
| 38. The Photograph | 337 |
| 39. Thief | 341 |
| 40. Marriage | 347 |
| 41. In Memoriam | 357 |
| 42. Constipation | 361 |
| 43. Latika Rani | 369 |
| 44. Hamid's Baby | 378 |
| 45. Blouse | 387 |
| 46. Mantra | 395 |
| 47. Outcry | 402 |
| 48. Taqi the Calligrapher | 410 |
| 49. Humiliation | 420 |
| 50. Mozelle | 437 |
| 51. Barren | 455 |
| 52. My Sahib | 469 |
| 53. Mummy | 484 |
| 54. Mahmooda | 517 |
| 55. My Marriage | 524 |
| 56. Recite the Creed | 537 |
| *Acknowledgements* | 545 |

## Translator's Note

This is the first of three volumes of my translations of Manto's short stories. Each volume contains stories selected for their geographical location; the idea was to distil the aura that Manto creates of a time, a place, and a moment. This compendium has fifty-four stories and two essays, 'My Marriage' and 'My Sahib', in which the action takes place in Bombay and Poona in colonial India. Manto wrote several Bombay stories after 1948, across the border in Lahore, Pakistan, which read like dystopian love letters to the city he claimed to embody, describing himself as, 'Bombay in motion'. Volume Two contains stories set in other parts of India before 1947, including some rather well-known stories of Partition in Punjab, such as 'Cold Flesh' (Thanda Gosht), the first story Manto wrote in Pakistan, although the narrative unfolds in India. Volume Three has all the stories set in Pakistan, but it opens with 'The Drawstring' (Khol Do), which begins in India and ends in Pakistan.

I am aware of the several English translations of Manto's stories and essays. These are significant contributions to the world of letters; without them, Manto would have remained inaccessible to anyone unable to understand Urdu or read the Urdu or Devanagri scripts.[1] Those irked by yet another English translation of Manto's stories should blame David Davidar, who suggested that I undertake this venture.

The project has its roots in my doctoral dissertation, *A History of the Cinema in Lahore, c. 1919-1947*.[2] I had turned to Manto for two reasons. First, quite simply the discovery that he had written the

---

[1] Hamid Jalal (trans.), *Black Milk: A Collection of Short Stories*, Lahore: Sang-e-Meel Publications, 1997; Aakar Patel (ed. and trans.), *Why I Write: Essays by Saadat Hasan Manto*, New Delhi and Bangalore: Tranquebar Press, 2014; Khalid Hasan (ed. and trans.), *Bitter Fruit*, New Delhi: Penguin Books, 2009; Saadat Hasan Manto, *Stars from Another Sky: The Bombay Film World from the 1940s*, New Delhi: Penguin Books, 2010; Muhammad Umar Memon, *My Name Is Radha: The Essential Manto*, New Delhi: Penguin Books, 2015; Matt Raeek and Aftab Alam (trans.), *Bombay Stories*, London: Vintage Books, 2014; Aatish Taseer, *Manto: Selected Stories*, New Delhi: Random House, 2003.
[2] Nasreen Rehman, 'A History of the Cinema in Lahore, c. 1919–1947', PhD dissertation, University of Cambridge, 2015.

screenplay for a Lahori film called *Jhumke*.³ Secondly, using ephemera, including film magazines and newspapers, I was able to reconstruct fragments of the lives of film stars, directors, and producers, people at the top of the film universe. Yet, I found nothing on the financially precarious and ropy everyday lives of men and women who worked lower down in a very hierarchal industry brimming with opportunities for social and economic advancement.

One evening, my wracked brain turned to 'Babu Gopinath', and I revisited the story. As I leafed through my Manto volumes, I encountered men and women extras, gaffers, spot boys, technicians, munshis (dialogue writers), lyricists, composers, choreographers, assistants, and assistants to assistants. In stories such as 'Mummy' and 'Janki', I found accounts of Poona studios.

Khalid Hasan had translated a selection of Manto's essays on film personalities, and I brought these to the attention of my supervisor Professor Sir C. A. Bayly.⁴ Furthermore, I selected fifteen stories and translated them for Chris, as he liked to be addressed by everyone, including his students. Chris Bayly was the pre-eminent historian of modern India. An architect of world history, he was among the pioneers writing intellectual history that included non-European and Indian perspectives.⁵ Chris and I had several conversations about Manto's engagement with history and his insistence on inserting himself into his fiction as a subject.⁶

A generous teacher with a singular ability to immerse himself in a student's work, Chris read the stories and, encouraged by him, I used Manto as an ethnographer in my thesis. I was surprised to find

---

³*Jhumke* (directed by J. K. Nanda, 1946). Although the film is lost, a booklet with details of the cast and synopses of the story survives. It was remade in Pakistan as *Badnaam* (directed by Iqbal Shahzad, 1966).
⁴Khalid Hasan, *Stars from Another Sky*, New Delhi: Penguin Books, 2010.
⁵C. A. Bayly, *Rulers, Townsmen and Bazaars: North Indian Society in the Age of British Expansion, 1770–1870*, Cambridge: Cambridge University Press, 1983; *Empire and Information: Intelligence Gathering & Social communication in India 1780-1870*; Cambridge: Cambridge University Press, 1996; *The Birth of the Modern World, 1780-1914, Global Connections and Comparisons*, New Jersey: Wiley, Blackwell, 2003; & *Recovering Liberties: Indian Thought in the Age of Liberalism and Empire*, Cambridge: Cambridge University Press, 2011.
⁶Included here are two obituaries of Chris Bayly by his colleagues. Faisal Devji, 'C. A. Bayly', *Past & Present*, Volume 237, Issue 1, November 2017, pp. 3–12; Richard Drayton, 'Sir Christopher Bayly obituary', *The Guardian*, 23 April 2015.

in Chris quite a movie buff, exceptionally well-read on the cinema. He agreed that he had not come across a magazine, or a journal, a narrative, or a film history that captured the everyday life and enduring allure of the cinema the way Manto does in his short stories and essays. The only remotely comparable example that comes to mind is Luigi Pirandello's novel, *Shoot*.[7]

Chris suggested that I write an introduction and get the fifteen stories published. I tried to convince David Davidar to publish my translations of Manto's fifteen cinema stories. Instead, he asked me if I would care to translate all of Manto's short stories. I agreed because Manto remains among my favourite short story writers and essayists. But the undertaking remains a daunting task; more so because, sadly, Chris passed away on 18 April 2015, a week before my PhD viva, as did my friend Asma Jahangir on 11 February 2018, for whom the dedication of this volume was meant as a surprise. My dissertation, dedicated to Chris Bayly, will be published at the end of 2022.

Before embarking on this project, I read and re-read Manto, including his translations of European literature from English into Urdu. His lexicon is everyday Urdu, and his style has the spontaneity of informal conversation, amplified by his regular appearance in his narratives. In translating, I have eschewed the literal and tried to internalize Manto's voice and imagine how he might have spoken and written in English. Occasionally, Manto uses English words, which I have retained. They are italicized in the text. There remains the exasperating issue of transliteration. The only way to reflect the long vowels (aa, ee, oo) and the palatal, dental, fricative, and guttural sounds is by using diacritics, which can be tedious. Besides notwithstanding the use of dots below, and accents above letters, the words, invariably, are mispronounced by non-Urdu speakers. I decided to eschew diacritics. I have doubled 'a' and 'e' for certain words where I thought it necessary—but not for all. For example, I have not doubled the 'a' in 'insaniyat', but have doubled the 'e' and

---

[7] Luigi Pirandello, *Shoot!: The Notebooks of Serrafino Gubio, Cinematograph Operator*, trans. C. K. Scott Moncrieff, with an introduction by Tom Gunning, Chicago: University of Chicago Press, 2005. First published in 1915, the novel is based on the absurdist journals of camera operator Serrafino Gubbio.

in 'Shaheed', which can be confused with the name 'Shahid' also spelt 'Shahed'.

Manto's world, including his humour and warmth, is dark and suffocating. The resonance with present times is terrifying. I have to keep coming up for air. His belief in a humanist imperative—insaniyat—has kept me going.

Nasreen Rehman<br>
October 2021<br>
London

## Introduction

On an unrecorded date in 1937, Sardar Begum bid farewell to Amritsar, a charming old town in the heartland of Punjab and boarded a train down to Bombay, the burgeoning new metropolis by the Arabian Sea. A widow of Afghan extraction, she was on her way to move in with her daughter, Nasira Iqbal, whom she had married off two years earlier to M. U. Khan, an officer in the railways. The widow had reason to mistrust her son-in-law, to whom she had ill-advisedly entrusted her meagre savings. Moreover, Khan's notoriety as a serial philanderer exacerbated Sardar Begum's aversion. Yet, she had little choice but to join his household.

Sardar Begum's late husband, Maulana Ghulam Hasan, who died on 25 February 1932, had retired as a munsif or a sub-judge with the colonial government and should have left her in considerable comfort, but she was his second wife. By the time the Maulana married Sardar, he had fathered nine children, of whom eight had survived and attained maturity.[1] Sardar Begum was not accorded the same status as Ghulam Hasan's first wife. Significantly, she was not of Kashmiri stock.

Ghulam Hasan (1855–1932) belonged to a clan of Kashmiri Saraswat Brahmans who had converted to Islam. The family name, Manto, derived from the word 'mant', referred to a weight measure the equivalent of which the clan elders were entitled to collect as rent from peasants.[2] In the nineteenth century, the Mantos gave up their thriving trade of pashmina shawls and turned to the legal profession. They moved down to Amritsar, where they took up residence in

---

[1] Sardar Begum's stepchildren: Amir Begum, Badshah Begum, Muhammad Hassan, Saeed Hassan, Saleem Hassan, Mehtab Begum, Saeeda Begum, and Shah Begum.
[2] Saadat Hasan Manto, 'Pandit Manto's First Letter to Pandit Nehru' (Pandit Nehru ke naam Pandit Manto ka pehla khat), *Manto Baqiyat*, Lahore: Sang-e-Meel Publications, 2004, pp. 411–99.

Kucha-i-Vakilan (Lawyers' Lane) in Katra Jaimal Singh.[3]

Sardar bore four children, of whom two survived—Nasira Iqbal, also known as Balaji, and her son, Saadat, who addressed her as Bibijan in the Afghan fashion. After Maulvi Sahib's death, Sardar Begum and her offspring continued to live in the family home. They survived on a monthly allowance of forty rupees, paid by Sardar's two stepsons, successful barristers who treated her and her children not as equals in a family but rather like poor relations. The indifference of other family members served to cement a bond between Sardar, Balaji, and Saadat. Until death parted them, the three remained unwavering in their commitment to each other.

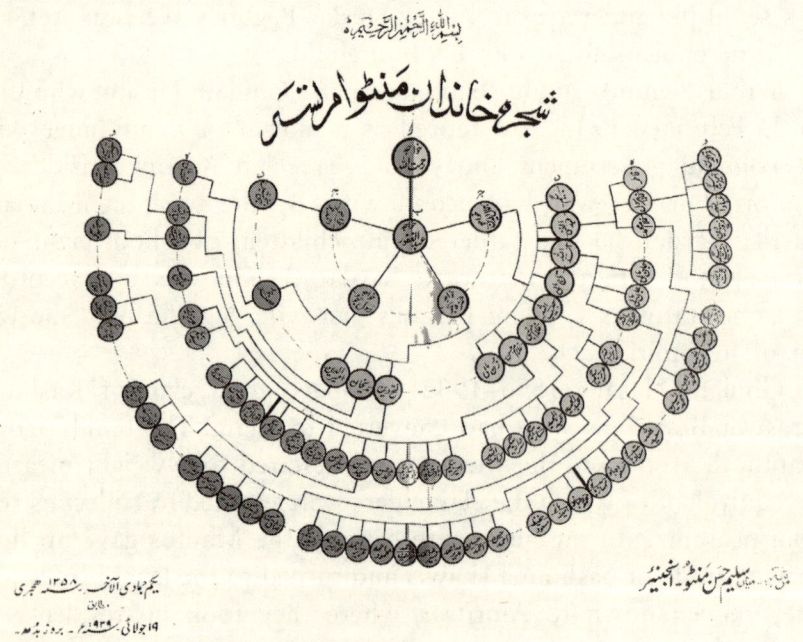

The Manto Family Tree (Source: Manto Family Archive).

---

[3] Ayesha Jalal, *Pity of Partition: Manto's Life, Times, and Work across the India Pakistan Divide* (Lawrence Stone Lectures), Princeton, N. J.: Princeton University Press, 2013, pp. 27, 29. The historian Ayesha Jalal is Manto's great niece. Her father, Hamid Jalal was Manto's half-sister's son, and her mother, Zakia, is Safia Manto's sister. Jalal's late brother, Shahid Jalal was married to Nusrat, Manto's youngest daughter. Jalal had special access to family accounts, and the Manto papers.

Saadat did not conceal his disapproval of his brother-in-law's shenanigans and consequently his entry to his sister's flat was barred, notwithstanding that Bibijan lived there. There is no record of M. U. Khan's version of events; Manto's take on the matter is there for posterity in his essay, 'My Marriage', included in this volume.

In part, Sardar Begum's relocation to Bombay was precipitated by Saadat's move to the city, a year earlier, to take up the role of editor of *Mussavir* (The Illustrator), an Urdu weekly film magazine. By the time Bibijan arrived in Bombay, Saadat had to his credit the screenplay and dialogue of *Kisan Kanya* (Village Girl, dir. D. N. Madhok, 1937), the first technicolour film released in India. Notably, in 1936, he had published to critical attention *Atish Pare* (Ring of Fire), his first collection of short stories.

From time to time, Saadat gave Bibijan whatever he could afford from his irregular income. Unlike other men of his family, he did not enter a stable bourgeois profession such as engineering or the law. Instead, he deployed his forensic insights to write short stories, essays, radio plays, screenplays, film dialogue, editorials, op-eds, and essays.

The concept of royalties was non-existent in the publishing and film industries in colonial India. Thus, Saadat was paid a meagre seven to twelve rupees for a short story and a paltry forty for his exertions as editor of *Mussavir*. The colonial government kept a sharp eye on the content of films but its concerns centred mainly on sedition, obscenity, and blasphemy. It looked away as publishers and particularly errant film producers habitually reneged on contracts. Technicians, scenarists, bit part players were often paid less than the agreed sum, and rarely on the due date.

Unlike film stars, the cohort of film professionals on the middle and lower rungs of the film industry could not afford legal action to enforce their contracts. Besides, their substantially lower earnings supported their families and, in some instances, subsidized their literary careers.[4] Saadat joined the ranks of these exploited men and women, some of considerable talent.

With Saadat's entry barred from Balaji's flat, mother and son communicated by post. Bibijan comes across as a genial woman

---

[4]Shaukat Kaifi, *Kaifi and I*, trans. Nasreen Rehman, New Delhi: Zubaan Books, 2010.

with considerable social skills, and one who, like many in her time, loved the movies. As editor of *Mussavir*, and working with the top studio in Bombay, Saadat kept her supplied with complimentary film passes. In an undated letter, Saadat enclosed, as per Bibijan's instructions, 'a pass for *Savitri*' (dir. Franz Osten, 1937), a Bombay Talkies production. He advised her 'to use the pass the following day and informed her that *Kisan Kanya* will be released at Diwali, which is about twenty-five days away.'[5]

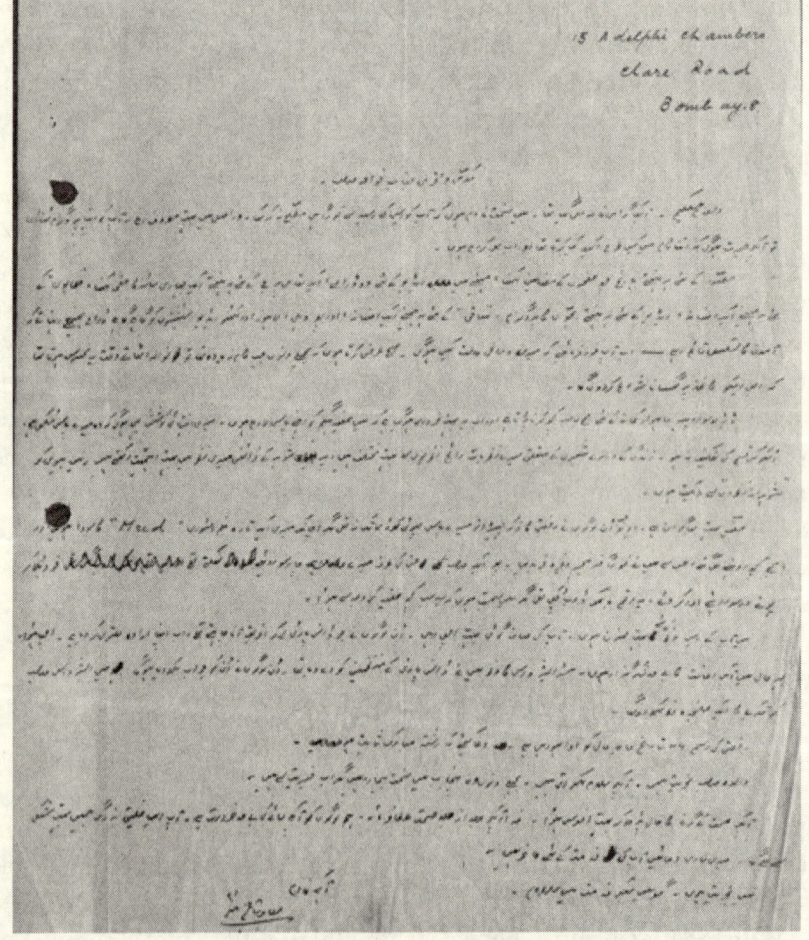

Saadat's letter to Bibijan (Source: Manto Family Archive).

---

[5]Saadat's letter to Bibijan.

In the essay on his marriage, Saadat recounts Bibijan's concern and curiosity about his lifestyle. He describes how on a visit to his lodgings one afternoon, Bibijan wept and lamented her son's fall from his nest of childhood privilege into a fleapit 'where bedbugs rained from the ceiling, and large mice ran across the floor, undeterred by human presence'. She berated Saadat for not completing his higher education.

Saadat did not launch into a tale of woe about the cunning Nazir Ludhianvi, proprietor of *Mussavir*, or of unscrupulous film producers. Instead, he declared with characteristic nonchalance, 'I make enough to look after myself. In a city like Bombay, higher education is not a must to earn good money. Besides, I live by myself; I can make a lot more should the need arise.' Indeed, he earned enough to live in comfort, but several Bombay film producers collectively owed Saadat substantial sums of money—typically, as they did so many others. Significantly for Saadat, his declaration propelled his mother on a course to arrange his marriage.

Bibijan adored Saadat and was his only consistent and unwavering ally. She did not understand Saadat's way of life but was a keen interlocutor. In a letter full of praise for his essay calling for Hindu–Muslim unity in the wake of communal riots, his mother cautions him on the wisdom of naming the ringleaders and thus making enemies.[6]

Saadat's emotional reliance on Bibijan was enormous. He has written that he fainted three times in his life: first, in 1939, when he slipped and sprained his ankle just before his marriage; again when he received news of Bibijan's sudden death in 1940; and yet again the following year when his beloved son, Arif, died in 1941.

SHADOW OF A PATRIARCH

Among the great short story writers of the world, Saadat Hasan Manto was born in Punjab in a village called Sambrala in district Ludhiana on 11 May 1912. His father, Maulana Ghulam Hasan, was a pillar of the Amritsar bourgeoisie and a prominent member of the Anjuman-i-Islamia, an influential Muslim civil society organization in

---

[6]Jalal, *Pity of Partition*, p. 57.

Punjab. According to Ayesha Jalal, in his leisure hours, the Maulana (her great grandfather) penned works on Islam and the real meaning of self-improvement (jihad).[7]

Paternal disapproval shadowed Saadat's life. I have not investigated Maulana Ghulam Hasan's professional decisions, but from his son's writings, he comes across as a harsh parent unable to confine his judgmental disposition to the courtroom. Manto grew up with what comes across in his writings as a profound lack of a father, which may well have fed and, in turn, possibly justified to him his addiction to alcohol.

Ghulam Hasan did not invest the same time, effort, or money to educate Saadat as he had expended on his older sons, whom he sent to England for further education. Nevertheless, he was not entirely disinterested in his youngest son. It might have been better for Saadat's emotional health had his father remained completely aloof and not forced the poor lad to study the sciences when he was naturally drawn to literature and the arts.

Saadat's grades at school were not merely poor; he failed his school Matriculation examination from the Muhammadan Anglo-Oriental (MAO) High School, for the third time in 1929.

In 1930, Saadat transferred to the Islamia High School, where the headmaster, Khwajah Muhammad Umar, who taught English, recognized the young man's proficiency in the subject. Khwajah Sahib took a keen interest in all his students, and under his guidance, the young Manto switched to the Arts. On 23 May 1931, he finally passed his Matriculation examination in the third division. The same year, Maulana Ghulam Hasan ensured Saadat's admission to the Hindu Sabha College in Amritsar, ostensibly to study English, Philosophy, and Economics for his FA from the Punjab University.[8] His dear childhood friend, Abu Saeed Qureishi, recalls how Saadat roamed around college sporting a red and white striped silk kurta with a short jacket. His ensemble duly finished off with a pyjama made of boski, a prized creamy Chinese silk stamped with a trademark of two red horses on both sides of the narrow outer edge of the fabric authenticate every yard.

---

[7] Ibid., p. 29.
[8] Ali Sana Bukhari, *Saadat Hasan Manto, Tehqiq*, Lahore: Manto Academy, 2006, p. 19.

> [Certificate image]
>
> سعادت حسن منٹو (تحقیق)
> ضمیمہ جات      ۲۷
>
> ضمیمہ نمبر ۲
>
> 6625.
>
> **The University of the Panjab.**
>
> The Matriculation Examination.
>
> SESSION 1931.
>
> This is to certify that Saadat Hassan son of M. Ghulam Hassan and a student of the Muslim High School, Amritsar passed in the Third Division, the Matriculation Examination of the Panjab University held in March, 1931.
>
> Passed also in Nil Additional Subject.
>
> Date of Birth 11th May, 1912.
> (Eleventh May, One Thousand Nine Hundred and Twelve).
>
> Senate Hall,
> Lahore:
> The 1st August, 1931.
>
> REGISTRAR,
> University of the Panjab.

Manto's Matriculation results, 1931 (Source: Manto Family Archive).

Saadat's rakish sartorial style, his taste for finely crafted shoes, an almost magnetic propensity for daring acts such as literally walking on coals, plus an attachment to music and theatre to the detriment of his studies horrified his father.[9] Unfortunately, Ghulam Hasan died a year after Saadat passed his Matriculation examination, most likely convinced that his youngest son was an irredeemable idler. Saadat was twenty and had not passed his Entrance (FA). More than twenty years later, he wrote of an episode that describes the chasm between

---

[9]Hamid Jalal (trans.), *Black Milk*, p. 14. Saadat's nephew, Jalal recounts an episode when he witnessed the teenaged Manto walk barefoot on coals, challenged by a fire walker. To everyone's astonishment Manto's feet remained unscarred.

Ghulam Hasan, the abstemious legal professional, and Saadat, his raffish youngest son.

> I got together with two or three professional layabouts and formed a Dramatic Club... Our activities lasted for a little more than a fortnight. But then my father and his wrath descended upon us; he broke our harmoniums and tablas and told us unequivocally that he disapproved of such 'useless pastimes'.[10]

Ghulam Hasan's visceral reaction is unsurprising in a parent who wanted his son to follow in the sturdy bourgeois footsteps of his older half-brothers. Besides, at the time, mistrust of theatre professionals and musicians was not uncommon among the bourgeoisie across the world.

If ever Bibijan tried, she failed to bring about a rapprochement. On the contrary, it is likely that to compensate for his father's harsh demeanour, she indulged Saadat and conveyed simultaneously contradictory messages, reinforcing his entitlement as a Manto while at the same time berating him for not competing with his older brothers.

Saadat was nineteen when his father died. In the essay on his marriage, he writes in an appeal for sympathy, 'I lost my father at a very young age.' His yearning for a filial and fraternal bond is apparent in his writings and several acts throughout his life. He dedicated his first collection of short stories, *Atish Pare*, 'To My Father'.

The love and approbation he craved from his father and older brothers are apparent in the warm conviviality with which he writes of his mentor, Bari Alig, 'Bari Sahib loved me.'[11] He makes the same claim for Professor Zia-ud-din, who taught Persian at Santiniketan. Yet again, he describes how, when he ran short of funds to furnish his flat before his marriage, he turned to Hakim Muhammad Abu Talib Ashk Azimabadi, 'an elder (buzurg), well disposed towards me.'

The economic gulf between four sons of the same father irked Saadat. In 'Ram Khelawan', Manto takes his usual autobiographical turn and deploys a buried photograph of his estranged and wealthy

---

[10] Saadat Hasan Manto, 'Agha Hashr se do mulaqaten', *Manto Numa*, Lahore: Sang-e-Meel Publications, 2003, pp. 30–43.
[11] Manto, 'Bari Sahib', *Manto Numa*, pp. 70–96.

older half-brother to reveal his sense of dissonance.

In 'Mantra', Manto describes how a barely eight-year-old precocious Ram confronts his parents' routine violence and his father's complacent strictures with humour and good cheer. Ram's father, Ramashankar Acharya, is a keenly observed lawyer who prides himself on his moral compass. He wants to do his best for his children, which includes an eye on their diet, a sound thrashing from time to time, and daily doses of moral education, peppered with references to the Indian Penal Code and Bhagwan the Almighty. The tale ends with Ram and his father on the Deccan Queen, an express train between Bombay and Poona. Little Ram's antics drive his father nuts, and lead to Ramashankar's quiet compromise with his conscience, in a story that is testament to why Manto's fiction continues to resonate across time.[12]

## AMRITSAR AND LAHORE IN THE EARLY TWENTIETH CENTURY

Amritsar, where Saadat spent his childhood and youth, was no backwater. A small yet modern city founded in the sixteenth century, it was the holiest site for Sikhs and home to the Golden Temple.[13] From 1919, it would not be an exaggeration to say that Amritsar is stamped on almost every South Asian heart and mind as the site of the brutal Jallianwala Bagh massacre, when the British colonial army gunned down, massacred, and maimed thousands of innocent Indians, including women and children.

The Grand Trunk Road (GT Road), built by Sher Shah Suri (1472–1545) in the sixteenth century, linked Amritsar to Lahore and Peshawar and beyond the northwest through the Khyber Pass to Kabul. In the east, the GT Road helped strategic and trade activity across the Indo-Gangetic plain to Dhaka and Murshidabad in the fabulously wealthy province of Bengal. Furthermore, the famed road connected with other roads leading to central India and kingdoms

---

[12]The story first appeared in *Manto ke Afsane* (Manto's Short Stories), his second collection of short stories, published in 1940.
[13]Shahla Rafi Matringe, *Les Discours Subversif dans L'oeuvre de Sa'adat Hasan Manto (1912-1955)*, Mémoire présenté en vue de l'obtention d'une Maîtrise de Littérature compare, Université des Sciences Humaines, Strasbourg, 1984. Rafi presents a succinct account of Manto's life, and contextualizes his writing in the wider political, social, and cultural milieus of his time.

of legendary wealth south of the Vindyas. In his compelling novel *Kim*, Rudyard Kipling (1865–1936) describes British imperial visions and life in Lahore and on the GT Road.

Forty miles apart, just an hour's tonga ride away, Lahore and Amritsar were almost twin cities before 1947, when the partition of Punjab put up between the two purged cities and their dwellers an increasingly impenetrable invisible but palpable wall of communal and nationalist suspicions—even hatred. The two cities and the province witnessed an orgy of communal violence and one of the largest ever migrations of people, with Muslims fleeing their home in India to go to Pakistan and Hindus and Sikhs from Pakistan running to India.

An ancient city, but famed from the sixteenth century, Lahore was the rotational seat of the fabulously wealthy Mughal court. Its patrons supported ateliers, guilds, and men and women artists, scholars, traders, bankers, artisans, architects, and engineers.[14] From 1799, Lahore was the seat of the prosperous and modern Sikh empire, until Punjab was sacked by the British in 1849. The city was plundered and stripped bare of its wealth.[15]

Nevertheless, during colonial occupation, Lahore gained significance as the capital of Punjab, the granary and recruiting ground for the British empire. As a result, the city became a strategic hub for playing the Great Game, which resulted in British misadventures in Afghanistan during the nineteenth and twentieth centuries, continuing into the twenty-first century.

After colonial occupation, Punjab supplied foot soldiers for imperial designs in India during the war against the British in 1857; again for waging the First (1839–42), Second (1878–80), and Third Afghan Wars (1919); and the two World Wars.[16] Due to systemic militarization in colonial times, after the emergence of Pakistan as an independent

---

[14] Muzaffar Alam and Sanjay Subrahmanyam, *Writing the Mughal World: Studies on Culture and Politics*, New York: Columbia University Press, 2011.
[15] Priya Atwal, *Royals and Rebels: The Rise and Fall of the Sikh Empire*, Oxford: Oxford University Press, 2020.
[16] William Dalrymple, *Return of a King: The Battle for Afghanistan*, New Delhi: Bloomsbury, 2012.

state in 1947, Punjabis strengthened and deployed the army to transform Punjab into the dominant province, quell democracy, and grab more than their fair share of national income.

Propelled by the military, the new country aligned itself with the US and became a frontline state to support US's strategic aims in the region, which further strengthened the army's role. Since Pakistan's birth, the US and its NATO allies, including the UK, have supported, financially and militarily, every dictator who has ruled Pakistan. Consequently, between 1979 and 1992, Pakistan played a pivotal role in the US fight against the Soviet Union in Afghanistan. The stated aim was to use jihad as a weapon and Islam as a buffer against communism. Thus, for example, the US supported Zia-ul-Haq, the military strongman between 1977 and 1988, responsible for Pakistan's civic, cultural, and religious turn away from the Sufi Islam imbricated in the everyday lives of Pakistan's Muslims. As part of the American project, Zia strengthened the foundations for the rise of religious fundamentalism and obscurantism in Pakistan.[17]

The fallout of the US jihad was the onset of a culture of drugs, heroin, and Kalashnikovs, and the training of foot soldiers to fight the Russians. In addition, the madrasa, once an ordinary vernacular school, was transformed into a seminary to train militant jihadists, the mujahideen. The money pumped in by the US and Saudi Arabia into the new madrasas, and military training camps fed a transformation of the practice and interpretation of Islam in Pakistan. The foot soldiers of militant Islam have multiplied and diversified into groups such as the Taliban, Al Qaeda, and ISIS, among others.

After forty years of catastrophic meddling in the region, US forces withdrew from Afghanistan in August 2021. They left behind an Afghanistan in chaos and in control of the Taliban—hard-line Islamists propagating and practising a reconstructed misogynist Islam that shuns all forms of pluralism, with little regard for learning and education—while the people of Afghanistan learn to survive in grinding poverty.

In the 1960s, Pakistan was what the World Bank considered a perfect model of economic growth, although the fruits of this growth

---

[17] Mohammad Hanif, *A Case of Exploding Mangoes*, Delhi: Penguin Random House, 2011.

largely benefitted twenty-two families, as highlighted the country's chief economist Mahbub ul Haq. Still, it is important to recognize that the problems were of distribution of wealth—the country was not perpetually on the brink of economic instability and collapse, as it has been for some decades now, with its citizens crushed by hyperinflation. Moreover, the country's social, cultural, and political fabric is in tatters. A debased ventriloquist military establishment (fuelled for decades by the US) holds itself unaccountable. It plays puppet master to equally corrupt politicians from religious and secular formations. With the judiciary and courts compromised—countless citizens, and human rights activists continue to struggle for the rule of law and voice dissent.

Manto was particularly alarmed by Pakistan's emerging role as a frontline state for the United States's strategic aims from the early 1950s. He recorded his concerns in his nine 'Letters to Uncle Sam', written in 1951.[18] Just as Saadat recognized the possibilities of a toxic fallout from Pakistan's alliance with the US, he was alert to the misuse of Islam by all and sundry, which he records in his story 'The Manufacturer of Martyrs' (Shaheed Saaz).[19]

In the story, a man from Kathiawar moves to Pakistan and becomes rich with fake property claims and allotments. His boundless greed twinned with a desire to gain favour with the Almighty inspires him to construct a substandard multistorey building designed to collapse. In this way, he ensures that all labourers and residents die as martyrs (shaheed). His conscience is appeased and he congratulates himself for assuring a place in heaven for them and, thus, himself.

Read together, the nine 'Letters to Uncle Sam', and 'The Manufacturer of Martyrs' stand as cautionary tales. The texts are essential readings for those who wish to understand the macabre beginnings and the fallout of the tragedy of Pakistan's alliance with the United States.

---

[18]First published in 1951, the nine 'Letters to Uncle Sam' appeared in Manto's collection called *Upar, Niche, aur Darmiyan* (Top, Bottom, and Middle). They are found in this volume, interspersed between pp. 259–449. For an English translation, see *Letters to Uncle Sam*, trans. Khalid Hasan, Islamabad: Alhamra Printing, 2001.
[19]Saadat Hasan Manto, 'Shaheed Saaz', *Manto Kahaniyan*, Lahore: Sang-e-Meel Publications, 2015, pp. 92–98.

It may be appropriate here to recall that for centuries the Bamiyan Buddhas were famous attractions in the safe custody of Afghan Muslims before the Taliban destroyed them in 2001. Moreover, present-day Afghanistan, Bangladesh, India, and Pakistan were part of a vast space where Muslim rulers patronized humanist learning. For centuries, Christians, Jews, Hindus, Zoroastrians, and others engaged in an exchange of ideas, including Vedic, Buddhist, Hellenic, and Sufi philosophy, mathematics, chemistry, medicine, history, literature, and the roots of social anthropology.

The great centres of scholarship patronized by Muslim kings and queens stretched from North Africa, and Spain in the West into parts of Europe, across what is referred to as the Middle East today, and through India, further towards the Far East. Significantly, Lahore's patron saint, Ali Hajveri (c. 1009–1072), a Sufi moral philosopher known to Lahoris as Data Sahib, was born in Ghazni in present-day Afghanistan.

Although plundered and stripped bare of its wealth by the British, colonial occupation and governmentality drawing on Lahore's Mughal and Sikh roots contributed to a modern efflorescence of diverse cultural practices and intellectual activity. The city saw the growth of highly regarded educational institutions of international repute. Music, dance, the arts and crafts, modern subjects such as psychology thrived, as did a small but vibrant film industry—in collaboration and competition with Calcutta and Bombay.[20]

During his youth, Saadat lived briefly in Lahore where he watched movies and hung around in coffee houses and courtesans' salons, while he tried to establish his career as a writer and a journalist. In an essay on Chiragh Hasan Hasrat (1904–55), an Urdu broadcaster, journalist, and a man of letters, Saadat compares the Arab Hotel in Lahore with the French Latin Quarter.[21]

In part, because of colonial policies, Lahore figured throughout Saadat's life. The Portuguese had introduced printing to India in the

---

[20]Nasreen Rehman, 'A History of the Cinema in Lahore'.
[21]Manto, 'Chiragh Hasan Hasrat', *Manto Namah*, pp. 306–19. Cf. K. K. Aziz, *Coffee Houses of Lahore: A Memoir, 1942-1957*, Lahore: Sang-e-Meel Publications, 2008.

sixteenth century, but the indigenous printing industry did not take off until the early nineteenth century, under the British in Bengal. Punjab, where the British had replaced Persian with Urdu as the official language of statecraft and education (along with English), saw an explosion of publishing houses. Lahore joined Lucknow as home to some of the most influential Urdu publishing houses, such as Dar-ul' Ish'at, and literary journals of the day, such as *Humayun*, and *Adab-i-Latif*, which published Manto's works.

After his move to Bombay in 1936, Lahore's importance in the world of Urdu letters brought Saadat back, invariably to face charges of obscenity. First, in colonial Lahore in 1944, for 'Black Shalwar' (Kali Shalwar) and 'Smoke' (Dhuan). Then, in 1946, Saadat faced charges for 'Scent' (Bu), along with his friend Ismat Chughtai, who was held up for 'Quilt' (Lihaf) her short story. Both were arrested without warrants in 1946 from their respective homes in Bombay but released on bail. They travelled to Lahore several times, and finally, were acquitted in 1947. Saadat spent his last years in Lahore, where he made literary and legal history as the defendant in Pakistan's first obscenity trial when pulled up for 'Cold Flesh' published in March 1949.

Two of Saadat's three daughters were born here—Nuzhat in 1948 and Nusrat in 1949. The sisters continue to live in the city, where their mother Safia brought them up with their elder sister, Nighat, born in Bombay in 1946. Significantly, Lahore is where Manto was most prolific as a writer and finally and quite literally laid to rest.

After his father's death, Saadat continued to live with Bibijan and Balaji in the family house in Amritsar's Lawyers' Lane but with a decline in their status and circumstances. In 1933, Saadat left Hindu Sabha College and enrolled in his old alma mater, now elevated to the MAO College under the aegis of the Anjuman-i-Islamia, his admission facilitated by the Manto family's strong ties with the Anjuman. His two childhood pals, Abu Saeed Qureishi and Hassan Abbas joined him.

Saadat's two years at MAO College train the spotlight on the diversity in Muslim subjectivity, social formations, political thought, moral philosophy, and literary production. Funded by the Anjuman-i-Islamia, MAO High School and College was a posting house for subversive young Muslim Marxist revolutionaries. It attracted teachers such as Mahmud-uz Zafar (1908–54), a member of the Communist Party of India. Zafar, who taught at MAO School between 1933–35 after his return from Oxford, had contributed to *Angare* (Embers), a collection of Urdu short stories that became the rallying call for the All-India Progressive Writers' Movement (PWM) in 1932, which Saadat must have read. In 1934, Zafar married Rashid Jahan (1905–52), a medical doctor and a short story writer, also a part of the *Angare* collective. Rashid Jahan's parents, Sheikh Abdullah (1874–1965) and Waheed Jahan Begum set up the Muslim Girls' School in Aligarh in 1906. They laid the foundations of the Women's College—alma mater of Saadat's friend, Ismat Chughtai, a pathbreaking feminist writer before the term feminism entered everyday usage. It is worth noting that like Manto, both Rashid Jahan and the trenchant Ismat were writing in Urdu, and therefore accessible to men and women from a wide social spectrum.

Another notable presence who taught English at MAO College was Faiz Ahmed Faiz (1911–84), a Marxist revolutionary modern Urdu poet and member of the PWM. In addition, Faiz was an essayist, a journalist, a legendary editor (in Urdu and English) and founder of the Arts Council of Pakistan. To this day, rights activists and dissidents chant his poems as anthems of resistance, hope, and freedom across the world.[22]

Manto described his encounters with these urbane intellectuals in an essay, 'The Compelling Nina' (Pur Israr Nina), about the film actress Nina, who was married, briefly, to Rashid Jahan's brother, Mohsin Abdullah. In the same essay, Saadat writes of his devotion to Faiz. Although the poet was but a year older, Manto ran errands for Faiz, particularly before the besotted poet embarked on his regular visits to Dehradun to meet Rashid Jahan.

Without paternal policing and fraternal guidance, the young Manto spent most of his time gambling in the company of friends, invariably

---

[22] An example is Faiz Ahmed Faiz's poem 'Hum Dekhenge' (We Shall See), composed in defiance of Zia-ul-Haq's military dictatorship in 1986. It was chanted by the women in Shaheen Bagh in Delhi during the protests against the Citizenship Amendment Act in 2020.

at Hotel Shiraz or Jeejay's Hotel (Jeejay ka Hotel). During these unsettled years, Manto cultivated a taste for alcohol, a passion for literature, and a reflective engagement with music and the cinema. His essays and stories, describing his visits to literary gatherings, drinking dens, and courtesans' salons in Amritsar and Lahore, are a compelling archive of artistic avant-gardes in early twentieth century Punjab.

Saadat relished the company of creative individuals and artists. When he heard that Agha Hashr Kashmiri (1879–1935) was in Amritsar, Saadat sought the playwright and screenplay writer, often referred to as the Shakespeare of modern Indian theatre. He met Hashr at the salon of the playwright's paramour, the legendary tawa'if, songstress, theatre, and film actor Mukhtar Begum (1911–82).[23] Similarly, the young Saadat went to Jeejay's Hotel searching for Akhtar Sheerani (1905–48), a popular romantic poet, scholar, publisher, and alcoholic surrounded by an air of tragic mystery. In an essay, Saadat recorded his rumbustious meetings with the desolate alcoholic poet, surrounded by devotees chanting his poems on the rooftop of Jeejay's Hotel.

Manto kept up with Sheerani, and in 1943 invited him to work as a lyricist for *Naukar*, a film directed by Shaukat Hussain Rizvi, married to the singing star Noor Jehan, who had a role in the film. In 1948, more than twenty years after their first meeting, Saadat met Sheerani at a literary gathering in Lahore. Not much later, his friend and publisher, and a well-regarded man of letters, Ahmad Nadeem Qasmi, and Saadat's nephew, the filmmaker Masood Parvez, dropped by to tell him that Sheerani was critically ill and under treatment in Mayo Hospital. The three men went to call on Sheerani Sahib to see what they could do to help. They found him in the general Sialkot ward in a coma, and not much later, Saadat heard of Akhtar Sheerani's death on 9 September 1948.

The modernist scholar and critic Hasan Askari has described how deeply affected Manto was by Sheerani's death.[24] In 1953, felled by

---

[23] Hashr whisked Mukhtar off to Calcutta where she found fame and fortune in Parsi theatre and the silent cinema with Madan Theatre. Unlike many stars, she made a successful transition to the talkies.
[24] Hasan Askari, 'Manto', *Majmuah*, Lahore: Sang-e-Meel Publications, 2015, pp. 434–46.

cirrhosis of the liver, Saadat was taken to Mayo Hospital by his much younger friends, Choudhury Rashid of Maktaba-e-Jadid, and Jamil Khan, a medical student at the time. Saadat was allotted the same bay number as the dying Akhtar Sheerani.[25] He recorded Sheerani's unattended death in the general Sialkot ward of Mayo Hospital.[26] Unable to combat his addiction to alcohol, in Sheerani's end Manto saw the rout of his spirit in his battle to support his family and live his life with dignity.

Saadat's literary education began in Amritsar in 1933. Manto writes that he was fortunate to meet Abdul Bari (Alig) at Jeejay's Hotel. Bari Sahib was with Haji Laq Laq, a well-known Urdu journalist and satirist of his time.[27] Bari Sahib had moved to Amritsar from Lahore to take up the editorship of *Mussawat* (Equity), an Urdu, socialist daily. He attached Alig to his name, an abbreviation for Aligarh University graduates, although he had not graduated from the university. At the time, Saadat was twenty-one, and he attributes his turn to literature and writing to Bari Sahib, and refers to him as 'the socialist writer, my friend, my mentor' and continues:

> Bari Sahib loved me and was proud of me but never expressed his views or feelings. I do not know if he ever claimed, 'I made Manto what he is today.' But, indeed, it is true that he put me on the path of writing and literature...if I had not met him in Amritsar, it is likely that by now, I would be lying in an unmarked grave or serving a lengthy prison sentence for dacoity or theft.[28]

In 1948, Bari Sahib wrote an essay on his time in Amritsar, including the days he spent with Manto and his friends—and claimed no credit for setting his protégé on his writing career.[29] Like the best teachers, Bari Sahib recognized a spark in his young friend and set him on

---

[25] Bukhari, *Manto Tehqiq*, p. 79.
[26] Manto, 'Akhtar Sheerani se chand mulaqaten', *Manto Numa*, pp. 44–55.
[27] Manto, 'Bari Sahib', *Manto Numa*, p. 88.
[28] Manto, 'A few encounters with Akhtar Sheerani', *Manto Numa*, pp. 44–55.
[29] Bari Alig, *Chand Mahine Amritsar Mein* (Few Months in Amritsar), reprint, in *Manto Mera Dost Mera Dushman*, edited by Ahmad Saleem, Lahore: Sang-e-Meel Publications, 2012, pp. 264–74.

his path to literary fame. In his essay on Bari Sahib, Saadat writes that although an avid reader, before he met Bari Sahib his palate was restricted to every translation into Urdu of English detective and crime fiction and essays by Tirath Ram Firozepuri (1885–1954).[30]

On the other hand, Bari Sahib drew Saadat's attention to English canonical texts and translations into English of Russian and French literature. Furthermore, he encouraged Saadat and his friends Abu Saeed Qureishi and Hassan Abbas to translate Oscar Wilde's *Vera*. Bari Sahib has described how he organized the printing of life-sized posters to publicize the book. Nevertheless, the republican thrust of the play meant that the colonial authorities cracked down and had the posters removed. The trio's translation faded.

The year 1934 set Saadat on his ascent to literary fame. Using an English translation, Manto translated Victor Hugo's *The Last Days of a Condemned Man* into the Urdu *Sarguzaasht-e-Aseer*. Impressed by Saadat's work, Bari Sahib helped get it published. He handed the manuscript to Yaqub Husain, owner of Urdu Book Stall, Lahore, who paid Saadat thirty rupees and published it immediately.

That year Saadat began to write a film column for *Mussawat*. His first published short story, 'Spectacle' (Tamasha), appeared in Bari Sahib's fly-by-night publication called *Khalq* (The Masses). The same year, Saadat edited a volume of his translations of Russian short stories with an introduction by Bari Sahib for *Humayun*.

Nightly soirées were held at Manto's house, where the writer would hang out with Bari Sahib, Abu Saeed Qureishi, and Hassan Abbas. Bari Sahib named the room where they met Dar-ul-Ahmar or the Red Den in a clever conceit that referred to the group's political leanings and red wine because it was also their watering hole. When *Mussawat* folded up, an unemployed Bari Sahib spent a few months in Saadat's family house in Lawyers' Lane, before his return to Lyallpur.

Bari Sahib has described the strict rules of engagement in the Red Den, where the four friends worked on their writing with a strict 'do not disturb' code of silence by day and drank through

---

[30] C. M. Naim, 'An Extraordinary Translator, Tirath Ram Firozepuri (1885–1954)', The Annual of Urdu Studies, No. 28, 2013, pp. 1–37. Firozepuri was translating the novels of George W. M. Reynolds and other writers of crime fiction. This essay sheds light on the popular choices of Urdu readers at the time.

the night. Manto recounts how Bari Sahib held forth on Hegel and Marx. Although he may not have been an expert on the two philosophers, Bari Sahib was erudite. As for many within similar social and political formations, Marx's name was emblematic of a desire for political liberation and social justice post the Russian Revolution. The legendary human rights activist, and journalist, I. A. Rehman Sahib (1931–2021), who had access to an excellent library growing up in Karnal in the 1930s, recalled Bari Sahib's book, *Kampani ki Hakumat* (The Rule of the East India Company), circulating in left-leaning circles in north India.[31]

Notwithstanding nightly encounters with friends and men of ideas, it became clear to Saadat that life in Amritsar had reached a cul-de-sac. Balaji, his beloved sister, who shared his love of literature, was married and living in Bombay. In a letter dated 20 February 1934, Saadat writes a heartfelt appeal asking her to keep in touch. He registers his pain at her criticism of him as 'uncivilized', 'rigid', and 'petulant', which he happened to read in her letter to their mother. Saadat feels her absence and declares his love for her. In the letter, he adds, 'I shall send your essay within three days to *Nairang-i-Khayal* (The Enchantment of Thought), a leading Urdu literary journal.' I have found no evidence of any published work by Nasira Iqbal Begum. Ayesha Jalal describes her great-aunt as a gripping raconteur and a bundle of warmth.

Saadat decided to continue his formal education and enrolled at Aligarh University in 1935. However, soon after he arrived at the university, he was diagnosed with tuberculosis and packed off home. Later, doctors diagnosed his malady as chronic pleurisy. Yet, Saadat published his second short story, 'Revolutionary' (Inqilaab Pasand), in the Aligarh University magazine and developed a bond with Ali Sardar Jafri (1913–2000), a Marxist poet and scholar who, in later years, became a luminary of the PWM. Although Jafri Sahib remained a fainthearted ally, Saadat's relationship with members of the PWM stayed fractious.

---

[31]Bari (Alig), *Kampani ki Hakumat*, Lahore: Maktaba-i-Urdu, 1938.

## THE ICONOCLAST AND THE PROGRESSIVE WRITERS

Manto's relationship with Ali Sardar Jafri and Faiz Ahmed Faiz reveals the tense standoff between two leading literary formations in colonial India and later in India and Pakistan—the PWM and the modernists. From the late 1930s, arguably, the PWM gained ascendency in Urdu literary circles.

Sardar Jafri Sahib's book, *Tarraqi Pasand Adab* (Progressive Literature), outlines the didactic underpinnings of good literature and reads like a manifesto of the PWM. But Saadat was an iconoclast not entrenched in any school of thought or ideology.

Yet Saadat's writings are a searing indictment of the bourgeoisie and reveal a loathing of the commodification of sacred and profane relations, with a keen awareness of historical materialism. Manto's focus shifts from the weakest in his immediate world—children, women, and domestic servants—to the most reviled, prostitutes and pimps: the 'ungrievable' in the colonial and nationalist moral calculus, and among the most violated members of society.[32] Furthermore, Marx is one of the few historical figures about whom Manto has written—and with admiration. The others include Joan of Arc, Mirza Asadullah Khan Ghalib, Maxim Gorky, and James Joyce.

Urdu literary fiction had a tradition of sexually graphic storytelling, particularly in the poetic masnavi tradition, which was suppressed in the late nineteenth and early twentieth centuries. Some argue this happened under the influence of Victorian prudery of the colonial government. Moreover, Tariq Rahman has demonstrated how Hindi nationalists' attacks on Urdu as the language of a depraved civilization also contributed to self-censorship and governmental proscription of Urdu erotica.[33]

Sexuality was the stumbling block between Manto and the Progressives who, with their didactic underpinnings, dismissed Saadat's oeuvre as violent and sexually explicit without social or political purpose, therefore not literature (adab). Indeed, Saadat's stark descriptions of bodily parts and fluids with performative sexuality and violence against

---

[32] Judith Butler, *The Force of Non-Violence: An Ethico-Political Bind*, London: Verso Books, 2020.
[33] Tariq Rahman, 'The language of love: a study of the amorous and erotic associations of Urdu', *Cracow Indological Studies*, Issue 11, 2009, pp. 29–65.

the backdrop of contemporary urban and rural everyday life shocked and outraged many. As a result, Saadat was charged with obscenity twice by the colonial authorities before 1947, but ultimately acquitted. Manto fell foul of the official censors three times in Pakistan.

In response to critics and reformists who attacked him for having an obscene and sick mind and the Progressive Writers who advised him to write fiction with a purpose, Saadat wrote, 'How can I strip the choli of a civilization that is already naked? I don't attempt to clothe it because this is a tailor's job—not mine.'[34]

Nevertheless, when Manto was tried for obscenity for 'Bu' in 1946, Sardar Jafri gave evidence extolling the literary merits of the story.[35] Therefore, it was unsurprising that in 1947, before he left for Pakistan in 1948, Saadat handed the manuscript of *Chughad* (Imbecile), a collection of short stories, to Jafri Sahib, who was working with Qutb Publishers.[36]

After a brief correspondence, which includes a letter from Jafri Sahib, hinting at some hesitation on his part, Manto followed with a request to publish the collection without an introduction. Nevertheless, *Chughad* was published in India with Sardar Jafri's introduction—with more than a sting in its tail.[37] Jafri Sahib described Manto's writing as 'an expression of the middle class' guilty conscience' and, taking a purple turn, added that 'Manto's brilliance is like a jewel that sparkles on the tip of his pen.'[38] Yet, forever the Progressive, he advised Manto to eschew vicarious sexuality and sordid subjects, mature as a writer, and produce great literature with a purpose.[39]

In 1949, Manto received his most brutal Progressive blow unexpectedly and uncharacteristically from his old-time friend and benefactor, the revolutionary poet Faiz Ahmed Faiz. When charged with obscenity for 'Thanda Gosht', unsurprisingly, Saadat named Faiz

---

[34]Saadat Hasan Manto, 'A Taste for Suffering' (Lazzat-i Sang), *Manto Rama*, Lahore: Sang-e-Meel Publications, 2015, pp. 613–41. Manto's introduction to the collection of short stories that contains 'Bu', p. 240.
[35]Manto, 'Bu', *Manto Namah*, pp. 641–48.
[36]Shams-ul Haq Usmani, 'Introduction', *Pura Manto*, Volume 3, Karachi: Oxford University Press, 2013, pp. 449–50.
[37]Ibid.
[38]Ibid.
[39]Ibid.

as a witness for the defence, to support his claim that his story was not obscene.

Faiz was an old friend from MAO College, and Saadat had spent time with him in Delhi during his stint at All India Radio (AIR) between 1941–43. Upon arrival in Lahore in 1948, Saadat encountered a purged city. Horrified, he was unable to write stories. The old Lahori film industry was almost dead, and thus he called on his old friends, Faiz and Chiragh Hasan Hasrat, who were busy laying the foundations of *Imroze*, a Progressive Urdu daily. Immediately, they appointed him to write daily sketches, which he later published as *Talkh, Tursh, aur Shirin* (Bitter, Acrid, and Sweet).[40]

Importantly, as editor of the English daily *Pakistan Times*, Faiz had chaired a Press Advisory Board meeting and declared that 'Thanda Gosht' was not obscene. At the trial, Faiz declared in court that he did not think 'Thanda Gosht' obscene. Nevertheless, in what must have hit Manto like a targeted barb, Faiz added that 'Thanda Gosht' was not a work of literature because it did not explore life's fundamental concerns in a satisfactory manner.[41]

The magistrate relied, in part, on Faiz's dismissal of the story, backed by opinions of other academics and scholars who thought 'Thanda Gosht' obscene and upheld the charges against Manto, his editor, and publisher. Manto was handed out three months rigorous imprisonment and a fine. Fortunately, the three defendants succeeded in getting bail and filed an appeal in the Sessions Court, where all three were acquitted on 28 January 1950.[42] However, matters did not end there, and the prosecution filed an appeal in the High Court, where Manto was found guilty. It is a bitter irony that scholars and writers now club Saadat Hasan Manto with the 'Progressive Writer'.[43]

THE WILL TO WRITE

On his return from Aligarh in 1935, a sickly Saadat, crushed in spirit and flesh, floundered in Amritsar. His lungs were weak, and

---

[40] Manto, *Manto Namah*, pp. 389–511.
[41] Manto, 'Zehmat-e-Mehr-e-Darakhshan', *Manto Namah*, pp. 366.
[42] Ibid.
[43] Priyamavada Gopal, *Literary Radicalism: Gender, Nation and the Transition to Independence*, London: Routledge, 2005.

he required proper medical attention. From his early twenties, Saadat battled chronic lung disease, escalating depression, alcoholism—and, unsurprisingly, cirrhosis of the liver in the last years of his life. Unfortunately, his older barrister half-brothers showed little interest in his education or deteriorating health. Consequently, Balaji and Bibijan organized funds and made arrangements for him to convalesce and regain his health in Batote, a tiny village in Jammu. In Saadat's letters home to keep his mother and sister informed of his health and constitution, there are early intimations of depression.[44] In addition, there are signs also of a love gone wrong.

Upon returning from Batote, Saadat immersed himself in the cinema, travelling to Lahore to watch films and work on his first collection of short stories. He managed to secure a post to write features for the weekly *Paras* (Touchstone), edited by Karam Chand, at forty rupees a month, of which he rarely received between ten to fifteen rupees.[45]

It was, perhaps, Saadat's native sense of justice that compelled him to explore, question, and reveal the world around him. He had ingested enough of the sanctimonious posturing of the Indian bourgeois milieu into which he was born, as well as the cruel duplicitous grandstanding and insatiable greed of British colonial authority and the equally specious posturing of local Indian nationalists.

He has referred to short story writing as his 'inheritance' (jaidad) and describes how persistent depression led him to writing.

> A few years ago, grappling with the pointlessness of existence in a reflective mood, I craved something to give meaning to my life. Some days were cloudless, but others so dark they aroused the envy of moonless nights... I was about to shut the door... but a short story entered my life and said, 'I can be of use to you...' Hard times made me a good short story writer.
>
> Bombay,
> 3 August 1940[46]

---

[44]Letter to his mother. Courtesy Nusrat Jalal, Manto Family Archive.
[45]Manto, 'Chiragh Hasan Hasrat', *Manto Namah*, p. 306.
[46]Shams-ul Haq Usmani, 'Zamima', *Pura Manto*, Volume 1, Karachi: Oxford University Press, 2013, pp. 365–66. The introduction to a collection of three short stories, 'Alcoholic' (Sharabi), 'Steps Towards Suicide' (Khudkashi ke Iqdaam), 'Student Union Camp'.

## HUMANISM, HISTORY, VIOLENCE, AND SEXUALITY

Saadat's engagement and preoccupation with Ghalib's humanism, reveals his desire to understand the human condition. This is what drew him to Freud and psychoanalysis; Marx and the commodification of human relations and historical materialism. His admiration of the anarchist Peter Kropotkin, points to his iconoclasm. His engagement with Freud is apparent throughout his oeuvre, perhaps, most strikingly in 'Miss Tinwallah'. Here Saadat records how his friend Zaidi, terrified of a tomcat, repeatedly beats him with a chilling ease that gestures to sexual abuse and post-traumatic stress disorder. Manto focused on the human will to cause harm and perform sexuality, together with an equally strong urge to hypocrisy, to deny and conceal, which he had witnessed in the milieu into which he was born, and in the world he discovered as an adult, through lived experience and reading. His ideas mark him out as an exemplar of autochthonous and global modernity. That Saadat Hasan Manto was a thoroughly modern man is evinced further in his everyday engagement with technologies such as electricity, telegraph, telephone, gramophone, film, and typewriter—particularly notable in South Asia, since the above-mentioned list of items was a rarity in the lives of most Indians and Pakistanis, even at the time of his death. Furthermore, his ability to indulge in old and new modes of dress, transport, and ideas, mark him out as a person who did not think of modernity as a project but rather a process where old ideas and practices can be adapted, transformed, overthrown, but, importantly, also persist.

In his local and regional contexts, Saadat lived his life on a knotty intersection of colonial brute force, contested nationalist politics, religious fault lines, class entitlement, and patriarchy laced with class, caste, and gendered exploitation. Manto witnessed the collapse of British colonial India, which culminated in the partition of Bengal and Punjab, amidst the violence that attended the emergence of two independent sovereign states: the Muslim majority Pakistan, and India with a Hindu majority, but avowedly secular claims.

For Saadat, writing was a balm for his troubled soul, and a way to assert his dignity. Furthermore, through writing, Saadat wished to recover the more humane aspects of the human condition (insaniyat).

The dedication to 'Cold Flesh' best illuminates Saadat's search for a redemptive humanism in a world—his world, where violence had descended into the quotidian and evil was banal:[47]

> To Ishar Singh, who did not lose his humanity after he became an animal.[48]

After a week's absence, Ishar Singh, a hardy, crass, and sexually voracious Sikh, goes to a hotel to visit his well-matched paramour, Kuldip Kaur. She questions Ishar Singh to understand her inability to arouse him. He describes the loot, killing, and rape in the city and how he killed six men but his realization that he was about to commit necrophilia makes him impotent. Finally, in a fit of jealous rage, Kuldip Kaur slits his throat. Ishar Singh's hands are cold as ice as he dies in Kuldip Kaur's arms.[49]

In 'The Drawstring' a father is looking for his daughter during the rapacious bloodbath of Partition in Punjab. It is a time when people refer to rape as a fate worse than death, and families refuse to accept rape survivors back into their fold. Instead, they ask, 'Why did you not die?' or say, 'It would have been better if you had died.' Yet, the father in the story is joyful to see signs of life in his daughter.

Often applauded for a gift of prescience, Saadat's writings reveal a non-linear understanding of history that forges links between past events, current affairs, and futurity, rather than articulations of a sixth sense or predictions based upon a study of the conjunction of stars. Furthermore, Manto had a grasp on how the logic of fiction and history are refined in the same crucible.[50] He does not write as a witness or an ethnographer but inserts himself into his stories and essays as a subject of history with conscious agency. For instance, in the opening sentence of 'Babu Gopinath', he writes:

> I met Babu Gopinath in 1940, and at the time, was editor of a Bombay weekly. I was writing the leader when Abdul Raffique

---

[47]Veena Das, *Life and Words: Violence and the Descent into the Ordinary*, Berkeley: University of California Press, 2007. Cf. Hannah Arendt, *Eichmann in Jerusalem: A Report on the Banality of Evil*; Manto, 'Zehmat-e-Mehr-e-Darakhshan', pp. 351–403.
[48]Manto, 'Thanda Gosht', *Manto Namah*, pp. 404–12.
[49]Ibid., p. 412.
[50]Jacques Rancière, *The Politics of Aesthetics: A Distribution of the Sensible*, trans. Gabriel Rockhill, New York: Continuum International Publishing Group, 2004.

Sando walked in with a short man. He greeted me in his distinctive manner and loud voice with an 'aadaab' and introduced me to his companion, 'Manto Sahib meet Babu Gopinath.'[51]

Manto is present throughout this story, as he is in countless others.

Furthermore, Saadat blurs the boundaries between art and life, fact and fiction, fantasy and reality. His stories often read like diary entries or essays, and his essays like stories or excerpts from his private journals. For example, 'Latika Rani' is a barely disguised account of film star Devika Rani and her husband, once actor, producer, and king at Bombay Talkies.[52] But, stylistically it reads like many of Saadat's essays.

Two essays that read like short stories are included in this volume: the first, 'My Marriage', is about Manto's marriage to Safia Qamar-ud Deen on 26 April 1939, included here because in it Manto recounts crucial aspects of his early childhood, later life, and his time in Bombay. The second essay, 'My Sahib', presages the subaltern turn to history; based on interviews in Bombay and Karachi with Azad, an aspiring actor, once employed between 1936 and 1937 as a driver by the Quaid-e-Azam Muhammad Ali Jinnah.

Saadat trained the twin lens of violence and sexuality on the world around him. Attention to violence is unsurprising in a sensitive person born in a militarized province two years before World War I, who lived through World War II, and saw the communal violence which accompanied the end of British occupation and Independence.[53] Moreover, he was raised under the critical eye of a stern patriarch in the context of constant colonial, racial, cultural, and intellectual degradation.

Manto's birth was coeval with the high noon of India's struggle for independence. Importantly, Punjab was not a mere comprador canal colony and a haven of opportunities for an emergent Indian bourgeoisie, new zamindars—local recruiting agents with land grants

---

[51] Manto, 'Babu Gopinath', *Manto Namah*, pp. 276–95.
[52] Manto, 'Latika Rani', *Manto Rama*, pp. 139–51.
[53] Das, *Life and Words*.

# Introduction

from the colonialists. On the contrary, the province was a hotbed of revolutionary radicalism: Lahore and Amritsar figured as centres of pulsating violent anti-colonial dissent.

Saadat was five at the time of the Russian Revolution, which inspired a rising tide of anti-colonial and revolutionary fervour across India. He was seven when British troops slaughtered hundreds of unarmed Indian men, women, and children and wounded countless more at Jallianwala Bagh in Amritsar on 13 April 1919. The sense of betrayal was hard felt in a province that had supplied cannon fodder for more than half a century to further British imperial aims—from quelling the rebellion in 1857 and then during World War I.

The massacre at Jallianwala Bagh spurred the Indian demand for freedom from centuries of colonial loot and brutality and left an indelible impression on Manto, as it did on the young and old across India. His first short story, 'Tamasha', was about the massacre.[54] The story records a seven-year-old boy's fear of the aircraft flying overhead lest they 'drop bombs' on his house; and his unsuccessful attempt to get a meaningful explanation from his father.

A mature Saadat returned to Jallianwala Bagh in 1951, in 'An Episode from 1919' (San 1919 ki Aik Baat).[55] He locates the story in the context of the burgeoning discourse of Gandhian non-violence and post-World War I pacifism. Manto rips apart the psychosocial dimensions of gendered violence to explore the horrifying entanglement of nationalist and colonial bourgeois hypocrisy. Thalia, a charming, handsome freeloader, is well-known in Amritsar as the brother and pimp of his two sisters—celebrated tawa'ifs. The siblings assume agency and dignity and heroically fight back in a stinging attack on British colonialists and Indian nationalists.[56]

The Communist Party of India was formed in 1920. Notwithstanding Mahatma Gandhi's call to non-violent non-cooperation, British brute force spurred many young women and men to revolutionary activity. The colonial regime responded with violence and a tightening of censorship. As a result, Punjab remained under martial law for much of the first half of the twentieth

---

[54] Manto, 'Spectacle' (Tamasha), *Manto Rama*, pp. 662–68.
[55] Manto, 'An Episode from 1919' (San 1919 ki Aik Baat), *Manto Namah*, pp. 151–58.
[56] Ibid.

century—a practice that continued in Pakistan after Independence.

Censorship codes imposed by the colonialists in 1920 remain the bedrock of censorship in Bangladesh, India, and Pakistan. The laws against sedition and terrorism in the post-colonial state are more repressive than those of the colonial era, with the explicit intention to expunge all dissent. In 'Women' (Aurat Zat), Manto writes about the circulation of blue movies to reveal the hypocrisy of the colonial government and the so-called respectable Indians. Colonial authorities were more interested in policing sedition than the erotic content of films.

As is evident from present times, it is not easy to resist the might of a brutal militarized government or state, with various surveillance mechanisms supported by law enforcement bodies like the police and paramilitary forces intent on violence. South Asian post-colonial states are propped up by legal systems increasingly more intent on policing sedition than acting as arbiters of the rule of law and fundamental rights. Yet, then as now, notwithstanding colonial and nationalist brute force, non-violent and armed dissent continued—the outrage against colonial brutality circulated through various means. For instance, Bhagat Singh's bust stood on the mantelpiece in the Red Den, in the house in Lawyers' Lane. And, of course, literature was a potent weapon in the arsenal of resistance.

Manto is widely known for exploring sexual violence, particularly around Partition. Nevertheless, his purview extends to routine, seemingly non-sexual abuse of and brutality against women and children. 'On My Way Sir' (Ji Aya Sahib), a story from his first collection, is a harrowing tale about young Qasim, a domestic child servant treated like a slave in his master's house. Adept at locating his characters in specific towns and cities, Manto uncovers Qasim's story in a bourgeois home that could be in any North Indian town. The master's cruelty is matched with that of the wife who invokes and acts in her husband's name to reveal a hideous masculinity underpinned by patriarchal entitlement, and class-, caste-, and gender-based violence.

It is instructive to place Manto's exploration of psychosocial violence and sexuality in a context of global patriarchies wherein fear of a woman's reproductive capacity instigated regimes of surveillance and male dominance over her. Central to this worldview was the indulgence of uncontrollable male libidos and the horror of a woman's ability to conceal or misrepresent the paternity of an offspring. Manto was writing before DNA testing was on the horizon. 'Hamid's Baby' (Hamid ka Bacha) is a disquieting story about a married man who must confront the fear that a woman he hires for sexual pleasure is about to give birth to his child.

In 'Offspring' (Aulaad), a harrowing tale about Zubeida, a middle-class woman, Manto explores the psychosocial violence inflicted on childless and infertile Zubeida. Although her husband is a devoted and generous man, it is her mother's questioning and imagined societal pressure that fuels her belief that she has failed to fulfil her role as a woman and casts a shadow on Zubeida's life.[57] The story also reveals how women are co-opted as the worst agents of patriarchy—a case of victims who become perpetrators.

In Manto's time, religious, social, and political institutions, custom and law, official and popular discourse converged to propagate a belief system that so-called upright, decent, and respectable men must regard wives strictly as breeding stock. For sexual and erotic pleasure, they were encouraged to seek elsewhere.

In more affluent Indian families, it was de rigueur for young men to visit courtesans for schooling in etiquette, a euphemism for erotic pleasures. At the top end were the courtesans, often granted land and property and precious jewels by their patrons—and many were among the highest taxpayers in several cities. Manto's sex workers are not from the higher echelons but rather the second, third, and even lower rungs of the profession, who charge from anything between a hundred rupees (for a private house) to fifty for a hotel room, and as little as ten or less for seedier joints. Considering that standard salaries and wages were not more than a hundred and fifty rupees a month, even ten rupees was a lavish outlay.

Furthermore, the colonial authorities considered the bazaars legitimate centres for the less wealthy, particularly libidinous soldiers. Pimps and prostitutes remained under a licensing regime and surveillance by civic authorities, who also provided clinics for sexually transmitted diseases for regular health check-ups for women in the trade.

---

[57]Manto, 'Offspring' (Aulaad), *Manto Kahaniyan*, pp. 455–60.

Saadat foregrounds the hypocrisy of the colonial authorities in 'Black Shalwar' (Kali Shalwar), a story he wrote in 1941 when living in Delhi and working at AIR, which was published in 1942, and in 'Smoke' (Dhuan), named after the first story in the collection. In 'Black Shalwar', Sultana moves from Ambala Cantonment to Delhi. She lives opposite the railway godowns in a flat reserved by the municipality for sex workers. Although exploited by Khuda Baksh, her pimp and partner, Sultana was happy in Ambala because he managed to get her a steady supply of gora soldiers as clients.[58] However, the move to Delhi draws Sultana into a sorry web of dual exploitation and betrayal after she meets Shankar.

Furthermore, Manto explored hypocrisy and transgression to reveal how laws, customs, and practices are challenged and violated, notwithstanding gatekeepers of society. The story 'Smoke' unfolds in a Muslim household and hints at shared sensual pleasure when a young and robust Kulsoom asks Masood, her adolescent brother, to massage her back and legs with his feet. One afternoon, when Masood walks into their shared bedroom, the story takes an unexpected turn with Kulsoom lying on her bed with her friend Bimla and staring at her bare breasts.

Not surprisingly, Saadat was charged for obscenity by the colonial authorities—with both the above-mentioned stories named in the summons. Nevertheless, in two accounts of his trial, Saadat recounts how the prosecution's focus was not on 'Smoke' but rather on 'Black Shalwar' and the poor light the narrative shed on colonial governance and the municipal authorities.[59]

MEN, WOMEN, SEXUALITY, AND VOYEURISM

Saadat's view of women is complex and contradictory. Like most male writers of his age, including his older European contemporaries, Bertolt Brecht (1898–1956), Jean-Paul Sartre (1905–80), and the Progressives, Manto often deploys the binary of the so-called respectable woman

---

[58] Saadat Hasan Manto, 'Kali Shalwar', *Manto kay Afsane*, Lahore: Sang-e-Meel Publications, 2018.
[59] Manto, 'Zehmat-e-Mehr-e-Darakhshan', *Manto Namah*, pp. 351–402; and 'White Lie' (Safed Jhoot), *Manto Namah*.

(mother, wife, and sister), and the 'respectable' harlot.

In Manto's everyday life, he witnessed how gendered violence was imbricated in an intersection of class entitlement, religious hypocrisy, colonialism, and nationalist politics. Bibijan and Balaji were the persons with whom he had his closest bonds from early childhood. He shared Bibijan's humiliation and grew up as her outraged and emasculated son.

Saadat understood what it meant to be a woman with no private income—and thus in economic bondage. He witnessed how his intellectually precocious sister Balaji remained tied in marriage to the obnoxious M. U. Khan because she too had no independent means or the luxury of an education to improve her life.

Invariably, Manto's women are cast in a sexual mould—as wives and potential wives, or harlots and actresses. The world in which Manto lived, men married women for their reproductive function, as breeding stock to propagate and raise a family, and to enhance a family's wealth. Like so many Manto characters, such as Babu Gopinath, Hamid, and Maqbool (in this volume), for erotic pleasure men turned to the world of the harlot where they expended and often lost their wealth.

Heterosexual marriage was the central institution to restrict a so-called decent (sharif) woman's sexuality. Religious, social, and political institutions, custom and law, official and popular discourse converged to propagate a belief system whereby sharif women were brainwashed from childhood by age-old ritual practices and narratives to construe sexual desire and agency as unnatural and taboo—even sinful. Their duty was to procreate, preferably sons, for their husbands and to strengthen the patriarchal family and ensure that ancestral property remains in the family.

Yet, in his writing, Saadat's sense of camaraderie with his wife comes across. Saadat shared his writing with Safia; and encouraged her to write—he ran errands for her and ironed her saris. In Bombay, their relationship withstood many strains, notwithstanding that Arif's tragic death precipitated Saadat's descent into alcoholism. The autobiographical turn in his writings reveals that he began to spend time in the company of sex workers—the extent of his pursuit is left to the imagination. In 'Mummy', in which both Saadat and Safia are present, he writes of Mummy's concern about the couple not having another child so many years after Arif's death.

Saadat's nephew Hamid Jalal writes that in family discussions, Manto always revealed himself as '...conservative and almost a reactionary on issues like women's education and mixed social gatherings.'[60] Indeed, in Bombay, there were no signs of Saadat expecting Safia to conform to social segregation. He wrote 'Mrs D'Costa' in the first person—in the sympathetic voice of a pregnant woman, who is Safia. In 'Mummy', Safia travelled with him to Poona and met his friends, but unsurprisingly, he kept her from his alcoholic binges

The gatekeepers of patriarchies, religious elders, and the government did not deny the existence of sexual desire and pleasure for men. On the contrary, they ensured that men could turn to the bazaar to find women to suit all tastes. Furthermore, families, society, the government, and the law looked away as libidinous men preyed upon women who worked as domestic helpers and cleaners in their homes or subordinate positions in offices and industries, including the film industry: women who resisted or complained could lose their livelihoods—and even their lives.

Additionally, although colonial and Indian bourgeois and other reformists decried pornography in their drawing rooms and the media, the elite and bourgeois certainly had access to blue films. In the story 'Women', watching blue movies elicits a bashful and hypocritical response, as both men and women watch them.

In Manto's stories, wives are often either domineering nags, such as the protagonist Mustaqeem's (whose name means righteous) wife in 'Mahmooda', or satirical and hapless creatures such as Mrs D'Costa and Mrs D'Silva. Wives with sexual agency, such as Zubeida in 'Suited Booted' (Kot Patlun), are temptresses or cast in a satirical mould like Izzat Jahan, an educated working woman. Marxist women come in for a fair bit of criticism. Perhaps, Hamid Jalal was right that Manto preferred his so-called 'respectable' women in the four walls of the home, the 'char divari'.

Even a sex worker such as Kuldip Kaur in 'Cold Flesh', who has an insatiable libido and sexual agency, is a murderous psychopath. She

---

[60]Hamid Jalal, 1997.

is not unlike the vamp in the film *Fatal Attraction* (dir. Adrian Lyne, 1987). It is worth commenting that almost forty years apart, in both narratives, the men are rescued and redeemed. Ishar Singh is almost sanctified with redemptive humanism in death. In *Fatal Attraction*, the faithful wife saves her unfaithful husband and marriage—in an act of vigilantism, she murders the violent interloper. Significantly, in Pakistan, when Manto wrote of erotic pleasure between two married couples from different social class backgrounds in *Top, Bottom, and Middle*, he was charged for obscenity and found guilty.

Manto rages against the commodification of human relations. In 'Babu Gopinath', the protagonist informs Manto that he likes to hang out at shrines and brothels, although he knows that in the former human beings barter their faith, and in the latter, parents trade their offspring. Manto has sympathy for sex workers, harlots, and street walkers. Saugandhi in 'Humiliation', Sarita in 'Ten Rupees', and Gungu Bai in 'Loser', are not mere sex objects compelled to sell their bodies (usually to bourgeois men from different walks of life), but nuanced human beings trapped in their profession. They seek agency and dignity.

Manto's stories compel a confrontation with questions of homophobia, the boundaries between pornography, obscenity, erotica, literary realism, and voyeurism. Saadat's matter of fact descriptions of two women making love in 'Smoke' implies a non-judgmental acceptance of same sex love. Nevertheless, in 'Mummy', Sen, a music director lures Ram Singh with promises to make him a singer. But when Sen does not keep his word Ram Singh murders him.

In 'Mummy', Manto's heroine, Mrs Stella Jackson advises Ram Singh to tell the truth at his trial. She continues, 'Without a doubt your hands are covered in blood, but it is the blood of something unclean and unnatural.' Ram Singh's testimony is accepted; and his acquittal is celebrated. Arguably, Manto is writing about different attitudes towards same sex love, since in the first instance ('Smoke') he is observing an act, while in the second ('Mummy'), he is reporting words spoken by Mummy—but she is an admired protagonist.

In his stories and essays, the woman who has to deal with a fair bit of misogyny and mockery is the actress. Included in this volume are three stories that illustrate this point. 'Latika Rani' is a searing onslaught on this figure—Manto has no sympathy for Latika, in a not particularly disguised description of Devika Rani. Nevertheless, 'My Name is Radha' is a complex story about female sexual desire, and Saadat has affection for his protagonist. While he writes with tragic irony of Paro Devi in 'Scissors from Meerut', all three stories satirize and lampoon women professionals in the studio. His essays on Naseem Bano and Noor Jehan bring into sharp focus the binary of the respectable wife on the one hand, and the harlot and actress on the other.

Manto accepted the charge of voyeurism and brushed it off lightly.

> People raise objections that modern writers focus on sexual relations between men and women. I cannot speak for everyone but can say this about myself—I am drawn to these matters... Just accept that I have a *perversion*... If you are unfamiliar with our times, then read my short stories. If you find my stories unbearable, it means our times are unbearable.

Bombay
February 1947

In the story, 'Suited Booted', Nazim is the ultimate voyeur, a peeping Tom who looks at his neighbour Zubeida through a hole in the bathroom door. Yet, in a misogynistic turn, it is Zubeida who invites his gaze. In 'Majeed's Past' (Majid ka Maazi) Majeed recalls his nightly visits to Miss Leena, his Jewish neighbour, sipping tea as he catches glimpses of her daughters Helen's and Esther's pubescent breasts, which remind him of small peaches. In the same story, Majeed recalls how he liked to sit on a bench at a railway platform to gaze up the skirts of Christian and Jewish girls. Today, the practice is referred to as 'upskirting' and, in some countries, is an offence.

Perhaps, Saadat's most controversial story is 'Scent', for which he was charged with obscenity. Set in Bombay, the entire story is told from the point of view of Randhir, a young professional, who is not sexually aroused by his fair, educated, and appealing young bride on their wedding night. Instead, his thoughts go back to a chance encounter with a Ghatan (a young tribal from the Western Ghats).

Sarah Waheed, in her insightful essay on 'Scent', writes that in her reading, 'the sexual desires of men, especially men of privilege, are as structured by misogyny as they are manufactured out of political convenience.'[61]

Certainly, for Randhir women are objects of sexual desire and are replaceable. He is upset that he does not have access to hoity-toity Hazel and is denied access to other Anglo-Indian girls, because he is not a white soldier. Moreover, Randhir's preference for the dark skinned Ghatan resonates with the romanticized bourgeois vision of tribal people, and, at the same time, is a repudiation of the racist privileging of white skin.

Not surprisingly, Manto was criticized by Sajjad Zaheer, a leading member of the Communist Party as well as the PWM, who described the story as 'the portrayal of the sexual perversion of a self-indulgent member of the middle-class, however realistic, is a waste of time of both writers as well as readers.'[62]

Whereas Saadat's friend Ismat Chughtai found that, 'In "Bu" there is only the body at first reading, but if you examine the story carefully you will find a soul inside the body: the soured, unsavoury soul of the rich, pleasure-seeking classes, and the unpretentious reality of the down-trodden class.'[63]

In 1946, Manto and his friend Ismat Chughtai drew the ire of the colonial government and self-appointed arbiters of morality: Ismat for her short story, 'Lihaf', and Manto for 'Dhuan', and 'Bu' published in the monthly *Adab-i Latif* under the aegis of Ahmed Nadeem Qasmi, a Progressive writer. They were arrested without warrant in Bombay. In February 1947, while still in Bombay, Manto wrote an account of his trial for obscenity (for 'Bu') in colonial Lahore.

Manto's harshest condemnation of bourgeois hypocrisy comes across with his heroic pimps—men such as Khushya and Sahai, both protagonists in stories of the same names. They are romanticized, generous, and sympathetic players in a market where they make a living, and are fair in their dealings with the women whose bodies they sell. Some are positively heroic like Thalia in 'An Episode from 1919'. And there is Sahai, with whose spirit Mumtaz (the narrator) wishes to commune forever, as he stands on the deck of the ship

---

[61]Sarah Waheed, 'Anatomy of an obscenity trial', *Himal Southasian*, 1 July 2013.
[62]Ibid.
[63]Ibid.

leaving for Pakistan with his friends who have come to see him off, in a thinly disguised autobiographical account of Saadat's last days in Bombay, and his farewell to the city he loved.

THE ALLURE OF THE CINEMA AND THE SEA

In 1936, Nazir Ludhianvi, a Bombay based publisher, invited Saadat to take over as editor of *Mussavir*. Saadat accepted Ludhianvi's invitation, and though he admonished himself in later years, left Bibijan on her own and set off for Bombay. He left Amritsar forever, only to return for a few brief visits to the house in Lawyers' Lane. Kucha-i-Vakilan and the Manto house in Amritsar were burnt down in the 1947 communal bloodbath in which Muslims and their properties were attacked.

Saadat Hasan Manto arrived in Bombay in 1936, where he lived until 1948, but for a spell in New Delhi between 1941 and 1943. Manto was happiest in this mesmeric and ghastly metropolis by the sea and described himself as 'Bombay in motion' (Chalta phirta Bambai). Manto's Bombay stories (in this collection) and his essays evoke multi-sensory encounters with the city, which breathes and comes alive through night and day—its sights, smells, sounds, textures, and people are palpable; it is sleazy and murky, rank with the stench of bodily fluids and effluence. Men, women, and children of different ethnicities, faiths, and no faith, speaking countless languages, and a distinctive Bombay lingo, pimps, and prostitutes, nawabs and housekeepers, Marxists and industrialists, beggars and hawkers live cheek by jowl with film stars, bedbugs, rats, and cats.

Like countless others, it was the allure of the cinema which drew Manto to Bombay. His life and writings are constitutive parts of the histories of Indian, Pakistani, regional, and world cinemas. He joined the international modernist literary avant-garde of writers and poets such as T. S. Eliot, Virginia Woolf, and James Joyce, who wove the cinema into their works.[64] Saadat read and relished world literature, particularly James Joyce, with whom he shared, perhaps to his gratification, the irksome experience of being charged for obscenity.

A film critic with a keen understanding of the cinema, Saadat

---

[64]David Trotter, *Cinema and Modernism*, Oxford: Blackwell, 2007.

had watched much of world cinema, particularly in the silent era when American, British, French, and Russian films (among others) were screened widely in India, with intertitles in local languages. Yet, ironically, a man who dismissed Indian cinema as a mere pastiche of Hollywood spent eleven years of his life working for a film industry for which he had little regard.[65] He did this along with many other poets and writers, often to subsidize his more literary work.[66] Saadat's friend Krishan Chandar has described the level-headed manner in which his friend Manto was willing to make significant changes to characters, storylines, and dialogue to indulge the whims of his producers. Saadat told Krishan Chandar:

> My friend, this is not literature but the cinema, with intelligent, educated literary connoisseurs, such as Maulana Salahuddin, Kaleemullah, or Hamid Ali Khan at the helm. So, feel free to change a mother into a sister, a sister into a lover, and a lover into a vamp in a film. Serve literature and earn money from films.[67]

Krishan Chandar adds that he was referring to a man who did not allow his publishers to edit a word of his writing or change the punctuation.[68]

Saadat worked as a film critic and editor of a film magazine but most importantly, he was of the industry. Immediately upon his arrival, Manto took over the editorship of *Mussavir*, and for this arduous task, Nazir Ludhianvi, the proprietor, paid him a paltry sixty rupees a month. Saadat slept in the office, and for this favour, Ludhianvi deducted two rupees from his salary. Nevertheless, his parsimonious employer introduced Saadat to the Imperial Film Company, where he was employed as a munshi or writer of screenplays and dialogue—after which Ludhianvi cut Saadat's salary by half.

Owned by Ardeshir Irani, Imperial had produced *Alam Ara*, the first Indian talkie, in 1931.[69] Irani wished to produce the first 'technicolour'

---

[65] 'Hindustan ki sannat-e-filmsazi' (India's Film Industry), *Manto Numa*, pp. 596–613.
[66] Shaukat Kaifi, *Kaifi and I*. In a memoir of her life with Kaifi Azmi, the communist poet and lyricist, Shaukat describes with an air of acceptance the family's budgetary challenges, mainly because producers did not pay Kaifi on time.
[67] Krishan Chandar, 'Saadat Hasan Manto', *Manto Mera Dost, Mera Dushman*.
[68] Ibid.
[69] *Alam Ara* (dir. Ardeshir Irani, 1931).

film, *Kisan Kanya*, for which Manto, who was a complete unknown, wrote the screenplay.[70] In an attempt to appease financiers, the name in the credits was of Professor Zia-ud din, who was complicit in the deception. The film was released in 1937 and was a box-office flop. Nevertheless, Manto's reputation was not particularly tarnished by the event, perhaps, because his name did not appear in the credits.

As a munshi writing screenplays and dialogue, Saadat was employed by well-known Bombay studios such as Imperial Film Company, Saroj Movietone, Filmistan, and Bombay Talkies. Besides, Manto was a friend of several stars, directors, technicians, and other journalists. He travelled between Bombay and Poona, and his stories 'Mummy' and 'Janki' provide rare insights into the film industry in Poona. Between 1937–48, Saadat penned the screenplays for nine films, of which all, other than *Kisan Kanya*, had varying degrees of success at the box office. They include *Apni Nagariya* aka *Mud* (dir. Gunjal, 1940); *Naukar* (dir. Shaukat Hussain Rizvi, 1943); *Chal Chal re Naujawan* (dir. Gyan Mukherjee, 1944); *Begum* (dir. Sushil Mazumdar, 1945); *Shikari* (dir. Savak Vacha, 1946); *Jhumke* (dir. J. K. Nanda, 1946), a Lahore production; *Ath Din* aka Eight Days (dir. D. N. Pai and Ashok Kumar, 1946), in which he even faced the camera.

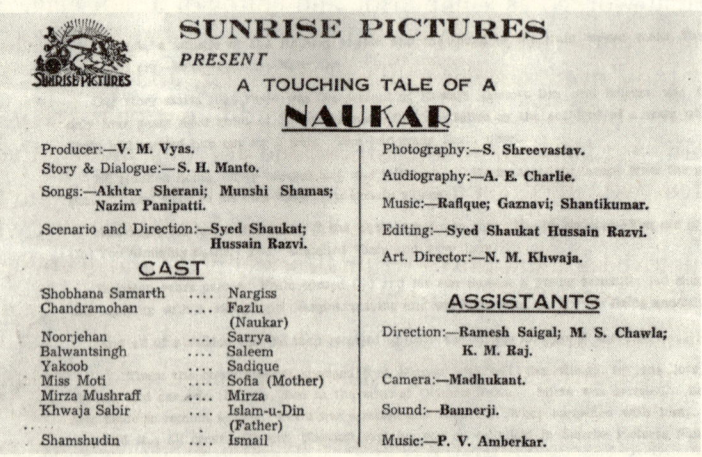

Credits from booklet of *Naukar* (dir. Shaukat Hussain Rizvi, 1943). Rafiq Ghaznavi appears as Shafiq Toosi in 'Babu Gopinath'.

---

[70] *Kisan Kanya* (dir. Moti B Gidwani, 1937).

In 1954, Sohrab Modi released *Mirza Ghalib* (dir. Sohrab Modi, 1954). The story was by Manto, based on his sketch, 'Ghalib and Chaudhvin' (Ghalib aur Chaudhveen).[71] The screenplay was by J. K. Nanda, who had directed Saadat's story, *Jhumke* in Lahore in 1946, with the dialogue by his friend Rajinder Singh Bedi. Although nominated for the award in Manto's lifetime, in 1955, the film won India's National Film Award for the best feature film—but after Manto's death. Undoubtedly, Manto would have been pleased but would have had something to say about the ironic turn of events, whereby a film on the life of his beloved Ghalib, the most renowned Urdu poet of all times, received a silver medal for the best Hindi language film.

After his move to Pakistan, Saadat found an almost non-existent film industry, and invested whatever little money he had in *Beli*, his nephew, Masood Parvez's first directorial venture. Released in 1950, *Beli* starred Shahina, the daughter of Saadat's friend Raffique Ghaznavi, and Anwari.[72] It was also the debut of Pakistan's rising star duo, Sabiha and Santosh, with the songs and score composed by the acclaimed composer Rasheed Attre. Yet, it flopped at the box office. However, Saadat's faith in his nephew was not entirely misplaced; Parvez became a very successful Urdu and Punjabi film director with a string of super hits such as *Intezar* (1956), *Koel* (1959), and *Heer Ranjha* (1970). Nevertheless, *Beli*'s flop left Saadat penniless.

Apart from his short stories, Manto wrote several critical essays on Indian and Pakistani cinema. After his move to Lahore, he published a collection of essays on film personalities, that apart from being a delightful read, remain an invaluable primary source for film scholars.[73] Saadat continued to write short stories centred on the cinema, where the action takes place in Bombay, Poona, and post-independence Lahore.

In 'True Love' (Ishq-e-Haqiqi), a powerful story about the complex allure of the cinema, Saadat deploys two conceits. First, he turns to Sufi mysticism and calls his story 'Ishq-e-Haqiqi', a term used for

---

[71] Manto, 'Ghalib aur Chaudhveen', *Manto Namah*, pp. 504–12.
[72] See also, 'Babu Gopinath' for a discussion on Raffique Ghaznavi, who appears as Toosi.
[73] Saadat Hasan Manto, *Stars from Another Sky: The Bombay Film World in the 1940s*, trans. Khalid Hasan, New Delhi: Penguin Books, 1998.

divine love or the truth, usually hidden (mahjoob). In the second, he juxtaposes the practice of purdah (where women are hidden from the male gaze) and the cinema screen, called screen of illusion (purdaah-i-seemeen) in Urdu.

The story begins with Ashfaq, the protagonist in love with Ingrid Bergman and watching *For Whom the Bell Tolls* for the umpteenth time.[74] In the auditorium, he falls in love with a purdah-observing woman sitting next to him, her face covered with a niqab. After the movie, Ashfaq follows the woman and manages to speak to her. An epistolary love affair begins, followed by an elopement. Like many of Manto's stories, 'True Love' has an unexpected end.

Another such story is 'In the Name of Allah' (Bismillah), the opening words of the Qur'an, which Muslims use before they begin any activity. Manto's protagonist is a young girl called Bismillah, a not uncommon name for girls and boys, almost invariably among South Asian Muslim families. Saadat explores a nascent film industry in a new nation and merges the gruesome realities of the casting couch with the abduction and recovery of women across the religious divide during and after Partition.

In Saadat's writings, the sea remains an alluring presence: his characters gaze at its endless vista and relish the salt breeze, alone or with friends, feeling the sand beneath their bodies and feet at Juhu beach. Some sit on a small promontory at Mahim with a woman, while others ogle strangers and passers-by promenade by the sea at the Gateway of India and Apollo Bandar. Yet others listen to the lapping of waves as they sit by the quayside outside Parisienne Bakery and observe hookers and bobbing sails. In several stories, Bombay appears as a character bejewelled in nightlights, glittering in the Arabian Sea.

In other stories, the sea and the birds soaring high allow him to decentre human subjectivity as he tries to make sense of events and the world around him. In 'Sahai', as Mumtaz bids farewell to his friends and his beloved city, in the wake of murderous communal riots, the sight of the sky and the sea merging into each other in the

---

[74] *For Whom the Bell Tolls* (dir. Sam Wood, 1943) based on Ernest Hemingway's novel of the same name.

distant horizon gives him hope for his vision for the human condition and a rapprochement between Hindus and Muslims.

MARRIAGE

In Bombay, the affable and outgoing Bibijan, struck up a friendship with Mairaj Begum Qamar-ud Deen, another widow, who lived in Mahim, around the corner from her, and was of Kashmiri extraction. The late Khwajah Qamar-ud Deen was a public prosecutor in the service of the Crown in Zanzibar. A Kashmiri with a fair complexion, Khwajah Sahib, was mistaken for an Englishman and killed by locals during a riot.[75]

After her husband's death, Begum Qamar-ud Deen received a comfortable pension from the Crown. She moved to Bombay with six of her seven offspring, where she set about to ensure that her three sons qualified as bourgeois professionals and her three daughters found suitable husbands. Finally, the two widows arranged a match between Saadat and Safia, Begum Qamar-ud Deen's eldest daughter.[76]

When Saadat and Bibijan arrived to meet Safia's family, they were greeted at the door by her cousin Malik Hasan, a fingerprint expert. Bibijan was ushered to the zenana, and Malik Sahib made Saadat feel at home and proceeded to regale him with stories about his love of horseracing, bridge, and crosswords. Saadat did not pretend to be wealthy, but Bibijan lived around the corner from the Deens, who had met his brothers in East Africa. Safia's family assessed the Mantos as Kashmiri bourgeois professionals, and as for Saadat, there was an allure of the cinema attached to him.

With two younger unmarried daughters, Begum Qamar-ud Deen was keen to get Safia married—she was twenty-two, and at the time, in danger of being considered on the shelf. So Saadat and Safia were married on 26 April 1939. It was a marriage between the offspring of two Kashmiri families. Apart from their Kashmiriyat and the fact that both were bespectacled, Saadat and Safia shared a birthday. Like

---

[75]Khwajah Zaheer-ud Deen, *The Memoirs of an Architect*, Lahore: Z. D. Khwaja, 1998.
[76]Safia Manto had two younger sisters, Rafia and Zakia; and five brothers: Khwaja Basheer-ud Deen (a teacher and business man), Khwajah Naseer-ud Deen (a barrister), Khwaja Zaheer-ud Deen (an architect and town planner), Khwaja Muneer-ud Deen (an engineer).

Saadat, Safia was born on 11 May, but in 1917 in Zanzibar. And they spoke to each other in Punjabi. Bibijan moved in with them.

Saadat has written that he informed Safia's family of his taste for 'a beer' every evening. Malik Hasan did not detect that Saadat's relationship with alcohol, even at the time, bordered on the addictive. Safia grew up in a family where the men around her were gainfully employed, qualified professionals. She had no idea that life with Saadat would be a challenge.

Yet, there is plenty of evidence that points to her family's affection for Saadat. In his memoir, Safia's brother, Zaheer-ud Deen Khwaja, writes with admiration of Bhai Saadat's erudition and knowledge of European literature. He mentions a generous gift of a set of short stories from around the world, made to him by his brother-in-law. Zaheer-ud Deen Sahib describes Manto's vast personal library, which sadly he had to abandon in 1948. He corroborates that Manto was earning good money from his work in the cinema and records his encounters with stars and visits to film studios, courtesy his brother-in-law.[77] The Qamar-ud Deen family and the Manto family strengthened their ties with the subsequent marriages of Safia's sisters, Rafia and Zakia, to Waheed and Hamid Jalal, respectively, the sons of Saadat's half-sister.

Indeed, Saadat's work in the cinema supported his family. He had published to critical acclaim a collection of twenty-two short stories, *Manto ke Afsane*—many are included in this volume.[78] The same year, he wrote the screenplay for *Apni Nagariya* (dir. Gunjal, 1940), a reformist tale about the evils of class exploitation, which became a box-office hit.

On 28 May 1940, Safia and Saadat's son was born, and they named him Arif. Saadat fussed over Arif and cossetted him—and gave him the love he did not receive from his father. Saadat had joined his friends Rajinder Singh Bedi (1915–84), Krishan Chandar (1914–77), and Ismat Chughtai (1915–91), among the top literary stylists in the world of twentieth-century Urdu and Indian fiction. He was courted by leading literary journals. Bibijan had arranged

---
[77]Ibid.
[78]'Khushya', 'Barren', 'Mantra', 'Outcry', 'Blouse', 'Humiliation', 'Ten Rupees', and 'Mrs D'Costa'.

Saadat's marriage; she witnessed his success as a writer. She lived to see her grandson but died a sudden death a month later—almost as though she thought her life's work done. Saadat fainted when he heard the news.

The same year, for unknown reasons, Nazir Ludhianvi fired Saadat. With a wife and child to look after and studios notoriously irregular at paying employees, Saadat went to see Baburao Patel, the influential and mercurial publisher and editor of *FilmIndia*, who immediately offered Manto a job in his Urdu weekly, *Karvan* (Caravan).[79]

In 1941, Manto went to Delhi to join AIR's Urdu drama department. Krishan Chandar recalls receiving a letter from Saadat to ask if he could stay with him for a few days. They had an ongoing correspondence but had never met.

Saadat left Safia and Arif in Bombay and travelled by train to Delhi, where his old Amritsari friends, Abu Saeed and Hassan Abbas, met him at the railway station. Saadat was Krishan Chandar's guest for a few weeks, and the host describes his guest as a slim man of medium height, with unusually large prominent eyes, and a fair complexion. He describes Saadat as a man always attired in impeccable white kurta pyjama, who insisted on neat and clean surroundings. With a steady government job on a fixed salary, Saadat soon found suitable accommodation, and Safia and Arif joined him. The Manto family lived a comfortable life in Delhi.

Saadat immersed himself in writing radio plays and short stories and spent his evenings drinking at Bhola Ram's bar with old friends from Amritsar, including Faiz Ahmed Faiz and Chiragh Hasan Hasrat.[80] Krishan Chandar has written of two years full of conversations and debates, which come across as landmarks in the history of broadcasting and modern Urdu literature. The AIR contingent included Rajinder Singh Bedi, N. M. Rashid, Ahmad Nadim Qasmi, Upendranath Ashk, and Devendra Satyarthi.

Some attribute Saadat's move back to Bombay to the departure of his friend Krishan Chandar and Upendranath Ashk's appointment as an adviser on drama.[81] Many remember Ashk as an abrasive

---

[79]Manto, 'Baburao Patel', *Manto Numa*, pp. 210–23.
[80]Manto, 'Chiragh Hasan Hasrat', *Manto Namah*.
[81]Ibid.

personality.⁸² Krishan Chandar describes how Manto wrote his early radio plays on his Urdu typewriter, and upon seeing this, Ashk promptly bought two typewriters—one for English and another for Hindi. Saadat promptly bought an English typewriter, which prompted Ashk to invest in an Urdu typewriter. When Saadat saw Ashk walk into the radio station with a peon carrying three typewriters, he stopped using a typewriter and went back to using his Sheaffer and Parker fountain pens and fine pencils.

Saadat and Safia were happy in Delhi, but Arif was suddenly struck down with a high temperature and seizures. He died soon after on 28 April 1941, one month before his first birthday. His death cast a dark shadow over Saadat and Safia's lives.⁸³ A small measure of Saadat's grief is palpable in 'Khalid Miyan'—a story written, perhaps, as a balm for the pain of abiding loss.⁸⁴ According to their daughters, Nuzhat and Nusrat, Safia never talked about the death of her son.⁸⁵ Nusrat, their youngest, believes that 'Abbajan never recovered from Arif's death.'⁸⁶ While Nuzhat, their second daughter, thinks that Arif's death was the cause of Manto's chronic depression.⁸⁷

Krishan Chandar has written how Saadat sobbed inconsolably at Arif's death; he considered this a defining tragedy in Manto's life. He believed that Saadat confronted losing Arif like a diver who delves into the inner depths of an ocean to recover a pearl; that his encounter with pain gave him a special insight into the pain of others.⁸⁸ It seems that Saadat did not discuss the pain of losing Arif even with Safia, and much to her chagrin, he left Delhi and his secure job at AIR. Moreover, the hostility between Saadat and Ashk, and also his squabbles with Satyarthi (referred to by Krishan Chandar), could not have made life easier for Saadat, and he left Delhi to move back to Bombay and his unpredictable life with the cinema in 1943. In her essay on Saadat, 'Manto, My Friend, My Enemy' (Manto, Mera Dost, Mera Dushman), his friend Ismat Chughtai recalls Saadat telling her

---

⁸²Upendranath Ashk, *Manto Mera Dushman*.
⁸³Manto, 'Mummy', *Manto Namah*, pp. 179–220.
⁸⁴Manto, 'Khalid Miyan', *Manto Namah*, pp. 72–81.
⁸⁵Nusrat Manto: email correspondence.
⁸⁶Ibid.
⁸⁷Conversation with Nuzhat Manto, Lahore, June 2019.
⁸⁸Krishan Chandar (2012).

that if he ever loved anyone, it was Arif.[89]

Bibijan's unexpected and Arif's untimely death cast a shadow on Saadat's life. In 'Mummy', a story written in Pakistan but located in Bombay and Poona of the 1940s, Manto has hinted of problems in his and Safia's conjugal relations. Their marital squabbles come alive in stories such as 'Green Sandals'.

On his return to Bombay, Saadat went back to work with Nazir Ludhianvi, who missed Manto's flair as an editor. In the following four years, Saadat published two and completed another collection of short stories and scripted six successful films—three, in 1946, the year his daughter Nighat was born. The same year Saadat purchased a life insurance policy with the Oriental Government Life Insurance Company Ltd.

Yet again, he revealed himself as a pragmatist, who settled for less than half the sums owed to him by Ardeshir Irani and Nanubhai Desai; and the screenplay and dialogue writer who most willingly changed his scripts to suit the whims of financiers.

MIRZA GHALIB AND MANTO

Arif's death and Saadat's move from Delhi, seemingly on a whim, draw attention to Saadat's affinity with the humanist poet Mirza Asadullah Khan Ghalib (1797–1869). The tragic irony of naming his son Arif and his death in Ghalib's city could not have been lost on Saadat. Ghalib, who spent a significant part of his life in Delhi, had several children, but none survived infancy. So instead, he adopted his nephew, Arif, whom he loved dearly. Arif died an early death, and a grief-stricken Ghalib composed a ghazal, known to Urdu poetry enthusiasts as 'Marsiya-e-Arif' (Arif's Elegy).[90]

There are other comparisons between Manto and the great poet, who lived in nineteenth-century metropolitan Delhi and raged against the religious establishment's hypocrisy. In his loathing of posturing and piety, Manto was not unlike Ghalib. And not unlike Manto, Ghalib, too, manoeuvred a tripartite balance between a lack of funds

---

[89]Chughtai, *Manto, Mera Dost, Mera Dushman*.
[90]Ralph Russell and Khurshid-ul Islam (trans. and ed.) *Ghalib: Life & Letters*, New Delhi: Oxford University Press, 1994.

to run his household, a sense of noblesse oblige, and his love of good whisky throughout his life.

After the rebellion of 1857, as a nominally free India became part of the British empire, Ghalib witnessed the political, military, economic, social, and cultural collapse of the Mughals and their other Indian allies—both Hindu and Muslim. It was the death of an entire way of life as the British relentlessly massacred Hindu and Muslim Indians. Ghalib's poetry and letters are full of descriptions of blood and gore and Delhi in flames.[91] A decade short of a century later, Manto witnessed and captured in his writing how Hindus, Muslims, and Sikhs massacred each other after the British looted, pillaged, divided, and quit India.[92]

Stylistically, Manto's prose has the same ring of the spontaneity of everyday Urdu conversation found in Ghalib's letters.[93] But, of course, the prose is distinguished by their times and the linguistic milieus to which they belonged. Manto's Urdu is from a distinctly modern urban bourgeois Punjabi milieu. Yet, he was a master at capturing local idioms: his characters speak distinct variations of Urdu/Hindustani, inflected with local diction, such as Venkat Atre with his Marathi usage in 'Mummy',[94] or the chaste Urdu spoken by Nawab Salimullah and Mrs Lovejoy.

Just as Ghalib was aware of his genius and singular style (andaz-e-bayan) and set new benchmarks for the Urdu ghazal, Saadat knew his measure as a writer of short stories, and wrote his epitaph:

> Here lies Saadat Hasan Manto, and with him are buried the secrets of short story writing. Under mounds of earth, he continues to wonder if he or God is the more extraordinary storyteller.

Balaji edited it—she feared that bigots might deface Saadat's tombstone or worse. Yet, in comparing himself with God, Saadat asked the age-old question about the relationship between art and life—perhaps, playing with the aphorism that truth is stranger than fiction.

---

[91] Ibid.
[92] Penderel Moon, *Divide and Quit*, Oxford: Oxford University Press, 1998.
[93] Russell and Islam, *Ghalib: Life & Letters*.
[94] Manto, 'Mummy', *Manto Namah*, pp. 179–220.

Others have commented and written about Ghalib and Manto. Most notably, in 2012, Arunava Sinha's *Conversations in Hell* translation of Rabisankar Bal's Bengali novel *Dozakhnama* came to the attention of an English readership. Rabisankar sets up an audacious and engaging conversation beyond the grave between the two masters on matters of mutual interest.[95]

PRELUDE TO DARKNESS

As the British fast-forwarded Independence and Partition to 1947, gruesome violence broke out across India, most horrifically in Bengal and Punjab. Still, violence in Bombay was no less chilling.[96] There was a family wedding in Lahore, and Safia and Saadat thought it sensible for her and Nighat to travel to Pakistan. So, while Saadat decided to wait it out in Bombay, his wife and daughter joined other family members and travelled by sea to Karachi, where they took a train to Lahore.[97]

Saadat was not a nationalist. His rejection of Hindu and Muslim nationalism and religious communalism and violence is powerfully summed up in 'The Privy' (Mootri). At the unforgettable end of the story 'Mozelle', a romance between a Jewish woman and Trilochan, a turbaned Sikh, Mozelle tells Trilochan, 'Take this away, this religion of yours.' Yet, Saadat decided to leave for Pakistan, a country that came into existence specifically for the Muslims of South Asia.

Partition narratives often focus on the partition of Punjab and Bengal. Saadat has written searing accounts of this historic moment in stories such as 'Cold Flesh', 'The Drawstring', and 'Toba Tek Singh'. Additionally, several essays, particularly on his friends Shyam and Ashok Kumar, and some of his Bombay stories reveal the dark underbelly of religious communalism in the beloved city where he spent the happiest years of his life.

In his story 'Ram Khelawan' Saadat writes how his genial, honest and honourable dhobi almost kills him after being brainwashed into

---

[95] Rabisankar Bal, *Dozakhnama*, trans. Arunava Sinha, Gurugram: Vintage Books, Random House, India, 2012.
[96] Moon, *Divide and Quit*.
[97] Nusrat Manto.

a frenzy fuelled by a free supply of alcohol and communal speeches delivered by politicians and gangs brought in from other areas.[98] Finally, 'Sahai' is a fictionalized autobiographical account of Saadat's emotions in the aftermath of Independence and Partition, and his views on communitarian identity politics and violence. This is his account of the ultimate blow that prompted him to leave India.[99]

In 1948, the year that Saadat left Bombay for Lahore, the most significant film personalities to migrate to Pakistan included the non pareil Noor Jehan (1926–2000), who by then was a household name, and a successful actor/singer, elevated from Baby Noor Jehan to Melody Queen (Malika-i Tarranum). Her husband, the successful film director Shaukat Hussain Rizvi, travelled with her by sea.

In 2001, in a telephone conversation, when asked to comment on Noor Jehan's departure for Pakistan, her friend Lata Mangeshkar, the greatest playback singer of all times, said, 'They had to leave. They had little choice. Matters got very bad for them.'[100] The *Times of India* and *FilmIndia* archives for 1947 attest to a nationwide uproar with communal overtones, orchestrated and led by Baburao Patel and members of the Hindu Mahasabha, against Rizvi's film *Jugnu*, starring Noor Jehan and Dilip Kumar.

*Jugnu* was declared obscene: allegedly for showing Indian youth, particularly students, in a poor light. At the heart of the matter was a scene in which a group of male and female students play a game with an orange tucked under their chins, which then has to be transferred without the use of hands to another member of the team. On the face of it, an innocuous matter. What proved incendiary was the fact that Jugnu, the protagonist played by Noor Jehan, was a Hindu girl, and the actress and director Shaukat Hussain Rizvi were Muslims. As a result, the film was sent back to the censors and re-released after several thousand feet of film were cut. Nevertheless, this did not stop Baburao's vitriolic campaign against Rizvi and Noor Jehan, whom he had praised in the past. Baburao turned more communal and poisonous by the day, and ultimately, the government banned *FilmIndia* in the 1960s.

---

[98] Manto, 'Ram Khelawan', *Manto Rama*, pp. 36–44.
[99] Manto, 'Sahai', *Manto Rama*, pp. 20–27.
[100] Telephone interview. Courtesy Javed Akhtar, 2001.

Furthermore, conversations with P. K. Nair Sahib (1933–2016) confirmed the communal atmosphere in Bombay during Independence. The founding director of the National Film Archive of India in 1964, Nair Sahib shared his encyclopaedic knowledge with boundless generosity. On hearing Lataji's remarks about Noor Jehan and Rizvi, and what the *Times of India* and *FilmIndia* archives revealed, he recalled:

> There were angry rumours about the Muslim directors and producers like Mehboob Khan and Kardar, who were making frequent trips to check the lie of the land in the other place. Finally, they decided to stay in India. Still, for many Muslims in the industry, the burning down of the studio of the producer Shiraz Ali Hakim was a signal that they should leave India.[101]

The actor Nazir joined Rizvi and Noor Jehan, as did Ghulam Haider (1908–53) 'Masterji' as his three famous protégés reverentially referred to him. Haider had introduced Shamshad Begum (1919–2013) as a playback singer to the film industry in Lahore in the late 1930s. He auditioned and recruited Noor Jehan into Pancholi's studio in 1937 in Lahore, where she rose to fame as a singing star before moving to Bombay in 1943. Ghulam Haider also recruited Lata Mangeshkar as a playback singer in Bombay. The grande dame of playback singers never failed to touch her ears and click her tongue as a mark of respect when she mentioned 'Masterji'.

In 1947, Saadat had joined Ashok Kumar and Savak Vacha in the newly configured post-Himanshu Rai Bombay Talkies. Hindu members of the studio accused Vacha and Ashok Kumar (the management) of recruiting Muslims with Manto's help and threatened to burn the studio if they did not redress the balance and get rid of Muslims. Not unreasonably, Saadat felt that his friends shared these stories with him because they wanted convey a message.

---

[101]Conversation with P. K. Nair, Pune, 2001.

In her essay, written after Saadat's death, Ismat Chughtai upbraided him for not saying goodbye.[102] She did not forgive him for choosing Pakistan and made no allowances for a possibility that either fear of what might happen if he stayed on or simply an inability to face the heartbreak of leaving Bombay made him slink away. And perhaps, what was most difficult for Ismat to accept was that Saadat, who was no nationalist, accepted the existence of Pakistan. She believed in the secularism espoused by the Congress Party.

Strangely, secular India's Constitution, passed by the Constituent Assembly in November 1949 and adopted on 26 January 1950, designated a substantial part of India's population as religious minorities: Buddhist, Christian, Jain, Muslim, Parsi, and Sikh. Arguably, after the Constitution was adopted, India became a secular state with a Hindu majority, and special protection for minorities. But in a bizarre step for a secular state, all religious groups could retain their personal laws, some of which were in contradiction of the fundamental rights and equality guaranteed by the Constitution—mainly when it came to women's rights of inheritance, divorce, and evidence.

From his essay 'My Sahib', included here, it seems that Manto admired Jinnah. Nevertheless, it is equally clear that he had no delusions about Pakistan and was critical of state policy and the dangers of rising religious obscurantism. Although he was not a nationalist, he accepted his lot as a Pakistani and celebrated national holidays with his daughters.

The only identity that Manto claims time and again is that of a Kashmiri. After Independence and his move to Pakistan, Manto wrote an open letter to Pandit Nehru, as one Kashmiri Pandit to another. He published this as the introduction to his 'Untitled' novel.[103] Forever aware of the tangled web of history, Manto points to the (unresolved) centrality of the Kashmir issue and the water dispute, as a hindrance to peaceful relations between India and Pakistan.

---

[102]Chughtai, *Manto, Mera Dost, Mera Dushman*.
[103]Manto, 'Untitled' (Beghair Unvan), 'Introduction' (Dibacha), *Manto Baqiyat*, pp. 411–16.

> I admire you as a great politician because you excel in going back on your statements.... I am astonished to hear that you are stopping the water of our rivers.[104]

Since 1947 in India, from time to time, subterranean lava has continued to erupt from volcanoes of communal hatred, mainly with Hindu mobs destroying the livelihoods and lives of Christians and Muslims. Usually, constitutional guarantees and courts stepped up to protect minorities. Nevertheless, since the late 1980s, with the movement to demolish the Babri Masjid, India's secular fabric has been under attack.

Since 2014, the Indian state has purposefully moved towards consolidating the idea of Hindutva—Hindustan for Hindus. As a result, the Babri Masjid is no more, and there are plans to demolish other signs of Muslim presence in India. The Citizenship (Amendment) Act, 2019 (CAA) guarantees the right to stay in India to all non-Muslim minorities and migrants, if they have entered the country before 31 December 2014; it gives a clear signal to Muslims that they are outsiders, or less than second class citizens at best.

A docile, and partly complicit, media occasionally carries stories of the lynching of Muslim men by cow protection vigilantes, in an echo of the practice in colonial times. For some years, there has been an increase in Muslim men being accused of love jihad when Hindu girls marry them with full and free consent. As a result, many Muslims fear their state, and Hindu co-citizens are being brainwashed by media and the education system to perceive Muslims as marauders who came to India to rape and pillage and stayed behind as enemies within. With slogans like the one below doing the rounds of the country, is it valid to ask if Saadat Hasan Manto was right to leave India?

> Mussalman ke do hi stan
> Pakistan ya Qabaristan
>
> For Muslims, there are just two stans,
> Pakistan or Graveistan

---

[104]Ibid.

## PAKISTAN

In January 1948, Manto set sail from Bombay to Karachi, where he took a northward bound train to Lahore on 7 or 8 January.[105] He wrote that he moved because 'all my near and dear ones were here.' Saadat lived for seven years in Lahore and died on 18 January 1955. These were his most productive years as a writer of short stories and essays. Yet, Manto's time in Pakistan was blighted by poverty, alcoholism, and consistent blows to his self-esteem by the state and his family. The former refused to face the mirror that Saadat held up to his times, and used the full force of the law to silence him. The latter, with little understanding of addiction, failed to recognize his tormented descent into alcoholism as a malady, and turned into a version of the ever-watchful moral police.

In Bombay, a substantial part of Manto's income, irregular as it was, came from the film industry. However, when he moved to Lahore in 1948, the old Lahori film industry was lifeless, and the new Pakistani industry had not found its feet. Additionally, *Beli*, his film venture in 1950, flopped and wiped out his finances.

With no film work to distract him or feed his family, Saadat wrote incessantly—short stories and essays continued to flow. His daughter Nuzhat believes, 'his last years in Lahore were his most prolific, precisely because he did not have opportunities to work for the cinema.'[106] Exploitative publishers who understood his need for alcohol paid him between twelve and twenty rupees for a story, with which he headed to a wine merchant or a bootlegger.

Upon arrival in Pakistan, Saadat was disoriented by sudden change in the political and sociocultural temperament of the new country. He had known Lahore as a small yet pluralist city, where Christians, Hindus, Muslims, Sikhs, and Parsis lived together—not always in harmony, but within negotiated boundaries.

Saadat could not bring himself to write short stories. He found work with *Imroze*, and began to write essays. His entertaining and insightful collection on film personalities published in *Ganje Farishte*

---

[105] Manto, 'Troubled by the Blazing Sun', *Manto Namah*, pp. 351–403.
[106] Conversation with Nuzhat Manto, Lahore, 26 March 2019.

(Bald Angels), remain favourites, particularly with scholars of Bombay cinema.

Finally, Saadat wrote 'Thanda Gosht', for his old friend Qasmi Sahib, who had started a literary magazine called *Nuqush* (Features). Qasmi Sahib turned the story down, saying it was too 'hot' for his publication. Saadat asked him to return the following day, which Qasmi Sahib did, just as Manto was writing the closing lines of 'Khol Do'. A visibly horrified Qasmi Sahib published the story and publication was proscribed for six months.[107]

After considerable toing and froing between publishers, Arif Abdul Mateen of *Javed* published 'Thanda Gosht' in March 1949. However, after a few days, *Javed* was proscribed, and after a few weeks, Arif Abdul Mateen, the editor, Naseer Anwar, the owner, and Manto were arrested and charged with obscenity, in independent Pakistan, under Section 292 of the colonial Indian Penal Code, 1860. They were released on bail.

The case lasted a year. The arguments presented by the prosecution and the defence, including the expert witness statements, are landmarks in the debates on what constitutes obscenity and whether courts should decide the nature of obscenity in literature. In the first instance, the three men were found guilty; a fine, and a sentence of three months rigorous imprisonment was imposed. Fortunately, they were granted bail.

The case dragged on, mainly because their lawyer did not turn up on the date set for the appeal. Nevertheless, in a Mantoesque turn, four young lawyers walked into court to represent him, led by Sheikh Khursheed Ahmed. As a result, Manto and the two other defendants were acquitted in the Sessions Court in July 1950.

This was the year the prosecution appealed, and the 'Thanda Gosht' case came before the High Court, before Justice Mohammad Munir, who overturned the lower court's decision in 1952 and declared 'Thanda Gosht' obscene; he imposed fines but waived the prison sentences.[108]

Perhaps, Manto's spirit might find some consolation in the fact

---

[107] Manto, 'Troubled by the Blazing Sun', *Manto Namah*.
[108] Crown v. Saadat Hasan Manto (sic) PLD 384 (1952) (Pak) at 388.

that six years later Justice Munir shamed himself and the Pakistani judiciary by declaring the doctrine of necessity and supporting the 1958 military coup that set the scene for eleven years of dictatorship, and the toxic poisoning of all institutions—including the steady descent into a dark space of unaccountability of the armed forces, judiciary, civil, civic, religious, secular, cultural, and financial institutions.

For his fifth and last trial, a tired and seriously unwell Saadat travelled by train to Karachi, in early 1953. In court, Saadat pleaded guilty and was fined twenty-five rupees for *Top, Bottom, and Middle*, published in February 1952.

In the story written as a radio play or film dialogue, a husband and wife get aroused as they discuss their son's interest in *Lady Chatterley's Lover*. Today the story seems innocuous, but clearly the reference to the proscribed and notorious book that was only ever mentioned in hushed tones, was inflammatory. Another couple who work for the first couple, get aroused by the first couple's activities. The magistrate who fined Manto, wrote about the proceedings several years later.[109] The stress of litigation broke Saadat's spirit. On his return from Karachi, he was admitted to the Mayo Hospital, with suspected jaundice, but diagnosed, unsurprisingly, with cirrhosis of the liver.

THE ASYLUM

The weight of on-going litigation, the failure of his film venture, no prospects for cinema work, exploitative publishers, the humiliation of grinding poverty, and the inability to support his family, pushed Saadat deeper into an abyss of alcoholism and depression. He borrowed money from friends and strangers, and even filched from Safia's meagre housekeeping cash.

In Bombay, Saadat and Safia had withstood the pain of losing Arif, and Saadat's heightened depression. In Lahore, Safia had to contend with Saadat's further descent into depression and reliance on alcohol for solace. Burdened by the humiliation of not being

---

[109]Mehdi Ali Siddiqi, 'Manto aur Main' (Panchva Muqaddama), *Dastavez*, June 1982. In 1983, Muhammad Umar Memon translated it: 'Manto and I', *Annual of Urdu Studies*, No. 28, pp. 177–381.

able to provide for her children she enrolled in evening classes at a secretarial college. Finally, after Saadat spent the money he had been given for little Nighat's medicine on liquor, Safia gave up and wrote to her brother in East Africa, saying she wished to file for divorce. He advised her against the move, reminding her that Saadat was very unwell. Outraged by friends and well-wishers who pandered to Saadat's alcoholism, Safia began accompanying Saadat whenever he stepped out of their flat in Lakshmi Mansions.

According to some family members and Hamid Jalal's account, in 1952, Manto had requested that he be admitted to the Lahore lunatic asylum (pagal khana).[110] Others have a more controversial account of these events. Saadat had three spells in the asylum. His first visit was between 25 April and 2 June 1951, and he returned for a few months. His second visit was on 27 December 1951 to 9 January 1952, and finally on 3 February 1952.

Saadat wanted no part of a vile, mad world where the person who spoke the most sense was brushed aside for spouting gibberish, and consigned to a lunatic asylum. He observed his beloved family visibly revolted by his presence; old neighbours had turned into combatant Hindus, Muslims, and Sikh, and much-loved places parcelled off between two enemy countries, Pakistan and Hindustan. His time in the asylum drove him to take his usual autobiographical turn, and his outraged spirit communed with Bhisham Singh in 'Toba Tek Singh', his alter ego.

Exhausted, Manto's repudiation of his times was the manner of his death. Saadat blurred his troubled world with alcohol, and willed himself to an early grave. On 18 January 1955, Safia rode with Saadat in the ambulance, and he died of multiple organ failure on the way to the hospital.

After Saadat's death, Safia and their three daughters lived with her mother Begum Qamar-ud Deen in a flat in Laxmi Mansions.[111] Safia Manto died in Lahore on 23 November 1977, twenty-two years after

---

[110]Conversation with Mrs Zakia Hamid Jalal (Safia Manto's younger sister), February 2020.
[111]Conversations with Nuzhat and Nusrat Manto.

Saadat. Their daughters, Nighat, Nuzhat, and Nusrat, continue to live in Lahore. They were hurt and amused in equal measure when the Pakistani state honoured their father, first in 2005 with his image on a postage stamp, and again in 2012 with the Nishan-i Imtiaz, the highest civilian honour for an artist—for he had predicted, tongue in cheek, the danger that this might happen.[112]

Today, Saadat Hasan Manto's soul must cringe at the attempts by Indian and Pakistani nationalists and progressives to consign him to their respective ideological straightjackets. Manto's stories continue to hold up a mirror as citizens of both countries outbid each other to manufacture imagined religious communitarian histories that fuel hatred, revenge, and violence. Nevertheless, it is important to look back on Manto's life and works to reclaim a politics of peace and humanism whereby citizens of both countries can rise above histories of communal bloodshed and attempt to live in peace within and outside their borders.

---

[112] Manto, 'The Shroud's Pocket' (Jaib-e-Kafan), *Manto Namah*.

# 1
## Women

Ashok met Maharajah 'G' at the races and in no time a spirit of camaraderie developed between them. The Maharajah travelled far corners of the world to fulfil his passion for racehorses and had some rare thoroughbreds in the stables of his palace, the domes of which were visible from the racecourse. On Ashok's first visit, Maharajah 'G' spent several hours showing him some prize stallions, colts, mares, and fillies—and a thoroughly impressed Ashok showered the young Maharajah with praise.

One day, Ashok turned up for a racing tip and found the Maharajah seated in his darkroom watching a 16 mm film he had shot on his camera. The Maharajah asked Ashok to join him, and screened an entire race from beginning to end, in which, of course, his horse had won. Ashok wanted to watch more films and Maharajah 'G' entertained him with many more. After an enthralled Ashok watched Switzerland, Paris, New York, Honolulu, Hawaii, and the Kashmir valley whizz past in technicolour, Maharajah 'G' switched on the camera light and walloped his thigh with an air of familiarity, 'Well then, my friend?'

Ashok, who owned a 16 mm camera and a projector, had neither a comparably rich collection of movies nor the time to indulge his passion. He lit his cigarette and said, 'So enjoyed watching those films.'

'Should I show you some more?'

'Thank you, but no….'

'Ah really, you must watch this one. You'll love it,' said the Maharajah, as he opened a small trunk, took out a can, loaded the film on the projector, and added, 'Just relax and watch this.'

'What do you mean?' asked Ashok.

'I mean, see everything carefully,' said the Maharajah as he switched off the light and the projector began to whir, a white light shimmered on the screen, and images began to roll. Ashok saw a stark-naked woman stretched out on a sofa, while another stood near a dressing table styling her hair. He watched the film in silence for some time, but suddenly a weird involuntary sound escaped his throat. The Maharajah laughed and asked, 'What's the matter?'

Ashok's words were stuck in his throat but he managed to call out, 'Stop it, yaar, stop it!'

'What should I stop?'

Ashok stood up but Maharajah 'G' gripped him by his shoulders and pushed him back into his seat, insisting, 'You must watch the whole film.'

The film continued, and an uneasy Ashok had no choice but to confront nudity and watch bodies of men and women engage in depraved sexual acts. When the film came to an end, and a white light shone on the blank screen, Ashok felt what he saw was projected through his eyes and not by a machine. Maharajah 'G' turned on the lights, looked at Ashok, and chuckled, 'What's wrong with you?'

As Ashok shrank into his seat and shut his eyes to block out the sudden glare, large beads of sweat appeared on his forehead. Maharajah 'G' whacked Ashok on the thigh yet again and roared with laughter as tears rolled down his cheeks. Ashok stood up, pulled out his handkerchief to wipe his brow, and said, 'Nothing, yaar.'

'Nothing? What? Didn't you enjoy yourself?'

Ashok's throat was parched; he swallowed some saliva and asked, 'Where did you find this film?'

An animated Maharajah sprawled out on the sofa and disclosed, 'In Paris...Pari, Pari,' he repeated, dropping the final 's'.

Ashok shook his head, 'I don't understand....'

'What don't you understand?'

'These people...I mean, in front of a camera, how can they?'

'Well, this is what's so extraordinary! Isn't it?'

'It sure is,' said Ashok, wiping his eyes with his hanky, 'I can feel all the images glued to my eyes.'

The Maharajah rose from the sofa, 'Once, I showed this film to some ladies.'

'To ladies...!' shrieked Ashok.

'Yes, yes, they loved it.'

'Lies!'

The Maharajah intoned with great solemnity, 'Seriously. They were squealing, yelling, and giggling, and wanted to see it again.'

Ashok shook his head in disbelief, 'This is the limit. I'd imagine they'd have fainted.'

'Exactly what I thought, but they had a great time.'

'Were they Europeans?' asked Ashok.

'No, my friend—from our country. They borrowed the film and my projector several times. Who knows how many of their friends saw it?'

Ashok paused for a while and asked, 'May I borrow this film for a couple of days?'

'Yes, of course—take it!' said the Maharajah, nudging Ashok's ribcage with the same air of familiarity he had demonstrated earlier, 'Saale, to whom will you show the film?'

'To friends.'

'Show it to whomever you please!' Maharajah 'G' took the spool off the projector, transferred it to a can, and handed it to Ashok. 'Here... have fun!'

As Ashok took the can, he felt a shiver run down his spine and forgot his racing tip; he chatted with the Maharajah about this, that, and the other and left.

Ashok used his projector and showed the film to several friends, making mental notes of their reactions. This exposure to naked humanity was a novelty for most of them. Some showed a hint of discomfort but remained absorbed in every frame. Others watched a tiny bit and closed their eyes, yet others could not see the film even though their eyes were wide open. One walked away, nauseated. After three or four days, Ashok thought he ought to return the film but decided to show it to his wife. That night, he summoned his wife to their bedroom and shut the door before he turned on the projector. Ashok fitted the film, turned off the light, and started the show. The white light shimmered on the blank screen for a fleeting second before images began to roll. Ashok's wife shuddered and shrieked before she jumped up from their bed, producing some bizarre sounds. He tried to calm her but she covered her eyes with her hands and shrieked louder, 'Stop it! Stop it!'

Ashok laughed and said, 'You must watch it. Why are you embarrassed?'

'No, no...!' She yelled emphatically and forced Ashok to let go of her hand. She loosened his grip and tried to run away, but Ashok held her tight and pulled her hand away from her eyes. In the tug of war that ensued, she began to weep, and stutter incoherently. Ashok felt someone had applied the brakes. He had shown the film to his wife as mere entertainment, but when she unlocked the door and left the room, his mind went blank. As he sat watching the naked images perform their depraved acts, the delicacy of the moment struck him, and he wanted to perish in a sea of shame.

Ashok thought about what had transpired and told himself, 'I've behaved in a most unsavoury fashion. How odd it didn't even cross my mind that it was all right for me to show it to my friends, but at home to my wife...to my wife...!' Tiny beads of sweat appeared on his brow as the film continued to run, and primeval nudity adopted different postures on the screen. Ashok switched the projector off. As the screen went blank, he looked away and sank deeper into the depths of shame. Plagued by his despicable behaviour, he wondered how he could ever look his wife in the eye. The room was pitch dark. He lit a cigarette to distract himself, but this random act did not dispel his sense of shame. Strange thoughts began to rear their heads, and he wanted the darkness of the room to envelop his mind.

Self-recrimination weighed down Ashok's spirit. 'Such despicable behaviour! What if my mother-in-law hears of it? And my sisters-in-law, who respect me...will be shocked to hear of my shallow and filthy mentality.' Ashok lit another cigarette, but when he imagined his wife's face beside the cavorting naked bodies, the weight of his sleazy conduct crushed his spirit further. Ashok shuddered. He began to pace up and down but there was no end to his restlessness. Eventually, he stepped out of his bedroom and quietly peeped into the spare room where his wife lay with her face covered. He wondered if he should beg her to forgive him but could not muster the courage to approach her. Instead, he walked into the living room, where he lay stretched out on the sofa for several hours before he could fall asleep.

The next morning, Ashok woke up early with the previous night's episode fresh in his mind. He did not think it appropriate to greet his wife and left for work without breakfast. At work, from time to time, thoughts of his vile behaviour lined up in his mind to chastise him. Each time he resolved to telephone his wife he replaced the receiver on the cradle before he finished dialling the number. In the afternoon, when their servant brought his lunch, Ashok asked him, 'Has Memsahib had her lunch?'

The servant answered, 'No. She has gone out.'

'Where?'

'I don't know, Sahib.'

'What time did she leave?'

'At eleven o'clock.'

Ashok's heart began to pound; he lost his appetite, and pushed away his lunch after a few mouthfuls. Chaotic thoughts flooded his mind. 'Eleven o'clock, and she's not back! Where is she? Has she gone to her mother's? Will she tell her everything? Perhaps, she has gone to see her sisters. What will they think when they hear of my behaviour? Who knows what they think of me now?'

Ashok left his office and drove aimlessly around the city in his car. Unable to figure out a course of action, he thought it best to go home and face the consequences. The lift began its ascent and his heart leapt into his mouth when it stopped on the third floor. Ashok stepped out and made his way to his flat but hesitated; he was about to beat a retreat when the front door opened and their servant stepped out to smoke a biri, which he concealed in his hand and greeted Ashok, who now had no option but to enter the flat. The servant followed him in, and Ashok asked, 'Where is Memsahib?'

The servant answered, 'In her room.'

'And who is with her?'

'Her sisters, Sahib; the Colaba Sahib's Memsahib and two Parsi Bais!'

Ashok proceeded towards the room; when he pushed the door, he found it locked. His wife's sharp shrill voice asked, 'Who is it?'

The servant answered, 'Sahib.'

Ashok heard an unexpected commotion in the room—banging, clanging, shrieking, squealing, and the sound of doors being locked. He made his way along the long corridor and entered the bedroom by the back door. In the dim haze of the projector light, he saw the same naked male and female figures engrossed in the same mechanical bestial acts. Ashok broke into irrepressible laughter.

## 2
## *Suited Booted*

When Nazim found work with a new film company as a munshi, I mean a dialogue writer, he was assured of a salary of two-hundred-and-fifty rupees a month. He decided to indulge himself and moved from the filthy neighbourhood of Dongri to Bandra. He thought himself lucky when he found three rooms to rent in a building with chawls—the local name for tenements inhabited by people from the lower classes. The rooms were not unusually large, but in the eyes of the other residents of the building, only a tycoon could afford such luxury. Besides, his neighbours considered Nazim well dressed, simply because he gave up his native kurta–pyjama for a Western suit after getting a job in a film company.

Nazim, who had just got married, was pleased with three rooms and he thought they were more than adequate for a couple. He did feel a bit cheerless when he discovered that a single bathroom served the entire building, but conditions in Bandra were an improvement on Dongri, where at least five hundred people had to make do with one bathroom. In Dongri, Nazim who was not an early riser, rarely got an opportunity to bathe. Here, in Bandra, most men in the tenement slept through the day, perhaps because they worked on a pali or a night shift—and this worked to Nazim's advantage. The bathroom was diagonally opposite his chawl, towards the left of his front door, but its entrance was in a passage on the right, facing a small room that looked directly into his chawl. He had no idea who lived in it.

One day, after he locked the bathroom door, Nazim noticed it had a hole that was not a natural crack in the wood but seemed drilled with a sharp metal instrument. He stripped and began to bathe when he had a curious urge to peep through the hole, and trained his eye on it: he saw a young woman in a brassiere with the lower part of her body encased in a sari petticoat sitting with her arms outstretched, as though inviting an unseen man to crush her in his arms and cure her ennui. Dripping wet and unable to take his eyes off the woman who was examining her taut body as though she wished to figure out its purpose, Nazim shivered. A recently married sissy, he was terrified of his wife; besides, he was not of a lascivious disposition.

Nevertheless, the hole in the bathroom door drilled several holes in Nazim's moral fibre, and he continued to peep at the woman every morning. When Nazim fixed his gaze on her, he experienced a peculiar sensation course through his body. After a few days, Nazim concluded that the woman, whose name was Zubeida, knew that he peeped at her through the hole in the door as part of his daily morning ritual. A man who locks himself up in a bathroom to peep at his neighbour through a fissure in the door cannot have good intentions, and there was nothing virtuous about Nazim's intentions—he was aroused by the woman who wore nothing but a brassiere and a sari petticoat. Any man who fixed his gaze on Zubeida as she stretched her limbs would find her seductive.

One day, Nazim noticed Zubeida wore a smile on her face and red lipstick on her luscious lips, her petticoat tighter, and her brassiere more taut than usual. Nazim was sure she knew he was looking at her dab powder on her face and rouge on her cheeks. He felt like the hero of a film for which he was writing the script; but thoughts of his wife, who was visiting her well-to-do brother in Worli, reduced him to an extra; he reckoned he should put an end to his antics.

Several months after he moved into the chawl, Nazim learnt that Zubeida's husband, a mill worker, who could not father a child spent all his leisure hours visiting holy men, shrines, doctors, and hakims. A quiet man not given to conversation, he had no facial hair—I mean, his face lacked a moustache or a beard. In Punjabi, such men are called 'diggers'. I am not quite sure how the tradition came about, but Zubeida's husband was a 'digger' digging his way to fulfil his desire for a child. Zubeida did not desire a child; she wanted someone to desire her and gratify her passion, of which her husband was completely unaware.

There was another young man who lived in the building, and he was a bachelor. Several other bachelors lived in the building, but this young man stood out because, like Nazim, he was suited booted. To Nazim's chagrin, he too was a 'peeping Tom' for whom Zubeida exhibited her body. Nazim was resentful. It is not unusual for men to be jealous in such matters, and Nazim was no different. After a month or so, the suited booted young man went off to a better job in Ahmedabad, and Nazim felt particularly buoyant. Although he continued to peep at Zubeida through the hole in the door, he could not muster the courage to speak to her. The fear of being discovered by his neighbours and his reputation plummeting to nought prevented him from taking matters any further.

Nazim's wife returned from Worli after a week, and he stopped peeping at Zubeida. His conscience troubled him, and he made unusually amorous advances towards his wife in direct proportion to his guilt. She was startled but delighted to find her husband more attentive than usual. Still, Zubeida's taut body had taken over Nazim's senses and soon, he returned to his peeping Tom antics. He wanted to possess Zubeida, and as she stretched her body, he longed to become one with her in an everlasting stretch.

Nazim received a regular salary from his film company and decided to treat himself to a new suit. Aware of Zubeida eyeing him through the open door of her room, he wanted to walk up to her and say, 'Hello madam!' One day, he mustered enough courage to take two steps towards Zubeida, but when he saw her bloom from a bud into a flower, he shrivelled up. The thought of his wife, combined with a sense of dignity, forced him to retract his steps. At home, his impassioned advances fuelled by his guilt made his poor wife blush.

Around this time, another suited booted man arrived in their building, and he too was a peeping Tom who looked at Zubeida through the hole in the bathroom door. A few days after he moved in, Nazim's second rival fell off an electric train and died. Although saddened by the young man's death, Nazim reasoned that God wanted to remove this obstacle from his path, and returned to his antics—peeping at Zubeida and longing for her with renewed fervour.

Nazim's wife had to attend a family wedding in Lahore; he wanted to tell her that such a long separation would be unbearable, but as thoughts of Zubeida crept into his mind, he encouraged her to go. Nazim could not start his day without two cups of tea first thing in the morning, and the matter of his bed tea began to trouble his wife, who hit upon an idea and said, 'Don't worry, I'll request Zubeida to organize your tea every morning.' Then she called out across the corridor to draw Zubeida's attention.

A fully clothed Zubeida walked across to see them; her head partially covered with a dupatta, she was the picture of modesty. Zubeida cast an electrifying sidelong glance at Nazim, who did not say or do anything to arouse his wife's suspicion. After a few minutes of polite conversation, they agreed that Zubeida would take charge of Nazim's morning tea. When his wife handed Zubeida a ten-rupee note on account, she declined, 'Behen, there's no need for such formality. Don't worry; your husband will get his morning tea at whatever time he wishes.'

Nazim's face flushed with pleasure, and he thought, 'I don't care for tea. Zubeida, all I want is you.' But with his wife standing next to him, his passion ran cold.

Nazim's wife departed for Lahore. The following morning, he was fast asleep when there was a knock on his door. He turned over and went back to sleep, thinking his wife was pounding coals in the kitchen. The knocking continued, and a female voice called out, 'Nazim Sahib, Nazim Sahib!'

Nazim recognized Zubeida's voice and leapt out of bed to open the door. He saw Zubeida holding a tray with both her hands, and she looked—oh so demure.

'Tea is ready, sir!'

Nazim felt utterly bewildered but pulled himself together and said, 'You've taken so much trouble. Please, give me the tray.'

Zubeida insisted, 'No trouble at all. I'll put it down on the table.'

Nazim was in his striped poplin night suit—an indulgence he had splashed out on for the first time in his life. Zubeida was in a shalwar–qameez of ordinary cotton, but it suited her. She carried the tray into the room and put it down on a side table, playing on Nazim's heartstrings, before she said, 'I'm so sorry your tea is late. I'm a late riser.'

Nazim sank into an armchair. He wanted to resort to poetry, 'Come, let us sleep. Sleep is manna from heaven,' but lost his nerve and his voice. Zubeida poured Nazim's tea like a devotee making an offering; he felt he consumed Zubeida with every sip. Still, all that the lily-livered Nazim could bring himself to say was, 'Zubeidaji, don't trouble yourself. I'll have the crockery washed and sent across to you.'

Zubeida brought Nazim's bed tea every morning; she poured it, and as he drank it, he continued to imagine he was consuming her. Thoughts of his wife set off alarms; yet, every night, Nazim fell asleep dreaming of Zubeida. This pattern continued for a fortnight. Zubeida gave Nazim every opportunity to crush the longing out of her bones, but somehow, the vision of her outstretched arms paralysed him.

Although Nazim owned two suits, he placed an order for a third at a shop on Charni Road, where the seth of his film company had his suits tailored and promised to settle the account as soon as he received his next pay cheque. Nazim walked past Zubeida's room in his new gabardine suit. She was in her usual brassiere and sari petticoat. The minute she saw him, she rushed to the door, and a thin smile flitted across her red lips as she chirped, 'Nazim Sahib, today you look like a prince.'

Nazim was transported on horseback to the Caucasus Mountains or perhaps, into the pages of some book packed with stories of princes and princesses. As his wife's face flashed before his eyes, he fell from his steed flat on his face and turned to her in Lahore, crying out, 'I'm in such pain.'

The pain of love is exquisite, and Nazim's agony was incurable because his decency and his wife stood in the way. And if this penalty was insufficient, Nazim received another blow. Not a soul knew what happened. One day, when he reported for work, he was told his film company was declared bankrupt. Five days earlier, he had sent two hundred rupees to his wife in Lahore, plus he had to pay another hundred rupees to the tailor and outfitter on Charni Road and settle other sundry debts.

The calamity of losing his job did not cure Nazim's longing for Zubeida. She continued to bring his tea every morning, but now every sip was infused with guilt and embarrassment because he had no idea how to pay for it. He thought up a scheme, and for a mere fifty rupees, pawned his three suits, including the gabardine one, and put five ten-rupee notes in his pocket. He planned to give two to Zubeida and unburden his heart to her. At Dadar Station, a pickpocket swiped his cash. Nazim contemplated suicide. As the trains whizzed up and down the platform, he reckoned he could pretend to slip and put an end to everything within seconds. He thought of his wife in Lahore—pregnant with their child.

Zubeida continued to bring Nazim's tea every morning, but now he did not find the same vitality in her eyes. The tea was of poor quality, the milk more like water, and Zubeida was not decked up as usual. In the bathroom, when Nazim peeped through the hole in the door, he did not see her. Preoccupied with thoughts of how to clear two months' rent arrears, the Charni Road tailor's bill, and other debts, Nazim felt like a failed bank and feared he could land up in a debtors' prison. Rather than confront this humiliation, he resolved to give up the three rooms in Bandra and found a man who agreed to take over his apartment and pay off his debts. Nazim retrieved his three suits from the pawnbroker. When moving his few belongings from the building in Bandra, he spotted Zubeida. She was eyeing the new tenant, suited booted in a sharkskin suit, with the same look she had cast on Nazim some months earlier.

# 3

## Miss Mala

The moment the lyricist Azim Gobindpuri signed his contract with ABC Studios, his thoughts turned to his friend Bhatsave, a Marathi music director with whom he had worked on earlier films. Poor Bhatsave remained in the recesses of anonymity since he had little opportunity to demonstrate his brilliance in stunt films. Azim recognized Bhatsave's talent and convinced his producer, a rich seth, to sign him up for a film for three thousand rupees. Bhatsave signed the contract and received an advance of five hundred rupees, which he distributed amongst his creditors. Thereafter, he received five hundred rupees every month to make up the balance. Ever grateful, he wished to repay his friend but held off because he knew Azim was an upright man with no base motives.

Both men immersed themselves in their work. Azim wrote lyrics for ten songs, of which the seth selected four. Bhatsave composed two much-admired melodies in close collaboration with Azim, and rehearsals continued for a fortnight. The first song was a chorus that required at least fifteen female singers, but the production manager failed on this front. So Bhatsave sent for Miss Mala, who had a good voice, and knew at least five or six other girls able to carry a tune.

Miss Mala Khandekar, as is evident from her name, was a Maratha from Kolhapur. Miss Mala was young, but her features were hard-baked. She conversed with an air that oozed experience and a familiarity with the ups and downs of life. Compared with others in the studio, her Urdu pronunciation was first-class, and she quite liked to speak the language. She was cordial with everyone in the studio and addressed every man as 'bhaijan' to mark him out as an older brother. Bhatsave tasked her with finding ten girls for the chorus, and the following day she turned up with twelve. Bhatsave selected seven and dismissed the others saying, 'Well, seven will have to do.'

Nonetheless, he consulted Jagtap, the sound recordist, who assured him, 'You don't need to worry, I'll handle everything. The recording will be perfect; listeners will get the impression of twenty girls singing!'

Jagtap, who understood his craft, gathered the musicians and singers in a room with concrete walls instead of a soundproof studio with soft cushioning that would have compressed the sound. Miss Mala proved a perfect assistant to Bhatsave. She directed the seven girls individually to ensure they did not sing a false note. Bhatsave was satisfied with the first rehearsal but decided to go for a few more to be doubly sure. When Jagtap heard the soundtrack for the first time on the studio headphones, he beamed as he gave a thumbs-up and shouted, 'Okay!' Each voice and instrument sounded perfect.

The owner of ABC Studios organized a muhurat of the film *Bewafa* (Unfaithful) with great fanfare, with many financiers and distributors from the industry among the countless guests. The celebrations kicked off with a chorus. The recording started, and as the technician switched on the headphones provided for every guest, Bhatsave's voice rang out on the microphone, 'Song number one! First take. Ready, one, two....' The chorus filled the air; it was a lovely composition, and of the seven girls, not one faltered. The guests were thrilled. The seth was overjoyed. He did not know the first thing about music but was delighted because his enthralled guests were raving about the song. Bhatsave thanked the orchestra and the chorus, with a special mention for Miss Mala for organizing the singers at such short notice.

Bhatsave had just turned around to embrace Jagtap, the sound recordist, when Seth Ranchod Das, the owner of ABC Studios, sent a flunky to summon Bhatsave and Azim Gobindpuri. Both hot-footed it to the corner of the studio, where the party was in full swing. In full view of the guests, Seth Sahib twirled a crisp green hundred-rupee note, which he handed to Bhatsave, and produced another for Azim. The small garden packed with guests resounded with applause. After the guests dispersed, Bhatsave said to Azim, 'Wealth must flow. Let's go *outdoor*!' Azim didn't quite get what he meant. Bhatsave smiled and added in half-Marathi, 'Maze malge, let's go for moj shok!' In other words, 'My boy, let's have fun and games!' He added, 'You have a hundred rupees, and I have a hundred. Let's go!'

Azim understood but was wary of Bhatsave's moj shok. He had a wife and two small kids and had never indulged in debauchery. Yet, blissfully content, he thought, 'Let's go and see what happens.'

Bhatsave sent for a taxi, and as they neared Grant Road, Azim asked, 'Where are we going, Bhatsave?'

Bhatsave smiled, 'To my aunt's house!'

They arrived at Miss Mala Khandekar's house. She greeted the two men with warmth and took them inside her lodgings before she sent for tea from a nearby hotel. After tea, Bhatsave said to her, 'We're out for moj shok. Arrange something.'

Mala understood. She was indebted to Bhatsave and promptly said something in Marathi, which meant, 'I'm always at your service.'

Beholden to Azim Gobindpuri for introducing him to ABC Studios, Bhatsave wanted to humour him and instructed Mala to procure a girl. She promptly changed her clothes and applied make-up. The three of them climbed into a taxi and drove to the playback singer Shanta Kurnakaran's house—she was out with someone else. They proceeded to Ansuya's place, but she was not up to their standards. Disappointed by two failed attempts, Miss Mala was determined to accomplish her mission. Now, the taxi headed towards Gol Petha to check out Krishna, a soft and nubile fifteen- or sixteen-year-old Maratha girl who sang in a fine pitch. Mala entered her house, and not much later, came out with Krishna, who joined her hands to greet Bhatsave and Azim with a namaste. Like an ace pimp tested in the art of sign language, Mala winked at Azim to say, 'She is for you!'

Bhatsave too signalled his approval with his eyes. Briefed by Mala, the pubescent Krishna began to seduce Azim, who responded like a bashful teenage girl. Bhatsave figured out Azim's inhibitions and asked the taxi driver to stop at a bar; he took Azim inside while the women waited in the car.

The lyricist had tasted alcohol a couple of times but always in the context of work. He told himself that this too was work. Egged on by Bhatsave, Azim downed two pegs of rum and, in no time, was smashed. Bhatsave bought a bottle, and the two of them returned to the taxi. Azim had not the faintest idea that his friend was carrying two glasses and a bottle of rum. Bhatsave informed him that Mala had told Krishna's mother that her daughter had to rerecord at night because of problems with all her previous recordings. As a rule, Krishna's mother kept a strict eye on her daughter's movements, but agreed when Bhatsave assured her that he would pay Krishna for the additional work. Nonetheless, she instructed her daughter, 'Come home as soon as you finish the recording and don't hang around the studio.'

The taxi arrived at Worli Sea Face and stopped on a small hillock. I'm not sure if it was man-made or natural, but it was at a fair height with a vast open vista and a view of the sea. Randy men in search of pleasure converged here with some woman or the other on their arms. There were rows of wooden benches; each bench stood at a fair distance from its neighbour, and an unwritten consensus operated between the couples: no more than one couple occupied a bench, and users did not trouble each other. Bhatsave, who wished to please Azim, left Krishna in his care, and walked off in the opposite direction with Mala.

Azim, who never desired a woman other than his wife, faltered when Krishna clung to him. And an inebriated Azim could not resist this typical sturdy dusky Maratha wench—ripe with all the delights a nubile and willing girl can offer. Frisky thoughts entered his mind, some on account of the rum he had consumed and others fired by the warmth of Krishna's body. Azim forgot his wife and wanted to make Krishna his wife, at least for some time. Usually, a reticent man of few words, tonight he tickled Krishna and shared several jokes with her in pidgin Gujarati. Heaven knows how the thought crossed his mind, but in jest, he shouted a warning for Bhatsave:

'Police.... Police!'

Bhatsave dashed across with Mala in tow and swore at Azim before he began to laugh. Although he knew Azim was pulling his leg, he thought it best to go to a hotel with no danger of the law turning up. As they headed back to the taxi, a yellow turban materialized and began to interrogate them in a typically officious manner, 'What are all of you up to at eleven o'clock in the night? Don't you know it's against the law to sit here after ten o'clock?'

Azim addressed the policeman in Bombay speak, 'Sir, we're filmwallahs.'

'And this lass?' The yellow turban pointed at Krishna.

'She works with us in that studio across the road. We are not here with any bad intentions. We work all day long, get exhausted, and come here for some air and to relax. Our shooting is about to resume at midnight.'

Azim's response satisfied the yellow turban, who turned to Bhatsave and asked, 'What are you up to?'

Bhatsave was caught off guard but pulled himself together and did not bat an eyelid as he lied, 'My wife and I came here for some air. Our taxi is waiting by the roadside.'

After a few more questions, the yellow turban let them off, and they headed back to their taxi. Bhatsave thought it pointless to consult Azim on the type of hotel where a man could take a woman for a one-night stand, but the Sea View Hotel in Duke's Yard came to mind, and he instructed the driver to take them there. Bhatsave booked two rooms; Azim and Krishna took one and Bhatsave and Miss Khandekar the other.

Krishna was the quintessence of an available girl, but after his two pegs of rum, Azim was in a philosophical mood. He looked at Krishna and wondered why this young girl had chosen a horrific path of sin. Why was this anaemic girl so hot and sexy? When will this frail girl with no meat on her stop selling her flesh? Azim's heart bled for Krishna; he assumed the role of her messiah and began to plead with her, 'Krishna, give up this life of sin. Selling your body is a terrible vice. I have taught you how to differentiate between good and evil—think of this as your night of deliverance.'

Krishna interpreted Azim's words as a declaration of love, and as she began to wrap her body around his, Azim forgot all his arguments about virtue and sin.

Late that night, a penitent Azim stepped out to the veranda of his hotel room where he found an edgy Bhatsave pacing up and down as though he had stirred a hornet's nest. Krishna followed Azim. When Bhatsave saw his sated expression, he grunted, 'That slut's left.'

Azim, who felt he was standing in an abyss of shame, mumbled, 'Who?'

'Mala.'

'Why?'

A restless Bhatsave elaborated, 'Here I was, kissing her all this time, but when I asked her to sleep with me, the slut pushed off, and do you know what she said? "You are my brother; I'm a married woman now." Saali! I thought, well then that sister...must have come home.'

## 4

## The Actress's Eye

The shooting of *Paap ki Guthri* (Bundle of Sins) had continued through the night, and some exhausted actors and technicians were gathered in the small timber hut commandeered as his make-up room by the tall villain of the film company. People dropped by to relax; they sank drowsily into sofas and chairs where they gossiped, invariably about the state of their seth's finances. In one corner, there was a small grimy table perpetually piled up with ten to fifteen teacups, consumed through the day by the same folk. Some cups were half full, and others were upturned or lay on their sides. Thousands of flies swarmed around this mess, and a person approaching the hut for the first time could easily mistake their buzzing for that of an electric fan.

The tall villain was stretched out on his sofa, snoring away with his eyes wide open and mouth half shut; sporting a silk shalwar-qameez, he resembled a Lahori tongawallah. An elderly actor with a long moustache had nodded off on an armchair. Another actor was trying to catch some sleep leaning against a free-standing plank of wood near the window. The company's dialogue writer, the munshi, was sitting with his feet on the dressing table, a biri between his lips. He looked busy; perhaps he was writing the song he had to submit to the seth at four o'clock that evening.

'Ooh, ooh! Aah, aah!' A distinct cry of anguish entered the hut through the window. The villain sat up and rubbed his eyes. The actor with the long moustache raised his left hand to one of his noticeably long ears, trying to recognize this female voice. Munshi Sahib removed his feet from the dressing table and looked at the villain as though he should know the answer.

'Ooh, ooh, ooh! Aah, aah!'

The villain, the munshi, and other half-asleep inhabitants of the room craned their necks to look out of the window.

'Arrey, what's up?'

'Is everything all right?'
'What has happened?'
'I say it's Devi!'
'What's the matter, Devi?'

The room buzzed with questions as people anxious to express their goodwill peered out of the window.

'Aaah...Aaah! Ooh...ooh...ooh! Aah...aah!' Cries and squeals of pain emanated from the rosebud mouth of the company's beloved heroine as she stamped her sandal-clad foot on the concrete floor of the studio's courtyard.

Devi was petite, with a well-rounded figure; she had a wheatish complexion, arched dark eyebrows, and a broad forehead adorned with a kusum bindi. Her long wavy black hair was combed back with a centre parting and rolled into a chignon that resembled a honeycomb. Her white cotton sari with a narrow border draped in the Bombay style hung in gentle folds that accentuated the sexy curvature of her body. Her bosom was spilling out of her sleeveless Gujarati style choli; imported Japanese bangles on her rounded wrists collided with those of solid gold to produce a pleasing tinkle. Solitaire diamond studs glistened like raindrops on the delicate earlobes of her perfectly shaped ears. Devi cried out; she squealed; she shouted; she stomped her foot and began to rub her right eye with a small handkerchief.

'Aah, my eye...ooh, my eye!'

Some necks craned to look out of the window began to shake; others withdrew amidst a babble of questions, comments, and suggestions. 'Do you have something in your eye?'

'There is so much dust and grit here...just flying around in the air.'

'The place is swept only every six months!'

'Come inside, Devi.'

'Yes, yes...do come inside...and don't rub your eye.'

'Arrey, baba, I've told you, you'll hurt yourself. You'd better come in.'

As Devi made her way to the door of the hut, still rubbing her eye, the villain leapt up and, in one clean sweep gathered all the teacups into a large handkerchief and shoved them out of sight behind the dressing table mirror. He pulled out a pair of old trousers from somewhere, and used it to wipe the table clean. Other actors straightened their chairs and sat up with as much grace as they could muster. Munshi Sahib threw away his half-smoked biri and he pulled out a half-smoked cigarette from his pocket and lit it. Devi walked in. The villain and Munshi Sahib stood up to greet her, and Munshi Sahib said, 'Devi, do sit down.'

The elderly actor rose from his chair, his long salt-and-pepper moustache quivered as he offered Devi his chair in his Gujarati accent, 'Seet here, Devi.'

Devi ignored his quivering moustache and continued to rub her eye as she stepped forward, crying, 'Aaah! Aaah! Ooh!'

A young man in a tight-fitting shirt, who looked like a hero, pushed a chair towards Devi and said, 'Do sit down.'

Devi sat on the chair and rubbed the top of her nose with her handkerchief. The very thought of Devi in pain drained the colour from all the faces in the room. More sensitive than others, Munshi Sahib removed his spectacles and began to rub his eye in solidarity. The young man who had offered Devi his chair looked worried and leaned forward to inspect her eye, 'The redness means you are in pain,' his strident voice cracked and reverberated across the room.

Devi squealed louder, and under her white sari, her legs shivered in perceptible anxiety. The villain leaned forward, bending his stiff back with concern: 'Devi, is the pain burning or piercing?'

Another gentleman, sporting a sola topi on his head, entered the room; he stepped forward and asked, 'Is it uncomfortable under your eyelid?'

After continuous rubbing, through the veil of her moist eyelashes, Devi's bloodshot right eye looked like the setting sun. She looked gorgeous and tragic, and she was in pain. Devi let her arms hang loose. She rolled her afflicted eye and cried out, substituting her 'f's for 'p's and 'b's for 'v's and vice versa, 'It's bery fainpul! Aah, ooh!'

The gentleman with the long moustache cried out from his corner, 'Don't ruv your eye. You bill habe more fain.'

'Yes, of course. See, you are doing it again,' said the young man with a voice like a blunderbuss.

The villain, who wanted immediate results, was most irritated, 'All of you are all talk and no substance. I mean, none of you has the good sense to call a doctor. Will serve you right if the same thing happens to your eye!'

He stuck his neck out of the window and shouted, 'Arrey, is anyone there? Can you hear me? Gulab! Gulab!'

He got no response and pulled his neck back in, muttering, 'God knows where all these hotel chaps disappear just when you need them! He must be sleeping in some corner of the studio...good for nothing....' Just then, he spotted Gulab and hollered, 'Gulab, hey Gulab!'

Gulab ran towards him, a teacup dangling from the ten appendages of his hands, and stopped by the window. The villain addressed him as though it were a matter of life and death, 'Quick! Fetch a glass of water. Quick!'

As Gulab peered through the window to see what was happening, the hero roared, 'Arrey, what do you think you're up to? Run! Run! Get a glass of water!'

Gulab dashed off across the road to the hotel with a corrugated iron roof.

By now, the pain in Devi's eye was a lot worse; her delicate chin shaped like a Banarsi mango began to quiver, and she began to squeal like a toddler. She stood up and stomped her feet, walked around the room, and sank back into the sofa. She took a compact out of her handbag and opened it to inspect her eye in its mirror. Munshi Sahib said, 'We should have told Gulab to put some ice in the water.'

'Yes, yes, cold water is a good idea,' said the villain before he stuck his neck out of the window to shout, 'Gulab! Arrey, Gulab, put some ice in the water!' He looked most thoughtful and said, 'I tell you, steam your hanky with your breath and compress it on your eye. Why, Dada?'

'Absolutely!' responded the man with the moustache.

The hero turned to the pocket of his coat, which was hanging on a peg on the wall, and pulled out a white handkerchief he handed to Devi. After he instructed her to blow on it to make it warm, he stepped back. Devi took the handkerchief, took a deep breath, puffed her cheeks, and blew hard before she put the warm compress on her eye. It did not make much difference.

'Any relief?' asked the man in the sola topi.

Devi replied tearfully, 'No. Nothing. I'm dying.'

That very minute, Gulab turned up with a glass of icy water. The villain and the hero rushed forward, and together they bathed Devi's eye. She sat back and began to blink her eyes.

'Any better?'

'No pain, now?'

'The grit must be washed out.'

'Now, you'll soon feel better.'

The intense pain in Devi's eye vanished, at least for a few moments, but soon she screamed out in agony.

'What's the matter?' asked a man who walked into the room, presumably to check what the commotion was all about. Although advanced in years, the newcomer, looked in command of the world around him, and could pass off as an ex-army man. His black hat was slightly awry, a necktie dangled around his open-collared khaki shirt, his khaki trousers sagged at the knees and hung loose on his buttocks and thighs as a telltale sign that he didn't have much flesh on his limbs. Old age had hollowed out his cheeks, and his sunken eyes scrunched up when he moved his shoulders. Years of exposure to biri smoke had given his grey moustache a yellowish tint. He moved around with the agility of a photographer, and addressed a question to everyone in the room, but it sounded more like a declaration: 'Grit in her eye?'

He stepped towards Devi to continue his examination and instructed the villain and hero to move out of his way. 'Water didn't make a difference? Does anybody have a handkerchief?' Half a dozen handkerchiefs appeared. With a theatrical gesture, he selected one, and commanded Devi to remove her hand from her eye. She followed his instructions. Like a magician, he produced a small case from his breast pocket, took out his spectacles, and placed them carefully on the bridge of his nose before he inspected Devi's eye through the lens, but from a distance. He moved closer to Devi, widened his legs, held her eyelids and stretched them open with his long slim fingers, almost as though he were shutting the aperture of a camera. He changed his posture quite dramatically two or three times, and finally, as the spectators looked on in silence, he dropped a corner of the handkerchief into Devi's eye. For five minutes, there was a death-like silence in the room. The gentleman, who was a photographer, cleared Devi's eye of the offensive particle and removed his spectacles. As he put them back into their small case, he turned to Devi with a dramatic air, 'The grit is out. Soon, you will feel better.'

Devi rubbed her eyelid with her hand and took out her compact to assure herself. A chorus erupted in the room, 'The grit is out?'

'You don't feel any pain now?'

'Saala must be out now...caused so much pain!'

'Devi, how do you feel now?'

Amidst the cacophony, the photographer shrugged his shoulders and said, 'You could have tried all day without any results. My twenty-five years in the army have not been wasted. I know about such matters. The grit is out—there is a bit of discomfort, but that too will go.'

As Devi inspected her eye in the mirror of her compact, she looked close to tears but burst into laughter. The box-like wooden hut seemed to fill with starlight, as she cried out, 'It peels good! It peels good!'

All eyes were fixed on Devi as she ran towards the hotel where the seth was waiting for her. Dumbfounded, the hero tried to sink into the sofa but landed on Munshi Sahib. The outraged dialogue writer cried out, 'Do you want to go back to sleep? You better rehearse the dialogue for tomorrow's scene.'

The hero, however, had another scene on his mind.

# 5
## My Name Is Radha

About eight or nine years ago, I was employed by a film company on a salary of forty rupees a month. There were no signs of war, and disruptions occurred with logical predictability—not in the chaotic, random manner they strike us today. My life was moving at a steady pace. I arrived at the studio at ten o'clock every morning, and as part of my daily routine, fed two paise worth of milk to the villain Niaz Mohammad's cats. Additionally, I wrote racy dialogue for a racy film, humoured the actress called the 'Nightingale of Bengal', and before heading home, I showered Dada Gore, perhaps the most revered film director at the time, with undeserved praise.

As I have said, my life was moving at a steady pace. The owner of the studio, Hormuzji Framji, was a fun-loving man with fat rosy cheeks. Although besotted with a Khoja actress well past her prime, he kicked off his day routinely fondling the breasts of a new female specimen. The shooting of *Ban ki Sundari* (Jungle Beauty) was in full swing. God alone knows why Niaz Mohammad, the villain, kept two pet cats. Every day, I fed them two paise worth of milk before sitting down to write dialogue for a film, although I had no idea of the story or the plot. I was a mere clerk who put pencil to paper to record anything that came to the director's mind, which he shared with me in his not-very-good Urdu.

A Muslim harlot from Calcutta's Boubazar, simultaneously conducted three love affairs to ensure that all three men (the director, the sound recordist, and the dialogue writer) focused their attention on her. However, a hot rumour doing the rounds informed us that Seth Hormuzji Framji had recruited a new actress to play the vamp. The hero was Raj Kishore, a robust young man from Rawalpindi, universally acknowledged as a magnificent specimen of manhood. I thought him athletic but did not find him attractive, perhaps because I inhabit such an emaciated frame. Besides, I tend not to reflect too much on the physique of the male of our species.

As a rule, I tend not to loathe human beings, but Raj Kishore did not appeal to me, and in due course, I shall give you the reasons. I loved Raj Kishore's diction—typical of Rawalpindi. If you wish to find sweetness in the Punjabi language, it is in the Rawalpindi idiom—in a male, it sounds tender, but when a woman from Rawalpindi speaks, you can feel the nectar of a sweet mango trickle into your mouth. Here, however, I am concerned with Raj Kishore, for whom my feelings do not match my love for mangoes.

At the risk of repeating myself, Raj Kishore was a handsome and robust young man, and this should suffice as a description of him. What harm can there be in being fit and handsome? However, Raj Kishore's pathological obsession with his good looks and vigour, particularly around those less well-endowed, was unacceptable to me. As God is my witness, I never use my several chronic ailments and weak lungs to gain cheap notoriety or sympathy. I loathed the coarse manner in which Raj Kishore flexed his biceps in the middle of an animated conversation or unbuttoned his khadi kurta to gaze at his broad chest during a serious discussion on swaraj. Raj Kishore was an ardent member of the Congress Party and was a regular at Congress rallies and literary gatherings. He favoured homespun, but I have no compunction in saying that he loved himself more than he loved his country. Almost everyone disagreed with me, in the studio and the world at large. His countless fans admired Raj Kishore's looks, his ideas, and the way he spoke in that delightful Rawalpindi diction that I, too, loved. He shared good and bad times with his acquaintances and was not reserved like other heroes.

It is no mean feat for a man or woman to survive in the film world and remain untainted by sin. Raj Kishore was a popular hero, and producers admired him for his flawless reputation; and in part, this had propelled him to fame in the first place. The public knew Raj Kishore as a man of lofty morals. On my regular visits to the local paan shop in Nagpara, the conversation often turned to the latest scandals attached to actors and actresses. Whenever Raj Kishore's name came up, Shyam Lal, the paan shop owner, declared in a voice tinged with personal pride, 'Manto Sahib, Raj Bhai is the only actor who never gives in to temptation!' I am not sure how Shyam Lal fancied Raj Kishore as his 'bhai'. Still, his sense of brotherhood did not surprise me because the most mundane acts of 'Raj Bhai's' life had great significance for his many fans. They knew the minutiae of his income and expenditure, including what he gave his father as a monthly allowance and how much he donated to charities and orphanages.

Once, Shyam Lal informed me, 'Raj Bhai is very generous to his stepmother. Although, when he was down and out, she ill-treated him, as did his father. But, hats off to him, Raj Bhai remained a dutiful son. He has ensured his elderly parents have all the comforts they desire. They rule his household. Every morning, he stands in obeisance before them; he touches his stepmother's feet, and his father's wish is his command.'

Yet, a suspicion skulked in my heart, telling me, 'Raj Kishore's entire life is false—he is fake.' You may think badly of me, especially when I tell you that in the days when nobody had much time for munshis and clerks, he chatted with me for hours. Not a soul agreed with me; people worshipped him like a god—and this irked me.

Raj had a wife and four children. He was a caring father and a considerate husband. You could lift the veil from any part of his life and find no dark secrets. Yet I remained suspicious. I swear by God, I rebuked myself routinely. I had no reason to condemn a universally revered man. Why should it matter to me if he admired his athletic body? Perhaps, if I had such a perfect body, I would do the same. There was not a breath of scandal attached to his life. He addressed all actresses as 'behen', or sister, to proclaim he did not desire them sexually, and this peeved me further.

The studio was abuzz with activity around *Ban ki Sundari*. Every day, a posse of extras arrived, and we spent our time with them, engrossed in inane chatter. One day, we were sitting and chatting over a round of tea in Niaz Mohammad's dressing room when Ustad, the make-up master, walked in to inform us that the actress selected to play the vamp had arrived and was about to give her opening shot. The arrival of a new girl in the studio tends to cause a thrill; warmed up by the hot tea and the news, we trooped out to inspect her.

It was evening. Seth Hormuzji Framji had stepped out of his office and was standing by the driveway; he helped himself to a tobacco-laced paan from the tabla player Isa's box and tucked it into his fat rosy cheek. That was when we spotted her—and the scene was over in a flash. Still, from what I could figure out, she was a dusky woman. She shook hands with the seth and drove off in the studio's limousine, and he headed towards the billiards room. Niaz Mohammad informed me that she had thick lips. Ustad, who probably had not caught a glimpse of her, shook his head in disappointment and wrote her off as 'Kundum!'

Five days passed before we saw the new girl in the studio again. On the sixth day, I was walking out of Gulab's hotel after a cup of tea when I bumped into her. I tend to steal looks at women, but when I find a woman right in front of me, I fail to see her. I did not see her until she bumped into me. All I could notice were her feet in delicate open-toed sandals in the latest fashion. I saw that they made it difficult for her to walk the short distance on the gravel path that led to the film studio.

Over time, Miss Neelam and I became friends. Nobody in the studio was aware of it, but an air of informality developed between us. Her real name was Radha. When I asked her why she had changed such a lovely name to Neelam, promptly she responded, 'For no particular reason,' but then she looked me in the eye and added, 'such a lovely name isn't suitable for a film actress.'

Her response may lead you to think that Radha was of a religious disposition, but she had no ties with any religion or its rituals. She loved the name Radha in the same way that I unconsciously write the numeric equivalent (786) of 'Bismillah' or 'In the name of Allah' before I begin a new piece of work. Since she did not like being called Radha, I shall refer to her as Neelam.

Neelam was the daughter of a tawa'if from Banaras and spoke Hindustani in the charming eastern UP diction. My name is Saadat, but she always called me Sadiq. Once, I asked her, 'Neelam, you know my name is Saadat. Why don't you call me by my name?'

A shadow of a smile appeared on her thin dark lips, 'Once I make a mistake, I never bother to correct it.'

Neelam was no ordinary actress but an individual with a singular disposition. Her eyes held a hint of sadness, and that shadow of a smile created an aura of inaccessibility. She had none of the racy traits required to play a vamp, and I fail to understand how she was assigned the role in *Ban ki Sundari*. When she appeared for her first shot, her tight-fitting choli offended my eyes. Quick at reading people's reactions, she explained, 'The director said, "You're not a decent woman, and must dress your part." I told him, "If you call this a dress, I am willing to go naked on the set!"'

'What did the director say?' I asked.

That usual shadow of a smile appeared, 'He began to imagine me in the nude. Foolish man. After seeing me in this outfit, where's the need to see me naked?'

In Bombay, the monsoon starts in June and continues well into September. In the first few weeks, the rain comes down in torrents and makes it impossible to get any work done. We started shooting *Ban ki Sundari* at the end of April and had completed our third set by the time the first rains arrived, and then, all work came to a halt. Everyone sat around idle for several weeks, with the rain cascading down on us.

I spent almost the entire day drinking tea in the company of flies at Gulab's unspeakably squalid hotel, with a corrugated iron sheet for a roof. Throughout the day, thoroughly or partially drenched people walked in seeking shelter from the rain. Gulab's hotel smacked of squalor. Soggy tea cloths lay unnoticed on the backs of chairs, just as knives smeared with sliced onion lay forgotten elsewhere. And Gulab stood surrounded by this mayhem, flashing his carnivorous teeth with particles of meat stuck between the gaps, spouting Bombay Urdu: 'Hey mother...can't gola there! Too much confuyionschh. Yaar, you wantla fight?'

Barring Seth Hormuzji Framji, his brother-in-law Edelji, and the heroine, everyone from the studio hung around at Gulab's hotel. Niaz Mohammad popped in several times a day to visit Chunni and Munni, his two cats. Raj Kishore dropped by at least once, and the moment his tall, athletic frame appeared in the doorway, all eyes but mine began to sparkle. Young actors stood up in deference and offered their chairs to Raj Bhai. When he accepted a proffered chair and sat down, people hovered around him like moths around a flame. Invariably, his conversation followed two drifts: one with young male extras, who praised Raj Kishore's acting in his earlier films, and another strand where Raj Kishore rambled on about how he left school and college to enter the film world. I had heard all his stories, so I said my goodbyes and exited the hotel the moment I spotted him.

One afternoon, when there was some respite from the rain Hormuzji Framji's terrified Alsatian ran into Gulab's hotel, fleeing Niaz Mohammad's two cats, who were hot on his chase. On my way to the recording room, I spotted Neelam and Raj Kishore deep in conversation, sitting on the circular concrete seat under the maulsari tree in the courtyard. Raj Kishore was swaying backwards and forwards, a sign that, in his opinion, he had something of immense importance to impart. At one point, I noticed he stopped swaying and took out a thick notebook from the khadi bag slung across his shoulder, and instantly, I recognized it as his diary.

Every night, after he completed his day's work and received his father and stepmother's blessings, Raj Kishore wrote his diary. Although he loved the Punjabi language, he penned his daily log in English with discernible touches of Tagore's delicate style, inflected by Gandhi's political thought, charged with Shakespearean drama. It held neither veracity nor insight into the writer's mind. If ever you come across this diary, you will read an account of two decades of Raj Kishore's life and learn how much he collected for and donated to charity, how many public meetings he attended, and what he wore. If my assessment of his diary is correct, you will find my name alongside the thirty-five rupees I borrowed from him. I did not return the money I owed him because I knew he would not record this second fact in his diary.

I saw Raj Kishore read a few pages from his journal to Neelam and could tell from a distance that he was delivering a paean to himself in the Shakespearean style. Neelam remained seated on the circular concrete seat under the maulsari tree. Raj Kishore's words had little effect on the eternally withdrawn and thoughtful expression on her face; her gaze was fixed on the dark hair on his heaving fair chest, visible through the unbuttoned collar of his kurta. I am not sure when Neelam and Raj Kishore first met, but Neelam knew him before she entered the film world. On at least two occasions, I had heard her admire his stunning body.

All around the studio, as far as the eye could see, everything looked bathed and clean. Niaz Mohammad's usually grimy cats lay freshly rinsed on a bench, wiping their mouths with their soft paws. Neelam was draped in a bright white georgette sari, and her white linen blouse presented an appealing contrast against her firm, dusky arms. A thought crossed my mind, 'Why does she look so different?' Our eyes met briefly, and I got the answer to my question. Neelam was deeply in love and spellbound. She waved her hand to summon me, and we made small talk. After Raj Kishore departed, she said, 'You must come home with me this evening.'

At six o'clock that evening, Neelam and I were at her place. The moment we entered, she tossed her bag on the sofa, and without looking at me, she said, 'Your thoughts are baseless.'

I understood what she meant and asked, 'How did you know what I was thinking?'

I saw that shadow of a smile cross her face. 'I know. Both of us are thinking about the same thing. I've thought about the matter, and I think we are wrong.'

'If I insist that both of us are right?'

She sat on the sofa and answered, 'Then, we are idiots.' Her dusky face darkened, 'Sadiq, how is this possible? Am I a child that I do not understand my heart? How old do you think I am?'

'Twenty-two.'

'Correct! But you do not know that I knew what love meant at the age of ten. Forget the meaning of love; I swear upon God, I have loved. I was imprisoned in a dangerous love, from the age of ten until I was sixteen. How can a new love take hold of my heart?'

She looked at my impassive face and continued, 'You will never believe me; even if I take my heart out and show it to you, you will not believe me. I know you too well. I swear upon God; may I drop dead if I am lying. It's no longer possible for me to love anyone, but I must say….' She did not complete her sentence.

I remained silent because she was deep in thought. The shadow of a smile reappeared on her lips and gave her eternally withdrawn face a mischievous look. She sprang up from the sofa, 'But I must say, this is not love; Sadiq, I assure you…call it by any other name….'

I responded with alacrity, 'You are trying to reassure yourself!'

Outraged, she retorted, 'You're depraved. In any case, why do I have to assure you? I am trying to convince myself, but the trouble is I can't. Can you help me?'

She sat down next to me on the sofa. Playing with the little finger of her right hand, she continued, 'What do you think of Raj Kishore? What I mean is, in your opinion, what is it that I like about him?' She let go of her little finger and, in quick succession, began to pull at each finger of her right hand.

'I do not like him…I do not like what he has to say. I do not like his acting. I do not like his diary. Who knows what rubbish he was spouting today!'

Unhappy with herself, she stood up, 'I can't figure out what's wrong with me. I want a huge upheaval—like cats fighting with dust in the air. Sadiq, what do you think? What sort of a woman am I?'

I smiled and said, 'Cats and women are beyond my comprehension….'

She interrupted, 'Why?'

I thought for a while and said, 'We had a cat; once a year she had a hysterical fit, and in response to her wails, a tomcat appeared on the scene. There was such a kerfuffle between them. Oh God, I tell you, such blood and gore. After this, she became the mother of four or five kittens.'

Neelam's mouth turned sour, 'Yuck! What a filthy chap you are….'

She sat quietly for a while and declared, 'Change the subject… I loathe the idea of children.' She opened her paandaan to prepare a paan for me. She applied cachetu and lime on a green leaf, from which she had removed all the veins, and folded it into a triangular gilauri with her slim fingers. As she offered it to me, she asked, 'What do you think, Sadiq?'

'About what?'

She cut roasted betel nut with a sarota as she said, 'About this nonsense that has erupted for no rhyme or reason. I mean, what else is this but nonsense? I rip the fabric apart, and I darn it. If this continues, who knows what will happen? You don't know what an astonishing woman I am.'

'What do you mean by astonishing?'

That same shadow of a smile appeared on Neelam's lips. 'You are shameless. You know what I mean, and yet you want to needle me.' The white of her eyes turned pink. 'Why don't you understand?

I am a passionate woman.' She stood up as she spoke, 'You better leave; I want to take a bath.'

I left.

Neelam did not mention Raj Kishore for several days, but since we could read each other's minds, our communication continued. One day, Kripalani, the director of *Ban ki Sundari,* was rehearsing a song with the heroine, and all of us had gathered in the music room. The lyrics were coarse, but the melody was catchy. Neelam was sitting on a chair beating time with her foot. As the rehearsal ended, Raj Kishore walked in with his khadi bag slung across his shoulder. He greeted everyone individually, starting with the director, Kripalani; music director, Ghosh; and sound recordist, P. N. Mogha. He turned to the heroine Eidan Bai, joined his hands, and swaying in his usual manner, said, 'Namaste, Behen. Yesterday, I was buying mausumis for your Bhabi at Crawford Market and spotted your car.'

Finally, his eyes fell upon Neelam, sunk in an armchair near the piano. As he swung around to greet her and joined his hands in a namaste, Neelam stood up and remonstrated, 'Raj Sahib, please do not call me behen!' Everyone in the music room was rendered speechless; Raj Kishore looked sheepish and could barely bring himself to ask why.

Neelam did not respond and left the room.

Three days later, I visited Shyam Lal's paan shop late in the afternoon and found it abuzz with gossip about the episode in the music room. Shyam Lal was holding forth, 'The bitch must have evil intentions; why else would she object to Raj Bhai calling her "sister"! Come what may, her wish will not be granted. Raj Bhai is fidelity personified!'

I was bored with Raj Bhai's fidelity and did not respond to Shyam Lal's rants. Instead I sat down and heard him and his friends exaggerate and embellish the episode in a manner with no bearing on reality.

In the studio, too, everyone wanted to know why Miss Neelam did not want Raj Bhai to call her his 'behen'. I did not hear Raj Kishore air his views on the matter. A mutual friend, who read an extraordinary account of the incident in Raj Kishore's diary, told me that the hero prayed to God to cleanse Miss Neelam's heart and mind of sinful emotions and intentions. For some weeks, nothing of great importance transpired. Neelam appeared more thoughtful than she did before the episode, and the buttons of Raj Kishore's kurta remained permanently undone, revealing his broad fair chest covered with dark hair.

It had not rained for a few days, and the paint dried up on *Ban ki Sundari*'s fourth set. Director Kripalani had an announcement put up on the noticeboard for shooting to commence. The scene in question was between Neelam and Raj Kishore. Since I had written the dialogue, I knew that Raj Kishore had to kiss Neelam's hand halfway through their conversation. There was no need for a kiss in the scene, but Kripalani was faithful to the old formula he and other directors deployed to titillate audiences.

I was present on the set when shooting commenced. I must add, as I was thinking about how Raj Kishore and Neelam would behave with each other, I felt a wave, like an electric current run through my body. The first scene finished with no untoward episode. Predictably, the lights were switched on and off after every dialogue. The air echoed with 'Start!' and 'Cut!' They shot the climax that evening. Raj Kishore held Neelam's hand in a courtly manner, turned his back on the camera, pushed her hand away and kissed his own. I waited for Neelam to plant such a tight slap on Raj Kishore's cheek that its echo would cause the sound recordist P. N. Mogha's eardrums to burst. Instead, I saw a controlled smile on Neelam's thin lips. There was no trace of feelings of a woman scorned. I was sorely disappointed but did not mention this to her. She, too, did not speak of the matter. I concluded that Neelam missed the intended slight because she was so overcome on hearing professions of love from Raj Kishore, a man known to address every other woman than his wife as his sister. I asked myself several questions: Why did Raj Kishore kiss his hand instead of Neelam's? Was he settling scores? Did he want to insult Neelam? I had no answers.

On the fourth day of the shoot, on my regular visit to Shyam Lal's paan shop in Nagpara, Shyam Lal upbraided me, 'Manto Sahib, you never tell us anything about your film company. Either you don't want to tell us, or you don't know what Raj Bhai did...' And he began to recount the story. 'There was a scene in *Ban ki Sundari* in which the director ordered Raj Bhai to kiss Miss Neelam on her lips. I ask you, is there any comparison between Raj Bhai and that hussy? Raj Bhai declined immediately, saying, "No, Sir, I'll do no such thing. I have a wife at home! How can my lips kiss my virtuous wife after I have kissed this fallen woman?" So the director had to change the scene. He told Raj Bhai, "Well then, don't kiss her lips, kiss her hand instead!" Aha! Raj Bhai is no greenhorn; he kissed his own hand with such finesse that everyone thought he had kissed that slut's hand!'

I did not mention this conversation to Neelam; I saw little point in adding to her misery.

I cannot recall the exact date or month, but *Ban ki Sundari*'s fifth set was under construction, and the monsoon continued to pour down on us. Neelam was gripped by a high fever; I had no work in the studio and kept her company for hours. Malaria added a deathly pallor to her dusky complexion, and the indescribable bitterness now discernible in her eyes and around the corners of her mouth gave her a hitherto unseen air of vulnerability. Moreover, large quantities of quinine had affected her hearing; when she raised her frail voice, perhaps, she thought I, too, had lost my sense of hearing.

Neelam began to receive visitors after her temperature returned to normal and remained so for over a week. One day, she was lying on her bed and very gracefully thanking the heroine, Eidan Bai, for visiting her when the sound of a car horn penetrated the air. I saw Neelam shiver and sensed a cold wave travel across her body. Not much later, someone pushed open the heavy mahogany door that led into her room. Raj Kishore entered, dressed in a white khadi kurta and a tight white churidar pyjama. His sharp-featured domesticated wife was with him; she looked cast in a mould from a bygone era. Raj Kishore greeted 'Eidan Behen', shook my hand, introduced all of us to his wife, and sat down on Neelam's bed. He gazed emptily into space before he turned towards her, and for the first time, I saw a dark expression in his usually bright eyes.

I was trying to figure out what was afoot when Raj Kishore said in a light-hearted tone, 'I've wanted to enquire after your health for some time, but my wretched car packed up and it was in the workshop for more than ten days. Just got it back today, and immediately, I said to Shanti, "Up Shanti, this very minute, we must leave now... immediately; someone else can handle the kitchen chores. What a coincidence, it's Raksha Bandhan today! Let's go and enquire after Neelam Behen so I can ask her to tie a rakhi around my wrist.'' He put his hand into the front pocket of his khadi kurta and pulled out a floral bracelet with two silk pompoms, which he had bought to perform the symbolic ritual that celebrates the bond between a brother and sister.

As the deathly pallor of Neelam's face heightened, Raj Kishore looked away from her and turned to Eidan Bai, 'What a happy occasion! But how will my frail sister have the energy to tie the knot? Shanti, put some lipstick on her. Where is her vanity case?'

Neelam's vanity case was on the mantelpiece. Raj Kishore reached for it, and in a few long strides, carried it to her bed. Neelam remained silent, with her thin lips pursed as though she wished to suppress a scream. Shanti rose like a dutiful wife who knows that her husband is her god and master on earth. Propped up by Eidan Bai, much like a corpse, Neelam did not protest when Shanti put on her make-up and smeared lipstick on her in a hasty manner. Neelam looked at me and smiled. Her smile was a silent scream.

I felt something would happen. Neelam's pursed lips would open, and the torrent of her repressed feelings would burst forth uncontrollably and push us into an unknown abyss. After Shanti completed her task, I was astonished when she remained silent and expressionless as though made of stone—her pallor concealed under a layer of make-up and lipstick. She turned to Raj Kishore and asked him courteously, 'Give it to me...now I'll tie the raksha bracelet.' She steadied her trembling hands and tied the knot.

As Neelam tied the knot of the bracelet of flowers with its soft pompoms firmly around Raj Kishore's wrist, once again, I noticed the intensity of the dark look in Raj Kishore's bright eyes, but he managed a contrived laugh. In keeping with the niceties of the ritual, Raj Kishore, who was now Neelam's brother, handed her an envelope with some paper currency; she accepted it with grace and tucked it under her pillow.

After her visitors departed, Neelam and I were on our own. She looked at me, and I could see she was devastated. Then, silently, she lay her head down on her pillow. Raj Kishore had left his bag on Neelam's bed, and she pushed it aside with her foot. I sat with her for another two hours, quietly reading the newspaper. She did not utter a word, and I did not take my leave before I left.

Three days after this episode, I was in my nine-rupees-a-month kholi in Nagpara, busy with my morning routine—shaving and listening to my neighbour Mrs Fernandez shouting and hurling abuses at whoever was within earshot. Someone rushed in, and I turned around. For a moment, I wondered who had barged in. It did not take me long to register that Neelam was standing before me. The lipstick smeared across her lips looked as though blood had dripped from her mouth and congealed. Not a hair on her head was in place. The white applique flowers on her white sari were in tatters, and through her unbuttoned white blouse, I could see bruises on her dusky breasts. I could not bring myself to ask what had happened or how she got to my place. My instant reaction was to shut the door. She leaned against my writing table. As I pulled up a chair to sit near her, she said, 'I've come here directly.'

I asked gently, 'From where?'

'From my place...I've come to tell you that the nonsense that had started has finished.'

'How?'

'I knew he would return to my house at a time when I would be on my own.' She continued to speak, and the same shadow of a smile appeared on her lips, now shapeless because of the smeared lipstick. 'He returned for his bag. I told him, "It's in the other room." I think my tone was odd because he looked worried. I said, "Don't worry." When we entered the other room, instead of returning his bag, I sat down in front of the dressing table and began to apply my make-up.'

She became silent. Neelam picked up the glass of water on my rickety old table and drank its contents. She wiped her mouth with the corner of her sari pallu and resumed her account. 'For an hour, I continued to apply my make-up; I smeared as much lipstick and plastered as much powder as I could on my face. He stood there, staring at me silently. I looked like a witch. Sure-footed, I walked to the door and bolted it.'

'Then, what happened?' I turned towards Neelam in search of an answer

As she wiped her lips with her sari pallu, the lipstick left eerie smudges. I thought she must have looked like a witch when she put on her make-up for Raj Kishore. Neelam did not respond to my question but moved away from my rickety desk and sat on my rope charpai before she continued, 'I held him by his shoulders and shook him and clung to him like a wildcat. I scratched his face, and he scratched mine as we wrestled with each other. Raj Kishore had the energy of the devil, but I've told you that I am an astonishing woman. Gone was the weakness that had overcome me after malaria; my body burned, and my eyes were full of fire. I have strong bones; I caught him and fought with him like a cat. I don't know why. We did not utter a word that could make sense to anyone. I continued to scream, but the only sound he produced was "hoonh...hoonh". I clawed at his white khadi kurta, and he pulled out clumps of my hair. He expended his full strength as he tried to overpower me, but resolute that victory would be mine, I had him there flat on the carpet like a corpse. As I ripped his kurta to shreds, I was so breathless I thought my heart would stop any minute. When I saw his broad fair chest, I got to the core of that nonsense—that nonsense both of us discussed but could not figure out.'

Neelam stood up hastily, tidied her hair, and with an equally swift movement of her head, she said, 'Sadiq, the wretch does have a beautiful body. I am not sure what happened to me; I leaned over him and started to bite him all over, and he whimpered. I planted my bloodied lips on him, and when I gave him a smouldering kiss, he collapsed like a conquered woman. I stood up and looked down at him—repelled. My blood and lipstick had left ugly marks that crept like ivy all over his body. I looked around my room; everything appeared false. I feared I might choke to death and opened the door and came directly to you.'

She finished her account and fell silent like a corpse. Terrified, I touched her limp hand that seemed to dangle from the edge of my charpai: it was on fire. I called her softly, 'Neelam...Neelam...!' And then somewhat louder, 'Neelam!' I called her name several times, but she did not respond. Terrified, I shouted, 'Neelam!'

She gave a start and stood up from the charpai, held my hand and squeezed it. Before she left, all she said was, 'Saadat, my name is Radha!'

# 6

## Scissors from Meerut

Finally, the shadow cast on Filmistan and our lives by the failure of *Chal Chal re Naujawan* (Onwards, Young Man) was about to lift. Gyan Mukherjee started work on a script for a propaganda film, but before the story took shape, the studio signed a one-year contract—I believe for twenty-five thousand rupees—with Nalini Jayant and her husband, Virendra Desai (from whom she is now divorced). The production controller, Shashidhar Mukherjee, typically dragged his heels. Still, Gyan Mukherjee tucked the bare outline of a story into his bag and set off for Delhi to get government approval.

As the shoot drew nearer, Virendra Desai demanded that his contract be extended for another year because the existing contract was about to end. Rai Bahadur Chunni Lal, the managing director, was a stubborn man and did not agree. In the court case that ensued, the judge ruled in Desai's and Nalini's favour. The bare synopsis of the propaganda film now faced a loss of both time and money. Rai Bahadur wanted a quick release, so he summoned the lyricist Wali Sahib and signed up his wife, Mumtaz Shanti, with an advance of fourteen thousand rupees—in black, without a receipt.

The shoot commenced and continued for two days. After various major and minor glitches, they shot a brief dialogue between Mumtaz Shanti and Ashok Kumar. At the screen test, everyone rejected Mumtaz Shanti's work. In part, the opposition stemmed from the fact that she turned up to work in a burqa. Besides, Wali Sahib had told Mukherjee quite categorically that no one was to touch any part of his wife's body. The producers declared Mumtaz Shanti unsuitable for the role, arguing that several scenes required the heroine to display certain parts of her body. In short, another fourteen thousand rupees went down the drain. With no heroine and an incomplete skeleton of a story buried under thirty-nine thousand rupees, Rai Bahadur Chunni Lal grew angrier by the day. After the flop of *Chal Chal re Naujawan*, he had propped up the company with loans from

Marwaris. His anger was justified.

One afternoon, Vacha, Pai, Ashok, and I were deep in conversation sitting in the studio courtyard, lamenting the litany of mistakes responsible for the company's losses. Ashok told us that he had loaned Rai Bahadur the fourteen thousand rupees lost on Mumtaz Shanti; he made this disclosure while scratching his shin in such a peculiar manner that the four of us broke into laughter. That very moment we saw our hefty hairdresser and an unknown woman making their way up the gravel path to the studio dressing room. Datta Ram Pai parted his thick black lips, revealing his scary uneven, filthy buck teeth, and nudged Vacha, 'Who is she?'

'You so-and-so, who are you to ask?' Vacha retorted and slapped the back of Pai's head. 'She'll run away if she sees you!

Pai could do little but clench his hideous teeth. Ashok, who had remained quiet throughout this exchange, passed his verdict in English, *'She's good looking!'*

I looked at her and responded in Urdu, 'Yes, doesn't go down bad on the eyes.'

'Doesn't go where?'

I explained, 'I meant that the woman who just walked by is pleasing to the eyes...spick-and-span, but a bit short.'

Yet again, Pai flashed his hideous teeth and added, 'She'll do.... Why, Vacha?'

Vacha ignored Pai and asked Ashok, 'Dadamoni, do you know who she is?'

'No, not really...although I did hear from Mukherjee that someone was coming for a screen test today.'

All of us were summoned for the screen and sound test and asked to give our opinions. Ashok and Vacha dismissed her outright; they thought her movements, expressions, and laugh were like a naach girl's. Pai had flipped for her and repeated himself several times in English, *'Vunderful screen face! Vunderful screen face!'* Datta Ram Pai was a film editor and an expert in his field. At Filmistan, a studio where all men and women were encouraged to express their points of view, Pai continued to spout his wanted and unwanted opinions with abandon, undeterred by my sarcastic jibes.

Rai Bahadur Chunni Lal ignored our objections and signed up

this woman on a meagre monthly salary. Her name was Paro. An agreeable, witty, and entertaining tawa'if, she was from Meerut, where all the local wealthy hedonists admired her. Paro had refined biting to an art form; her teeth left such distinctive marks on her victims' flesh that they named her 'Scissors from Meerut', in a play on the Urdu word 'kaat', which means to cut and to bite. Paro had plenty of money—it was her love of the cinema that brought her to Filmistan. In the many conversations with her, I learnt that Josh Malihabadi, Saghar Nizami, and other poets were regulars at her salon. Her diction was as smooth as her skin, and I admired both. Her tight-fitting short-sleeved blouses showed off her firm, creamy arms shaped like elephant tusks, which glowed like the polished bark of a willow tree.

Every morning, Paro arrived at the studio, surrounded by a wholesome aura. Freshly bathed, impeccably turned out, invariably clad in a white or pastel sari, she looked like an advertisement for a superior soap. She appeared as well groomed at the end of the working day as she did in the morning. Datta Ram Pai fell deeper in love with her. Since the shooting was on hold, he had no work and spent his time chatting with Paro. I am not sure what she thought of his coarse manner, his crooked buck teeth, and his overgrown fingernails with dark deposits of grime underneath. A simple explanation comes to mind—a tawa'if can endure a lot.

I was assigned the task of reviewing and tweaking the synopsis of the propaganda film. I looked at it and concluded that rarely had I come across such a disjointed script. Since it was a test of my ability, I immersed myself in a new treatment. Besides, I had recommended my friend Savak Vacha as director, so the film took on an added significance for me. When the 'full bench' at Filmistan gathered to hear the new outline, I felt like an accused in the dock. Shashidhar Mukherjee's judgement was brief: 'All right but needs amendments.'

Gyan Mukherjee's face puckered as usual, 'Almost there.'

Here was the gentleman whose name appeared in the credits as director of all the films directed by Shashidhar Mukherjee, although he had not directed a foot of celluloid in his entire life. The modus operandi at Filmistan was curious: You could direct the film, but my name appeared on the screen! The story is mine, and your name appears in the credits. I suppose you could call it a 'real' team effort. Imagine the chaos: my adviser was Datta Ram Pai, who did not know the first thing about storytelling. Only someone familiar with the craft can appreciate the challenges involved in writing a propaganda film.

The trickiest task was how to introduce Paro in the film. Her lovely face came with two handicaps. She had no idea of what it meant to be an actor, and she was short. Nevertheless, the story took shape, and we began to shoot. Everyone agreed to schedule Paro's scenes at the end of the shoot because this would give her time to soak in the studio's atmosphere and feel comfortable before the camera. Regardless of the shooting schedule, Paro hung around with us. Datta Ram Pai became very informal and engaged her in pointless banter, which irritated me no end. In Paro's absence, I took sarcastic digs at him, and the idiot responded, 'Saale, are you jealous?'

Paro was not your standard flashy tawa'if. She could hold her own in polite circles and conversed in chaste Urdu that she had picked up most likely because the cognoscenti and not the riff-raff visited her salon in Meerut. Paro soon became part of the studio. Her courteous disposition won her the respect of the junior staff, who referred to her as 'Paro Devi'. The name caught on, and she appeared as 'Paro Devi' in film credits too.

I am not aware of the tricks Pai deployed, but his relationship with Paro progressed. One day, he was invited to her house and experienced her gracious hospitality. After that, Pai became a regular and turned up at Paro's several times a week. In the canteen, he bragged about his visits, infusing his account with a hint of romance. Vacha and I pulled his leg, but he was too thick-skinned for our barbs to deter him. Occasionally, in Paro's presence, I mocked Pai about his unrequited love. She sat there with a composed smile and revealed the pearly white scissors, which had shredded who knows how many hearts in Meerut.

Pai's predicament became more comical by the day. One evening, when he was at her place, Paro poured him two pegs of Johnnie Walker whisky, after which he got a bit drunk. Then, Paro being Paro, asked him very affectionately to recline on her sofa. Now convinced that Paro was madly in love with him, Pai thought all of us were about to die of jealousy. I am not sure what Paro thought about all this. She did not live on her own but with an older man who was twice her height. I had seen Paro with him a couple of times. He was not her wedded lord and master but seemed more of a minder or keeper.

The producers selected Veera, a Parsi actress, as the heroine, and Paro played a supporting role of a fiery girl from a rebellious Burmese tribe. As her schedule approached, I dreaded Paro would prove to be a disappointment. Finally, on the morning of her first shot, she arrived before the camera, all made-up and dressed in a rather garish short choli that revealed a bit of her stomach above the belly button. A short lehnga swirled around, about six inches above her knees. She did not look nervous before the camera or the mike, and we had made sure she knew her dialogue, but when it came to her first take, her entire body turned into a plank of wood. She delivered her dialogue in a flat monotone. Several rehearsals followed, but nothing could breathe life into that dead wood. When she tried to act, she raised her eyebrows like a professional dancer eager to fix her price. After several retakes, I lost all faith in her ability to act. Finally, Vacha asked Gyan Mukherjee to 'fix' her. How could Mukherjee fix her—she was formed of a clay immersed in the art of dance and mime. Finally, in a take where her performance was just about acceptable, Mukherjee locked the shot. All of us tried to help her lose the stylized body and facial movements she had picked up over the years, but Paro did not improve.

Disappointed by her lack of talent, I decided to edit and cut out her scenes. She heard about this from Pai and began to sit with me between takes. Often, we chatted for hours, and in her refined diction she praised me without a hint of flattery, and invited me to her house a couple of times. I may well have visited her, but the propaganda film's screenplay was on my mind, although by now I had three assistants, namely Raja Mehdi Ali Khan, Mohsin Abdullah, and Dixit. Raja Mehdi Ali Khan was perpetually engrossed in writing love letters to his perpetually peeved wife. Mohsin Abdullah (the inscrutable Nina's husband) was cementing his ties with Veera, and Dixit, who was Paro's coach, was occupied in helping her memorize her dialogue.

In the film world, it is not unusual for a man to grab a new actress the moment she arrives at the studio, rather like a cricket ball hit by a bat and caught by one of the many fielders awaiting his prize. Nobody pounced on Paro; perhaps, Filmistan was not as predatory as other studios, or perhaps it was simply that Paro was not in a hurry to get caught. Mohsin Abdullah was busy trying to strike a marital relationship with Veera. He stopped travelling to work with us because we travelled in second-class carriages, and Veera travelled first class. To win her, he followed the rules of *etiquette* and often walked around with her pet dog's leash wrapped around his wrist. After all, Laila's bitch was dear to Majnun, the imam of all lovers.

Vacha, who had recently divorced his horrid French wife, had no interest in Neelam. Shashidhar Mukherjee was besotted with the fairylike Naseem Bano; Gyan Mukherjee was content with his wife and not in the count. All I can say about myself is that I liked Paro's skin. One day, I mentioned this to Shahid Latif (a film director and producer). He smiled, and responded with an Urdu pun, 'You love her jild [skin], that's fine, but do you know what lies inside the jild [cover] of the book?'

Paro was playing an independent, headstrong, and passionate tribal girl who loves Ashok, but he loves Rita (Veera). When Paro and Ashok faced each other on set, she looked at him with such passion that it seemed Paro wanted Ashok to accept the dialogue as reality and not mere acting. Ashok was a rather bashful kind of guy who couldn't express his love for any woman. I knew Ashok fancied Paro but did not have the nerve to have a physical relationship with her. Hundreds of girls had entered Ashok's life—not hundreds but thousands. If he wished he could have styled himself on Lord Byron, but restrained by his natural reticence, he disappointed all the butterflies who longed to be captured by him. Those were the days when any actress would be Ashok's for the asking. Many were ready to throw themselves at him. I told myself, 'Nothing surprising if Paro's heart is aflutter.' Moreover, she was new in the field, and an attachment with Ashok could propel her to stardom.

The film provided Paro plenty of opportunities to express her love for Ashok. We were shooting indoors and outdoors, and one day, we were on location on the sea. There were two boats—one for

Ashok and one for Paro. Paro had to jump into Ashok's boat the moment her boat approached his. The water was deep. Paro jumped as directed but misjudged the distance between the two boats and fell into the sea. Vacha shouted for help, and instantly some fishermen on the shore jumped into the sea and rescued Paro. Although a woman, Paro remained undaunted by this episode. She dried her clothes, put on her make-up, and in no time, was ready for the next take. As she squeezed her clothes dry, Ashok and I caught an enticing glimpse of one of her rather lovely legs. On our way home from the location, Ashok said, 'Manto, Paro's leg looked delicious. I wanted to roast it and eat it.'

I was stunned. Ashok was so conventional, and a sissy. Perhaps this was an expression of his repressed emotions.

Every day, Ashok and I returned home from the studio in his MG, and on the way, we chatted about all manner of things. Every day, we drove down a road from where a turn led to Paro's flat. One evening, we were driving past Paro's lane as usual when Ashok stopped the car. I asked, 'What's up?'

Ashok turned around to look at the lane, 'This morning Paro invited me to celebrate Holi. Should I go?'

What objection could I have? 'You must go,' I said.

'Then, you must come along.'

I said, 'How can I? She hasn't invited me.'

'Never mind,' said Ashok and turned his car around swiftly. We reached Paro's flat, and he applied the brakes. When he blew the horn, Vacha and Pai appeared on the balcony. Pai spotted me and flashed his hideous teeth, 'Arrey, you're here as well.'

Vacha turned to Ashok, 'Come, Dadamoni, we were waiting for you.'

Paro was dressed uncharacteristically as a bride and had draped her sari in the Parsi style. She greeted us graciously and regretted that she had forgotten to invite me. Rounds of drinking began, and Pai was tipsy after his first peg. Vacha requested Paro to sing a few songs. Paro looked at Ashok as though about to devour him, and asked, 'Ashok Sahib, would you care to hear something?'

Ashok blushed. 'If you sing, I shall listen.'

Paro commenced with a few bazaari thumris, followed by a ghazal, followed by a film song, and as she continued to sing, Paro's husband or whatever he was, continued to replenish everyone's glasses with soda and whisky. Pai's eyes were about to close after his second peg. A moderate drinker, Ashok stopped at a peg and a half. Vacha covered his glass after his third. Thumris, ghazals, and geets continued for a while, and finally, Paro sang a bhajan. After this, probably to please me, she began to sing a na'at in praise of the Prophet Muhammad, and I stopped her, 'Paro Devi, we're assembled here for pleasure and drinking; I don't think it appropriate to mention the one in the black cloak.'

She apologized and acknowledged her mistake. The food was excellent, but Ashok ate quite fast. Paro stood up to take him to wash his hands. He looked agitated when he returned and hurriedly begged his leave. He took me along and drove off; we remained silent, and he dropped me home.

Several evenings after Holi, we were halfway through the film shoot, and Ashok was dropping me home. When we drove past Shivaji Park where Paro lived, he slowed down and turned to me. 'Manto, let me tell you something interesting....' His voice had a distinct tremor.

I recalled how agitated he was the night of the Holi party, and urged him, 'Yes, please do....'

He continued, '...that evening when Paro handed me a towel in the bathroom, she said, "Come alone tomorrow at six-thirty in the evening." I was so shocked I dropped the towel and stepped out.' He stopped the car by the kerb.

I asked him, 'Did you go?'

'Yes,' said Ashok. Lifting his hands off the steering wheel, he rubbed them hard, 'But I ran away.'

I wanted to know the details, 'What happened? Recount the whole scenario.'

'I am a coward. I'm not sure what happens to me on such occasions. She invited me to sit on the sofa and gave me two pegs. She had a little something herself before she lowered herself down on the carpet, leaned her head on my knees, and embarked on a declaration of love. I began to tremble. When she squeezed my hand, something compelled me to push her aside. Her eyes welled up with tears that disappeared in no time; she smiled and said, "Ashok Bhai! I was testing you." My head began to spin, and I stood up. She continued, "Ashok Sahib, you are like a brother to me." I did not respond and climbed down the stairs, sat in my car, and drove home, where I had half a peg of whisky. When I thought about what happened that evening, I felt dejected. Would it be wrong if I had…?'

I said, 'Of course not, nothing wrong.'

I sensed a profound sense of loss in Ashok's voice and recalled an outdoor shoot. On a bitterly cold night of celebration, I had seen Ashok and his heroine Veera on the dance floor with their arms around each other. Across the floor, a statuesque Paro stood alone—a quintessence of sorrow.

## Cause for Concern

Naim entered my room and sank into a chair. I did look up but thought I'd continue my piece for the evening edition of my newspaper. When I noticed his unusually troubled expression, I took off my spectacles and studied his face, 'What's up, Naim? You look unwell.'

Naim ran his tongue across his dry lips, 'I don't quite know what to say. Out of the blue, I'm in an unimaginable mess. I can't show my face to anyone.'

I collated the various slips of paper with different news items for the day and set them to one side before turning to him with genuine concern, 'A mess...with some girl in the film company?'

Naim responded, 'No, my friend, nothing with an actress-vactress. It's another mess. If you have time, I'll relate the full story.'

Naim has been my friend since he first moved to Bombay some years ago. He began work for my paper soon after he arrived in the city and proved himself a man of many talents. He was from a distinguished family, and we had many mutual friends. Within a brief period of six months, my regard for him had increased and a spirit of amity developed between us. Naim worked hard to make my paper newsy for our readers and wrote an attention-grabbing story every week. After I had read four or five of his tales, I concluded that a more extended stint at the newspaper would cramp his style and used my influence to get him a permanent contract as a dialogue writer in a film company.

I'm a busy man and did not follow up to check the impression Naim made on various producers and directors, but he told me several times that they were pleased with his work. Naturally, I wondered what had happened to drain the colour from his face. Naim was a downright decent man, and it was impossible to attribute any inappropriate behaviour to him. What could he possibly have done that made him ashamed to show his face at his company? I finished my editorial in a rush, handed a sheaf of papers to the copy editor, and moved closer to Naim.

'Do forgive me; I couldn't give you my undivided attention. But what happened? I want the full story.'

Naim pulled out a pack of cigarettes from his pocket, lit one, and began, 'What can I say, except that whatever happened was down to my stupidity. There is an extra in our film company, Ashiq Hussain—a first-rate idiot. He is besotted with me because I don't pull his leg as others do. I use the word "besotted" because he speaks to me in the manner I would to a beautiful woman.'

I laughed, 'And, you are not beautiful!'

Naim's pallor turned crimson as he blushed and laughed, 'He is devoted to me because from time to time I help him with his pronunciation. He doesn't quite know how to express his sentiment, and his appreciation takes on the same form as the fidelity he has towards his wife. Incidentally, Ashiq Hussain Sahib is a superb dancer, but he doesn't know the first thing about anything other than dance. The day before yesterday, he sidled up to me, and in flowery Urdu, he said, "Naim Sahib, I have a humble submission."

'I responded in a similar register, "Do go ahead."

'Ashiq Hussain had given the matter some thought, and he said, "Let's go on a junket!"

'Now here, I must admit to a weakness. If the weather is agreeable and my mood capricious, nothing pleases me more than a good junket. That afternoon, a lovely soft evening breeze filled me with longing—you know the kind that often grips the hearts of lonely bachelors. My body tingled when I thought of Juhu Beach and the balmy breeze that moves like the women who stroll along the seaside in their heavy silk saris. I agreed promptly. "Let's go. But where will we go?" I asked.

'Ashiq Hussain drifted into a reflective mode and responded as though he had a revelation, "Anywhere! We can go anywhere; but first, let's get out of here." We walked out of the studio to the bus stop around the corner and awaited our ride.'

Naim stopped. A hint of colour had crept back to his face. I helped myself to one of his cigarettes and lit it before I clarified, 'Both of you walked out of the gate and were waiting for a bus?'

Naim nodded, 'It was our bad luck that Ashiq Hussain spotted his Marwari friend driving past in his car. He hollered in Marwari to draw his friend's attention. The car stopped. Ashiq Hussain ran to the car and said something to the Marwari, and ran back to me, "Now that we have found a car, let's go."

'I said, "Let's go!" and climbed into the car. Ashiq Hussain introduced me to his Marwari friend and his companion, who looked like the driver. He went into characteristic hyperbolic overdrive: "This is a wealthy seth from Marwar. He is here on some business. I owe him zillions." Then he introduced me to his friend, "He is a writer—Hindustan's greatest." The wealthy seth from Marwar and Hindustan's most illustrious writer shook hands as they exchanged polite smiles, and the car set off.'

I laughed, 'Naim, you seem to have a rather low opinion of this Marwari seth! He is not the villain of the story, is he?'

'First, hear the entire story and then decide who is the hero and who the villain. But there is no doubt in my mind that the heroine of the story is Zehra, whom I first set eyes on when I stood as an accused in a criminal court in Dadar.' Naim's earlobes turned crimson with embarrassment when he mentioned Zehra.

Struck by her sudden appearance in the story, I said, 'Naim, this sounds like a short story by Edgar Allan Poe. Zehra has appeared unexpectedly in your story like one of Poe's characters. Who is she?'

'I have no idea,' said Naim. 'May the hand of God strike me down if I know anything about her. What I do know is that she has filed a criminal case against us. Our crimes? Burglary and robbery!' Naim's voice acquired a dark sonority as though about to reveal a spiritual injury, and he repeated, 'Yes…burglary and robbery! I don't remember the exact sections of the law. All I know is that we stand accused of breaking into Zehra's house and removing some valuable goods. But this is the end of the story—let me complete the opening episodes before I return to it. Where was I?'

'You were in that Marwari's car,' I answered.

'Yes, at Ashiq Hussain's behest, I got into that cheapskate Marwari's car. He was driving with another equally worthless man sitting next to him in the front seat. If I recall correctly, Ashiq Hussain had told me that this man was a car mechanic. As we made our way through various bazaars, I felt content, lost in thoughts of Juhu Beach, where I go from time to time to lie on the soft, moist sand. I love to watch the waves turn with the ebb and flow of the tide in the grey light of the evening. As the light changes and the stars begin to twinkle, I contemplate the distant horizon where the sea and sky merge shapelessly in a faint, ephemeral glow as alluring and distant as an unknown woman. Ashiq Hussain's voice interrupted my ruminations. He asked his friend to stop the car in Dadar. He turned to me and said, "Come, let's have a drink."'

Naim continued, 'God knows how, but just as he knew I love junkets, Ashiq Hussain knew I love beer. Well, we entered a bar, where I ordered a beer, as did Ashiq Hussain. The Marwari seth and the car mechanic did not drink anything. We finished our beer in no time, went back to the car, and headed towards Juhu. But unexpectedly, Ashiq Hussain remembered, "Oh, I have to go to my student Zehra's house; I promised to meet her. Naim Sahib, if you don't mind, it will only take five minutes. Her house is just around the corner." What objection could I possibly have? Ashiq Hussain asked the Marwari to stop the car in an alley and went into a house.'

'Where was this alley?' I asked.

'In Dadar,' Naim answered, 'around countless Parsi homes.... I believe they call the place Parsi Colony.'

He continued, 'Ashiq Hussain walked across a garden towards a small double-storeyed bungalow with flats, and knocked on a door. He didn't get a response, so he knocked again. A woman's voice called from inside, "Who is it?"

'Ashiq Hussain responded in a loud and clear voice, "Ashiq!" The woman bellowed, "I'll Ashiq..."

'When Ashiq Hussain heard the abuse, he turned around to look at us before he banged the door harder and shouted, "Open the door! I said open the door!"'

I laughed, 'I think the woman misconstrued the word "Ashiq". She took it in its literal sense, which means "lover". But you just told me she was Ashiq's student.'

Naim responded, 'Who knows what the hell she was or is. Maybe Ashiq Hussain lied and the thought of seeing Zehra entered his head after he had downed a bottle of beer. Someone must have told him that a woman called Zehra lives in such-and-such a place. Leastways, Ashiq began to kick up a racket, and a barrage of expletives continued to bombard him from inside. Before I could say or do anything to stop him, Ashiq Hussain had forced open the door. Hearing the hullabaloo, many Parsi residents of the area gathered around the house.

'I resolved to bring Ashiq back and got out of the car. Ashiq's mates followed me. I peeped into all three rooms, but there was no sign of Ashiq or Zehra. I searched a pathway at the back of the bungalow and checked the three rooms again but found no trace of them. I returned to the car and sat down in the back seat, aware of the countless dirty looks from the Parsis gathered in the alley. By now, my drunkenness had travelled down from my head to my ankles, and my anxiety ratcheted.

'It crossed my mind that I should make a run for it and abandon Ashiq the lover and his companions, but I knew I was trapped. If I tried to escape, the Parsis would cook my goose. They kept their eyes on me as they would on a monkey escaped from a zoo. Fifteen minutes passed in this state of confusion before Ashiq and his two friends came out of the house and got into the car. I did not ask Ashiq any questions. As we drove out of Dadar, I said, "Just drop me here, and I'll take a bus home." Ashiq asked his Marwari friend to stop the car. I said goodbye to them and headed home and pushed the episode out of my mind.'

Naim lit another cigarette and fell silent for a while. Curious to know how matters developed, I asked, 'And what happened next?'

'I was arrested.' Naim declared in a bitter voice and continued, 'When the police cross-examined Ashiq and asked who was with him, that son of a gun named his Marwari friend, the car mechanic, and yours truly...and we were arrested within the hour.'

'When did all this happen? Why didn't you inform me?' I asked.

'Yesterday. The warrants for our arrest were issued around two-thirty. I would have called you if I had my wits about me. By God, I was worried out of my mind. The police inspector put us in a taxi and took us to the police station where they took our statements. I discovered that Ashiq Hussain's Marwari friend who had come to Bombay on some business had made off with Zehra's electric fan, which the police found on him.'

When I heard this, I commented in a troubled tone, 'But this is clear proof of theft!'

'It is proof of theft, and that is why I am so nervous. Even if there were no proof, I'd be equally concerned. Imagine being bundled off to a police station and appearing in a criminal court—it's disgraceful! I have no choice but to face the consequences. There's no way I can wash this stain off my character, although I am blameless. I mean, I don't even know Zehra. I went to her house because Ashiq Hussain took me there, and it is because of this nincompoop who cannot hold a bottle of beer that I have to face this ignominy.'

For some reason, the mixture of anger and hatred in Naim's expression made me laugh uncontrollably, 'Buddy, you're stuck!'

Naim responded bitterly, 'Yes. Laugh and pay the price! The first time I saw Zehra was in court, yesterday!'

Dying to know more, I asked, 'What's she like?'

Naim's response was perfunctory, 'Not bad, I mean as far as looks go, she's not bad. She has an oval face. As a teenager, she must have had acne. She has long black hair, a narrow forehead, and is youthful—looks like she's just entered the trade.'

I did not give the matter much thought and asked, 'What trade?'

Naim looked embarrassed, 'You know, whatever it is that women do...you can see the trademark on Zehra's face from a distance. I would not have been so furious with her, but when the magistrate pointed at me and asked her, "Do you know this man?" Zehra looked at me with her large bright eyes and said, "Yes, sir, he is the one who stole my heavy silver tea set."

'When she said this, I swear upon God, I felt like pulling a slat out from the dock and shoving it down that hussy's throat. What a monstrous lie!'

'Well, obviously she's going to lie,' I declared, 'how else will she build her case? Now you have to face the music.'

Naim looked distressed, 'Of course, I have to bear the brunt of what happens. I'm so stressed. If a man had filed this case against me, I would not be so outraged. Imagine! She is a woman, and I revere women!'

'Why?' I asked.

Naim responded quite simply, 'I suppose because I don't know them. I've never had the opportunity to chat with women in a relaxed atmosphere. Now, a woman enters my life for the first time, and she does so as a plaintiff.'

I couldn't contain my laughter, and this angered Naim, 'It's okay for you to laugh, but I am in real trouble. I haven't been to the film company for two days. They must have heard the news by now. How am I going to face Seth Sahib? How am I going to explain matters to him?'

'Tell him exactly what happened,' I suggested.

'I'll tell him, but think about it, I respect Seth Sahib because he is my boss. What if he thinks I'm immoral and dismisses me? My reputation will be stained for the rest of my life! I am more worried about the loss of face than losing my job—my good name and social standing are mud. Seth Sahib will lose all faith in me and will always suspect me of telling lies, although everyone in the film company is prone to lying, even Seth Sahib himself. What should I do? I can't figure out what to do.'

I tried hard to make Naim feel more confident, but he was a coward, particularly when it came to women, and this was a grim matter. If the police had not recovered the electric fan from the Marwari's car, the case was baseless, but to that extent, Zehra's account had a ring of truth to it. Naim did not sit around for much longer and left.

The following day, Naim returned looking more anxious than ever, and said, 'Now I'm in a real soup!'

Concerned, I asked, 'What's happened now...another case?'

'No, not another case, but there is a new development; it's most unexpected.' He looked wan and on edge and began to shake his right leg. 'This morning, Seth Sahib sent his car to pick me up. I had resolved never again to step inside the film company, but I had to go. I felt like a convicted thief. My throat was parched, and my head weighed down on me with shame. I walked into Seth Sahib's office with my eyes lowered. Seth Sahib stood up and greeted me with great warmth; he extended his hand for a handshake and chuckled, "Munshi Sahib, you've turned out to be quite a dark horse! Do take a seat."

'I could have withered away with shame, but I sat down. Seth Sahib began to chat with such bonhomie. As he rambled on, I felt someone was shredding my brain. On and on he went, "Why do you worry? All will be well. Tell me, what is this Zehra like? Is she any good? I hear that you put on such a tamasha that the whole Parsi colony gathered to watch. Somebody told me you unwrapped Zehra's sari and took off with it. I don't understand—you must be a regular, then why did the haramzadi file a report with the police? Who knows what mischief you were up to?" He chuckled and carried on endlessly in this vein before he ordered tea.

'Seth Sahib continued to chat and poured me a cup of tea before he added, with a glint in his eye, "If you give me the silver tea set you carried away, I shall take you to my lawyer this very minute. He will plead your case with such skill that Zehra will not know what hit her. I hear she is not bad looking. After the case, why don't you bring her here, we'll give her some small role in one of our films. But why did you take a dozen men with you? Poor girl must have lost her nerve." He punctuated each comment with a hearty laugh. He had hit upon a droll topic of conversation. It's extraordinary. Before now, he'd never even bothered to acknowledge my presence.'

I said, 'So what; you should be pleased he's not displeased with you.'

Naim was exasperated, 'What do you mean? Pleased! He thinks I am a thief—which I am not! What could I say? I had to remain silent, as he chatted away for some time before he summoned his cashier and asked him to give me a hundred rupees as an advance, when nobody in the studio has seen a paisa for the last two months.'

'Well, then what's wrong with that?' I asked.

'Why don't you listen to what I'm saying?' an irritated Naim continued, 'he handed me an advance of a hundred rupees and said, "keep this. You will need it for your legal costs. Let me organize a lawyer for you." Seth Sahib picked up the telephone receiver and spoke to his attorney. He walked me to his car and accompanied me to the lawyer. After he had explained everything to the lawyer, he concluded, "Put your heart and soul into this case. The matter is very straightforward because Munshi Sahib and Zehra's relationship goes back several years." What could I say? I remained silent.'

I laughed and added, 'Good, remain silent. What do you have to lose?'

An agitated Naim stood up and began to pace up and down in my office. Turning to me, he added, 'I have to state on oath in court that Zehra is my mistress and I have known her for years! And you want to know what I have to lose? To crown it all, Seth Sahib has invited me out this evening. "Let's go to Greens for some light entertainment," he said. My life is chaos. I don't know what to do.'

# 8

## Uncouth

I was dejected when I moved back to Bombay from Delhi, where I had friends who quite liked me and, most importantly, a job that lived up to my wife's expectations. I was earning two hundred and fifty rupees a month sitting at home; but without forewarning, a perverse sense of unease drove me back to Bombay. My wife wept and wailed to little avail. I have a wide social circle in Bombay, and quite enjoyed catching up with some old acquaintances after several years. I was particularly pleased to meet Izzat Jahan. You must know Izzat Jahan because who has not heard of this young woman's name, especially if you are a socialist and live in Bombay. You may well have met her on several occasions.

You must know that Izzat Jahan dedicated several years of her life to socialist pursuits and recently married a rather nondescript man. His name is Nasir, and I know him well from the dim and distant past when I called him Naso. We were in the same year at Aligarh Muslim University. A combination of ill health and poverty forced me to quit education, but Nasir, who was merely poor, managed to scrape through his BA and took up employment with a large mill in Bombay, where I met him a few times. Alas, a combination of factors forced me to leave Bombay and head to a well-paid but soul-destroying job in Delhi.

When I was in Delhi, I had kept up with Izzat Jahan's whereabouts and ideas through her writings in several newspapers and periodicals, and they left a deep impression on me. I, too, am a socialist and have written many essays on socialism. I wanted to meet the woman behind the ideas. Now, for God's sake, don't think I was in love with Izzat Jahan, but like any young school or college boy who can't resist an opportunity to talk about his puppy love, I wanted to meet her to discuss my deep commitment to socialism.

It took me some time to find and furnish a place to live in Bombay, and until then, I was putting up with a friend. I had left my wife in Delhi with the promise that she would join me the moment I found suitable accommodation. Most of my film director friends were bachelors who didn't wish to pursue a relationship with an actress or the daughter of an actor. Most of them had rather curious views on the role of women. Some told me that when they felt the urge, they asked one of their pimps to procure a girl, whom they kept for a night and sent off at dawn. They remained single, convinced that no wife could be happy with them. One such friend explained, 'I'm a film director, and if I have a day shoot, I'm out the whole day; if I have a night shoot, I'm out all night. If I work through the day, I must rest at night, and if I work through the night, I must catch up on sleep during the day. A wife will demand her rights. Tell me, can an exhausted man fulfil them? A new woman every night is a good idea. If I'm sleepy, I can tell her to go and sleep; if bored, I can pay her taxi fare and ask her to leave. The moment a woman becomes a wife, she becomes a duty, and because I like to do my duty, I abstain from marriage.'

One evening, the friend at whose flat I was putting up hailed a taxi and took me along in search of a girl. The pimp, who was an old acquaintance of his, procured two pubescent girls from farming families of the Deccan. When my friend saw my perplexed expression, he explained, 'Don't worry, what's the difference between one or two.'

The taxi drove off, and the film director, the two girls, and I headed home. We climbed three flights of stairs and arrived at his flat on the third floor. As we walked in, I was surprised to see Nasir ensconced in an armchair, inspecting my Urdu typewriter. He was with a bespectacled woman and, when she turned around to look at us, I saw it was Izzat Jahan. My film director friend was taken aback to find two strangers in his flat. The girls from the Deccan had entered the room; he had little choice and saw no point in trying to conceal matters. I introduced my friend to Nasir, who in turn introduced us to his wife. I sat down and turned towards Izzat Jahan and said to my director friend, who was lighting his cigarette, 'She is among Hindustan's great women socialists. You must have read her articles.'

My friend was not in the least bit interested in socialism. Later,

I discovered he had never even heard the word. With a wave of his hand, he ushered the two girls into the other room and turned to us, 'Do forgive me. I'll be back soon.'

Izzat Jahan fixed her eyes on the girls, I mean, she scrutinized them from head to toe, inspecting their bodies and attire. After they left the room and my friend shut the door firmly behind him, she turned to me and said, 'So pleased to see you…. Nasir talks about you every day, but I have been busier than usual. Now you have relocated here—the accommodation is not bad.' She inspected the four corners of the room with approval.

I responded, 'Yes, it's nice and airy.'

'It's not in the least bit airy!'

'When the interconnecting door is open, there is a lot of air.'

'Yes, I think there was….'

For hours, Nasir, Izzat Jahan, and I talked about various matters, but I sensed that Izzat was restless—she was itching to find out what my friend was up to in the other room with the two girls. After all, he had promised to return soon. She asked me rather formally, 'May I have a glass of water, please?'

The kitchen had two entrances—one through the sitting room where my friend had disappeared, and another at the back. I did not think it wise to ask my friend to open the door and headed to the back door. When I returned with a glass of water, I noticed that husband and wife were whispering to each other. Izzat Jahan took the glass from me and said, 'Sorry to trouble you.'

I responded, 'No, it's really no trouble at all.'

After she drank the water, she scrunched up her eyes behind the thick lens of her spectacles and enquired in a rather pompous tone, 'I understand this flat has two entrances.'

'Yes.'

We talked about this and that for a while, and finally, an excited Izzat Jahan and I turned to socialism. I turned literally and metaphorically red and began to expound my views, 'Socialists claim that all human activity, for example, religion, history, politics, and so on, are mediated by social and economic relations. In current social relations, the means of production are in the hands of a limited class of people for their personal use and gain. When this is abolished, do you think a socialist era will begin, one in which the people will control the entire means of production?'

'But, of course.'

She was spot on to interpret my question as an assertion. I continued, 'The power of the proletariat will devolve to a special party, which will be called the socialist government.'

Izzat Jahan repeated, 'Yes, of course.'

'But it is noteworthy that even in a socialist system, all power will be in the hands of a limited circle. This representative group will work for the upliftment of all people, in line with socialist principles. This party will not permit any personal or private gain. But how many of us can place our hands on our hearts and say that in time this party will not resort to cruelty and oppression like the capitalists—can these people not become oppressors?

Izzat Jahan smiled, 'You sound like Bakunin's brother!'

I responded with added vigour, 'I accept that after he clashed with Karl Marx, Bakunin could not lay the foundation of a philosophically sound argument. However, he was not wrong when he asserted that democracy is also a form of oppression of smaller parties by larger parties. I am in favour of a political system where society is free of all types of pressure from the state.'

Izzat Jahan smiled, 'So, you want anarchy, which is impractical. Between them, Bakunin and Kropotkin could not make it acceptable.'

I responded, 'At one time, many said that socialism did not have a philosophy we could put into practice. People referred to it as a hazy dream of madmen, but in the nineteenth century, Karl Marx presented it as a system we can practice. Perhaps, anarchy will find its Karl Marx.'

Izzat Jahan looked at the locked door as though she had not heard me, and said, 'Your friend promised he'd return before long.'

I thought it best to explain everything to her and said, 'He was standing on ceremony; actually, he had no intention of coming back.'

Izzat Jahan asked with great innocence, 'Why?'

Now, Nasir began to take an interest in our conversation. I looked at him and smiled, 'How can he leave those girls and join our dry gathering?'

Izzat looked at me and asked, 'Were those girls film actresses?'

'No.'

'They must be his friends?'

'No. He met the girls for the first time tonight.'

Gently, I explained the entire matter to Izzat and outlined my friend's views on sexuality. She listened to me with rapt attention and started as though about to deliver a fatwa: 'This,' she asserted, 'is the worst form of anarchism. If your friend's views prevail, the world will turn into darkness. A man and a woman's relations will be restricted—restricted to the bed. Does your friend think a woman is a loaf of bread, a cake or a biscuit, a cup of coffee or tea…take a sip and discard her with other soiled dishes? I fail to understand why people give so much importance to sex. Can't your friend live without a woman? Why does he need a woman every day? To hell with women who put up with such humiliation.'

I expressed my opinion: 'Every man feels the need for a woman; some think it more important than others. My friend is among those who consider it an everyday necessity. If eating, drinking, and sleeping are important for some, for him, a woman is equally important. He may well be misguided, but he has never concealed his need.'

Izzat Jahan's tone hardened further, 'That he does not conceal his need does not make it right. Prostitutes sell their bodies in the bazaar, but that does not mean that their bodies are pure artifice. Such behaviour happens because our entire system is artifice. Your friend's basic bodily system is flawed, and that is why he sees no difference between food and a woman. Human beings cannot live without food, but they can live without sex.'

I said, 'Yes, of course, human beings can live without sexual relations, but it's not a question of life and death. Not all men can get a woman, but the ones who can include her among the necessary commodities of everyday life.'

By now, Nasir had lost all interest in our conversation and proclaimed his boredom, 'Forget it, yaar, it's late, and we live nineteen miles from here. Izzat, let's go.'

Izzat ignored her husband's intervention and said to me, 'Whatever his views, I must say your friend is very uncouth. I mean, what does he mean…the three of us are here in this room and, in the other room, sir is…. Oh, to hell with him…'

Nasir was sleepy, 'Arrey, for God's sake, stop this conversation and let's head home.'

Izzat looked stung, 'Arrey vah! Arrey vah! Slowly but surely, he has transformed into my husband.'

I began to laugh, and as Nasir joined me, Izzat's face broke into a smile. 'Of course, this is what it's all about; slowly, he becomes a husband so that he can boss me around!'

Nasir and Izzat took their leave not long after our exchange. I did not get an opportunity to discuss Hindustan's left-wing movement with her at any length. Nevertheless, I enjoyed my first encounter with Izzat Jahan, and it gave me plenty of ideas to explore in my mind. She fascinated me. I was sure that future meetings would prove intellectually productive.

When we met, Izzat Jahan and I discussed philosophy and the beginnings of socialism from Hegel to Karl Marx, and we analysed the ideas of Lenin, Trotsky, and Stalin. I was expansive about my views on progressive movements in India, and she shared her thoughts with me. I regaled her with stories of young men who strutted around with a copy of *The Communist Manifesto* tucked under their arms to impress others. I told her a tale of a friend who had every book published on socialism in the English language. He dropped Karl Marx's name in conversations just as people with family connections to the municipal commissioner mention his name after every other sentence to impress their listeners. Notwithstanding this unsavoury habit, he was a genial fellow who could not bear to hear a word against socialism.

Occasionally, Izzat Jahan and I shared our thoughts about those young men and women who professed socialist ideas merely in search of sexual encounters. I regarded half the young men in various socialist movements as lascivious predators whose eyes preyed upon the opposite sex with an insatiable hunger. I thought young women from capitalist families often joined the movement in search of some distraction. After reading a few foundational texts, they became committed party workers. Over time, some conceded to sexual relationships while others crossed the farthest limits of freedom in the name of the nation—and served its leaders. In short, I enjoyed talking about India's socialist movement with Izzat Jahan, whose brilliance I had assessed through her articles. I knew she shared my views on important issues.

After I found a flat and my wife joined me, Izzat and Nasir came to see us. Izzat and my wife struck up an instant friendship. Izzat came to town every day to go to her office, and often on her way home in the evenings, she would drop by to see us. I wanted to sit and talk to her about Hegel, Karl Marx, Engels, Bakunin, Kropotkin, and Trotsky, and exchange views on every stage of the development of socialist thought. However, my wife and Izzat retreated to our bedroom, and goodness alone knows what they talked about as they lazed on the bed. If I broached the topic of socialism or the effect of Stalin's current war policy with Izzat, she ignored me and turned to my wife to discuss the price of white wool. If I wanted to talk of M. N. Roy's hypocrisy, she launched into ecstatic praise of the songs from the film *Khandaan*. And if ever I succeeded in making her discuss Russia's war policy, before long, she made her way to the kitchen to help my wife chop onions.

Izzat spent the entire day working at the party office about twenty-five miles away from where she lived. Every day, she travelled an hour in each direction on the electric train and returned home knackered. Her husband was employed in a mill and did a fifteen-hour night shift, but Izzat seemed content. She told my wife, not once but several times, 'The real meaning of marriage is not confined to a bed, and a husband is not merely a companion for the night.'

My wife was deeply affected by Izzat Jahan's ideas. I admired Izzat's commitment to her work and did not resent the fact that she preferred my wife's company to mine. I thought it very likely that soon Izzat would convert my wife's capitalist middle-class mentality to a socialist outlook.

One afternoon, I returned home from office earlier than usual, at around two o'clock. I knocked on the door, and it was opened not by my wife but by Nasir. A creature of habit, I walked to my desk and put down my bag. Nasir went and stretched out on my bed; he covered himself with a blanket and announced, 'I have a temperature.'

I saw Izzat Jahan reclining on the sofa opposite him, and enquired, 'And you…?'

She responded, 'Thank you, no, I was just lying down.'

'Where is Ruqqaiya?'

Izzat answered, 'She is sleeping in the other room.'

'What's up...everyone's sleeping...?'

I called my wife, 'Ruqqaiya...Ruqqaiya....'

A sleepy voice answered, 'Yes!'

'Arrey, come here, how long are you going to sleep?'

Ruqqaiya entered, rubbing her eyes, and sat down on the sofa with Izzat. Nasir did not stir under the blanket. I pulled up a chair and sat down next to my wife. For a while, we discussed deep sleep because Ruqqaiya sleeps as if there is no tomorrow. Next, Izzat Jahan and my wife launched into a discussion on crochet needles. When tea arrived, Nasir drank his reclining in bed. I gave him two sachets of Aspro to cure his fever. Nasir and Izzat Jahan sat for another two hours or more and left.

That night, I slipped into bed, and as usual, doubled up my top pillow but noticed that the other did not have a pillow cover. I turned to Ruqqaiya, who was standing near me, changing her clothes, 'You forgot the pillow cover on this?'

Ruqqaiya looked at the pillow. Taken aback, she said, 'Hoonh? Really, where's the pillow cover? Your friend....'

I smiled, 'Has Nasir taken it?'

'Who knows?' Ruqqaiya answered with some hesitation and continued, 'Hai, how shameless. I didn't tell you; I was asleep in the other room and they—I mean your friend and his wife...they can go to hell...they're so uncouth.'

The following day, the missing pillow cover turned up under the bed. Mice had eaten holes through it. When Ruqqaiya turned it inside out, she found the two sachets of Aspro I had given Nasir for his headache.

# The Psychoanalyst

Today, I'll tell you an absurd and entertaining story. It was the age of curfews, and by that, I mean the days when communal riots had started in Bombay. Every morning, newspapers arrived to inform us how many Hindus and Muslims had lost their lives. The house felt empty because my wife had gone to Lahore to attend her sister's wedding. I should not call it a house because it was just an apartment with two rooms, plus a bathroom with sparkling white tiles and a dark kitchen around the corner from it.

We had two young servants who were brothers, but I could not stand the younger chap, a smooth talker too crafty for his years. Taking advantage of my wife's absence, I sacked him and employed another fellow called Iftikhar. I regretted my decision because he turned out to be a fox. The moment I sat down to conjure a short story, he darted in from the kitchen and asked, 'Sahib, you called me?'

I asked myself, 'When did I call the imbecile?' and pounced on him, 'Iftikhar, your ears must be ringing. Come only when I call you.'

Iftikhar responded, 'But, Sahib, I heard your voice.'

I told him firmly, 'No, Iftikhar, I did not call you. Go, do your work.'

He left. Nonetheless, it became a daily routine for Iftikhar to walk in and ask, 'Sahib, you called me?'

Finally, one day, I lost my temper and snarled at him, 'Don't talk nonsense! You're too clever for your own good. Get lost now!' And he got lost.

Since I was on my own, my friend Raja Mehdi Ali Khan moved in with me. He liked Iftikhar's manner and was full of praise for him, 'Manto, I like this servant of yours; he's so efficient.'

I turned around and said, 'Raja, my dear man, you'd do me a great service by taking him away to your place. I don't need such an efficient servant.'

I'm not sure why Raja didn't employ him. One evening, I told him, 'Look here, this chap is treacherous. I know he's a thief and one day he will rob me.'

Raja laughed at me, 'Now, now Manto! You think you're Freud. Such good servants are a rare commodity. You haven't got the measure of him.'

I reflected on the matter and questioned my opinion of Iftikhar, telling myself, perhaps, Raja was right and Iftikhar was an honest fellow after all. Still, the more I dwelled on the subject, the more I was convinced that I was right. I am an expert in human psychology, and I knew my opinion of Iftikhar was spot on, but—and this 'but' is at the heart of the story.

Every evening, after I returned home from Bombay Talkies, as a routine I tucked any paper money in a celluloid wallet with my monthly rail pass, which I kept with all loose change on a tray on my desk. One evening, I returned home loaded, with sixty rupees in six ten-rupee bills. As always, I tucked the sixty rupees into the celluloid wallet which I left on the tray on my desk. Then, I drank my brandy, had dinner, and fell asleep. That evening, Iftikhar laid the table with added speed. When I finished dinner, he said, 'Sahib, do you want me to get some cigarettes?'

Furious, I bellowed, 'I don't want cigarettes,' and asked, 'where do you think you'll get cigarettes? Don't you know there is a curfew from nine at night to six in the morning?'

Iftikhar remained silent.

I tend to wake up early, around five o'clock. The following morning, I woke up, as usual, but there was no newspaper because of a curfew, and the servants were asleep. In Bombay, newspapers arrived around five-thirty, so I sat aimlessly on the sofa. I was about to nod off but decided to walk up to the window and look down at the deserted bazaar that usually came to life every morning at three o'clock, with a rumble of trams and the clamour of mill workers. On the morning in question, by the time I had finished with the newspapers, the clock had struck six and I headed for a bath.

The room had just one window, and my desk stood near it. Coincidentally, my gaze fell on the tray where I had kept my rail pass and money. However, I could not see the pass or the celluloid wallet in which I had tucked the six ten-rupee notes. I kept my wallet on the tray with such regularity that it had become a part of my personality. At first, I thought perhaps, I might have hidden it under some papers, but when I lifted the wad of papers, I did not find anything. Perplexed, I sifted through the documents one by one but did not find the pass. Both the servants were asleep in the kitchen. Mystified, I tried to figure out what might have happened. I thought if I had consumed alcohol before I came home, the matter would make sense, but I had not touched a drop of alcohol on my way home from Bombay Talkies because I knew I had a full bottle of brandy at home. Perhaps, my memory was failing, or I might have dropped the money while taking my handkerchief out of my pocket.

I rummaged around and found the rail pass with the six ten-rupee notes between some files in the lower drawer of my desk. I could not figure out what had happened because I had not hidden the pass. I realized Iftikhar was up to his tricks. He had taken the pass from the tray while I was asleep and hidden it between the files in the lower drawer since he could not leave the flat because of the curfew. His scheme became clear to me—he would wait for the curfew to end in the morning, remove the pass from the drawer, and disappear. Nevertheless, I was no less cunning. I wanted to catch the worried expression on Iftikhar's face when he failed to find the pass under the papers, and I put the celluloid wallet back on the tray.

That night, I had to go to Bombay Talkies. As usual, I took out a kurta–pyjama, put the drawstring through the pyjama, took a fresh towel, and went to the bathroom, with just one wish: to catch Iftikhar red-handed. Knowing he would look for the pass in the bottom drawer of my desk, I imagined him seeing it on the tray, tucking it into his waistband, and walking away. The bathroom was right opposite my room, and I thought I would leave the door slightly ajar, lie in wait, and catch Iftikhar in the act of stealing. I had no intention of handing him over to the police. All I wanted was to summon him before Raja and have my credentials as a psychoanalyst validated.

I entered the bathroom and left the door slightly ajar. Elated, I poured two mugs of water on my body, rubbed soap all over, and peeped into the room several times. Although the curfew had lifted, there was no sign of Iftikhar. I sat under the steady cold flow of water, and as I washed my body, I began to mould my scheme into a short story. Soon, the water, my story, and I, became one. Thoroughly rinsed with soap and water, the entire story became crystal clear. I was thrilled. In the climax, I catch my servant in the act and my reputation as a psychoanalyst spreads far and wide! I was so pleased with myself that I smothered my body with more soap than usual and poured more water than necessary, but the story was luminous in my mind.

I emerged from my bath on a high. I had written the entire story in my head with soap and water. Now, all I had to do was put pen to paper and send it off to some publication. I went into the other room to change my clothes. The first room held the entire story—I mean my railway pass and the six ten-rupee notes. When I came out of the second room, or should I say when I emerged from the world of fiction, I recalled my scheme in a flash. To be a writer of fiction is a curse. I had forgotten the task at hand. I leapt back into the room with the tray and the pass. The moment my eyes fell on the tray, my entire world of storytelling crumbled. My railway pass and the six ten-rupee notes had vanished. I hollered for my decent servant, 'Karim, where is Iftikhar?'

He said, 'Sahib, he's gone to get some coal.'

I said, 'Ah well then, he's blackened his face.'

Karim tried to find Iftikhar. I returned to my bathroom and tried to wash the human condition clean with soap and water. Iftikhar had cleaned me out. My journey to Bombay Talkies was a series of bilingual puns in Urdu and English. I did not have a 'pass', 'on my person' in Urdu (Mere paas pass nahin thaa). When the ticket checker came, I lost my paas ('self-respect' in Urdu) and had to pay a hefty fine.

# 10

## *Empty Bottles and Empty Boxes*

To this day, I continue to wonder why unattached men are obsessed with empty boxes and bottles. By unattached men, I mean those bachelors who are not interested in getting married and, invariably, are eccentrics with odd habits. Even so, I fail to comprehend their obsession with empty bottles and boxes. It makes sense for them to crave a friend or to keep a pet because they are lonely. What possible consolation can empty boxes and bottles provide? It is easy to ascribe reasons for eccentricities, but a challenge to understand the real psychological motivation behind such traits.

I am quite close to someone who is about to enter his fiftieth decade. He likes to keep pet dogs and pigeons. I find nothing peculiar about this because he has not one but several outlandish habits. As part of his daily routine, he buys full-cream milk and reduces it since he considers this the best way to prepare pure ghee for a unique curry he makes for himself. He keeps his drinking water in an earthenware pot with a fine muslin cloth tied around its mouth to let the air in and keep flies and insects out. He strips before he goes to the lavatory, ties a towel around his midriff, and puts on wooden clogs. Now, who can solve the psychological riddle behind his full-cream ghee, the muslin tied around the mouth of his earthenware water-pot, the towel around his midriff, and his wooden clogs?

Another unattached gentleman friend, who on the face of it appears quite normal and is a Reader at the High Court, imagines a perennial nasty smell under his nose. Consequently, his handkerchief is always attached to his nose. For some reason, he likes to keep pet rabbits. There is another unattached friend, who keeps a keen eye on international politics and excels in teaching parrots how to talk; he is perfectly sane but likes to offer his prayers whenever he finds a moment. There is also an elderly retired Major, quite well-to-do, and he collects all types of hookahs—those with long curvaceous pipes as well as upright ones. He owns many houses but lives in a rented room in a hotel, and he will stake his life on pheasants. There is a retired Colonel Sahib, who lives in a large house with ten or twelve large and small dogs. He has every conceivable brand of whisky; he consumes four pegs a day and loves to share his drink with one of his darling dogs.

All the bachelors I have referred to share an interest in empty bottles and empty boxes, obviously shaped by their different circumstances. My friend who prepares ghee from full-cream milk washes the empty bottles and displays them in a cupboard because he thinks one day they will come in handy. The High Court Reader with a perennial bad smell under his nose only keeps bottles and boxes after he rules out any danger of foul odours. The man who likes to offer prayers has collected countless empty bottles to wash after going to the toilet and uses the empty cans to perform his ritual ablutions. He considers these items inexpensive, and therefore, pure. The Major who collects hookahs also collects empty bottles and boxes and sells them, while the retired Colonel restricts his collection to empty whisky bottles.

If you visit Colonel Sahib, you will see a small, neat, and tidy room with several glass-fronted cupboards full of empty whisky bottles displayed in rows. He has some rare old brands and is obsessed with his collection, like any dedicated philatelist or numismatist. Colonel Sahib has no close associate or relation—at least, I do not know of any such person. He is alone in the world and does not seem to mind it in the least. He treats his dogs like his children; he spends his entire day with these animals, and in his spare time, he arranges and rearranges his cherished empty whisky bottles.

You may well ask, empty bottles are understandable, but why have I added empty boxes to the equation? Is it necessary that men who enjoy the single state should fancy empty boxes as well as empty bottles? And why just empty bottles and boxes? Why not full bottles and boxes? I am equally perplexed by this question, but notwithstanding my best efforts, I have not come up with an answer. If there is a logical connection between empty boxes and empty bottles and single men, it must be that boxes and bottles represent a void in these men's lives. The first question that comes to mind is: do these men wish to fill one void with another? Dogs, cats, rabbits, and monkeys can be pleasant companions, and to some extent, fill an empty life; they can get up to exciting antics and return the love they receive. What possible joy can empty boxes and bottles bring? Perhaps, you will find an answer to these questions when I recount the following incident.

Ten years ago, when I moved to Bombay, a movie produced by a famous film company was in its twentieth week. The heroine was old, but the hero was new, and he looked young, at least in the newspaper advertisements. I had read good reviews of his performance and went to see the film. The story held my attention, and the new hero performed well, especially since this was his first time before the camera. It is difficult to tell the age of an actor or actress on screen because make-up can make an older person appear young and a young person, old. Undoubtedly though, this new hero was very young, fresh, and alert, like a college student. His name was Ram Swaroop, and although not handsome, with his slim physique, he looked perfect on screen. I watched many of his films, and over time, he acquired polish. Age and experience matured the childlike quality of his features and now he was ranked amongst the top stars of his time.

Scandals are commonplace in the film world. Every other day you get to hear that X actress is involved with Y actor; this actress left that actor and went off with Z director. It is unexceptional for rumours of some romance or the other to be attached to an actor or actress. Ram Swaroop's life, however, was unsoiled by scandal, and there were no sordid stories about his sexual exploits in the press. Quite honestly, I had never given the matter much thought because I have no interest in the personal lives of actors and actresses. I watch a film and form a positive or negative opinion of it—that is about it.

I happened to meet Ram Swaroop eight years after I had watched his first film and discovered many curious facets of his personality. When Ram Swaroop entered the film world, he lived in a village at some distance from Bombay. After a string of successful movies, he rented a four-room middle-class apartment by the seaside in Shivaji Park. Ram Swaroop lived here with seven other members of his family, which included his servant, who doubled up as his cook, three dogs, two monkeys, and a cat. Ram Swaroop, his servant, the dogs, and the cat did not have partners of the other gender, but there was a male monkey and a female monkey, who spent most of their time locked up in a wire-gauze cage.

Ram Swaroop adored these half a dozen creatures. Although he was kind to his servant, there was no evidence of an emotional bond between them. It seemed Ram Swaroop had given him a list of all the rules and regulations governing his life, which this efficient man committed to memory and performed with mechanical regularity and due diligence. The moment Ram Swaroop took off his work clothes and put on his shorts, his servant knew that Sahib was ready to have some rum and play with his dogs, and he laid out a few sodas and a flask of ice on the glass-topped side table. He understood that now, if the telephone rang, he must say, 'Sahib is not at home.'

The servant also knew the protocols he had to follow when the contents of a bottle of rum or a packet of cigarettes finished. He could not throw away or sell an empty bottle, box, or carton, but had to put them away carefully in the room designated for this purpose. If a woman came to call on Sahib during the day, the servant turned her away from the door and told her that Sahib returned home late from his shoot last night and was asleep. Lady visitors who turned up in the evening or at night were told that Sahib was away on a shoot.

Ram Swaroop's home was not unlike that of most bachelors who live on their own. I mean, it lacked the order and taste inherent in the feminine touch. It was clean but stark. The first time I entered his flat, I had an overpowering feeling that I had walked into the section of a zoo where lions and cheetahs live because it exuded a similar odour. Apart from the kitchen, the flat had a bedroom and a living room. A third room that reeked of stale cigarettes and rum was full of countless empty boxes, bottles of rum, and packets of cigarettes. There was no order in the way boxes stood on bottles, and bottles lay on boxes, some lined up in rows, and others piled high—all coated with layers of dust. Astonished, I asked Ram Swaroop, 'I say, what's going on here?'

'Going on?' He asked.

'This...this rubbish tip...' I responded.

'It piled up.' He added.

'So much!' I exclaimed, '...it must have taken at least seven to eight years to accumulate so much rubbish.' I was way off the mark. This treasure trove had accumulated over ten years—and Ram Swaroop had brought it with him when he moved to Shivaji Park. One day, I suggested, 'Ram Swaroop, why don't you sell all these bottles and boxes? I mean, you should have sold them over the years; you have a stockpile, and you'll get a good price because of the war. Get this rubbish tip cleared.'

All he said was, 'Forget it, mate, who's going to go through the hassle!'

His response suggested that he was not in the least bit interested in the bottles and boxes, but I gathered from his servant that there was hell to pay if Ram Swaroop discovered that somebody dared to move a bottle or a box from its place.

Ram Swaroop was not in the least bit interested in women. But, over time, we became rather informal with each other, so one evening, I asked him, 'I say, when are you thinking of getting married?'

He responded with a question, 'What will I do with *marriage*?'

He's quite right, I thought. 'What will he do with *marriage*? Will he lock his wife up in the room full of empty boxes and bottles? Or will he take off his clothes, put on his shorts, and play with her?' From time to time, I brought up the subject of marriage with him. Nevertheless, when I reflected on the matter, I found it difficult to imagine him in a relationship with a woman.

Over several years, I met Ram Swaroop regularly. I heard he had fallen in love with an actress called Sheela but paid little attention to the rumour. Primarily, I did not expect such behaviour from Ram Swaroop. More importantly, I thought no young man in his right mind could fall in love with the lifeless Sheela, whom you could mistake for a patient in the last stages of tuberculosis. When she started her film career, Sheela was just about acceptable in a few films, but after some years, she became so lacklustre that her studio relegated her to C-grade films. Once, I asked Ram Swaroop about Sheela, and he retorted, 'Why? Is she the only woman left for me?'

Around this time, Stalin, Ram Swaroop's most beloved dog, developed pneumonia; he got him the best veterinary attention and nursed him round the clock, but Stalin did not recover. Ram Swaroop was devastated by Stalin's death, and for several days, his eyes continued to well up. I was surprised when I witnessed how the pain of Stalin's death compelled Ram Swaroop to give his other dogs away to a friend. When he bade farewell to the male and female monkeys, I realized that he did not wish to confront the pain of another death.

Now, he sat in his shorts, drank rum, and played with Nargis, his cat, who became attached to him because now she had Ram Swaroop's undivided attention. His home stopped smelling of lions and cheetahs. Instead, there was a visible sense of order and cleanliness in his flat and a glow on his face. These events transpired at such a slow pace that it was difficult to identify the exact point in time when the transformation began.

And as the days rolled by, Ram Swaroop's new film was released. I noticed a renewed energy in his acting and congratulated him. In response, he handed me a glass, smiled, and said, 'Here, have a whisky!'

Taken aback, I asked, 'Whisky?'

Ram Swaroop only drank rum. His smile returned to his pursed lips, and he said, 'I'm sick of drinking rum.'

I did not question him further. A week later, I visited him in the evening and found him sitting not in his usual shorts, but a qameez and pyjamas, drinking whisky, not rum. We sat together for hours, drinking whisky and playing cards. I noticed how he grimaced after every sip and asked, 'Whisky doesn't go down well on your palate?

He smiled and said, 'It will, in time.'

Ram Swaroop's flat was on the second floor. One day, I was passing by his building and saw mounds of empty bottles and boxes piled up on the driveway and three or four rag-and-bone men loading them on two rattletrap trucks parked nearby. I knew that this treasure belonged to none other than Ram Swaroop. Utterly surprised, I felt a twinge in my heart at seeing the collection go. I ran upstairs and rang the bell. As I tried to step in, the servant stopped me and said, 'Sahib was shooting last night; he is asleep.'

Taken aback and furious, I mumbled something under my breath and left.

That evening, Ram Swaroop came to my place with Sheela, who was draped in a sari. He gestured towards her and said, 'Meet my lawfully wedded wife.'

If I had not consumed four pegs of whisky, I would have fainted. Ram Swaroop and Sheela did not stay long. After they left, I sat around, deep in thought for hours. 'Whom does Sheela remind me of, her skinny body wrapped up in a beige Banarsi tissue sari, fluffy here and pressed down there?' Suddenly, I had a vision of an empty bottle wrapped up in brown paper. Sheela was a vacuous woman. I thought, 'Perhaps, one void will fill the other.'

# 11
## Sahai

'Do not say a hundred thousand Hindus have died, or a hundred thousand Muslims have died, but two hundred thousand human beings have died. The real tragedy is not the death of two hundred thousand human beings, but the missing scorecard for those who killed and those who died. Muslims killed a hundred thousand Hindus and thought they had erased Hinduism, but it is alive and will continue to live. Hindus slaughtered a hundred thousand Muslims and celebrated; they believed they had wiped out Islam, but the truth is there for everyone to see—they have not damaged Islam in the least. Those who think violence can exterminate religion are foolish. Doctrine, religion, faith, dharma, belief, devotion—call it what you may—is not in our bodies but in our souls. How can knives and bullets destroy souls?' Mumtaz was impassioned that evening. We had gathered to see him off because he was leaving us and going to Pakistan for an indefinite period. Pakistan—a place about which none of us knew anything.

Juggal's remark had triggered Mumtaz's decision to leave us. Three of us were Hindus, who knew that many of our relatives had confronted death and looting in West Punjab. Juggal had received a letter from Lahore with news that his chacha was killed in a riot. He had turned to Mumtaz under a pall of grief and said, 'I was wondering what I'd do if a riot were to start in our area.'

'What would you do?' Mumtaz had asked him.

Juggal had responded in a sombre tone, 'Most likely I'll kill you.'

Mumtaz fell into a spell of silence that continued for eight days. Suddenly, one morning, he informed us that he was leaving for Karachi by a ship set to sail at a quarter to four that evening.

None of us questioned his decision. Juggal was the quietest amongst us; he knew that his remark, 'Most likely I'll kill you,' had impelled Mumtaz to leave Bombay. Juggal had reflected on the matter and asked himself if he could kill his cherished friend in a fit of rage.

Oddly enough, Mumtaz was unusually chatty, particularly in the few hours before his departure. That morning, he woke up and began to drink and supervised his packing as though he was going off on vacation. He may have fooled a stranger, but we knew his ceaseless talk and laughter was as much an attempt to distract us as it was to divert his thoughts.

I wanted to discuss the matter with him and asked Juggal to do so as well, but Mumtaz gave us no opportunity. Juggal consumed more than three pegs and retreated into silence and his room. Brij Mohan and I decided to hang around Mumtaz, who had to pay the doctor's fees and collect his laundry, which he did in a light-hearted mood, but when he went to the local paan shop next to the hotel around the corner, his eyes brimmed over. Heading back, he placed a hand on Brij Mohan's shoulder and said, 'Remember, yaar, ten years ago when we were down and out, Gobinda loaned us a rupee.'

We walked back in silence, but the moment we reached home, Mumtaz launched into a ceaseless torrent of inane banter that was so amiable that Brij Mohan and I were forced to respond in the same vein. When the time for Mumtaz to leave our flat drew near, Juggal joined us.

As our taxi wound its way towards the port, Mumtaz's eyes bade farewell to Bombay's bustling streets and markets. All of us remained silent. Huge crowds had gathered at the port to see off thousands of refugees, most of whom looked quite wretched—very few had an air of prosperity about them. Although surrounded by a sea of people, I felt Mumtaz was the only one who was leaving—leaving us to go to a place he had never set eyes upon, which would remain alien even if it were to win him over. I cannot say what was going through his mind. Mumtaz had his luggage dispatched to his cabin and took us up to the deck. He leaned silently against the rails and fixed his eyes on the distant horizon where the sea and sky meet. After some time, he turned to Juggal and held his hand, 'This union of the sea and sky is an illusion—but what a compelling illusion.' Juggal remained silent; his remark, 'Most likely I'll kill you,' continued to disturb him.

Mumtaz ordered brandy from the ship's bar because this was what he had been drinking all day. The four of us carried our glasses back to the deck, where we stood together, leaning against the rails.

Countless refugees piled onto the ship, and seagulls continued to fly over an almost still sea. Juggal finished the contents of his glass in one big swig and awkwardly turned to Mumtaz, 'Forgive me, Mumtaz—I hurt you.'

Mumtaz hesitated before he turned to Juggal and asked, 'When you said, "Most likely I'll kill you," did you actually mean it at the time?'

Juggal nodded in the affirmative and added, 'But I regret it.'

Mumtaz responded in a very philosophical tone, 'If you had killed me, your regret would have been far deeper, but only if you stopped to think that you have killed Mumtaz, not a Muslim, not a friend, but a human being. If the person you kill is a bastard, you do not kill his illegitimacy—you kill a human being. If he is a Muslim, you do not kill the fact that he was a Muslim—you exterminate his being. If some Muslims chance upon his corpse, there will be one more grave in a Muslim cemetery, but one less human being in the world.'

Yet again, Mumtaz drifted into silence, deep in thought before he added, 'My co-religionists might proclaim me a martyr, but by God, if I could, I'd tear my grave asunder and shout, "I have no desire to embrace martyrdom. I don't want this accreditation for which I have not taken an exam." A Muslim killed your chacha in Lahore; you heard the news in Bombay and killed me. Tell me, what laurels do your chacha, and I deserve? And your chacha's murderer in Lahore and you, what badges of honour will you earn? All I can say is that those who died—died a monstrous death, and those who killed coloured their hands with blood for no reason.'

Mumtaz continued his monologue, brimming with goodwill. His words touched my heart. Indeed, religion, faith, belief, dharma, and devotion are in our souls and not our bodies; violence, bullets, or knives cannot annihilate them. I said, 'You are right.'

Mumtaz stopped to reflect on what I'd said and responded with visible impatience, 'No, not right—I mean all this is fine, but perhaps, I have not expressed my thoughts adequately. By religion and dharma, I do not mean that which ninety-nine per cent of us are involved with, but rather the quality that brings out an individual's humanity and makes one human being different from another. Sadly, it's not a commodity—I cannot hold it up and show it to you.'

I noticed a glow in Mumtaz's eyes and heard him ask himself, 'What was that special quality about him? He was a diehard Hindu; his profession was totally base, but he was enlightened.'

'Who?' I asked.

'A pimp....'

The three of us were astonished, but Mumtaz did not vacillate, so I asked, 'A pimp?'

Mumtaz nodded. 'What continues to astonish me is the kind of person he turned out to be. Universally known and referred to as a pimp, his conscience was pure.' Mumtaz hesitated for a few moments as though to refresh his memories, before he continued, 'I don't recall his full name...something Sahai. He was from Banaras and was obsessed with cleanliness. He lived in a tiny but extremely orderly room divided into different sections, with appropriate arrangements for purdah. There were no beds or charpais, just mattresses on the floor covered with sparkling clean sheets and bolsters lined up against the walls. He had a servant, but Sahai did the cleaning and all his chores himself. Quick to action, he did not indulge in duplicity or lies. If he had nothing but diluted alcohol to hand late at night, he would say, "Sahib, don't waste your money." If he had doubts about a girl, he did not hide them. Over time, in various conversations with him, I gathered that he earned two-and-a-half-thousand rupees in commission from every ten thousand. He had managed to save twenty thousand rupees in three years, and needed another ten. I'm not sure why just ten thousand and not more, but he planned to return to Banaras with thirty thousand rupees in his pocket and set up shop as a cloth merchant. Can't say why.'

I responded, 'What a peculiar man.'

Mumtaz continued his account, 'At first, I thought him a complete fake, a big fraud. Who could believe that he looked upon the twelve or thirteen girls on his books as his daughters, that he had opened post office savings accounts for his girls to deposit their monthly earnings? He even paid for their food from his pocket. Everything about him seemed fake. Once, I went to see him, and he said, "Amina and Sakina are on leave. I give them leave to go and eat meat in a local hotel once a week. Here, as everyone knows, everything is Vaishnava—vegetarian." I smiled to myself, "Saala, he's having me on!"

'Once, Sahai told me of a letter he received from a Hindu girl he had helped marry a Muslim client from Lahore. She wrote to tell him that she had gone to the shrine of Data Sahib where she made a pledge and asked the saint to intercede to help Sahai earn thirty thousand rupees so he could return to Banaras in no time and open his cloth shop. When Sahai finished his account, I laughed out loud because I thought he was spinning a yarn to please me. After all, he knew I am a Muslim.'

'Were you wrong?' I asked.

'Absolutely! There was no contradiction between his words and his actions. I'm sure he had some flaws and may well have committed several misdemeanours in his life, but he was a fine human being.'

Juggal asked, 'How did you find out?'

'When he died.' Mumtaz gazed at the horizon before picking up the thread of the story again, '...the riots had started. Early one morning, I was walking through the deserted streets of Bhendi Bazaar; there was a curfew and barely any traffic on the roads. Trams were suspended. As I approached J. J. Hospital, on the lookout for a taxi, I saw a man lying on the footpath curled up beside a basket. I thought, perhaps, a labourer had fallen asleep, but when I saw the flagstones near him covered in blood, I stopped. It was a clear case of homicide. I thought I had better make my way but stopped when I detected a movement.

'Not a soul was around, so I stooped to look and saw Sahai's familiar face covered in blood. I sat beside him on the footpath and saw his usually pristine white twill shirt drenched in blood. Perhaps, the wound was in his ribcage. When I heard him moan, I held him very gently by his shoulders, as you would somebody you wished to arouse from sleep. A couple of times, I addressed him by his incomplete name and was about to leave when he fixed his half-shut eyes on me.

'As he recognized me, his entire body became stiff, and he said, "You...You?" In haste, I asked him a muddle of questions: how did he happen to be here? Who attacked him? For how long had he been lying on the footpath? "There is a hospital in front of us—should I inform them?" He did not have the strength to speak. I finished questioning him, finally he managed to say, "My days have come to an end. Perhaps, this was Bhagwan's will." I was not quite sure of Bhagwan's will, but it was not my will as a Muslim in a Muslim area to stand beside a Hindu and watch him die, knowing that his killer was a Muslim.

'I am not faint-hearted, but at that moment, I was worse than a coward. Petrified that I'd be arrested or hauled up for interrogation, a thought flashed across my mind: if I take him to hospital, he could implicate me to seek revenge. He would think "I have to die why not take him with me?" With a jumble of such thoughts in my head, I turned to run for my life when Sahai called me. I stopped, even though I had no intention of doing so. I gave him a look that said, "Come on, man, I must leave." Sahai doubled up with pain but managed to unbutton his shirt and said, "In the right pocket of my waistcoat, you will find some jewellery and twelve hundred rupees that belong to Sultana. I had kept them with a friend and was going to send them to her today. There's danger all around. Please tell her she must leave at once. And look after yourself!"'

As Mumtaz fell silent and gazed into the distance where the sea and the sky had merged in a blurred union, I felt his voice had joined Sahai's on the footpath in front of J. J. Hospital. We heard the ship's horn as Mumtaz told us, 'I met Sultana. She was inconsolable when I handed her the jewellery and cash.'

We said goodbye to Mumtaz and walked down to the quay. When we turned around to look at him, we could see him standing on the deck by the railing, waving to us. I turned to Juggal almost questioningly, 'It seems Mumtaz wants Sahai's soul as a companion for life.'

Juggal responded, 'I wish I were Sahai's soul.'

## Toto

Lost in thoughts of the first woman ever to become a mother, I wondered if the first man in the world had looked at the sky with a gleam in his eyes as he addressed the universe in the first language of the world, and declared with great pride, 'I, too, am a creator!' The telephone rang to break the chain of my wayward thoughts, and I left my seat on the balcony to head towards the room where the phone continued to shriek like an errant child. A phone is a useful machine, but I dislike it because it tends to ring at awkward moments. I lifted the receiver quite half-heartedly and said, 'Four-four-five-seven.'

'Hello, hello,' started the voice at the other end.

'Who is it?' I asked, irritated.

'Ayah, is Memsaab there?' said the voice.

'Hold on...' I said as I put the receiver down and called my wife, who most probably was asleep in our bedroom, 'Memsaab, Memsaab!'

My wife woke up, walked into the room, yawned, and asked, 'Is this some joke?'

I smiled, 'Memsaab is fine...do you remember, you told your first ayah to call you Begum Sahiba instead of Memsaab, and she called you Baingan Sahiba, or Aubergine Sahiba!'

My wife's yawn turned into a smile, and she asked, 'Who is it?'

'Find out for yourself.'

She lifted the receiver with a 'Hello, hello....'

I returned to the balcony. Women tend to ramble when it comes to the telephone, and for the next twenty minutes, their 'hello, hello' continued.

I wonder why it is necessary to say, 'hello, hello' after every two to three words during a telephone conversation. Is there a lack of confidence concealed in the persistent repetition of 'hello, hello?' The only people who should resort to 'hello, hello?' are those who fear that the person at the other end is bored and wishes to end the conversation. Perhaps, the pointless deployment of 'hello, hello?' is just a habit.

My wife returned with a worried expression on her face, 'Saadat Sahib, this time the matter looks serious!'

'What matter?'

She ignored my question, and proceeded, 'The matter has become serious and reached the point of divorce. There is a limit to madness. I bet they've made a mountain out of a molehill. Both are nuts.'

'But, my dear, who are nuts?'

'Haven't I told you? They—it was Tahira on the telephone.'

'Tahira, which Tahira?'

'Mrs Yazdani.'

Immediately, the whole matter made perfect sense to me, and I said, 'Must be some new disagreement.'

'New and major; Yazdani Sahib wants to talk to you.'

'What does he want to say to me?'

'I have no idea…he snatched the receiver from Tahira, and simply said to me, "Bhabijan, please call Manto."'

'I don't see why but I'll have to put up with his rant,' I muttered and headed for the telephone to speak to Yazdani, who said, 'The situation is very delicate. Jump into a taxi with Bhabi and get here immediately.'

My wife and I rushed to change our clothes and headed to the Yazdanis. En route, we had a long chat about them. Tahira was the beautiful daughter of a musician whose real profession was 'falling in love'. Ata Yazdani, the son of a worthy Pathan, first dabbled in poetry, then turned to playwriting, and finally to screenwriting. One day, Yazdani's roving eye collided with Tahira's. He stayed up the whole night, penned a long love letter, and had it delivered to her. An epistolary romance continued for a few months, and finally, they got married without any obstacles. At the time, Tahira's father was immersed in his eighth love affair, and Ata Yazdani was writing a play, called *The Shovel,* for Allama Mashriqi's Khaksar Party.

Ata Yazdani felt cheated that his love affair had concluded without any drama. Tahira, too, had a taste for histrionics. She was a clever young woman with some outlandish traits. Once, she had to go somewhere but did not have a sari petticoat, so she simply tied a drawstring around her waist and tucked her sari into it—and off she went. Before her courtship and marriage, Tahira often embarrassed her friends because the moment she saw a bald man, she wanted to sprinkle dirt on his head—and she proceeded to do just that. I am not so sure if Tahira fell in love with Ata Yazdani, but although she was a flirt when it came to her virginity, she was a girl with moral fibre. When she received Yazdani's first love letter, her attitude was, 'Love is a curious game, why not play it?' She had a similar approach to marriage. Even the tiffs she had with her husband were like parts of a serialized story.

Nevertheless, when the two of us arrived at their flat and observed the drama, we discovered that the game had acquired a dangerous character. An inordinate din greeted us as Tahira and Yazdani hurled high-pitched and voluble accusations at each other. They dug up long-dead matters to expose skeletons in each other's closets. When they were exhausted, the heart of the matter began to emerge. Tahira complained that Ata was roaming around town in taxis with a third-rate actress from his studio. Yazdani wrote this off as mere slander. Tahira was ready to swear on the Qur'an that Ata had illicit relations with the actress. When Ata denied the allegation, Tahira shrieked, 'Trying to be holier than thou! The ayah who is standing here, didn't you try to kiss her? It's just that I arrived just in time.'

Yazdani roared, 'Stop talking rot!'

And once again the same unholy noise erupted. I tried to calm matters; my wife tried to calm matters. I took it upon myself to tell Yazdani off, 'You have exceeded all limits…apologize and finish the matter.'

Ata turned to me in a sombre tone, 'Saadat, this is a serious matter, and it will not end like this. This woman has made all manner of accusations, but I have not uttered a word against her. Do you know Inayat?'

'Inayat?'

'The playback singer, her father's student?'

'Yes, yes….'

'A crook of the highest order, but this woman invites him here every day. Her excuse….'

Tahira cut him off, 'There's no excuse-shexcuse…say what you have to say; what do you want to say?'

Ata's tone was full of loathing, 'Nothing!'

Tahira pushed her fringe away from her forehead. 'Inayat is devoted to me, that's all.'

Ata let out a volley of oaths—harsh words for Inayat and milder ones for Tahira—and a barrage of furious invective broke loose. Once again, they flung the same old accusations at each other. My wife and I tried to calm them, not that our efforts made a difference. I got the impression that Ata and Tahira had not bombarded each other to their heart's desire. After a brief lull in hostilities, the flames of war erupted again and cooled down without a satisfactory outcome. The stalemate continued while the combatants continued to stoke the fire.

I took time to reflect upon on what Ata and Tahira wanted as the outcome of their war but drew a blank and was exasperated. We talked a lot, quite aimlessly, and I could not see an end to the problem, so I said, 'Well if the two of you can't work this out, perhaps you should separate.'

Tahira remained silent, but Ata gave the matter some thought, and said, 'Not separate…but divorce.'

Tahira shrieked, 'Talaq, talaq, talaq…why don't you divorce me? I am not going to fall at your feet and beg you not to divorce me!'

Ata responded firmly, 'I will divorce you—and very soon.'

Tahira pushed her fringe back from her forehead, 'Today! Divorce me today.'

Ata stood up and went to the telephone, 'I'll call the qazi.'

I thought matters were getting out of hand, and restrained Ata, 'Don't be foolish and sit down calmly.'

Tahira said, 'No, Bhaijan, don't stop him.'

My wife told Tahira off, 'Don't talk rubbish.'

'This rubbish will only end with a divorce,' said Tahira.

'Did you hear that?' Ata addressed me as he leapt towards the telephone, but I barred his way.

Tahira turned to my wife, 'He will divorce me and marry that tarty actress.'

Ata turned to Tahira, 'And you?'

Tahira's pushed back her fringe, now soaked in the sweat of her brow. 'Me? With your handsome Joseph—Inayat Khan!'

'This has crossed all limits. Move out of my way,' yelled Ata as he picked up the telephone directory and began to search for the qazi's number.

When he started dialling the number, I did not think it appropriate to stop him. He tried the number a couple of times but did not get through. I found the opening I was looking for and told Ata Yazdani quite emphatically that he should exercise restraint. My wife pleaded with him, but he ignored her, and when she saw this, Tahira cried out, 'Safia, don't say anything. This man has a heart of stone. I'll show you the letters he wrote to me before we got married. In those days, I was the joy of his heart, the light of his eyes; one word from me was enough to give life to his dying body; he was ready to die happily for a mere glimpse of me, but today, he does not care an iota for me.'

Ata tried to dial the number yet again. Tahira continued, 'He was even in love with my father's music. He was proud that such a great artist was ready to accept him as his son-in-law. When he went to see my father with his proposal, he even touched my father's feet to win his approval. But today, he has forgotten him.'

Ata continued to dial the number. Tahira turned to me, 'He calls you his brother and says he respects you. He says, "I shall do whatever Bhaijan says", but you see what he's up to...trying to call the qazi to divorce me.'

I pushed the telephone aside and said, 'Come on, Ata, forget it....'

'No,' he said, as he pulled the telephone towards himself.

Tahira said, 'Forget it, Bhaijan. How can he have a place in his heart for me when he doesn't think about Toto?'

Ata shouted, 'Don't take Toto's name.'

Tahira flared her nostrils and said, 'Why shouldn't I take Toto's name?'

Ata slammed the receiver, 'Toto is mine!'

Tahira stood up, 'When I am not yours, how can Toto be yours? You can't take his name!'

Ata gave the matter some thought, and then said, 'I shall make all the arrangements.'

The colour drained from Tahira's face. 'Are you going to snatch Toto away from me?

Ata replied very firmly, 'Yes.'

'Ruthless man!' Tahira let out a scream and was about to swoon when my wife caught her.

Visibly concerned, Ata rushed to her and sprinkled water and eau de cologne on her. He produced some smelling salts; he telephoned doctors, tore his hair out, and wrenched his collar. When Tahira recovered, he patted her hand and declared, 'My life, Toto is yours, Toto is yours.'

Tahira burst into tears, 'No, he is yours.'

Ata kissed away the tears from Tahira's eyes, 'I am yours, you are mine, Toto is yours, and he is mine!'

I signalled my wife, and we decided to leave. As we got into the taxi that was waiting for us, I asked her, 'Who is this Toto?'

My wife responded amidst a ripple of laughter, 'Their son!'

Surprised, I asked, 'Son?'

My wife nodded.

Taken aback, I asked, 'When was he born?'

'He's not born yet; she's in her fourth month.'

Four months after this episode, I was sitting aimlessly on the balcony when the telephone rang; I was about to get up half-heartedly when it stopped. Not much later, my wife arrived, and I asked, 'Who was it?'

'Yazdani Sahib.'

'A new battle?'

'No…Tahira had a baby girl…stillborn.' A tearful Safia left the room.

I could not help but wonder if Tahira and Ata were to fall out, who would make peace between them now.

## 13

## *Ram Khelawan*

After I had killed an army of bedbugs, I was looking for some papers in my trunk when I found Saeed Bhaijan's photograph and slipped it into an unused frame standing on my desk. I sat down on a chair to await the dhobi—an exercise I repeated every Sunday because by Saturday I ran out of my stock of laundered clothes. I should not refer to it as a 'stock' because in those hard times I had just enough clothes to keep up appearances for a week. A couple of weeks earlier, I got engaged and had started visiting my fiancée's family every Sunday. The dhobi was a decent man; although I had not settled his bill, he turned up with my laundry every Sunday on the dot. Yet, I lived in fear that he might go off and sell my clothes at Chor Bazaar, the local thieves' market, and I would have to participate in my marriage discussions in an unsavoury state of undress.

My fleapit of a room reeked of dead bedbugs, and I was thinking of ways to get rid of the horrible smell when the dhobi arrived, and said, 'Salaam, Saab,' before sitting on the floor and opening his bundle to account for my laundry. When he stood up to put my clothes on my desk, he spotted Saeed Bhaijan's photograph and stepped back, stared at the image, and emitted a strange sound, 'Wa, wa, wa, what!'

'What's the matter, Dhobi?' I asked.

'This is Saaed Shaalim balishter!'

'You know him?'

Dhobi gave a firm nod of his head and continued, 'Two brothers...them...have kothi here in Colaba...Saaed Shaalim balishter, I wash his clothes.'

I reckoned this was at least two years ago because Saeed Hassan Bhaijan and Mohammad Hassan Bhaijan had a law practice in Bombay for about a year before they left for the Fiji Islands. So, I said, 'You are talking about two years ago.'

Dhobi nodded his head vigorously, 'When Saeed Shalim balishter left, he gives me one pagri, one dhoti, he give me one kurta, all

brand new…very good people, them. One have beard…that long….'
He stretched his hand out under his chin to indicate the length of
the beard before pointing at Saeed Bhaijan's photograph. 'This be
small one…he has three babalog, two boys, one girl…they play a
lot with me. They have kothi in Colaba…very big.'

I said, 'Dhobi, he is my brother.'

Dhobi emitted the same strange sound, 'Wa…wa, wa, what? Saeed
Shalim balishter?'

I tried to dispel his doubts and said, 'Dhobi, this is Saeed Hassan
Bhaijan's photograph; the bearded one was Mohammad Hassan, the
eldest amongst us.'

Dhobi stared at me before he reviewed my miserable room—a
small dump without electricity where the only furniture consisted of
a table I used as a desk, a chair, and a ropy charpai infested with
bedbugs. Dhobi could not believe I was Saeed Shalim balishter's
brother. After I shared many facts about my older brother, he shook
his head and added with more than a hint of disbelief, 'Saeed Shalim
balishter live in Colaba and you in hole!'

I responded in a philosophical tone, 'Such are the ways of the
world, Dhobi…in some parts there's light and in others darkness.
Five fingers are never the same.'

'Yes, Saab, what you say is barobar, right….'

Dhobi lifted the bundle of clothes and was ready to leave. I
thought I should settle his account. I had eight annas in my pocket,
and that was barely enough to take me to Mahim and back. To
assure him of my good intentions, I said, 'Dhobi, do keep a tab.
God knows how many clothes you've washed.'

Dhobi adjusted his dhoti, and in his typical Awadhi, he said, 'I
don't keep tab. I work one year for Saeed Shalim balishter…what
he give, I take. I don't know account.'

He said what he had to say and left, and I got dressed to go to
Mahim to discuss preparations for my wedding.

The deliberations progressed well, and I got married. Generally,
matters improved, and I moved from the dump on Second Peer Khan
Street, where I had paid nine rupees a month, to a flat on Clare
Road at a rent of thirty-five rupees a month. And Dhobi got paid on
time for the laundry. Delighted that my lifestyle had improved vastly,

Dhobi said to my wife, 'Begum Saab, Saab's brother Saeed Shalim balishter very big man. He live very big kothi there in Colaba. When he left, he give me one pagri, one dhoti, one shirt...your Saab also become one type very big man.'

I shared the episode of the photograph with my wife and told her how Dhobi stood by me during hard times. He took what I gave, never questioned, never asked, never complained. However, my wife paid little attention to my words, and after some time, began to complain that Dhobi did not provide an account. I said, 'He has washed my clothes for four years; and has never kept an account.'

She responded, 'Why should he have kept an account? He was making more than twice or four times as much as what you owed him.'

'How?'

'You don't know. Such people take men who don't have wives for a ride.'

Almost every month, my wife nitpicked and asked Dhobi why he kept no account of our clothes. He responded, 'Begum Saab, I don't know account. I not lie. Saeed Shalim balishter your Saab's brother, and I work for him for one year. Begum Saab said, "Dhobi, this your money," I say, "Okay."'

One month, we sent two hundred and fifty items, and my wife decided to test Dhobi. She told him, 'Dhobi, this month's tally is sixty.'

He said, 'Sure, Begum Saab, you will not lie.'

My wife paid him for sixty items; he took the money, touched it to his forehead, said salaam, and was about to leave, when my wife stopped him, 'Wait a minute Dhobi...not sixty, two hundred and fifty items...here, take the rest of your money.'

All he said was, 'Begum Saab, you will not lie.' And touching the extra cash to his forehead, he said salaam and left.

Two years after my marriage, I moved to Delhi. When I returned to Bombay after a year and a half, we found a place in Mahim, and within three months, we changed four dhobis because we found them dishonest and confrontational. Every week I witnessed altercations, sometimes about missing clothes, at others about substandard washing. We missed our old dhobi. One day, when we were without a dhobi, he appeared without warning and said, 'I saw Saab on bus and said, "How this possible? Saab gone Dilli"; I asked in Byculla; the man at the local stall said, "Look in Mahim." In the building next door, Saab has friends; I asked them and arrive.'

We were delighted, and immediately our everyday life and that of our clothes progressed into happier times.

The Congress government came to power in Bombay and proscribed the making and selling of local alcohol, although Western or imported alcohol was available. It was common knowledge that ninety-nine per cent of the dhobi community was addicted to alcohol. After spending the entire day standing in water, a dhobi consumed at least a quarter litre of local ale. It was during this time that our dhobi picked up an infection. He tried to cure himself with whatever he could lay his hands on and consequently developed severe complications in his stomach that took him to death's door.

I was swamped with work and left home at six-thirty every morning and returned at ten at night, but when my wife heard that Dhobi was critically ill, she took a taxi to his house. Our servant and the taxi driver carried Dhobi to the taxi, and she took him to a doctor. The doctor was very touched and refused to charge a fee, but my wife said, 'Doctor Sahib, you can't earn all of God's favours.'

The doctor smiled and accepted half his fee. Dhobi got proper medical attention, and he recovered after a course of a few injections. Some discomfort remained, but that settled down with restorative medicines. Dhobi was fit and well after a few months and blessed us night and day, 'Bhagwan make Saab into Saeed Shalim balishter. Saab go live in Colaba, have babalog and tons of money. Begum Saab come to fetch dhobi…in car…and take me big doctor in Fort, Bhagwan keep Begum Saab happy.'

Several years passed, and we witnessed many political upheavals. Now healthy, Dhobi came every Sunday without fail. He did not forget our goodwill and continued to pray for us and ask Bhagwan to bless us. Dhobi gave up alcohol. Although initially, he missed it occasionally, in time, he forgot the word. Now he could spend the entire day standing in water without the need for a drink to drive away his fatigue.

Hindu–Muslim riots flared up at Partition, and matters reached a critical point. In the darkness of night and the light of day, Hindus slaughtered Muslims in their neighbourhoods, and Muslims killed Hindus in theirs. My wife left for Lahore. When matters looked critical, I said to Dhobi, 'Look here, Dhobi, I think you'd better stop working here. We live in a Muslim area—what if someone kills you?'

Dhobi smiled, 'Saab, no one kill me.'

Several incidents occurred in our neighbourhood, but Dhobi continued his regular rounds.

One Sunday, I was checking the scores of different cricket matches listed on the sports page of a newspaper; and the front page of the same daily carried the death toll of the Hindu–Muslim riots. As I reflected on the eerie symmetry between the two, Dhobi arrived. I took out the laundry notebook and began to tick off the clothes, and Dhobi started his usual cheerful chatter, 'Saeed Shalim balishter was good man. Going from here he give me pagri, dhoti, kurta; your Begum Saab is too good person. She gone for work? To her land? When you write letter say my salaam. She brought car to my kholi; I had such runny tummy; doctor jabbed me needle, I was fine. You write there, say my salaam. Say, Ram Khelawan says, "Write to me…".'

I interrupted his drift and asked, 'Dhobi, you've started drinking again?'

Dhobi laughed, 'Drink? Where do you find drink, Saab?'

I didn't think it appropriate to pursue the matter. Dhobi tied my dirty laundry into a bundle and left.

After some days, matters got a lot worse, and a string of telegrams arrived from Lahore with the same message: 'Drop everything and leave at once.'

On a Saturday, I decided to leave the next morning. My clothes were with Dhobi, and I thought I ought to collect them since he usually dropped them off on Sundays. That evening I took a victoria and set off for Mahalaxmi, an hour before the curfew. There was traffic on the roads, and trams were running. As my victoria reached the Mahalaxmi bridge, I heard a loud din and saw people running helter-skelter. Two bulls were locked in combat. When the crowd dispersed, a horde of dhobis surrounded the bulls wielding lathis and spears and producing strange noises. The coachman refused to move forward. I paid his fare and set off on foot. As I approached the dhobis, they fell silent. I walked up and asked one of them, 'Where does Ram Khelawan live?'

A lathi-wielding dhobi sauntered up to the dhobi I had questioned and asked, in typical Awadhi, 'What does he ask?'

'He asks, "Where does Ram Khelawan live?"'

Drunk blind, the lathi-wielding dhobi walked right to me and asked, 'Who are you?'

I said, 'Ram Khelawan is my dhobi.'

'Ram Khelawan is your dhobi, and which dhobi's son are you?'

Another dhobi shouted, 'Hindu dhobi or Mussulman dhobi?'

I was surrounded by dhobis, some with clenched fists, others with lathis, trishuls, and spears. I had to respond to one question: am I a Hindu or a Muslim? Petrified, I knew there was nowhere I could run. I could see no police constable at hand whom I could call upon for help. Unable to think of anything to say, I responded in jibberish, 'Ram Khelawan is a Hindu; I ask, where he live? Where his hut? For ten years he our dhobi, he very ill, we take him doctor. My Begum, my Memsaab, come here in a car....'

I stooped so low that I embarrassed myself and wondered, 'How low can a human being stoop to save his life?' This feeling stirred some courage in me, and I said, 'I am a Mussulman.'

Cries of 'Kill him...kill him!' rose in the air.

A dhobi who looked drunk to the point of being brain-dead turned towards a man and shouted, 'Wait! Ram Khelawan will kill him.'

I turned around and saw Ram Khelawan leaning on a stout stick and swaying. He raised his stick to his head and began to walk towards me, shouting vile abuse at Muslims in his Awadhi idiom. I called out in an authoritative tone, 'Ram Khelawan!'

Ram Khelawan snarled, 'Quiet...you Ram Khelawan's....'

My last hope was dashed. When he came near me, I asked him in a dry tone, 'Don't you recognize me, Ram Khelawan?'

Ram Khelawan was about to strike me when he scrunched his eyes, then opened them wide and scrunched them again. He threw the stick to the ground, and as he stared me in the face, he cried out, 'Saab!' He turned to his comrades, 'This is not Mussalman, he my Saab; Begum Saab's Saab; she bring car...take me to doctor... cure my diarrhoea.'

Ram Khelawan tried to calm his companions, but they were drunk.

As an altercation broke out between them, some dhobis joined Ram Khelawan. Soon there was a punch up. I took this as an excellent opportunity to run.

The following morning at around nine o'clock, with my luggage packed, I was waiting for a friend who had gone to get me a ticket on the black market. Overwhelmed with all manner of emotions, I wished I could set off for the port because I feared that further delay could transform my flat into a prison. I heard a knock and opened the door, but instead of my friend, I saw Dhobi.

'Saab salaam!'

'Salaam.'

'May I come in?'

'Do.'

He entered silently, untied the cloth bundle, laid my clothes on the bed, and wiped his eyes with the corner of his dhoti. Then he asked, 'You leave, Saab?'

'Yes.'

He began to weep, 'Saab, forgive me; it all fault of liquor. And these days, liquor free. The seths distribute free with instructions, "Drink and kill Mussalman." Saab, you tell me, who turn down free liquor, Saab? Forgive me, Saab. I drink. Saeed Shalim balishter very good to me. He give me pagri, dhoti, kurta. Begum Saab save my life; take me to doctor...spend so much money. You go country, don't say to Begum Saab that Ram Khelawan....' His voice cracked as he folded the cloth in which he had brought my clothes and slung it across his shoulder.

I tried to say something to him, 'Ram Khelawan....' He did not wait to hear what I had to say but adjusted his dhoti and hastily stepped out.

# 14

## Shanti

They were enjoying measured sips of piping hot tea, sitting outside Parisienne Dairy under a striped-green umbrella by the seaside, with the hum of waves in the background. Opposite them, seated on a chair next to the main door, was the familiar figure of a round-faced Jewish woman with dark eyebrows, a sharp nose, and thick lips reddened with carelessly applied lipstick. Maqbool turned to look at her and said to Balraj, 'She's sitting here to cast her net.'

Balraj did not look at the woman with the dark eyebrows and said, 'Hmm...she'll catch some fish or the other.'

Maqbool shoved an entire pastry into his mouth, 'This business is strange—one opens a shop, the other walks around selling her wares, and another waits for her customers in such restaurants. Selling one's body is an art and a difficult one at that. So how does this one with the dark eyebrows draw a client's attention? How does she let a man know she is for sale?'

Balraj smiled, 'Take some time out one day and sit here for a few hours, and you'll learn how eyes seal deals and communicate rates.' He had just finished his sentence when he grasped Maqbool's arm with some urgency, 'Look, look here.'

Maqbool looked at the woman with the dark eyebrows, but Balraj pressed his arm again, 'No, yaar, here, under the umbrella in this corner.'

Maqbool turned around and saw a slim, fair girl about to sit on a chair. She had short hair, regular features, and wore a pale lemon georgette sari. Maqbool asked Balraj, 'Who is she?'

'Arrey, the same one...the one I said was unusual.'

Maqbool thought for a while and said, 'Which one, yaar? As far as you are concerned, every girl you meet is unusual.'

Balraj smiled, 'This one is rather special. Look at her carefully.'

Maqbool scrutinized the girl, who had strawy light brown hair. She wore a pale lemon sari and a short-sleeved blouse that revealed her slim pale arms. When she turned around, Maqbool noticed the red lipstick smeared across her thin lips and said, 'All I can say is that your unusual girl doesn't know how to apply lipstick. And now that I've had a good look, she doesn't know how to tie her sari, and her hair's a mess.'

Balraj laughed, 'You always look for defects. Unfortunately, your eyes never see the good points.'

Maqbool retorted, 'Why don't you list the good points, but before you do, tell me, do you know her?'

When the girl saw Balraj, she smiled, and Maqbool interjected, 'I've got my answer, but now, please recount madame's qualities.'

'Number one: she is very forthright, doesn't lie, and abides strictly by the rules she has set for herself. Second, she's very particular about personal hygiene. And third, she's not into love and romance; on this front, her heart is cold as ice.' Balraj took the last sip of his tea and asked, 'Well then, what do you think?'

Maqbool sized up the girl and said, 'Men visit such girls with a desire to lose themselves in make-believe, if not real love. If this girl does not help a man in his delusions, I think her very foolish.'

'This is what I thought at first. This creature is forthright to the extent of being insipid. Try having a conversation with her, and you'll get a jolt. I'm not sure how to explain it, but once she told me, "It's more than an hour, and you haven't said anything worthwhile. I'm off..." and she took off. On another occasion, she told me, "Your mouth's reeking of alcohol; please leave...and don't touch my sari, it will get soiled."'

Balraj lit his cigarette and continued, 'But she is an unusual girl. When I first met her, by God, my head went into a spin. The moment we got up to leave, she declared, "Not a penny less than fifty. If you have it in your pocket, let's go; otherwise, I have other things to do."'

Maqbool asked, 'What's her name?'

'Shanti...she's a Kashmiran.'

Maqbool, a Kashmiri, was startled and asked, 'She's a Kashmiran?'

'Your compatriot!'

Maqbool looked at the girl. Sure enough, she had Kashmiri features. So he asked, 'How did she land here?'

'I don't know.'

Maqbool began to show an interest in the girl, 'Does she have any relatives?'

'If there are any in Kashmir, I can't say. Here in Bombay, she lives on her own.' Balraj put out his cigarette on the ashtray.

'She rents a room in a hotel on Hornby Road. I discovered this quite by chance; otherwise, she doesn't tell anyone where she lives. She meets her clients here at the Parisienne Dairy and comes here every day, exactly at five o'clock.'

Maqbool was silent for a while, but just as he signalled the waiter to get the bill, a well-dressed young man came up and occupied the chair next to the girl. Maqbool turned to Balraj, '...should meet her sometime.'

Balraj smiled, 'Certainly, certainly, but right now, she's busy. Come back another evening.'

Maqbool settled the bill, and they left.

The following evening, Maqbool returned on his own; he ordered some tea and sat down. At precisely five o'clock, the girl got off a bus and walked past Maqbool with a handbag dangling from her wrist. Her gait was sloppy; when she sat down on a chair at some distance from his, Maqbool thought, 'She doesn't have a tiny bit of sex appeal. How on earth does she run her business? The way she has applied her lipstick and tied her sari leave much room for improvement.'

His tea arrived, and he began to drink it, wondering how to approach her. Finally, he made a gesture which the girl noticed; she hesitated but walked up and sat on the chair opposite his. Maqbool was nervous but managed to ask her, 'Would you care for some tea?'

'No,' she responded rather dryly.

After a brief pause, he continued, 'Kashmiris are very fond of tea.'

The girl asked awkwardly, 'Do you want to come with me?'

Maqbool felt somebody had pushed his face down to the ground. A trifle tense, all he could bring himself to say was, 'Ya....'

The girl responded in English, 'Fifty rupees, yes or no?'

It was her second assault, but now Maqbool was more at ease, 'Let's go!' He settled his bill, and they headed to the taxi stand in silence. Once inside the taxi, she asked Maqbool in a strange slang,

'Where d'ya wanna go?'

Maqbool replied, 'Wherever you take me.'

'I dunno, you say, where d'ya wanna go?'

Maqbool could not think of an answer and responded in her idiom, 'I dunno....'

The girl moved her hand to open the taxi door, 'What sort of man are you, cracking rubbish jokes?'

Maqbool caught hold of her hand, 'I'm not joking. I want to talk to you.'

Visibly miffed, she asked, 'You said fifty rupees, yes...?'

Maqbool put his hand in his pocket, took out five ten-rupee notes, and handed them to her, 'Here...why are you nervous?'

She took the money, 'Where d'ya wanna go?'

Maqbool said, 'Your house....'

'No.'

'Why not?'

'I said no! No muck around.'

Maqbool smiled, 'All right, no muck around.'

She looked astonished, 'What kind of chap are you?'

'I am the way I am. You said, "Fifty rupees, yes or no?" I said, "Yes," and handed you the money. You said, "No muck around," I said, "Absolutely not." Now, what else do you have to say?'

The girl looked thoughtful. Maqbool smiled, 'Look here, Shanti, I saw you yesterday, and a friend told me a bit about you, and I find you interesting. Today I caught you...now, let's go to your house. I'll chat with you for a while and leave. Isn't this acceptable to you?'

Shanti looked perplexed, 'No. Here, take back your fifty rupees.'

'You're obsessed with the fifty rupees. There are things in the world other than money. Come on, give your address to the driver. I'm a decent man; I won't deceive you.'

Maqbool's voice had a ring of truth that touched Shanti. She hesitated for a bit, then said, 'Let's go.... Driver, Hornby Road.'

As the taxi moved forward, she slipped the money into Maqbool's pocket. Maqbool did not resist, 'It's up to you.'

The taxi stopped by a five-storeyed dank and dark building. Maqbool noticed massage parlours on the first and second floors; a hotel occupied the third, fourth, and fifth floors. Shanti's room was on the fourth floor, directly opposite the staircase. She took a key out of her handbag and opened the door. They walked into an uncluttered room. Maqbool saw a cast-iron bed with four trunks under it and a sparkling clean sheet on top. Pillowcases are often grimy, but hers had spotless covers. A dressing table stood in a corner, and a table fan rested on a stool. He was impressed. Everything was immaculate. Maqbool was about to sit on the bed, but Shanti stopped him, 'No. Nobody has permission to sit on my bed. Sit on the chair,' she asserted as she sat down on the bed.

Maqbool smiled and planted himself on the chair. Shanti tucked her handbag under her pillow and turned to him, 'So then what d'ya want to ask?'

Maqbool looked at Shanti and said, 'The first thing I want to say is that you do not know how to apply lipstick.'

Shanti did not seem to mind and said, 'I know.'

'Here, get up and give me your lipstick. I'll teach you how to apply it,' and Maqbool pulled out his handkerchief.

Shanti said, 'You can pick it up; it's on the dressing table.'

Maqbool picked up the lipstick, and as he checked it out, he said, 'Come here, let me wipe your lips.'

'Not with yours; take mine,' said Shanti as she opened a trunk and handed him a clean handkerchief.

Maqbool wiped her lips and very delicately reapplied the lipstick; he proceeded to comb her hair with a fine-toothed comb and said, 'Here, now look in the mirror.'

Shanti stood before the dressing table to inspect herself; she scrutinized the change with approval and turned to Maqbool, 'Yes, it's good now,' and returned to sit on her bed, before she asked, 'you have a wife?'

Maqbool replied, 'No.'

She lapsed into silence. Maqbool wanted to chat and started a conversation, 'I know you are from Kashmir. Your name is Shanti, and you live here. Tell me, how did you get into this "fifty rupees" business?'

Shanti responded without hesitation, 'My father is a doctor in Srinagar. I was a nurse in his hospital; a boy spoilt me, and I ran away and came here. Here, I met a man who gave me fifty rupees and said, "Come with me." I went. That's it. Work started. I came here to the hotel, but I don't talk to anybody here; all harlots here—they don't allow anybody on their patch.'

Maqbool did not dig any further. They chatted for a while, and it became evident that Shanti was not interested in sexual matters. When the subject came up, she said in English, 'I don't like vot is bad.' For her, the fifty rupees matter was business. The boy who spoilt her in the hospital in Srinagar had the gall to offer her ten rupees; Shanti was furious and tore up the money. The episode left a deep imprint on her mind. As far as she was concerned, there was no question of gratification. When Shanti started her business, sheer coincidence fixed her fee at fifty rupees. She had trained and worked as a nurse and was meticulous about hygiene.

Shanti had been in Bombay for a year, and by now, she could have saved ten thousand rupees, but she had developed a passion for horse racing and lost five thousand rupees. Yet, she had faith that she would win in future and cover her loss. Shanti kept an account of every single paisa. Every day, she earned one hundred rupees and banked it at the first opportunity. She could make more but was very conscious of her health. When two hours passed, she looked at her watch and said to Maqbool, 'Now, you go. I eat and then sleep.'

As Maqbool got up to leave, she said, 'If you come for a chit-chat, come in the morning; evening time I make a loss.'

All Maqbool said was, 'Okay,' and he left.

The following morning, Maqbool arrived at Shanti's at around ten o'clock. He thought she would disapprove of him turning up unannounced, but she did not seem to mind. Maqbool sat with her for a long time, and they chatted away. He taught Shanti how to drape a sari; she was an intelligent girl and learned quickly. She had some beautiful clothes in her wardrobe and showed Maqbool her entire collection. Shanti was not childlike, nor did she look as though she had aged before her time, but she lacked a glow. It seemed someone or something had applied the brakes just as she was about to come into her own. It was impossible to form an opinion about her. Shanti was neither beautiful nor ugly, neither woman nor girl; she seemed undefined.

Maqbool tried to learn more about Shanti and to understand

her but often felt very frustrated. He wanted to discover the point in her life where she had wavered, and he began to visit her every other day. She did not offer him any food or drink but permitted him to sit on her pristine bed. On one visit, Maqbool was taken aback when Shanti asked him, 'You want a girl?'

Maqbool, who was lying on the bed, sat up as he exclaimed, 'What did you say?'

Shanti said, 'I ask if you want girl, I get you.'

When Maqbool asked her what made her ask this strange question out of the blue, she remained silent, but when Maqbool insisted, Shanti explained that she had figured out that he considered her a worthless woman. Indeed, she was surprised why so many men visited her when she was such a cold fish. She knew that Maqbool chatted with her simply because he looked upon her as an object of curiosity. She had given the matter some thought and told herself, 'All women are not like me and if it is a woman that Maqbool needs, let me get one for him.'

For the first time, Maqbool saw tears in Shanti's eyes. She got up and cried out, 'I nothing…go…go away…why you come to me? Leave. Go away.'

Maqbool did not say a word, and he left.

The following week, Maqbool went to Parisienne Dairy every day but did not find Shanti there. Finally, one morning, he headed for her hotel. She opened the door but remained silent. Maqbool walked in and lowered himself down on a chair. He noticed the lipstick smeared on Shanti's lips, her hair a mess, and her sari draped in the old sloppy manner. He asked her, 'Are you angry with me?'

Shanti sat on her bed but did not respond. Finally, Maqbool asked in a firm voice, 'Have you forgotten what I taught you?'

Shanti remained silent. Maqbool persisted. His anger apparent in his tone, 'Answer me, or else, remember, I shall hit you.'

Shanti merely said, 'Hit….'

Maqbool got up and slapped Shanti's face. She shuddered as tears began to flow from her horrified eyes. Maqbool took his handkerchief out of his pocket and furiously wiped off the distasteful lipstick. She tried to stop him, but he continued to wipe the colour off her lips and applied fresh lipstick. Finally, he took her comb and restyled her hair and said, 'Fix your sari.'

Shanti stood up to fix her sari, but as she did, she began to weep inconsolably and threw herself on her bed. After she had steadied herself, Maqbool said, 'Get up, Shanti. I am leaving.'

Shanti trembled as she turned on her side and cried out, 'No, no…you can't leave.' She ran and stood with her back against the door and spread her arms out as she said, 'If you go, I'll kill you.'

Shanti was breathless and her breasts, which Maqbool had never paid any attention to, looked as though they wanted to wake up from a deep sleep. Maqbool was astonished as he witnessed her transformation. Her tearful eyes began to sparkle, and her red lips began to quiver. Maqbool stepped forward and enveloped her in a tight embrace, and squeezed her close to his chest.

They went and sat on the bed, and Shanti put her head on Maqbool's lap. It seemed nothing could stop her torrent of tears, even though Maqbool kissed them away and asked her not to weep. Shanti choked as she sobbed, 'There in Srinagar, a man killed me… and here a man brings me back to life.'

After two hours, when Maqbool was about to leave, he took fifty rupees out of his pocket, put them on Shanti's bed, and said, 'Here, take your fifty rupees.'

Shanti flung the money aside. Then, her face flushed with rage, she opened her dressing table drawer and turned to Maqbool, 'Here… look at this.'

Maqbool saw several shredded hundred-rupee notes. Shanti picked up a fistful, and as she tossed the confetti of money in the air, she said, 'Now, I no want these.'

Maqbool smiled. He patted Shanti's cheek gently and asked, 'And now, what you want?'

Shanti replied, 'You.' She walked up to Maqbool and stood so close that she seemed glued to him.

Maqbool ran his fingers through her hair, and as he pushed it away from her face, he said in a tender voice, 'Don't cry. You've got what you want.'

## 15

## Babu Gopinath

I met Babu Gopinath in 1940. I was editing a Bombay weekly at the time and was engrossed in writing the leader when Abdul Rahim Sando walked in with a squat man and greeted me with an aadaab. As Sando began to chant paeans to me in his distinctive loud voice, I stood up to shake hands with the squat man, and Sando bumbled on, 'Babu Gopinath, you are shaking hands with Hindustan's number one writer. People go "dharan takhta" when they read his writings, and his "continutelies" knock them out. Manto Sahib, what was the piece you wrote a few days ago, "Miss Khursheed Bought a Car?" Why Babu Gopinath, what do you think? Allah is the Great Facilitator! "Anti ki panti poo".'

Abdul Rahim Sando's diction was unique—words and phrases such as 'continutely', 'dharan takhta', and 'anti ki panti poo' were his coinage, and he used them with abandon. After he introduced me to Babu Gopinath, who looked suitably impressed, Sando turned to him, 'And, this is Babu Gopinath, the Star Crossed. After wasting his life in Lahore, he's come to Bombay with a Kashmiri dove.'

Babu Gopinath smiled, but Abdul Rahim Sando clearly thought his introduction inadequate because he continued, 'If there is a number one fool, it is his highness. People massage his ego and fleece him. Merely for making small talk, my daily supply of two packs of Polson's butter is fixed. Seriously, Manto Sahib, he's a real "anti-flujustine" kind of man. You must grace his flat with your presence this evening.'

Jolted out of his reverie, Babu Gopinath said, 'Yes, please do us the honour...' He turned to Sando and continued, 'Why Sando, does he indulge a bit?'

Abdul Rahim Sando laughed uproariously, 'Uh, all sorts of indulgences. Manto Sahib, do join us this evening. I, too, have started drinking because it's free.' Sando shared the address of Babu Gopinath's flat with me, and they left.

As agreed, at six o'clock that evening, I arrived at Babu Gopinath's large, clean, and tidy three-roomed flat with brand new furniture. Babu Gopinath and Sando were sitting in the living room with two men and two women, whom Sando introduced to me. The first, Ghaffar Sain, was an impressive specimen of a Punjabi godman, clad in a tehmad with a string of large beads around his neck. 'He is Babu Gopinath's legal adviser—get what I mean?' asked Sando, adding, 'In Punjab, any man whose nose and mouth dribble can claim a direct connection with God. Well, he is connected or about to get connected and decided to tag along with Babu Gopinath. After all, what hope did he have of finding another sucker in Lahore? Here, he manages to sponge his daily quota of Craven A cigarettes and Scotch whisky and spends his time in prayer.' Ghaffar Sain smiled.

Sando then introduced the other man as 'Ghulam Ali, my disciple; he follows in his master's footsteps.' I observed the tall young man with an athletic body and a pockmarked face, as Sando continued, 'A famous Lahori tawa'if's virgin daughter fell in love with him, and many 'continutelies' were set in motion to entrap him. He said, "Do or die, I'll remain true to my bachelorhood!" He bumped into Babu Gopinath at a shrine, and from that day has clung to him like a leech. His daily quota of Craven A, plus food and drink are fixed.' Like Ghaffar Sain, Ghulam Ali broke into a smile at Sando's introduction.

When I entered the room, I had noticed a woman with a round face and rosy cheeks and recognized her as the Kashmiri dove Sando had referred to in my office. Immaculately turned out, her clear, bright eyes added to the refreshing air around her; her hair looked cropped but was not. Her features revealed her obdurate and naïve disposition. Sando turned to her and said, 'Zeenat Begum, whom Babu Sahib affectionately calls Zeeno. An irascible tawa'if plucked this apple from Kashmir and brought her to Lahore. Babu Gopinath heard about her through his CID and took off with her one night. A string of court hearings continued for some time. The police made hay. Ultimately, Babu Gopinath won the case and brought her here— dharan takhta!'

Next, he turned to the other woman, dark and brazen, with shamelessness oozing out of her red eyes. She continued to smoke as Babu Gopinath turned towards her and said, 'And something about her....'

Sando slapped the woman's thigh and continued, 'Sir, this is Tin Tin Pooti Fil Fil Footi, Mrs Abdul Rahim Sando, nicknamed Sardar Begum. Her Highness is also a product of Lahore. In 1936, she fell for me, and within two years reduced me to dharan takhta. I fled Lahore but Babu Gopinath called her here to humour me. She, too, gets a packet of Craven A as part of her daily ration and a morphine injection worth two-and-a-half rupees every evening. I admit her complexion is dark, but still...she's a real "tit for tat" type of woman.'

Sardar interjected, 'Don't talk rot!' Her manner smacked of a woman well-rehearsed in the trade.

After he introduced me to everyone in the room, Sando began his usual hymn to me. I cut him short and said, 'Forget it, yaar, let's talk about something else.'

Sando yelled across the room, 'Boy, whisky and soda! Babu Gopinath, twirl a hundred.'

Babu Gopinath pulled out a wad of hundred-rupee notes from his pocket and handed one to Sando, who eyed it wistfully and rasped, 'Oh God, Oh Master of the Universe, when will I see the dawn when I can conjure banknotes into existence? Off you go, Ghulam Ali, and get two bottles of Johnnie Walker Still Going Strong.'

The bottles arrived and a bout of drinking continued for the next two or three hours. As usual, Abdul Rahim Sando talked the most. Downing his first peg in one gulp, he cried out, 'Dharan takhta, Manto Sahib, what a whisky! As it makes its way down from the throat to the stomach, it cries out "Long Live the Revolution!" but I say, long live, Babu Gopinath, long live!'

The mild-mannered Babu Gopinath remained silent through most of the evening but occasionally added a word or two to agree with Sando. I felt this man didn't have a mind of his own. When Sando referred to Ghaffar Sain as Babu Gopinath's legal adviser, he meant that Babu Gopinath revered Ghaffar Sain. I saw this as further evidence of Babu Gopinath's feeble mind. As our conversation continued, I learnt that in Lahore, Babu Gopinath spent most of his time in the company of faqirs and dervishes. I noticed he looked lost in his thoughts and asked, 'Babu Gopinath, what are you thinking?'

He gave a start, 'Me? Nothing, really nothing,' but then he gave Zeenat a look that radiated affection and responded, 'I am thinking about these beauties. What else can us ordinary mortals think about?'

Sando added, 'He's impetuous, Manto Sahib, really impetuous, and I don't think there is a tawa'if in Lahore with whom Babu Sahib hasn't had a continutely.'

Babu Gopinath added with gauche modesty, 'Now the loins don't have that old vigour, Manto Sahib.'

The conversation took on a tasteless turn with a focus on the pedigrees of various Lahori tawa'ifs and their salons. The exchanges, mainly between Sardar, Sando, Ghaffar Sain, and Ghulam Ali, were in the unexpurgated language of Hira Mandi, Lahore's red-light district. They discussed the most prized gem in the market and recalled how much Babu Gopinath paid to deflower this or that girl. I managed to follow the drift of the conversation, but many expressions eluded me.

Zeenat remained silent, occasionally she smiled at something, but I got the impression that she was indifferent to the conversation. She did partake of a chhota peg, but that too in a disinterested manner. She smoked, it seemed, without a taste for tobacco or an interest in the smoke rings she continued to blow throughout the evening. Yet, she lit the most cigarettes. I could not tell if she loved Babu Gopinath. It was clear that he had great sympathy for her and provided for all her comforts. Yet, I sensed a curious tension between them; they seemed estranged.

At around eight o'clock, Sardar went off to Dr Majeed's for her nightly morphine injection. Ghaffar Sain consumed three pegs, and clinging to his rosary, fell asleep on the carpet. Ghulam Ali was sent to the hotel to fetch dinner. When Sando stopped his curious banter for a bit, Babu Gopinath, by now quite drunk, gave Zeenat a doting look and asked me, 'Manto Sahib, what are your thoughts about my Zeeno?'

Quickly, I considered the matter and turned to look at Zeenat, who blushed. I said in an offhand manner, 'Very worthy thoughts....'

Babu Gopinath looked pleased, 'She is a very worthy person, I swear upon God! She does not care for jewellery or fripperies. How often have I asked her, "Love of my life, should I build a house for you?" Do you know what she says, "What will I do with it? Who do I have?" Manto Sahib, for how much can I get a car?'

I told him, 'I haven't the faintest idea.'

Taken aback, Babu Gopinath said, 'Manto Sahib, what are you saying? You don't know the price of a car! Come with me tomorrow, and we'll buy a car for Zeeno. I've realized that a car is a must in Bombay.'

Zeenat's face remained blank.

After several hours, an inebriated Babu Gopinath turned to me again, 'Manto Sahib, you are a man of the world, and I'm an ass. Do tell me how can I be of service to you. When Sando mentioned your name yesterday, immediately I sent for a taxi and said, "Take me to Manto Sahib." If I have offended you in any way, forgive me. I am a sinner. Should I get some more whisky for you?'

I said, 'No, no...we've had a lot to drink.'

He responded in a maudlin tone, 'Do drink some more, Manto Sahib,' and again, he pulled out a wad of hundred-rupee notes from his pocket and began to separate them. I took all the bills from his hand and stuffed them back where they came from, 'You just gave Ghulam Ali a hundred-rupee note, what happened to that?'

At first, I thought Babu Gopinath was an ass, but over the course of the night, I observed how his companions bled him like leeches and began to sympathize with him. He appreciated my concern and responded with a smile, 'Manto Sahib, the change from that hard cash has either fallen out of Ghulam Ali's pocket or....'

He had not completed his sentence when Ghulam Ali entered the room wearing a pained expression and informed us that some bastard in the hotel had cleaned out his pocket. Babu Gopinath looked at me and smiled. He handed Ghulam Ali another hundred-rupee note and said, 'Hurry and get some food.'

I know it is not possible to know a person completely. Still, after five or six prolonged encounters with Babu Gopinath, I discovered some curious facets of his life and formed an impression of his personality. First, I must confess I was way off the mark to think him a fool of the highest order. Babu Gopinath knew that Sardar, Sando, Ghaffar Sain, Ghulam Ali, and company were self-seeking toadies; yet, he put up with their scolds and taunts without a hint of anger. He told me, 'Manto Sahib, to this day, I never ignore anyone's advice. When somebody gives me a piece of advice, I say, "God is great!" They think me a fool, but I think them smart to understand that my frailties can be of use to them. I have spent a lifetime in the company of pimps and faqirs, and have grown to love them. I cannot live without them. When my wealth runs out, I shall retire to sit in the shade of some shrine—a harlot's salon and a saint's shrine are the two places where my heart finds a measure of peace. Soon, my pocket will be empty, so the harlot's salon will be barred to me, but there are thousands of shrines in Hindustan, and I shall take myself to one of them.'

I asked him, 'Why are you so drawn to harlots' salons and shrines?'

He reflected for a while and responded, 'Both places are immersed in deception from ceiling to floor. What better place for a person who wishes to deceive himself?'

I followed his answer with another question, 'I've noticed that you enjoy listening to tawa'ifs sing. Do you understand music?'

'Not in the least,' he said, 'and this is no bad thing because I can listen to the most tuneless tawa'if and shake my head in appreciation. Manto Sahib, I have no interest in singing. I get a thrill in pulling out a hundred-rupee note from my pocket and waving it at a tawa'if; when she approaches me with a coquettish air, I tuck the note away into one of my socks, so she has to bend down to pull it out, and this tickles both of us. There are many such pointless rituals that voyeurs like us enjoy; otherwise, who doesn't know that in a harlot's salon mothers and fathers exploit their daughters and in shrines and sanctuaries human beings their God.'

I know nothing about Babu Gopinath's lineage, except that he was the son of a very wealthy and miserly bania. On his father's death, he inherited an estate of ten lakh rupees, which he squandered at will. He arrived in Bombay with fifty thousand rupees. In the time that I am referring to, everything was comparatively inexpensive. Even so, he spent a hundred or one-hundred-and-fifty rupees every day. Besides, he purchased a Fiat car for Zeeno, I think for three thousand rupees, and employed a driver, who was also a bit of a hustler—Babu Gopinath liked such men.

I was merely interested in Babu Gopinath, but he was devoted to me and held me in higher esteem than he did most other men. We began to meet frequently. I arrived at Babu Gopinath's flat early one morning and was startled to find Shafiq there. Perhaps, if I say Mohammad Shafiq Toosi, the name might mean something to you. Shafiq was a rather well-known man, in part for his distinctive musical compositions and equally, if not more, his inimitable personality.

One aspect of Shafiq Toosi's life remained hidden. Very few people knew that before he kept three sisters serially as his mistresses, for two to three years each, he'd had a relationship with their mother. It was even less well known that he did not like his first wife because she did not have the wiles or airs of a tawa'if. She died soon after they were married. Nevertheless, every person acquainted with Toosi knew that in the forty years of his life, many tawa'ifs had retained his services. Shafiq's wardrobe was of exceptional quality; he ate the choicest food and drove the best car in town but did not spend a penny from his purse on a tawa'if. Women, particularly professionals, were drawn to his inimitable personality, which had more than a hint of a mirasi—a member of a hereditary community of musicians, barbers, and genealogists rolled into one.

I was not in the least bit surprised when I saw him laugh and flirt with Zeenat, but I did wonder how he had turned up at Babu Gopinath's. Sando was the only person who knew him, but they had cut off diplomatic relations some time ago. Later, I heard they had patched up, and Sando had brought him to the flat. The entire evening, Babu Gopinath sat quietly in a corner with his hookah. Perhaps, I have not mentioned this earlier, but he did not smoke at all. When I entered, I found Mohammad Shafiq Toosi recounting jokes about mirasis, which Sardar appreciated more than Zeenat. When he saw me, Shafiq quipped, 'Bismillah, Bismillah! Why, I see you spend your time in this valley as well?'

Sando said, 'Do grace us, Izrail Sahib.'

I knew why Sando was referring to me as the angel of death. We continued to make small talk, but I noticed Zeenat and Shafiq Toosi's eyes were saying something to each other. Although Zeenat drew a blank in the art of coquetry, Shafiq's expertise masked her inadequacies. Sardar observed this interaction with the interest of a tout sitting by the ringside to watch his top prize-fighters' manoeuvres.

Over several months, an air of informality had developed between Zeenat and me. She called me 'bhai', and I did not object to her addressing me as her brother. Zeenat was a genial, unpretentious, not very talkative, tidy, and well-turned-out woman. I did not much care for the flirtatious exchange of glances between her and Toosi, mainly because she was inept, but she called me 'bhai' and that had something to do with my intervention.

Shafiq and Sando stepped out of the room for a bit. I lost no time in taking up the matter of the exchange of glances with Zeeno. Her eyes welled up with tears, and she walked out of the room. Babu Gopinath stopped smoking his hookah, left his seat in the corner, and followed her. Sardar tried to say something with her eyes, but I could not follow the drift. Shortly, Babu Gopinath returned to the room and said, 'Come, Manto Sahib,' and he took me to the other room.

I saw Zeenat sitting on her bed, her face covered with both her hands, but when she saw us, she lay down. Babu Gopinath and I sat down on the two armchairs by her bedside, and he began in a solemn tone, 'Manto Sahib, I love this woman. She has been with me for two years. I swear on Hazrat Ghaus-i-Azam Gillani that she has never given me cause for complaint. Her sisters, I mean other women from her profession, have robbed me blind, but she has never taken an extra penny from me. If I was lying around at another woman's for weeks, this poor creature sold or pawned a piece of her jewellery. I have told you that very soon, I shall cut ties with this world. My wealth will run out, and I don't want her life ruined. I tried to explain this to her in Lahore and said, "Look at other women and learn from them. I am wealthy today, but tomorrow I will be a beggar. It is not enough for you girls to have just one rich man in your lives. If you do not trap somebody after me, how will matters work out for you?" But Manto Sahib, she did not pay the slightest attention to my advice. She sat at home like a sharifzadi—a girl from a decent family. I consulted Ghaffar Sain, who said, "Take her to Bombay." His reasons made sense to me because two tawa'ifs known to him have become actresses in Bombay. I sent for Sardar to teach her all the tricks of her trade.

'We've been in Bombay for two months, and she can learn a lot from Ghaffar Sain, but she is worried, "Babu, it will be humiliating for you." Nobody knows me here, so I said, "Forget about it; Bombay is a huge city. There are tens of thousands of rich men. I have bought you a new car. Now, find a suitable man." Manto Sahib, I swear upon God, my greatest wish is to see her stand on her own two feet. I am ready to deposit ten thousand rupees in her bank account today, but I know that Zeenat will be destitute within ten days, and Sardar will pocket everything. So you must try to explain to her the importance of being shrewd. Now that I've bought her a car, Sardar takes her to Apollo Bandar every day, but they return without any success. Sando brought Muhammad Shafiq Toosi here with great difficulty. What do you think of him?'

I did not think it appropriate to air my views, but Babu Gopinath continued, 'He looks pretty well-off and is handsome. Why, Zeeno darling, does he appeal to you?'

Zeeno remained silent.

When Babu Gopinath explained why he had brought Zeenat to Bombay, my head went into a spin. I did not believe such things were possible, but later events proved me wrong. Babu Gopinath desired with all his heart to see Zeeno as some rich man's mistress or for her to learn the tricks of her trade so she could continue to earn money from different types of men. If Babu Gopinath wanted to get rid of Zeenat, he could have done so in a day. His intentions were worthy, and he had tried every possible ploy to secure her future. To facilitate her entry into the film world as an actress, he entertained many impostors who posed as film directors and had a telephone line installed at home. Alas, nothing worked.

Mohammad Shafiq Toosi's visits continued for almost a month and a half; he spent several nights with Zeenat but was not the kind of man who could be a source of comfort to any woman. One day, Babu Gopinath declared dolefully, 'Shafiq Sahib turned out to be a hollow gentleman. Look at the cheek of that man—he swiped four bedsheets, six pillow covers, and two hundred rupees in cash from poor Zeenat! I've heard these days he is romancing with some girl called Ilmas.'

He was spot on; Ilmas was Nazir Jan Patialay Wali's youngest daughter, and before her, her sisters were Shafiq's mistresses. I know that the two hundred rupees he took from Zeenat he spent on Ilmas, who later fell out with her sisters and consumed poison. When Mohammad Shafiq Toosi stopped his visits, Zeenat telephoned me several times and begged me, 'Please find him and bring him to me.'

I did look for him, but nobody knew of his whereabouts. One day, I bumped into him at the radio station; he looked distracted. I told him, 'Zeenat wants to see you.'

He shrugged his shoulders, 'I've received several such messages. Sorry, I have no time these days. Zeenat is a perfect woman, but alas, very decent. I'm not interested in women who are like wives.'

Disappointed by Shafiq, Zeenat resumed her trips to Apollo Bandar. In fifteen days, after they burnt several gallons of petrol, Sardar ensnared two men. Zeenat earned four hundred rupees from them. Babu Gopinath thought matters looked auspicious because one of them, an owner of a silk cloth mill, had told Zeenat he would marry her. A month passed, but this man did not return to visit her. One day, I cannot recollect why, but I was going past Hornby Road and saw Zeenat's car parked by the pavement. Mohammad Yasin, the owner of Nagina Hotel, was sitting in the back seat. I asked him, 'Where did you get this car from?'

Yasin smiled, 'You know the lady of the car.'

I said, 'Indeed, I know her.'

'Well then, figure it out. She's a nice girl, yaar!' Yasin winked at me, and I smiled.

Four days later, Babu Gopinath came to my office in a taxi, and I heard from him how Zeenat met Yasin. One evening, Sardar and Zeenat picked up a man at Apollo Bandar and took him to Nagina Hotel. For some reason, that man did not work out, but Zeenat and the owner of the hotel became friends. Within a fortnight, he had bought her six exquisite, expensive saris. Babu Gopinath was delighted. He thought he should allow a few more days for Zeenat and Yasin's friendship to take root before he could return to Lahore, but this did not happen. A Christian lady hired a room in Nagina Hotel, and her young daughter, Muriel, caught Yasin's eye. Yasin had a great time roaming around town with Muriel in Zeenat's car while she sat around in the hotel night and day.

Babu Gopinath was dismayed by Yasin's antics. He turned to

me and said, 'Manto Sahib, what sort of people are these? I mean, if your heart has switched off, why don't you say so? But Zeeno is also strange. Why doesn't she say, "Sir, if you are conducting a romance with this Christian girl, please, why not arrange for a car of your own? Why are you using my car?" Manto Sahib, I don't know what to say, she's a very decent and good woman. She must acquire some crafty traits.'

Zeenat showed no signs of regret when her relationship with Yasin ended, and nothing new transpired for some time. One afternoon when I telephoned, I heard that Babu Gopinath had left for Lahore to arrange for some money because the fifty thousand had run out. He took Ghulam Ali and Ghaffar Sain with him, and told Zeenat he would be away for some time because he had to sell off some property.

Sardar needed her morphine injections and Sando his Polson's butter, and they worked hard. Every day they trapped two or three men and brought them to Zeeno. They told her Babu Gopinath had no plans to return from Lahore, so she must look after herself. They managed to collect hundred to one-hundred-and-twenty-five rupees every day, of which Zeenat got half, and Sando and Sardar pocketed the rest.

Exasperated by the turn of events, one day, I turned to Zeenat and asked her, 'What do you think you're up to?'

She revealed her stubborn streak and said, 'I don't know, Bhaijan, I go along with whatever these two say.'

I wanted her to understand what was going on and said, 'Zeenat, what you're doing is not right. Sando and Sardar are only in this for their gain.' I saw little point in saying anything because Zeenat was a tediously vacuous, disheartened, and lifeless woman. The wretch did not value anything, not even her life. After all, she had to sell her body and she should have picked up some traits of the women who do. I swear by God, she infuriated me. She had no interest in the cigarettes, alcohol, and food she consumed, or for that matter, the house and telephone at her disposal, or even the sofa on which she spent most of her time.

Babu Gopinath returned after a month, and he found strangers living in his flat in Mahim. He came to see me, and I gave him Zeeno's new address. On Sardar and Sando's advice, Zeeno had rented the upper storey of a house in Bandra. When he asked after Zeenat, I told him what I knew, but not that Sardar and Sando had put her to work. Babu Gopinath had left Ghulam Ali and Ghaffar Sain behind in Lahore. He had with him a mere ten thousand rupees, which he had collected with great difficulty. He had a taxi waiting downstairs, and insisted I accompany him. It took us an hour to get to Bandra. As the car climbed up Pali Hill, we spotted Sando in a narrow side alley. Babu Gopinath hollered, 'Sando!'

When Sando saw Babu Gopinath, all he could say was, 'Dharan takhta!'

Babu Gopinath said, 'Come, join us in the taxi...' but Sando said, 'Please, park the taxi by the roadside. I have something confidential to say to you.'

The driver parked the taxi. Babu Gopinath joined Sando and walked with him about two hundred yards. They continued to talk for some time. When Babu Gopinath returned to the taxi, he looked happy and told the driver, 'Take us back.' As we approached Dadar, he said, 'Manto Sahib, Zeeno is getting married.'

Amazed, I asked, 'To whom?'

Babu Gopinath responded, 'A rich landowner from Hyderabad Sindh. I pray to God for their happiness. Just as well, I arrived at the right time. We can make Zeeno's trousseau with the money I have brought with me. Why, what do you think?'

I did not have any thoughts on the matter but had one question: who was the wealthy landowner from Sindh? Was this some stratagem organized by Sardar and Sando? My fear was ill-founded.

The man was a real zamindar from Sindh, who was introduced to Zeenat by her music teacher who was from Hyderabad Sindh and had made many unsuccessful attempts to teach Zeenat how to sing. One day, he brought Ghulam Hussain, the zamindar, who was his patron, to meet Zeeno, and she entertained them lavishly. When Ghulam Hussain urged her, she sang Ghalib's ghazal, *Nukta chin hai gham-e-dil us ko sunae na bane.* (I must share my heartache with my beloved.) An enamoured Ghulam Hussain was willing to die a hundred deaths and more for Zeenat, and wanted to marry her. The music teacher mentioned this to Zeenat. Sardar and Sando stepped in to finalize a date for the wedding.

Masquerading as Sando's friend, an overjoyed Babu Gopinath went to visit Zeenat. He was indescribably happy when he met Ghulam Hussain, Zeeno's prospective husband, and told me, 'Manto Sahib, what a handsome and competent young man! Before heading back to Bombay, I had visited the shrine of Hazrat Data Ganj Baksh, and made an offering; the saint has granted my prayer. I pray to Bhagwan that the two of them will be happy.'

Babu Gopinath made all the arrangements for Zeenat's wedding with extraordinary generosity and attention to detail. He spent two thousand on jewellery and two thousand on clothes and gave her five thousand in cash. Mohammad Shafiq Toosi, Mohammad Yasin, proprietor, Nagina Hotel, Babu Gopinath, and I were the wedding guests. Sando, who was the bride's vakil or legal representative, murmured 'Dharan takhta!' after the nikah namah was signed and sealed.

Ghulam Hussain wore a suit of fine blue serge. Everyone congratulated him and extended their good wishes, which he accepted with grace. Ghulam Hussain was an impressive man, and standing beside him Babu Gopinath looked like a little rotund pheasant. Yet, Babu Gopinath rose to the occasion. He provided all the fare for the wedding feast and after everyone finished eating, he poured water for all the guests to wash their hands. When it was my turn, he said, 'Manto Sahib, just go in and see how lovely Zeeno looks in her wedding finery.'

I lifted the curtain, and we walked into the bridal chamber where Zeenat sat dressed in a red and gold brocade shalwar–qameez; her dupatta of the same hue had an embroidered border. She had light make-up on her face. I dislike lipstick, but Zeenat's lips looked lovely. When she blushed and greeted me with an aadaab, I thought her ever so pretty. I spotted a bridal bed adorned with flowers in one corner of the room, and unable to repress my laughter, I turned to Zeenat and asked, 'What is this farce?'

She looked at me like an innocent dove and asked, 'Bhaijan, you think this a joke?' Her eyes brimmed over with tears.

Before I could make amends, Babu Gopinath stepped forward and tenderly wiped away Zeenat's tears. He turned to me and said in a voice full of regret, 'Manto Sahib, I did not expect this of you. I considered you an exceptional and compassionate human being. You should have given the matter some thought before you mocked Zeeno.' It was clear from his tone that I had fallen from the position of reverence where he had placed me. Before I could respond, Babu Gopinath placed his hand on Zeenat's head and said, 'May Khuda always keep you happy.' He looked at me with eyes full of sad reproach and left the room.

## Dr Sherodkar

Renowned in Bombay as a first-class specialist of women's ailments, Dr Sherodkar had a healing touch. His clinic occupied two floors of a grand building and had many rooms. The lower level was for middle-class and working-class women, the top floor was reserved for wealthy ladies. There was a laboratory with an adjoining room for a compounder and a separate X-ray facility. The clinic which was also a maternity home, boasted excellent catering facilities outsourced to a Parsi lady, the wife of a friend. Although Bombay has countless government hospitals and maternity homes, you can imagine that with the city's population being what it is, Dr Sherodkar's clinic was always full. He had to turn away several cases because no bed was available. He inspired confidence, and that was why people left their wives and daughters in his hospital. Dr Sherodkar's monthly income was around three thousand rupees.

The hospital had ten or twelve diligent and amiable nurses who took great care of their patients. Dr Sherodkar selected the nurses after a rigorous process and never employed an unattractive or ungainly nurse. Once, four nurses decided to get married around the same time and left at short notice. A worried Dr Sherodkar placed advertisements in various newspapers. Several women responded, but they did not measure up to his standard of training or comportment. He stood his ground, placed more advertisements, and finally recruited four efficient and attractive nurses with good taste. Now, satisfied on the nursing front, he returned to work with enthusiasm. His women patients were delighted because they felt they were getting the specialized care they expected.

In Dr Sherodkar, the new contingent of nurses found a considerate employer who paid them well and on time. The hospital provided their lunch and uniforms. Dr Sherodkar had a sizeable income and did not skimp on these minor expenses. In the early days, after he resigned from his job at the government hospital and started his clinic, circumstances forced him to keep a tight fist, but no sooner did his business stabilize than he loosened his purse strings. He did intend to get married some day but could not spare a minute because he spent night and day at his hospital. He snatched a few hours of sleep in a small room on the top floor but was often woken by his staff when a patient required his immediate attention. All the nurses sympathized with him and frequently asked, 'Doctor Sahib, why don't you keep an assistant?'

Dr Sherodkar had a standard response, 'When I find someone competent enough, I shall.'

And they gave their standard response, 'You want someone to measure up to you! Now, where will we find someone like that!'

'We shall find....'

The nurses could do little but remain silent, but amongst themselves, they discussed their worries, 'Dr Sherodkar is ruining his health...what if he *collapses* one day?'

'Yes, his health has deteriorated. He has lost weight.'

'He doesn't eat or drink much.'

'It's because he's always so busy.'

'Now, who can reason with him?'

The nurses had this conversation almost every day. They sympathized with Dr Sherodkar because he was an extremely decent man.

Every day, hundreds of young and beautiful women came to his clinic for treatment; Dr Sherodkar did not look at them as objects of desire but through the eyes of a professional doctor. The truth was that Dr Sherodkar was obsessed with his work; he took care of his patients like a ministering angel. In his days at the government hospital, he had developed a reputation as a surgeon who did not dig open his patient's bodies with scalpels but healed them with a delicate touch. Ninety per cent of his surgeries were successful, and countless certificates were testament to his skills. His supreme self-confidence, perhaps, was the biggest secret of his success.

One day, after he had examined a woman who could not have babies, he returned to his office to find a gorgeous girl waiting to see him. Dr Sherodkar was stunned; he had never seen such a specimen of feminine beauty. The girl was about to stand up to greet him, but Dr Sherodkar said, 'Please remain seated,' and sat down on his revolving chair. He lifted the glass paperweight on his desk and observed the bubbles in it before he asked the girl, 'Tell me, what brings you here?'

The girl lowered her eyes and said, 'I wish to have a private conversation.'

Dr Sherodkar looked at her devilishly beautiful eyes and said, 'You can have the private conversation later, but first, tell me your name.'

The girl said, 'I…I do not wish to give my name.'

Her response aroused the doctor's interest further, and he asked, 'Where do you live?'

'In Sholapur. I arrived here today.'

The doctor put the paperweight down on his desk and asked, 'Why have you come here from such a distance?'

The girl answered, 'As I said, I want a private conversation.'

She had just finished her sentence when a nurse entered the room, and the girl began to look anxious. The doctor gave a few instructions in response to the nurse's questions and added, 'Now, you can go. Ask an attendant to stand outside the door and instruct him not to allow anybody in.'

'Yes, sir,' said the nurse and left the room.

The doctor locked the door, sat down on his chair, and addressed the gorgeous girl, 'Now, tell me about your private matter.'

The girl from Sholapur looked distressed and found it difficult to speak. Finally, she mustered some courage, but all she could bring herself to say was, 'I have…I have made a big mistake and am worried.'

Dr Sherodkar understood, but even so, he said to the girl, 'Human beings make mistakes. What was your mistake?'

After a brief silence, the girl responded, 'The one…the one that all foolish young women make.'

Dr Sherodkar said, 'I understand…but now what do you want?'

The girl got to her point immediately, 'I want to get rid of it… it's just been a month.'

Dr Sherodkar thought for a while and responded in a solemn tone, 'This is a crime. Don't you know?'

The girl's light brown eyes brimmed over with tears, and she said, 'So, then I will take poison.' She began to weep uncontrollably.

The doctor felt great sympathy for her. She had made the first mistake of her youth. Who knows how she lost her virginity to a man in a moment of weakness? Now she regretted it, and naturally, she was worried.

In the past, Dr Sherodkar had encountered many such cases but had turned them away with a firm response, 'I cannot commit foeticide; it is a sin and a crime.'

However, the girl from Sholapur cast such a spell on Dr Sherodkar that he agreed to commit the crime. He organized a private room for her, which not even a nurse could enter because he did not want to reveal the girl's secret. Abortion is painful. After he administered all the medicines and finished the task, the Maratha girl from Sholapur fainted. When she woke up, she felt so weak that she could not even drink a glass of water without help. She wanted to return home at the earliest, but how could the doctor permit her to leave when she was not in a fit state to walk? He said to Miss Lalita Khamtekar (the beauty from Sholapur had eventually told him her name), 'You must rest for at least two months. I shall write to tell your father that you fell ill at your friend's house, and currently are under treatment in my hospital. There is no need to make any special arrangements.'

Lalita agreed and remained under Dr Sherodkar's care for two months. When it was time for her to leave, she felt the same problem had occurred again. She informed Dr Sherodkar. The doctor smiled and said, 'You have nothing to worry about; we shall get married today.'

## Burmese Girl

Gyan was at his shoot, and Kifayat decided to have an early night. His wife and children had left for Rawalpindi, and like most people in Bombay, he had little interest in his neighbours with whom he rarely interacted. So Kifayat drank four pegs of brandy, had dinner, dismissed the servants, locked the front door, and went to bed.

He heard a thud and opened his eyes. It was around five o'clock in the morning, and down in the bazaar, he could hear a tram thundering by. After a few seconds, he heard a loud knock on the door. Kifayat sat up and climbed out of bed to find his bare feet immersed ankle-deep in water. Astonished, he wondered how so much water had come into the room. He found even more water in the corridor, and the loud knocks continued. He stopped thinking about the water and opened the door.

Gyan hollered, 'What on earth is this?'

Kifayat replied, 'Water.'

'Not water...a woman,' said Gyan as he entered the corridor in semi-darkness, followed by a petite girl.

Gyan did not notice the water, but the girl lifted her pyjamas as she walked behind him, taking short, measured steps.

Thoughts of the girl taking dips in a pool of water flooded Kifayat's mind. 'Who is she? From her face and her attire, she looks Burmese. Where did Gyan find her?' Gyan went into the bedroom and fell on his bed without changing his clothes. Kifayat tried to talk to him, but he responded with incoherent 'hoonhs' and 'haanhs' without opening his eyes. The girl sat down on the other bed, and Kifayat left the room. He went to the kitchen, where he discovered the rubber hosepipe had slipped off the faucet. When the water supply came on at three o'clock, it flooded the flat instead of filling the large kitchen drum.

Kifayat woke up the three servants, who were fast asleep on the balcony, and put them to work to get rid of the water. He joined them as they cupped the water with their palms and poured it into buckets. When the Burmese girl saw them at work, she took off her sandals and joined them. She had small fair hands with long unpainted fingernails. Her short, trimmed hair, was slightly wavy, and she wore printed flared silk pyjamas with a black silk kurta that concealed her small breasts. Kifayat turned to her and said, 'Please, don't trouble yourself; this work will get done.'

She did not say anything but broke into a delicate lipstick-adorned smile and continued to work. Within half an hour, they had cleared all three rooms of water. Kifayat thought, 'Ah well, this was a good excuse to wash and clean the whole flat.'

The Burmese girl went to the bathroom to wash her hands. After a disrupted night, Kifayat stretched himself on his bed and fell asleep. He woke up around nine o'clock; the first thoughts to enter his mind were about the water and the Burmese girl who had arrived with Gyan. He asked himself, 'Was it a dream? But Gyan is fast asleep right in front of me, and the floor looks washed.'

Kifayat observed Gyan lying face down with his coat, trousers, and shoes on and woke him up. Gyan opened one eye and asked, 'What?'

Kifayat asked, 'Who is this girl?'

Startled, Gyan responded, 'Girl? Where is she?' and immediately turned flat on his back. He said, 'Oh, don't talk nonsense. All's well,' and went back to sleep.

Kifayat had to be at work by nine o'clock and he tried to rouse Gyan, who did not budge. So he rushed to the bathroom to shave, after which he headed to the living room, where he found an artistic spread on the dining table. Breakfast at Kifayat's place was usually a simple matter of two boiled eggs, two slices of buttered toast, and tea...but this morning, the boiled eggs looked like flowers, and there was salad creatively arranged on another plate. Even the toast looked like an ornament. An astonished Kifayat made his way to the kitchen where he found the Burmese girl seated on a low stool before a stove, with the three servants gathered around her, laughing and chatting away. When they spotted Kifayat, they stood up. The Burmese girl turned her eyes towards him and smiled. Kifayat wanted to talk to her but did not know what to say. He did not even know her, so he asked one of his servants, 'Bashir, who prepared breakfast today?'

Bashir looked at the Burmese girl and said, 'Baiji did.'

Kifayat rushed through his eye-catching breakfast and left for office.

That evening, when Kifayat returned home, he found the Burmese girl in his only night suit pyjamas. He stepped back because that was all she was wearing while ironing her kurta.

'Please, come in...' she said.

Kifayat thought, perhaps, somebody else had spoken but the Burmese girl's diction was clear. She smiled and greeted him with a salaam and was not in the least bit embarrassed by Kifayat's presence. She continued to iron her kurta. Kifayat noticed the tiny beads of perspiration between her small round breasts. He wanted Bashir to check on Gyan but checked himself because he did not think it appropriate since the girl was almost naked.

Kifayat took off his hat and put it aside. He continued to look at the girl with what he thought was tepid indecency, but he was not aroused. Her body was without a blemish, and her skin so smooth that his eyes slipped off it. When she finished ironing her kurta, she switched off the iron. He noticed another neatly folded ironed white boski kurta on top of her pyjamas. She picked up her clothes and announced, 'I'm off to take a bath.'

A rattled Kifayat scratched his head and wondered, 'Who is she?'

Thoughts of the doll-like girl kept returning to Kifayat's mind. He recalled how he had woken up in the middle of the night to find water everywhere, opened the door and said, 'Water,' but Gyan had said, 'Girl, not water.' Kifayat told himself, 'Forget it, my friend, when Gyan returns you'll find out everything. She's a curious lass. She's so tiny I wish I could keep her in my pocket. Ah well, time for brandy.'

Bashir had kept a glass, brandy, and ice, in the living room on a teapoy. Kifayat changed his clothes and began to drink. He had just finished the first peg when he heard the bathroom door creak. He poured his second peg and waited because he expected the Burmese girl to join him. He finished his regulation four pegs, but she did not turn up, and neither did Gyan.

An infuriated Kifayat went to the bedroom to find the girl fast asleep in her freshly ironed clothes with one hand resting on her tiny breasts. She had folded Kifayat's night suit and kept it on the ironing table. He returned to the living room, poured himself a double brandy, and downed it neat. Not much later, his head began to spin. He tried to push away thoughts of the Burmese girl, but thoughts of her filling her cupped hands with water and pouring it into the bucket invaded his mind. He gave dinner a miss, lay down on the sofa, and fell asleep thinking of her.

In the morning, Kifayat found himself on his bed instead of the couch. He taxed his memory, 'When did I come to my room last night? Did I eat dinner?' He found no answer.

The bed opposite his was empty. He shouted for Bashir, who came running. Kifayat asked him, 'Where is Gyan Sahib?'

Bashir responded, 'He didn't come home last night.'

'Why?'

'I don't know.'

'Where is that Baiji?'

'She's frying fish.'

Kifayat felt someone was frying fish inside his head. He went to the kitchen and found the Burmese girl seated on a low stool, frying fish on the stove that stood on the floor. When she saw Kifayat, a hint of a smile appeared on her lips as she lifted her hand to greet him with a salaam before returning to work. Kifayat noticed the three servants looked cheerful and busy. For several days Bashir had been pestering Kifayat because he wanted to go home on leave, 'Sahib, please give me my pay. I've received many letters from home. My mother is unwell.'

Kifayat had ignored Bashir's request last night but remembered it now and said, 'Hey Bashir, take your pay. I brought the money from my office yesterday.'

As Bashir took the money, Kifayat said to him, 'There's a train at nine o'clock, you can take that.'

'Yes, sir,' said Bashir and trotted off.

Before sitting down to breakfast, Kifayat sent Bashir to call the Burmese girl, but he returned and said, 'Sir, she says she will have her breakfast later.'

Breakfast was delicious—especially the fried fish.

Kifayat's finances were tight, and neither was Gyan too comfortable on this front; they made do from here and there. Gyan organized the brandy and, somehow, they managed food and sundries. Gyan's film company was on the verge of bankruptcy, but he liked to fool himself into thinking that a miraculous bailout was around the corner. Shooting was in progress, and this was the reason for Gyan's absence the night before. After Kifayat finished breakfast, he peeped into the kitchen, and as usual, found the Burmese girl engrossed in her work, laughing and chatting with the three male servants. Kifayat said to Bashir, 'The fish was great.'

The girl turned around to look at him with a quiet smile on her lips.

Kifayat set off for work hoping that he could organize a bit of money but returned empty-handed. The Burmese girl was in the bedroom flicking through the pages of an illustrated magazine. She sat up and greeted Kifayat with a salaam; he returned her greeting and asked, 'Did Gyan Sahib return?'

'He did in the afternoon, ate lunch, and left. He came back this evening for a few minutes.' She lifted a cushion and pulled out a bottle wrapped in paper, and handed it to Kifayat, saying, 'He told me to give this to you.'

Kifayat took the bottle from her. Gyan had written a few words on the wrapper, 'Somehow we manage to get this wretched stuff, but never any money. Well, have a blast! Yours, Gyan.'

The Burmese girl unwrapped the bottle; it was brandy. She looked at Kifayat and smiled.

'Do you drink?' he asked.

The girl shook her head firmly, 'No.'

Kifayat enveloped her in his gaze, thinking, 'What a cute little doll!' He wanted to sit and chat with her, so he said, 'Come, let us sit in the other room.'

'No... I'm going to wash my clothes.'

'At this hour?'

'This is a good time...wash them at night, and they are dry by the morning...wake up and iron them.'

Kifayat lingered for a while, but since he could not think of anything else to say, he went to the living room and poured himself a brandy. It was dinner time; he asked the Burmese girl to join him, but she said, 'I'll eat with Gyan Sahib.'

Kifayat ate his dinner and went to bed. He woke up around one o'clock at night. It was a moonlit night, and a pleasant breeze filled the room. He turned over. His gaze fell on the bed opposite his, where he saw a small shapely doll attached to Gyan's broad hairy chest. Kifayat closed his eyes. After a while, he heard Gyan's voice, 'Go now. Let me sleep. Put on your clothes.'

Kifayat heard the creak of the spring bed and a rustle of silk. After a while, he fell asleep.

Kifayat woke up at six o'clock the next morning because he had to go on a long train journey to meet a man with the possibility of some good luck. He got out of bed and saw the Burmese girl fast asleep on the floor, her head resting peacefully on her shapely round arm. She was wearing his only night suit again. Kifayat woke her up, and as she opened her jet-black eyes, he asked, 'Why are you sleeping on the floor?'

She gave a shy smile and said, 'Gyan doesn't like sleeping with anyone.'

Kifayat was aware of this trait and said to her, 'Go and sleep on my bed.'

The girl went and lay down on Kifayat's bed.

Kifayat went to the bathroom where the Burmese girl's clothes were hanging on a clothesline. As he rubbed soap on his body, his thoughts turned to the girl's soft body on which his gaze had slipped several times. He finished his bath and put on his clothes. He was running late and did not have time to talk to Gyan, who was still asleep.

Kifayat left at daybreak and did not return home until eleven o'clock at night, but with empty pockets. He went into the bedroom, where he saw Gyan and the Burmese girl in bed. Exhausted, he returned to the living room, where he sat by himself and drank his brandy. He had returned with his hopes thwarted and dropped off to sleep on the sofa, with the Burmese girl on his mind. He woke up at five o'clock in the morning to find his stale fourth peg mixed with water lying on the teapoy. Kifayat went to the bedroom and again found the Burmese girl asleep on the bare floor, with Gyan standing in front of the wardrobe, fixing the knot of his necktie. Kifayat lifted the girl in his arms and lay her down on his bed. When Gyan turned around, he saw Kifayat and asked, 'Why, my dear, did you manage to arrange for some money?'

Kifayat responded in a defeated voice, 'No.'

'Then I'd better go...perhaps something will work out.'

Before Kifayat could stop him, Gyan rushed out of the room, saying, 'You must give it another try, Kifayat.'

Kifayat turned around and looked at the bed. The Burmese girl was sleeping peacefully, her small, round breasts aglow. He left the bedroom and went into the bathroom where the Burmese girl's clothes were hanging out to dry. When Kifayat came out of the bathroom, the girl was busy with the servants preparing his breakfast, which he ate before leaving the flat.

Four days passed in this manner, but Kifayat remained ignorant about the girl. Gyan often returned late at night, and at times he left at the crack of dawn. Kifayat's timings were no different. Both were worried. The fifth morning when Kifayat woke up, Bashir handed him a note from Gyan, which said, 'For God's sake, find ten rupees from somewhere and give it to the Burmese girl.'

The girl was ironing her clothes, finishing off a sleeve with great care. Kifayat looked at her, and as their eyes met, the girl smiled. Kifayat thought hard about ways to procure the ten rupees. Bashir, who had figured out the problem, said, 'Sahib, please may I have a word.'

Kifayat asked, 'What is it?'

'Sahib, I want to say something.' Bashir moved to a corner, took a ten-rupee note out of his pocket, and handed it to Kifayat, 'Sahib, I haven't gone home.'

Kifayat took the note from him and began to think, 'No...no... you keep this. But why haven't you gone?'

'Sahib, I'll go tomorrow or the day after. You keep the money for now.'

Kifayat put the note in his pocket and said, 'Okay. I'll return it to you in the evening.'

After the Burmese girl got dressed and finished her breakfast,

Kifayat gave her the ten rupees, 'Gyan Sahib said I should give this to you.'

The girl took the money and called Bashir, 'Go, bring a taxi.'

After Bashir left, Kifayat asked her, 'Are you leaving?'

'Yes,' said the girl as she returned to the bedroom. She had forgotten to iron her handkerchief. Kifayat wanted to talk to her, but the taxi arrived, and she was ready to leave with the hanky in her hand. She bid farewell to Kifayat with a salaam and said, 'Well, I'm off. Do say salaam to Gyan from me.'

She shook hands with the three servants and left. Everyone looked sad.

Gyan returned after forty-five minutes and immediately asked, 'Where is that Burmese girl?'

'She left.'

'How? Did you give her ten rupees?'

'Yes.'

'That's perfect, then…just perfect!' Gyan sank into an armchair.

Kifayat asked, 'Who was this girl?'

'I don't know.'

Kifayat looked astonished, 'What do you mean?'

Gyan responded, 'I mean, I don't know who she was.'

'Lies!'

'I can swear by you, it's true.'

Kifayat asked, 'Where did you find her?'

Gyan stretched his legs, put his feet up on the table, and smiled, 'It's a strange story, yaar…the night of the flood, I had gone to Shankar's place and ended up drinking too much. I took the train at Andheri station and fell asleep. I found myself at Churchgate, where the watchman woke me up. I said, "I have to go to Grant Road, Bombay." The watchman laughed and said, "You're five stations ahead." I got off and went to the other platform where I boarded the last train to Andheri. When the train began to move, I fell asleep again and arrived at Andheri.'

Kifayat asked, 'But what does that girl have to do with your falling asleep?'

'Just let me finish,' said Gyan as he lit a cigarette and continued, 'when I reached Andheri, I mean when I woke up, I found myself stuck to a tiny lass. At first, I was terrified. She was awake. I asked, "Who are you?" She smiled. I asked again, "Who are you?"

'"You have been kissing me for hours, and now you want to know who I am."

'Surprised, I exclaimed, "Really!" She began to laugh. I did not see any reason to tax my mind and squeezed her tight. Until three o'clock in the morning, we slept on a bench on the platform at Andheri station. At three-thirty, the first train arrived, and we took it. I thought, somehow, I'll arrange for some money and give it to her. When we got here, there was a deluge. Isn't that so? Interesting tale....'

Kifayat responded, 'Quite interesting, but why did she stay here for so many days?'

Gyan flung his cigarette on the floor. 'She didn't stay. I kept her. Essentially, she stayed because I didn't have anything to give her, and the days went by. I was embarrassed. Last night I told her plainly, "Look here, the days are passing, why don't you give me your address and I'll make sure I send you what's due to you. These days I'm rather tight for money."'

Kifayat asked, 'What did she say?'

Gyan shook his head. 'She is a strange girl; she said, "What are you saying? When did I ask you for money? But do give me ten rupees. I live far from here. I'll take a taxi, but I don't have a single paisa."'

Kifayat asked, 'What was her name?'

Gyan gave the matter some thought.

'Have you forgotten?'

Gyan removed his legs from the table, 'No, yaar, I didn't ask her name,' he added, 'this is the limit,' and began to laugh.

## 18

## *Fobha Bai*

The moment Shahab stepped on the platform at Bombay Central, he turned to Hanif and said, 'Look here, my friend, remember we must have that business tonight, or else I'm heading back to Hyderabad.'

Hanif knew what that business entailed, and the same evening took Shahab along and hailed a taxi. When they reached the Grant Road crossing, he summoned a pimp and told him, 'My friend is here from Hyderabad. We need a prime lass.'

The pimp removed the biri tucked behind his ear, and as he squeezed it between his lips, he asked, 'Will a Deccani do?'

Hanif cast an enquiring look at Shahab, who said, 'No, my friend. I want a Muslim.'

'Muslim?' repeated the pimp questioningly as he pulled on his biri and said, 'let's go!' and after giving some instructions to the driver sat next to him on the front seat. The taxi wound its way through various bazaars and finally entered a very steep alley on a hillock near Forjett Street. When the driver put the car into the first gear, Hanif feared that any moment it would stall and start to roll backwards, but that did not happen. The pimp asked the driver to park the taxi at the top of an incline abutting a square. Hanif had never been here before; the hillock was fairly high, and to its right, he noticed another steep incline with tall four-storeyed buildings. There was one two-storeyed block of flats, which the pimp entered. Later, Hanif discovered the building in question had two other levels below the slope which could be accessed by a lift.

The pimp sang high praises of the girl, 'She's from a decent family. I am getting her out as a *special* favour to you.'

Hanif and Shahab sat quietly in the back of the taxi, thinking of the *special* favour. Not much later, the pimp appeared on his own. He told the driver to reverse and got back into the front seat. They drove past three or four buildings before the pimp hollered, 'Stop!'

He turned to Hanif and said, 'She's on her way. When she asked me, "What sort of men are they?" I said, "Numero Uno!"'

About fifteen minutes later, the back door opened without warning, and a woman got into the taxi, sat next to Hanif, and said, 'Off we go!' It was night, and the alley was not well lit. Consequently, Hanif and Shahab could not see her face.

The taxi began to speed downhill. The pimp took a hundred rupees and got off at the Grant Road crossing. Since Hanif did not have access to a place where such 'business' could happen, Shahab had telephoned their friend, Dr Khan, who worked at the local military hospital, where he had two rooms in the staff accommodation.

Shahab informed Khan that Hanif and he would visit in the evening and bring 'the stuff' with them. They headed to the military hospital but could not see the woman clearly or have a proper conversation with her. Shahab asked her, in his typical Hyderabadi accent, 'What is your good name?'

The woman replied, 'Fobha Bai.'

'Fobha Bai?' Hanif asked himself, 'What sort of name is that?'

Dr Khan was expecting them. Shahab was the first to enter the room, and as the two men embraced each other, they exchanged some choice expletives. But when Dr Khan saw a young woman in the doorway, he fell silent. After a brief pause, he said, 'Do come in,' and placed his right hand on his chest before adding, 'Dr Khan... and you?'

He looked at Shahab, who looked at the woman, who replied, 'Fobha Bai.'

Dr Khan stepped forward and took her hand, 'Such a pleasure to meet you.'

Fobha Bai smiled, 'For me too, a great pleafure.'

Hanif and Shahab looked at each other. Dr Khan shut the door before he turned to his friends and said, 'Please feel free to use the other room; I have to wind up some tasks.'

Shahab turned to Fobha Bai, 'Let's go!'

Fobha Bai caught Dr Khan's arm and said, 'No. Pleafe, you muft join uf.'

Dr Khan released his arm gently and responded, 'Why don't you go ahead, and I'll join you shortly.'

Shahab and Hanif took Fobha Bai to the other room. After a brief conversation, they learnt that she had a swollen tongue and could not pronounce 'sh' and 's'—the sibilant sounds—which she substituted with 'f's'. Her name was Shobha Bai, but this was not her real name. She was a Muslim from Jaipur who had fled to Bombay four years ago. She did not say more about her life. Her face was quite ordinary—there was nothing special about her eyes, and neither was her nose particularly attractive. A scar left by an old wound on her upper lip expanded when she spoke. She wore real gold bangles on both wrists and a necklace studded with precious gems around her neck. Shobha Bai was a talkative woman. The moment they sat down, she began to chatter about this and that. Hanif and Shahab merely 'umm-ed' and 'ahh-ed', but she launched an inquisitorial probe. What do they do? Where do they live? How old are they? Are they married or single? Why is Hanif so thin? Why does Shahab have two artificial teeth? If he is a carnivore, why didn't he ask Dr Khan to treat him? Why does he feel shy? Why doesn't he recite couplets? Shahab came up with a few couplets, and Shobha Bai appreciated them volubly. When Shahab came up with:

Water your fields before the Ganga flows away
Act, O young ones, before your youth blows away!

Shobha Bai jumped up on her seat and exclaimed, 'Vah! Fahib, vah! What a great couplet; efpefially "before your youth blowf away!"'

When Shahab finished, Shobha came up with many couplets without rhyme, metre, or meaning. After she finished her recitation, she asked Shahab, 'Fahab Fahib, did you enjoy yourfelf?'

Shahab replied, 'A lot.'

Shobha looked bashful and said, 'They were mine. I love poetry.'

Shahab and Hanif exchanged looks. Shobha recited another couplet,

Do afk after my heartache, fometime
You are fo familiar with my pain.

Hanif had heard this couplet several times; perhaps he had even used it during a conversation, but Shobha said, 'Hanif Fahib, thif couplet if alfo mine.'

Hanif showered her with effusive praise and said, 'Mafallah, Fobha Bai, you're a wizard!'

Taken aback, Shobha said, 'Forgive me, fomething if wrong with my tongue, but why did you fay mafallah inftead of mafallah?'

Hanif and Shahab roared with laughter, and Shobha joined in. Just that moment, Dr Khan walked in. He turned to Shobha and asked, 'Well, madam, what makes you laugh so?'

Shobha broke into a ripple of laughter, and as she wiped away her tears, she turned to Dr Khan, 'Fomething happened that made uf laugh a lot?' She added, 'Do fit down.' She shifted to the edge of the charpai, held Dr Khan's hand, and drew him to sit by her side.

Another session of poetry followed. Shobha recited some banal ghazals, and everyone praised her, but Shahab was bored; he wanted that business. Hanif noticed the change in his mood and said, 'Ah well, I'm off; inshallah, I'll see you tomorrow.'

As he got up from his chair, Shobha caught hold of his hand and said, 'No, you can't leave.'

Hanif answered, 'My apologies, but my wife must be waiting for me.'

Shobha insisted. 'Oh…but really, you muft fit with uf a little longer; it's juft eleven o'clock.'

Shahab yawned, 'It's very late.'

Shobha smiled as she looked at Shahab and said, 'I'm with you for the reft of the night.'

Shahab's boredom disappeared, and Hanif sat a little longer before he took his leave.

The following morning, Hanif arrived at around nine o'clock and Shahab began to tell him about the night. 'Fobha Bai is a strange woman. There is a scar the size of my palm on her stomach…as the result of an operation. She told me she was the mistress of a seth who traded in timber, and he opened a film company for her. She was a signatory on all the cheques, and he bought her a car, which she has to this day. The timber merchant loved her dearly. When she had her operation, he gave one thousand rupees as charity to an orphanage.'

Hanif asked, 'Where is the timber merchant now?'

'He's selling timber in the other world,' said Shahab. 'She is an extraordinary woman, Fobha Bai. After I fell asleep, she slipped into Dr Khan's bed. At five o'clock in the morning, Khan asked her to leave, so she said, "Okay, I'm off, but keep my jewellery. I don't go out on my own in this finery."'

Hanif asked, 'Did Khan keep the jewellery?'

Shahab shook his head, 'Yes. He thought it was fake, but when he saw it in the clear light of day, he realized it was real.'

'And she left?'

'Yes. She said that she'd return for it.'

'What an unbelievable story!'

'I swear upon God it's true.' Shahab lit a cigarette, 'This is why I said Fobha Bai is an extraordinary woman.'

Hanif asked, 'But what sort of a woman was she?'

Shahab blushed, 'Well, I don't really know much about this stuff; ask Khan; he's the expert.'

That evening they went to visit Dr Khan. The jewellery was in his custody, but Shobha had not come to collect it. Khan said, 'I think she is the victim of some trauma.'

Shahab said, 'You mean she's mad.'

Khan replied, 'No. She is not mad, but certainly, her mind is not what you would call *normal*.'

Hanif asked, 'Why do you think her mind is not normal?'

Khan replied, 'Well, I think if she were normal, she would not leave jewellery worth more than two thousand rupees with a total stranger. Besides, she has to take morphine injections.'

Shahab asked, 'It's a form of addiction, isn't it?'

Khan said, 'Yes, a hazardous kind…much worse than alcohol.'

'How did she get into the habit?' asked Shahab as he picked up the paperweight from Dr Khan's desk and balanced it on the inkpot.

'Her operation was botched up. She was in extreme pain; the doctors kept injecting her with morphine to cope with the pain. This routine continued for almost two months, and she became an addict.' Dr Khan then launched into a brief lecture on morphine and its after-effects.

A week passed, but Shobha did not return. Shahab left for Hyderabad.

Dr Khan came to see Hanif with the jewellery and said, 'Come, let's find her.'

They headed for the Grant Road junction but could not find the pimp who had taken Hanif and Shahab to her house. Hanif recalled the name of the building and the alley, and the doctor said, 'This is good enough; we'll find it. I don't wish to hang on to this jewellery. What if it's stolen from my place...she's a strange and irresponsible woman!'

They arrived at their destination in a taxi. Hanif explained the exact location to Dr Khan and added, 'I'm not going in there. You better find her.'

Dr Khan entered the building and asked a couple of men, but nobody could tell him anything about Shobha. Finally, as the lift came up, a hotel boy stepped out carrying empty teacups, and Khan asked him. The boy directed the doctor to the flat at the end of the corridor in the basement; Khan took the lift down and pressed the doorbell. After a minute or so, an older woman opened the door. Khan asked her, 'Is Shobha Bai in?'

The woman replied, 'Yes, she is.'

Khan said, 'Go tell her Dr Khan is here.'

Shobha called from inside, 'Come on in, Dr Fahib, come on in.'

Dr Khan entered a small, carpeted drawing room packed with kitschy furniture. The woman went into the other room, and instantly Shobha called out, 'Come in, Dr Fahib, I cannot come out.'

Dr Khan entered the other room, where Shobha was lying in bed, her body hidden underneath a sheet. Khan enquired, 'What's the matter?'

Shobha smiled, 'Nothing, Dr Fahib, I waf having an oil maffage.'

The doctor sat down on an armchair near the bed. He took the small bundle of jewellery out of his pocket, untied the handkerchief, and placed it beside her. 'For how long do you expect me to guard your jewels? You left and didn't bother to return.'

Shobha laughed, 'I had too much work. But why did you take the trouble? I would have collected it myfelf.'

She turned to the old woman, 'Order fome tea for Dr Fahib.'

The doctor said, 'I have to go now.'

'Where?'

'To the hospital.'
'Have you come by taxfi?'
'Yes.'
'If it ftanding outfide?'
The doctor nodded, 'Yes.'
'Pleafe, go ahead, I'll follow you.' She shoved the jewellery under her pillow and returned the hanky to Dr Khan.

Dr Khan returned to Hanif, who asked, 'Did you find her?'

The doctor smiled, 'Yes, I found her, and she's on her way!'

After fifteen to twenty minutes, Shobha opened the back door and hastily got into the taxi.

They had a long poetry session in Dr Khan's room, where Shobha recited many pedestrian couplets about obsession and love, union, and parting, claiming them as her own. Dr Khan and Hanif showered her with praise.

'Yaqoob Feth would fit and hear my refitation for hourf.'

Yaqoob Seth was the same timber merchant who had opened a film company for Shobha, and as Dr Khan and Hanif chortled, Shobha joined them.

Dr Khan and Shobha became friends. At first, she visited him twice a week, but in time she began to visit him almost every evening: she stayed the night and left early the following morning. Every evening, Shobha Bai took a morphine jab. She loved the cold feel of the medicine the doctor applied to desensitize her before he injected the morphine into her body. Three months passed, and Shobha got ready for a trip to Jaipur. She left her car with Khan, with instructions to look after it. The doctor went to the station to see her off. They continued to chat for a long time, and as the train was about to leave, Shobha clutched the doctor's hand and said, 'Fuddenly, why have I got thif feeling that fomething is about to happen....'

The doctor asked, 'What is about to happen?'

Shobha looked terrified, 'I'm not fure; I have a finking feeling in my heart.'

Dr Khan reassured her. As the train pulled out of the station, Shobha continued to wave until she was out of sight.

Shobha wrote two letters from Jaipur to tell Dr Khan that she had reached safely and would bring back many presents for him when she returned. And then, a card arrived, saying, 'Yesterday, God extinguished the only lamp in my dark life. Bless him.'

Dr Khan's eyes welled up with tears. He knew the 'Bless him' was suffused with endless sorrow.

Several months went by. There was no letter from Shobha. The months drifted into a year, and Dr Khan had no news of her. She had left her car with him. He went to the building and her basement flat. He found a man who looked like a pimp living there. Finally, Dr Khan gave up. He stopped making enquiries and had the car parked in a garage.

One day, a pale and troubled Hanif arrived at the hospital looking for Dr Khan. The doctor was on duty, but he sent for him and told him, 'I saw Shobha today.'

The doctor grabbed Hanif by his arm and asked, 'Where?'

'At Chowpatty. I didn't recognize her—she was a bag of bones.'

Dr Khan repeated in a hollow voice, 'A bag of bones....'

Hanif's sigh was icy. 'It was not Shobha. It was her shadow. Her eyes were sunken, her hair dishevelled and dirty. She was not walking but dragging herself as she came up to me and said, "Give me a fiver." I did not recognize her and asked, "What will you do with five rupees?" But when she said, "I'll get a morphine fot," I felt someone had slapped me. I peered at her and saw the mark on her upper lip, and yelled out, "Shobha!" She looked at me with tired vacant eyes and asked, "Who are you?" I said, "Hanif." She said, "I don't know any Hanif." I mentioned your name and told her that you had looked for her everywhere. A quiet smile appeared on her lips, and she said, "Tell him not to fearch for me. Look at me. For fo long I've been roaming around fearching for my loft darling. Fearching is pointleff. You don't find anything. Give me five rupeef." I gave her five rupees and said, "At least take your car back from Dr Khan." She laughed out loud and walked away.'

Khan asked, 'Where?'

Hanif said, 'I don't know. She must have gone to some doctor.'

Dr Khan searched everywhere but found no sign of Shobha.

## Old Fogey

The Great War had just ended when my dear friend Lieutenant Colonel Mohammad Saleem Sheikh (AB) arrived in Bombay via Iran from Iraq and other fronts. At the time, he was just a lieutenant. He knew the whereabouts of my flat since we had corresponded from time to time. I should add, there was little joy in that correspondence since the authorities censored every letter, posted from here or sent from there, which was a real bother. So, there is little to be gained by going on about those annoying matters. Billeted at the BB & CI (Bombay Baroda and Central India Railways), Saleem invited me for a drink at the buffet of the grand terminus. Known as a professional Romeo since our college days, he regaled me with stories of his amorous encounters in Iran, Iraq, and goodness knows where else. I could fill a hefty volume with stories of Saleem's peccadillos, but one was particularly gripping.

I should inform you about another aspect of Saleem's personality that has some bearing on the story I shall tell you. He had a knack for attracting young girls. In Gordon College, Rawalpindi, he was known as Raja Inder, and all the fairies in his durbar danced to his tune. He was beautiful—yes, a lovely specimen of the male of our species with a sharp and pointed nose that played its part in his appeal. His small dark brown eyes looked perfect; if any larger, perhaps the complete charm of his face would be marred. Saleem was a flirt, a Byronic figure who liked to trap a girl and move on. I thought this a rather cruel trait, but he was nonchalant about it: 'Son of a gun, read Ghalib and see what he says.' Saleem, who could never recall a couplet but managed to convey its essence in his own words, continued, 'Ghalib says, just one houri in paradise! By God, life would be unbearable. Be like the honeybee. Don't suck nectar from one flower.' He finished his beer and turned to a couplet by Iqbal, 'O naive soul sated by a few buds....'

Before I get to the real story, I must take another detour and relate a very odd tale about Sheikh Saleem. We were in the final year of our BA at Gordon College, Rawalpindi. During our Christmas break, we heard that our classmate Rukmani was getting married. We had seen her head over heels in love with Sheikh Saleem. She was pretty ordinary looking, but my friend was a honeybee, and their romance continued for two months, after which, in pure Byronic mode, Rukmani became a stranger to Saleem. Yet, some of his cronies mocked him, 'Drown yourself, the girl on whose account you picked so many fights—that Rukmani is getting married to someone else! You will survive but think of our loss of face.' Invariably, such talk irritated Sheikh Saleem, but this time he twirled his pencil thin moustache and said, 'Ah well, let's wait and see!'

A boy asked him, 'What will we see?'

Sheikh Saleem cut him short, 'Wait and see on the day of the wedding.'

On the wedding day, the bridegroom entered the gate of the bride's house, astride an exquisitely adorned horse, and in keeping with tradition, his face concealed by the strands of jasmine and rose of the traditional floral sehra tied around his head. As he entered the marquee, also festooned with flowers, the bride's father and relatives stepped forward to greet him and took him to the mandap prepared for the bride and bridegroom to sit together for the marriage rituals. The sacred fire was ablaze. A bare-chested priest rose to bless the bridegroom and said to the bride's father, 'Sardarji, please hurry. Call the bride. The auspicious hour is here.'

Rukmani arrived and sat next to the groom; the priest began to recite some sacred verses that I did not understand. Suddenly, the wedding ceremony halted because another bridegroom alighted from a car. The new arrival bellowed at almost a thousand people gathered for the ceremony, 'I've been deceived. I will file a case.'

When the new bridegroom stepped forward and took the bride's hand, Saleem lifted his sehra and roared, 'Abay, get lost! You will file a case, will you?'

When Sheikh Saleem revealed his face, a blend of hums, haws, and laughter filled the air. The stupefied spectators included guests and members of the bride and the real bridegroom's families. A mortified Rukmani remained silent when Saleem asked her in a booming voice,

'Do you wish to marry this imbecile?' He took her silence as a cue and continued, 'Ah well, go to hell then. You worshipped me not for one day but three months.'

Saleem took off his garlands and stepped forward to put them around the neck of the real bridegroom incandescent with rage, and got back on his horse, spurring it on. He galloped out of the bungalow gate as every member of the bridegroom's party turned to stone. I darted to match the speed of Saleem's horse and caught up with him. He smiled at me and said, 'Why, you son of a gun, what did I say! Did you see what I just did?'

I said, 'What a prank! Nobody could have done what you just did, my friend, but what if Rukmani's father files a warrant for your arrest?'

He expanded his chest and said, 'Father! Her father's father will not. Do you think he will ask his daughter to appear in court? I am willing to get arrested right away! Let them put me in the lock-up, and I shall reveal the hussy's secrets. I have dozens of her letters.'

The entire city was abuzz with rumours that Rukmani's father wanted Sheikh Saleem to get a sentence he would remember for the rest of his life, but nothing happened. A few days later, Saleem came to see me, crooning a Ghalib ghazal:

> The news of Ghalib's destruction was spread far and wide
> I went to witness the spectacle, but there was none.

∽

Now, I shall turn to the story I set out to recount in the first place, and it has far more appeal than the Rawalpindi incident. I heard it from Sheikh Saleem and am convinced of its veracity because he does not spin yarns. So here it is in his words:

'I was in Iran, where the girls are no different from European girls when it comes to fashion and physique. Still, they are quite different when it comes to beauty. And very few countries can compete with the kind of shenanigans that go on in Iran, where I made several killings. Now, I had a senior officer called Colonel Usmani. Although far senior to me, he was very well disposed towards me. Whenever he saw me, he hollered, "Ahoy Sheikh! Here, come and sit with me."

We'd start a round of whisky and chat about this and that.

'Colonel Usmani loved to crack jokes at my expense and was delighted when he scored a point. He was quite elderly; besides, he was a senior officer. Naturally, I remained silent. The Colonel took great interest in the Polish nurses who worked in the Ambulance Corps. These Polish girls were devilishly fit, with large firm calves, ample bosoms, and fleshy and firm buttocks solid like steel. Several were my friends, but when I met Irene, I forgot everyone. If you saw her breasts and calves, you'd imagine that her hands to be like loaves of bread, and her fingers thick as breadsticks—but no, my friend, her hands were soft and delicate and her slender fingers tapered like those of a woman in a Chughtai painting. I was besotted with her. Within a few days of knowing each other, we became quite informal.'

Sheikh paused and fixed himself another peg of whisky, which he downed in one gulp, and continued, 'Don't remind me of this story....'

I said to him, 'But, Lieutenant, you were the one who started it.'

The furrows on his brow deepened as he poured himself another peg and proceeded to pour the remaining three or four into my glass. He drank his neat and almost choked to death. He coughed and said, 'Damn you! I mean, seriously, was this any occasion to send me to perdition?'

'Don't ask me, sweetheart!' said I.

He continued, 'The following night I met the Colonel, who said in a rather sarcastic tone, "I say, my son, you think me an old fogey." I submitted, "Colonel Sahib, there is no comparison between us," but thought to myself, "The delusional wretch; knee-deep in his grave, and he's out romancing!"'

Sheikh continued, 'The Colonel and I chatted for some time about Irene, my darling Irene. I told myself, I swear by God if I reach his age, I will commit suicide. I mean, what with a mouth in which half the teeth are not his own, he's eyeing my Irene. He is welcome to be a colonel in his own home! If ever he refers to her again, I shall punch his face and knock out the rest of his teeth. Regardless of my thoughts, the Colonel continued his sarcastic jibes. We were on our fourth round of whisky, and I said to him in a most solicitous manner, "Colonel Sahib, whoever calls you an old fogey is an old fogey himself! Mashallah, you are very fit." Boy, was I happy when this session came to an end!'

Sheikh Saleem continued, 'Irene had promised to meet me the following evening at seven o'clock at a hotel popular with army personnel. It was a Sunday, so I put on a well-tailored suit instead of my uniform and arrived for our rendezvous. It was nine minutes to seven when I walked into the dining room. My feet came to a halt. You could say I was transfixed—glued to the ground, as it were. Oblivious to the crowd of people around him, Colonel Usmani was kissing Irene; it was a long passionate kiss. I could feel myself mutate into an old fogey, far older than the Colonel.'

## Miss Tinwallah

I was polishing my white canvas shoes when my wife walked in and said, 'Zaidi Sahib is here!'

I handed her my shoes, washed my hands, and went to the other room to meet Zaidi. I saw his expression and asked, 'Arrey, what's up with you?'

Zaidi made an unsuccessful attempt to look cheerful and responded, 'I've been unwell.'

I sat on a chair near him, 'You've lost a lot of weight, yaar. I didn't quite recognize you. What's the problem?'

'I don't know.'

'What do you mean?'

Zaidi rolled his tongue over his parched lips.

'Can't you figure out the illness?' I asked.

'You could say so.'

'Consult a good doctor.'

Zaidi remained silent, so I persisted, 'Have you consulted a good doctor?'

'No.'

'Why?'

Zaidi did not respond to my question but took a cigarette case out of his pocket. I noticed his fingers were trembling.

'Zaidi, I think your nervous system is affected. Start vitamin D injections, and soon you'll be fit as a fiddle. Last year, I was in a similar state—overindulging in whisky, but after twelve injections, my weakness faded. Why don't you consult a good doctor?'

Zaidi took off his spectacles and began to wipe them with a hanky. He had dark circles under his eyes. 'Can't you sleep at night?' I asked.

'Very little.'

'Your brain's exhausted.'

'Don't know what it is...' he said, looking thoughtful, 'look,

Saadat, let me tell you something very odd. I don't have any illness-shillness. I can't sleep at night because I'm scared.'

'Scared...Why?'

'I'll tell you why...' His hands continued to tremble, but he lit a cigarette and proceeded to break up the extinguished matchstick. 'I'm not quite sure what you'll make of it when I tell you, but this story is about a tomcat....'

I might have smiled inadvertently because Zaidi's tone became solemn as he turned to me, 'Don't laugh...it's a fact. I've come to you because you're interested in human psychology. Perhaps you can figure out why I'm so scared.'

I said, 'But here, it's a question of an animal.'

A peeved Zaidi turned around, 'Ah well, poke fun at me, and I won't tell you anything.'

'No, no...forgive me, Zaidi. I'll pay full attention to what you have to say.'

Zaidi remained silent for some time and lit another cigarette before he began. 'You know I live in two rooms, and the main room has a small balcony with a wrought-iron railing. April and May are such hot months, I roll out my bedding and sleep on the balcony. We're in June now. It was an April morning when I finished breakfast and opened the front door to head to work. I saw a fat tomcat lying right in the middle of the doorway with his eyes closed. I prodded him with my shoe. He opened his eyes for a split second, gave me a cursory look as though I was of no consequence, and closed his eyes. Taken aback, I poked him hard in his ribcage. He opened his eyes to give me an equally dismissive look, walked a few steps forward, and lay down a few feet away by the stairs. The way he walked made it clear that he did not fear me in the least. I was furious. I stepped forward and kicked him hard. He took off and limped down fifteen steps before he steadied himself on all fours. He looked up at me with his deep yellow eyes, turned his head, and walked away silently. Are you interested in what I have to say?'

'Yes, yes, why not!'

Zaidi flicked the ash from his cigarette and continued his account, 'Immersed in work, I forgot the entire matter, but when I returned home and approached the front door where I had seen the tomcat that morning, the entire episode came back to me. As I bathed, drank my tea, and ate my dinner, I asked myself several times, "I kicked him hard—in fact, three times in his ribcage! Why wasn't he scared of me? Not even a meow—and what a gait! He opened and shut his eyes with complete disregard. I began to think about this tomcat more than was necessary, and this irritated me to no end. After all, why was I giving such importance to an ordinary animal? I can't find an answer to this question, and three months have passed.' Zaidi became silent.

'Finished?' I asked.

'No,' said Zaidi, as he rested his cigarette on the ashtray. 'I want to understand why I have given so much importance to this tomcat. Why am I so terrified? I can't solve the mystery. Perhaps you can understand it better than me.'

I said, 'First, I must have the full picture.'

Zaidi picked up his cigarette from the ashtray and took a puff before he said, 'Let me tell you...after the first encounter, several days passed and I didn't see the tomcat again. Perhaps, it was a Saturday night, and I was asleep in the balcony. At about two o'clock, a noise in the living room woke me up. I switched on the light and saw the same tomcat on the dining table. He had removed the net cover from a dish full of rice pudding and was helping himself to it. I tried to shoo him away, but he paid no attention to me. I aimed my slipper at him, and it struck him hard on his belly, but he continued to lap up the pudding, ignoring his injury. Furious, I grabbed a pole from the mosquito net and whacked him on his spine. He looked at me with complete indifference and skipped lightly onto a chair, from where he jumped down to the floor without making a sound and made his way to the balcony, slunk through the wrought-iron rails, and leapt down to a ledge. I stood there and wondered why violence did not affect this animal. I tell you, Saadat, he's scary—that tomcat with his fat head. He is white but always covered in dirt; I've never seen such a filthy tomcat in my life.' Zaidi extinguished his cigarette and fell silent.

I said, 'Cats and tomcats usually keep themselves clean.'

'Yes, they do,' Zaidi stood up, 'I think this tomcat enjoys being filthy; he loves to hang around rubbish dumps. If his ear is covered in blood, he does not lick it clean like other cats. If his head is injured, he doesn't seem to care but roams around aimlessly the whole day.'

'But what's there to be terrified of?' I asked.

Zaidi sat down, 'That's it…that's what I am trying to understand. Well, I have thought of at least one reason. For the past ten days or more, he has woken me up every night, and each time, I've given him a real thrashing. He should never return to my flat. After all, even animals have some intelligence. I am terrified he might leap on me while I'm asleep and scratch one of my eyes out. I've heard that if you thrash a cat or tomcat, one day, she or he will seek revenge.'

I said, 'Well, this is a perfectly valid reason for your fear.'

Zaidi stood up again, 'But it doesn't satisfy me.'

A thought crossed my mind, 'Why don't you try to show him some love and affection?'

'I tried that,' said Zaidi, 'after such terrible thrashings, I thought he wouldn't let me touch him, but it was quite the opposite. I shouldn't call it the opposite because the wretch is equally indifferent to any display of affection. One day, I was sitting on the sofa, and he came and sat near me. I extended my hand towards him and cautiously began to stroke his back gently. Saadat, he sat there with his eyes shut. Usually, cats and tomcats wag their tails in response to love and affection, but the wretch—not a hair in his tail moved! Fed up, I hit him on his head with a book. He looked at me without a hint of concern in his yellow eyes before he jumped down and slunk through the wrought-iron railing on the balcony onto the ledge. Well, from that time onwards, he began to live in my thoughts twenty-four hours a day.'

Zaidi sat down on the chair opposite mine and began to shake his right leg vigorously. It was clear to me that his fear was not unreasonable, but all I said was, 'I can't make head or tail of this.'

Zaidi bit his nails and said, 'I can't figure it out either, and that's why I have come to see you.' He began to pace up and down the room. After some time, he picked up another matchstick from the ashtray, proceeded to break it up into pieces, and added, 'Now I'm in such a bad state that I lie awake the whole night. If I hear the slightest sound, I think it's that tomcat. He's been missing for the past eight days. For all I know, someone might have killed him.

Maybe he's sick or has gone somewhere else.'

'Why do you think about him?' I asked and added, 'It's good he's disappeared.'

'I'm not sure why I think of him; I've tried hard to forget the wretch but can't get him out of my mind.' Zaidi lay down on the sofa and put a cushion under his head. 'If someone else were to hear this, he'd laugh at the thought that a tomcat has reduced me to this state. At times I laugh at myself, but the laughter hurts.'

As Zaidi was speaking, I realized that to see me laugh in the face of his vulnerability was very painful for him. His account had a comical side to it, but it was clear that a traumatic moment from Zaidi's past was concealed somewhere in that tomcat's being, a moment wiped out from his consciousness. I asked him, 'Zaidi, is there any episode from your past that you can associate with this tomcat? I mean, an episode that has terrified you in the past, and the tomcat has reminded you of it?'

Just as I finished what I had to say, I thought, how is it possible for an episode to resemble a tomcat?

Zaidi responded, 'I have given the matter a great deal of thought. I can't recall any such episode.'

I said, 'Perhaps, you might recall something still.'

'It's possible...' said Zaidi as he got up from the sofa. He talked about an assortment of things and left after inviting my wife and me for lunch the following Sunday.

The following Sunday, my wife and I went to Santacruz. I have not told you that Zaidi is an old friend. We were in the same school until our entrance. Even at college, we were together for two years. I failed, and he passed his FA and left Amritsar for Lahore, where he did his MA. Unemployed for four to five years, he came to Bombay and found a job with a shipping company, where he had been working for over a year. After lunch, we continued to chat about old and new films. Zaidi's wife and my wife watched a lot of films. Naturally, they were the most enthusiastic participants in this conversation.

Our wives decided to chat on their own, and just as they stood up to go to the other room, a fat tomcat entered the living room through the wrought-iron railing on the balcony. Zaidi and I turned simultaneously to look at him, and from Zaidi's expression, I knew he was the tomcat in question. I scrutinized him. He had a deep wound on his head between his ears, and someone had applied a turmeric ointment on it. His coat was filthy, just as Zaidi had described, and I noticed a peculiar insouciance in his gait. There were four human beings in the room, but he did not pay the slightest attention to us. When he passed by my wife, she screamed, 'What sort of tomcat is this, Saadat Sahib?'

'What do you mean?' I asked her.

My wife replied, 'He looks like a real pervert!'

Puzzled, Zaidi repeated, 'A pervert!'

My wife looked embarrassed, 'Yes, he looks like a pervert.'

Zaidi drifted into his thoughts, and both women went into the other room.

After some time, Zaidi stood up, and as he walked towards the balcony, he said, 'Saadat, come here.' Once on the balcony, he turned around to face me and said, 'The mystery is solved!'

'How?'

'Your wife solved it. Think about it, doesn't this tomcat look like Miss Tinwallah?'

'Yes, yes, that pervert who sat outside our school, the one that Mustafa referred to as "Miss Tinwallah".'

I recalled that Miss Tinwallah always had an eye on Zaidi, a beautiful young boy, but wondered how this cat resembled Miss Tinwallah. Oh, no...suddenly it struck me that he did. Miss Tinwallah had the same laidback gait and often walked around with an injured head. Several times, Headmaster Sahib had various people beat the hell out of him to stop him from hanging around the school gate, but this did not deter him. One boy's father struck him so hard with a hockey stick that many thought he would die in the hospital, but within two days, he was back at the school gate. All these incidents sprang to mind within a split second, and I turned to Zaidi, 'You're right. Miss Tinwallah also remained silent after he was thrashed.'

Zaidi did not respond. He was trying to recall something. After a while, he looked at me and said, 'I was in Class Eight and had gone on my own to Company Bagh to study. I was sitting under a tree and reading when suddenly Miss Tinwallah appeared from nowhere, holding a piece of paper in one hand. He said to me, "Babuji, please read this letter out to me." I almost died of fright. There was not a soul around, and Miss Tinwallah unfurled the letter on my thigh. I ran for my life, and Miss Tinwallah pursued me. I ran fast; he couldn't catch up with me. By the time I reached home, I had a high temperature and was delirious for two days. My mother thought the tree I was sitting under was possessed by an evil spirit.'

As Zaidi continued to speak, I saw the tomcat wind his way around our legs. He took a few measured steps and turned around to look at us with a practised insouciance in his yellow eyes before he slid through the wrought-iron railing of the balcony and jumped down to the ledge. I smiled and said, 'Miss Tinwallah!' and Zaidi blushed.

## Peeran

This story is about a time when I was destitute and living in Bombay in a nine-rupees-a-month fleapit without electricity or running water, where bedbugs rained down on me from the ceiling and armies of rats ran around with abandon. I have never seen such enormous rats in my life—even cats were terrified of them. The tenement had one bathroom, which had a door with a broken latch. I made sure I had my bath before an assortment of Jewish, Marathi, Gujarati, and Christian women lined up to fill their buckets and canisters with water at daybreak.

One morning, I woke up late and rushed to the bathroom. I had just started my bath when the door opened with a thud, and I saw my neighbour with a brass pitcher tucked under her arm. She stared at me for a split second, petrified as though she had spotted a tiger lying in wait for her. As she turned to flee for her life, her brass pitcher fell and rolled on the floor. I laughed out loud, got up to shut the door, and returned to my bath. Not much later, as I was getting dressed, the door opened again. This time, it was Brij Mohan, who said, 'Hey Manto, it's Sunday.'

Of course, it was Sunday. Every Sunday, Brij Mohan took eight annas from me for his train fare and headed to Bandra to meet his friend Peeran, a plain Parsi girl with whom he had been having an affair for the past three years. They chatted for half an hour or so, and Brij solved the *Illustrated Weekly of India* crossword puzzle for her before he returned. Brij was unemployed at the time and spent his entire Sunday scratching his head, solving crosswords for Peeran. He had won several small prizes, but, of course, the winnings were hers—and he never asked her for a single paisa.

Brij Mohan had a stash of more than a hundred photographs of Peeran dressed variously in shalwar–qameez, churidar–pyjamas, sari, frock, bathing costume, and in fancy dress. Peeran was not good looking in the least. I would say she was positively ordinary, but I did not share my views with Brij Mohan. I had no idea how Brij Mohan met her, how their romance started, or if he intended to marry her. He never told me, and I never asked. It was just that every Sunday after breakfast, Brij Mohan took eight annas from me for his return fare to Bandra, headed out to see Peeran, and returned late in the afternoon. I went to my fleapit and returned with eight annas, and he left. When Brij Mohan returned that afternoon, quite unexpectedly, he said, 'Today, the matter is over.'

'What matter?' I asked.

Brij Mohan responded with light-hearted relief, 'Today, I distanced myself from Peeran. I told her, "You're unlucky for me. Whenever I meet you, either I lose my job, or I can't find any work". She said, "Very well, then stop meeting me. I'll see if you find work! I'm unlucky, but you are a layabout and a champion malingerer." So now that this story is over, I think, inshallah, tomorrow I'll find work. Give me four annas; I want to meet Seth Nanubhai Vakil. I'm sure he'll employ me as his assistant.'

Seth Nanubhai Vakil was a film director who had refused to give Brij Mohan a job on several occasions. Yet, the following day, Brij Mohan took four annas from me and returned that afternoon with the excellent news that a delighted Nanubhai had employed him on a salary of two-hundred-and-fifty rupees a month and he had signed an annual contract. Brij Mohan pulled out a hundred-rupee-note from his pocket and said, 'I want to go Bandra and wave my contract under Peeran's nose: "Here, look, I have found work!" but I'm terrified; I know the moment I see her Nanubhai will fire me. It's happened to me not once but several times. I find employment, then I meet Peeran, and everything falls through. God knows from where this girl has inherited her lousy luck. I don't plan to set eyes on her for at least a year. I've barely any clothes left, let me build up a new wardrobe, and then I'll reassess matters.'

∫

Six months passed. Brij Mohan went to work every day. Several new additions graced his wardrobe. He treated himself to at least a dozen handkerchiefs and all the accoutrements a bachelor needs to make his life comfortable. One day, a letter addressed to Brij arrived at the tenement; he was at the studio, and I forgot to give it to him that evening but handed it over the following morning at breakfast. The moment he took the envelope from me, he cried out, 'Bad luck!'

'What's happened?' I asked.

'It's Peeran...and I was doing so well in life!' He opened the envelope with the edge of a spoon and said, 'It's that wretch, Peeran. Could I ever forget her handwriting!'

'What does she say?' I asked.

'Nothing! "You must meet me this Sunday. I must tell you something".' Brij Mohan put the letter back in the envelope and tucked it in his pocket. 'Ah! Well then, Manto, inshallah, tomorrow I'll be sacked.'

'Don't talk nonsense!'

Brij Mohan insisted with an air of finality, 'No, Manto, you will see. It's Sunday tomorrow. Seth Nanubhai is bound to come up with some grievance against me.'

I said, 'If you are so sure, don't meet her.'

'That's impossible...if she summons me, I must go.'

'Why?'

'Actually, I'm a bit fed up with work. It's been more than six months now.' He smiled and left.

The following morning, Brij Mohan set out for Bandra after breakfast. When he returned, he did not utter a word about his meeting with Peeran, so I asked him, 'Well then, after all, you met your unlucky star?'

'Yes, my friend, and I told her that very soon I'll lose my job.' He stood up from the charpai and said, 'Come, let's get something to eat.'

We had dinner at Haji's Hotel, and for the rest of the evening, we did not mention Peeran. Before he went to bed, Brij Mohan said, 'Let's see what tidings the dawn brings.'

I was sure nothing untoward would happen, but Brij Mohan returned from the studio earlier than usual the following day. When he saw me, he laughed out loud and said, 'Free, Manto Bhai!'

I didn't think he was serious. So I said, 'Forget it....'

'It is forgotten. Seth Nanubhai has been declared bankrupt and has to sell his studio—and it's all because of me that poor Nanubhai has to face disaster.' Brij Mohan laughed out loud.

All I could say was, 'How very odd....'

'There you are...the wise don't need praise.' Brij Mohan lit a cigarette, took his camera, and went off for a stroll.

Now, Brij Mohan was unemployed, and after he ran through his savings, he returned to his old routine: every Sunday, he asked me for eight annas for his trip to Bandra and back. Brij Mohan was a great conversationalist, but I have no idea what he and Peeran talked about, especially since he believed she had the power to bring him bad luck. One day, I asked him, 'Brij, does Peeran love you too?'

'No. She loves somebody else.'

'Why does she meet you?'

'Because I'm intelligent. My words have the power to transform her ordinary face into a thing of beauty. I solve crossword puzzles for her, and occasionally I win prizes. But, Manto, you don't know these girls; I understand them very well. All the attributes she thinks are missing in that chap she finds in me and fills the void. She's a real 420.' Brij Mohan smiled as he referred to the section of the Indian Penal Code that relates to fraud.

Perplexed, I asked him, 'But why do you meet her?'

Brij Mohan laughed and scrunched his eyes behind his spectacles, 'I enjoy myself.'

'With what?' I exclaimed.

'I test her; test her as a harbinger of bad luck, and she's always passed the test. Whenever I start visiting her, I lose my job. Now I have just one wish: I want to dodge her spell.'

'What do you mean?' I asked.

Brij Mohan looked solemn, 'I want to hand in my resignation before my boss sacks me. I want to say, "Sir, I'm leaving because I know you want to fire me. But let me tell you, you are not dismissing me—it's my friend Peeran, whose nose pierces the lens of my camera like an arrow."'

Brij Mohan smiled, 'It's an insignificant wish...let's see if it will be fulfilled.'

I said, 'What a peculiar wish.'

'Everything about me is peculiar. Last Sunday, I photographed Peeran for the friend she loves. The idiot is going to enter my work in a competition. No doubt, he'll win a prize.' Brij Mohan smiled.

Brij Mohan was a peculiar man. He had taken several photographs, which appeared in the *Illustrated Weekly of India*, credited to Peeran's friend, and his false fame was a source of great joy for her. Brij Mohan had no idea what Peeran's friend looked like. All he knew was that the chap worked in a factory and was very handsome. One Sunday, Brij Mohan returned from Bandra and said, 'Hey, Manto, the matter's over!'

I asked, 'Peeran's matter?'

'Yes, my dear. I was running out of clothes and thought I should put an end to this matter. Inshallah, in a few days, I'll find some work. I plan to meet Seth Niaz Ali, who has announced a new film. I plan to see him tomorrow. Yaar, do find the address of his office for me.'

I got the new telephone number for Niaz Ali's office from a friend and gave it to Brij Mohan, who went off to see him the following morning. He returned that evening with a satisfied smile on his face. 'Here you are, Manto,' he said, throwing some typed papers at me, and added, 'A contract for a movie! Salary, two hundred rupees a month—it's not a lot, but Seth Niaz Ali said he'll increase it. So what do you think?'

I laughed, 'When are you going to meet Peeran?'

'When will I meet her? Hmm...exactly my thoughts on the subject. Manto, my friend, I have a small wish, and I want it granted; I don't think I should rush into anything. Let me get a couple of suits tailored; I've taken an advance of fifty rupees. You keep twenty-five.'

I took the twenty-five and paid off my running debt at Haji's Hotel.

Our days were cruising along comfortably. I earned a hundred rupees a month, and Brij Mohan brought home two. For five months, we had fun, but then Brij Mohan received a letter from Peeran. He smiled as he slit open the envelope. 'Ah well, Manto, Izrail Sahib has arrived,' said Brij, referring to the angel of death as he unfolded the paper. The letter was very brief.

I asked Brij, 'What does she say?'

'She says, "We must meet this Sunday. Something urgent has come up."' Brij Mohan folded the letter and tucked it in his pocket.

'Will you go?' I asked.

'I must go,' he said, singing the film song, 'Don't forget, Oh, traveller, you must go....'

'Brij, don't go to meet her.' I begged him, 'We're having such a good time. You've no idea; God alone knows how I gave you those eight annas every Sunday.'

Brij Mohan smiled, 'I know all too well, but sadly those days are about to return when God alone knows how you will give me eight annas every Sunday.'

On Sunday, Brij went to Bandra to meet Peeran. When he returned, all he said was, 'I told her, "This is the twelfth time I'll lose my job because of your ill luck. May Zarathustra bless you.'

'And what did she say?' I asked.

'Quite simply, "You're a silly idiot!"'

'One hundred per cent!' I agreed and laughed out loud.

'Now, the first thing tomorrow morning, I'll hand in my resignation. I wrote it at Peeran's place,' and he showed me the letter. The following morning, Brij gobbled his breakfast in an unusual rush and left for office. When he returned that evening, he looked crestfallen.

I felt compelled to ask, 'Why Brij, what happened?'

He shook his head hopelessly and said, 'Nothing, yaar, the whole matter has come to an end.'

'What do you mean?'

'When I handed in my resignation to Seth Niaz Ali, he smiled and handed me an official letter, which said he had raised my salary the previous month—from two hundred to three hundred rupees a month!'

Brij Mohan lost all interest in Peeran and told me, 'My interest in her and all my hobbies came to an end when she lost her power to cast a bad spell on me. I wonder who will assume charge of my laziness now.'

## Janki

The Poona racing season was about to begin when Aziz wrote from Peshawar to say, 'I am sending Janki, a female acquaintance. Please help her find work in a film company in Poona or Bombay since you have connections in the right circles. I hope it will not be too much trouble.'

It was no trouble, but I had never done anything of this sort. I was in two minds because a man who wants to fix up a woman with a film company usually wants to live off her earnings. Still, Aziz had invested so much faith in me, and I felt I could not let him down. Besides, I knew that the doors of a film company are always open for a young woman, and asked myself, 'What's the big deal? I'm sure she will get a job in some company or the other with or without my help.'

Four days after I received Aziz's letter, Janki reached Poona, where she had to find me on a crowded platform. She had travelled thousands of miles from Peshawar to Bombay, where she took the train to Poona. As the train pulled in, I peered into each carriage and did not have to walk far before I saw a woman of medium height step out of a second-class carriage, holding my photograph. She stood on tiptoe with her back towards me; I approached her and said, 'I think I am the person you are looking for.'

She turned around, 'Oh, you...?' She cast a quick look at my photograph and continued in a very matter-of-fact manner, 'Saadat Sahib, the journey was arduous. Waiting for this train at the Bombay railway station after I got off the Frontier Mail has wiped me out.'

'Where is your luggage?' I asked.

'Just bringing it,' she said and climbed back into the carriage. I hailed a coolie as she dragged out two suitcases and a holdall. As we stepped out of the station, she announced, 'I am staying in a hotel.'

I found her a room in a roadhouse opposite the station. She had to bathe, change, and rest. I gave her my address, asked her to meet me at ten o'clock the following morning, and left.

She had difficulty in finding the place and arrived at Prabhat Nagar at ten-thirty. I was putting up at a friend's compact new flat and writing a screenplay. My friend was out and the only other person around was Majeed, an imbecile of a servant who added to the vacuity of a place. I had worked through the night and had woken up late. When Janki entered unannounced at ten-thirty, I was drinking a cup of tea after my bath still in my pyjamas and regulation vest. On the station platform and at the hotel, despite her fatigue, I met a robust woman, but in Flat Number 11, Prabhat Nagar, a worried and broken person stood before me. Janki looked as though she had just donated fifteen ounces of blood to charity or had a miscarriage.

I poured a cup of tea. 'You must have had your breakfast at the hotel. Do have some tea.' She looked distracted and bit her lip as she lifted the cup. She sipped her tea in silence and began to shake her right leg quite vigorously. I noticed her lips quiver and gathered she wished to say something to me but was hesitating. Perhaps, a traveller had made a pass at her in the hotel. 'I hope you didn't have any trouble at the hotel,' I asked.

'Oh, oh, no.'

I assumed I should remain silent, but since we were about to finish our tea, I thought it best to talk about something and asked, 'How is Aziz Sahib?'

She did not respond to my question but put her teacup down on the teapoy and stood up. She strung her words in rapid succession and asked, 'Manto Sahib, do you know a good doctor?'

'In Poona? I don't know anybody.'

'Oh!'

'Why? Are you unwell?' I enquired.

'Yes.' She sat down on the chair.

'What's your problem?' I asked.

When she smiled, her thin lips shrank or, perhaps, she had pursed them. She could not bring herself to say anything, and as she stood up, she picked up my tin of cigarettes and helped herself to one, lit it, and added, 'I beg your pardon, but I smoke.'

In time, I discovered that Janki did not smoke cigarettes—she consumed them. She held her cigarette in her fist in a masculine manner and inhaled hard. In a day, she smoked approximately seventy-five cigarettes. I asked, 'Why don't you tell me about your illness?'

Janki blushed like an unmarried girl and stomped one foot on the floor, 'Hai Allah! How can I tell you?' she stuttered and smiled, revealing her extraordinarily spotless and sparkling teeth through the arch of her thin lips. Then, she sat down and averted my gaze because her eyes had brimmed over with tears. 'The fact is that it's been more than fifteen days, and I am scared....'

At first, I did not get her drift, but when she stopped mid-sentence, I figured what was up and asked, 'Does this happen often?'

She took a deep manly puff and exhaled hard, 'No, it's something else. I fear it might have stopped.'

'Oh...' I responded.

She drew the last puff from her cigarette, stubbed it out in the saucer, and continued, 'If this is the case, I'm afraid it's going to be a real nuisance. Once the same problem occurred in Peshawar, but Aziz Sahib procured a terrific medicine from some hakim friend of his, and everything cleared out within days.'

'You don't like children?' I queried.

She smiled, 'I like them...but who's going to bother with looking after them?'

I said, 'Do you know that it is a crime to get rid of a baby in this manner?'

Her expression turned solemn, and she added in an astonished voice, 'Aziz Sahib says so as well. I ask you, Saadat Sahib, what's criminal about this? After all, it is one's possession. Do these lawmakers have any idea how painful it is to abort a child? How easy it is to say, "It's a big crime!"'

I laughed and said, 'You're an extraordinary woman, Janki.'

She responded, 'Aziz Sahib says so as well.' Then, Janki opened her handbag and took out a handkerchief to wipe away her tears and turned to me like a naïve child, 'Saadat Sahib, tell me, do you find my conversation interesting?'

'Very.'

'Lies!'

'Do you have proof?'

She lit a cigarette, 'Well, one thing I know for sure, I am foolish. I talk too much; I overeat; I laugh too much. I mean, you can see how my tummy has expanded. Aziz Sahib always says, "Janki, eat less." As you can see, I have not paid the slightest attention to him. But, Saadat Sahib, the fact is that if I don't satisfy my appetite, I feel I have forgotten to say something to somebody.' She began to laugh, and I joined her. Janki had a distinctive laugh, like the tinkling of bells.

She was about to discuss her miscarriage when my friend and host arrived. He was working as an assistant to a director who had a new film in production. I introduced Janki to him, saying she wanted to join the film line. He took her to his studio, confident that his director had a suitable role for her in his new film—but he was proved wrong. I tried all the studios in Poona with help from different quarters. Some took Janki's sound test, others a camera test, one film company dressed her up in various costumes—but without a favourable outcome. She was anxious about missing her days, and her anxiety increased after she had spent four to five mind-numbing days visiting different film companies.

In her attempt to abort the foetus, Janki ingested a daily dose of twenty green quinine tablets, which dampened her mood. Furthermore, her concern about how Aziz Sahib was managing without her in Peshawar added to her anxieties. Janki had sent Aziz a telegram the moment she arrived in Poona and subsequently wrote to him every day. Every letter was full of advice on how to look after his health and take his medicines regularly. I did not know anything about Aziz Sahib's health, but Janki informed me that he paid serious attention to what she had to say because he was in love with her. Janki recounted how Aziz quarrelled with his wife when she nagged him for not taking his medication but never said anything to her. At first, I thought her concern for Aziz was twaddle, just an act, but over time I realized that Janki cared for Aziz. She read and reread several times every letter that he wrote and wept copiously.

Janki's rounds of film companies in Poona resulted in nought, but the one fear that haunted her proved ill-founded. Now, Janki had been in Poona for twenty days and was writing letter upon letter to Aziz, who wrote back long lovesick letters. In one of his letters, Aziz suggested that if nothing works out for Janki in Poona, I should try Bombay, a city with countless studios, and his suggestion made complete sense to me. I was busy writing a screenplay, and could not accompany Janki, so I telephoned my friend, Saeed, who was the resident hero in a film production company in Bombay. He was not in his office, but when our mutual friend Narayan heard I was calling from Poona, he took the call and roared down the line, 'Hello Manto, Narayan speaking from this end,' before switching to Hindustani, 'tell me, what's up? Saeed is not in the studio. He's at home settling the final account with Razia.'

'What do you mean?' I asked.

'They've had a tiff. Razia connected with another man.'

'But what's this settling of the final account?' I asked.

Narayan said, 'Well, Saeed is petty. He's taking back the clothes he bought for her.'

'Ah well…I'm calling because a friend in Peshawar has sent me a woman who is keen to work in the movies.'

Janki was standing near me, and I realized my turn of phrase was tasteless and was about to rectify matters when Narayan's voice pierced my ears, 'A woman from Peshawar! Kho send 'er 'ere soon!' he said, dropping his aitches. 'Kho, I am also a Patan from Kusur!'

'Don't talk nonsense, Narayan,' I stressed, 'and pay attention. I am sending her to Bombay on the Deccan Queen tomorrow. So either you or Saeed…one of you please meet her at the station—tomorrow on the Deccan Queen!'

Narayan bellowed, 'But how will we recognize her?'

'She will recognize you,' I said and added, 'but seriously, do get her fixed up somewhere.'

Three minutes were up. I put the receiver down and turned to Janki, 'Tomorrow, you leave for Bombay on the Deccan Queen. I shall show you photographs of Saeed and Narayan. They are tall, handsome youngsters with fine physiques. You'll have no trouble recognizing them.'

In an album lying around, I found several photographs of Saeed and Narayan, and as Janki scrutinized them, I noticed that she showed more interest in Saeed. She put the album aside but failed in her attempt to look disinterested and asked, 'What sort of men are they?'

'What do you mean?'

'I mean, what sort of men are they? I've heard that men in the film line are unusually wicked.' She looked unmistakably serious.

I responded, 'That's quite right, but is there even a need for virtuous men in the film industry?'

'Why?'

'There are two types of human beings in the world. Type one reflects on his misery to understand pain. Type two reflects on the sorrow of others to do so. In your opinion, which type gets to the bottom of human pain and suffering?'

Janki looked thoughtful and said, 'Type one, who has suffered pain.'

I said, 'You're right. Only a person who has experienced heartbreak can enact a tragic scene. Do you think a pious woman, who considers love an unclean emotion, can express her love for a man in front of a camera?'

Janki remained silent for a while and asked, 'Do you mean that a woman should know all these things before joining the film industry?'

I said, 'It's not necessary. You can join the industry and get to know these things.'

She reflected on what I had said and repeated her first question, 'What sort of men are Saeed Sahib and Narayan?'

'Do you want a detailed analysis?'

'What do you mean by detailed?'

'That of the two, who will be better for you?'

Offended by my response, she retorted, 'What sort of talk is this?'

'The sort you want....'

'Stop it,' she said and smiled, 'I'll never ask you anything.'

I smiled and said, 'If and when you ask me, I shall promote Narayan's case.'

'Why?'

'Because he is a better human being.'

And to this day, I have not revised my opinion.

Saeed is a poet—a cruel poet. If he has to slaughter a hen, he will not cut its jugular as prescribed by Muslim law but twist the creature's neck, rip off its feathers, extract a broth, drink it, and chew the bones before taking himself to a secluded corner to write a tearful poem on the death of a hen. Saeed drinks but never gets drunk, which irritates me to no end because it destroys the meaning of liquor. He takes his time to get out of bed every morning. His servant brings him a cup of tea, and if he has some rum left over from the previous night, he pours it into his tea and drinks this vile mixture sip by horrid sip, oblivious to anything called taste. If a boil on his body erupts and turns septic, Saeed will not consult a doctor. If you comment on the matter, you will get the following response, 'Often, maladies become part of the person. When this wound is not troubling me, why should I seek treatment for it?' He will turn his wound into an opportunity to write a tragic verse. Saeed is incapable of subtle emotions and will never make a good actor. I saw him in a film which became a hit because of its heroine's songs. In one scene, he had to hold his beloved's hand and express his love for her. By God, he held her hand as you would a puppy's paw. I have told him several times that he must forget the idea of becoming an actor: 'You're a good poet; sit at home and write poems.' But the acting bug has infected him.

I am fond of Narayan and quite like the rules he devised to guide his life in a studio. Known as his Ten Commandments, he inscribed them in a notebook, and they provide a ready assessment of Narayan's character. Of course, people say he does not abide by all his rules, but I think he does, and here they are, as transcribed by him:

1. An actor should not get married; if he does, he should divorce the film world, open a dairy business, and sell milk and yoghurt. If famous, he will make a lot of money.
2. If an actress addresses you as her brother, 'Bhaiya' or 'Bhai Sahib', whisper into her ear and ask her, 'What's your bra size?'
3. If you fancy an actress, do not waste time thinking of ways to attract her. Instead, ask to meet her for dinner à deux and tell her that you wish to make a proposition. If she does not fall for that, shower your wealth on her.
4. If an actress becomes a part of your life, do not take a single penny from her earnings. An actress's earnings are only kosher for her brother or her husband.

5. Make sure she does not bear you any children while she is your wife. After you win swaraj, or freedom, you can father her children.
6. An actor must live up to a reputation instead of building it at the barber's salon on mere looks, try something less flashy; for instance, an act of charity.
7. At the studio, be kind to the Pathan watchman, and you will benefit hugely, if not in this world, then definitely in the next.
8. Do not get addicted to alcohol and actresses. It is likely that one day, the Congress government will impose a ban on both.
9. A businessman can be a 'Muslim businessman', but an actor must not be a 'Muslim actor' or a 'Hindu actor'.
10. Do not lie.

I did not share Narayan's commandments with Janki but told her what I thought of him and Saeed as simply as I could and added, 'If you join this line, you will have to rely on the support of some man or the other. I think Narayan will prove a friend.'

Janki heard me out and left for Bombay. When she returned the following day, she looked most chuffed. Narayan had fixed her up at his studio at five hundred rupees a month. We had a long conversation about how she got this work, and I asked her, 'You met both Saeed and Narayan. Of the two, who liked you more?'

Janki smiled, and with her eyes full of excitement, she said, 'Saeed Sahib!' and on a more serious note, she asked, 'Saadat Sahib, why did you praise Narayan to the skies?'

I asked, 'Why?'

'He's a dreadful man. Last night, I was having a drink with him and Saeed Sahib; I wanted to ask him something and had just said, "Narayan Bhaiya," when he brought his face very close to mine and whispered in my ear, "What's your bra size?" Bhagwan knows I was livid. What a lecherous man!' Janki looked outraged, and tiny beads of perspiration appeared on her forehead.

I chuckled in response, and Janki asked, 'Why on earth are you laughing?'

'At his foolishness,' I said and applied the brakes on my chuckle.

After Janki decimated Narayan's character, she began to voice her concerns for Aziz. She had not received a letter from him for many days and was worried he might have caught a cold. 'Aziz Sahib is careless when riding around on his bicycle.' She wondered if he had met with an accident, or even if he was on his way to Poona because when seeing her off at the Peshawar railway station, he had told Janki, 'One day I'll turn up unannounced!'

Janki seemed less agitated after we had chatted for a while, and her concern for Aziz changed into a shower of praise. She described what good care he took of his children as part of his daily routine, how he made them exercise, helped them bathe and change, and took them to school. He did all this and kept up with relatives because his wife was slothful. Once, when Janki had typhoid, he looked after her for twenty days like a professional nurse, etc., etc., etc. The following morning, Janki thanked me most graciously and left for Bombay, where the doors of a new and iridescent world had opened for her.

I spent almost two months in Poona, completed a scenario for a new film, collected my dues, and headed back to Bombay, where a new contract awaited me. At around five o'clock next morning, I reached Andheri, where Saeed and Narayan shared a modest bungalow. I crossed the veranda but found the front door locked. I knew they would be asleep and went around to the back door, often left open for the servants. I walked in and found the kitchen and the adjoining room filthy as usual, even though Saeed and Narayan used the latter as their dining room. Opposite this room was the guest room; I opened the door and walked in. There were two beds. On one, Saeed was fast asleep with another person under a quilt; the other was unoccupied.

Overwhelmed by sleep, I did not bother to change, but lay down, looking forward to getting some good rest, and had just pulled the blanket lying at the foot of the bed over myself when an arm with bangles emerged from under the quilt on the other bed. As Janki stretched out to grab a white lattha–shalwar thrown across the back of a nearby chair, I picked it up, threw it at her, and went to Narayan's room to wake him up.

Narayan told me he had finished shooting at two o'clock that morning. I was sorry to disturb the poor chap. Still, surprised to see me, he wanted to indulge in a tasteless gossip session, and that is what we did until nine o'clock in the morning. Janki's name came up several times during the course of our conversation. When I told Narayan the story about the bra, he laughed and said, 'What's interesting is that when I asked her the size of her bra in a whisper, she responded promptly, "Twenty-four." But the moment it struck her that my question was coarse, she told me off. Janki's like a child. Whenever she sees me, she covers her bosom with her dupatta, but Manto, she is a forthright woman.'

'How do you know?' I asked.

Narayan smiled, 'A woman who tells a total stranger the correct size of her bra can't be two-faced.'

Narayan's logic was strange, but he tried to convince me in all seriousness that apart from being sincere, Janki was also an honest and devoted ayah, 'Manto, you've no idea how well she looks after Saeed. I mean, to take care of such a self-centred man is not an easy matter. And Janki does this with such good cheer. She wakes up at eight in the morning and spends half an hour waking up this pig of a man. She helps him as he brushes his teeth and gets dressed, assists with preparing his breakfast, and at night, when he is ready to sleep after drinking a fair bit of rum, she shares his bed. In the studio, she gabbles endlessly about Saeed: "Saeed Sahib is a perfect man. Saeed Sahib sings very well; Saeed Sahib has put on weight; Saeed Sahib's pullover is ready; I sent for Peshawari chappals for Saeed Sahib; Saeed Sahib has a headache, and I'm getting some Aspro for him; Saeed Sahib wrote a couplet to praise me." She always frowns when she bumps into me because she recalls the bra episode.'

I enjoyed Saeed and Narayan's hospitality for almost ten days. Not once did Saeed mention Janki; perhaps, for him, their affair was quite old. On the other hand, in the many conversations I had with her, Janki made it clear that she quite fancied Saeed. She complained about his cavalier attitude towards his health, 'Saadat Sahib, he doesn't look after himself. Everything happens for a reason. You may well laugh, but every day I have to ask him if he has been to the toilet or not.'

Narayan was right. Janki had nothing but Saeed's welfare on her mind and attended selflessly to all his needs. I was most impressed, although I did wonder what was to become of Aziz. I recalled Janki's concern for him. Had she forgotten him after she found Saeed? A few more days in Bombay could provide an answer to this question, but I fell out on a minor matter with the producer with whom I was to sign a contract and returned to Poona to get rid of the stress. Two days after I reached Poona, I received a telegram from Aziz, informing me that he was coming to Poona, and five or six hours later, he was with me. The following morning, Janki was at the door.

Aziz and Janki did not reunite with the passion of long-lost lovers. Perhaps, the reason for their restraint was the very formal nature of my relationship with Aziz; we had not discussed his ties with Janki. He wanted to move into a hotel, but since my friend was in Kolhapur for an outdoor shoot, I asked Aziz and Janki to stay with me. There were three bedrooms—Janki could use one and Aziz the other. I should have given them one room, but I was on reasonably formal terms with Aziz as I have said earlier. They went to the cinema that night. I wanted to get down to writing a new screenplay and did not join them but gave Aziz a set of keys and was comfortable on that front.

I was up until two o'clock and then fell asleep. No matter what time I go to bed at night, I wake up between three-thirty and four to have a glass of water. That night too, I woke up as usual, but Aziz was asleep in the room where I kept my earthenware pitcher. I did not want to disturb him, but my throat was parched because of the whisky I had drunk the night before. I knocked on the door, and Janki opened it. She rubbed her eyes and said, 'Saeed Sahib!' but when she saw me, a soft 'Oho,' slipped from her mouth. I saw Aziz fast asleep on the bed, and as my face broke into an irrepressible smile, so did Janki's. I took the pitcher of water and left.

Next morning, I woke up to a room full of smoke and rushed to the kitchen, where I found Janki trying to light a fire with a scrunched-up paper because she wanted to heat water for Aziz's bath. Her eyes were watering, but when she saw me, she smiled and continued to blow on the fire as she informed me, 'Aziz Sahib catches a chill if he takes a cold bath. I was not in Peshawar, and he was sick for a month. So naturally, that was bound to happen. He stopped his medicines, and you can see how much weight he has lost.'

After his bath, Aziz stepped out for some errands, and Janki asked me to send Saeed a telegram, 'I've made a big blunder. I should have wired him yesterday, the moment I got here. He must be so worried.' She asked me to compose a text to inform him of her safe arrival, expressing concern for his welfare and instructions not to forget his injections. Four days passed, and Janki sent five telegrams to Saeed, but there was no response. She was planning to leave for Bombay when quite suddenly Aziz fell ill. She asked me to compose another telegram to Saeed and stayed up the whole night, tending to Aziz. It was an ordinary fever, but Janki was anxious. Saeed's silence added to her worries. She shared her thoughts with me several times. 'Saadat Sahib, I'm sure Saeed Sahib is unwell; otherwise, he would have responded to my telegrams and letters.'

On the fifth day, I was sitting and chatting with Janki and Aziz, and she was laughing at something I had said when Saeed's telegram arrived. It read, 'I am very unwell. Come immediately.' Janki became silent. Visibly annoyed by Janki's silence, Aziz's voice acquired a sharp edge, and I left the room. When I returned that evening, Aziz and Janki were sitting together, and the trace of tears on her cheeks was a telltale sign of their quarrel. Janki talked about this and that for a while, but then she picked up her handbag and said to Aziz, 'I'm leaving but will be back soon.' Then she turned to me and said, 'Saadat Sahib, please look after him; he has a fever.'

I accompanied Janki to the station, where I managed to buy her a ticket on the black market and put her on a train. I returned home to find Aziz had a mild fever. We talked late into the night, but there was no mention of Janki. Three days later, at five o'clock in the morning, I heard the front door open, followed by Janki's garbled voice asking Aziz about his health and if he had taken his medicine in her absence. I did not catch Aziz's response, but half an hour later, although my eyes were overwhelmed by sleep, I could hear Aziz making his displeasure known to Janki. I could not figure out his words, his muffled tone was suffused with anger.

At ten o'clock, Aziz had a cold bath as the bucket of hot water heated by Janki stood nearby. When I mentioned this to Janki, her eyes welled up with tears. Aziz went out after his bath, and Janki stayed in bed. At around three o'clock, I checked on Janki, and discovered she had a high temperature. I stepped out to call a doctor and saw Aziz getting his luggage loaded on a tonga.

'Where are you going?' I asked.

He shook hands with me and said, 'To Bombay. Inshallah, we'll meet again.' He got into the tonga and drove off. I did not get an opportunity to inform Aziz that Janki was running a high temperature.

The doctor examined Janki and told me she had bronchitis; he advised complete rest, saying her condition could develop into pneumonia, gave his prescription, and left. Janki turned to me to ask about Aziz. At first, I thought I should not tell her that he had left, but upon reflection, I could not think of a good reason to withhold this information from her. Deeply upset, Janki nuzzled her face in her pillow and began to weep. The following morning, around eleven o'clock, when Janki's temperature was a degree lower, and she felt slightly better, a harshly worded telegram arrived from Saeed, saying, 'Remember, you have not kept your word.' I tried hard to stop her, but Janki left for Bombay on the Poona Express with a high fever.

After five or six days, I received a telegram from Narayan: 'Urgent work. Come to Bombay immediately.'

I thought Narayan was referring to a contract with a producer, but when I reached Bombay, I discovered that Janki's condition was critical; her bronchitis had developed into pneumonia. When she got off the Poona train at the Bombay terminus, she ran to catch a moving train to Andheri and fell. Janki had bruised her thighs badly, yet she confronted the injury with great courage. But her spirit wilted when she reached Andheri, and Saeed pointed to her luggage and said, 'Please, leave.'

Narayan told me, 'Saeed's words were as cold as ice, and for a moment, Janki turned to stone. I am sure she asked herself, why did I not come under the Andheri train and die? Saadat, whatever you say, Saeed's conduct with women is most unmanly. Poor thing, she had a fever; she had fallen off a moving train, and that too because she was in a hurry to get to this swine—but without a care for her suffering, Saeed repeated, "Please, leave." Manto, there was no emotion in his voice. It was like a line from a newspaper coming out of a linotype machine. I felt miserable, so I just left the room. When I returned that evening, Janki was not there. Saeed was sitting in bed, nursing a glass of rum, and writing a poem. I remained silent and went to my room. The next day, at the studio, I heard that Janki was at some female extra's house and critically ill. I spoke to the proprietor of the studio and had her sent to a hospital. She's been there since yesterday. Tell me, what can we do? I can't go there because she loathes me. You better go and check on her.'

I went to the hospital. The first thing I did was ask Janki how both Aziz and Saeed had ill-treated her, and was touched by her ability to forgive. The doctors told me that Janki's lungs were inflamed, and her life was in danger, I was amazed at the courage with which Janki confronted her sickness. On my return from the hospital, I went to the studio to find Narayan. I heard that no one had seen him since the morning. That evening, when he returned home, he showed me three small glass phials with rubber bands tied around the mouths. 'Do you know what this is?'

I said, 'I don't, but they look like injections.'

Narayan smiled, 'They are injections...of penicillin.'

I was surprised because penicillin was gold dust. The authorities had earmarked the entire supply that came from America and England for military hospitals. I asked Narayan, 'How did you get these?'

He smiled, 'As a child, I was an expert at opening the safe at home and stealing money. Today, I used my expertise to open the refrigerator of a military hospital and stole these three phials. Hurry, let's go and take Janki from the hospital to a hotel.'

I took a taxi to the hospital and rushed Janki to the hotel where Narayan had booked two rooms. In a weak voice, Janki asked me several times why I was taking her to a hotel. Each time I told her, 'You'll soon find out.'

When Narayan entered her room with a syringe in his hand to inject her, she turned her face away in disgust and said to me, 'Saadat Sahib, please ask him to leave.'

Narayan smiled, 'My heart's delight, forget your anger. It's a matter of your life.'

Janki was furious. Despite her weakness, she sat up and said to me, 'Saadat Sahib, I'm leaving if you don't get this parasite out of here.'

Narayan pushed her back and turned her around, smiling as he said, 'This bastard will give you an injection, come what may. Don't you dare try to stop me.'

He handed the syringe to me and grabbed Janki's arm with one hand and with the other, dipped the cotton swab into some surgical spirit and wiped her arm. He handed me the swab, took the syringe, and pierced the needle into Janki's arm. She screamed, but penicillin entered her body. When Narayan released Janki's forearm from his firm grip, she began to weep. Narayan ignored her tears, wiped her arm with the swab dipped in surgical spirit, and went to the other room.

Narayan gave the first injection at nine o'clock at night and the second after three hours. He explained that if three hours lapse into three-and-a-half, the effectiveness of the penicillin is nullified. Narayan kept awake. At around eleven-thirty, he turned on the stove, boiled the syringe, and filled it with penicillin. I could hear Janki's lungs crackle as she breathed with her eyes closed. Narayan cleaned her other arm with spirit, and as he pushed in the needle, she emitted a soft scream. Narayan injected the medicine into her body, pulled the needle out, wiped her arm with spirit, and said to me, 'Now, the third at three o'clock.'

I have no idea when Narayan administered the third and fourth injections, but I woke up to the hiss of the burning stove and heard him ask the waiter for some more ice because the penicillin had to be kept cold. He had to give the fifth injection at nine o'clock. When we went into her room, Janki was lying in bed, wide awake. She looked at Narayan with eyes full of loathing but remained silent. Narayan stood by her bedside and asked, 'Why, my heart's delight, how are you?' He continued, 'These injections are shots of love that I've stolen from the military hospital with great cunning. They will cure your pneumonia. Here, now lie flat on your tummy and lower your shalwar from your buttock.' He poked his finger at a spot on Janki's buttock and asked, 'Have you ever had a jab here?' When a furious Janki turned on her stomach, Narayan said, 'Well done!'

Before Janki could protest, Narayan lowered her shalwar with one hand and turned to me, 'Apply the spirit.'

Janki began to kick her legs about, and Narayan said, 'Janki, stop moving your legs-vegs. I shall give you the injection come what may.'

By nine o'clock, Naryan had administered five injections, and fifteen remained. The entire course was to take forty-five hours, and after the first five injections, there was no visible improvement in Janki's condition. Yet, convinced of the superior powers of penicillin, Narayan had total faith that she would survive. For several hours, the two of us sat and talked about this new medicine. At eleven o'clock, Narayan's servant brought a telegram for me. A film company had ushered me to Poona, and I left immediately. I returned to Bombay after a fortnight and reached Andheri late that evening. I heard from Saeed that Narayan had not returned home from the hotel, in the city centre, and I decided to spend the night in Andheri.

The following morning, I took a train to Colaba and was at the hotel by eight o'clock. I found Narayan's room unlocked and walked in, but he was not there. So I opened the door that led to the adjoining room and walked in upon some unusual activity. The moment Janki spotted me she hid under the quilt. I turned to leave, but Narayan, who was snuggling in bed with her, said, 'Hey Manto, I always forget to lock the door. Come on in, yaar, and take this chair; just hand me Janki's shalwar.'

## Mrs D'Silva

We lived opposite each other. Our flat was Number 13, and hers 14. When someone knocked on her front door, I would think it was on ours. One day, I opened our front door under a similar misapprehension, which was when I first met her. I had seen her on the stairs, in the bazaar, and on the balcony but never spoken to her. She looked at me and smiled, 'You thought somebody had come to see you.' I smiled back. For a few moments, Mrs D'Silva stood in her doorway, and I stood in mine. This encounter led to a feeling of conviviality between us. Her name was Mary, and God alone knows what else, but since her husband's name was P. N. D'Silva, I called her Mrs D'Silva. I could have called her Mary, but she was a lot older than me.

Mrs D'Silva had a plump face with a broad flat nose like a pakora. Her small head with a crop of perpetually dishevelled short hair rested on a stumpy neck. I have no idea what her eyes looked like when she was asleep, but whenever I saw her—awake, that is—she kept them wide open like the mouth of an inkpot. Her husband was an ordinary-looking man who worked in some office. Every evening, on his way back from work, if Mr D'Silva spotted me on our balcony, he doffed his hat by way of greeting. He was a thorough gentleman. Mrs D'Silva, too, was an agreeable lady, and both husband and wife led a peaceful life.

Mr and Mrs D'Silva had a son who was four or five years old. At times, he looked like a mini version of his father, and at others, it seemed his mother had shrunk into his body. The boy's face was such a hotchpotch of his parents' features that it was difficult to say whether he looked like his father or his mother. In the five years of their marriage, the D'Silvas had produced one child. One day, Mrs D'Silva told me in pidgin Hindustani, 'My mother also give children like this. Behind five years, first I born; behind another five years, my brother born; behind him my one more sister.'

Now that her five-year cycle had ended, Mrs D'Silva was pregnant with the second D'Silva offspring, and her husband was delighted.

The several dates inscribed in Mrs D'Silva diary included the birthday of her first child, an approximate due date for the new arrival, and the year in which their third child would arrive. From his wife's ceaseless chatter, I understood that Mr D'Silva didn't much care for the restrictive five-year cycle. He failed to understand why his wife should take a vacation for five years after the birth of a child. Mrs D'Silva was equally confused about the matter but was proud to follow in her mother's footsteps. I, too, was surprised about Mrs D'Silva's five-year cycle and often wondered, 'Almighty, what is this five-year cycle? Why doesn't one of them forget to count? How come she's all set to produce a child at the end of the five-year cycle? God alone knows His ways.'

We heard that a woman in our neighbourhood had carried a baby for a year and a half. Her doctors thought there was nothing wrong with her uterus—the foetus was there for sure, but it was not ready to make its entry into the world. When Ammijan heard about these matters from me, she made the routine declaration she relied upon when matters were either beyond her comprehension or not to her taste, 'The Day of Judgement is upon us. God knows what has happened to the world. Never in my life have I heard of such things. Women always delivered babies after nine months; that was that. There were no discussions. Now, when women get pregnant, the news spreads like wildfire, and you see them roaming around town with their potbellies, with the whole world watching. I ask you, are they in the least bit embarrassed? These days, the very concept of shame is dead.'

I chuckled to myself because Ammijan had developed a potbelly several times, and she had carted it around, doing her household chores and making daily trips to the market. Of course, she had forgotten.

I fail to understand why Ammijan wants to promulgate a regime of shame. If a woman is pregnant, how is it her fault? When God has ordained that it is a woman's function to carry a baby in her stomach for a fixed time, why should she feel embarrassed? Besides, why should a pregnant woman give up everything and sit around and twiddle her thumbs? Why should all outdoor activities be curtailed? I must say, I found my mother's philosophy very odd. Ammijan liked to lecture on every subject under the sun. Of course, if the matter concerns her daughter, her lips were sealed. When I was expecting Arif, I went to Apollo Bandar for a walk every day. I swear to you, not a word against me came out of her mouth. Now that it was Mrs D'Silva's turn, Ammijan found a perfect opportunity to hold forth, prefaced by an 'I tell you...' or 'I must say'. And that too, about Mrs D'Silva, the poor dear who only ever went out with her husband to buy groceries in the evenings or to church on Sundays.

A woman's stomach tends not to expand as much with the first child as it does with the second because, by this time, it is more pliant. When Mrs D'Silva moved around her flat, I could see her weird little body through her kaftan. Her tummy and skinny legs reminded me of a large round clay pot standing on two stilts; she looked like a cartoon character. In the early days of her pregnancy, Mrs D'Silva was nauseous and vomited all day long. The moment she heard the ice cream vendor, she called out excitedly, but after Mrs D'Silva had eaten her ice cream, she would become sick, and the poor dear spent the rest of the day licking a lemon.

One afternoon, I went across to ask how she was doing and found her lying in bed with her legs raised. I smiled and asked, 'Mrs D'Silva, are you doing some exercise?'

She looked exasperated and said, 'I feel fed up; I lift the leg like so and have better feeling.' She had rested her feet against a cold wall for some respite. Occasionally, when overcome, she banged her fists on her bed or a nearby table or chair, and if this did not ease her discomfort, she began to weep. It tickled me to see Mrs D'Silva in this condition, but, of course, I had forgotten my pregnancy. I asked her several times, 'Mrs D'Silva knowing everything, why did you take on this trial?'

She gave a standard irate response, 'Where I take? This saala wants to arrive behind five years.'

'Mrs D'Silva, why didn't you go to Bangalore in the fifth year?' I asked.

And she said, 'I go...truly. I think I stay there, and my sahib stay here. I ready to go, but this war it start. Too much expense, and thinking like this, I stay here, and this saala, this terror land on my head.'

The early weeks of her pregnancy did feel like terror to Mrs D'Silva, but with time she began to look forward to the birth of her second child. Her nausea and sickness stopped, and after the first two months, the need to put her legs up also disappeared. She had no ailments, just a bit of stiffness in her stomach now and again and a bit of discomfort when the child moved. Mrs D'Silva was ready for the new arrival. She had stitched tiny frocks and prepared towels and nappies, which she kept in a mini bag. Her husband bought a steel cot, and Mrs D'Silva made a mattress and stuffed it with fillings from old cushions. Much of the paraphernalia for a layette was ready. All that remained was for Mrs D'Silva to go to the hospital and deliver her baby.

Two months before the due date, Mr D'Silva booked a room in a hospital and paid a five-rupee advance to ensure a bed was available and to avoid last-minute glitches. Mr D'Silva was a prudent man; he had made equally comprehensive arrangements when their first child was born. Mrs D'Silva was even more prudent than her husband. In nine months, she had organized everything for the first two years of the child's life—a rubber mat to protect the mattress, feeding bottles, pacifiers, rattles, and various Japanese toys along with other items that she had packed carefully in a trunk. Every other day, Mrs D'Silva opened the trunk and rearranged everything in a more orderly fashion. She counted the days to when she could hold her baby in her arms, nurse her baby, sing lullabies, and rock her baby to sleep in the cradle. She was as excited as a student going back to school after a five-year break.

As Mrs D'Silva's due date drew closer, Mr D'Silva took a sample of his wife's urine to the Parsi doctor's clinic opposite our building every morning. The D'Silvas had heard that doctors could determine the baby's time of arrival in the final days of pregnancy by examining a urine sample. Mrs D'Silva thought she was full-term, but the Parsi doctor thought there were more days to go.

One day, I was taking a bath when I heard Mrs D'Silva cry out in pain. I heard her front door open and heard her cry out again. After my bath, I peeped through the window into the hallway and saw

Mrs D'Silva holding on to her husband's arm as she climbed down the stairs. She was yellow as turmeric; when she saw me, she tried to smile. I adopted the demeanour of an elder and said, 'Stay safe.'

When Mr D'Silva heard my voice, he doffed his brown hat and greeted me. I called out to him, 'Mr D'Silva, do inform us as soon as the baby arrives.' The smile on Mr D'Silva's lips spread wider.

The whole day, I thought of little else but Mrs D'Silva. I opened the door several times to check on her, but there was no sign of the servant or Mr D'Silva. By the evening, I thought to myself, 'God knows where these people have disappeared.'

There was no news from the hospital, and someone had come to pick me up for a planned visit to my sister in Mahim. When I returned after three days, instead of going to my flat, I knocked on Mrs D'Silva's door and found her standing before me with her potbelly. Shocked, I asked her, 'What happened?'

She took me inside and said, 'I feel the pain, I think time up. I go hospital the nurse people lay me down and pain it go. I feel too much shock. Nurse people laugh too much and ask, "Why you come here so early. Now go home for some more time." I feel too much shame.'

Mrs D'Silva had gone to the hospital in a taxi, and she described in some detail how at the hospital they took her name and particulars, how two nurses made her strip and lay her down on a bed, and how she could hear another woman scream from the adjoining room. She bathed, they gave her an enema, and a third nurse arrived to give her an injection. Finally, after all the fuss, when the doctor arrived and examined Mrs D'Silva's stomach, she looked irritated and said, 'Why have you come here so early? Go home and rest.'

The nurses laughed their hearts out. A mortified Mrs D'Silva put on her clothes and came out to meet her husband, who was waiting for her.

Mr and Mrs D'Silva felt thwarted. Mr D'Silva had taken the day off, so they decided to catch a matinee at the Regal Cinema. The events of the day took Mrs D'Silva by surprise. Her first baby had arrived bang on time. She could not understand why her estimate was so off the mark this time. Six days after Mrs D'Silva returned from the hospital, I was sitting out on our balcony, at around seven o'clock in the evening, when her servant arrived with a ten-rupee note in his hand and said, 'Memsahib has asked for change. She is going to the hospital.'

I rushed to get the change and ran to Mrs D'Silva's flat. Both husband and wife were ready. Mr D'Silva and I supported Mrs D'Silva and helped her down the stairs and into the taxi. 'Stay safe,' I said before I went back upstairs and began to mark time.

That night, I sat up until midnight with my ears trained on the stairs, but there was no sign of the D'Silvas. Burnt out, I fell asleep. When I woke up the following morning, the dhobi had arrived, and I got busy accounting for the laundry and forgot about Mrs D'Silva. As the dhobi took our bundle of clothes and stepped out, he left the door ajar. I saw and heard him knock on Mrs D'Silva's door. When it opened, who did I see but Mrs D'Silva with her potbelly. I let out a half scream, 'M-r-s D'Sil-va! You're back again!'

When I walked across to her flat, she took me to a room. Notwithstanding her dark complexion, her face was a deep crimson. Haltingly, she said to me, 'I understand nothing. The pain exactly like the before, and the nurses them say, "Go home." Just now a long time. What on earth happening!' Mrs D'Silva's could not contain her tears. It seemed this time the nurses had told her off rather harshly. A combination of shock, shame, and bewilderment had reduced poor Mrs D'Silva to a sorry state. I felt a wave of sympathy for her, and we chatted for what seemed like an age; I reassured her that there was no reason for her to feel ashamed. 'False alarms happen; they are not unusual. It's the nurses' job to deliver babies. People go to them under all sorts of circumstances for comfort and reassurance. They had no right to poke fun at you. And when the fees, etc., have been paid in advance, there was no need for such insensitive talk.'

Mrs D'Silva's anxiety did not subside. The real issue was that by now, her husband had taken two days off work. From his boss to the peon, everyone knew that a baby was on the way; Mr D'Silva felt he could not show his face to anyone. Similarly, the entire neighbourhood knew that Mrs D'Silva had made two visits to the hospital and returned without delivering her baby.

Several women visited her, and for each visitor, she had to fabricate a new story about why the baby had not arrived. As a devout Christian, it caused her great spiritual pain to tell a lie, but what else could she have done? On the seventh day, with my thoughts on Mrs D'Silva, I ate my lunch and lay down for a siesta. I was about to fall asleep when I heard a baby cry. What on earth was that? I ran and opened my front door and saw Mrs D'Silva's servant rushing out of her flat. He looked anxious, 'Memsahib has...Memsahib...baby.'

I rushed in and saw Mrs D'Silva lying on her bed, semi-conscious. Terrified that she'd have to face further indignities, the hapless woman had delivered her baby at home—all on her own.

## 24

## Sickness

'It is peculiar, but whenever a girl writes to me, she addresses me as "bhai" or brother before she continues, in rather curious and charged emotional prose, to inform me that she is seriously unwell. The account of her ill health is followed by endless praise of my writing. I cannot understand why all women who write to me suffer from some sickness, perhaps because they know that I, too, do not keep good health. Perhaps they want my sympathy. I cannot think of any other reason. Invariably, I do not respond to such letters, but occasionally I do. After all, it is part of my duty as a human being to respond to a heartfelt note.

'A few days ago, I received a longish letter, yet again from a woman whose name I do not wish to disclose. She wrote to say that she admired my writing and informed me that she had been unwell for some time, adding that her husband also suffered from some ailment. She thought he was the cause of her sickness. I did not respond to this letter and received another in which she chastised me for my silence. Compelled, I put pen to paper and expressed my sympathy for her. She wrote back to say that her health had deteriorated, and she was about to die. I composed a very sympathetic response, in which I told her, "...to give up on life means spiritual death. Build your resolve; your sickness will disappear without a trace. Not that long ago, I too was at death's door—doctors had given up, but I did not contemplate death. As a result, my doctors released me from the hospital." I added, "Belief in yourself will make the impossible possible. Convince yourself that you are healthy."

'Her five-page response made it amply clear that my sermon had not affected her in the least. She informed me that she had arrived at a logical philosophical conclusion that God did not wish her to live in this world for long. She also asked me to send her my latest books, which I did. I received an acknowledgement with thanks and another burst of praise, which infuriated me. In my opinion, the books I had sent had little merit since I had put them together merely to earn a living. I wrote back, "...your praise is unmerited; these books are drivel; read my earlier work, where you will discover the real me."

'In the letter, I discussed my views on the art of short-story writing at some length and later asked myself why I did not write such a long and considered exposition for a literary journal. Yet, now that it was written, I had to post the epistle. Her response arrived three days later, and in it, she addressed me as, "Dear Bhaijan." She managed to find my earlier work and was reading it, but her illness was getting worse by the day. She asked if she should consult a hakim because she had lost faith in her doctors. I wrote another long sermon and advised her to consult either. Importantly, I reminded her, "Remember, you are your own best messiah. If you confront your anxiety, you will recover in no time."

'She wrote back to me after a month to say that she had taken my advice but did not see the desired outcome. She informed me that she was on her way from Hyderabad to meet me and would be in Bombay within three days, hoping to spend some time at my place. Astounded and worried, I wondered what I would do if the lady were to turn up. An inveterate loner, I lived in a two-room flat. I gave the matter some thought and concluded the lady could spend a few days in one of the rooms, and I could fix a consultation for her with a very respected hakim who was very considerate towards me.

'For the next six days, I remained on edge. If the newspaper boy knocked on the door, I jumped, thinking the lady had arrived. When the houseboy in the kitchen scrubbed dirty utensils with ash, I mistook it for the sound of her sandals. By the seventh day, convinced that there was no chance of her turning up, I was sitting and reading accounts of Hindu–Muslim riots in the *Hindustan Times* when there was a loud knock on the door. I thought it must be the milkman and hollered for the servant, "Rahim, check who's there."

'Rahim, who was making tea, left the kettle to boil over on the stove and stepped out to open the door. He returned shortly and said, "A woman is here."

'Stunned, I asked, "A woman?"

'"Yes. A woman. She is standing outside and wants to see you."

'I realized this must be the same sick woman who had been writing to me and said to Rahim, "Make her comfortable in the living room; tell her Sahib will be with you shortly."

'"Very well," said Rahim and went off.

'I put the newspaper aside and went to the bathroom. I gave some thought to the woman and imagined her suffering from tuberculosis or some form of paralysis. I asked myself why she had come to see me and recalled she had to consult a doctor. I took my time to bathe and wondered if she was good looking. Several faces flashed before my eyes, and I concluded she was physically disabled and in need of financial assistance. As it happened, it was the third of the month; I had disbursed several sundry bills from my salary and had a balance of three hundred rupees in my pocket. Not stretched on the financial front, if the woman needed help, I would give her a hundred rupees. It crossed my mind that if she had some vile contagious disease, I should get her admitted to a hospital. I had several doctor friends at J. J. Hospital, who would never refuse if I were to ask them to help an impoverished woman.

'I am not comfortable in the company of women, to the extent that I had agreed to a nikah about a year and a half ago but had not made any arrangements to bring my bride home. I had never been close to a woman and had no idea how to behave with my wife. I poured jug after jug of water on my body to prepare myself to meet this unknown woman, waiting for me in the living room of my tiny flat. I took my time to get dressed; I oiled and combed my hair and lay down on my bed to think. More time elapsed before Rahim came in and said, "The woman wants to know how long you will be."

'I said, "Tell her he says he'll be with you in five minutes; he's getting dressed."

'"Very well," said Rahim and left.

'After our prolonged correspondence, it was pointless to ponder further over this matter. Besides, the woman had travelled a long distance, and human decency demanded that I meet her and look after her.

'I got up from my bed, put on my slippers, and entered the living room. The woman was in a burqah. I greeted her and sat down in a corner. All I could figure out through the black niqab was her sharp nose. I felt uncomfortable but taxed my mind to start a conversation, "I'm sorry you had to wait so long. It's my habit..."

'The woman interrupted me, "It doesn't matter. There is no need to stand on ceremony. I am accustomed to waiting."

'I was not sure how to respond, and the first thing that came to my mind was a question, "Have you been waiting for someone?"

'She lifted her niqab ever so slightly to wipe away her tears with a tiny hanky and said, "I beg your pardon?"

'A glimpse of her chin, as lovely as the tip of a Banarsi mango, left me mesmerized and speechless.

'Eventually, she broke the silence, "You asked me if I was waiting for someone. Do you want to know?"

'"Yes...do tell me, but let it not smack of despair."

'The woman threw back her niqab; I felt the moon had emerged from behind a dark cloud. She lowered her eyes and said, "Do you know who I am?"

'"No," I said.

'"I am your wife.... Remember, you had a nikah a year and a half ago? I have been writing to you to tell you that I am sick, but if you keep me waiting in this manner, I know I will die."

'The following day, I brought her home with great fanfare, and now I am most content.'

A friend who is a short-story writer and a poet shared this story with me, and I wrote it down in my way.

## Nawab Salimullah Khan

Nawab Salimullah Khan was a man of great discernment and refinement. Counted amongst the wealthy in his town, he was neither decadent nor a celebrant of luxury. Nawab Sahib, who was around fifty-five years old, led a quiet, sober life. He met a few select people hosted regular parties, and served alcohol, but with restraint. In fact, in all matters, he favoured moderation. He was forty when his wife died of a heart attack. Although grief-stricken, he endured this sorrow as the will of the Almighty. They had no offspring, and now Nawab Sahib was alone in a grand house. Four retainers attended to his comfort and looked after his guests. Fifteen years after his wife's death, his heart was weary. He summoned his favoured munshi, Muazzam Ali, and said, 'Find an agent who can sell my entire estate for a good price.'

Muazzam Ali was taken aback and said, 'Nawab Sahib, your honour, I beg your pardon, what does your worship lack that you wish to sell your entire estate? You don't carry the burden of debt.'

Nawab Sahib responded with great solemnity, 'Muazzam Ali, my heart feels burdened in this milieu—each moment seems like a year. I want to go away from here.'

'Where would your worship go?'

'I think I shall go to Bombay; I recall I stopped there on my return from England and liked the city. I have decided to live there; organize the sale of my estate.'

It took a month to sell the estate. Nawab Salimullah Khan received ten lakh fifty thousand rupees from the proceeds and had about two-and-a-quarter lakhs in his bank. He deposited the sale receipts in his account, gave generous gifts to his retainers, bid them farewell, and left for Bombay with his personal effects.

In Bombay, Nawab Sahib stayed at the Taj Mahal Hotel. He was accustomed to spacious surroundings, and within a few days, he purchased a house in Bandra, had it refurbished and furnished suitably to his taste. Within a month or two, Nawab Salimullah Khan acquired a large social circle. He became a member of the Radio Club, where he and other members of Bombay high society spent many leisurely hours. Every evening, Nawab Salimullah Khan played bridge and returned home in his new car. Nawab Sahib did not like to eat out but preferred a fare prepared at home by his excellent chef to suit his palate. At least once a week, he invited friends to dine.

One day, Nawab Sahib reflected on the needs of his household and decided to hire a housekeeper. He thought women had more grace than men in such matters; they brought better taste and added a flair to the art of housekeeping. He placed an advertisement for 'A Good Housekeeper' in the *Times of India* and a few other publications. Several women responded. He interviewed a few, but none came up to his expectations. Some were loud and tasteless, others batted their eyes and wriggled their hips. One by one, Nawab Sahib sent off all the women, informing them most graciously, 'I shall let you know very soon. For the moment, I have not arrived at a decision.'

One morning, Nawab Sahib was seated in his favoured armchair; he had lit his Havana cigar and was picking up a newspaper to peruse it for the second time. Just then an attendant came to inform him that a woman had arrived in response to the job advertisement. Nawab Sahib put the newspaper down on a side table and said, 'Send her in.'

The woman was of medium height with a firm body and a dark complexion. From her features, it seemed she was from Goa. She greeted Nawab Sahib in Urdu, speaking in a well-modulated voice as he stood up and offered her a chair. Then, much like the English, he made a few comments about the weather before asking her, 'Have you worked anywhere else before this?'

The woman responded in chaste Urdu, 'Yes, in two or three very respectable households. Here are their references.' She opened her handbag and handed Nawab Sahib a few papers, 'Please, do look at them.'

Nawab Sahib cast an obligatory eye at the papers and returned them. He turned to the woman and asked, 'Your name?'

'My name is Mrs Lovejoy.'

'Lovejoy is your...?'

'My husband.'

Nawab Sahib drew in a deep puff of his cigar and asked, 'What does he do?'

'He was a second lieutenant in the army, but he died in the war three years ago, which is my reason for taking on this employment.'

Nawab Sahib scrutinized Mrs Lovejoy through the cigar smoke for his final assessment and asked, 'When can you start?'

'I could start right away, but I have to bring my luggage. I can report tomorrow morning.'

'Perfect. For the time being, you will get a hundred rupees a month. If your work is good, it will increase.'

Mrs Lovejoy thanked Nawab Sahib using the most appropriate words. Then, she bid him goodbye and departed. Nawab Sahib began to wonder what he would do if his choice were to prove wrong. Ah well, after a month's probation, he could give her the second month's pay and get rid of her.

Who knows what time Mrs Lovejoy arrived the following morning, but when Nawab Sahib stirred, there was a gentle knock on his door. He thought it must be his bearer with his bed tea and called out, 'Come in, the door is not locked.'

The door opened, and Mrs Lovejoy entered. She wished him good morning and continued, 'The bearer will bring your tea. I have run the hot water for your bath. Once you have done with your tea and bath, I'll lay out your clothes. Your wardrobe is unlocked, isn't it?'

Nawab Sahib responded, 'Yes, it's unlocked.'

Mrs Lovejoy inspected Nawab Sahib's wardrobe and asked, 'Perhaps, you might want to wear the gabardine suit today....'

Nawab Sahib thought for a moment and said, 'Indeed, I was thinking of wearing it.'

The bearer brought tea, which Nawab Sahib drank, and then he proceeded to the bathroom where the white tiles shone like mirrors—never had they sparkled so. Nawab Sahib was most pleased. No doubt Mrs Lovejoy had a hand in this transformation. After his bath, when he returned to his dressing room, he saw his clothes neatly laid out, with the tie he usually chose with his gabardine suit. When he finished dressing, Mrs Lovejoy arrived and said, 'Your breakfast awaits you.'

Mrs Lovejoy accompanied Nawab Sahib to the dining room. She had organized a breakfast of devilled kidneys, cheese, perfectly crisp toast, cream, eggs, and a glass of milk.

In next to no time, Mrs Lovejoy acquired a presence in Nawab Sahib's house. She won over his friends; she knew what they liked—who preferred a particular cut of the chicken and who loved a specific wine. When Nawab Sahib hosted a dinner party, she laid the table and waited on the guests. Her standards were exacting. Nonetheless, she treated the staff with great civility. She was quick but did not scurry about like a squirrel. Each task was accomplished with great finesse and within the appointed time. Whenever a friend praised her, Nawab Sahib responded with great pride, 'The choice was mine; I interviewed a hundred women but selected her.'

Members of the household staff were most pleased with Mrs Lovejoy because she reduced their workload. On Sundays, however, they had to bear the full burden of responsibility because Mrs Lovejoy took a break. She attended mass, went out to the cinema with a group of friends, and stayed the night at the house of an old acquaintance. She reported back on duty the following morning. Nawab Sahib felt her absence, but he was a man of principles and did not want any member of his household to be a slave on duty twenty-four hours a day. If Mrs Lovejoy took off one day in the week, it was her right.

Day after day, Mrs Lovejoy created a place for herself in Nawab Sahib's and his friends' hearts. Everyone valued her. One afternoon, a friend said to Nawab Sahib, 'I have a request.'

'Do tell me.'

'If you release Mrs Lovejoy for me, I'll remain indebted to you for the rest of my days. I need her quite urgently.'

Nawab Sahib drew on his cigar as he shook his head vigorously and said, 'No, sir, this is out of the question. Where will I find such a housekeeper?'

His friend tried to lay it on, 'Nawab Sahib, your eye will find one even better. Where do we have such discernment?'

Nawab Sahib drew another puff from his cigar and said, 'No, sir, I cannot hand over Mrs Lovejoy to anybody.'

That night when Mrs Lovejoy brought Nawab Sahib his freshly ironed pyjamas, he studied her carefully. He did not wish to go to bed early, and said, 'Mrs Lovejoy, tonight I shall sleep late. I feel like going to a late-night movie. In your opinion, what are the good movies showing in town these days?'

Mrs Lovejoy mulled over the question, 'I have heard great praise for *Mutiny on the Bounty*. It's been running to packed houses at the Metro for the past six weeks.'

Nawab Sahib wished to thank her and asked, 'Will you join me?'

'It is kind of you. If you take me, I shall join you.'

Nawab Sahib stood up and examined himself in the full-length mirror before he turned to Mrs Lovejoy, 'Let's go then...we shall dine out tonight.'

Mrs Lovejoy replied, 'With your permission, I think I should change. It's not appropriate to accompany you in these clothes. It will take me, at the most, ten minutes. I'll be back.'

A stylishly turned-out Mrs Lovejoy returned in no time. Nawab Sahib said to her, 'Let's go.'

Mrs Lovejoy walked ahead of him, but when they arrived at the front door, she stopped. Nawab Sahib understood the implication—she was no longer his employee. He was a courteous man, so he stepped forward in the English way, and as a mark of respect opened the door for Mrs Lovejoy. She stepped out, and Nawab Sahib followed her. His car was parked in the porch; the chauffeur was on duty but Nawab Sahib discharged him. He made Mrs Lovejoy sit in the passenger seat in front, settled himself in the driver's seat, and started the car. When they drove past Marine Drive, Nawab Sahib turned to Mrs Lovejoy, sitting quietly beside him, and asked, 'Where would you like to dine?'

'I think the restaurant above Eros Cinema should be good. You will find things of your choice on the menu.'

Nawab Sahib said, 'Perfect...but why don't we relax—dine upstairs and then watch a film at Eros?'

Mrs Lovejoy thought for a while and said, 'Yes...there is a good film on at Eros, *The Good Earth*. Some of my friends have seen it and were full of praise for it. I hear Paul Muni's acting is brilliant.'

Nawab Sahib and Mrs Lovejoy arrived at Eros and took the lift to the top floor. They could hear the strains of Western music from the ballroom. Nawab Sahib looked at the menu and ordered the food, which was served to them after he drank two pegs of whisky and she a glass of sherry. Both were in a state of tender intoxication, and they finished dinner, couples appeared on the dance floor. Nawab Sahib recalled his time in England when his young heart was carefree. He had taken lessons in ballroom dancing and this recollection stirred in him a wish to dance. He turned to Mrs Lovejoy and said, 'Will you give me the pleasure?'

Mrs Lovejoy said, 'I wouldn't mind.'

They danced for a long time. Nawab Sahib was charmed by Mrs Lovejoy's nimble grace.

After they danced, they went down to see the film, and after the show, they headed home along Marine Drive. The necklace of lights twinkling along the seaside and a gentle, mildly chilly breeze enhanced the enchantment of the night. When they arrived home, Nawab Sahib opened the door for Mrs Lovejoy and inadvertently slipped his arm around her waist. Mrs Lovejoy did not object. Next morning, Nawab Sahib woke up unusually early, at six o'clock. He sat up and looked at his bed as though he had lost something and was searching for it.

There was a chill in the air, but suddenly, beads of moisture broke out on Nawab Sahib's forehead. The pillow next to his had a dip left by Mrs Lovejoy's head. A contrite Nawab Sahib asked himself why he had stooped so low when everyone held him in such high esteem. Troubled by these thoughts, he was about to sink to the depths of shame when Mrs Lovejoy entered and said, 'I have prepared hot water for your bath. The bearer will bring your bed tea. After you finish your tea and bath, I shall lay out your clothes.' Nawab Sahib felt a lightness in his breath; he skipped his tea but went to the bathroom, where a hot bath awaited him.

## Miss Faria

It was merely a month after his wedding, and Suhail was worried. Anxious by day, he lay awake at night. When he discovered that the baby he had never thought about had made its presence felt, he felt unsteady on his feet. Suhail had not thought it likely that any such event would occur for another three years. Besides, his wife had been in no hurry to become a mother; she was still a child—how else would you refer to a girl of fourteen or fifteen? Not that long ago, Ayesha was playing with her dolls. It was not more than five months ago that Suhail had spotted her in their alley, her face flushed as she quarrelled with a dishonest street vendor who had given her less than her money's worth of channas.

Now, Suhail imagined Ayesha on a train, on her way to see her family, like so many women he had seen, breastfeeding an infant who was producing the same suckling sounds, like all other babies, and wailing. At one point, he heard himself ticking Ayesha off, 'The baby is crying his heart out, and instead of pacifying him, you're looking out of the window.' Suhail's throat felt parched as he continued with his internal monologue. 'A baby at my age will be my ruin. It will spell the end of my poetry. She will become a mother and me, a father. What will remain of our marriage? We've barely lived together for a month as man and wife. I can't understand why babies are a must in a marriage. I'm not saying they are a terrible idea, but they should arrive as and when desired, not like uninvited guests. The time immediately after our marriage was packed with social commitments; we've just started to make sense of our lives together and to enjoy married life. Now, this imp will descend upon us, and who knows how many others will follow?'

Suhail panicked, terrified he was losing his equilibrium. 'It's bad enough for me to become a father, but Ayesha can't become a mother at her age. What will happen to her sparkle, which distracts me even today? Will her innocence disappear with motherhood? I can see her playing with household objects and singing nonsensical lullabies in her tuneless voice, trying to soothe the tiny puppy wailing in her arms. By God, I'll go mad.' The catastrophic news of Ayesha's pregnancy drove Suhail to the edge of madness. For three or four days, nobody noticed his condition, but as his face grew more pallid, his mother asked, 'Suhail, what's the matter? You look very worried these days.'

Suhail said, 'Nothing, Ammijan, it's the weather.'

The weather was perfect, the breezes balmy and light. On their regular walks to Victoria Gardens, Ayesha and Suhail revelled in the glory of flowers of brilliant hues surrounded by luxuriant trees of different shades of green. And here was Suhail, holding the weather responsible for his anxiety. His mother said, 'Suhail, you're hiding something from me.... Tell me the truth...what's happened...has Ayesha said or done something wrong?'

He wanted to cry out, 'Something wrong! Ammijan, she's ruined my life. She has decided to become a mother without consulting me!' He refrained, knowing his mother would disapprove of his sentiments. Instead, he said, 'No, Ammijan, Ayesha has not said or done anything. She's a lovely girl and loves you, dearly—and Ammi, I'm pleased with life.'

Reassured, his mother declared in a benedictory tone, 'May Allah keep you happy, always.' She continued, 'It's true, Ayesha is a lovely girl. I think of her as my daughter. Now tell me, when will my heart's desire be fulfilled?'

Suhail pretended not to understand her, 'I don't understand, Ammijan.'

'You understand everything. I want to know when will I hold your little boy in my lap. Suhail, Allah fulfilled my heart's desire to see you as a bridegroom. Now, I pray to Him—I want to see your family grow.'

Suhail put his hand on his mother's shoulder and said with a sheepish laugh, 'Ammijan, you never tire of saying this; I don't want children for the next two years.'

'For two years...you don't want children? I mean, you don't want a baby girl or a baby boy? Vah! Is this possible? To give or not to give a child is in His hands, and He will give. Most certainly! By Allah's command, I will hold my grandson in my arms, and I will play with him—tomorrow!'

Suhail did not respond. What could he say? If he told his mother that Ayesha was pregnant, it would put an end to his taking any steps to prevent the baby's arrival.

When Ayesha first mentioned that she was late by a fortnight, he thought the whole business a mistake. He consulted several married friends, who told him that it was not unusual for women to make mistakes in their calculations. He latched on to this idea, and he believed the cloud would lift even after the matter was confirmed. Another fortnight passed, but he could think of no way out of the darkness. Suhail's anxiety ratcheted. When he looked at Ayesha, she reminded him of a magician's bag. 'Today, she is standing before me looking innocent and gorgeous, but in a few months, her stomach will become a sack; her hands and feet will swell up, she will walk around sniffing strange odours, she will vomit. God knows what she will turn into.'

Suhail hid his anxiety from his mother. He did not even tell his sister, but obviously, his wife was aware of his fears. One night, she asked him, 'You've been looking very worried for the past few days…what's the matter?'

It was ridiculous, but Ayesha had no idea what the changes in her body signified. When she consulted Suhail, he sidestepped her questions by saying that the female body undergoes many changes after marriage.

Ultimately, he had to tell her the truth. 'Ayesha, I'm worried because you are about to become a mother.'

Ayesha blushed, 'You say such strange things.'

'I say strange things! To tell you the truth, it might be good for you, but I swear upon God, the news is driving me nuts.'

When Ayesha saw Suhail's worried expression, she asked, 'Then… truly?'

'Yes, yes…truly, you are about to become a mother. I swear upon God that when I think that you will become something else in a few months, my brain begins to spin. I don't want you to produce a child so quickly. Now for God's sake, do something about it.'

Ayesha withdrew into herself. She felt nothing but a need to conceal herself. She knew that a baby was likely after marriage, but had no idea it would be such a source of anxiety for Suhail. He noticed her silence and said, 'Now, what are you thinking? Do something so we can get rid of this nuisance of a baby.'

Ayesha was thinking about her baby's layette, but Suhail's comment jolted her. She asked, 'What did you say?'

'I'm saying, make some arrangements, so the baby is not born.'

'Tell me, what should I do?'

'If I knew, would I ask you? You're a woman. You meet women all the time. When we got married, your married friends must have given you endless advice. There must be some way out of this.'

Ayesha rummaged through her memory bank but could not recollect a remedy.

'Nobody has ever said anything about this to me. What I want to know is, why didn't you say anything to me for so many days? Whenever I said something to you about my condition, you changed the subject.'

'I did not want to worry you, plus I thought, what if I am mistaken? Now that it is confirmed, I must tell you. Ayesha, do something about this. I swear upon God, it will be a disaster. A person gets married to have a few years of fun, not to have a baby right away. I must consult a doctor.'

Ayesha began to share Suhail's anxiety, 'Yes, we must consult a doctor. I don't want to have a child so soon.'

Suhail's thoughts darted in all directions. He knew a Polish doctor who would have obliged him. Suhail had procured whisky from him just a few months earlier when there was prohibition but the authorities had sniffed out his activities, and the doctor was in the lock-up in Deolali. Apart from the Polish doctor, Suhail knew a Jewish doctor, who had treated his chest pain. He could have consulted him, but this doctor looked so venerable that Suhail did not have the nerve to seek his advice on such matters. There were thousands of doctors in Bombay, but it was impossible to discuss such issues without a proper introduction. Suhail taxed his memory, and finally, an image popped up of Miss Faria, a fat bulky Christian woman in rather odd clothes.

Miss Faria practised in Nagpara, where several Jewish, Christian, and Parsi girls lived and did all the things that made a girl a girl.

They dressed in bright tight-fitting clothes with their skirts just below their knees to show off their bare calves. Sporting high-heeled shoes, they styled their short hair with waves in the latest fashion, applied layers of make-up, wore lipstick, and dabbed rouge on their cheeks. They plucked and shaped their eyebrows into sharp arches, and they attracted Suhail's attention.

When Suhail first moved to Bombay, he was mesmerized by these colourful butterflies flitting around Nagpara, and he longed to capture at least one. His desire remained unfulfilled, and he remained hopelessly miserable until he met Miss Faria. Unlike the butterflies he desired, Miss Faria wore a long ankle-length robe and outmoded shoes with long thick socks that hid her calves. She did not curl her short hair, and this lack of attention made it appear brittle and lifeless. She had a very dark complexion, but at times her skin managed to look dusky.

∽

Ayesha's response to worries was sleep, and for the next few nights, she fell asleep talking to Suhail and thinking about the baby. On the other hand, Suhail stayed awake, thinking about the first time he met Miss Faria precisely a year ago—in this very room, before he married Ayesha and the new bed arrived with her dowry. Suhail's sister was about to have a baby; the family wanted to know when she would go into labour, and they had summoned Miss Faria. She had arrived wearing a black lace cap with three or four colourful pompoms that looked like plums resting on a bit of sludge on her head. Her limp, shabbily tailored dress of good quality floral georgette hung down to her ankles. The aesthete in Suhail was hurt, and he had thought, 'What an awkward woman...what hideous clothes...and with her height—very soon she's likely to transform into a buffalo.'

After Miss Faria finished examining his sister, she had asked Suhail in English, 'Where is the bathroom? I want to wash my hands.'

Suhail had escorted her to the bathroom and got an opportunity to have a closer look at Miss Faria. He had wanted to like her and found several feminine qualities in her. 'She's not bad. Her eyes are beautiful—and so what if she doesn't wear make-up? She's just fine... what lovely hands.'

Miss Faria had been exhausted after a full day's work, and the tiny drops of sweat trembling on the light down on her upper lip appealed to Suhail, who by now had begun to fancy her. He had wanted to do something that would cover her entire body in similar tiny drops of sweat. After she washed and dried her hands, Miss Faria had turned to Suhail's mother and said, 'Please send him with me. I'll prepare the medicine and send it back with instructions on how to use it.'

On their way to Nagpara where Miss Faria lived, Suhail did not say very much in the victoria. First, he had asked a few basic questions about how much quinine a person suffering from malaria should take. Then he had quizzed her about dental hygiene. Soon, they had reached a building where a board hung by a door with 'Miss Faria MBBS' emblazoned on it. Miss Faria's clinic was on the first floor in a room split into two sections. One part had her desk, and the other was the dispensary where, apart from two cupboards for medicines, there was a small takht that looked like an improvised table for examining patients. Miss Faria had taken off her cap and hung it on a nail hammered into the wall, and Suhail had sat down on a bench near her desk. Miss Faria then called out in a blend of a half-English and half-Hindustani accent, 'Boay! Come here....'

An emaciated man had emerged from the other section of the room, and saying, 'Yes, Memsaab,' he left the room.

Memsaab had not uttered a word but went to dispense the medicine. In the meantime, Suhail had been thinking of ways to befriend Miss Faria. She returned with the medicines and sat down on her chair, glued a label on the bottle, and had begun to number some sachets, telling him, 'Here are the medicines. Give her one sachet as soon as you get home and one dose of the mixture after half an hour. Then, follow the same pattern every three hours.'

Suhail had put the sachets in his pocket, and as he picked up the bottle, he had looked at Miss Faria in a rather odd manner. She had been nonplussed, 'You haven't forgotten, have you?'

Suhail had looked at her in the same odd manner and said, 'No. I haven't forgotten. I remember everything.'

Miss Faria had been at a loss for words and muttered, 'Then... then...fine.'

Suhail drew courage and fixed his gaze on her. As Miss Faria busied herself to arrange some papers, he had asked, 'The payment for these...?' and had taken out his wallet. 'How much?' he had asked as he proffered her a five-rupee note.

Miss Faria had taken the five rupees and opened the drawer of her desk to keep it inside. Swiftly, she had taken out some change and gave Suhail an account. As she handed the balance to him, Suhail had grabbed her hand, 'Your hand is so beautiful.' He had placed his other hand on his heart and continued like a greenhorn, 'I am in love with you.'

At first, Miss Faria was nonplussed, but she pulled herself together and had said, 'What on earth do you mean?'

Suhail had noticed a hint of rejection in her tone and had been surprised because he had heard that Anglo-Indian and Christian girls are easy to catch. He rushed to pick up the bottle and had said, 'I beg your pardon. I should not have spoken to you in this foolish manner. I'm not sure what nonsense just came out of my mouth. Please forgive me.'

Miss Faria had stood up; her temper somewhat cooled by his apology, 'I was livid. Now when I look at you, you seem so raw—raw to the point of stupidity. Go. And never do something like this again.'

Miss Faria had transformed into a schoolteacher, and a mortified Suhail had bumbled, 'Please, have you forgiven me?'

The smile Suhail had wanted to see on Miss Faria's lips did not appear. 'Leave. I have told you not to behave in this manner ever again. In the future, get your medicine from somewhere else. And you have not paid my fare.'

'How much is it?' Suhail had managed to ask.

'Twelve annas.'

Suhail had put twelve annas on the table, but when he reached the bazaar, he recalled paying the victoria driver twelve annas. An extra twelve annas seemed like a small price to pay for his escape from further humiliation. Suhail had experienced rejection in the past; in Amritsar, several girls had put him in his place with far more punishing words, but, but this episode continued to trouble him for several hours. The following day when he had gone to Miss Faria's clinic to collect the prescription, she spoke to him as she did to all her clients and the residue of his embarrassment disappeared. For ten to twelve days afterwards, Suhail visited Miss Faria's clinic every day, and nothing transpired to make him relive that moment of utter humiliation. His sister recovered, and Miss Faria disappeared from his world.

After a little over a year, Suhail found himself thinking of Miss Faria, and he decided to consult her. He thought, 'This woman is greedy, and she will help us in this matter. Besides, the two matters are not related, and if she agrees to do my work, I'll pay her whatever she demands.'

The following evening, he went to Miss Faria's clinic. When she saw Suhail, she remarked in a business-like manner, 'It's been a long time.'

Suhail had changed after his marriage. He sat down on the bench, confident and relaxed, and said, 'Nobody's been sick, so we didn't need to trouble you.'

Miss Faria smiled, 'What brings you here?'

'I have come for some advice about my wife.'

Miss Faria showed some interest and asked, 'You got married?'

'Yes...I'm married.'

'When?'

'A month ago.'

'Just a month?'

Miss Faria turned around on her chair, 'What's your wife like?'

'Lovely,' said Suhail, much as a matter of form.

'I mean, is she beautiful? She must be beautiful. I mean, girls from Punjab are beautiful.'

Suhail looked at Miss Faria, who had powdered her face. He found her lifeless complexion and brittle hair most unattractive. In her shabby dress, she looked like a charwoman in comparison with Ayesha. Suhail laughed to himself and thought now was the time to even the score. He said, 'My wife is stunning. Wait till you see her!'

I'm not sure if Miss Faria heard Suhail's comment; she was lost deep in her thoughts and said, 'Ah, so this past month you've been having a great time.'

To needle her further, Suhail said, 'It's a chance of a lifetime, why not take full advantage of it?'

'Yes, of course, of course, you should take advantage, but not too much. You must be taking full advantage.' There was a hint of envy in her voice.

Suhail was beginning to enjoy this conversation. He smiled and said, 'Why shouldn't I take full advantage; after all, this is the time to indulge myself. I have a gorgeous wife and our temperaments are compatible—youth, a pleasant home, and lovely weather are on our side.'

To hide her emotions, a ruffled Miss Faria asked, 'What sort of advice are you seeking?'

'I have come to ask you something about my wife.'

Overcome, Miss Faria said, 'Certainly...certainly, I'll examine her. I'd be delighted. Who would have thought that you'd get married so soon? There must be a huge change in your life.'

Suhail answered, 'No real change...What difference can there be? It's just that I'm delighted with life. Marriage is great.'

Miss Faria gulped, 'Is marriage great?'

'In fact, I'd say you too should get married.'

Miss Faria leaned towards her desk to pick up a Japanese fan with painted butterflies and began to fan herself. 'Tell me something about your wife. I mean, how is your marital life? What are her views...?'

There was a hint of a nervous smile on Miss Faria's lips. Her open mouth parted in a way that reminded Suhail of a big gaping wound, with its stitches coming apart. He looked at her carefully, and his thoughts drifted back to the time when he had found some beauty in this woman, and he had tried to befriend her with callow intentions. Now, the same woman was sitting before him, fanning herself to calm her troubled spirit. One year had left its mark on her dark face and brittle hair. Suhail was lost in his thoughts when Miss Faria said, 'How much you have changed! Now, you are a man.'

Suhail looked at Miss Faria, but now the tiny beads of perspiration on the down above her upper lip did not arouse his passion.

Miss Faria flicked her fan to close it and rested her elbows on the desk, much like a nightingale that returns in spring to sing sad songs. Suhail leaned forward and stretched his hand to pluck out a thin stray reed from her fan. Miss Faria looked at him and held his hand, 'Do you remember once you clasped my hand like this?' There was a tremor in her voice.

Suhail pulled his hand away and said in a dry tone, 'Miss Faria, this is very inappropriate behaviour. Make sure it never happens again.' He took out his wallet, his hands quivering as he put twelve annas on the table, and said, 'This is the return fare for your visit.'

Suhail climbed down the stairs and walked through the bazaar, lost in his thoughts, 'I shall come here to show off our baby to Miss Faria.' He felt utterly pleased with life and went over the episode several times in his mind for sheer pleasure. He recalled the twelve annas he had put on Miss Faria's desk with an unsteady hand and thought, 'Hey, why did I give her twelve annas? What was that fare for?' Unable to find an answer, Suhail smiled.

## Loser

Most people love to win, but he got a kick out of losing. Success was never a problem for him, but he struggled to fail, and it took him time. In the old days, when he held an ordinary post in a bank and decided to build a fortune, his near and dear ones had mocked him, but he gave up his job. He moved to Bombay, where several doors were open to him; he stepped into the film world, where he found riches and fame. He reached such heights that he could extend financial assistance to friends and relatives in no time. He earned and lost at will not lakhs but crores. Once, he earned a lakh in cash for writing lyrics for a film. Although it took a while, he blew it up at the races, in gambling dens, and on pimps and brothels. Finally, he went on to produce a film and made a profit of ten lakhs.

His dilemma was how to wipe out his gains; he invested in several reckless projects and expended a tidy sum on three cars—one flashy new specimen and two old rattletraps. He knew the latter were write-offs and parked them outside his house to rot and rust while he locked the new limousine in a garage on the pretext that petrol was scarce because of the war. He made do with taxis; he hired a cab in the morning, drove around all day and asked the driver to drop him off at some gambling den, where he lost two to three thousand rupees and came out the following morning to find the taxi waiting. He headed home and forgot to pay for the ride. When he stepped out in the evening and found the same cab waiting, he admonished the driver, 'You useless chap, why the hell are you still here? Come with me to the office so I can settle your account.' And at the office, yet again he forgot to close the tab.

In quick succession, he produced two or three films that broke all box-office records and stockpiled mountains of wealth and endless fame. Exasperated, he released one terrible film after another, each a case study on how not to make a movie. In his quest for failure, he brought down several others but immediately pulled himself up and produced a film that generated a gold mine. Of course, he rescued all those he had ruined.

When it came to women, his instincts were similar—to attain and then to lose. He picked up women at social gatherings or courtesans' salons and showered them with jewels. He transported them to the pinnacle of fame. After he had stripped them of everything that constituted their femininity, he gave them every opportunity to seduce several top industrialists and handsome lotharios, whom he looked upon as his rivals. He loved to gamble with his conquests and gave his competitors every opportunity to snatch away his trophies.

Not long ago, in a single sweep, he lost a gorgeous actress and ten lakh rupees on a film. Yet, these two episodes did not gratify his longing to lose. Perhaps he did not comprehend the full measure of his losses. Perhaps this was the reason he headed to Poon Bridge every evening, with some cash in his pocket, determined to lose at least two hundred rupees in the gambling dens on Faras Road.

At times, he lost this sum in two or three hands, but occasionally, he had to wait until dawn. One evening, cruising along Faras Road, his taxi stopped by a lamp post next to a row of shops set behind a wrought-iron railing. He stepped out, settled his horn-rimmed spectacles on the bridge of his nose, adjusted the folds of his dhoti, and made his way up to the gambling den. He spotted a hideous woman sitting on a wooden takht behind the wrought-iron railing to his right. She was preening herself in front of a cracked mirror.

He visited this gambling den every evening. On the eleventh evening, when his taxi stopped by the lamp post, and he went through the ritual of adjusting his horn-rimmed spectacles and the folds of his dhoti, it struck him that he had been seeing this woman for the last ten nights. He walked up to the wrought-iron railing and peered at the aged woman sitting on the takht, preening herself in front of a cracked mirror. Her dark skin glistened; the tiny black circles tattooed into her chin and cheeks had almost merged with her complexion. Tobacco and paan had caused her teeth and gums to rot. He thought, who on earth would want to visit this woman? As he walked towards the repulsive woman, she smiled, set aside the mirror, fixed her eyes on him, and asked in a manner that smacked of her trade, 'Why, Seth, you want to hang out?'

He looked at the woman, amazed that she entertained hope of hooking a punter even at her age, and asked her, 'Bai, how old are you?'

The woman scrunched her face in anger and under her breath swore at him in Marathi. He responded with great sympathy, 'Forgive me, Bai, but I am curious. I see you sitting here all decked up every evening, but does anyone ever approach you?'

The woman did not respond. Again, without letting on that he realized his question was misplaced, he asked her, 'What's your name?'

The woman had lifted a tattered curtain to go inside, but she turned around and said, 'Gungu Bai.'

'Gungu Bai, how much do you earn every day?' There was compassion in his voice.

Gungu Bai walked up to the wrought-iron railing, looked at his face, and said, 'Six-seven rupees...and sometimes...nothing.'

He thought of the two hundred in his pocket. 'Look here, Gungu Bai, you earn six-seven rupees every day; take ten from me.'

'To hang out?'

'No. You can imagine it's for hanging out.' He put his hand in his pocket and pulled out a ten-rupee note. As he handed it to her through the wrought-iron railing, he said, 'Here...take it.'

Gungu Bai took the money but gave him a questioning look.

'Look here, Gungu Bai, I'll give you ten rupees every day—on one condition....'

'Condeesun?'

'Yes. The condition is that after you take the ten rupees, you will eat something, then go inside, and go to sleep. I don't want to see your light on at night.'

He noticed the weird smile that lit up Gungu Bai's face and said, 'Don't laugh. I shall prove true to my word.' As he climbed up the stairs to the gambling den, he thought, 'I have to lose this money, if not two hundred, why not a hundred and ninety.'

Every evening, his taxi stopped by the lamp post, and as he opened the door to step out, he looked to the right through his horn-rimmed spectacles to find Gungu Bai sitting on her wooden takht, behind the wrought-iron railing. He adjusted his horn-rimmed spectacles and the folds of his dhoti, walked up to her, took out a ten-rupee note from his pocket, and handed it to her. She took the money, touched it to her forehead, and greeted him with a salaam. He climbed up the stairs to the gambling den to lose the one-hundred-and-ninety rupees in his pocket. Usually, he did not lose the requisite amount before eleven o'clock; at times, it took till two or three o'clock in the morning. By the time he made his way down the stairs, Gungu Bai had closed her shop.

One evening, he gave her ten rupees and climbed up the stairs, but that night, the cards fell in a manner that one-hundred-and-ninety rupees were wiped out by ten o'clock. As he made his way down to his taxi, he saw Gungu Bai sitting on the wooden takht behind the wrought-iron railing, on the lookout for a punter; her shop was open. She looked nervous when he walked up and asked, 'What's up, Gungu Bai?'

Gungu Bai did not respond.

'What a shame you didn't keep your word. I told you I didn't want to see your light on at night, but here you are, sitting with your shop open.'

His tone was sad. Gungu Bai remained silent, but she looked thoughtful.

As he walked away, he added, 'You're wicked.'

Gungu Bai called out, 'Stop, Seth.'

He stopped.

Gungu Bai chewed every syllable and said, 'I am wicked, but Seth, who's good around here? You give ten rupees to turn off one light. Just look around and see how many lights are on.'

He looked, through the thick lens of his horn-rimmed spectacles, at the naked light bulb glaring at Gungu Bai's head and her grimy face. He hung his head down, and all he could say was, 'No, Gungu Bai, no.' He turned around and walked to the waiting taxi with a heart as empty as his pocket.

## The Urinal

Not far from Congress House and Jinnah Hall, there is a urinal, generally referred to as a mootri in Bombay. All the filth of the local neighbourhood piles up outside this foul-smelling little shed. The stench is so overpowering that those forced to walk past it must cover their noses with their handkerchiefs.

One day, he had no option but to use the urinal. He held his breath, covered his nose with a handkerchief, and entered the fetid hellhole to urinate. He found its floor smeared with rank faeces and the walls covered with sexually explicit graffiti. In front of him, somebody had written: 'Screw the Pakistan of the Sisters of Mussalmans!' These words intensified the putrid stench, and he rushed out.

The government has control over all the activities in Jinnah Hall and Congress House, but the urinal around the corner is free to spew its filth, as mounds of garbage from the local neighbourhood grow higher by the day.

One day, yet again, he had to use the urinal; he covered his nose with his hanky, held his breath, and entered the hellhole. Streaks of runny faeces had dried on the floor. Emissions of semen had multiplied on the walls. Below 'Screw the Pakistan of the Sisters of Mussalmans!' somebody had inscribed these vile words: 'Screw the Akhand Hindustan of the Mothers of Hindus!' The inscriptions added a noxious heat to the stench of the urinal, and he rushed out.

Mahatma Gandhi had been released unconditionally. Jinnah lost in Punjab, and Jinnah Hall and Congress House remained under government control. Around the corner, the urinal remained under the sway of that fetid stench as the mounds of rubbish from the local neighbourhood rose higher.

He had to visit the urinal yet again, for the third time. This time, it was not just to urinate. He covered his nose, held his breath, and entered the house of filth. Revolting creatures swarmed around the floor. Images of shameful parts of the human anatomy covered the walls, leaving no room for graffiti. The words 'Screw the Pakistan of the Sisters of Mussulmans!' and 'Screw the Akhand Hindustan of the Mothers of Hindus!' had faded. Below, someone had written in white chalk: 'Screw the Hindustan of the Mothers of Both!' For a moment, these words blocked out the stench of the urinal. As he walked out from the foul-smelling house of filth, he thought he caught a whiff of an unnamed perfume.

## Siraj

Dhondu was leaning against the tall lamp post by the small garden opposite the Irani hotel, next to the Nagpara police station. He arrived here every evening at a fixed time after sunset and plied his trade until four o'clock in the morning. I do not know his real name, but everyone called him Dhondu, with two hard 'd's' meaning 'the one who finds'. It was an apt name for someone in his line of work. For over a decade, he had dealt with countless girls of every faith, race, and temperament, and matched them with the needs of his clients.

The lamp post by the small garden opposite the Irani hotel, next to the Nagpara police station, was Dhondu's hangout ever since he started his trade. It was symbolic of him—to me, the lamp post was Dhondu. It did not matter what time of day I passed this way, but when my eyes fell on the lamp post splattered with red paan spittle, I thought of Dhondu standing there, chewing his paan with black camphor-coated Mysore supari.

A web of wires spread out from the lamp post's head, making connections far and wide; one entered a building, another a shop, and yet another got lost in a tangle. Since the telephone department had installed a box next to the lamp post, the wires were inspected from time to time. Together with other such lamp posts, it held sway over the entire city. The tall and lanky Dhondu was another such hub, connecting men with their sexual preferences. His clients included not just men from local neighbourhoods but several seths from further afield. His regulars came after long and short intervals whenever they felt the need to fix the taut or limp wires of their sexuality.

Dhondu knew all the girls on his beat; he understood their bodies and their moods. He could match any filly from his stable to suit a client's needs at any time of the day. Siraj was an exception; Dhondu could not reach the depth of her personality. Dhondu had told me several times, 'Saali Siraj, her head is skewed. Manto Sahib, I don't understand the hussy. She blows hot and cold; at times, she's fire, and at times water; one moment, she is laughing, talkative, and suddenly she starts weeping. Saali doesn't get along with anybody. She is so combative, fights with every passenger. Saali, I've said to her several times, "Fix your head or else go back where you belong. You don't own a rag to cover your body and can't put a morsel in your mouth. My darling, all this carrying on won't work...." But she doesn't heed anybody's advice; she's like a misguided sperm....'

When I first saw the very skinny yet gorgeous Siraj, I was irked by her more-prominent-than-necessary eyes, which seemed to fill her fair-complexioned oval face merely to flaunt their size. I wanted to say, 'Hey, why don't you go away for a while? I want to see Siraj.' Petite yet striking, Siraj reminded me of an earthenware pitcher filled beyond capacity with debased wine. I use the term 'debased' because Siraj exuded a bitterness, not unlike a fine wine diluted with water by a trickster who wished to increase its volume. Her luxuriant black hair, her sharp nose, her delicate pursed lips, and fingers that tapered like a draughtsman's pencils added to the aura of feminine beauty that surrounded her.

I figured she was angry with everything around her—with Dhondu, with the lamp post that he leaned against, with her punters, and with her big eyes that filled more than their rightful share of her gorgeous oval face. She also seemed angry with her fingers that tapered like a draughtsman's pencils—perhaps because they could not draw her desired blueprint. Still, a writer of fiction can convey on a grain of sand the power of Sang-e-Aswad, the black stone that wipes out sins.

Here, it is worth recounting what Dhondu told me about Siraj: 'Manto Sahib, yesterday, the saali created chaos again. Perhaps, some good turn came to my rescue. Thanks to your good wishes, all the officers at the Nagpara checkpost are kind to me; otherwise, your Dhondu would have been in the lock-up. What a ruckus she created! All I could do was invoke my father, "Baap re baap!"'

'What happened?' I asked.

'The same as always, what else! I cursed seven generations of my forefathers and asked myself, "Bastard, when you know this hussy so well, why do you finger her? Why do you bring her out? Is she your mother or sister?" My brain has stopped functioning, Manto Sahib!'

We were sitting in the Irani hotel. Dhondu poured his usual mixture of tea and coffee into a saucer and began to slurp it before he continued, 'The fact of the matter is that I have sympathy for the saali.'

'Why?' I asked.

Dhondu pushed his head back and said, 'Don't know. If I knew the answer, wouldn't this saala everyday chaos come to an end?' He put his empty cup face down on the saucer and asked, 'Do you know that she is still a virgin?'

For a second, my head went into a spin, 'Virgin?'

'I swear on your life.'

I turned to him but addressed myself, 'No, Dhondu....'

Dhondu ignored my reservations. 'I will not lie to you, Manto Sahib...full sixteen annas...she's a virgin...we can bet on it.'

All I could do was ask the obvious question, 'How is that possible?'

Dhondu responded like an expert witness, 'Why is it not possible? A girl like Siraj can be in this trade and remain a virgin all her life. Saali doesn't allow anybody to touch her. I don't know her full *history*, but I know she is a Punjaban. She was with a memsahib on Lamington Road, where saali fought with all the passengers. Two to three months passed without a problem because that madam had between ten to twenty other tarts on her books. Eventually, the madam threw saali out with just the three items of clothing on her back. Manto Sahib, how long will someone go on feeding a dead horse? Saali went to another madam on Faras Road, and a couple of months passed by without incident. Still, saali's temperament is so fiery. Here too, she was equally pig-headed. Nobody has the patience to indulge her and cool her down all the time. God be with you, she moved to a hotel in Khetwadi, but here too, she did not give up her antics. Finally, the exasperated manager sent her packing. What can I say Manto Sahib, saali doesn't care for food or drink! Her clothes are infested with lice; she doesn't wash her hair for months on end. She likes to smoke if she can lay her hands on a couple of marijuana cigarettes, or she likes to hang around various hotels and cafés listening to film songs.'

I shall skip the details of how Dhondu's account played on my mind because it is inappropriate for a writer of fiction to do so. But, to keep the conversation going, I asked Dhondu, 'Why don't you send her back if she is not interested in this trade? Take the fare from me.'

Dhondu found my question unpalatable. 'Manto Sahib, it's not about the saala fare. Do you think I can't give it?'

I wanted to needle him, 'Then why don't you send her back?'

Dhondu was silent for a while. He took the cigarette butt tucked behind his ear and lit it. After exhaling the smoke through his nostrils, he said, 'I don't want her to leave.'

I thought, 'One end of the tangled thread is in my hand now,' and asked him, 'Do you love her?'

Dhondu looked appalled, 'What are you saying, Manto Sahib!' He touched both his ears before he pulled them, 'I can swear upon the Holy Qur'an that this unclean thought never crossed my mind.' He stopped before he added, 'It's just that I like her.'

'Why?'

I had asked the obvious question, to which Dhondu gave a spot-on response, '...because she is not like all the others. All the others are worshippers of money, bastards of the first degree, but she is—what can I say—she is unique. I take her out, she agrees to come, and we strike a deal. She stays put in the taxi or victoria. Now Manto Sahib, the saala passenger is out to have fun and games and is spending his earnings, but the moment he gropes or touches her, that's it. The commotion starts. She starts to lash out; if the man is decent, he runs away, but if he is a gangster or is drunk, there's mayhem. It's happened time and again. I have to come to the rescue, return the money, and join my palms to beg forgiveness. I swear upon the Qur'an, Manto Sahib, I swear on your life, Siraj has reduced my traffic by half.'

I do not wish to describe the image of Siraj I had conjured in my mind, but it had little semblance with what Dhondu told me. One day, I decided to meet Siraj without him as an intermediary. From several conversations with Dhondu, I had figured out where Siraj lived. Before I set out to find her, I changed out of my stylish clothes—but this account is not about me. I arrived at the squalid slum near Byculla Station, where the corporation has built countless tin shacks for the poor amid open sewage drains and mounds of rubbish. It is pointless talking about the grand tall buildings that stand near this abode of filth because they have nothing to do with this story. Besides, is this not the way of the world?

The goat tied outside Siraj's shack spotted me and began to bleat. An old crone stepped out, leaning heavily on her stick. She reminded me of a terrifying old creature from an old tale. I was about to turn back but stopped when I spotted two large eyes behind a jute curtain riddled with holes. I recognized Siraj's gorgeous oval face and as always was furious with her astonishing eyes. When she saw me, she dropped whatever she was doing, came out, and asked me, 'What brings you here?'

'Meeting you,' I answered briefly.

Siraj ignored the old crone and responded with equal brevity, 'Come inside.'

I said, 'No. You come with me.'

The miserable old crone standing by the fetid mounds of waste said, 'That will be ten rupees.'

I took out my wallet, gave ten rupees to the old crone, and said, 'Come, Siraj.'

For a moment, Siraj's large eyes looked away so I could see her face, and once again, I concluded she was lovely. With her lissom figure and perfect features, she was the embodiment of eternal beauty. For a moment, I felt I was in Egypt, in charge of an archaeological dig. Here, I do not wish to go into too much detail, but Siraj accompanied me to a cafe.

She sat opposite me, and I noticed that her clothes were filthy as usual. Not only did her large eyes take over her face, they concealed her whole being. I had paid the price demanded by the old crone but gave Siraj another forty rupees. I did not utter a word that smacked of comfort or love because I wanted her to fight and spar with me like she did with others. Her large eyes remained blank. Although they saw me and took in the entire world around us, she remained silent. I wanted to provoke her and consumed four pegs of whisky to induce lascivious heat in my mind and body. I teased her like any ordinary passenger, but she did not object. I did something profoundly objectionable and unmentionable to provide the necessary fire to cause the gunpowder inside her to explode, but she surprised me and remained calm. She stood up, gathered me into the expanse of her eyes, and said, 'Get me a joint.'

'Will you have a drink?'

'No, I'll smoke some hash.'

I procured a joint for her, which she smoked like a professional addict. Every feature on her face told a tale of emptiness—of a wasteland—or a wrecked empire. My mind went into a spin, but I do not wish to rehearse my problems since they are of little interest to my reader. I had no interest in knowing if Siraj was a virgin or not, but through the tobacco smoke, I caught a glimpse of something in her sad intoxicated eyes that my pen cannot describe. I tried to talk to her, but she showed no interest. I wanted her to spar with me, but here too, she disappointed me, and I took her home.

Dhondu was furious when he heard of our secret meeting. I had crossed the line between friendship and business. He gave me no opportunity to explain, but as he walked away from the lamp post, he said, 'Manto Sahib, I did not expect this of you.'

Oddly, the following evening, I did not see Dhondu at his usual hangout, and he was not there the following morning. A week passed, and I walked past the lamp post every day at dawn and dusk, on the lookout for Dhondu. I went to the squalid shantytown near Byculla Station to search for Siraj, and all I found was the wizened old crone. When I asked her about Siraj, she gave a toothless grin that encapsulated a wellspring of knowledge of the carnal trade that stretched back a thousand years before she announced with an air of finality, 'She's gone. There are others. Should I get?'

I wondered where Dhondu and Siraj had gone, particularly after my secret meeting with her. They did not exactly love each other. Besides, Dhondu was above such matters; he had a wife and children whom he loved dearly. I could not figure out why they were missing. Perhaps, Dhondu had decided that Siraj should return home. He could never make up his mind about this matter; maybe, now he had. About a month after their disappearance, one evening, quite unexpectedly, I spotted Dhondu leaning against the lamp post. I felt as though some power had restored the electric supply after an extended power cut and rejuvenated the lamp post, the telephone box, and the tangled web of wires.

I walked up to Dhondu; he looked at me and smiled. I did not ask him any questions, and we walked in silence to the Irani hotel, where he ordered his usual tea mixed with coffee and a tea for me. I noticed how he settled in his chair and turned on his side; his manner indicated he was about to reveal some great secret, but all he said was, 'So, what's new, Manto Sahib?'

'What can I say, Dhondu...it's passing.'

Dhondu smiled, 'You're right! It is passing—and it will pass. But this saala passing and what has passed is a strange business. Everything in this world is strange.'

'You're right, Dhondu.'

Our tea arrived. I began to sip mine, and Dhondu poured his tea mixed with coffee into a saucer, looked at me, and said, 'Manto Sahib, she told me everything. She said, "That seth, your friend, his nut is loose."'

I laughed, 'Why?'

'She said, "He took me to a hotel and gave me loads of rupees but didn't do any of the things that seths do."'

Embarrassed by this revelation of my ineptitude in such matters, I said, 'The situation was such, Dhondu.'

Now, Dhondu laughed heartily, 'I know...forgive me, I was angry with you that day.'

There was a certain familiarity in the way he spoke, 'But now, that matter is—finito!'

'What matter?'

'This saali Siraj's matter, what else?'

'What happened?' I asked.

Dhondu began to hum a tuneless song and continued, 'That evening, after she went with you, she came to see me and said, "I have forty rupees. Take me to Lahore." I said, "Saali, what the hell has come over you all of a sudden?" She said, "Nothing. But swear by me." And Manto Sahib, you know I cannot deny that saali anything. I like her. So I said, "Let's go."

'We purchased our tickets, boarded the train, and arrived in Lahore, where we stayed in a hotel. She said, "Dhondu, get me a burqah." I bought her a burqah. She put it on, and for several days we roamed every street and alley of the city. I asked myself, "Dhondu, where on earth have you landed yourself? Saali's nut was always loose, but saala, have you lost your mind as well?" Manto Sahib, finally one day, when we were roaming the streets of Lahore in a tonga, she asked the tongawallah to stop. She pointed towards a man and said to me, "Dhondu, bring this man to me. I'm heading back to the hotel."

'My brain had ceased to function, and by the time I got off the tonga, the man had disappeared around the corner, but I managed to tail him. With your good wishes and the grace of God, I understand men. In a short exchange, I figured that he enjoyed fun and games, or "moj shok", as we call it here in Bombay. I told him, "I have special goods from Bombay." He said, "Let's go." I said, "No. First, let's taste the takings." He produced a wad of notes. I thought to myself, well Dhondu, why not ply your trade in Lahore? I failed to understand why the saali Siraj had to select this man in the whole of Lahore. I hailed a tonga, and we arrived at the hotel.

'I asked the stranger to wait in the hotel lobby and went to inform Siraj. She asked me to wait for a while before taking the handsome young man to her room. The moment he set eyes on Siraj, the saala tried to bolt like a horse, but Siraj grabbed hold of him.' Dhondu stopped and finished his tea mixed with coffee in one gulp and lit a biri.

'Why did Siraj grab hold of him?' I asked.

Dhondu's voice acquired a sharper edge as he continued, 'Yes, my dear, she caught hold of the saala and said, "Now, where will you go? Why did you make me leave my home and bring me here? What did you want of me? I loved you. You told me that you loved me too. Do you remember how I left home? I left my mother and my father and ran away with you. We came here from Amritsar and stayed in this hotel, but you ran away and abandoned me that night. Why did you bring me here? Why did you make me run away from home? I was ready for everything. Come into my arms. My love remains the same; Come...." And with these words Manto Sahib, she enveloped him.

'Saala, his eyes filled with tears. He wept and begged her, "Forgive me, I made a mistake. I lost my nerve. I swear I'll never leave you."

He cowered and produced strange sounds. Siraj signalled to me to leave the room.

'In the morning, I found Siraj trying to wake me up, "Let's go, Dhondu."

'"Where?" I asked.

'"Back to Bombay," she said.

'"Where is that saala?" I asked.

'"He's upstairs. Asleep." Siraj smiled and said, "I covered him up with my burqah."'

Dhondu had just turned around to draw the waiter's attention to order another tea mixed with coffee when Siraj walked in. Her gorgeous face was radiant, and her large eyes looked expectantly into the future.

## Majeed's Past

Majeed earned two-and-a-half thousand rupees a month. He had a car, a grand house, and a wife, and he was carrying on with at least fifteen other women. Despite his hectic but comfortable life, time and again, especially after three or four pegs of whisky, Majeed liked to sink into a chair and dwell on the good old days, when life was full of cheer and without any of his current headaches. He loved to drift back fifteen years to a time when he struggled to earn a paltry sixty rupees a month. But, of course, he did not have a house or a car and forget a wife with whom to share his life. Majeed had no idea what it meant to be intimate with a woman.

Two-and-a-half thousand rupees was a substantial sum of money by any standard, yet Majeed had endless worries. He spent most of his time seeking expert advice on creating fake receipts, bribing revenue officers to avoid income tax, resolve problems with sales tax, and launder his earnings to turn black money white. All this wheeling and dealing often ended up in court hearings. On the home front, he had to mollify his wife and indulge his children. Majeed was a workaholic absorbed in his new life, but he was unhappy. He felt fine when he was busy, but the blues set in when he took time out to relax with a couple of pegs of whisky. To dispel his bad mood, Majeed shut out the present and ushered in memories of the good old days, when no uncertainties bedevilled his existence.

Majeed was a self-made man—from his car to his house and its furnishings, he owed everything to himself. Yet, his insecurities multiplied. When he was out with one woman, another telephoned to complain, invariably at an inappropriate moment. Stress about financial matters mingled with the fear of his wife learning of his sexual antics was enough to turn his blood cold. There was comfort in dwelling in the past, when he had earned just two rupees a day, yet his nights were restful. He slept better stretched out on his old wooden bench than he did on his luxurious bed with a spring mattress.

Majeed knew the age of the bench because the man who sold it to him had owned it for ten years, and he, in turn, had purchased it from a shopkeeper who picked it up eleven years earlier from a junk shop. Only God knew the age of the mature bedbugs that infested Majeed's old room. There was no equivalence between the indulgences of Majeed's current life and the good old two-rupee days.

Today, Majeed owned hundreds of different kinds of footwear from all the leading brands. In the old days, all he had was a single pair of canvas shoes. Every night before falling asleep on the wooden bench, Majeed would take off his canvas shoes and clean them with Blanco. Every morning, before he headed for the hammam where he paid one anna for his bath, he would call the errand boy to fetch his breakfast from the hotel across the road. Scrubbed, clean, and cheerful, Majeed would sit down to a fresh hot buttered brown pav with a cup of tea. After breakfast, he smoked a Passing Show, ate a paan, and would begin work. Lunch at Haji's Hotel in Bhendi Bazaar was mouth-watering khari dry dal with a pure ghee baghaar and some sautéed meat. After a glass of icy cold water and another Passing Show revived every part of his being, Majeed would enjoy a short nap before sitting down to work once more.

Majeed would finish work at six o'clock and take a one-anna tram ride to Apollo Bandar to enjoy the cool breeze and simply to look at the assortment of men and women out for their strolls. He used to love listening to them chatter in so many different languages. He recalled these simple pleasures and the fun in observing cars, victorias, and bicycles moving up and down the road against a backdrop of grand tall buildings on one side and the vast unending ocean with its undulant waves on the other—the bobbing of boats and the occasional strains of a boatswain's song.

Majeed remembered the Gujarati and Marathi beauties with fresh flowers wound around their chignons and how he watched the different Parsi, Jewish, Anglo–Indian, and European women but never desired them. Now a veteran in sexual relations, every beautiful woman was an object of desire. Majeed reminisced about the good old days and how he alternated between going to Apollo Bandar and Chowpatty, where he sat on the wet sand and ate chaat, gazing at the boundless sea that sparkled like silver in the golden sunlight.

And he reminded himself, 'If I had my heart's fill there, I headed to Malabar Hill and the Hanging Gardens.' These days, he walked in well laid-out gardens, but flowers seemed to have lost their glory. Majeed barely noticed the choicest blooms skilfully arranged in vases and replaced before they wilted in his house.

Majeed had no enemies in the old days. The whole world seemed an ally, including the tram, the sky, the roads, and the footpath where he had slept before he found the bench infested with bedbugs. Now, wherever Majeed turned, he encountered adversaries—at work and in his romantic entanglements. In those magical days, free from all cares and woes, simple things gave Majeed immeasurable pleasure. A short one-mile taxi ride was the height of indulgence, and his spirit lifted when he gave a paisa to a beggar. He gave away thousands in charity but had no spiritual fulfilment because he made donations to impress others. In the good old days, he thought of novel ideas to amuse himself. He took the electric train to a random village, where he drank the local brew or bought a kite to fly on Chowpatty with kids he did not know. He remembered his childish thrills, ogling young schoolgirls at Dadar Station in the mornings or the times when he perched himself at an angle at the bottom of the footbridge to look up the skirts of Anglo–Indian girls.

At other times, Majeed got a kick out of saving an anna or two by walking all the way home and spending it on something else. Occasionally, he wrote love letters to imaginary girls and laughed at his silliness when posting them to the first address that came to mind. Majeed grew a fingernail at other times and went to a cosmetic store and applied Cutex on the pretext of testing the colour. He got a giddy thrill from smoking cigarettes he had scrounged off others. When the bedbugs on the wooden bench made his life miserable, instead of losing his cool, Majeed spent the entire night out on the streets. When skint, he skipped lunch and imagined he had eaten it.

After Majeed figured out how to make money and riches came his way, the razzle-dazzle of silver and gold obscured the simple pleasures of life. Now, he attended parties pulsating with dancing and merrymaking. He had lost the simple pleasures of the good old days when he spent long nights alone. Now, every evening, Majeed had a woman by his side. He had lost the peace of bachelordom that had sheltered him through the night. Now, several what-ifs dogged his life—what if his wife finds out; what if a woman becomes pregnant; what if he catches a disease; what if a woman's husband turns up? In the good old days, there were no fears. Now, he had access to the best alcohol, but he had lost the nightly kick he got from drinking the 'Made in Japan Ab Hi Beer'.

Occasionally, when Majeed ventured into the past and talked to himself, he recalled Keki Mistry, 'the kindly man I asked for an Aspro, and he gave it for free, saying "I'm hardly going to ask you to pay for this." Just a few days before this episode, he had helped me out of a tight spot and loaned me five rupees—and he never mentioned it again.'" Majeed's mind had a logjam of memories about the simple joys of life: 'That afternoon on the tram, when I gave up my seat to the Marathi girl, how sweetly she smiled to acknowledge my gesture and said, "Thank you."'

He recalled the thrill he had experienced when he caught a glimpse of a pair of perfect legs at Apollo Bandar as a sharp gust of wind lifted a Jewish girl's silken skirt. Or the fun-filled Sundays at the Parsi hotel, where he had slurped while eating a fresh hot naan dipped in delicious hot shorba and payas—trotters and gravy. He reminded himself, 'I got thrills simply thinking about how much I enjoyed a technicolour film, or how well the girl extras danced. The kick I got from my cigarette and the joy of seeing the happy husband and wife cooing like lovebirds at Dadar Station! How wonderful if I could experience such simple pleasures every day!'

In the old days, after work and his trip to Apollo Bandar or Chowpatty, he would head home around eight in the evening, and would stop to wash his face at a municipal tap by the roadside before walking to the bar near Byculla Bridge. Here, he would greet the proprietor, an obese Parsi seth with a disproportionately large nose, 'Well, Seth, kem chho?' That was the extent of his Gujarati, but it pleased him no end to speak even as much, especially when the seth smiled at him and said, 'Saru chhe, saru chhe.'

He would stand at the counter and chat to the Parsi seth about the war before he sauntered to his favourite white marble-topped table in a corner.

The waiter would arrive and wipe the table with a damp cloth before he asked Majeed, 'Tell me, Seth...?'

Majeed had felt like a seth at a time when he had one rupee and four annas in his pocket. He would turn to the waiter with a grand air, smile and say, 'You know exactly what I want, yet you ask me...bring the usual.'

The waiter would give the table another quick, instinctive swipe with the wet cloth and walk away, and return with a glass, a large plateful of kabuli channa and another of khari sing—chickpeas and salted peanuts. And Majeed would say, 'You always forget to bring the papad.'

The nibbles came free with the beer, and Majeed had devised a formula: he would ask the waiter to bring a second plate of the delicious kabuli channa, sprinkled with salt and black pepper. The generous portions of channa and salted peanuts with a beer were Majeed's dinner. When the beer arrived, he would pour it slowly into his glass and savour every sip, as its cooling sensation permeated his heart and mind.

He would observe the obese Parsi and think, 'Why does he have such a prominent nose? What crime has he committed that God has paid so little attention to his nose?' He recalled how wretched he felt on a tram when he saw a woman with a firm figure, an ample bosom, beautiful eyes, a spotless complexion, and lovely lips, but her nose was like a parrot's beak. Throughout the journey, he kept asking himself, 'Is there no way of fixing her nose?' As he recalled this episode, he thought of every lovely nose he had seen in his life.

In the old days, Majeed would sit in the bar for ages, thinking of all manner of things. For instance, he would tell himself, 'Although this Parsi has a very prominent nose, he is a very virtuous man. He gives me credit when I am broke.' He recalled the many times he had leaned against the counter and said, 'Seth, no maal paani today...tomorrow?'

And in response, the seth would smile and say, 'No vanda!' meaning, 'No problem.'

In the old days, a bottle of beer set him back fourteen annas. After he polished off his beer and nibbles, he summoned the waiter with an elegant wave of his hand to ask for the bill. He put one rupee on the plate and declared, 'Keep the change.'

The waiter would salute him and called him 'Sahibji'. Majeed would then stand up and head off, happy and content.

Every night, on his way back to his fleapit after his beer, Majeed would make a routine stop in a neighbouring alley to meet Miss Leena and her two daughters—Esther, who was sixteen, and Helen, thirteen. Once upon a time, Miss Leena had been a famous cabaret dancer. Before turning into her alley, Majeed would order three teas from the hotel on the corner. The moment he put his foot in through the door of their tiny room, he would holler, 'Assalaam alaikum!'

The mother and daughters would respond in an unadulterated Arabic accent, 'Wa'alaikum salaam!'

The only light in Miss Leena's hovel was a dim flicker from an old oil lamp. Usually, Majeed found Esther and Helen stretched out on the solitary double bed, in their long kaftans, which often climbed up, leaving them half-exposed. He would sit on a steel chair near Miss Leena, who sat cross-legged on the floor on a rush mat on which she slept. He would inform her that he had ordered tea, and Esther would say, 'Thank you,' in her reedy voice. As Helen wriggled around on the bed, Majeed would catch several glimpses of her breasts that reminded him of ripe peaches. While the mother and daughters drank tea, Majeed would sit in silence in the confined dark space, where he felt strangely at peace. Majeed recalled his debt of gratitude to the three women for their company and to everything around them, including the metal chair and the small oil lamp that emitted a lot of smoke and exuded a gentle light. Majeed usually drifted into a mild stupor, and after some time, would pull himself up on his unsteady feet to make his way back to his fleapit, where he changed his clothes, lay down on the bench, and immediately descended into the depths of sleep.

It became almost a routine that after three or four pegs of whisky, Majeed forgot all his cares and woes and sank into memories of the good old days, but as his intoxication wore off, pressing concerns lured him back to the present. With time, as he conjured new schemes to play the black market and hook women whom he wished to bed, old memories of the years before the war began to fade. Majeed's preoccupation with his wealth erased those that remained.

## Mrs D'Costa

Nine months were up. My stomach did not feel too uncomfortable but Mrs D'Costa was having kittens. I gave up worrying about the impending event and began to feel sorry for my neighbour. Nothing but a plank of wood riddled with holes stood between the balconies of our flats. My mother-in-law, God bless her, and I loved to watch the entire D'Costa clan at their meals through the holes but fled when the vile smell of dried prawn curry reached our nostrils. To this day, I continue to wonder why they ate something so foul-smelling. Alas, human beings eat things that smell far worse.

Mrs D'Costa had a chronically swollen right foot. She must have been around forty. Her short frizzy hair with countless grey streaks had lost its dark shine and sat on her head like a hat made from a worn-out doormat. Occasionally, she put on a shabby flashy tailor-made dress, plastered the hair on her head, and covered it with a net studded with tiny red beads, which looked like pins stuck in her head and made her look like a mannequin in an auction house.

Every morning, Mrs D'Costa served breakfast to her husband and their four sons. Mr D'Costa worked for the railways, and one of their sons, who had just joined the army, counted himself among Hindustan's leaders. Every morning, another son ironed his starched white trousers and put them on before heading downstairs to flirt with pubescent Christian girls. After breakfast, Mrs D'Costa stood on the balcony to wave 'bye-bye' to her husband before she put curlers in her uncontrollable frizzy hair and started to worry about my baby's arrival.

Mrs D'Costa had produced half a dozen babies, of whom five (her four sons and a daughter) had survived. I have no idea if she marked the days leading to her deliveries with impatience or sat around beatifically awaiting the appointed hour. I had to endure Mrs D'Costa's keen interest in the occupant of my stomach. Several times a day, she leaned across the balcony and spoke to me in her peculiar English. She had little regard for grammar, but for her not to speak the language constituted a grave insult to the British Raj.

Mrs D'Costa's characteristic cross-examination included questions such as, 'I ask, where you go today?'

When I told her I had merely gone out shopping with my husband, she forgot her English and broke into Bombay Urdu, with the sole intention of finding out how many days were left for my baby to arrive. If I knew the answer, I would have told her and saved myself from the daily barrage of questions and Mrs D'Costa from anxiety. I had no idea how to calculate the due date. All I knew was that when nine months are up, the baby arrives!

According to Mrs D'Costa, nine months were up, although my mother-in-law thought I had some time. I taxed my brain, unsuccessfully, to figure out how Mrs D'Costa had counted the days to complete the nine months. I was the one who got married and was about to have a baby, but Mrs D'Costa had the full tally. At least, I knew that I got married on 26 April—I mean on the night of 26 April, I left my mother's home for my husband's. With all the events jumbled up in my mind, it was a challenge to arrive at an exact conclusion, and I reckoned I should have written all the dates down in a little notebook, or at least in the dhobi's account book. To this day, I fail to understand how Mrs D'Costa knew that nine months were up and my baby was overdue.

One day, she said to my mother-in-law in an anxious tone, 'Your daughter-in-law's baby is late—should be born last week.'

Stretched out on the sofa inside, thinking about the baby's arrival, I could hear their conversation. My mother-in-law and Mrs D'Costa reminded me of two biddies waiting at a platform for a late train. God bless my mother-in-law, who was not as anxious as Mrs D'Costa, and tried to reassure her several times a day, 'This is nothing to worry about, by God's grace, a few days here and there is not unusual.' But Mrs D'Costa had done her calculations and stood her ground. How could she be wrong! When Mrs D'Silva had her babies, she knew the exact time of their arrival. Besides, Mrs D'Costa had given birth to six babies and not one of them was late. And to add the proverbial icing on her cake—she was a nurse. It is quite another matter that she did not train as a midwife, but everyone called her

'Nurse'. A small wooden plaque hanging by the front door of her flat had 'Nurse D'Costa' painted on it. If she did not know how to calculate the time for the arrival of a baby, then who did?

When Mr Nazir in No. 14 was unwell, and his nose began to swell, it was Mrs D'Costa who sent for cotton wool from the bazaar and applied a hot compress. She loved to recount this episode as evidence of her competence as a nurse. Whenever she did, I had a standard response, 'How fortunate we are to have as our neighbour a lady who cares about the welfare of her fellow human beings and is also a nurse!'

Mrs D'Costa beamed with delight, and her pleasure worked to my advantage. Once, my husband had a high temperature, and without hesitation, Mrs D'Costa loaned me her rubber cold-compress bag. It remained with us for more than a week and came in handy for several malaria victims in our family. Mrs D'Costa was a very thoughtful person, but her do-good instinct was driven in no small measure by prurience—she wanted to know her neighbours' most intimate secrets.

Mrs D'Costa knew a lot about Mrs D'Silva's frailties because they shared the same faith. She knew Mrs D'Silva got married during the Christmas season, but her first baby arrived in July, which meant that her 'real' marriage took place before Christmas! Moreover, she knew that Mrs D'Silva liked to visit a dance hall where she earned a lot of money. No longer as beautiful as she was in her prime, now Mrs D'Silva made less money than she did several years ago.

In her vast inventory of local gossip, Mrs D'Costa also had several stories about the Jewish family that lived on our floor. She regaled us with stories about 'that fat Mozelle who came home late every night because she was out gambling'. There was another that concerned 'the old shorty, who leaves the flat every morning with his thumbs tucked under his suspenders, and his jacket thrown over his shoulder, and returns every evening—he is Mozelle's old friend'. Mrs D'Costa made some enquiries and discovered that this short old Parsi was a manufacturer of a fiery soap with aphrodisiacal properties.

One day, Mrs D'Costa told us that Mozelle had betrothed her young daughter Flori to a man who drove the short old Parsi to his flat every day. I saw Flori every morning on her way to school in her gymslip. And I know enough about the old Parsi to add that his car was always parked downstairs, and he spent the night at the flat, as did Mozelle's daughter's fiancé. According to Mrs D'Costa, Flori's fiancé was the short old Parsi's driver, and the old Parsi was in love with his driver's sister, Leyli, who also lived in the flat with her sister, Violet. According to Mrs D'Costa, Violet was, '*a bad character*'. The baby she dandled all day long was not the abandoned child of some Parsi woman, as per neighbourhood gossip, but Violet's sister Leyli's baby. I have related everything I remember, but I doubt anyone could recall the long and convoluted genealogies presented by Mrs D'Costa.

Mrs D'Costa's store of tittle-tattle extended way beyond the men and women of our neighbourhood; she held information about many people from other localities. She went for regular treatment for her swollen foot and returned laden with intelligence. One day, I saw Mrs D'Costa busy chatting with her two older sons, daughter, and two female neighbours. I was miffed and moved away from the balcony, convinced that she was chatting to them about my overdue baby. But, alas, she spotted me and headed towards our front door; I had no choice but to let her in. I invited her to sit on a bamboo moorha, and the moment she sat down, she started, 'You heard something? What's Mahatma Gandhi gone and done? Saali Congress wants to pass new law. My Frederick brings news that it will be *prohession* in Bombay. You understand what is *prohession*?'

I professed my ignorance and confessed that my English vocabulary did not extend to the word. Mrs D'Costa explained, '*Prohession* is when alcohol stops. I ask you, this Congress, what we have done to it that it want to stop alcohol? What rubbish government! I don't like. How our celebration will happen? How we have Christmas? Christian people never agree to this law! How they agree? In my house, twenty-four o'clock need for brandy. If this law pass, how we will function? All this is done by Gandhi...saala, not drinking himself and stopping others. He is very thick with Mammadan people—and you know he is a huge enemy of the government of us people.'

It seemed that Mrs D'Costa had embraced the entire British establishment. She was a dark-complexioned Christian woman from Goa, but when she talked in this vein, I imagined her with white skin as a newly arrived Englishwoman who had nothing to do with

Hindustan. Indeed, she had nothing to do with Mahatma Gandhi, who began the movement to extract salt from the sea and taught Indians to use the spinning wheel and wear homespun with pride—along with many other unusual things.

Perhaps, Mrs D'Costa's aversion to Mahatma Gandhi fuelled her belief that the sole purpose of Prohibition in Bombay was to target the British. Besides, she had compressed her opinions of the Congress and the Mahatma in one item of clothing: the Mahatma's loincloth. After cursing Mahatma Gandhi and seven generations of his ancestors and progeny, she came to the real point of her visit: 'And yes, why your baby is not arriving? Come, I take you to doctor.' I did not pay much attention to her, but before she left, she said, 'Look here, if something happen you don't blame me.'

The following evening at around six o'clock, I was sitting with my Sahib (my name for my husband), who was busy writing. I thought it an excellent time to call Mrs Kazmi, who was also was very concerned about the baby's arrival. I got up to go downstairs to Nazir Sahib's office to make the call since not a soul would be there at this time. Besides, doctors and experienced women had recommended climbing up and down the stairs to make childbirth easier. I was breathless and in pain. I felt I had a rubber ball stuck in my midriff. My mother-in-law had explained that, at times, when a baby moves around, an arm or leg can get trapped somewhere. I stood up with my soon to be born baby to begin my slow climb down the stairs, but before I walked past Nurse D'Costa's door, she popped out and whisked me into her flat.

I told Mrs D'Costa I could not sit with her for long since I had to make an urgent phone call. Of course, without paying the slightest attention to what I had said, she held my arms and forced me down into a sofa with greasy upholstery. I was not sure why she shooed her two younger sons out of their bedroom rather unceremoniously and did the same with her unmarried daughter, whose shorts were not much longer than the Mahatma's loincloth. Mrs D'Costa ushered me into the vacated room and locked the door from inside. She limped around and accomplished everything at such speed that I did not have time to collect my thoughts.

When Mrs D'Costa looked me up and down before she shut and

bolted the three windows in the room, she reminded me of Aladdin's chacha, who had trapped him in a cave. She almost scared the life out of me. I was terrified and wanted to open the door and run. After all, what was Mrs D'Costa doing? What did she want? What was the need for such aggressive action? She was my neighbour, and we owed her several favours, but she was an outsider. And what about her sons, the one in the army and the other who wore starched trousers and flirted with pubescent Christian girls? After all, family is family, and outsiders are outsiders.

In several romantic Urdu novels, I had come across the character of a busybody called a kutni. For me, as she rushed around the room, Mrs D'Costa transformed from a nurse into a kutni. I was filled with horror when she bolted the door and windows and drew the curtains, and the room with four iron beds became dark. She switched on the light and looked resolute as she walked to the fireplace and picked up a bottle that contained a runny white substance. Mrs D'Costa turned to me and said, 'Take off your blouse. I want see something.'

Terrified, I asked, 'What do you want to see?'

She could see everything below the blouse, so why did she want me to undress? What right did she have to call a woman into her house and ask her to undress?

'Mrs D'Costa, I will not take off my blouse.' My tone was anxious but firm.

Mrs D'Costa turned pale, 'Then how I will know when you have baby? This bottle have coconut oil. I pour this on your stomach to see when baby born, and this tells exactly when baby born and if baby boy or girl.'

My anxiety vanished, and once again, Mrs D'Costa was Mrs D'Costa. Coconut oil is harmless. Even if she poured the entire bottle on my stomach, it would do me no harm, and I quite liked the idea. Besides, my refusal would disappoint her, and I'm not particularly eager to hurt anybody. I wanted to put on my clothes and walk away. To take off my blouse in the presence of a stranger was embarrassing enough. Besides, on the lower half of my protruding belly, I had red marks that looked like crumpled silk and these added to my inhibition—but I coped. Mrs D'Costa had lifted the hand that held the bottle and looked, delighted as a line of cold oil ran down my stomach.

As I put on my blouse and tied my sari, she questioned me in a measured tone, 'What's date today? Eleventh! That is it, the baby arrives on fifteenth, and it be a boy.'

My baby boy was born on the twenty-fifth. From time to time, when he pats my stomach with his little hands, I recall how Mrs D'Costa had poured a bottle full of coconut oil on it.

# Khushya

Khushya was deep in thought, chewing a tobacco-laced paan he had scrounged off the flower seller whose shop abutted the small platform he used as his hang-out. This is solid slab of concrete heaved with spare parts of old cars, discarded motor tyres, and nuts and bolts throughout the day. Around eight-thirty at night, the vendors cleared their goods and shut down shop, leaving the space free for Khushya.

He relished the flavour as he crunched his paan and his thoughts between his molars. Khushya allowed the paan spittle to gather in his mouth as he continued to think about what had happened to him just half an hour earlier. Before he came to his hang-out, he had gone to a filthy alley in Khetwadi to check on Kanta, the new hussy from Mangalore, because his informants had told him she was moving out. When he knocked on her door, she called from inside, 'Who is it?'

Khushya responded, 'It's me, Khushya.'

Not much later, the door opened. Khushya stepped in, and Kanta locked the door from inside. He turned around and was astounded to find her naked. She hid her body with a small towel, but everything she should have concealed from view was exposed to Khushya's astonished eyes.

'Tell me, Khushya, what brings you here?' she asked and added, 'I was about to take a bath. Sit…sit. You could have asked the chap outside for a cup of tea. Do you know that wretch Rama has run away?'

Khushya felt awkward. Confronted by nudity, his gaze wanted to hide. He had never seen a woman so casually naked and stumbled on his words, 'Go…go have your bath…' but found his tongue and continued, 'you were naked. Why did you open the door? You could have told me, and I would have come back later…go…have your bath.'

Kanta smiled, 'When you said it's Khushya, I thought, what's the harm? After all, it's only our Khushya.'

Kanta's smile touched Khushya's heart and mind; her gorgeous naked body reminded him of a wax figurine—and he could feel it melt and enter his body. Khushya knew that women who sell their bodies are often perfectly formed, but he failed to understand how Kanta could stand naked before him and feel no shame. Even though she had told him, 'When you said it's Khushya, I thought, what's the harm? After all, it's only our Khushya.'

Kanta and Khushya shared the same profession. He was her pimp, and by that measure, he was hers. Yet, this was not a good enough reason for her to stand stark naked in his presence. He wanted to unravel Kanta's straightforward yet complicated words and continued to think of her naked body, taut like leather stretched across a frame drum. Khushya tried to recall the number of times he had fixed his gaze on her. Yet, she remained indifferent and continued to stand before him like a statue devoid of feeling, not conscious that she was standing before a man, a creature whose gaze could penetrate a woman's clothes and her body. Kanta's eyes did not turn red with shame but remained bright and clear; she did not lower her gaze but looked Khushya directly in the eye. Granted, she was a harlot, but even harlots don't just stand around stark naked.

In ten years of pimping, Khushya had come to know all the secrets of the girls who worked for him. He knew that the girl who lived at the far end of Pydhonie loved to play her broken harmonica for the young boy who lived with her and she claimed was her brother—especially that song from the film *Achhut Kanya*, 'Kisey karta murakh pyar, pyar, pyar' (O foolish heart, who do you love, love, love!). She was madly in love with Ashok Kumar, and from time to time, fell prey to crafty lads who made false promises to introduce her to him.

Khushya knew all there was to know about the Punjaban who lived in Dadar and wore a man's suit simply because her lover had told her, 'You have legs like the actress in *Morocco*, also known as *Khun-e Tamanna*.' She saw the film several times. When her lover informed her that Marlene Dietrich had insured her stunning legs for two lakh dollars and wore trousers to hide them, the Punjaban took to wearing pants that would get stuck between her buttocks.

Khushya knew that the girl who lived in Mazgaon was from the Deccan, and she knew she was barren. Yet, she liked to hook handsome young college boys because she wanted to give birth to a beautiful child. There was little difference between her and the dark Madrasan, who wore diamond botiyan in her ears and knew her skin would never turn pale. Yet every other day, she continued to waste money on countless skin whitening remedies. Khushya knew all the secrets of all the girls who worked on his circuit. Yet, it never crossed his mind that one day Kanta Kumari—whose real name was so complicated that he would fail to recall it even if he tried till the end of his life—would stand stark naked before him.

Khushya was so preoccupied trying to understand what had happened that he overlooked the paan spittle collecting in his mouth. And was finding it difficult to chew the tiny slivers of betel nut swivelling through the gaps between his teeth. Beads of sweat dripped from his furrowed brow like murky paneer water through muslin. The whole episode was an insult to his manhood. He felt humiliated. Time and again, he asked himself, 'Now tell me if this is not an insult, what is? I mean, the hussy stands in front of you stark naked and asks, "What's wrong with it? After all, you're only Khushya." So, saali, I'm nothing but the tomcat lying in a stupor at the foot of your bed—what else!'

Khushya considered himself a victim of a great injustice. He knew at a subliminal level that any woman, decent or a harlot, would think him a man and be aware of the primal limits of caution between a man and a woman. He had gone to see Kanta to discuss his bonus and to check on her plans. Before he knocked on her door, he had thought about what she could be up to, and several possibilities came to mind. She could be in bed with a bandage tied around her head, or picking fleas from her cat's coat, or removing the hair from her underarms with that vile pongy powder, or playing patience. Since nobody was allowed entry to Kanta's shack, the thought of finding her with a man did not cross his mind—but there she stood, stark naked before Khushya, who had always seen her fully dressed. Yes. Imagine her stark naked because her small towel barely concealed anything. Khushya felt he was holding a banana peel, from which the banana had fallen out. No. Khushya felt he was naked. Perhaps, he might have brushed aside his astonishment had the hussy not turned around and said, 'When you said it's Khushya, I thought, it's only our Khushya, let him in.' And he recalled, 'Saali was smiling.'

Khushya continued to mutter to himself. He recalled Kanta's barefaced smile. It reminded him of her naked body, which stirred lustful thoughts in his mind. His memory travelled back to his childhood when his neighbour would yell out for him from her courtyard every other day, 'Khushya, son, run and fill this bucket with water!' When he returned with the bucket, she would invite him behind the temporary dhoti curtain. 'Put the bucket near me. I have soap all over my face and can't see a thing.' When Khushya lifted the curtain to put the bucket down near her, he would see the woman's naked body covered with soapsuds but felt no sexual excitement. 'Well,' he thought, 'I was a child at the time. There is a difference between an innocent child and a man. Who observes purdah from children? I am almost twenty-eight years old! Now I am a mature man; even an old woman will not stand stark naked in the presence of a young man.'

What did Kanta think of him? Didn't he have all the qualities of a young stud? Caught off guard when he saw Kanta stark naked, he had not gazed at her whatnots, but he had noticed that even with the use she put them to every day, they looked untouched. He thought it curious that as a man, it had never crossed his mind that what was on offer was not a bad deal for ten rupees. He recalled how on Dussehra, a bank munshi turned Kanta down, even though Khushya offered him a two-rupee rebate. The bank munshi was an ass, a perfect ass. Khushya felt a strange tension in his body. Why did the dusky girl from Mangalore not think him a man but simply Khushya? Khushya was furious. He spat out the thick paan spittle that had collected in his mouth, and as it created numerous patterns on the footpath, Khushya decided to take a tram home.

At home, Khushya bathed and changed into a fresh, clean dhoti. He went to the salon in the tenement where he lived. He looked at himself in the mirror before combing his hair and sat down on a chair. He asked the barber for a shave in a rather sombre voice. It was his second shave of the day, and the barber asked, 'Arrey, Khushya, have you forgotten, I shaved your beard this morning?'

Khushya rubbed the back of his hand across his face and responded very thoughtfully, '…didn't get rid of the spikes.' The barber got rid of the spikes. Khushya dusted his face with powder and stepped out. He found a taxi parked in front of the barber's salon, and called out, 'Chhee Chhee', in typical Bombay fashion, to alert the taxi driver and raised his finger as a signal. As he got in, the driver turned around and asked, 'Sahib, where to?'

The three words, especially 'Sahib', thrilled Khushya to bits. He smiled and responded amiably, 'I'll let you know, but first go towards Pasmira House, from Lamington Road…understood?'

The driver pressed the red button to start the meter. *Ting ting* it beeped, and the taxi was on its way to Lamington Road. When they reached the end of Lamington Road, Khushya instructed the driver, 'Turn left now.' The taxi turned left, and the driver did not get a chance to change the gear when Khushya said, 'Park near the lamp post in front of you.'

The driver parked the taxi next to the lamp post. Khushya got out and walked towards a paan shop where he bought a paan. He exchanged a few words with a man standing nearby, and the man walked back with him to the taxi and sat on the passenger seat in front. Khushya told the driver, 'Drive on, straight!'

The taxi drove on for a while, with Khushya giving directions as they wound their way through colourful, crowded bazaars. Finally, they drove through a dimly lit alley without much traffic, where some men were lounging around on charpais parked on the street while others were getting a champi or a head massage. They reached a bungalow-like structure, constructed mainly of wood. Khushya told the driver, 'That's it…just stop here.'

He turned to the man who had accompanied him from the paan shop and said sotto voce, 'I'll wait here….'

The man gave Khushya a moronic look before he stepped out of the taxi and entered the wooden bungalow.

Khushya sank deeper into his seat and crossed one leg over the other. He took out a biri, lit it, and took two puffs before throwing it out on the road. He was agitated and suspected the taxi driver of running the engine to burn petrol and raise the fare. He protested, 'How much more money will you make by running the engine for no rhyme or reason?'

The driver turned around and said, 'Seth, the engine isn't running.'

Khushya's chest was rattling. When he realized his mistake, his tension escalated. He did not respond to the driver but bit his lips. Unthinkingly he put on his black boat-shaped hat, tucked under his arm all this time. Still, he patted the driver's shoulder and said, 'Look, soon you'll see a girl; the moment she gets in, start the car. Understand? Nothing to worry about; there's nothing fishy happening here.'

Just as Khushya finished his instructions, his friend walked out of the bungalow with Kanta draped in a rather garish sari. Khushya slid across the back seat to the other side. His friend opened the door for Kanta, and after she got in, he slammed it shut but heard her shriek, 'Khushya…you?'

'Yes, me…but did you get your money? Look, driver, take us to Juhu.'

The driver started the car. The purr of the engine drowned Kanta's response. The taxi juddered forward and disappeared, leaving Khushya's astonished friend standing in the middle of the dimly lit alley. Nobody ever again saw Khushya hanging around at night by the concrete platform that was a spare parts shop by day.

## Ten Rupees

Sarita was playing with little girls at the corner of an alleyway near a garbage dump. Her mother made Kishori comfortable in their chawl and asked the tea boy to make tea mixed with coffee for him before she started looking for her daughter in the tenement. She searched all three floors of the building. Where on earth had her daughter disappeared? Sarita had just recovered from dysentery without taking medicines, yet her mother looked for her in the toilet and called out, 'Sarita...O Sarita!'

Sarita's mother was on edge. Kishori had told her of the three seths waiting in a car in the big bazaar. Seths with motor cars did not turn up every day, but Sarita was nowhere to be found. Forget seths—nobody wanted to come to this filthy neighbourhood reeking of the sickly stench of burnt biris that Kishori loathed and its walls and pavements sprayed with paan spittle. Sarita's mother thought it most considerate of Kishori to bring two fat Assamese men every month. The shrewd Kishori never brought punters to Sarita's fleapit but dressed her up and took her out to meet them. He advised the men in a confidential tone, 'Sahib, these are sensitive times; the police are always on the prowl. They've caught two hundred hussies plying the trade. I have a case running in court. You must tread carefully.'

Sarita's mother was furious. She rushed down the stairs and found Ramdai sitting by the landing, making biris as usual. Sarita's mother asked her, 'Have you seen that Sarita? Where in hell's name has she disappeared? Wait till I find her; I'll beat the living daylights out of her. Fully mature and frisking around with boys the whole day!'

Ramdai continued to cut biri leaves and did not feel the need to respond. Sarita's mother had not addressed her but had walked past muttering under her breath, as she did every other day. Every day, Ramdai sat by the landing all day long, with her basket in front of her, cutting leaves, filling, and then winding white and red threads around the biris. Ramdai was familiar with Sarita's mother's routine search for her daughter and her pronouncements to the women in the tenement, 'I am going to marry my Sarita off to some gentleman. That is why I tell her she must learn to read and write a bit. The *moonsipulty* has opened a small school near here. How often do I ask myself, why don't I send Sarita there? Her father was very keen on his daughter's education.'

Sarita's mother invariably heaved a deep sigh after her pronouncements and before she embarked on the saga of her dead husband that all the women in the tenement could repeat verbatim. If you were to ask Ramdai to recount what happened to Sarita's father when he worked in the railways, she would tell you, 'His boss swore at him, and Sarita's father began to froth at the mouth. He shouted, "I am not your servant; I work for the *gorment*! Don't you boss me around! Watch it! If you swear at me, I'll knock all your teeth out." Ah well, the boss erupted and swore at him again. Now incensed, Sarita's father thwacked his boss so hard on the neck that the chap's head spun around, and his cap flew off and landed at least ten yards away. But he was the boss sahib; he stepped forward and kicked Sarita's father so hard in the stomach with his heavy boots that Sarita's father split his spleen and dropped dead by the railway track. The *gorment* filed a case against the boss sahib, and Sarita's mother got five hundred rupees as compensation. Unfortunately, she liked to gamble, and within five months, all the money evaporated.'

Sarita's mother recounted this story ad nauseam, but everyone questioned its veracity. Not a soul in the tenement had an ounce of sympathy for Sarita's mother, perhaps because all of them deserved sympathy themselves. They lived cheek by jowl, but no bond of friendship existed between the people who lived in the tenement. Almost all of them slept all day and staayed awake all night, mainly because they worked on night shifts in the nearby mill. Nearly everyone in the neighbourhood knew that Sarita's mother put her daughter to work, but no one was interested in calling her to account when she said, 'My daughter doesn't know anything about the world.'

Nonetheless, one morning after Tuka Ram made a pass at Sarita near the municipal tap, Sarita's mother shouted her lungs out, 'Why doesn't someone control this baldy! I pray with all my heart that Parmatma strikes him blind in both eyes with which he lusts after my pure, innocent daughter. I tell you, one day, there'll be real trouble when I smash his brain with my shoe. He can do what the hell he wants outside, but here, he should live like a decent man! Do you hear me?'

When Tuka Ram's squint-eyed wife heard Sarita's mother, she came out of her chawl in her dhoti and retorted, 'Watch it, you witch! One more word from you and...! Your goddess plays hide-and-seek with boys from the hotel. Do you think all of us are blind, and we don't know about the babus who come to see her and where your Sarita goes all dolled up, regularly? Hunh! Look who's talking about decency. Get lost!'

Many stories about Tuka Ram's wife were doing the rounds of their neighbourhood. The whole world knew that when the kerosene oil seller did his rounds, she called him in and locked the door. Predictably, Sarita's mother laid great emphasis on this matter, 'And what about your kerosene oil seller? What were you up to, locked up with him for two hours? Sniffing kerosene oil!'

The hostilities between Sarita's mother and Tuka Ram's wife did not last long. Soon after their heated exchange, Sarita's mother caught her neighbour exchanging sweet nothings with someone in the dead of night; and the following morning, Tuka Ram's wife saw Sarita going off in a car with a *genterman* chap. These two episodes formed the basis of a truce between the two women, and now, Sarita's mother felt she could ask Tuka Ram's wife, 'You haven't seen Sarita, have you?'

Tuka Ram's wife looked at the corner of the street with her squint eye, 'She was playing there with the patwari's daughter near the rubbish dump.' She lowered her voice and added, 'Kishori just went upstairs. Did he meet you?'

Sarita's mother looked around her and whispered as she headed to the rubbish heap, 'I've asked him to sit upstairs, but this Sarita always disappears at critical moments. She doesn't understand anything. She wants to play around the whole day.'

A crestfallen Sarita spotted her mother approach the concrete urinal and stopped in her tracks. Her mother gripped her arm. 'I want to drag you home and kill you. You don't have anything else to do but play, do you?' As they walked home, Sarita's mother's tone became gentler, 'Kishori's been waiting for a while. He's brought a seth with a motor car. Run up now and get dressed. Listen, wear the blue georgette sari. And yes, your hair's dishevelled. Hurry and get dressed. I'll comb it.'

Sarita too was delighted when she heard that a seth with a motor car had arrived. She was not interested in the seth but the motor car. Sarita loved the thrill of sitting in a car as it sped along an open road, and the breeze caressed her face. Enveloped in the breeze, Sarita felt as weightless as the air flying along the highways.

Sarita was around fifteen but behaved more like a naïve thirteen-year-old. She loathed sitting around gabbling with older women and preferred to spend her time playing silly meaningless games like hopscotch with much younger girls. Sarita could spend the entire day drawing criss-cross lines with white chalk on the tarred road of their alley. When she couldn't join them, Sarita loved to stand behind the gunny curtain of her chawl and observe her little friends bending down to draw and wipe out chalk marks as they played their mindless game of hopscotch.

Sarita was not beautiful. Her complexion was wheaten and tended towards a darker shade, but Bombay's damp climate gave her smooth skin a constant shine. The edge of her lips was the colour of a chikoo, and often tiny beads of sweat glistened on her upper lip. Sarita lived in squalor but was healthy. Puberty had visited her with reckless abandon. Her taut rounded body was well formed, and her petite frame added to her vigour. When she walked by the roadside and the movement of her body lifted her grimy ghagari, many male passers-by turned to look at her smooth, youthful calves that shone like freshly rubbed down teak. The mottled skin around certain parts of her body was reminiscent of tangerine peels concealing a luscious fruit.

Sarita's ill-tailored ungainly blouses revealed well-rounded arms, and her long thick hair exuded the scent of coconut oil. Her plait, which dangled on her back like a heavy whip, infuriated her to no end because she had tried out all sorts of ploys to control it: yet it was always in her way, especially when she was playing with her friends. Sarita's heart and mind were free of all cares and woes. She ate two square meals every day, and her mother did all the housework. Still, for several years now, instinctively, she performed the two chores assigned to her. Every morning Sarita filled two buckets of water and carried them upstairs, and every evening she picked up one paisa from the bowl full of change, took the oil lamp to the bazaar, and had it filled with oil.

Four or five times a month, Kishori brought various seths who took Sarita to a hotel or some other dark destination. She did not like to dwell on every aspect of these outings but learned to see her trips as fun-filled adventures. Perhaps, Sarita thought that men like Kishori visited other girls—and they too went out with seths—and whatever happened to her on the cold benches in Worli or the wet sand of Juhu Beach happened to them as well. One day she said to her mother, 'Ma, Shanta is mature now, why don't you send her with me? The seths feed me eggs, and Shanta loves eggs.'

Her mother fobbed her off, 'Yes, yes, I'll send her along one day; let her mother return from Poona.'

The following day Sarita passed on the good news to Shanta when she bumped into her at the urinal, 'Just let your mother return from Poona, and my mother will fix everything. You too will go to Worli with me.'

Often, Sarita recounted tales of her nocturnal trips as though they were beautiful dreams. Shanta, who was two years younger, felt tiny bells tinkle in her body. She never seemed to get enough of Sarita's stories and often tugged at her arm and insisted, 'Let's go downstairs; we'll talk there.'

And downstairs, they talked about things that sent shivers down their spines, sitting near the urinal on jute mats on which Girdhari the bania spread filthy pieces of coconut out to dry.

⌒

Sarita stood behind a temporary dhoti curtain strung up by her mother, and as she wrapped the blue georgette sari around her body, its soft texture tickled her thoughts. A drive in a car felt like the wings of a dove aflutter in her heart. What will the seth be like this time? Where will he take her? Several such and other questions crossed her mind. What if the car stops at a hotel after a short drive, and the seth starts drinking alcohol in a locked room, and she finds it difficult to breathe? Sarita disliked locked hotel rooms, usually with two steel beds, clearly not meant for sleeping to your heart's content.

Sarita wrapped her georgette sari around her body in a rush and came out from behind the curtain, adjusting its pleats. She stood in front of Kishori and turned her back to him, saying, 'Look, Kishori, is the sari all right from behind?' She did not wait for his answer and fixed a cloudy mirror between the window's steel bars before moving towards a broken wooden box where she kept her Japanese make-up. Sarita leaned forward, dusted her face with powder, and applied lipstick before looking at Kishori with questioning eyes. In her bright blue sari, with red lipstick on her lips, and pink powder daubed on her dusky cheeks, Sarita looked like one of the brightly coloured clay dolls sold in toy stalls on Diwali. As she finished her toilette, her mother arrived and fixed her hair. 'Look, beta, talk nicely; agree to whatever he says. The seth who is here today is a very big man; he owns a car.' Sarita's mother turned to Kishori and said, 'Now, take her quickly. The poor gentleman has waited too long.'

Out in the bazaar, three young men waited for Kishori in a yellow car parked by a small board that said, 'Urinating Not Allowed Here' on a wall that seemed to go on forever. They were holding their handkerchiefs to their noses. Kifayat, the young man sitting with one hand on the steering wheel, had tried to park the car further along the factory wall. But along the unending wall was an unrelenting line of men urinating. When he saw Kishori at the corner of the alley, Kifayat turned to his companions and said, 'Well guys, here comes Kishori...and...and,' and added, 'arrey, she's a little girl. Look, arrey, that one in the blue sari.'

Kishori and Sarita approached the car, and the two young men sitting in the back seat moved their hats and other paraphernalia to make some space. Kishori stepped forward to open the back door, pushed Sarita in, and hurriedly slammed it shut. He turned to the young man behind the steering wheel and said 'Forgive me for taking so long. She had gone out to meet a friend...so...so....'

Kifayat looked at Sarita and interrupted Kishori, 'It's all right, but look here...' He slid across to the other side, stuck his head out of the window, and whispered in Kishori's ear, 'She won't kick up a fuss, will she?'

Kishori put his hand across his heart and said, 'Seth, you can count on me.'

The young man took two rupees out of his pocket and handed them to Kishori, 'Have a ball!'

Kishori raised his hand to say salaam, and the engine of the car began to purr.

It was five o'clock in the evening. Bombay bazaars were teeming with cars, trams, buses, and people. Sarita looked around her as she sat silently between the two men. She clenched her thighs and held them tight. She wanted to say to the young man who was driving, 'Seth, drive faster, I feel I'm going to suffocate.'

For quite some time, nobody uttered a word. The two young men in the back seat buttoned up their achkans to conceal the agitation they were experiencing, like so many young men who find themselves near a young girl for the first time—a young girl who is their very own and, they can tease without fear.

Kifayat had moved to Bombay two years ago and had spent time with several girls of various temperaments and different ethnicities by day and by night, and he was not particularly restless. On the other hand, his friends were visiting from Hyderabad, and one, whose name was Shahab, wanted a full tour of Bombay. As a gesture of goodwill, Kifayat, the owner of the car, had procured Sarita through Kishori. His other friend, Anwar, could not bring himself to admit that he wanted a girl. Although Kishori had provided a new girl after ages, Kifayat took no interest in Sarita. Perhaps, he could focus only on one thing at a time and was concentrating on his driving.

As they passed the city limits and drove into a suburb, Sarita felt the car had begun to fly. With the cool breeze blowing around her, she lost all sense of restraint and turned into a bundle of energy. Electrified, her legs tapped, her arms danced, and her fingers quivered as she watched the trees whiz past on both sides of the car. By this time, Anwar and Shahab were more relaxed, but Shahab, who thought he had proprietary rights over Sarita, tried to put his arm gently around her waist. Sarita was ticklish. She began to giggle, and as she fell on Anwar, her laughter spread far into the night air through the open windows of the car. When Shahab made another attempt to put his arm around her waist, Sarita rolled over with laughter. Anwar slid into a corner and tried to lubricate his dry mouth. Shahab's imagination brimmed over with exciting possibilities, and he said to Kifayat, 'By God, what a scrumptious lass!' He pinched Sarita quite hard on her thigh, and in response, Sarita tweaked Anwar's ear because he was closest to her.

The car filled with laughter. Although Kifayat could see everything in the rear-view mirror, he turned around to observe the scene from time to time. He increased the speed to keep up with the peals of laughter. Sarita wanted to sit on the bonnet with the flying fairy made of steel, and as she leaned forward, Shahab tickled her again. To steady herself, Sarita put her arms around Kifayat's neck, quite unintentionally. Kifayat kissed her hands, and a shiver ran down Sarita's spine. She jumped across to the front seat, sidled up to Kifayat, began to play with his tie, and asked, 'What's your name?'

'My name?' Kifayat asked. 'My name is Kifayat,' he said and popped a ten-rupee bill into her hand. Sarita paid no attention to his name and tucked the ten rupees into her choli. Delighted like the child she was, she said, 'You are a perfect gent, and this tie of yours is very nice.'

At that moment, everything looked 'very nice' to Sarita. She wanted all manner of nice things to happen, especially for the car to keep flying and for everything to turn into a ball of air. Suddenly, she had an urge to sing and stopped playing with Kifayat's tie as she crooned:

*You've taught me love*
*You woke my sleeping heart.*

Sarita continued to sing the film song for a while before she turned around and saw that Anwar was silent and asked him, 'Why are you so quiet? Say something. Sing a song.'

Sarita jumped back onto the back seat and began to run her fingers through Shahab's hair. 'Come, let's sing. Do you remember that song sung by Devika Rani, "My heart sings like a bird in the forest?" Devika Rani is so nice.'

She clasped her hands and put them under her chin, fluttered her eyelids, and continued, 'Ashok Kumar and Devika Rani were standing next to each other, and Devika Rani said, "My heart sings like a bird in the forest!" Ashok Kumar asked, "Why don't you sing?"' And Sarita began to sing, '*My heart sings like a bird in the forest!*' Shahab raised his tuneless voice, '*My heart sings like a bird in the forest!*'

As their duet progressed, Kifayat provided another line of percussive accompaniment, and the hooting of the car horn joined Sarita's claps and her high-pitched voice, along with Shahab's foghorn mingled in an ensemble, accompanied by the whistle of the wind and the rumble of the car engine. Sarita was happy, Shahab was happy, Kifayat was happy. With so much happiness around him, mortified by his self-restraint, Anwar felt his dormant emotions stir; he decided to partake in Sarita's, Shahab's, and Kifayat's happiness.

Sarita took off Anwar's cap and put it on her head. Once again, she jumped to the front seat to check how she looked in the rear-view mirror and slapped Kifayat's thigh before she asked, 'If I wear your trousers and your shirt and put on your necktie, wouldn't I become a full sahib?'

Anwar wondered if he had been wearing the cap when he got into the car. Shahab, who could not make head or tail of Sarita's question, shook Anwar's arm and said, 'By God, you are a total imbecile.' And for some time, Anwar felt he was the biggest imbecile on earth.

Kifayat asked Sarita, 'What is your name?'

'My name?' asked Sarita as she tucked the strap of Anwar's hat under her chin. 'My name is Sarita.'

Shahab said, 'Sarita, you're not a woman; you're a sparkler!'

Anwar wanted to say something, but Sarita began to sing on a high pitch, '*I shall make a home in the land of love and set the whole wo...o...o...rrr...ld afff...flame.*'

Somehow, Sarita's plait began to unravel, and as it broke loose from its coil, her hair began to whirl around like thick smoke in the wind. Sarita was happy. Shahab was happy, Kifayat was happy, and now, Anwar had every intention to be happy. When they finished their song, it felt as though a downpour had stopped. Kifayat turned to Sarita and said, 'Sing another song.'

Shahab shouted from the back seat, 'Yes, yes, let's have another. Give these filmwallahs something they will never forget!'

Sarita sang, '*My friend came to my courtyard, and I was walking on air!*' She felt as though the car was riding on air.

Finally, they reached the end of the road and were by the seaside. The sun was about to set. As soon as the car stopped, Sarita opened the door and ran out. She ran far along the shore, wanting to feel the cool breeze blowing across the sea. Kifayat and Shahab joined her. Wafted by the breeze, so near the endless sea and the tall palm trees with moist sand beneath her feet, Sarita wanted to dissolve in this heaven. She wanted to absorb the moist sand through her feet and merge with the sea or rise so high that she could look down on the palm trees from above. Sarita wanted more of the same car ride, the same flight, the same breeze, and the constant hooting of the horn. She was deliriously happy as she sat down to drink beer on the wet sand by the seaside with the three young Hyderabadi men.

She snatched a bottle from Kifayat's hand and said, 'Stop! I'll pour…' and as she tipped the contents of the bottle into a glass, she watched with delight as it fizzed. She dipped a finger into the soft foam, stuck it in her mouth, and pulled a long face because she found it bitter. Kifayat and Shahab laughed uncontrollably. When they stopped laughing, Kifayat noticed that Anwar had joined their laughter. Of the six bottles of beer, the sand absorbed some, and Kifayat, Shahab, and Anwar's stomachs received the rest. Sarita continued to sing. Anwar looked at Sarita and thought that she too was made of beer. The sea breeze moistened her dusky cheeks. Sarita was ecstatic. Now, Anwar, too, was happy. He wanted the entire sea to turn into beer so that he could dive in—and he wanted Sarita to join him. Sarita picked up two empty beer bottles and banged them together, and there was a ring in the air. She began to laugh, and Kifayat, Shahab, and Anwar joined in. She turned to Kifayat and said, 'Come, let's go for a drive in the car.'

They stood up and ran towards the car, leaving the empty bottles standing face down on the sand. Once again, Sarita revelled in the hoot hooting of the car horn, and as her hair whirled like smoke in the chilly breeze, she began to sing. The men joined her and their songs fused into a hallucinatory vision. Sarita continued to sing as the car forged its way through the breeze. She was sitting in the back between Shahab and Anwar, who seemed to be falling asleep. Sarita began to run her fingers through Shahab's hair, and this put him to sleep. She turned towards Anwar, who was fast asleep. She climbed over to the front seat, sidled close to Kifayat, and whispered, 'I have lulled both your friends to sleep. Now, you should go to sleep as well.'

Kifayat smiled, 'And who will drive the car?'

Sarita smiled as well, 'It will keep on driving.'

Kifayat and Sarita continued to chat. Finally, they reached the bazaar where Kishori had introduced Sarita to the three men. When they reached the wall with the many boards which said 'Urinating Not Allowed Here', Sarita said to Kifayat, 'Stop, just stop here.'

Before Kifayat had time to collect his thoughts, Sarita was out of the car. She raised her hand in a salaam and was about to head off. Kifayat rested his hands on the steering wheel and was trying to relive the entire episode in his mind when Sarita stopped. She pulled the ten-rupee bill out of her choli, and with a flick of her hand, left it on the passenger seat. An astonished Kifayat asked, 'Sarita, what's this?'

'Why should I take this money?' asked Sarita as she walked away.

Kifayat looked at the ten-rupee note and glanced over his shoulder at the back seat where Shahab and Anwar lay listless like the ten-rupee note.

## Mammad Bhai

If you enter the alley on the right at a right angle to Faras Road, you will find another lane towards the right, and at the end of that lane, which is called Safed Gali or the White Alley, you will find a few hotels. Faras Road is a road, but the name is associated with a more expansive area where each alley has a name, but as shorthand, people refer to every alley either as Safed Gali or Faras Road. There are hotels and restaurants in every nook and cranny of Bombay, but the ones on Faras Road stand out because this locality is home to all kinds of hookers. Almost twenty years ago, I lived here and hung around the local cafeterias for endless rounds of tea and all my meals.

Walking through Safed Gali, you pass by Play House, where films are screened from morning until late at night, and a hullabaloo reigns supreme round the clock every day of the week. If I recall correctly, there are four film auditoriums in this area. Theatre proprietors hire men to ring loud gongs at regular intervals to alert prospective audiences. Zealous hired hands push passers-by into theatres, and voices blare from loudspeakers urging passers-by to 'Come and see, for two annas, come and see, *fust-class film* for just two annas!'

Everywhere you look, you find men offering a champi, the name for an energetic head massage in Bombay, which involves a very scientific method. A champi is no bad thing, but to this day, I have not figured why people in Bombay are addicted to it. Night and day, any time of day if you so wish, you can summon a champiwallah. Even at three o'clock in the morning, you can hear the call of a champiwallah in the remotest corner of Bombay.

Faras Road has thousands of shops that are cordoned off from the main thoroughfare by wrought-iron railings. Countless women sit behind the railings, on the lookout to sell their bodies. A punter will find an assortment of females of different generations, castes, complexions, and creeds. Jewish, Punjabi, Marathi, Kashmiri, Gujarati,

Bengali, Anglo-Indian, French, Chinese, Japanese—what I mean is that all types are available here. You can find a woman at prices that range from eight annas to eight rupees and from eight rupees to a hundred or more. Do not ask me to describe these women, but it is important to add that on Faras Road, most manage to find punters.

Faras Road has male and female entrepreneurs from every nation under the sun. Many Chinese live in this area, but again, do not ask me to expand on their work. Some run restaurants with signboards with who knows what written vertically in a script that to me looks like insects. An alley called Arab Gali, I believe, was named by the people who came and settled here a long time ago. When I lived in the area, there were more than twenty Arab families, and they described themselves as traders of pearls. The rest of the population consisted of Punjabis and Rampuris, and it was here that I found a place to live. The rent was seven-and-a-half rupees a month for a room with an embargo on natural light, and I had to keep the electric bulb on twenty-four hours a day.

If you have never lived in Bombay, you will find it difficult to believe that there is no give-and-take between people in this city. You could be on your deathbed in your kholi; nobody would bother to ask after you. You could die without knowing that someone had murdered your neighbour. But in Arab Gali lived a man who took an interest in the lives of all those who lived around him. His name was Mammad Bhai, and he was from Rampur. A swordsman of the first order, he was equally skilled in the art of wrestling and wielding a lathi. I heard his name when I first moved to Arab Gali and continued to hear about him from time to time. I left my kholi at the crack of dawn and returned in the dead of night, which meant I never had the opportunity to bump into Mammad Bhai.

Arab Gali was abuzz with stories of the great Mammad Bhai, and I wanted to see him at close quarters. I heard that even if ambushed by twenty or thirty men armed with lathis, Mammad Bhai could knock the lot out in a trice, without the slightest harm to a hair on his head. Not a man in Bombay could match his artistry in throwing a knife; his victims continued to walk a hundred steps before they figured out what had hit him and collapsed in a heap. In Arab Gali, Mammad Bhai was like a colossus. You could call him the godfather, dada, or ghunda of the area.

It was common knowledge that he never eyed people's daughters and daughters-in-law. A true friend, he stood with the poor in times of sorrow, not merely in Arab Gali but neighbouring streets as well. All the women knew Mammad Bhai because he helped them out financially in their hour of need. He did not visit them, but he sent an associate or a protégé to enquire after their welfare at regular intervals.

I don't know much about Mammad Bhai's means, but he lived, ate, and dressed well. He owned a sturdy mare and a small tonga which he drove with skill, usually with two or three deferential disciples in tow. On a trip back from Bhendi Bazaar or a shrine, he would head to an Irani hotel where he loved to lounge around, surrounded by his devotees, discussing the finer points of wrestling and other martial arts. I heard endless stories about Mammad Bhai from Ashiq Hussain, a Muslim Marwari dancer who lived in the kholi next to mine. He told me that Mammad Bhai was worth at least one hundred thousand rupees. Ashiq described how Mammad Bhai came to the rescue when he had cholera, and had summoned all the doctors of Faras Road to Ashiq's kholi and pronounced, 'Look here, if anything happens to Ashiq Hussain, I will wipe all of you out!' Ashiq Hussain recounted this tale in a tone dripping with devotion, 'Manto Sahib, Mammad Bhai is an angel…an angel. When he threatened the doctors, they began to shiver and treated me with such commitment that within two days, there I was, fit as a fiddle!'

In the filthy restaurants of Arab Gali, I heard countless other tales of Mammad Bhai's accomplishments. One of his devotees, who fancied himself a great fencer, told me that Mammad Bhai roamed around with a naked—I mean, an unsheathed—fine-edged dagger tucked in his cummerbund, right next to his stomach. The slightest tilt of its razor-sharp blade could spell the end of Mammad Bhai, and my desire to see him increased by the day. I can't recall how I conjured him in my mind's eye, but yes, I imagined a muscular, hefty man, the type that appears on ubiquitous advertisements for a Hercules bicycle.

Alas, there was little chance of my running into Mammad Bhai because such was my schedule. I juggled with ideas of skipping work with the sole purpose of hanging around Arab Gali the whole day so that I could see Mammad Bhai, but my worthless job did not allow such liberties. Around the time I was thinking of ways to meet Mammad Bhai, I was struck down by a vile attack of influenza; a doctor in Arab Gali feared it could turn into pneumonia. The man who shared my room had found a job in Poona, and it was not in my stars to enjoy the gift of friendship or companionship. The fever devoured me. Usually, I can look after myself, but this illness broke my back. My throat and mouth were parched, and the water supply to my kholi was a mere trickle. For the first time in my life, I felt a need for someone to comfort me.

I longed to see a human face, any face, even for a split second, and even though I knew no one could hear me, I cried out to reassure myself that someone out there was looking out for me. I lay in bed writhing with pain; two days passed, and nobody came. Indeed, who would come to see me? The hotel boy informed me that the dancer Ashiq Hussain had left for his watan because his wife was unwell. I had no other acquaintances. The two, three, or four people I knew in Bombay lived so far away that it would be difficult even for news of my death to reach them. In any case, at the risk of repeating myself, you can live or die for all anyone cares in Bombay. On the point of collapse, I was thinking of dragging myself to a doctor when I heard a knock on the door, and managed a faint, 'Come in.'

I thought it was the hotel boy, but a very slim man walked in. The first thing I noticed about him was his moustache. It gave life to his body; without it, he would be pretty ordinary. He walked in, twirling his Kaiser Wilhelm moustache, and stood by my charpai. Two or three rather anomalous-looking chaps followed him in. In a daze, I wondered why this ensemble had dropped by to see me. The man with the Kaiser Wilhelm moustache and slim body said in a very gentle voice, 'Vimto Sahib, you are the limit, saala, why didn't you inform me?'

The transformation of Manto into Vimto was not new to me, and I was in no mood to correct his mistake. I addressed his moustache and asked in a weak voice, 'Who are you?'

He gave a short answer, 'Mammad Bhai.'

I sat up. 'Mammad Bhai...so...so you are Mammad Bhai, the

famous dada?' The words were out before I could censor my indelicate tongue.

Mammad Bhai lifted the sharp point of his moustache with the little finger of his right hand and smiled, 'Yes, Vimto Bhai, I am Mammad Bhai, the famous local dada. I heard you are unwell. Saala, this is no way to behave. You did not inform me! Mammad Bhai's head goes into a spin when something like this happens.'

I was about to say something, but he turned to one of his flunkies and said, 'Arrey, what's your name? Run...run and get—what's that doctor's name? You understand, no? Tell him Mammad Bhai is calling you. Pronto. Quick! Pronto! Drop everything and rush. Rush and tell that saala to bring all the necessary medicines.'

The flunky rushed off.

As I looked at Mammad Bhai, all the tales I had heard about him whizzed through my mind. I continued to look at him and concluded that it must be his moustache that mesmerized everyone. It was impressive. I thought he had cultivated it to invest an aura of invincibility to his delicate face with its unusually fine features. Although overcome by a fever, it did not take me long to figure out that this man was not as terrifying as he made himself out to be. There was no chair in my kholi, and I asked Mammad Bhai to sit on my charpai, but he declined and said in a dry tone, 'It's fine. We can stand.' He continued to pace up and down in my tiny kholi. At one point, he lifted the hem of his kurta and pulled out a gleaming dagger from his cummerbund. I thought it was silver, and it looked sharp. He flicked it across his wrist and shaved clean any hair that came in its way; he seemed gratified and began to pare his nails.

I am sure his arrival brought my temperature down by several degrees. Somewhat recovered from my delirium, I asked him, 'Mammad Bhai, you keep this knife unsheathed in your cummerbund right next to your stomach. Aren't you scared?' He shaved off a sliver of a fingernail and responded, 'Vimto Bhai, this dagger is for others. Saali, she knows she is my very own. How can she harm me?' The bond he claimed with his dagger reminded me of a father who claims his offspring can do him no harm.

The doctor arrived. His name was Pinto, and it resonated well with Vimto. He greeted Mammad Bhai with a European Christian greeting and enquired how he could be of service. Mammad Bhai briefly explained the matter to him, but in stark words that sounded more like a command. 'Look here, if you don't look after Vimto Bhai properly, it won't be good for you.' Dr Pinto transformed into a dutiful offspring and checked my pulse and blood pressure before examining me with his stethoscope. He asked me for details of all existing medical conditions, but instead of addressing me, he turned to Mammad Bhai and said, 'Nothing to worry about; it is malaria. I'll give him an injection.'

When Mammad Bhai heard what Dr Pinto had to say, he swiped his dagger, shaved some more hair off his arm, and said, 'I don't care what you do, if you must give an injection, then do, but if something happens to him....'

Dr Pinto trembled visibly, 'No, Mammad Bhai, everything will be all right.'

'All right then,' said Mammad Bhai before he tucked the dagger away in his cummerbund.

'All right then, I'll give the injection,' said the doctor as he opened his bag and took out a syringe.

'Wait! Wait!' shouted Mammad Bhai. Immediately, the doctor shoved the syringe back into his bag and asked obsequiously, 'Why?'

'I can't bear to see a needle jabbed into anyone's body.' Mammad Bhai turned around and left my kholi with his companions.

Dr Pinto gave me a quinine injection very skilfully. I know malaria jabs can be very painful. When he finished, I asked him about his fees, and he said, 'Ten rupees.'

I was about to take out my wallet from under my pillow when Mammad Bhai returned. Just as I was handing Dr Pinto ten rupees, Mammad Bhai glared ferociously at him and roared, 'What's happening here?'

I said, 'I am paying the fees.'

Mammad Bhai turned to Dr Pinto, 'Saale, what are you taking the fees for?'

Dr Pinto replied, 'I was not taking it; he was giving it!'

'Saala, you dare take fees from us. Return that money!'

Mammad Bhai's tone was as sharp as his dagger. Dr Pinto returned the ten rupees to me, closed his bag, begged Mammad Bhai's leave, and rushed off.

Mammad Bhai smiled as he twirled the tip of his pointed moustache with one finger, 'Vimto Bhai, it's not allowed for local doctors to charge you fees. I swear by your head, I would have shaved off my moustache if that saala had taken a paisa from you. All of us here are your humble servants.'

I hesitated before I asked him, 'Mammad Bhai, how do you know about me?'

Mammad Bhai's moustache quivered noticeably, 'Who doesn't Mammad Bhai know? I am the king of this area, sweetheart, and I look after my subjects! Our CID keeps us informed. We know who is doing well and who is in trouble, and we know everything about you.'

I was curious and asked, 'What do you know about me?'

'Saala, what is it that I don't know! You are from Amritsar, but you are a Kashmiri. You work for newspapers, and you owe Bismillah Hotel ten rupees—that is why you have stopped going near that place. A paanwallah in Bhendi Bazaar is after your life because you've smoked cigarettes worth twenty rupees and ten annas on his account.'

I wanted to drown in shame. Mammad Bhai stroked his pointed moustache with one finger and said, 'Vimto Bhai, don't worry. Consider all your debts settled. Now you can start anew. I have told those saalas to watch it and not to bug you. Mammad Bhai assures you, inshallah; nobody will trouble you.'

I was feeling unwell, and the quinine jab caused a persistent ring in my ears. I crumbled under the weight of Mammad Bhai's goodwill and could barely bring myself to say, 'May God grant you a long life and happiness, Mammad Bhai.'

Dr Pinto visited me every evening. Each time I mentioned his fees, he touched his ears and said, 'No...no...Mr Manto...this is Mammad Bhai's business. I cannot take an anna from you.'

I thought this Mammad Bhai was a big shot—of the dangerous type—when an upright man like Dr Pinto didn't have the guts to take money from me and was spending money from his pocket on my injections.

During my illness, Mammad Bhai visited me every day, randomly in the morning or evening, but always with six to seven hangers-on. He boosted my morale and reassured me that I had a very straightforward case of malaria, and Dr Pinto's treatment, inshallah, would make me very well very soon. I recovered within a fortnight. During this time, I observed several facets of Mammad Bhai's personality.

Mammad Bhai must have been between twenty-five or thirty years old at the time. As I have said earlier, he was a man with a slim physique and slender limbs. His hands were deft as the devil's, and several residents of Arab Gali had told me how he used them to aim his sharp-edged knife to pierce his enemy's heart. Each story contributed to Mammad Bhai's fame; someone told me he had killed countless men, but now that I knew him, I found this hard to believe—even though thinking of his dagger made my body quake. Why did he keep the horrific weapon tucked in his cummerbund?

One day, after I recovered from malaria, I bumped into Mammad Bhai in a third-class Chinese restaurant in Arab Gali. He was paring his fingernails with that same horrific dagger. I asked him, 'Mammad Bhai, this is an age of pistols and guns, why do you walk around with a dagger?'

Mammad Bhai stroked his pointed Kaiser Wilhelm moustache with a fingertip and said, 'Vimto Bhai, there is no thrill in pistols and guns—any child can fire them; press the trigger and bang! Where is the thrill in that? But this dagger—by God, what pleasure it gives! I mean, it is an art, sweetheart. Art! He who does not know the art of blades and daggers is *kundum*, worthless. What is a pistol? A toy that can cause harm; where is the thrill? None whatsoever. Now, look at this dagger and its sharp edge.' He kissed his thumb and rubbed it across the dagger. 'It is silent, unlike a gunshot, and it enters the stomach ever so gracefully; *saala* doesn't even know firearms are rubbish.'

Soon after I recovered from my illness, I began to meet Mammad Bhai every day at some point in the day. I felt hugely indebted to him, and he felt slighted by my gratitude. He reminded me that he had done me no favour but merely his duty. After some enquiries, I discovered that, indeed, he was among the godfathers of Faras Road—a godfather who kept an eye on everyone. It was the job of his CID to keep him informed, and if a person was sick or needy, Mammad Bhai was there to help. He was the acknowledged dada or godfather of his area, but I fail to understand by what yardstick he was a ghunda. With God as my witness, I saw no signs of ghundagardi in him—just his terrifying moustache that he loved as a parent loves a child, and cared for much in the same way. Once, someone told me that Mammad Bhai lubricated his moustache with full cream and liked to twirl it with a finger dipped in rich gravy because his elders had told him this is the best way to boost hair growth.

I hate to labour a point, but his moustache was terrifying; his moustache and the dagger tucked in the cummerbund of his narrow-cut shalwar exemplified Mammad Bhai. I am not quite sure why, but I was equally terrified of both. Mammad Bhai was indeed the big dada of Faras Road, but he had everyone's welfare at heart. As I have said earlier, I am not sure about his means, but he helped people in their hour of need. All the hookers of the area revered him as their pir or spiritual leader. It was logical to assume that as a celebrated ghunda, he had dealings with local tawa'ifs, but I discovered he was not remotely associated with that sort of business.

Over time, Mammad Bhai and I became good friends. He was uneducated, and I have no idea why he held me in such high esteem, but his regard for me invited the envy of all the inhabitants of Arab Gali. One morning, I was on my way to work when someone in the Chinese hotel told me that the police had arrested Mammad Bhai. I was astounded because all the police personnel were either his friends or in his pocket. When I asked my informant, he gave me the reason for Mammad Bhai's detention, 'There is a woman called Shireen Bai, who lives here in Arab Gali. Yesterday, somebody spoilt her young daughter, I mean stole her virginity. Shireen Bai came to see Mammad Bhai in tears, and said, "You are the dada here. Such and such man did this and that with my daughter. And you were sitting at home. May you rot in hell!" Mammad Bhai let out a choice expletive and asked the old woman, "What do you want?" She said, "I want you to rip that bastard's innards apart." Mammad Bhai put down his qeema pau, pulled out his dagger from his cummerbund, stroked the edge of its blade with his thumb, and said to the old woman, "Go. Your work will be done." And it was done.'

To cut a long story short, the man who robbed Shireen Bai's daughter of her innocence is no more. Mammad Bhai accomplished his deed with finesse, and there were no eyewitnesses; even if there were, who would give evidence against him? Yet, he was arrested and kept in the clinker for two days, where he was pretty comfortable. From police constables to sub-inspectors and inspectors, everyone knew him. Mammad Bhai had countless friends in Arab Gali, and most reassured him that this was not a serious matter. Again, there were no eyewitnesses, but they reckoned his moustache could set the magistrate's heart against him. As I have said earlier, the moustache made him look fierce; without it, he did not look remotely like a dada. Mammad Bhai was released on bail at the police station, and now he had to appear before a magistrate in court.

I ran into him at the Chinese hotel and was startled to see that his moustache that always pointed fiercely upwards was drooping, and his ever-pristine clothes were filthy. I did not mention the murder, but he said, 'Vimto Sahib, I am sorry about one thing. Saala, I made a mistake in throwing the saala knife, and that too was that saala chap's fault. My hand was at an angle, and unfortunately, he turned around without warning; that is why the whole thing was kundum. I regret he died in pain.'

Imagine my reaction when I realized that Mammad Bhai was lamenting the fact that he could not kill a man without causing him pain.

As the date for his hearing drew closer, Mammad Bhai became more apprehensive by the day. In his entire life, he had never set eyes on a courtroom. The court proceedings gave Mammad Bhai the biggest jolt of his life. I do not believe he had ever killed anybody before this incident, nor had he dealt with a magistrate, a lawyer, or a witness. He had no understanding of legal procedures. He continued to run a finger across his moustache and told me several times, 'Vimto Sahib, I'd rather die than go to court. Saali, I don't know that sort of place.'

I met him at the Irani hotel a few days after his bail hearing, and he was palpably nervous, convinced that if he appeared in court with his moustache, the magistrate would find him guilty. You think I have made up this story, but I have not. His disciples were in a state of disbelief because they had never seen him so nervous. Most of his close friends advised him, 'Mammad Bhai, don't go to court with this moustache, the magistrate will lock you up.' Mammad Bhai asked himself if his moustache had murdered the man but drew a blank on that front. He pulled the blade out from his cummerbund and flung it out into the alley. Astounded, I asked, 'Mammad Bhai, what was that?'

'Nothing, Vimto Bhai. The whole thing is a scam. I must appear in court, and all my friends tell me that when the magistrate sees my moustache, he will find me guilty. Now, you tell me, what should I do?'

I looked at his frankly terrifying moustache and said, 'Mammad Bhai, they are quite right. Your moustache will influence the magistrate's decision, and the entire proceedings will not be against you but your moustache.'

'So, should I shave it off?' Mammad Bhai asked as he stroked his beloved moustache with a tender touch.

I asked him, 'What do you think?'

'Don't ask me what I think. Everyone thinks I should shave it off if I want the saala magistrate to look upon me with favour. I think I should have it shaved off, Vimto Bhai.'

After some hesitation, I said, 'Yes, have it shaved off if you think it appropriate. It's a question of the court, and quite frankly, your moustache is terrifying.'

The following day, Mammad Bhai had his moustache shaved off. It was dearer to him than life, but his honour was at stake, and he did so solely on the advice of others. The case came up in Mr F. H. Tag's court. Mammad Bhai appeared sans moustache, and I was there. There was no evidence against him, but the magistrate sahib declared him a dangerous ghunda and passed an order to expel him from Bombay. Mammad Bhai had to leave Bombay Presidency. The court gave him one day to wind up his affairs. He did not speak a word as he left the court, but I saw his fingers continually feeling the clean-shaven area above his upper lip, now without a moustache.

The court had exiled Mammad Bhai, and he had until nightfall to leave Bombay Presidency. I went to see him at the Irani hotel where he was drinking tea in the company of twenty or so disciples, who had pulled up their chairs around him. He remained silent in response to my greeting. He looked like a perfectly respectable man without his moustache, but I could see he was disconsolate. I drew my chair close to his and asked, 'What's the matter, Mammad Bhai?'

He let out a humungous expletive directed God alone knows at whom and said, 'Saala, Mammad Bhai is no more.'

I said, 'Never mind, Mammad Bhai, if not here then somewhere else.'

He came up with a string of obscenities against all the places he could think of, 'Saala, I don't care if I live here or somewhere else, but why did I have this saala moustache shaved off!' He continued with a barrage of a hundred thousand or more expletives at all those who had advised him to shave off his moustache, 'Saala, if exile it had to be, why not with my moustache!'

I chuckled. Mammad Bhai was incandescent with rage and said, 'Saala, what sort of man are you, Vimto? Truly, I swear upon God, they could have hanged me, but I am responsible for this foolish act. To this day, I have never feared anyone. Saala, I was frightened of my moustache.'

He slapped both his cheeks in turn and said, 'To hell with you, Mammad Bhai, saala, frightened of your moustache! Now get lost, and...your mother.' His eyes brimmed over with tears, which looked out of place on his moustacheless face.

## Sharda

Nazir set out in the morning to find whisky on the black market. He knew he didn't have to go far and could find a bottle at the cigarette vendor's kiosk. It was eleven o'clock by the time he paid thirty-five rupees for a bottle of Scotch. As a rule, he drank in the evenings, but tempted by the clement weather, he thought why not start right away and continue until night. Nazir headed to the Bori Bunder taxi rank in an ebullient mood, planning to have his first peg before heading home in a state of blissful intoxication. He knew his wife would try to stop his drinking, and he would say, 'Look at the lovely weather,' and recite a meaningless couplet. She would protest but ultimately give up and head off to make the qeema parathas he so enjoyed. Nazir had not walked more than twenty yards from the cigarette kiosk when a man greeted him. He didn't have the faintest idea who the fellow was, but without letting the stranger figure out this lapse of memory, he asked courteously, 'Well, then my friend, where are you these days? Haven't seen you around.'

The man smiled and said, 'Why, sir, I am around; it's just that you haven't been around.'

Nazir failed to recognize him. He said, 'Well now, here I am.'

'Well, then come with me.'

Nazir was in a marvellous mood and said, 'Let's go.'

The man looked at the bottle wrapped in newspaper and asked with a meaningful smile, 'You have all the "other stuff"?'

The moment he heard this phrase, Nazir figured the man was a pimp and asked, 'What's your name?'

'Karim...you'd forgotten?'

Nazir recalled that he had known this chap in his bachelor days. Indeed, Karim had supplied him with some great girls. Nazir looked him up and down, and as old memories revived, he recalled Karim as an upright pimp and apologized, 'Yaar, I didn't recognize you. I think it must be at least six years since I last saw you.'

'Yes, sir.'

'Wasn't your hangout around Grant Road?'

Karim lit a biri and said with a degree of pride, 'I've left that area. With your blessings, now I carry out my trade from a hotel around the corner.'

Nazir complimented him, 'You've done well.'

Karim continued, 'I have ten hussies—one is brand new.'

Nazir mocked him, 'You guys always use the same line.'

Karim was irked, 'I swear on the Qur'an, I never lie. May I eat swine flesh if this girl isn't brand new!' He lowered his voice and whispered in Nazir's ear, 'The first passenger came eight days ago. May I perish if I lie.'

Nazir asked, 'Was she a virgin?'

'Yes, sir! I took two hundred rupees from the passenger.'

Nazir nudged Karim in his ribcage, 'Look at that...already trying to fix the price!'

Karim was offended, 'I swear on the Qur'an! May I rot in hell if I play the market with you. Come with me, sir. I'll accept whatever you give. Karim owes you his livelihood.'

Nazir had four-hundred-and-fifty rupees in his pocket. His mood was as balmy as the weather, and as his thoughts drifted back six years, he felt chipper even without a drink. He said to Karim, 'Come on, yaar, let's give in to all pleasures today. You'll have to arrange another bottle.'

Karim asked, 'How much did you pay for this one, sir?'

'Thirty-five rupees.'

'What brand?'

'Johnnie Walker.'

Karim put his hand on his heart and said, 'I'll get another for you for thirty?'

Nazir took out three ten-rupee notes and handed them to Karim. 'Would I look a gift horse in the mouth? Here you are. After you settle me down, it's the first thing you must do. You do remember that at such times I don't drink on my own.'

Karim smiled, 'And, sir, you know I never drink more than a peg and a half.'

True. Even six years ago, Karim did not consume more than a

peg and a half. Nazir smiled, 'Two for today.'

'No, sir, not a drop more than a peg and a half.'

Karim stopped by a third-rate building. Nazir saw a small, smudged board hanging towards the left on the corner of the outer wall with 'Marina Hotel' written on it. The name was lovely, but the building was horrid and mouldy. At the entrance, near a rickety wooden staircase, several Pathan moneylenders clad in flared white shalwars were sprawled out on charpais. Karim informed Nazir that a colony of Christians lived on the first floor, many laid-off sailors occupied the second, the proprietor of the hotel kept the third floor, and Karim had a room in one corner of the fourth floor. Nazir spotted several girls sitting like hens in a coop.

Karim got a key from the proprietor and unlocked a large room with countless folding wooden windows on three sides, instead of walls. Some windowpanes were broken, while others were missing altogether, consequently, there was plenty of air. The space was sparsely furnished, with a steel bed, an armchair, and a teapoy. Karim wiped the grimy armchair with an even grimier cloth and said to Nazir, 'Do sit down, sir. might I inform you, with respect, the rent for this room is ten rupees.'

Nazir inspected the room, 'Yaar, ten rupees is a bit much!'

Karim responded, 'Too much, but what to do...saala, the proprietor of the hotel is a bania...he will not reduce a paisa. Besides, Nazir Sahib, men who like the good life don't care.'

Nazir gave the matter some thought and said, 'You're right. Should I pay the rent in advance?'

'No, sir, at least check out the lass.'

Karim went to his coop and returned with a timid Hindu girl with a white dhoti wrapped around her. She had a homely appearance and was no beauty. Yet, no more than thirteen or fourteen, she had an air of innocence. Karim turned to her, 'Sit down. Sir is my friend; he is our own.'

The girl sat down on the steel bed; she looked downcast. Karim continued, 'Check her out, Nazir Sahib,' and added, 'I'll get a glass and some soda,' before he left the room.

Nazir left the armchair and moved to the bed to sit next to the girl, who shrank to one side. Nazir asked her with an ease he had perfected over six years, 'Your name?'

The girl did not respond. Nazir moved closer and held both her hands and asked, 'What's your name, my dear?'

The girl pulled her hands away and said, 'Shakuntala.'

Nazir thought of the Shakuntala with whom Raja Dushyanta had fallen in love. Determined to indulge in all manner of hedonism, he said, 'My name is Dushyanta.'

The girl smiled at his response, just as Karim returned waving four bottles of soda sweating because they were so cold. He said, 'I remember you like Roger's soda and brought some chilled!'

Nazir was delighted. 'You're a magician!' He turned to the girl and asked, 'And mademoiselle, would you care for some?'

The girl remained silent. Karim said, 'Nazir Sahib, she does not drink. She's only been here for eight days.'

This information cast a damper on Nazir's spirits, 'How awful!'

Karim opened the bottle of whisky and poured a peg for Nazir, winked at him, and said, 'Why don't you persuade her?'

Nazir downed a peg in one gulp. Karim drank half a peg, and his voice promptly acquired a hint of intoxication. He began to sway gently and asked Nazir, 'Do you like the filly?'

Nazir mulled over the question but could not make up his mind. He scrutinized Shakuntala, whom he might have fancied if she had a different name. The Shakuntala to whom Raja Dushyanta had lost his heart while hunting in the forest—that Shakuntala—was gorgeous. According to the old texts, she was like the moon, with doe-like eyes. Nazir looked at this Shakuntala again. Her eyes were passable, although not doe-like, they were black and large and had character. He did not tax his mind further and said, 'She's fine, yaar. Tell me, where do we fix the matter?'

Karim poured himself another peg and said, 'A hundred rupees!'

Nazir had stopped thinking, 'Okay!'

Karim drank his half peg and disappeared.

Six pegs of whisky cast an agreeable spell on Nazir. He locked the door and returned to sit next to Shakuntala. She looked terrified. When he tried to kiss her, Shakuntala jumped up. An offended Nazir made a second attempt. He held her arm, pulled her closer, and forced a kiss on her. Full of regret that such an expensive item should prove so unyielding, Nazir tried all sorts of manoeuvres with a girl who was not even a beginner. Shakuntala was headstrong. Finally, he gave up and opened the door and called Karim, who was in the coop with his hens. He arrived promptly and asked, 'What's the matter, Nazir Sahib?'

Nazir answered in a defeated tone, 'Nothing, yaar, she is of no use to me.'

'Why?'

'She doesn't understand anything.'

Karim took Shakuntala aside and tried to explain matters to her. Diffident and withdrawn, she clutched her dhoti and left the room. Karim said, 'I will just bring her back.'

Nazir stopped him, 'Let her be, bring someone else...' but immediately he had a change of heart. 'That money I gave you, use it for another bottle and send all your girls who drink, but not Shakuntala, send them to me. Today we shall have no other activity, but we shall drink. I'll sit and chat with them. That's it!'

Familiar with Nazir's ways, Karim sent four girls into the room. Nazir sized them up in a cursory manner. He had decided to restrict today's activities to alcohol and began his drinking spree. Nazir sent for lunch from the local hotel and indulged in pointless conversations with the girls until six o'clock in the evening. Time spent with the girls assuaged the frustration triggered by Shakuntala's behaviour, and he was left with half a bottle of whisky to take home.

After a fortnight, yet again, the weather stirred in Nazir a desire to spend the whole day drinking. He thought, instead of the cigarette kiosk, why not ask Karim to procure a bottle for thirty rupees, and he headed towards Marina Hotel. Fortuitously, he bumped into Karim on the road. Before Nazir could say anything, Karim whispered, 'Nazir Sahib, Shakuntala's older sister is here. She arrived by the morning train and is tenacious, but I am sure you'll win her over.'

Nazir thought there was no harm trying. He pulled thirty rupees out of his pocket and said to Karim, 'Yaar, first get the whisky.'

Karim took the money and left, saying, 'I'll bring it in no time, sir.'

Now, Nazir had ten rupees in his pocket and thought he should take the bottle of whisky from Karim, have a quick look at Shakuntala's sister, and head home. He asked Karim to open the room with windows on three sides, sat down on the grimy armchair, lit a cigarette, stretched his legs, and rested his feet on the bed when he heard footsteps. Karim walked in, and before he went off, he whispered in his ear, 'Nazir Sahib, she is on her way; only you can win her over.'

Five minutes later, a girl walked in wearing a white dhoti and a frown on a face almost a replica of Shakuntala's. She greeted Nazir with a couldn't-care-less aadaab and sat down on the steel bed. Nazir felt she had come to pick a fight with him. He took a cue from his six-year-old rule book and asked, 'You are Shakuntala's sister?'

She responded with a biting 'Yes.'

Nazir remained silent as he sized up the girl, who found his behaviour most annoying. About three years older than Shakuntala, she sat shaking her right leg and turned to Nazir, 'What do you wish to say to me?'

A six-year-old smile appeared on Nazir's lips, and he asked, 'What makes you so angry, my dear?'

She snarled at him, 'Why shouldn't I be angry! This Karim of yours whisked my sister away from Jaipur. Tell me, shouldn't my blood boil when I know that he's offered her to you as well?'

Never in his life had Nazir confronted such a dilemma. He gave the matter some thought and turned to the girl very gently, 'The moment I set eyes on Shakuntala, I knew she was not the girl for me. She's very stubborn, and I don't like such girls. You may not like what I'm saying, but it is the truth. I prefer women who understand men's needs.'

She did not respond. Nazir asked her, 'What's your name?'

Shakuntala's older sister gave a crisp answer, 'Sharda.'

Nazir asked her, 'Where are you from?'

'Jaipur.' Her tone was sharp.

Nazir smiled and said to her, 'Look here, you have no right to be angry with me. If Karim has been remiss, punish him. I haven't done anything to harm you.' He walked up to her, enveloped her in his arms, and kissed her on her lips. Before she could say anything, Nazir added, 'This is my fault, and you can punish me.'

Several expressions registered on the girl's brow before she spat on the floor three or four times, and she was about to swear at him when she changed her mind. She stood up but immediately sat down again. Nazir wanted her to respond and asked, 'Tell me what punishment lies in store for me?'

Before she could respond, they heard a baby cry. The girl leapt up. Nazir stopped her, 'Where are you going?'

Sharda transformed into a mother and left the room saying, 'Munni is crying for milk.'

Nazir tried to focus on Sharda but could not picture her in his mind's eye. Soon, Karim walked into the room with a bottle of whisky and some soda. He poured a drink for Nazir, finished his, and asked in a conspiratorial manner, 'Did you manage to have a conversation with Sharda? I thought you'd have won her over by now. She's a very angry woman.'

Nazir smiled, 'She is a very angry woman.'

'Yes. Sharda arrived this morning, and she's after my blood. Please win her over. Shakuntala came here of her own accord because their father had left their mother. Sharda was also in a mess because God knows where her husband took off soon after their marriage. Now she lives with her mother and her baby daughter. Why don't you try to win her over?'

'What's there to win over?' Nazir asked.

Karim winked at him, 'Saali doesn't care about what I say. She has been shouting at me from the moment she arrived.'

Just as Karim finished speaking, Sharda walked in, dandling her one-year-old daughter on her hip. She glared at Karim, who gulped down his peg and left the room. Munni had a bad cold and a runny nose. Nazir summoned Karim and gave him a five-rupee note, after which he wrote the name of a medicine on a piece of paper and handed it to him, saying, 'This is a medicine for a cold; you'll find it in any shop.'

'Yes, sir,' said Karim and dashed off.

Nazir enjoyed the company of children and instinctively warmed towards Munni. She was not good-looking, but she was a toddler, and Nazir picked her up. Nazir managed to lull Munni to sleep where her mother had failed, combing his fingers gently through her hair. He turned to Sharda and said, 'Actually, I am her mother.'

Sharda smiled, 'Give her to me. I'll take her inside.'

Sharda took Munni away and returned after a few minutes, and sat down on the bed without a hint of anger on her face. Nazir sat down beside her. He remained silent for a while and then asked Sharda, 'Will you allow me to become your husband?' He did not wait for an answer but drew her close. Sharda showed no sign of anger. He persisted, 'Answer me, my dearest.'

Sharda remained silent. Nazir stood up, and as he poured himself a peg of whisky, Sharda scrunched her nose and said, 'I hate this stuff.'

Nazir prepared another peg and sat next to Sharda, 'Why do you hate this?'

'I just do.'

Nazir touched the glass to Sharda's lips and said, 'Well, from today, you won't. Here....'

'No way will I drink this!' Sharda responded firmly.

'And I say, no way will you say no.'

Sharda took the glass and looked at it with an inexplicable expression in her eyes. She turned to Nazir with a defeated look, held her nose with her fingertips, and gulped down the contents of the glass. She was about to throw up but managed to stop herself. As she wiped her tears with a corner of her dhoti, she said to Nazir, 'This is the first and last time...but why did I drink?'

Nazir kissed her moist lips and said, 'Don't ask why,' and he shut the door.

Nazir opened the door at seven o'clock in the evening. When Karim walked in, Sharda lowered her gaze and left the room. Karim was delighted. He said to Nazir, 'You have worked wonders. I shan't ask you for a hundred—just give fifty.'

Nazir was content with Sharda, so content that he forgot all previous women. She was one hundred per cent the right answer to all his sexual desires. He said to Karim, 'I'll settle it tomorrow, with the bill for the hotel. Today, I have just ten rupees left after paying for the whisky.'

Karim said, 'Not a problem, sir. I'm thrilled that you struck a deal with Sharda. She addled my brain. Now, she won't say anything to Shakuntala.'

Soon after Karim left the room, Sharda returned with Munni in her arms. Nazir gave her five rupees but Sharda refused. Nazir smiled and said to her, 'I am her father; why are you refusing?'

Sharda took the money quietly. Nazir took Munni from Sharda and gave the little girl a peck on her cheek, saying, 'Well now, Sharda, I am off, but if not tomorrow, I'll come back day after...definitely.'

Nazir returned the following day. During their first sexual encounter, Sharda talked so much that it seemed a river of words was flowing from her mouth. Now, she did not wish to speak, her body responded with sympathy to Nazir. He paid off Karim's outstanding dues, sent for another bottle of whisky, and sat down with Sharda. When he asked her to drink, she said, 'I told you, that was my first and last glass.' Nazir drank by himself.

Nazir was with Sharda in the hotel room from eleven o'clock in the morning until seven o'clock in the evening. He returned home more gratified than the previous day. Despite her ordinary face and inability to make conversation, Sharda stirred his primal instincts. Nazir could not get her out of his mind and asked himself, 'What sort of woman is she? Never in my life have I met a woman who is so quiet and has such an expressive body.'

Nazir began to visit Sharda every other day. She had no interest in money but he handed Karim sixty rupees, from which the hotel proprietor took ten, and from the balance of fifty, Karim took a cut of around thirteen as commission. Sharda did not mention this transaction to Nazir. Two months passed, and Nazir's budget buckled. Besides, he felt that Sharda was destroying his married life. When he slept with his wife, he felt a lack, and thought it awful that he wanted to be with Sharda. As Nazir became more conscious of this feeling, he felt that somehow the Sharda business should come to an end. And one day he spoke to her, 'Sharda, I am a married man, and now I've run through all my savings. I don't know what to do. I cannot stop seeing you, although I keep hoping I never head in this direction again.'

Sharda heard him out and remained silent for a while before she said, 'You can take all the money I have. Just leave enough for our fare to Jaipur so I can take Shakuntala back.'

Nazir kissed her and said, 'Don't talk nonsense. You didn't understand what I meant. The problem is that I have spent a lot of money. I'm broke and was trying to figure out how I can continue visiting you.'

Sharda did not respond. The following day, Nazir borrowed money from a friend and arrived at the hotel. Karim told him that Sharda was ready and packed to leave for Jaipur. Nazir sent for her, but she did not come to see him; instead, she sent a wad of money with a message which said, 'Take this money and give me your address.'

Nazir gave Karim his address but returned the money. Sharda came in carrying Munni. She greeted Nazir with an aadaab, and added, 'I am leaving for Jaipur this evening.'

'Why?' asked Nazir.

Sharda's answer was a short, 'I don't know,' and walked out of the room.

Nazir asked Karim to fetch her but she did not return, and Nazir left. He felt the warmth of his body had vanished and with it the answers to all his problems. Sharda left Bombay. Karim was very distressed, and he admonished Nazir, 'Nazir Sahib, why did you let her go?'

Nazir said, 'Look here, I'm no seth! I was spending fifty rupees every other day—ten for the hotel, thirty for the bottle, and then other expenses on top. I am bankrupt. I swear upon God, I am in debt.'

Karim was silent. Nazir said to him, 'Look here, I had no choice. How long could I have carried on like this?'

Karim said, 'Nazir Sahib, she loved you.'

Nazir had no idea what love meant. All he knew was that Sharda's body was sympathetic. She was a one-stop solution to all his male conundrums. He knew nothing about Sharda, other than the brief account she had shared with him. Her husband was a degenerate, who left her merely because she did not have a child for two years. But nine months after they separated, Sharda delivered Munni, who looked exactly like her father.

Nazir picked up several facets of Sharda's life from Karim. She adored her sister and had brought Shakuntala to Bombay because she wanted her to get married and lead a decent life. Yet, Karim tried hard to induct Shakuntala into the trade. Several passengers had agreed to give two hundred rupees for her, but Sharda did not agree. She also quarrelled with Karim about Nazir, and told him, 'If you were not the go-between, I would never have agreed to this bargain. I would not have allowed Nazir Sahib to spend a penny.'

Once, Sharda asked Nazir for his photograph, and he brought one for her. Sharda never expressed her emotions in words. When they were together in bed, she remained silent, even when he urged her to speak. Nazir craved the sympathy of Sharda's body; for him, she was the embodiment of compassion; but she had caused a breach in Nazir's family life. With her departure, a burden lifted from his heart. If she had stayed a little longer, in time, Nazir would have drifted away from his wife. It took a few days for him to return to his usual self, and gradually his body began to forget Sharda's touch.

A fortnight after Sharda's departure, Nazir was working from home when his wife walked in with the morning post. Since she read all the mail, she opened a letter, looked at it, and handed it to Nazir, saying, 'Don't know if it's in Gujarati or Hindi.'

Nazir took the letter but could not decipher the script. He put it away in a separate tray and returned to work. Nazir's wife shouted for her younger sister, Naeema, and handed the letter to her, 'Read this, since you can read Hindi and Gujarati.'

Naeema looked at the letter and said, 'It's Hindi,' and began to read, 'Jaipur, Dear Nazir Sahib,' after she had read these four words she hesitated, and Nazir gave a start. Naeema read another line, 'Aadaab, you must have forgotten me, but ever since I returned to Jaipur, I can't stop thinking of you.'

Naeema's face turned crimson as she turned the paper over and said, 'It's some Sharda.'

Nazir leapt up and almost snatched the letter from Naeema's hand. He turned to his wife and said, 'God knows who she is...I'm going out, I'll get someone to read the letter and write it out in Urdu, and bring it back.' Without waiting for his wife's response, he set off to see a friend.

At his friend's place, they sent for some paper and ink to match those used by Sharda. His friend wrote another letter with the first few lines precisely as in the original, while the rest described how Sharda was so thrilled to meet such a great artist at Bombay Central. When Nazir returned home that evening, he handed the fake letter to his wife and read out its Urdu translation. When his wife asked him about Sharda, he said, 'Ages ago, I had gone to the station to see off a friend, and he introduced her to me on the platform. She's interested in painting.' And he thought that was the end of the matter.

The following morning, another letter arrived from Sharda. Somehow Nazir managed not to arouse his wife's suspicion but immediately sent Sharda a telegram asking her to stop writing to him and to wait for a new address. He rushed to the local post office, where he instructed his postman to hold on to all letters from Jaipur, adding that he would collect them personally every morning. Nazir received three letters through the postman's good offices, and all subsequent letters from Sharda arrived at his friend's address.

Sharda was not very talkative, but she wrote long letters. She had never spoken to Nazir of her love for him, but her letters were full of all the mundane matters found in love letters, with professions of adoration and plaints of longing and separation. Nazir was not in love with Sharda in the way that writers describe the emotion in short stories and novels. He had no idea what he could write back to her and handed this task over to his friend, who penned the response in Hindi and read it out for Nazir's approval. Sharda longed to return to Bombay, but she did not want to stay with Karim, and Nazir could not find affordable accommodation for her in Bombay. The thought of a hotel crossed Nazir's mind, but he knew that if his secret assignations came to light, the fallout would be nothing short of cataclysmic. He asked his friend to write to Sharda and ask her to bide her time.

Meanwhile, communal riots broke out, just before Partition, and an eerie restlessness infiltrated the atmosphere. His wife announced that she wanted to leave for Lahore, and added, 'I'll stay there for some time. If matters improve, I'll return, or else you join me there.'

Nazir tried to stop her, but he had to agree when her brother and sister-in-law also decided to leave for Lahore.

Nazir was by himself in the flat, and he wrote a quick note to Sharda, who wired back to say that she was on her way. By the time Nazir read the telegram, she had left Jaipur. The news astonished Nazir and thrilled his body; he needed the quiet sympathy of Sharda's body and longed to return to those days when he did not notice the hours pass from eleven in the morning to seven o'clock in the evening. He thought, 'I'll take my servant into confidence, and all will be well. Ten or fifteen rupees will seal his lips, and he won't breathe a word to my wife when she returns.'

The following day, by the time Nazir reached the station, the Frontier Mail had arrived but he could not find her on the train or the platform. He thought, perhaps, she's delayed for some reason, and wanted to send her another telegram. The next morning, on the usual train to his office, he got off at Mahalaxmi Station and saw Sharda on the platform. He shouted, 'Sharda!'

Startled, Sharda looked at him, 'Nazir Sahib!'

'You...here?'

Sharda said petulantly, 'You didn't come to pick me up, so I went to your office. They told me you hadn't arrived. I was waiting here for you on the platform.'

Nazir gave the matter some thought before he said, 'You wait here. I'll get leave from work.'

He left Sharda on a bench and rushed to his office, where he wrote an application and left it with a chaprasi. Nazir returned to Sharda, and they sat in silence on the train as their bodies drew closer.

At his flat, Nazir said to Sharda, 'You take a bath, and I'll have breakfast arranged.'

Sharda went to bathe, and Nazir told the servant, 'She is a friend's wife. She has come to stay. Hurry and prepare breakfast.'

Next, Nazir took a bottle out of the cupboard and poured himself a double peg, added some water, and drank it. He wanted to recreate the atmosphere of the old hotel. Sharda had her bath before they sat down to breakfast. She talked incessantly about here, there, and everywhere.

Nazir felt Sharda had changed. She was a quiet type. Usually, she remained silent for hours, but now she declared her love with desultory ease. Nazir asked himself, 'What is love? Why did she have to bring it up? I preferred her silence. I understood so much about her through her silence. Goodness, what on earth has happened to her now? She sounds as though she is reading out a love letter.'

After they finished breakfast, Nazir prepared a peg and offered it to Sharda. When he insisted, she held her nose and drank it. When she pulled a horrid face and rinsed her mouth with water, Nazir felt a hint of sadness and wished she had refused the whisky but did not give the matter too much thought. He sent the servant on an errand to some faraway place and locked the door. Nazir lay down in bed and turned to Sharda. 'You had written, "When will those days return?" Well, here you are, not just the days, but nights too. Those days were just days with no nights, in that seedy hotel. Here we are with everything sparkling clean, no rent for a hotel room, no Karim—we are our own masters.'

Sharda began to recount how she spent her days full of longing and continued with the same pointless talk lifted out of books and stories—about moans and sighs, and nights spent counting stars. Nazir downed another peg and wondered, 'Who on earth counts stars? How can you count stars? Count stars, indeed! What pointless piffle!' As these thoughts went through his mind, Nazir drew Sharda close to his body. The bed was clean; Sharda was clean; he was clean; the atmosphere in the room was clean. Why were his senses not stirred in the way they had been when he lay close to Sharda in that seedy hotel room on the steel bed?

Nazir thought, perhaps, he had not had enough to drink. He got up and fixed himself another peg, which he demolished in one gulp. He lay down next to Sharda, and she began to chant the same old words about separation, longing, and meeting. Nazir was irked, and this made his body tense. He felt the centre of Sharda's being had withered away. She no longer aroused the same fire in his body; she was of no use to him. Nazir lay with Sharda for a long time and ultimately wanted to hail a taxi and go home to his wife. Troubled by the realization that he was at home and his wife in Lahore, he wanted his flat to transform into Marina Hotel.

The sympathy of Sharda's body was the same but all the elements which had combined to create a distinctive mood had vanished—the buying and selling of a human body, the giving with one hand and taking with the other, and the squalid seediness of Marina Hotel. Nazir was at home. He was sleeping with another woman on the same bed on which he slept with his guileless wife. Drifting from thought to thought, a feeling of disquiet permeated his being. Perhaps, the whisky was substandard; Sharda did not satisfy him—if only she had not talked so much. But then he thought, the poor soul had missed him; she had not seen him for so long, and in a couple of days, she'll be the same old Sharda.

A fortnight passed, but Nazir did not find the same old Sharda from their days at Marina Hotel, when Nazir sent for medicines for Munni's colds, rashes, and sore throats. Now Munni was in Jaipur, and Sharda was on her own. In Nazir's mind, Sharda and Munni were one. He recalled how he experienced a strange pleasure when tiny drops of milk oozed out of Sharda's full breasts and stuck to the hair on his chest. He thought, how satisfying it must be to become a mother. Milk—what a significant lack in men who eat, drink, and consume everything, whereas women eat and drink, but they feed as well—what a splendid act to nurture another life, albeit your child. Without Munni, Sharda was incomplete. Her breasts were incomplete without milk, the white elixir of life. When Nazir squeezed her close to his chest, she did not stop him.

For Nazir, Sharda was no longer the same Sharda, although she was the same old Sharda and a little more. The generosity of her body had increased after their long separation. Sharda's love for Nazir was almost spiritual, but for Nazir, she no longer held the same allure. After a fortnight with Sharda, Nazir reckoned that fifteen days' absence from his office was enough. He woke up the following morning and went to work and returned in the evening, and this became his pattern. Sharda began to serve him much like a dutiful wife. She bought wool from the bazaar and knitted a sweater for him. When he returned from office, a ready supply of soda and ice in the thermos awaited him. Every morning, she laid out his shaving kit on the table and heated water for him, and after he finished shaving, she cleaned the paraphernalia. She had the house cleaned and swept the place herself. Nazir was more irked than ever.

They slept together at night but Nazir began to make excuses. He told Sharda that he was thinking of something and needed to sleep on his own. Sharda moved to the other bed, which upset Nazir further because she lay sound asleep while he was tossing and turning, thinking, 'After all, what is all this about, and why is Sharda here? I spent a wonderful time with her in Karim's hotel, why is she clinging to me? I mean, how will this entire matter end? Love, etc., are meaningless. Now that there is no spark between us, she should return to Jaipur.'

From time to time, it crossed his mind that he was continuing to sin just as he had sinned in Marina Hotel. Before his marriage, he had committed countless such indiscretions, but he had forgotten them. Now, he was overwhelmed by a profound sense of disloyalty to his naïve wife, whom he had deceived several times on the matter of Sharda's letters. Sharda became unattractive to Nazir, and his attitude towards her changed to one of indifference. Yet, her generosity remained undiminished. She knew that artists were moody and did not complain.

A month passed. When Nazir counted the days, he was furious and asked himself, 'What! Has this woman been here for a full month? What a despicable man am I! Here I am, writing to my wife every day, like a faithful husband telling her how concerned I am about her; how my life is impossible without her. What a big *fraud* I am! I am betraying my wife and Sharda. Why don't I tell her, "Look here, I no longer feel anything for you", but the question is, do I not feel anything for Sharda or is Sharda no longer as attractive as she used to be?'

Nazir did not find a ready answer to his questions, and his mind was in turmoil as he began to reflect on ethics. He was cheating on his wife. An omnipresent sense of guilt became sharper with time. 'I am contemptible. Why has this woman become my second wife? I do not need her. Why is she glued to me? Why did I permit her to come here when she sent me a telegram? But by the time I received the telegram, I couldn't stop her.'

At times, Nazir drifted into thoughts which made everything Sharda did seem artificial. Did she want him to separate from his wife? Sharda fell further in his estimation, and Nazir grew even more indifferent towards her. Sharda noticed his indifference and became more pliant and conscientious about Nazir's comfort. Her attention annoyed him further. He began to hate her.

One day, his wallet was empty since he had forgotten to withdraw money from the bank, and he was late for his office. Besides, he was not feeling too well. As he was leaving the flat, Sharda said a few words to comfort him, and he descended upon her, 'Don't talk nonsense! I am fine. I forgot to get money from the bank. I've run out of cigarettes.'

Nazir managed to get a packet of Gold Flake from a shop near his office. Although he disliked the brand, he felt compelled to smoke a couple since he had bought them on credit. When he returned home that evening, he noticed a tin of his favourite cigarettes on the teapoy. Nazir knew it was empty but checked it on the off chance there were some left. He opened the tin and found it full. He asked Sharda, 'Where did this come from?'

She smiled and said, 'It was in the cupboard.'

Nazir did not say anything. He thought, perhaps, he had kept it there and forgotten about it. The following day there was another tin full of cigarettes on the teapoy. When Nazir asked Sharda, she smiled and said, 'It was in the cupboard.'

Nazir erupted, 'Sharda, you're talking nonsense! I don't care for this habit of yours. I'm not a beggar that you supply me with cigarettes every day.'

Sharda responded very tenderly, 'You forget, and so…I dared.'

Nazir exploded, 'I might be a fool, but I loathe insolence.'

Sharda responded in a very gentle tone, 'I beg your pardon; I'm sorry.'

It did occur to Nazir that Sharda was not at fault, and he should step forward to kiss her because she took such good care of him, but simultaneously he remembered that he was betraying his wife. Consequently, he roared at Sharda in a tone permeated with disgust, 'Don't talk rubbish! I should pack you off tomorrow. Tomorrow morning, I'll give you all the money you need.'

Sharda remained silent. She slept with Nazir and caressed him all night long but Nazir did not respond. The following morning, she prepared an elaborate and delicious breakfast. Nazir did not speak to Sharda. He finished his breakfast, and before he headed out, he informed her in clipped tones, 'I am going to the bank. I'll be back soon.'

The branch of the bank where he held his account was nearby. Nazir withdrew two hundred rupees and returned home. He wanted to give the entire sum to Sharda to buy her ticket and other sundries before packing her off to Jaipur. When he returned home, the servant informed him that she had gone. He asked, 'Where?'

The servant replied, 'Sir, she didn't say anything to me. She took her trunk and holdall.'

Nazir went into the bedroom and saw a tin of his favourite cigarettes on the teapoy. It was full.

## Scent

They were the same old monsoon days, and beyond the window, the rain poured down on the peepul leaves in the same old way. On the spring mattress of a teak bed pushed away from the window, a Ghatan clung to Randhir. In the night's radiant darkness, the moist peepul leaves shimmered like jhumkas, and the Ghatan clung to Randhir like a relentless shiver down his spine.

It was early evening. Randhir had finished scanning all the news and advertisements in an English newspaper and stepped out on to the balcony in a leisurely mood when he spotted the Ghatan standing under a tamarind tree to escape the rain. It seemed she worked in the rope factory next door. Randhir coughed and cleared his throat to attract her attention and finally, called her upstairs with a wave of his hand.

For several days, Randhir had felt an oppressive sense of loneliness weighing down on him. He recalled a time when almost all the Christian girls in Bombay were available to him at affordable rates. Now, some had joined the Women's Auxiliary Force because of the war, while others had opened dance schools in the Fort area with entry restricted to gora soldiers. Randhir was miserable, primarily because Christian girls had turned into gold dust. Knowing that he was far more cultivated, educated, fit, and handsome in comparison with gora men made matters a lot worse. Before the war, Randhir had enjoyed a steady string of sexual relationships with Christian girls in Nagpara and around the Taj Hotel, but now most pleasure houses in Fort had barred their doors to him because of the colour of his skin. He knew he was far better informed about the minutiae of such matters than the Christian lads with whom these girls had brief flings before they married some imbecile or the other.

Randhir had summoned the Ghatan upstairs with a wave of his hand to seek quiet revenge on Hazel for her new-found haughtiness. Hazel, who lived in the flat below, stepped out every morning in her uniform with a khaki cap set at a cocky angle on her head of cropped hair. She strutted along the pavement, expecting every passer-by to fall at her feet like a doormat she could walk all over. Randhir mulled hard to understand his weakness for Christian girls. Perhaps, it was because they had no qualms in displaying their bodies to their advantage, discussing the chaos in their lives, or chatting about their old beaus. Moreover, they loved to shake a leg the moment they heard a dance tune. All this was very well, but Christian girls did not have a monopoly of these traits.

When Randhir summoned the Ghatan upstairs, he had no intention of sleeping with her. But when he saw her drenched clothes, he thought, what if the poor girl catches pneumonia, and told her, 'Take off these clothes. You'll catch a chill.'

It was clear from the shame reflected in her eyes that she understood what Randhir was after. When he handed her his clean white dhoti, she gave the matter some thought, and carefully untied and threw away her kashta, which looked filthier after being drenched in the rain. Hurriedly, she covered her thighs with Randhir's white dhoti, and she struggled with her chipped fingernails to undo the knot that fastened her tight-fitting choli, but it had sunk into the grimy cleavage of her small firm breasts. She accepted defeat, and turned to Randhir to say something in Marathi, which meant, 'What should I do? I can't undo it.'

Randhir wrestled with the knot. Exasperated, he held the two ends in either hand and pulled hard. The knot gave away, and his hands fell back to reveal two pulsating breasts. For a moment, he felt like a nimble potter who had kneaded and shaped this girl's young breasts into two exquisite bowls that had the ripe moisture of yielding, fresh clay as it leaves the hands of a master potter. The undulation of the girl's unblemished breasts exuded a peculiar lustre, like dark wheat lit from below by a faint flicker of light creating a startling and elusive glow, which reminded Randhir of lamps aflame in the muddy waters of a pond.

Yes, they were the same old monsoon days, and beyond the window, the peepul leaves continued to shimmer. The Ghatan's filthy clothes, drenched in the rain, lay in a pile on the floor, and she continued to cling to Randhir. The heat of her grimy naked body stirred in Randhir a sensation akin to the one he experienced in deep midwinter when he bathed in the equally filthy piping hot hammam run by the local nais, or barbers.

All night long, she clung to Randhir as though their bodies had merged into each other. They barely exchanged a few words because their breath, their lips, and their hands communicated whatever they wanted to say or hear. Randhir's hands moved across the Ghatan's breasts like a gentle breeze, her small nipples and areolae awakened to his touch to create such tremors of ecstasy in her body that, for a moment, Randhir found himself shivering. Randhir was familiar with these sensations. He had spent many such nights close to the firm and soft breasts of many girls. He had slept with tenacious girls who wrapped themselves around him as they shared intimate secrets that should have remained hidden. He had physical relations with girls who did all the hard work and gave him no trouble, but this Ghatan, whom he had summoned with the wave of a hand as she stood getting drenched under a tamarind tree, was different.

All night long, Randhir could smell an unfamiliar scent from her body, a scent that was both agreeable and distasteful. All night long, it permeated every breath that he took. It came from her underarms, her breasts, her hair, her stomach. Every part of her body exuded this scent, and it overwhelmed his senses. All night long, Randhir lay thinking that he would not have felt so close to the Ghatan had this scent not drifted from her naked body and crept into his heart and mind to penetrate his old and new thoughts.

The scent had fused Randhir and the girl into one for the night. They descended into the innermost recesses of each other's beings, where they melded into a sensation of pure human ecstasy, that although transient was eternal, as it stood still in mid-flight like a bird flying high, so high that it seemed immobile. Randhir understood the scent which ensued from every pore of the Ghatan's body, but he could not describe it. It was a bit like the smell of the earth with water sprinkled on it—but no, that was different. There was nothing synthetic about it; it was real and eternal like the intimacy shared between a man and a woman.

Randhir could not stand the odour of sweat, and after his bath, he dusted his underarms, etc., with powder or used some other preparation to repress the smell of sweat. Yet, several times, yes, several times when he kissed the hair on the Ghatan's armpits, he was not repelled but experienced a curious pleasure because the soft, moist hair exuded the same scent. Randhir knew the scent, he recognized it and understood what it meant but he could not describe it to anybody.

They were the same old monsoon days when he had looked out beyond the same window at the peepul leaves shimmering in the rain. The air was full of the same rustle and bustle of sounds. The darkness of the night had the same glow because starlight had descended to touch the raindrops. Randhir remembered the same old monsoon days when his room had just one teak bed. But now another stood next to it, with a new dressing table in the corner.

They were the same old monsoon days, and the starlight had descended to touch the raindrops. The air was full of the strong scent of the attar of henna. Randhir lay face downwards and looked out of the window at the dance of the raindrops on the shimmering peepul leaves. A pale white girl lay beside him. She seemed to have failed in her attempt to conceal her naked body before she fell asleep. On the other bed, her red silk shalwar, with a bauble dangling from its crimson drawstring, lay together with a floral gold brocade shirt, a bodice, knickers, and a dupatta—all red—very red and steeped in the attar of henna.

The girl's black hair glistened with tiny particles of stardust. Her cheeks dusted with rose-red rouge and particles of stardust made her look wan and lifeless. The raw dye of her bodice had bled, leaving red marks on her bosom. Her white breasts reminded him of milk with a hint of blue; her shaved underarms were a cloudy grey. Each time Randhir turned to look at this girl with scratches all over her body, she reminded him of a book frayed at the edges, or a piece of grazed old vintage china. She looked as though he had found her in an old trunk which he struggled to open after wresting out the long nails that secured it.

When Randhir untied the strings of her tight-fitting bodice, he found lacerations under her soft breasts, and the drawstring of her shalwar had cut into the flesh around her waist. The pointed pendants of her heavy gem-studded gold necklace had bruised her bosom, which looked as though long sharp nails had scratched her. They were the same old monsoon days and raindrops fell on the soft and smooth peepul leaves to create the same sound that Randhir had heard all through that night. It was the same old season with the same gentle breeze but filled with a smell of the attar of henna.

When Randhir's hands moved across the pale breasts of this white girl, he felt various responses, including shivers through several parts of her pale white body. When Randhir pressed his chest close to hers, every pore of the girl's body responded to his touch. But where was the cry that Randhir had sensed in the scent of that Ghatan's body? A call, more compelling than the cry of a baby thirsting for milk, which crossed the barrier of sound and became soundless. Randhir looked out of the window. Near him, the peepul leaves continued to shimmer, but his gaze was fixed far beyond them into the distance where, mixed with clouds the colour of mud, he could see a faint glow like the one he had seen in that Ghatan's bosom—a hidden light like a secret revealed.

By Randhir's side lay a girl whose pale white body yielded to his touch like dough kneaded with milk and ghee. Now fast asleep, her body continued to exude a stale smell of the attar of henna, and there was something strangely sour about it. Randhir felt sickly—like reflux caused by indigestion, and he looked at the girl lying beside him. Her sensuality was stagnant like rancid milk with white particles which had risen to the top and stood still. The natural scent of the Ghatan's body had permeated Randhir's entire being. Far lighter yet more invasive than the attar of henna, it had reached its destination and taken over his senses.

Randhir made one last attempt and stroked the girl's pale white body, but he did not sense a hint of movement. His new bride was the daughter of a first-class magistrate. A graduate and the heartthrob of countless boys in her college days, she did not make Randhir's pulse race. In the fading smell of henna, he longed for the same old monsoon days when beyond the window, the peepul leaves shimmered in the rain, and the Ghatan's grimy body exuded that same scent.

## Green Sandals

'I can't put up with you any longer. Please divorce me.'
'What fiendish words! From time to time, you get these fits and lose all self-control. This is your biggest failing.'
'And you have complete mastery over your mind—in an alcoholic stupor twenty hours of the day!'
'Of course, I drink alcohol, but unlike you, I don't lose my mind and spout such claptrap without drinking.'
'Ah, so I spout claptrap!'
'Did I say so? But think about it. What's this about getting a divorce?'
'I've had enough, and I want a divorce. What else can I ask of a husband who doesn't care an iota for his wife?'
'You can ask me for anything but a divorce.'
'What in the world can you give me?'
'This is a new allegation. Is there another woman in the family as lucky as you?'
'To hell with such luck!'
'Don't send it to hell. I'm not sure what I've done to make you so angry, but I can assure you with all my heart that I love you.'
'God save me from such love.'
'Okay...but forget this horrid talk and tell me, have the girls gone to school?'
'Why do you want to know? For all you care, they can go to school or hell. I just wish to God that they die!'
'One day I'll have to pull your tongue out with hot tongs. Aren't you ashamed of saying such horrible things about your children?'
'I've told you not to argue with me. You should be ashamed of yourself for talking in such a crude and low manner to a woman, and that, too, to your wife, when you know that you must respect me. It's all because of the bad company you keep.'
'And the madness in your brain? Who is responsible for that?'

'You! Who else?'

'For you, everything is my fault. I don't understand what's happened to you.'

'What's happened to me? What has happened has happened because of you. You drive me mad. I have told you, please divorce me.'

'Why? Do you want to get married again? Are you fed up with me?'

'I spit on you! What sort of woman do you take me for?'

'What will you do after you get a divorce?'

'I'll go where fate takes me. I'll work hard and look after my children.'

'You work hard? You wake up at nine o'clock and rest after breakfast, and sleep for at least three hours after lunch. Don't deceive yourself.'

'Yes, of course, I sleep all day long, but you are always awake. Just yesterday, the man who came from your office was saying, "Whenever we see our sahib, he is asleep with his head resting on his desk."'

'Who was that bloody son of an imbecile!'

'Hold your tongue!'

'Bhai, I lost my temper. It's difficult to control one's tongue when angry.'

'I am furious with you, but I have not used a single inappropriate word. A person should always remain within the bounds of propriety. You use this vile language because of the terrible company you keep.'

'What bad company do I keep, I ask you....'

'Who is that chap, who describes himself as a big cloth trader? Have you ever seen his clothes? Some strange woollen variety and that too—filthy! Although he has a BA, look at his slothful appearance!'

'That man is an ascetic!'

'What the devil is that?'

'You won't understand it. I'll be wasting my time.'

'Your time is very precious! Always being wasted in the shortest conversation!'

'What is it that you wish to say?'

'I don't wish to say anything. I have said what I had to say. Just divorce me so I am free. My life is unbearable with these everyday wrangles.'

'Your life becomes unbearable at the smallest profession of love. What is the cure for that?'

'The only cure is divorce.'

'Then summon some maulvi. If this is your wish, I shall not deny it.'

'Where will I get a maulvi from?'

'Bhai, you are the one who wants a divorce. If I wanted a divorce, I'd snap my fingers and produce a maulvi. Don't hold out any hope from me on this matter. It's your business and it's up to you to make the arrangements.'

'You can't do this much for me?'

'Oh, no.'

'You claim that you love me beyond measure.'

'That's to the point of friendship, and never to forsake.'

'Then, what should I do with that?'

'Do whatever you like. And look here, stop getting on my nerves. Call some maulvi who can draw up the divorce papers, and I'll sign them.'

'What will happen to my divorce settlement, my haq mahr?'

'Since you are asking for the divorce, the question of haq mahr doesn't arise.'

'Vah ji vah!'

'Your brother is a barrister; write to him and ask him. When a woman asks for a divorce, she cannot ask for her haq mahr.'

'Then...you divorce me.'

'Why should I do anything so foolish? I love you.'

'I don't care for this sweet talk. If you loved me, you wouldn't be so cruel to me.'

'Of what cruelty do I stand accused?'

'As if you don't know. Just the other day, you wiped your shoes with my new sari.'

'I did not, I swear upon God.'

'Then who did...the angels?'

'All I know is that your three little girls were wiping the dirt off their shoes with your sari. I told them off.'

'They are not so ill-mannered.'

'Pretty ill-mannered...because you haven't brought them up

properly. When they return from school, ask them if they made inappropriate use of your sari.'

'I'm not going to ask them.'

'I am not sure what's happened to your brain today. If you tell me the real reason for your anger, I may well find a solution.'

'Keep looking for your solutions, but I have arrived at mine. Please, divorce me. What's the point of living with a husband who doesn't care for his wife?'

'I have always cared for you.'

'You know it's Eid tomorrow.'

'Of course, I know. Why? Yesterday I bought shoes for the girls, and eight days ago, I gave you sixty rupees for their frocks.'

'You didn't do me a favour by giving me sixty rupees.'

'Who is talking of a favour? What's the matter with you?'

'The fact of the matter is that sixty rupees were not enough to pay for three frocks. The organdie was for forty rupees, and the tailor charged seven rupees a frock. Now tell me, what big favour have you bestowed upon these girls and on me?'

'Have you paid the balance?'

'How could I collect the frocks if I hadn't?'

'Then take the extra money from me. Now I understand what all your anger was about.'

'I'm telling you, it's Eid tomorrow.'

'Yes, I know; I've heard you. I am getting two chickens and seviyan as well. Have you made any arrangements?'

'Forget the arrangements....'

'Why?'

'I wanted to wear my green sari and ordered green sandals. How many times did I ask you to go to the Chinese shop to check if my sandals were ready or not? If you took the slightest interest in me, you would have gone.'

'The devil take your green sandals! All this fuss was about your green sandals? My dear, I picked up your green sandals from the shoemaker day before yesterday, and they're in your cupboard. Since you spend all your time sleeping, of course, you didn't bother to check your cupboard.'

## The Photograph

'Where are the children?'
'They're dead!'
'All of them?'
'Yes, all of them. How come you bothered to ask?'
'I am their father.'
'Please, God, never again should a father like you be born!'
'Why are you so angry today? I don't understand why your moods are always oscillating. I've just returned from work. I'm dog tired, and you've started your nagging. Might as well have stayed in the office and relaxed under the fan.'
'There's a fan here as well. You always find time to relax elsewhere; you can grace us with your presence and relax here.'
'There's no end to your sarcasm. I think it came with you as part of your dowry.'
'I tell you, don't talk such nonsense with me all the time. You've transformed into a most shameless person.'
'Everything transforms. Where's the bloom of your youth? And I feel I'm a hundred-year-old man.'
'It's all because of your antics. I've never felt old.'
'My antics are not so sinister. And as your husband, don't I have the right to feel that your bloom is fading?'
'Please speak to me in a language I can understand. What's this talk of fading?'
'Forget it. Let's talk about love and adoration.'
'You just said that you feel like a hundred-year-old man.'
'Yes, but my heart is young.'
'What can I say about your heart! You call it a heart? Let someone ask me, and I will tell them, "This man who claims his heart is full of love has a heart of stone." What do you know of love? Only a woman can love.'
'Ah, examine world history and tell me how many women have

loved men. It's always men who've loved women and been true to their love. Women are always faithless.'

'Lies! Lies from the beginning and lies to the end. Faithlessness is always the preserve of men.'

'And that king of England who gave up his crown and throne for an ordinary woman...is that an ordinary fictitious story?'

'Hah! Trying to impress me with one example!'

'There are several such examples in history. When a man loves a woman, he never steps back. The wretch will sacrifice his life but not let the slightest harm near his beloved. You don't understand how much power there is in a man's love.'

'I understand everything about power. You couldn't open the cupboard door that was stuck. Eventually, I was the one who had to use my strength to force it open.'

'Look here, my love, you are unfair. You know that my right arm suffers from rheumatism. I didn't even go to work at the time and was lying in bed, moaning with pain night and day. You didn't pay the slightest attention to me and went off to the cinema with your friends.'

'You were malingering.'

'La hol wa'llah! The Almighty protect us from the Devil! Malingering? I was dying of pain, and you say I was malingering. To hell with such a life.'

'Now you are sending me to hell!'

'You've lost your mind. I am moaning about my life.'

'All you do is moan.'

'Well, at least you always find some cause for laughter because you don't give two hoots for anybody. As far as you're concerned, the children can go to hell, I can die, this house can burn to ashes, and you will continue to laugh. I've never ever seen such a heartless woman in my life!'

'How many women have you seen to date?'

'Thousands, millions...these days all you see are women on the roads.'

'Don't lie. You've seen some woman or the other—especially!'

'What do you mean by especially?'

'I don't wish to reveal your secrets. I'm off now.'

'Where?'

'To a friend's...to share my pain. I shall weep buckets with her, and she will weep with me, to lighten the pain in my heart.'

'Why don't you tell me? I promise to share the pain you wish to share with your friend.'

'Your promises...have you ever kept a promise?'

'You are very unfair. To this day, I have fulfilled every promise that I ever made to you. Just the other day you asked me for a tea set; I borrowed money from a friend and bought you a wonderful service.'

'You did me a great turn! You bought that for your friends. Tell me, who broke two cups?'

'Your son broke one cup, and your little girl broke the other.'

'You always blame the children. Well, now let's stop arguing. I have to bathe and change and do up my chignon.'

'Look here, I've never been firm with you and always speak gently to you, but today, I order you, if you leave the house....'

'Aji vah! Just look at you, who are you to order me around?'

'Hasn't taken you long to forget! I am your husband.'

'I don't know what it means to be a husband...I shall live my life as I wish, and I'll go out. Certainly, I will go out. I'll see who can stop me.'

'You will not...and this is my final decision.'

'This will be decided in a court.'

'How does a court come into this? I don't understand the ridiculous things you're spouting today. Talk sense. Have a bath so you cool down a bit.'

'Living with you has turned me into ice from head to toe.'

'No woman is content with her husband, no matter how decent the poor chap might be. It's part of the female temperament to find fault with a husband. I have overlooked so many of your flaws and misdemeanours.'

'God forbid...what misdemeanours have I committed?'

'Last year, rather grandly, when you decided to cook a turnip shabdegh and put a massive pot on the stove in the evening. And you fell into such a deep sleep that when I woke up the following morning and went to the kitchen, I found all the turnips had burnt to cinders. I removed the pot and lit the stove to make tea, and you continued to sleep.'

'I don't wish to hear this nonsense.'

'Because there is not an iota of a lie in it. Why are women so allergic to facing reality and the truth? If I tell you that your left cheek is slightly fatter than your right cheek, perhaps you won't forgive me for the rest of my life, but it's true, and perhaps, you too are aware of this. Look, please put the paperweight back from where you picked it up. Aim it at my head, and this matter will get out of hand.'

'I picked up the paperweight because it is exactly like your face. The bubbles of air inside are your eyes, and this red thing is your nose that's always red. When I saw you for the first time, I thought the dark bags under your eyes looked like cockroaches sitting face downwards.'

'Does your heart feel lighter now?'

'My heart will never feel lighter. Let me go. I'll have a bath, change, and perhaps, go away forever.'

'Before you leave at least tell me why you're going away forever.'

'I don't want to tell you. You are one of the most shameless people in the world!'

'Bhai, I haven't understood a word of what you've said. I don't know why, quite out of the blue, you've started haranguing me.'

'Just check the inside pocket of your jacket.'

'Where's my jacket?'

'I'll bring it...I'll bring it!'

'What on earth can there be in my jacket? A bottle of whisky? But I finished that before I came home and threw it away. Maybe it's still there.'

'Here's your jacket.'

'Now, what should I do?'

'Put your hand in the inside pocket and take out the photograph of the girl with whom you are having a love affair these days!'

'La hol wa'llah! I thought I was losing my mind! My darling, the girl in this photograph is my sister. You haven't met her. She lives in Africa. You haven't seen the letter with it—here.'

'Hai, what a beautiful girl! Perfect for my bhaijan.'

## Thief

I had to settle many debts—debts that had mounted up because of alcohol. They say that an alcoholic is without a conscience but my conscience taunted me every day and left me with a profound sense of degradation. I owed money to more than twenty people, and every night, the moment I lay down on my charpai, I imagined all my creditors standing around me. One night, before I fell asleep—you could say before I started my futile effort to sleep—I began to calculate my debts that stood at one thousand five hundred rupees. I tried to work out how to return this vast sum and felt besieged. My income of almost twenty-five rupees a day is barely enough to cover my daily consumption of alcohol. To place this matter in perspective, I should remind you that a bottle of third-class rum a day costs sixteen rupees. To put sixteen rupees in my pocket, please add three rupees for the tonga ride to work and back. On the days I have no work, I survive on credit.

The moment my exasperated creditors catch sight of me, some come up with excuses to explain why they no longer can lend me money, while others simply vanish. After all, for how long can they extend credit without sight of a rupee in repayment? Nonetheless, I continue to put my trust in God and invariably succeed in getting a small loan of ten to fifteen rupees from some source or the other. But this trend could not continue for long because people who once had some respect for me now flee the moment they catch sight of me.

Those who witnessed my plight lamented the decline of a master mechanic. I am a great technician who can fix any malfunctioning machine in no time after a cursory look. You could describe me as a 'play one musical note and identify the raga' sort of person. In my school of mechanics, the most defective machine should take no more than a week to fix unless the required spare parts are not readily available—then, of course, nothing can be done. Not a mechanic in the country can match my skills. I am in high demand and work nearly every day of the week, but my talent is contingent entirely upon my need for alcohol.

Before I take on work, I calculate how 'X' number of rupees will sustain my drinking for 'Y' or 'Z' number of days. My clients exploit my unique skill and subsidize my alcohol consumption. I consider myself a thief because I think I clear out their pockets, since I do not value my skill as a mechanic and consider it a rudimentary everyday activity such as eating food or drinking alcohol. I can turn my hand to any task at hand with the utmost ease. Still, at times, matters become dicey. When it draws close to six o'clock in the evening, I begin to feel restless, and even though I have completed the job in hand, I misplace a screw or two to guarantee work for the following day. This bastard alcohol is a terrible curse because it can make human beings dishonest.

My preoccupation with my debts is in direct proportion to my consumption of alcohol, and it has a catastrophic effect on my life. It interferes with my sleep because I lie in bed, concocting schemes to pay off my debts. In one scenario, I wanted ten thousand rupees to begin life anew. I planned to take a taxi to see every creditor, and before repaying my debt, beg him to forgive me. After paying off the one-thousand-five-hundred-rupee debt in full, with the balance, I buy a second-hand car—and of course, stop drinking alcohol.

In another plan, I reckoned, ten thousand was not enough, and decided to start with at least fifty thousand. As my first step, I distributed one thousand to the destitute to start small businesses. From the balance of forty-nine thousand, I gave ten thousand to my imaginary wife, who had an equally fictitious fixed deposit. Now, after spending eleven thousand rupees, the balance of thirty-nine thousand was more than enough for me. I thought this unfair and doubled my imaginary wife's share to twenty thousand. Now, I had twenty-nine thousand rupees and thought I should give fifteen thousand to my widowed sister. From the balance of fourteen thousand, almost two thousand goes towards clearing my debts and leaves me with twelve thousand rupees. I can spend one thousand on good alcohol but I spit at the thought and resolve to spend a month in the mountains to repair my health and addiction, and drink milk instead.

I spend night and day immersed in such thoughts. I have no

idea how I'd get the fifty thousand, but I did think up a couple of schemes that include sitting down to solve the crossword in *Shama*, Delhi, and winning the first prize. Another plan involved buying a lottery ticket for the Derby. My ultimate scheme was to steal, and that, too, with great finesse. It was challenging to figure out which of these should be my first plan of action, but I resolved that by fair means or foul, I must have fifty thousand rupees. My brain was in a tailspin, and sleepless nights proved calamitous. Although my luckless creditors did not mention my debts, their demeanour was enough to make me break into an embarrassing cold sweat. At times, I thought I should put an end to the torturous situation and kill myself. I am not quite sure how or when I decided to turn to theft, or how I came to know of an immensely wealthy Parsi woman who lives on her own in our neighbourhood.

I arrived at her block of flats at two o'clock at night and put my scheme into action. I managed to dodge the Pathan watchman downstairs. I knew her flat was on the second floor, and if I recall correctly, I might have climbed up a pipe and found myself in this Parsi lady's flat. I used my torch to look around me and spotted a huge safe but I had never opened or closed a safe in my life. Some source instructed me to open the safe with an ordinary wire, and I found it full of jewels—precious jewels. I had with me a yellow handkerchief adorned with images of Mecca and Medina, and I used it to tie up the stash of valuable jewels I had looted, which must have been worth at least fifty or sixty thousand rupees. How fortuitous—that was the amount I had planned to steal. As I was on my way out, the old Parsi woman walked in. When she saw me, her wrinkled face stretched into a toothless grin. Stunned, I took out a loaded pistol from my pocket and aimed it at her. Her toothless grin expanded, and she asked me tenderly, 'What brings you here?'

I gave a straightforward answer, 'Robbery!"

'Oh,' she said and all the wrinkles on her face transformed into a smile. 'Then, do sit down. All I have in the way of cash is one rupee. You've stolen jewellery but I'm afraid they will inform the police because only a very big jeweller can buy these jewels, and every big jeweller in town and elsewhere will recognize them.'

She sat down on a chair. Worried out of my mind, I thought,

'Oh God Almighty, what's happening? Here I am robbing her, and there she is, smiling and chatting to me. Why?'

Almost instantly, I had the answer when Old Mother Hubbard ignored the pistol, stepped forward, and planted a kiss on my mouth. When she put her arms around my neck, I swear upon God, I wanted to throw the jewels to one side and run for my life, but she was a determined woman with a grip so tight that I couldn't move. A strange fear permeated my being because, for me, she transformed into a witch who wanted to tear out my liver and devour it. I thought to myself, 'There is no woman in my life. I am unmarried. In the three decades of my life, I have never looked at a woman, but on the first night I set out to rob, I meet this old crone who is making love to me.'

I swear upon your life, I lost my senses. She terrified me, and I folded my hands before her to plead, 'Dear mother, forgive me. Here are your jewels. Please release me.'

She responded in a commanding tone, 'You can't leave. I have your pistol. If you make the slightest move, I'll shoot you or telephone the police and hand you over. But the light of my life, I won't because I've fallen in love with you. I'm unmarried. I think that all these years I have remained a virgin just for you. You can't leave.'

I was about to faint when the ring of a distant clock told me it was five o'clock in the morning. I held Mother Hubbard's chin, and as I kissed her shrivelled lips, I lied, 'I have seen hundreds of women in my life, but God is my witness, I've never met a woman like you. You are a rare gift for any man. What a pity that the first robbery of my life was from your house. Here are your jewels. I'll return tomorrow, but on the condition that we'll be alone in your house.'

The woman was delighted. 'You must return. I'll make sure not a mosquito will be here to trouble your ears. I'm sorry, but all I have is one rupee eight annas. Before you return tomorrow, I'll draw more than twenty thousand rupees for you from the bank. Here, take your pistol.'

I took my pistol and ran for my life.

My first attempt at robbery failed but I had to implement my plan to repay my debts. It was six o'clock on a winter morning—a time when the whole world is sound asleep. I knew of a house owned by a stingy tycoon who did not keep his money in a bank but at home. It made sense to visit him, and I arrived at his house. I don't want to describe the problems I encountered but I got in. Allah be praised, the master of the house, a very young man, was fast asleep. I picked up the keys from his bedside table and unlocked his cupboards. I found some old papers and *French letters*, in the first wardrobe, although I failed to understand what use this man had for *French letters* since he was a bachelor. I found the second cupboard packed with clothes, and the third was bare—I couldn't figure out why it was locked. There were no other cupboards.

I searched the whole house but did not find a single paisa. I thought this man must have hidden his wealth somewhere, so I placed the loaded pistol on his chest and woke him up. Startled, he bolted, and my weapon fell on the floor. I picked it up, and aimed it at him, 'I am a robber and have come to rob your house. I haven't found a penny in your cupboards, although I have heard you're immensely wealthy.'

The man, whose name I cannot recall, smiled as he stretched his arms and said to me, 'Yaar, you are a thief, you should have informed me earlier. I love thieves. The people I deal with claim they are upright, although they are peerless thieves and black marketeers. If you are a thief, why didn't you conceal yourself? I'm so pleased to meet you.'

He shook my hand and proceeded to open his refrigerator. I thought he was going to be hospitable and offer me a soft drink, but he summoned me to the open fridge and said, 'My friend, this is where I keep all my money. Here, do you see this safe, it has nearly one lakh rupees in it. How much do you want?' He opened a strongbox that had wads of green notes, and handed me a bundle, 'Will this be enough, it's ten thousand?'

I did not know how to respond. I had come to rob him. I handed the money back to him, 'Sir, I don't want anything. Forgive me. I shall return to pay my respects another time.' Terrified, I ran all the way home. By the time I reached my doorstep, the sun was up. I thought I should give up the idea of robbery. I had made two unsuccessful attempts, and there was no guarantee of success in a third. Nevertheless, my debts continued to plague my conscience, a bit like a fishbone stuck in my throat.

Finally, I thought I should get some proper sleep, wake up, and end the matter by committing suicide. I was about to drop off when I heard a knock on the door and answered it to find an elderly gentleman standing before me. I greeted him respectfully with an aadaab. He responded, 'Do forgive me, it seems I have woken you up, but I troubled you because I had to give you this envelope.'

I took the reasonably hefty envelope from him. He bid me goodbye with a salaam and left. I shut the door and opened the envelope to see countless hundred-rupee notes. I counted them and found a staggering fifty thousand rupees, together with a brief handwritten note which said, 'I owed you this money for some time. I am sorry I was not in a position to return it before.'

I exercised my mind but could not recall this gentleman, or when and where he had borrowed so much money from me. I concluded that at some point, someone had borrowed money from me, and I had forgotten about it. In no time, I chalked out a plan to give twenty thousand rupees to my imaginary wife, fifteen thousand to my widowed sister, and two thousand towards my debts. From the balance of twelve thousand, I earmarked one thousand for first-class alcohol and abandoned the idea of going to the mountains and drinking milk.

There was another knock on the front door. I opened it and found myself confronted by one of my creditors. I owed him five hundred rupees. I leapt inside and reached under my pillow for the envelope of money and found nothing there.

## Marriage

Jameel had to take his Sheaffer Lifetime fountain pen for repair. He knew that Messrs D. J. Smithyer, the agents for the Sheaffer Company, had an office near Green Hotel and looked up the telephone directory for their number. He called them up and hailed a taxi to head to Fort. Once at Green Hotel, finding Messrs D. J. Smithyer's office was no trouble. It was nearby, in a building on the third floor, and he took the lift.

When Jameel entered the premises, he saw a good-looking Anglo–Indian girl with an unusually prominent bosom seated behind a small window in a wooden wall. He slid his pen silently through the window; the girl took it from him, opened it to examine it briefly before she wrote something on a chit, and silently handed it to Jameel. He inspected the chit, which was a receipt for the pen. Before leaving, he turned to the girl and said, 'I suppose it will be ready within ten or twelve days.'

The girl laughed. Jameel gave her a sheepish look and asked, 'I didn't quite get the meaning of your laugh.'

The girl leaned her face against the window, and said, '*Mister*, there is *a war* on these days, *a war*...this pen will go to America. You should enquire after nine months.'

'Nine months!' said Jameel, astounded.

The girl nodded her head of cropped hair. Jameel turned towards the lift.

This nine-month business was curious: a woman can produce a chubby-cheeked baby in nine months. Besides, who on earth can look after a scrap of paper for nine months or, for that matter, say with a degree of confidence that after nine months he would remember he had given a pen for repair? Besides, the poor wretch could be dead before the nine months were up. Jameel thought this smacked of a racket. His pen had a tiny fault: its feeder was supplying too much ink. Sending it to an American hospital seemed a mere ruse. He thought, 'To hell with this pen; it can go to America or Africa for all I care.' Jameel had bought it on the black market for a hundred and seventy-five rupees and for over a year, made good use of it, writing thousands of pages. These reflections transformed him from a pawn into a king, and instantly he recalled he was in Fort. Jameel knew he would not find whisky with any of the countless wine merchants in the area but could surely lay his hands on some excellent French cognac. And he headed to the nearest wine merchant.

Jameel was on his way home with a bottle of brandy when it crossed his mind that he should stop to see his friend, Pir Sahib, owner of a carpet showroom with French windows on the ground floor of Green Hotel. In no time, Jameel was inside the showroom, happily chatting and laughing with its proprietor, who was considerably older than him. He laid the bottle of cognac, carefully wrapped in tissue, on its side on a thick piled Persian carpet. Pir Sahib pointed to it and said, 'Yaar, unveil the bride! Let's tease her a bit.'

Jameel responded in good cheer, 'Well then Pir Sahib, send for some glasses and soda and watch how the world changes its colours.'

The glasses and chilled soda arrived in no time. They finished the first round and were about to embark on the second when a Gujarati friend of Pir Sahib's walked in and sat down on the carpet, without standing on ceremony. Fortuitously, the hotel boy had brought three instead of two glasses. Pir Sahib's Gujarati friend chatted about a few random matters in simple, chaste Urdu and poured himself a large peg brimming with soda. After three to four large swigs, he wiped his face with a hanky and said, 'Take out the cigarettes, yaar.'

Pir Sahib was guilty of the seven deadly sins but he did not smoke. Jameel took his cigarette case out of his pocket and kept it on the carpet with a lighter. Pir Sahib introduced his Gujarati friend to Jameel, 'Mr Natwar Lal—he trades in pearls.'

Jameel asked himself, 'A person who trades in coal metaphorically blackens his face, what happens to a person who trades in pearls?' Pir Sahib turned to Jameel and added, 'Mr Jameel, famous lyricist!'

Both men shook hands. Another round of brandy followed with such zest that soon the bottle was empty. Jameel thought to himself, 'This wretch of a pearl trader, he drinks like the devil, and he's downed the brandy I bought to indulge myself and enjoy with Pir

Sahib. God give him cataract!'

Still in good cheer, the moment the final swig of the last round reached his stomach, Jameel forgave Natwar Lal and said to him, 'Come on, Mr Natwar Lal, let's find another bottle!'

Natwar Lal sprang up, ironing out the creases of his white dagla before he fixed his dhoti, and said, 'Let's go!'

Jameel turned to Pir Sahib, 'Back at your service soon.'

Jameel and Natwar Lal stepped out and took a taxi to a wine merchant. When Jameel asked the taxi driver to stop, Natwar said, 'Mr Jameel, this shop is no good. He is very expensive.'

He turned to the taxi driver, 'Look here, let's go to Colaba.'

In Colaba, Natwar took Jameel to a small shop where they could not find the brand Jameel bought in Fort but settled for another recommended by Natwar, who declared it 'Number One!' Jameel paid for Number One, and they stepped out. Natwar stopped near a bar and said, 'Mr Jameel, what do you think, two pegs here before we head back?'

Jameel had no objection because he wasn't quite drunk, but he was under the impression that bar owners did not permit customers to bring their alcohol, and he said, 'Mr Natwar, how can we? They will not allow you to drink this inside.'

Natwar winked at Jameel, 'Here, everything goes,' and he entered a cabin. Jameel followed him. Natwar put the bottle on a marble-topped table, hailed a waiter, and winked at him as well, 'Look here, two Roger's sodas…' and added, 'chilled, and two glasses—aik dum clean!'

The waiter took his order. He left and returned almost immediately as though he had conjured the soda and glasses out of thin air. Natwar placed his second order, '*Fust class chips* and *tomayto soce* and *fust class cutlace*!' The waiter took off.

Natwar gave Jameel a foolish smile, and without so much as a 'by your leave', uncorked the bottle and poured a double peg into Jameel's glass, and a more substantial measure into his own. When the soda settled, they raised and clinked their glasses. Jameel was thirsty. He downed half a peg in one gulp. The sharpness of the soda caught his throat, and he produced some bizarre sounds. After around fifteen minutes, some piping hot French fries and cutlets arrived, and

Jameel fell on them. Natwar joined him. Within two minutes, they had wiped the platters clean and sent for some more cutlets with extra French fries. Two hours passed and they had consumed three-fourths of the bottle, and Jameel thought it pointless to return to Pir Sahib.

In their cups, Natwar and Jameel felt they were astride winged horses. Usually, such equestrians dream of a paradise full of beautiful naked damsels and abracadabra. Jameel longed for the valley where he could sweep up a stunning damsel into his arms and fly off with her, squeezing her oh so tight, so close to his burning heart that his bones would crack. He knew he was in an area famous for its brothels, frequented by decadent men seeking pleasure, and girls who wanted to ply the trade in a discreet manner. He turned to Natwar, 'I say, Natwar won't we find any lovelies in this area?'

Natwar poured a large peg into his glass and laughed, 'Mr Jameel, not one but thousands…thousands…thousands…thousands!'

The refrain of 'thousands' would have continued had Jameel not interrupted to say, 'Just one will work wonders, and I shall sing in praise of Natwar Bhai!'

By now, Natwar Bhai had reached seventh heaven, and he began to sway, 'Jameel Bhai…not one but thousands…let's go…finish this.'

They finished the contents of the bottle within half an hour. Plastered, they settled the bill and stepped out after thanking the waiter with a hefty tip. It was dark inside the bar, but outside, the bright sunlight dazzled Jameel's eyes. For a minute or two, he could not see a thing, but as his eyes became accustomed to the bright light, he turned to Natwar, 'Let's go, my friend.'

Natwar looked at Jameel with enquiring eyes, 'You have money?'

An intoxicated smile appeared on Jameel's lips as he nudged Natwar hard in the ribs, 'Plenty…Natwar Bhai, plenty!' He pulled out five one-hundred-rupee notes and asked, 'Is this enough?'

Unable to contain his grin, Natwar chimed, 'Enough? It's more than enough! Come on, first, let's get another bottle; we'll need it.'

Jameel approved of Natwar's suggestion because where else would they feel the need for a bottle if not in a mosque! So, they purchased a bottle, sat in the waiting taxi, and set off on their travels in search of the magical valley.

From the thousands of brothels in the area, they checked out around twenty-five girls, but Jameel did not fancy any of the specimens on offer. He did not want a girl concealed in thick layers of make-up, looking like a house refurbished by an amateur architect who had restored chunks of missing plaster with powder and paint. Several women paraded before them, and each time an exasperated Natwar put his hand on Jameel's shoulder and asked, 'Jameel Bhai, will she do?'

And each time Jameel Bhai stood up, and responded with a double entendre, 'Yes, yes she will do, but I must do something else.'

They checked out two other places, and a disappointed Jameel reflected on the men who visited these women, who reminded him of old ham past its sell-by date. He found their demeanour foul and their language obscene and wondered how these creatures passed off as 'private'—a term used for women who conducted their trade without walking the streets—and remained in 'purdah'. Jameel failed to understand the meaning of purdah in a context where the goods on sale were women's bodies. Jameel was deep in thought when Natwar remembered some essential unfinished business and asked the driver to stop. He took off and now, Jameel was on his own. The taxi was cruising at thirty miles per hour, and it was four-thirty in the afternoon. He asked the driver, 'Will I find a pimp here?'

The driver responded, 'Yes, you will, sir.'

'Well, then take me to him.'

The driver drove on, and after taking several sharp turns, he stopped the car at a building on a hillside and blew the horn a couple of times. Jameel was very drunk; his head felt leaden, and his eyes were misty. He could not figure out how he found himself sitting on a bed, near a nubile girl sitting on a chair and combing her cropped hair. She had a small pimple on the tip of her nose. Jameel stared at her and tried to figure out how he got here in the first place but thought it a pointless exercise and gave up. He rummaged inside his pocket to count his money and checked the bottle of brandy lying near him and felt reassured. A complete greenhorn, Jameel walked up to the girl and smiled before he asked her, 'Madam, how do you do?'

The girl put her comb down on the table and said, 'And you, sir?'

'Okay!' he said and put an arm around her waist, 'What's your name?'

'I did tell you once, but I don't think you remember it. You came here in a taxi. Who knows where you've been roaming? Your bill was thirty-two rupees, and you paid it. You kept swearing at a man called Natwar and called him all sorts of names.'

Jameel thought it pointless to try to get to the bottom of this matter, although he recalled settling the thirty-two rupees taxi fare. The girl got up from the chair, walked up to the bed to sit next to Jameel, and said, 'My name is Tara.'

Jameel pushed her down on the bed and attempted to flirt with her. After some time, he was thirsty and said to Tara, 'Two ice-cold sodas and two glasses!'

Tara promptly arranged for the two items. Jameel opened the bottle, poured a peg for himself and another for Tara, and they began to drink. After three pegs, he felt gratified and thought it time to stop kissing and canoodling Tara. To cut the story short, he said, 'Take off your clothes!'

'All?'

'Yes, all!'

Tara took off her clothes and lay down. Jameel had a cursory look at her naked body and found it attractive but several other thoughts lined up in a queue in his head. Some months ago, Jameel had a nikah ceremony, but the rukhsati, or the ritual sending off of the bride from her childhood to her marital home, had not happened. He had only met his wife a couple of times. Now, Jameel began to wonder about her body and asked himself if she would take off all her clothes at one order from him. Would she take off her clothes and lie down with him? Would she drink brandy with him and cut her hair short? His conscience had stirred. He knew a nikah meant that he was married. All he had to do was to go to his in-laws' house, take his bride's hand, and bring her home. Was it legitimate for him to indulge in such promiscuity with a bazaari woman and allow her to warm his bed?

Unable to confront his transgressions, Jameel fell asleep, and so did Tara. Jameel had many disconnected, meaningless dreams. Two hours later, a nightmare jolted him out of his slumber, and as he tried to find his bearings, he found himself in an unfamiliar room with a stark-naked girl lying beside him. As the fog began to lift, all the day's events played out before him. Astonished to find himself stark naked, he put on his pyjamas inside out, wore his kurta, and once again, rummaged through his pockets to check his money, and found it there. Jameel popped a soda and drank a peg before tapping Tara very gently, 'Wake up!'

Tara rubbed her eyes. Jameel said to her, 'Put on your clothes.'

Tara put on her clothes. The dark evening was turning into night. Jameel thought it was time to leave but he wanted to ask Tara a few questions to make sense of his clouded thoughts. 'Tara, when we lay down, I asked you to take off your clothes…. What happened after that?'

Tara answered, 'Nothing. You took off your clothes and fell asleep, stroking my arm.'

'Is that all?'

'Yes, but before you fell asleep, you mumbled two, three times, "I'm a sinner. I'm a sinner."'

Tara stood up and began to comb her hair. Jameel also stood up. To suppress the thought that he had sinned, he glugged a double peg, wrapped the bottle in a newspaper, and went to the door. Tara asked, 'Going?'

'Yes, I'll be back another time.'

Jameel climbed down the winding iron staircase and headed towards the big bazaar when he heard a car horn. He turned around and saw a taxi parked near the house. Thinking, 'Good, found one here; saved from having to walk,' he asked the driver, 'Why mate, are you free?'

The driver bellowed, 'What do you mean by, "are you free?" The meter's on.'

'Then…' Jameel asked him and turned away.

The driver called out, 'Seth, where do you think you're going?'

'I'll look for another taxi,' replied Jameel.

The driver stepped out, 'Have you lost your mind? You hired this taxi!'

Taken aback Jameel asked, 'I have?'

The driver turned rough, 'Yes, saala drinking daru…and he's forgotten.'

An exchange of hot words started, and a crowd gathered. Jameel opened the door of the taxi and got in, 'Let's go!'

The driver started the engine, 'Where?'

'Police station!' said Jameel.

The driver hurled who knows what filthy abuse at him.

Jameel thought hard. He had paid thirty-two rupees for the taxi he hired. How did this second taxi appear on the scene? Although drunk out of his mind at the time, he could say with absolute conviction that this taxi was not that taxi, and this driver was not that driver who brought him here. They reached the police station. Jameel was very unsteady on his feet. It did not take long for the sub-inspector on duty to figure out the matter, and he asked Jameel to take a seat. The driver began his saga, which was a catalogue of lies. Jameel wanted to contradict him but he did not have the strength to say too much. Instead, he addressed the sub-inspector and said, 'Sir, I don't understand what is happening here. I settled a fare of thirty-two rupees for the taxi I hired. Now, I don't know who this person is and why he is asking me to pay a fare.'

The taxi driver said, 'Respected Inspector sir, this man is under the influence of daru,' and as evidence, he put Jameel's bottle of brandy on the table.

Jameel was exasperated, 'Arrey, bhai, which swine says that I have not been drinking? The question is, where have you appeared from?'

According to the driver, the fare was forty-two rupees. The sub-inspector was a decent man and settled the matter at fifteen rupees. The driver created an uproar but the sub-inspector told him off and sent him packing from the police station. He instructed a constable to get another taxi for Jameel and assigned yet another constable to take him home. Slurring, Jameel thanked him and asked, 'Sir, is this the Grant Road Police Station?'

The sub-inspector roared with laughter and patted his belly, '*Mister*, you have provided perfect proof that you're completely drunk. It's the Colaba Police Station. Now go…go home.'

Jameel arrived home. He did not eat his dinner or change his clothes but fell asleep with the bottle of brandy lying next to him. The following day, he woke up around ten o'clock and every joint in his body ached. His head felt like it was carrying the weight of several large boulders, and he was left with a bad taste in his mouth.

Jameel drank at least three glasses of ENO Fruit Salt and five cups of tea. By evening, he felt somewhat revived and was able to reflect on what had transpired the previous day and managed to complete some parts of the long saga, but the rest remained hazy. The time with Pir Sahib in Green Hotel and from there to Colaba was quite clear but his mind was hazy about what had happened after he began his trip with Natwar to the beautiful valley. How had he got to that girl's house? Her name had slipped Jameel's mind but he remembered some of her words, and, of course, her face. Much as he tried, he could not piece together that part of the story. And the business about the taxis? He had paid off the first one. How did the second taxi descend on the scene? Jameel began to think. His brain was in turmoil; his thoughts clashed together and crumbled.

Determined to clarify how events unfolded, Jameel drank three pegs of brandy. He was unable to figure out if he should assign his incomplete sin to his debit or credit account—he wanted to complete the sinful act but the house by the hillside remained a mystery. Exhausted and defeated, he gave up the fight and filed away the entire episode as a dream. But how can a man spend so much money in a reverie? Jameel had spent at least two-hundred-and-fifty rupees. After a few days, Jameel visited Pir Sahib who informed him that the day after they met at the carpet showroom, Natwar had set off on a long sea voyage, apparently something to do with pearls. Jameel sent a thousand scourges his way and set out on his search. He taxed his memory, and in his mind's eye, he saw a brass nameplate hanging from the wall of a bungalow, with something written on it. Perhaps, Dr Bairamji, and something else.

Late one afternoon, roaming the streets of Colaba for hours, Jameel arrived in an alley with several two-storeyed bungalows that looked familiar. Several brass nameplates hung outside each building, three on some and four or five on others. Jameel began to check them out. At the forefront of his mind was the letter he had received that morning from his mother-in-law; her ultimatum was categorical. She would not countenance any further delays, 'I have fixed a date; come and take away your bride.'

And here he was, lost and wandering the streets of Bombay, wanting to complete his unfinished sin. Jameel pushed aside the thought of the letter and mumbled, 'Forget it. Let me wander the streets....'

Just as the words left his mouth, Jameel saw a small brass nameplate with 'Dr M. Bairamji, MD' written on it, and felt his body quake. It was the same building—the very same—the same colour and the same winding iron staircase. Jameel climbed up the stairs. Now, everything around him looked familiar. He walked through the corridor and knocked on the front door, and it was opened by the same boy who had brought the ice and soda that afternoon. Jameel brought a fake smile to his face and asked, 'Sonny, is Baiji at home?'

The boy nodded, 'Yes, sir!'

'Tell her that sahib is here to see you.'

There was an air of familiarity in Jameel's tone. The boy shut the door and went inside.

The door opened after a while, and Tara appeared. Jameel recognized her as the same girl but the pimple on her nose had disappeared. 'Namaste!' said Jameel.

'Namaste. Tell me, how are you?' asked Tara as she gave a gentle flick to her cropped hair.

Jameel answered, 'Well, thank you. I was swamped with work for the past few days; that's why I could not come back. Tell me, what's up?'

Tara's voice was grave, 'Forgive me, I was busy with my marriage.'

Jameel was flabbergasted, 'Marriage...when?'

Tara responded with the same gravity, 'This morning. Come, let me introduce you to my husband.'

Jameel felt dizzy. He did not wait to hear or say anything. He climbed down the steel staircase, his shoes producing a familiar clickety-clack on the staircase. Jameel was walking away when the driver of a taxi parked nearby called out, 'Seth Sahib, taxi?' Exasperated, Jameel responded, 'No, you wretch—marriage!' He quickened his pace and walked towards the big bazaar.

## In Memoriam

All through the night and by the early hours of the morning, news had reached every corner of the city—Kamal Ataturk was dead. Lottery players verifying their numbers over cups of tea in various Irani hotels heard this emotional news on radio waves, and forgetting everything, began to concentrate on sharing eulogies of Mustafa Kamal. A journalist who was sitting at a marble-top table in one of these hotels heard the news and said to his companion in an unsteady voice, 'Mustafa Kamal is dead!' His pal's teacup almost fell out of his hand, 'What did you say? Mustafa Kamal is dead?'

The journalist set the tone as they began to discuss Ataturk, 'Sad. Now, what's going to happen to Hindustan? I heard Mustafa Kamal was about to attack India, and we'd be free! The Muslim nation would have progressed. Sad. Nobody can win against Fate.'

The hair on his friend's body stood on end. Overcome by a hitherto unknown emotion, he articulated the first thought that came to his mind, 'From tomorrow, I must start offering my Friday prayers.' Later, he ascribed this thought to Mustafa Kamal Pasha's grand stature as a good Muslim.

In a narrow alley in a bazaar, a few cocaine peddlers were sitting on a charpai. One spat out his paan spittle, aiming it skilfully at a lamp post, and said, 'Mustafa Kamal was a great man but Muhammad Ali was no less. Just here in Bombay, people have named three or four hotels after him.'

Another turned to his companions and added, as he continued to scrape the dirt off his exposed calves with a blunt knife, 'There was a massive strike when Muhammad Ali died.'

Another man nudged one of his companions, and asked, 'And why not? Arrey, such a big Mussulman dies, and no strike!'

A passer-by heard this exchange and repeated it to his friends at the next crossroad. Within the hour, all those people who slept by day and roamed the bazaar at night knew about the strike the next morning.

Abu, the butcher, entered his kholi at two o'clock at night. He searched through several odds and sods lying in a recess in the wall and pulled out a small paper sachet before he filled a large pot with water, emptied the contents of the sachet into it, and began to stir the mixture. His wife was fast asleep on a jute mat, exhausted by her daily chores, but when she heard her husband's activities, she sat up and asked, 'You're back?'

'Yes, I'm back,' said Abu as he pulled off his shirt and tossed it into the pot and continued to stir.

His wife asked, 'What on earth are you doing?'

'Mustafa Kamal is dead. There is a strike tomorrow.'

His wife sprang up. She looked anxious as she said, 'There's bound to be violence. I'm sick and tired of these riots every day.' She held her head and added, 'I've told you a thousand times that we should move from this Hindu neighbourhood. Who knows when you'll pay attention to what I say?'

Abu laughed in response, 'Arrey, silly woman, this is not a Hindu–Muslim matter. Mustafa Kamal has died—the same one—the one who was a very big man. It's a strike to mourn his death.'

'I couldn't care less about a big man. Tell me, what are you up to?' his wife asked, 'Why don't you go to bed?'

'I'm dyeing my shirt black. We have to organize the strike tomorrow morning.'

He squeezed the water out of his shirt and hung it out to dry on a string tied to two nails hammered into the wall.

The following morning, groups of Muslim Black Shirts were roaming the streets of Bombay waving black flags and forcing shops to shut down, shouting, 'Long live the Revolution! Long live the Revolution!'

A Hindu on his way to open his shop heard these slogans, and when he saw the people chanting them, he got on a tram and vamoosed without a word. When other Hindu and Parsi shopkeepers heard a group of Muslims hotheads screaming, shouting, and chanting slogans, they shut down their shops.

Ten or fifteen Black Shirts walking through the bazaar were

chatting away. One turned to a companion, 'That was quite a strike, but it was nothing compared to the one when Muhammad Ali died. Trams are still running like they always do.'

The most hot-headed among them waved the black flag he was carrying and responded sharply, 'Well then, no trams will run today either!' He marched off towards a tram that was dropping off passengers at a stop with a wooden shelter, and his companions followed him. Within seconds, they had surrounded the red tram and forced all the passengers off.

That evening, there was a sizeable commemorative jalsa in one of the largest maidans in Bombay. Rabble-rousers from across the city had gathered. Vendors walked around selling paan, biri, and other treats from small trays slung across the back of their necks held by two canvas straps on the left and right. Scores of people were milling around, and it looked like a mela. Temporary stalls had mushroomed everywhere; chaat, channa, and boiled potatoes were selling out fast. There was a massive crowd inside and outside the perimeter of the maidan. In this multitude, many people were roaming around simply to find out why so many people had assembled. One gentleman had run a fair distance from his house with binoculars around his neck because he thought it was an assembly of wrestlers and was dying to get close to the action. Two men were standing near the wrought-iron railing of the maidan, and one said to the other, 'I tell you, this Mustafa Kamal was a big man. I am going to name the soap I am about to make Kamal Soap! Do you think that will work?'

The other responded, 'But the first name you thought of wasn't bad either—Jinnah Soap. This Jinnah is a big leader of the Muslim League.'

'No...no, I think Kamal Soap will be better. Look here, Mustafa Kamal is a bigger man than Jinnah.'

He placed a hand on his companion's shoulder and added, 'Let's get going, the meeting is about to begin.'

The jalsa kicked off with the chanting of poems and eulogies to celebrate Mustafa Kamal, the great man. A gentleman stood up to deliver a panegyric in praise of Kamal Ataturk. Members of the audience heard him in silence; whenever he repeated the words, 'Mustafa Kamal kicked the British out from the Dardanelles' or

'Kamal slaughtered the Greek wolf with the sword of Islam', the air reverberated with cries of 'Long live Islam! Islam Zindabad!' These cries stirred the speaker, who began to salute Ataturk's might and stature with even more enthusiasm. Each word intensified the zeal in the hearts of his audience. 'Till history remembers Gallipoli, Britain's head will remain severed in Turkey's eyes. Turkey is the only country that has defeated Britain successfully. Mustafa Kamal was the only Muslim who revived memories of the legendary military leader Ghazi Salahuddin Ayubbi, who raised his sword and forced the Europeans to recognize his greatness. Turkey was called the Sick Man of Europe but Mustafa Kamal instilled strength and vigour and made it the Man of Steel!'

These words echoed across the maidan and met cries of, 'Long live the Revolution! Long live the Revolution!' The slogans aroused the speaker's passion further. He raised his voice and continued, 'I cannot sum up Kamal's stature in a few words. We need time to talk about the services he has performed for his country. He cleaned out ignorance in Turkey, made education universal, and spread the light of new learning. He did all this by the sword. When he separated religion from politics, many conservatives opposed him, and they were sent to the gallows, publicly. When he passed an ordinance that nobody can wear a Turkish cap, many ignorant people wanted to raise their voices against him but he throttled their cries. He ordered that the call to prayers be in Turkish and killed many mullahs who violated the law.'

A man raised his voice from the audience and shouted out, 'This man is a blasphemer!' Suddenly the entire congregation was aroused, and the air was full of cries of 'He is a kafir! He is a liar!'

The cries and slogans drowned the speaker's voice, and before he could clarify his position, a stone hit his forehead, and he fell on the stage in a daze. There was pandemonium in the jalsa. On stage, the speaker's friend wiped the blood off his brow, and a rumble rose from the maidan, 'Mustafa Kamal Zindabad! Mustafa Kamal Zindabad! Mustafa Kamal Zindabad!'

## Constipation

I was sitting near the camera behind the actors and the director, holding a sheet of paper with freshly written dialogue. We were waiting for the soap factory next door to finish its shift and for the camera to roll. Every day, some noisy machine in the factory started without warning while we were in the middle of shooting a scene, and we had to reshoot it as several thousand feet of celluloid went to waste. Director Sahib was standing between the hero and heroine and smoking. I was sitting on a chair with my legs tucked under its seat. Several people have questioned this habit of mine but I find it most comfortable because I can shift my weight from my back to my legs.

Naina from the factory, with a squint in both eyes, walked up to Director Sahib and said, 'Sahib says, little work left, then noise finish.'

We knew that for the next half hour the machinery would be in use for cutting bars of soap and pasting labels. Director Sahib left the studio with the hero and heroine. I continued to sit on my chair and was contemplating how the weak light of the ceiling lamp made the props look stunted and the set appear further away than it was, when I heard someone say, 'Assalaam alaikum!'

'Wa'alaikum salaam!' I responded and turned around to see a new face. My eyes appeared to ask, 'Who are you?'

The clever chap replied, 'Sir, I joined your company today. My name is Abdur Rahman, from Dilli shahr proper. Delhi, perhaps, is also your native land.'

I responded, 'No, sir, I am a native of Punjab.'

Before the shoot, Director Sahib had asked us to remove our spectacles, so Abdur Rahman took his out of his pocket and tucked them neatly behind his ears. 'Do forgive me,' he said as he sized me up. I saw admiration in his eyes, 'By God, I thought you are from Delhi. I mean, your diction doesn't have a hint of Punjabiyat. Mashallah, what dialogue you've written! Fantastic! You put everyone to shame—and this story is also yours, isn't it?'

As Abdur Rahman continued in this toadying vein, his stature diminished in my eyes. 'No,' I said. My response was as stiff as the three planks of plywood used for the walls of the set.

Now, he became more unctuous, 'Strange times...nobody appreciates talent. I don't understand the city of Bombay at all. People here speak a strange gibberish. I've been here for fifteen days and what can I say, sir, I was most distraught, but meeting you today....' As he continued to rub his hands together, dried shavings of the residue of his face cream fell to the ground.

I responded with a 'Yes, of course.' After a brief pause, I unfolded the sheet of paper, put on a grave expression, and took out my pen to correct a few mistakes. Abdur Rahman continued to hang around. It was clear from his manner that he wished to say something to me, so I turned to him, 'Do tell me....'

'Do I have your permission to say something?'

'With pleasure....'

'Sir, please don't sit with your legs pulled up and tucked under your chair in this manner.'

'Why?'

He leaned forward, 'The point is that sitting like this causes constipation.'

'Constipation!' I asked, stupefied, 'How can sitting in a particular way cause constipation?' I wanted to add, 'Miyan, are you out of your mind? What have you eaten? I have been sitting like this for years. And I'll get constipated today because you say so!' I remained silent because I did not wish to prolong the conversation and take on an unnecessary headache.

He smiled, and the flesh around his eyes scrunched up behind the lens of his spectacles as he went on, 'You think I'm joking, but it's true, sitting with your legs joined together and pulled up is bad for your stomach. I have given my humble advice. Now it's up to you to take it or leave it.'

I took some time to think over my response. I mean, I had not suffered from constipation in the last twenty years and was not going to get constipated because of this joker. Constipation is caused by eating and drinking and not by sitting on a chair or a couch! I have no idea what it does for others but the way I sit on a chair gives me great pleasure. Indeed, I get a kick out of joining my legs and pulling them up to my chest. There is a lot of standing around on a set during a shoot, and it can get very tiring—this is how I get rid of my fatigue. I will not give up this habit simply because someone tries to instil a fear of constipation in me.

I would not have given up my posture even if Abdur Rahman had threatened me with the spectre of a tumour. I am not stubborn but sitting with my legs tucked under the seat of my chair remains not merely a habit but something my body demands, and nobody can influence me on this matter. I was outraged when Abdur Rahman ticked me off and thanked him in a tone that meant, 'To hell with you!' He acknowledged my appreciation and conjured a slimy smile on his thick lips and shut up. Not much later, the director, hero, and heroine returned, and shooting began. I thanked God I was spared Abdur Rahman's lecture on constipation and made the following mental notes to remind myself that the new extra recruited into the company was an imbecile, was ill-mannered, was a windbag in the premier league, and was loathsome.

I am an expert when it comes to hate. You may well ask why hate requires expertise, and I will tell you that every task has its protocols. Hate requires fervour, and therefore, a skilled practitioner. In comparison, love is a pedestrian sentiment. Through the ages, from Hazrat Adam to Master Nisar, humans have practised love, but very few have understood the protocols of hate, which has an acuity more pleasurable than love. Love has a sweetness that if tasted for too long can leave a bad taste in the mouth. I agree with the lesson of hatred taught by religion: We must hate the devil. It is a form of hatred that does not diminish the devil's stature. Universal hatred of the devil is proof of his existence. If we were taught to hate the devil with less fervour, this would diminish our idea of his immense presence. I began to hate Abdur Rahman, and he became a significant presence in my life.

Whenever and wherever I bumped into him, I enquired after his welfare, and we had a long conversation. Abdur Rahman was of medium height with a slim body, but when he wore shorts, the bulge of his firm tummy and the smooth, shiny flesh of his hairless calves reminded me of a brand-new football with a leather band around it. His nose and features were broad and puffy. The mark of an old injury on his broad forehead reminded me of a small cavity carved in a desk by a naughty schoolboy. He was a hafiz-i-Qur'an, by that I mean he had committed the entire Holy Qur'an to memory. Of course, at the drop of a hat, he chanted verses from the Qur'an, an infuriating intervention because everyone present had to stop their conversations as a mark of respect.

I informed Director Sahib that Abdur Rahman has a good command of Urdu, free from usual errors, and he began to rely upon him more than was necessary. In one film, Abdur Rahman was cast in ten different roles, which included standing around as a waiter in a hotel and acting a sadhu wearing a long-haired wig holding a chimta in one hand. When a scene required a clerk, the costume department pasted a beard on his face and glued a dark moustache on his upper lip to transform him into a ticket collector on a railway platform—and all this happened because I hated him. Abdur Rahman was delighted that in no time he had become so popular, and I was gratified that he invited the envy of other extras. I put in a word with the proprietor of the film company, and within three months, he received an increment of ten rupees and the twenty-five other extras in the company began to loathe him. It thrilled me that Abdur Rahman had no idea I was responsible for his good fortune.

Apart from my work with the film company, I edited a local weekly newspaper. One day, Abdur Rahman walked in holding my magazine in one hand, singing its praises, 'Munshi Sahib, this magazine…only you….'

I responded immediately, 'Yes….'

'Mashallah! What a wonderful magazine! I got hold of it last night, quite by coincidence. Riveting. Now, I'll buy it every week.'

His tone and manner suggested he was doing me a favour. I thanked him, and that was that. A few days passed, and I was sitting on a broken chair under a neem tree, writing a column for my paper. Abdur Rahman walked up and stood obsequiously near me. I looked at him and asked, 'Yes…?'

'When you're free….'

'I'm free…do go ahead….'

He opened a multicoloured envelope and handed me his photograph; I looked at it and broke into an involuntary laugh. Abdur Rahman was visibly upset, and as a gesture of appeasement, I said, 'Abdur Rahman Sahib, what a coincidence, just this morning, I was wondering how to fill the page after the title page, and I identified blocks for two images, but one is missing. I was thinking about this when you handed me your photograph! It will make a perfect block!'

Abdur Rahman pursed his thick lips. 'It's so kind of you...really... will you publish this photograph?'

I looked at the photograph and said, 'Why not?'

Abdur Rahman thanked me again and rubbed his hands as he added, 'If a note were to be included with the photograph, I'd be ever so grateful to you. Whatever you think appropriate...but...forgive me, I am disturbing your work.' He continued to rub his hands as he walked off.

I scrutinized the photograph. Abdur Rahman was looking straight into the camera, with his eyes wide open, and his slightly flared nostrils betrayed an effort to expand his chest. He looked like a cartoon character, with his hair parted on the right at an angle. In one hand, Abdur Rahman held a hefty directory; clearly a prop the photographer had purchased for one or two annas in 1916 to give his subjects a more professional appearance. In the other hand, he held a large pipe with the bit pointing towards his mouth like a teacup. A residue of tea had left a discernible imprint on his lips. We should remind ourselves that Abdur Rahman did not know how to read or write English and shunned tobacco.

I found the money for a photo block, and true to my word, published his photograph with a complimentary note. The following morning, around ten o'clock, I was sitting and drinking a cup of bitter tea in the company's filthy restaurant when Abdur Rahman entered carrying the latest issue and sidled up to me. He greeted me, 'Aadaab 'arz', and as he pursed his lips in gratitude, the flesh around his eyes scrunched up. He tucked the newspaper under his arm and began to rub his hands. I asked him, 'Your photograph was published...have you read the note?'

'Yes...sir...it was so kind of you.'

I felt a stab of pain in my chest, and the colour drained from my face. I have chronic chest pain and have tried thousands of remedies for it but none has worked. I was drinking my tea and could feel the pain spread through my chest. Abdur Rahman looked distraught and asked, 'I don't wish to tempt fate, but are you well?'

I was in a rotten 'couldn't care less' mood but said, 'I'm fine… it's nothing, really nothing.'

'Oh no, you are not, sir. You're unwell.' He looked anxious, 'I can be of assistance to you…'

'I am fine…please don't worry about me…just a mild pain in my chest…I'll be fine in a minute.'

'A pain in your chest…' he looked thoughtful, 'A pain in your chest means you are suffering from constipation, and constipation….'

Outraged, I wanted to hurl a few choice profanities at him but managed to control myself. 'You are the limit…the limit! What on earth does chest pain have to do with constipation?'

'Sir, you're wrong. Constipation can cause a hundred and one different ailments, and unquestionably chest pain is one of them. The chest and the stomach are so close. Constipation can lead to an onset of headaches. The yellowish tinge in your eyes indicates that you have been suffering from constipation for some time now. Sir, constipation does not mean that you do not evacuate your bowels for a few days. No, sir…it's possible that what you think is an evacuation, is in fact constipation. In your case, your weak constitution is related to constipation.' Abdur Rahman was silent for a minute or so, but introducing some more slime into his tone, he continued, 'You must have consulted several doctors. Please try a simple remedy of mine, and by God's will, it will cure your illness.'

I asked, 'What illness?'

Abdur Rahman rubbed his hands vigorously, 'Constipation….'

'La hol w'allah! God save me from the devil,' I thought, 'Who has told this idiot I have constipation?' I had chest pain for some time, and every doctor I had ever consulted thought so, but this half-baked doctor is insisting that I have constipation…constipation! I tried hard to control my temper and not hurl my teacup at him. What an idiotic man who refuses to pay attention to what I have to say! I was furious, and I shut up.

Abdur Rahman took advantage of my silence and began to list remedies for constipation, and continued to spout God alone knows what, 'The problem is that you have turds lying around in your stomach. Every day, you evacuate your bowels but not all the turds because your stomach is not functioning properly; consequently, your intestine is dehydrated. Phlegm, I mean mucus, which helps the excrement go down, is greatly reduced in your body. And that's why I think you have to apply more pressure than usual when you evacuate your bowels. The usual English medicines to open your bowels cause more problems than cures, and they are addictive. Think about it; if you developed an addiction, you'd have to spend two to three annas every day merely to shit. Unani medicines are compatible with people's temperaments. Secondly....'

Exasperated, I cut him short, 'Would you care for a cup of tea?' Without waiting for a response, I turned to the proprietor, 'Gulab, a double tea for sir!'

The tea arrived, and just as Abdur Rahman pulled a chair to sit down, I stood up, 'Forgive me, I have to discuss a scene change with Director Sahib. We'll chat another time.'

The constipation saga on the tip of Abdur Rahman's tongue came to a halt. The pain in my chest was troubling me, and his chatter made me feel worse. The problems with my health were common knowledge, and he could have told me about my weak lungs, my inflamed intestine, the growth in my stomach, my terrible teeth, and rheumatism, but to insist that I had constipation made no sense whatsoever. I failed to understand why he wanted to turn me into a victim of constipation.

I left the hotel and went to Director Sahib's room, where I found him sitting and chatting to the hero and heroine and a couple of other actresses. Cloudy weather had forced him to postpone the outdoor shoot, and everyone was free. It took me a few minutes to figure out that the conversation was about Hafiz Abdur Rahman, and I became all ears. One extra spewed invective against him, and another mimicked the way he delivered his dialogue. The hero complained to Director Sahib that Hafiz Abdur Rahman took it upon himself to correct his pronunciation all the time, and added, 'He is a weird chap, sir! Yesterday, he told somebody that my acting is rubbish. Do tell him off, at least once, just to teach him a lesson.'

Director Sahib smiled and said, 'All of you have complaints against him but he has a complaint against me.'

Three or four voices asked in unison, 'What is his complaint?'

Director Sahib's face lit up in a smile, 'According to him, I suffer from lifelong constipation and have never tried to cure it. I've reassured him several times that I do not have constipation-vonstipation but he refuses to accept my assertion and is wedded to the idea that I have constipation. He has prescribed several remedies. I think he wants me to be indebted to him.'

'How?' I asked.

'What else can it mean? The point is that he only has remedies for one ailment—constipation. And because he wishes to ingratiate himself to me, he is on the lookout, and the moment I get constipated, he will start administering his remedies and cure me. Interesting man.'

Finally, I had reached the heart of the matter and laughed out loud. 'Director Sahib, yours truly is also a recipient of Hafiz Sahib's favours. Yesterday, I published his photograph in my newspaper. A few minutes ago, he tried his best to repay my debt in Gulab's hotel and tried to convince me that I suffer from chronic constipation. Thank God I escaped his assault because I do not have constipation.'

Four days after this conversation, I got constipated, and my constipation persists. Come to think of it, I think I have been constipated for the past two months. I have used several patented drugs but none has had the desired effect. Perhaps, I should put Hafiz Abdur Rahman to the test. It should not matter if his remedies prove false. I am not in love with him.

## Latika Rani

She was not beautiful; nothing was striking about her face or appearance. Yet, she captured the hearts of filmgoers, who swarmed like flies even around her illuminated cinema hoardings. They were drawn to her flirtatious airs and loved to watch her flitting around on the silver screen. If you were to ask someone to describe the one trait that held Latika Rani apart from other female stars, without hesitation the person would say, 'Her innocence.'

Her innocence touched the hearts of all those who saw her on screen. Her studio presented her in locations away from city lights, where she lived in a simple village hut as the naïve daughter of an uneducated man—a farmer, a labourer, or a railway linesman—and she fit these roles perfectly. When somebody mentioned Latika Rani, the image that came to mind was of a petite barefooted young peasant girl with her hair pulled back from her face in a short plait. Imagine her playing with an equally innocent lamb as her ghagra swirls around showing her calves, and her tight bodice reveals the gentle protrusion of her breasts with artistic reserve.

Latika Rani's eyes and nose were pleasing. Imagine her in your mind's eye as someone immediately recognizable as a summation of all things wifely. She became famous with her first film, and although she left the film world ages ago, her celebrity abides. Latika gained both fame and fortune. In her measured way, she was aware of every single penny that came into her pocket, and she climbed every rung of the stairway to stardom in a similar calculated manner with apparent dignity and confidence.

Latika Rani was a great actress and a most curious woman. When twenty-one and studying in France, instead of learning French, she started learning Hindustani. A young man from Madras fell in love with her. She decided to marry him, but when she went to London, where she met a much older Bengali man struggling to pass his bar exams, Latika Rani changed her mind and decided to marry him instead. She took a considered step because she saw in this much older Bengali a man who could participate in the realization of her dreams. Latika was in love with the man from Madras but he was specializing in lung diseases, and the most she could gain from marrying him was a lifetime guarantee of healthy lungs. Prafulla Rai, the much older Bengali man, was a dream maker, who could spin everlasting dreams and with her charm, Latika Rani wove everlasting webs around him.

A hardworking man from a middle-class family, Prafulla Rai could have qualified as a lawyer with top honours had he wished but he hated the profession and was pursuing it to please his parents. He ate his dinners and perused his books from time to time but his heart was drawn to a different unknown path, and he seemed lost. Prafulla hated crowds. Disinterested in parties, he spent hours on his own in some teahouse or sitting with his old landlady in her flat discussing his imaginary castles. Nevertheless, he knew that one day he would create something that would lift his spirits.

When Latika Rani met Prafulla Rai, it took her time to figure out that this Bengali studying for his bar exams was no ordinary man. Other men were interested in her because she was young; several had even complimented her on her looks, but she knew she was no beauty and the compliments she received were just a matter of form. The doctor from Madras loved her and thought her truly beautiful but Latika felt he did not admire her but her lungs, which he had described as flawless. She grappled with a profound sense of imperfection and wanted to improve herself.

Latika was an intelligent woman, and she saw in Prafulla a man who would set her on a path to fame. Prafulla Rai was a chain-smoker, and the cloud of cigarette smoke that surrounded him gave him an absent-minded air. Yet, he deconstructed Latika's face in his imagination and saw and heard her through the eyes and ears of others. He gave her speech a new resonance, and her eyes and lips a new passion and vitality. She delighted him. In her, he saw the potential for laying the foundation of his future triumphs. She understood that Prafulla was an architect who would not reveal his blueprint.

Prafulla and Latika were content because they came to depend on each other. One was incomplete without the other. Latika could evaluate her every move in Prafulla's eyes that gazed silently into a void, and his quiet verdict became a touchstone for her thoughts and comportment. Soon, Latika discovered that the passion she saw in Prafulla's eyes that gazed silently into a void was missing from his embrace, which proved to be a bed of abrasive nettles. Still, she remained content because the desire in Prafulla's eyes was all that she needed to spread her wings.

Latika was a woman who calculated every permutation and combination on her road to success. In the first two months of knowing Prafulla, she knew that the doorway to the realization of her dreams would open within the year, and she ought to leave everything to Prafulla Rai's agile mind. On their return to India, they stopped in Berlin, where Prafulla's friend introduced him to UFA Film Studios. It was here that Latika had a clear sight of her future in Prafulla's eyes as he looked into the void. When she saw Prafulla deep in conversation with a famous German actress, she knew that this was how he wished to chart her future.

In Bombay, at the Taj Mahal Hotel, Prafulla Rai met a down-and-out English knight with a large social circle. A little over sixty, Sir Howard Pascal was well-spoken and well-bred. Although Prafulla Rai was unable to figure him out, the shrewd Latika Rani was quick to appreciate that this man could be of use to them. She began to cultivate him and fussed over him. She expected him to play a role in the drama of their lives. One evening, yet again as though preordained, two guests invited to dinner by Sir Howard became directors of the film company Prafulla Rai was about to create. Within a few days, they had cleared all the hurdles encountered in laying the foundation of a limited company.

Prafulla found Sir Howard to be a very worthwhile person, but from the very first moment she met him, it was Latika who realized this man would prove useful. Latika ignored Prafulla's hints of jealousy when she showered Sir Howard with attention. Proximity to Latika was a source of vicarious sexual thrills for Sir Howard, and she did not seem to mind in the least. She understood that many of his wealthy Marwari guests pledged their capital simply because they wished to be seen with her in the studio. Latika had no objections.

For her, access to their money was what mattered.

Once they had formed the limited company and sold all its shares, Latika reckoned everything was going according to plan. They acquired land for the studio in a most pleasant location—again because of Sir Howard Pascal's influence and his large social circle. With the company registered and launched, the directors advised Prafulla Rai to go to England to procure the necessary paraphernalia.

One day, before his departure, Prafulla proposed to Latika in typical European fashion. She accepted promptly. They were married the same day and left for England for their honeymoon, which was a matter of formality since they had been sharing the secrets of each other's bodies for some time. Now, they had one preoccupation: to procure equipment for the company they had created, and then head back to Bombay and get down to work. Latika had never given much thought to how Prafulla was going to run a studio since he knew absolutely nothing about film-making. Yet, convinced of his brilliance, she knew he would become a successful film producer. She knew that with his eyes that gazed silently into the void, he had worked out everything for her. She knew that whenever he launched her as a heroine in his first film, there would be a commotion across India.

Prafulla Rai knew nothing about the technique of film-making. He made a cursory inspection of the UFA Film Studios, but when he returned to India accompanied by a cinematographer and a director, everyone in the studio was impressed by his flair. A man of few words, Prafulla arrived at the studio early in the morning and spent the entire day overseeing the dialogue, sets, and scenario. Shooting progressed methodically according to plan, and every department had a head who worked under Prafulla's supervision. All indulgences were forbidden. The atmosphere in the studio was civil.

The first film was completed and released. What was projected on the screen was what Prafulla Rai's eyes wanted to see. Prafulla Rai's first film was released in an age of excess, when film romances were set in milieus not remotely connected to reality—heroines dressed in flashy clothes, associated with high society, and spoke the language of stage dramas. Prafulla Rai's film eschewed existing practice, and for film audiences, this was a revolution—a change they relished. The film was successful all over Hindustan, and Latika Rani created a place in the hearts of the public.

Prafulla Rai was pleased with his success and delighted when he read press reviews praising Latika's beauty, her innocence, and her childlike acting because he was the creator. For the shrewd Latika, her success was not a surprise, and it had no visible effect on her. All her accolades were like pages of a book she had written some time ago. She planned every move, from the clothes she wore to the premiere of her film, to the scripted conversation she thought was appropriate for her to have with her husband in the presence of others. She rehearsed which corner of her mouth to raise in a smile and earmarked the recipients of the garland she took off at a film premiere.

Prafulla had allotted space for Sir Howard Pascal to live on a floor above the studio, and Latika and Prafulla built their house nearby. Every morning, Latika spent half an hour chatting about flora and fauna with the geriatric knight, who was a keen gardener. She returned home to indulge in a bit of lovemaking to satisfy her husband's needs, and Prafulla pushed off to the studio. Latika busied herself with her make-up in a method devised entirely by her husband.

They completed the second film and then the third, and likewise the fourth and the fifth. All these films were hits, hits that compelled other producers to follow the protocols of production set in place by their studio, India Talkies. With each film, Latika's fame spread far and wide. Wherever you turned, India Talkies had left its mark, but very few people knew Prafulla Rai—Latika's creator and her *better half*. Prafulla did not give this matter a thought. His eyes that gazed silently into the void were busy, continually seeking new roles for Latika.

Early India Talkie films gave little importance to the hero, who stood up, sat down, and moved around in the narrative at Prafulla's direction. In the studio, too, his stature was of little importance. Everyone knew that Mr Rai was numero uno and next in line was Mrs Rai—everyone else was an extra. The cumulative effect was that the hero began to claim his right, and it became mandatory to have his name on the screen credits with Latika's. He too wanted to benefit from the studio's success. He loathed Latika because she did not give the slightest thought to his rights. Over time, he began to talk about this in the studio, with the result that Prafulla Rai dropped him from his next film. A minor crisis ensued but immediately died down. Rumours buzzed around when a new hero arrived, but gradually died down.

Latika did not agree with her husband's decision on the matter of the new hero but did not try to make him change his mind. In keeping with her designs, the new film was not a success and neither was the one that followed. Latika feared her fame was dying out, and one day, we heard she ran away with the new hero. There was a furore in the newspapers. It was remarkable that in all these years, Latika's reputation had remained untainted. When news spread that she had run away with the new hero, their love affair became the talk of India.

Prafulla Rai collapsed. Those close to him disclosed that he fainted several times. Latika's flight proved an unsurmountable tragedy in his life. For him, her body was the canvas on which he had painted his dreams. Where would he find anything remotely similar? Crushed under the weight of sorrow, several times he wished to set fire to the studio and throw himself into the flames, but this required the kind of courage he did not possess. Finally, the old hero stepped forward and offered to help sort matters out.

He stunned Prafulla when he revealed certain aspects of Latika's personality. 'Latika is a woman devoid of delicate emotions such as love. She hasn't run away with the new hero because she is in love with him; it's a mere stunt to fix her falling popularity ratings. She wants to raise her profile, and the new hero is her partner in crime. He is not headstrong like me, and she has taken him along as a servant. If she had chosen me, her scheme would not have worked because I do not follow her orders. She is ready to return. Her return is long overdue. I am following her instructions in conveying all this to you.'

Like many creative artists, Prafulla Rai was an eccentric, and the old hero's argument made perfect sense to him. When Latika returned, Prafulla moaned as a spurned steadfast lover and accused her of infidelity. Latika remained silent. She did not put up a defence. She did not even comment on whatever the old hero had said to her husband. On her advice, the old hero returned, and his salary doubled;

she talked to him but maintained the usual distance between them.

The next film was a success, as was the one after, but in the interim several new production houses began to follow the new pathways for film-making chalked out by India Talkies. Several new faces, far more attractive than Latika's, were introduced to the screen. The old hero expected Latika to leave her husband and go into the arms of another film producer, who would explore new aspects of her body, but this did not happen.

For ages, nothing noteworthy came to pass in India Talkies. Nevertheless, with the dawn of every new day, a new rumour about Latika entered the studio. Everyone speculated about her relationship with her husband. Among the several stories in circulation, one started by the old hero claimed she was having an affair with her syce, Ram Bharosay. The old hero believed that Latika satisfied her sexual desires with Ram Bharosay because her relationship with her husband was limited to a mere boudoir pageant. The old hero asserted that 'A woman like Latika can only have sexual relations with a servant—a man indebted to her and who will, therefore, do her bidding. If capable of love, she would not have returned after she ran away with the new hero. That was a mere stunt, and it unmasked her. Her days are over. With Fate stacked against her, she knows that Mr Rai's powers to fuel her rise to fame are over. She is like a mango seed sucked of all its juice—the nectar of her life has dried up. Wait and see, before long she will go off with another producer to create another turnaround in her fortune.'

Latika did not go off with another film-maker. This turn was not on her road map. After she ran away with the new hero, there was no visible change in her conduct. Yet again, every morning, she was seen busy gardening with Sir Howard Pascal. Although aware of the gossip in the studio, she maintained a meaningful silence. Two other films were released, and they flopped. India Talkies' brilliant reputation began to wane. These events did not have a visible effect on Latika but everyone in the studio knew that Mr Rai was anxious. The old hero, who felt concerned for his boss, counselled him to hand over the ropes of production to his junior and lead a quiet and peaceful retired life, but was ignored. Yet again, Prafulla Rai began to exercise his dream factory of a brain to create another enduring vision. He tried to rejuvenate Latika's tired body.

News of their household matters leaked out through the servants, who reported that Mr Rai was irritable and grumpy all the time. At times, he lost his temper and called Latika foul names but she remained silent. At night, when Mr Rai was unable to fall asleep, she stroked his head, massaged his feet, and put him to sleep. In the old days, Mr Rai never insisted that Latika sleep with him, but now he woke up several times every night to look for her and forced her to his bed.

The old hero's heart was full of sorrow, 'Mr Rai is a big man, but sadly, he has thrown his heart at the feet of a woman who is not worthy of him. She's not a woman; she's a witch. If left to me, I would get rid of her…put a bullet through her! The biggest tragedy is that now Mr Rai is even more in love with her than ever.'

Those able to get to the heart of the matter knew that a thwarted Prafulla Rai wanted to ruin Latika because he no longer had the strength to add flavour to her life. Not that long ago, he had held her in his heart as something sacred. He had not allowed a tiny particle of dirt or filth to settle on her, but now, he wanted to smear her with excrement. His spirit no longer cringed when people told him they had heard about Latika's involvement in 'X' or 'Y' filth. For years, he had lived in an illusory and tender world of dreams, but now he wanted to smash his own and Latika's heads against hard reality.

Time passed. The shooting of the twenty-second production of India Talkies was ongoing. Prafulla Rai was trying out a new experiment but even he did not know how it was meant to unfold. The light in Rai's office stayed on late into the night. Instead of going home, he often fell asleep in the studio. The stacks of paper on his desk became higher. When the servants cleaned his ashtray, they found heaps of cigarette butts. He had commissioned a story but the scenario department had no idea how it would progress.

The costume department was almost idle. One day, Latika walked in and ordered that they stitch a long-sleeved black blouse for her. The assistants purchased the cloth of her choice; she settled on the design and asked for a black georgette sari. She had a detailed discussion about her new hairstyle with Miss D'Silva, the hairdresser. When news of Latika's new wardrobe leaked, everyone in the studio began to speculate about the film in production.

The old hero thought Mr Rai was going to present the tragedy of his life. To everyone's disappointment, when the production department posted the details of the first shoot and work began on the set, it was the same old atmosphere and the same old clothes. The shoot continued in the usual organized manner, but one day, there was an uproar in the studio. Prafulla Rai arrived on the set and observed the shooting for a while. Suddenly, without further ado, he descended on the cameraman and slapped him so hard on his ear that the man fainted. At first, the studio staff remained silent, but when they saw that Mr Rai was like a madman possessed, they restrained him and took him home.

The best doctors were summoned but Prafulla Rai's madness escalated. Time and again, he yelled for Latika, but when she appeared, his ferocity increased, and he wanted to tear her apart. He swore at her and referred to her by such obscene names that bystanders exchanged horrified looks. For four days, Prafulla Rai remained hysterical and dangerously psychotic. On the fifth morning, Latika was gardening with Sir Howard Pascal and discussing her husband's tragic illness in a soft voice, when news reached her that Mr Rai was breathing his last. Latika swooned. Sir Howard and other studio staff were trying to revive her when further news arrived: Mr Rai had gone to heaven. At around ten o'clock that morning, when pallbearers arrived to lift his coffin, Latika appeared with her eyes swollen and her hair ruffled, dressed in a black sari and a black long-sleeved blouse. The old hero looked at her and said in a voice spiked with hatred, 'The wretch, she knew when this scene was to be shot.'

## Hamid's Baby

The moment Babu Hargopal arrived from Lahore he said to Hamid, 'Well then, arrange for a taxi.'

Taken aback, Hamid suggested, 'Why don't you rest for a while; you've just arrived after such a long journey. You must be tired.'

Babu Hargopal did not budge, 'No, my dear chap, I am not tired-wired at all. I've procured ten days with great difficulty, and have come for pleasure, not rest. For the next ten days, you are at my disposal. You will have to agree to whatever I say. I want to reach the height of decadence. Get some soda!'

Hamid tried to restrain him and asked, 'Babu Hargopal, is it wise to start drinking first thing in the morning?'

He ignored Hamid's question that was more of a comment, and taking out a bottle of Johnnie Walker from his suitcase, he said, 'If you can't get some soda, let me have some water. Now, don't tell me you won't give me water!'

Babu Hargopal was forty years old and older than Hamid, who was thirty and had great respect for Babu Sahib, an associate of his late father. Immediately, he sent for some soda but added gently, 'Please, don't force me. You know my wife is very hard on these matters. Of course, I'll keep you company.'

After four pegs, Babu Hargopal turned to Hamid and said, 'Well now, let's go. Look here, do get hold of a taxi on the luxurious side. I prefer private hire; I loathe these meters.'

Hamid arranged for a new Ford with a good driver, and Babu Hargopal was delighted. He sat in the taxi and inspected the contents of his wallet. Eyeing several hundred-rupee notes, he heaved a satisfied sigh and muttered under his breath, 'It's enough,' before adding, 'well then, driver, let's go!'

The driver cocked his cap at an angle, and asked, 'Where to, Seth?' Babu Hargopal turned to Hamid, 'You tell him....'

Hamid gave the matter some thought and told the driver where to go, and within a few minutes, they were with the ace pimp of Bombay, who took them to several establishments and produced several girls. Hamid, who appreciated refinement and cleanliness, did not approve of any. Notwithstanding their make-up, these girls looked unclean; besides, they had prostitution written across their faces, and this offended Hamid's sensibilities. He believed that even if a woman was a whore, she should remain a woman and not hide her womanliness behind the mask of her profession.

On the other hand, Babu Hargopal was turned on by smut; he traded in millions and if he so wished he could have the entire city of Bombay washed with soap and water. Yet, he paid little attention to his hygiene. When Babu Hargopal bathed, it was with little water, and often he did not shave for days. He could drink the finest whisky from a grimy glass and fall asleep holding the filthiest beggar close to his heart—and on waking up, say, 'Wow! I enjoyed that. What a woman!'

Babu Hargopal never ceased to amaze Hamid; often, he turned up wearing an exquisite sherwani over such a dirty vest that if you were to set eyes on it, you would retch. Babu Sahib carried a handkerchief but wiped his runny nose with the hem of his kurta and was equally relaxed when eating chaat out of an unwashed plate. He would rest his head on the oiliest pillow covers with a horrible stench without ever thinking that he could have them changed. Over the years, Hamid spent several hours thinking about Babu Hargopal's personality but failed to arrive at a satisfactory understanding. He had asked him several times, 'Babuji, why aren't you disgusted by squalor?'

In response, Babu Hargopal smiled, 'Of course, it disgusts me... but there's so much squalor all around us, and I can't fix it!'

Hamid would retreat into silence although Babu Hargopal's disregard for squalor irked him.

They roamed around Bombay for hours, and finally, the pimp realized that Hamid was finicky about such matters. After taxing his mind before he turned to the driver, 'Press onwards to Shivaji Park, and if she is not up to the mark, I swear upon God, I'll give up pimping!'

The taxi stopped at a bungalow-like building in Shivaji Park, where the pimp jumped out and went upstairs. He returned shortly for Babu Hargopal and Hamid, and together they walked up the stairs to an immaculate room. The floor was shining, and there was not a speck of dust on the furniture. An image of Swami Vivekananda hung on a wall to their left, and on the opposite wall were two photographs, one of Gandhiji and the other of Subhas Bose. The pimp invited them to sit, and as they lowered themselves into the sofa just below Vivekananda, Hamid spotted some Marathi books on the coffee table; he was impressed by the uncluttered cleanliness of the house. Its solemn air was nothing like the usual seedy surroundings of prostitutes; he could not wait to see the girl. A man walked in from through the door of the adjoining room towards their left, and spoke to the pimp in a soft, measured tone before he turned to Babu Hargopal and Hamid, 'She's on her way. She was having a bath and is getting dressed.' His job done, he disappeared.

Hamid began to inspect all the accoutrements of the room. A vase full of fresh flowers stood on a corner table to the right of the sofa, and near it was a bright jute carpet. On the left was another table with magazines neatly stacked, and against the wall near Gandhiji's photograph was a glass-fronted bookcase with neat rows of books. Facing them, near the door to the adjoining room, a pair of delicate sandals lay on the floor, looking as though someone had just left them there. Babu Hargopal stubbed his cigarette butt on the floor with the sole of his shoe, and a furious Hamid wanted to throw it out of the window, but just then he heard a familiar rustle of silk. He turned slightly and saw a fair-skinned girl walk in, barefoot.

She had a centre parting and had covered her head with a brand-new kashta. When she came closer and joined her hands to greet them with a pranam, Hamid saw an almost white leaf tucked into her thick, lustrous black hair skilfully coiffed into a chignon, and he stood up in response to her greeting. Of medium height, she looked diffident as she sat down on a solitary armchair and lowered her large black eyes. She had a fair complexion with a hint of pink and was no older than seventeen—like her new sari, she looked crisp. Hamid felt her take over his being.

Babu Hargopal said something and Hamid gave a start, as though jolted out of sleep. 'What did you say, Babu Hargopal?'

Babu Hargopal said, 'Say something, then,' and added in a soft voice, 'I don't much care for her.'

A furious Hamid looked at the girl draped in silk and all aglow. Her unblemished youth was within reach for a price, and he could possess her not for one or two, but several nights. Her beauty stirred Hamid, and he wondered why this girl should be an item for sale, but if this were not the case, how would he obtain her? 'Well then, my friend, what do you think?' Babu Hargopal asked in an uncouth manner.

'Think?' asked Hamid startled. 'You don't like her, but I...' Before he could complete his sentence, Babu Hargopal, who was a very generous friend, stood up and asked the pimp in a very business-like manner, 'Well, what do we have to pay?'

The pimp responded, 'Inspect the lass. She's fresh on the market.'

Babu Hargopal interrupted him, 'Forget her...talk business.'

The pimp lit his biri, 'It will be a hundred rupees. Keep her for a full day or a full night—not a penny less.'

Babu Hargopal turned to Hamid, 'Why, my friend?'

Hamid thought Hargopal's exchange with the pimp was not merely in poor taste but an insult to the girl. He was outraged that this stunning paragon of Marathi beauty, innocence, and sensuality was on the market for a mere hundred rupees. Nonetheless, the thought that he could pay a hundred rupees and attain this prize for a day or a night caused a twinge in his heart. He felt a man could spend a lifetime with her. Babu Hargopal repeated his question, 'Why, my friend, what do you think?'

Hamid had no wish to share his thoughts. Babu Hargopal smiled as he took his wallet out of his pocket and handed a hundred rupees note to the pimp, 'Not an anna less or more...' He turned to Hamid, 'Let's go, my friend, the matter's settled.'

They descended the stairs in silence and waited in the taxi for the pimp to bring the girl down. She blushed as she sat between them. Babu Hargopal booked a room in a nearby hotel for Hamid and took off to find a girl for himself.

When Hamid walked into the room, he saw the girl sitting on the bed with her eyes lowered, and his heartbeat quickened. Babu Hargopal had left half a bottle of whisky for him, and Hamid sent for some soda. He drank a sizeable double peg to build his courage, and sitting next to the girl he asked, 'What is your name?'

The girl lifted her eyes and said in a dulcet voice, 'Lata Mangalaonkar.' Hamid drank another double peg. When he removed the kashta from Lata's head and caressed her lustrous hair, she fluttered her long black eyelashes. Very gently, Hamid lowered the pallu of her sari from her shoulder and shuddered when he caught a glimpse of her throbbing breasts enclosed in her body-hugging choli. He wanted to turn into a choli and cling to Lata's body and fall asleep in its sweet warmth.

Lata had been in Bombay for just two months and only spoke Marathi. Hamid thought it a very harsh language but it sounded sweet on her lips. When she tried to speak to Hamid in broken Hindustani, he said, 'No, Lata, speak to me in Marathi, it sounds very "changli" to me.'

Lata laughed when she heard the word 'changli' and corrected his pronunciation. Hamid could not enunciate the medial sound between the 'ch' and 's', and they burst into laughter. He could not understand her but Hamid got a kick out of this lack of comprehension and kissed her on the mouth. 'Pour these sweet words from your mouth into mine, I want to drink them.'

Lata did not understand a word but she laughed. Hamid drew her close to his heart. For him, everything about Lata was lovable, including the short sleeves of her tight-fitting choli that encased her rounded white arms, and Hamid kissed them.

When Hamid dropped Lata off at nine o'clock that night, he sensed a void inside his being. He tossed and turned all night long. Without her soft touch, he felt as though someone had removed a layer of his skin. The following morning, Babu Hargopal arrived and asked him conversationally, 'Why, how was it?'

All Hamid said was, 'Fine.'

'Like to go again?'

'No, I have some urgent business....'

'Don't talk nonsense. I told you when I got here that for the next ten days you are mine.'

Hamid managed to convince Babu Hargopal that he had to meet someone to resolve an urgent business matter in Poona, and Babu Sahib set off on his own on his round of debauchery.

Hamid took a taxi to the bank, drew out money, and headed to Lata's house. In the sitting room, he found the same man who had ushered Lata into his life. While he waited for Lata to finish her bath, Hamid chatted to the man and handed him a hundred-rupee note. Lata walked into the room; she looked unsullied. When she brought her hands together in a pranam, Hamid stood up and addressed the man, 'I'm off, you bring her down. I'll drop her back on time.'

Hamid went downstairs. When Lata joined him in the taxi, he felt gratified by her touch. He wanted to squeeze her close to him but she stopped him with a wave of her hand. Lata stayed with him until seven-thirty that evening. When he dropped her back, he felt bereft and spent yet another unsettled night.

Hamid knew his behaviour was imprudent; he was a married man and a father of two toddlers. If his wife were to learn of his antics, he would get his comeuppance. She could possibly discount a one-night stand but he envisaged this matter heading towards something more prolonged. Hamid resolved to stay away from Shivaji Park. Yet, the following morning, he was back in the hotel with Lata by his side. For the next fortnight, Hamid visited Lata every morning. He wiped out two thousand rupees from his bank account. His business suffered on account of his neglect but Hamid was obsessed.

After considerable effort, Hamid found the determination to bring the matter to an end. Babu Hargopal completed his spell of debauchery and returned to Lahore, and Hamid immersed himself in his business and tried to forget Lata. Resolute for four months, one day, Hamid happened to find himself in Shivaji Park. Quite unintentionally, he turned to the taxi driver and said, 'Stop here.' The taxi stopped, and Hamid told himself, 'No, this is not it. Tell the taxi driver to drive on.' But he opened the door, stepped out, and went upstairs. When Lata walked in, Hamid noticed she had put on weight. Her breasts were fuller, and her face had filled out. He paid for her and took her to the hotel.

Hamid lost his equilibrium when he heard that Lata was pregnant. His intoxication vanished, and he asked, 'Whose foetus are you carrying?'

Lata did not understand a word but Hamid persisted and managed to explain his question to her. She responded with a simple, 'I do not know.'

Hamid broke out into a cold sweat, 'You have no idea!'

She shook her head, 'No.'

Hamid swallowed his saliva and asked, 'It isn't mine, by any chance?'

'I do not know.'

After he questioned her at length, Hamid discovered that her minders had tried their best to abort the foetus. No remedies had worked, and one had such nasty side-effects that Lata was laid up for a month. Hamid spent some time thinking about the matter and decided to consult a top-notch doctor before Lata's keepers packed her off to a village. He dropped Lata home and went to see a friend who was a doctor, who told him, 'Look here, this is a dangerous undertaking. It's a matter of life and death.'

Hamid turned to him and said, 'Here, it is a matter of my life and death. The foetus is most certainly mine. I've calculated; I've asked her. Please, for God's sake, think of the delicate position I am in...my children. A shiver goes down my spine when I think of it. If you do not help me, I will go mad.'

Hamid's doctor friend gave him some medication, which he passed on to Lata. He waited anxiously to hear some good news but Lata informed him that it did not have the desired result.

Hamid managed to find another drug, but that too proved ineffective. Lata's belly began to protrude, and her minders thought it best to send her off to her village. Hamid asked them to give him some more time to make some arrangements. His exhausted brain could not figure out what course of action to take. He cursed Babu Hargopal and called God's wrath upon himself for indulging in such idiocy. If the baby turned out to be a girl, she too would ply the trade like her mother. Hamid wanted to die of shame. He began to hate Lata. Her beauty and grace no longer evoked the same tender passion in his heart.

Hamid wanted Lata to die before she gave birth to his child. She had slept with other men; why did her body have to accept his sperm? At times, he wanted to plunge a knife in her inflated belly or do something to kill the baby she was carrying. Lata was distraught.

In the early days of her pregnancy, nausea made her weak, and with time, the weight she was forced to cart around caused horrible cramps in her stomach. Although she had no desire to give birth, Hamid thought she did not care, and told himself, 'If nothing else, the wretch should think of the state I am in and vomit the child out.'

Finally, everyone gave up on medicines and turned to alternative remedies and chants but the baby was determined to fulfil its destiny. A defeated Hamid permitted Lata to go to a village, but before he sent her off, he went to organize a house for her. According to Lata's calculations, the baby was due in the first week of October.

Hamid concluded that the only solution was to have the baby killed, and with this plan in mind he began to gourmandize and entertain Dada Karim, one of the big godfathers in Bombay. This ate up a lot of cash but Hamid thought nothing of it. As the due date drew close, he presented his scheme to Dada Karim. They agreed on a sum of a thousand rupees, but as Hamid handed the money to him, Dada Karim said, 'I won't be able to kill such a tiny baby. I'll bring it to you, and how you deal with it is up to you. Your secret will lie buried in my heart. Don't worry.'

Hamid agreed. He thought he would put the baby on the railway track or find some other way to get rid of it.

Hamid took Dada Karim to the village, where the latter discovered that the baby had arrived fifteen days earlier. Hamid experienced the same emotion as he did when his first son was born but suppressed it; he turned to Dada Karim and emphasized, 'Look here, you must do the deed tonight.'

At midnight, Hamid waited at a secluded place with his heart and mind in turmoil as he tried to transform himself into a murderer. He lifted a small boulder that lay in front of him to test if its weight was enough to crush a baby's head. At twelve-thirty, Hamid heard footsteps and felt his heart would burst. Dada Karim became visible in the darkness. He was carrying something in his arms, and as he came closer to Hamid, he thrust a small bundle into his hands, and said, 'My work is done. I'm off.' And he left.

Hamid shivered uncontrollably. The baby wriggled its hands and feet. Hamid put the bundle on the ground and tried to steady his trembling hands. He felt around for the baby's head and lifted the weighty boulder, and was about to do the deed when overwhelmed by a desire to catch a glimpse of the child, he tossed the rock aside, reached for a matchbox in his pocket, and lit a matchstick with his trembling hands. It went off before he could muster the courage to lift the swaddle. He took charge of his heart and lit another matchstick. First, he had just a glance and then a proper look but the flame flickered away. Hamid had seen this face somewhere. Where? When? Hurriedly, he lit another match, and as he held it over the baby, he smiled as the face of the man with whom Lata lived in Shivaji Park appeared before his eyes. 'Son of a gun! Ditto, the same face, the same features.' Hamid laughed out loud and walked away.

## Blouse

Momin was restless. For some time now, his entire body had been feeling like a festering sore. All his waking hours, he experienced a peculiar persistent pain. At times, it startled him, and at others, it triggered unclear yet troubling thoughts to run in and out of his mind. At times, he felt ant-like creatures crawling all over his body, and the usually easy-going Momin's heart and soul began to tingle. This unfathomable sensory strain made him want to lie in a huge mortar and ask someone to pound him. When he was pounding garam masala in the kitchen and iron hit iron to create a loud boom that resounded from the ceiling to the floor, the vibrations ran from Momin's feet through his taut calves to his thighs, and the sensation made him quiver. Momin was fifteen years old; perhaps, the sixteenth had started. He was not sure of his age but he was a hearty young man whose childhood had raced into puberty.

Momin had no understanding of the several changes apparent in his body. His neck, once very slim, was now thick, and his Adam's apple had become prominent. The muscles of his arms were taut, and the hair on his chest was thicker. He became aware of unusual lumps in his breasts that felt like little round marbles, and when he tapped them, he experienced excruciating pain. Sometimes, he touched them inadvertently and gave a start; the thick, rough material of his shirt caused a similar ache. At times in the bathroom and sometimes in the kitchen, when no one else was around, Momin undid the buttons of his shirt to observe the lumps. If he rubbed them with his hands, he felt a sharp twinge of pain and trembled. Yet, he continued to indulge in this activity. At times, if he pressed hard on his breasts, he saw a strange sticky fluid. His entire face, including his earlobes, turned crimson, and Momin thought he had sinned.

Momin's knowledge of sin and virtue was minimal. As far as he understood such matters, any act that a human being cannot perform in the presence of another is a sin. Hence, when shame turned his face crimson, he rushed to button up his shirt and vowed in his heart never to do this again. Notwithstanding his vow, within two or three days, he was back at his secret game. Momin had no idea how to cope with all the changes in his body—several times during the working day, a feeling of restlessness compelled him to hold on to a ledge with both his hands and pull himself up. He wished someone could hold his feet and pull him so hard that he would stretch and turn into a thin wire. All these thoughts occurred in such an obscure corner of his mind that he found it hard to grasp them.

Everyone in the house was pleased with Momin; he was a diligent and efficient lad. Indeed, why would anybody have reason to complain? In a short span of some months at Deputy Sahib's house, he had impressed every member of the household. Hired at six rupees a month, the following month he received a two-rupee increment. Although delighted by this unexpected gesture of appreciation, for the past few days, a strange waywardness had entered his mind—all he wanted was to roam bazaars or relax in some secluded spot all day long. Momin did not enjoy his work but he was not indolent. Nobody in the household had a hint of his inner turmoil.

Deputy Sahib had two daughters: Razia, who either read magazines or played her harmonium, practising tunes of the latest film songs all day long; and Shakila, who asked Momin to do random chores and run errands, and occasionally told him off. These days, she was engrossed in making paper patterns of the eight blouses she had borrowed from a friend who loved to dress up in the latest styles, and for several days, she had not paid much attention to Momin.

Deputy Sahib's wife was not a demanding woman. Besides, they had two other servants in the house. Apart from Momin, there was an older woman who worked mainly in the kitchen, and occasionally, Momin was told to lend her a hand. Perhaps, Deputy Sahib's wife might have noticed some slackening in Momin's work but she did not tick him off. As for the upheaval in his body, Deputy Sahib's wife did not have a son, and could not understand Momin's emotions or figure out the changes in his body. Besides, Momin was a servant, and who can be bothered with servants and their problems? They walk through all stages of life, from childhood to old age, without their employers noticing what they are going through.

At a subconscious level, Momin wanted something cataclysmic to happen. He imagined the neatly stacked crockery dancing around him, with the lid of the boiling kettle flying off, and the water dripping from the tap turning into a fountain. As Momin's restless joints felt taut and limp in turn, he wanted to experience something he had never felt before.

Razia had immersed herself in learning a new tune, and Shakila was busy making paper patterns for her blouses. When she finished this task, she chose the smartest of the lot and sat down to stitch a purple satin blouse for herself. Razia felt she had to put aside her harmonium and copybook full of film songs to observe her sister. Shakila was methodical and meticulous in whatever she did, unlike her boisterous younger sister. When she sat down to her sewing tasks, she was surrounded by an aura of calm as she applied every stitch with great forethought, leaving no room for mistakes. She took her time but the finished item was always a perfect fit, and this was because she worked with a paper pattern before she cut the cloth.

Shakila was a full-bodied healthy girl; her soft, plump hands had tiny dimples on every joint of her fleshy conical fingers. When she operated her sewing machine, the movement of her hand caused these dimples to disappear. Shakila worked the sewing machine with the care that she brought to all her tasks, and rotated its handle with two or three fingers, very slowly, with precise movements that created a curvature on her wrist. As she tilted her neck a little to one side, an unruly wisp of hair would slip out, and immersed in her work, Shakila never tried to brush it back.

When Shakila spread the purple satin in front of her and began to cut the blouse to her size, she realized she needed a measuring tape. Their old tape had disappeared; they had a steel yardstick but she could hardly measure her chest with it. She had plenty of blouses, but now that she had put on weight, she had to measure herself again. She took off her shirt and shouted for Momin. When he arrived, she said, 'Momin, go...run to Number 6 and get a tape for measuring cloth. Tell them Shakila Bibi wants it.'

Momin's eyes collided with Shakila's white vest. Although he had seen her in similar garments several times, today he felt a strange unease in his body. He looked away and asked, 'What sort of a measuring tape, Bibiji?'

Shakila responded, 'A measuring tape for cloth…the yardstick you see here is made of steel…there is another type…made of cloth; go to Number 6…run and get this measuring tape from them…say that Shakila Bibi wants it.'

Flat Number 6 was nearby, and in no time Momin ran back with the measuring tape. Shakila took the tape from his hand and said, 'Wait here…and take it back.' She turned to Razia and said, 'If we hang on to something of theirs, that old woman will drive us nuts and go on about it. Come here. Take the tape and measure me.' As Razia measured Shakila's waist and bosom, there were several exchanges between them. Momin stood in the doorway and overheard their conversation in uncomfortable silence.

'Razia, why don't you stretch the tape when you take measurements? You did this last time and ruined my blouse. If the cloth does not sit properly on the top, you get creases around the armholes.'

'What should I measure? You always create problems. I started measuring from here, and you said, "A little lower down." If there's a slight difference here or there, it's not the end of the world!'

'Vah! All the beauty is in the fitting. Look at Suraiya, what tight-fitting clothes she wears, and there's not a single crease. How beautiful her clothes look! Come on, then, take the measurement.' Shakila finished what she was saying and exhaled. She expanded her chest as much as she could, and held her breath, before she added in a muffled voice, 'Come on then…hurry, take the measurements.'

When Shakila exhaled the air from her chest, Momin felt as though several rubber balloons had exploded inside him. Restless, he said, 'Bibiji, give me the measuring tape. I'll return it.'

Shakila told him off, 'Hold on a bit.'

As she spoke, the measuring tape wound itself around her bare arm. When Shakila tried to unwind it, Momin caught sight of a clump of black hair in her white armpit. Although Momin had similar hair in his armpits, he was very attracted to the clump of hair in hers, and he felt a shiver run through his entire body as a strange desire took over his heart.

Momin recalled how, as a child, he had removed the golden hairs from corn on the cob and fashioned it into a moustache. When he held it down on his upper lip, he had a tremulous feeling around his lips and in his nose. He wanted to experience similar sensations again. Shakila lowered her arm, and although he could not see it, Momin continued to imagine the clump of black hair. After a few minutes, Shakila handed the measuring tape to him with instructions, 'Go and return it. And thank them profusely.'

After Momin returned the measuring tape, he went to sit out in the courtyard, and a jumble of thoughts flooded his heart and mind. He tried his utmost to understand what they meant but remained unsuccessful. Momin had no intention to open the tiny trunk which held his new Eid clothes, but when he lifted the lid, and the smell of new lattha reached his nose, he wanted to have a bath, put on his new clothes, and go directly to Shakila Bibi and say salaam to her. Momin smiled at the thought of how his lattha-shalwar would crackle. When his eyes fell upon his new fez cap, almost concealed underneath his clothes, he imagined its black tassels transformed into clumps of black hair in Shakila's underarms. He took the hat out and began to stroke its tassels, and just then he heard Shakila call from inside, 'Momin!'

He put the hat back in the trunk, closed its lid, and went inside, where Shakila had finished cutting several pieces of satin. She put the shiny and smooth pieces to one side and turned to Momin. 'I called you so many times. Were you asleep?'

He answered her with a nervous, 'No, Bibiji.'

'Then, what were you doing?'

'Nothing...nothing at all.'

'You must be doing something.'

Although Shakila was cross-examining him, her mind was on the blouse she had to hand stitch before she ran the machine on it. Momin gave an awkward laugh and said, 'I opened my trunk to check my new Eid clothes.'

Shakila gave a bubbly laugh, and Razia joined her. Shakila's laughter gave Momin indescribable pleasure, and he wished with all his heart to do something silly that would give Shakila more reason to laugh. He began to mimic the expressions of a bashful girl, and said in a coy tone, 'I'll take money from Bari Bibiji and get myself a silk hanky.'

Shakila laughed and asked him, 'And what will you do with the hanky?'

Momin looked bashful, 'I'll tie it around my neck, Bibiji...it will look so nice.'

Both Shakila and Razia bubbled with laughter. 'If you tie it around your neck, remember, I'll strangle you with it,' said Shakila as she tried to suppress her laughter.

She turned to Razia, 'The wretch...made me forget why I sent for him. Razia, why did I send for him?'

Razia did not respond and began to hum the latest film song she was trying to memorize.

'Look here, Momin, I'll take off this vest and give it to you...the new shop that has opened near the chemist, na...where you went with me the other day? Go there and ask them how much they will charge for six of these. Tell him it's us enquiring and he must give a discount. Understood, na?'

'Yes, Bibiji.'

'Now, move.'

Momin stepped out and stood behind the door, and not much later, the vest landed at his feet with Shakila's voice instructing him, 'Tell him that we want the same design—the same thing. There should be no difference.'

'Very well,' said Momin as he picked up the slightly damp vest, infused with the sweet, warm, and pleasant smell of Shakila's body.

Momin left for the bazaar rubbing the vest between his hands, and it felt as soft as a kitten. He returned after he made enquiries about the price of vests and saw that Shakila had started sewing a purple satin blouse, far shinier and more tremulous than Momin's fez hat. Shakila wanted the blouse ready. Eid was around the corner. She summoned Momin several times. His ears buzzed as he carried out her instructions, 'Momin, get some thread'; 'Get the iron out!'; 'Go...get a new needle for the sewing machine; the old needle broke.'

As evening fell, Shakila asked Momin to clear all the pieces of yarn and purple satin because she had to fold her work away for the day. Momin cleaned up thoroughly and threw away all the rubbish but unthinkingly kept the small pieces of purple satin in his pocket. He had no idea what he was going to do with them.

The following day, Momin took the pieces of purple satin from his pocket and began to pull out stray skeins of thread, and for some time kept himself busy with this game—so much so that the skeins formed a ball of yarn, which he began to stroke. He imagined it was Shakila's underarm with a small clump of black hair. That day too, Shakila called him several times. He had seen every stage of the creation of the purple satin blouse. First, she basted the satin in place, after which she pierced it with small and even white stitches. When she ironed the cloth to remove every crease, it began to shine even more, and Shakila tried it on to show it to Razia. When completely satisfied, Shakila took off the blouse and marked wherever it was tight or loose; she removed all its flaws and tried it on again. When she thought it a perfect fit, she ran the sewing machine over it.

Here, Shakila was stitching the satin blouse and there, Momin was unpicking stitches from the strange thoughts in his mind. Whenever he went into the room in response to a summon, his gaze fell on the shiny satin blouse. Momin wanted to touch it—not just feel it but stroke its familiar soft downy surface with his rough hands. Now, the discarded threads Momin had shaped into a ball were softer, and when he squeezed them, they sprang back. When summoned inside, Momin saw the blouse and imagined the black hair in Shakila's underarm and wondered if it was as soft as satin.

Finally, the blouse was ready. Momin was mopping the floor of her room when Shakila entered. She took off her shirt and flung it on the bed, revealing her white vest, similar to the one that Momin had taken to the bazaar as a sample. She wore the blouse over the vest and fastened the hooks in front and stood before the mirror. Momin continued to clean the floor but looked at the mirror and saw the blouse come to life. In some places, it shone so much it seemed the satin had turned white. Shakila had her back towards him, and her spine stood out in the tight-fitting blouse. Momin could not control himself, 'Bibiji, you have outdone tailors!'

Although delighted to hear this praise, she wanted to hear Razia's opinion, so all she said was, 'It's good, isn't it?' and ran out. Momin was left gazing at the mirror where the image of the shiny blouse lingered for a while.

At night, when Momin returned to the room with a pitcher

of water, he saw the blouse hanging from a wooden hanger on a clothes peg. He was alone, so he stepped forward and gazed at the garment. Terrified, he began to stroke the blouse, and as he did, he felt someone gently stroking the softness on his body. That night, Momin had chaotic dreams. In one, Deputy Sahib asked him to crush a large quantity of coals. He picked up a small lump and hit it with a hammer, and it transformed into a ball of soft hair. In another, stray narrow strands of black sugarcane turned into cylindrical pieces that turned into black balloons and started to fly in the air. They rose higher and higher before they burst. In yet another, he found himself caught in a gale, which blew away the tassel of his fez cap. He set out in search of the tassel and roamed around in seen and unseen places. In the middle of this dream, the smell of new lattha filled the air. Then goodness knows what happened, his hand found a black satin blouse. For a while, he continued to stroke something that was throbbing. Suddenly, Momin woke up. Startled, he sat up amazed but could not fathom what had happened. He felt fear and a distinct sharp pain he had never experienced before—at first, it was warm, but soon a cold wave began to creep through his body.

## 46

## *Mantra*

In keeping with his name, Nanha Ram was a little boy, but he was big on mischief. No expression or feature on his face betrayed the slightest hint of how naughty he was. Ram was barely eight years old, but devilishly sharp and intelligent, although this was difficult to assess from his appearance. Fat to the point of being obese, when Ram walked, he looked like a football rolling along. Mr Ramashankar Acharya MA LLB, Ram's pitaji, often said, 'The aphorism, "Chant Ram Ram, dagger in underarm!" was coined especially for Ram.'

No one had ever heard Ram chant, 'Ram Ram', and instead of a dagger, he carried a small stick tucked under his arm, which he loved to deploy when he mimicked the swordsmanship of Douglas Fairbanks, from *The Thief of Baghdad*.

One afternoon, Ram's mother, Mrs Ramashankar Acharya, dragged a silent Ram by his ear and brought him before his father, who was busy at work in his study. Ram's eyes were dry, and the ear in his mother's hand looked more elongated than the other. His mother's face was flushed with anger, while Ram's beatific smile seemed to announce to the world how much he enjoyed the game in which he handed his ear over to his mother. Mr Ramashankar Acharya sat down on his chair, intending to pull the imbecile's other ear. Routine pulling had stretched Ram's ears considerably but did not reduce his pranks.

In the courtroom, Mr Ramashankar Acharya used the force of the law to significant effect, but at home, his strictures had little effect on his brat of a son. Some months ago, after Ram had been particularly naughty, Mr Ramashankar Acharya tried to instil the fear of God in him, and said, 'Look here, Ram, you must be a good boy, or else I fear Parmeshwar will be angry with you.'

Ram responded, 'You, too, get angry with me, but I win you over.' And after giving the matter some thought, he asked, 'Bapuji, who is this Parmeshwar?'

Mr Ramashankar Acharya attempted an explanation, 'Bhagwan. Who else? Bigger than all of us.'

'As big as this house?'

'Bigger...now, look here...don't be naughty, or else he'll kill you.'

Mr Ramashankar Acharya tried his utmost to present a terrifying image of Parmeshwar because he thought fear would reform his son. Ram remained quiet as he weighed Parmeshwar's might in his mind. After a while, he asked in all innocence, 'Please show me Parmeshwar.'

Mr Ramashankar Acharya's vast experience and knowledge of the law were of no use. If Ram had raised a legal point, he could cite a case and show his son a reference. If he had asked a question about the Indian Penal Code, Mr Ramashankar Acharya would refer to the weighty tome on his desk, on the cover of which Ram had etched floral patterns with a knife. How on earth could he conjure Parmeshwar, about whom he had little to no knowledge? Just as he knew that Section 379 was about theft, he knew that the one responsible for death and life was called Parmeshwar. And just as Mr Ramashankar Acharya had not seen the being who made the laws that he referred to every day, he did not know Parmeshwar. Mr Ramashankar Acharya had no idea where Parmeshwar lived. He was an MA LLB and did not obtain his legal qualifications to get embroiled in these convoluted matters but to earn a fortune. He could not give Ram a glimpse of Parmeshwar; neither could he give him a logical answer. Ram posed the question in such a random manner that his father's brain felt drained. All he could say was, 'Now, off with you Ram! Please stop pestering me.'

It was true, Mr Ramashankar Acharya had a massive case load. He wanted to forget some of his old losses and crack the hefty new cases ahead of him. He looked at Ram with questioning eyes and turned to his lawfully wedded wife, 'What new pranks has he been up to today? Tell me quickly. Today I shall give him an extra harsh punishment.'

Mrs Ramashankar Acharya let go of Ram's ear and said, 'This fatso is the bane of my existence. He runs around all day with no concern for who is coming or going. He's been getting on my nerves since morning. I've spanked him several times, but does he stop his pranks! He's gobbled two raw tomatoes from the larder. Now, what am I going to use for salad, my head?'

Mr Ramashankar Acharya was nonplussed. He expected a serious allegation but all Ram had done was to swipe two raw tomatoes. His plans to scold Ram and send him to hell ran out of steam, and he felt deflated, a bit like one of his car tyres suddenly emptied of air. It was no crime to eat a tomato. Besides, just yesterday, a friend who had returned from Germany with a post-graduate qualification in medicine, had told Mr Ramashankar Acharya that he must ensure his children eat raw tomatoes with every meal because they were full of vitamins. He was all set to tell Ram off since this was what his wife wanted, but instead, he pondered over the matter and came up with a legal point, which rather pleased him. He turned to Ram and said, 'Come here, Ram, and give truthful answers to whatever I ask you.'

Mrs Ramashankar Acharya had left the room. Ram came and stood before his father, who cross-examined him, 'Why did you eat two raw tomatoes from the larder?'

Ram answered, 'There weren't two…Mataji was lying to you.'

'You tell me how many were there.'

'One and a half,' said Ram, as he indicated the half with his fingers, 'Mataji made chutney in the afternoon with the other half.'

'Okay, let's accept one and a half; but why did you take those tomatoes?'

'To eat,' Ram responded.

'Right. You committed theft,' Mr Ramashankar Acharya presented his legal argument.

'Theft! Bapuji, I am not guilty of theft. I've eaten tomatoes! How is that theft?' Ram squatted on the floor and looked his father straight in the eye.

'It was theft. To take somebody else's property without the person's permission is theft,' Mr Ramashankar Acharya hoped his son would understand the crux of the matter.

Ram responded immediately, 'But the tomatoes were ours…my mataji's.'

Nonplussed by his son's response, Mr Ramashankar Acharya tried to clarify what he meant, 'Your mataji's…that's fine, but they were not yours. Something that belongs to her—how can it be yours?

Look, there in front of us is your toy on that table. Bring it here, and I shall explain the matter to you.'

Ram leapt up and ran to pick up the wooden horse, which he handed to his father. Mr Ramashankar Acharya said, 'Now look here, this horse is yours, isn't it?'

'Yes, sir.'

'If I pick it up without your permission and keep it, that will be theft.' To clarify matters, he added, 'And I a thief.'

'No, Pitaji, you can keep it. I shall not call you a thief because I have an elephant to play with. You haven't seen it. Munshi Dada bought it for me just yesterday. Wait, I'll show it to you.'

With these words, Ram ran into the other room, joyfully clapping his hands while Mr Ramashankar Acharya was left blinking his eyes.

The following day, Mr Ramashankar Acharya had to go on urgent business to Poona, where his elder sister lived. She had not seen little Ram for some time and longed to see how he had grown. Ramashankar thought he could fulfil two objectives and decided to take his son along, but on the condition that Ram would promise to refrain from mischief. Little Ram was able to keep his word until they reached the platform of Bori Bunder Station, but when the Deccan Queen left the platform, wayward thoughts wriggled and reached Ram's little heart.

Mr Ramashankar Acharya was sitting on a spacious berth of a second-class compartment and reading a newspaper he had borrowed from his neighbour. Ram was seated at the other end of the seat, his neck sticking out of the window. As he felt the full force of the wind on his face, he thought what fun it would be if he were to fly off with it. Mr Ramashankar Acharya was keeping an eye on Ram through the far reaches of his spectacles, and when he saw the new cap on Ram's head, he tugged his son's arm, 'Will you sit still and let me have some peace or not? Take this cap off and put it away before the wind blows it away. Imbecile!' He pulled the cap off Ram's head and kept it on his lap. Before long, the cap was back on Ram's head, which was once again sticking out of the window as he gazed at the trees whizzing past. The speeding trees seemed to be playing hide-and-seek.

A gust of wind folded the newspaper backwards, and once again

Mr Ramashankar Acharya caught sight of his son with his head sticking out of the window. Furious, he pulled Ram by his arm and drawing him close, intoned sternly, 'If you move an inch from here, you've had it.'

Once again, he took the cap off Ram's head and put it on his lap. After he dealt with Ram, he picked up the newspaper and began to look for the line where he had stopped reading. Once again, Ram slid towards the window and stuck his head out. Mr Ramashankar Acharya spotted the cap on Ram's head and aimed for it like a furious and ravenous eagle. In one swipe, the cap was under his seat. He acted so fast that Ram did not have a chance to figure out what had happened. He turned around to look at his father, whose hands were empty. Ram looked anxiously out of the window, and far away along the railway track, where he saw a brown paper bag flying in the air. He mistook it for his cap, and the thought broke his heart. He looked at his father with repentant eyes, 'Bapuji, my cap?'

Mr Ramashankar Acharya remained silent.

'Aah, my cap!' Ram cried out.

Mr Ramashankar Acharya remained silent.

A tearful Ram wailed, 'My cap!' He grabbed hold of his father's hand. Mr Ramashankar Acharya pushed his son's hand away and said, 'It must have fallen off your head. Why are you weeping now?'

Two large tears began to swim in Ram's eyes, 'But you pushed me,' he said as he began to cry.

Mr Ramashankar Acharya admonished his son, and Ram began to weep his heart out. His father tried hard to soothe the inconsolable Ram and realized that the only way to stop his son's tears was to produce his cap. 'The cap will return, but on the condition that you will not wear it!'

Ram's tears dried up in his eyes like raindrops on burning sand. He snuggled close to his father, 'Bring it back, please, sir.'

Mr Ramashankar Acharya said, 'It won't just come back. I'll have to recite a mantra.'

All the passengers in the compartment were observing this exchange between father and son.

'Mantra!' said Ram, as he recalled a story in which a little boy chanted a mantra and made people's belongings disappear.

'Chant, Pitaji!' Ram looked at his father very carefully, as though Mr Ramashankar Acharya was about to sprout horns. Mr Ramashankar Acharya tried to recollect the words of a mantra he had committed to memory from *The Complete Indra Jal*, but before he began to chant, he extracted a promise from Ram, 'Well, then will you desist from mischief?'

'Yes, Bapuji,' said Ram.

Mr Ramashankar Acharya recalled the words of the mantra, and silently complimented his memory before he said to his son, 'Well then, shut your eyes.'

Ram shut his eyes. Mr Ramashankar Acharya began to recite the mantra, 'Om nama kashmiri mad madesh autama de bhar yang para, svaha.' In concert with 'svaha', one of his hands went under his seat, and the very next instant, Ram's cap fell on his chubby thighs. When he opened his eyes, Ram saw his cap under his fat flat nose. The tip of Mr Ramashankar Acharya's sharp straight nose quivered under the grip of his spectacles, much like it did after he won a case in court.

'The cap is here!' was all Ram could say before he fell silent.

Mr Ramashankar Acharya returned to the newspaper. He immersed himself in a sensational news item and forgot all about the mantra. The Deccan Queen was flying at the speed of lightning, and the regular rumble of its iron wheels imbued solidity to every line of the astonishing news: 'There was pin-drop silence in the courtroom when suddenly the accused shouted "Bapuji".'

At precisely this point Ram cried out, 'Bapuji...' and Mr Ramashankar Acharya thought the words had leapt off the newspaper. Ram's trembling lips were a clear indication he wished to say something.

Mr Ramashankar Acharya asked in a sharp tone, 'What is it?'

He was relieved when through the corner of his spectacles, he spotted Ram's cap on the seat. Ram slid closer to his father and said, 'Bapuji, please chant that mantra.'

Mr Ramashankar Acharya looked at Ram's cap and asked, 'Why?'

'Your papers—the ones you'd kept here—I just threw them out.'

Ram said something else, but as darkness fell before Mr Ramashankar Acharya's eyes, he seemed to have turned deaf as well. He stood up with the speed of lightning and looked out of the window but could see nothing but pieces of paper flying around like butterflies.

'You've thrown away the papers I had kept here?' He asked, pointing towards the seat with his right hand.

Ram shook his head in agreement as he added, 'Chant that mantra, sir.'

Mr Ramashankar Acharya knew no such mantra that could bring back things that were lost. He was worried beyond belief. His son had thrown away the brief of his new case, with legal documents for goods worth forty thousand rupees. Checkmated by this move, countless thoughts about the papers flashed through Mr Ramashankar Acharya MA LLB's legal brain. His client's loss was his loss, but then, what could he do? The only option was to leave the train at the next station and walk back along the railway track to look for the papers like a headless chicken—and let Fate decide if they would turn up or not. Many more ideas whizzed through his mind before he arrived at a decision. If he did not find the papers, he would refuse point-blank that his client ever handed them to him. Reprehensible from a legal and moral standpoint, but what other option did he have? Notwithstanding this palliative thought, there was a bad taste in Mr Ramashankar Acharya's mouth. He wanted to pick Ram up and throw him out of the window like the papers, but he suppressed this wish and turned to look at Ram, who had a peculiar smile on his face as he said to his father, 'Bapuji, chant the mantra, sir.'

Mr Ramashankar Acharya bristled and said, 'Be quiet, or else just remember I'll wring your neck.'

A meaningful smile played on the face of a passenger who was observing the father and son's conversation. Ram snuggled close to his father, 'Bapuji, shut your eyes, sir. I'll chant the mantra.'

Mr Ramashankar Acharya did not shut his eyes. Yet, Ram began to chant the mantra, 'Om mayang shayang, lad maga, farodama svaha', and with the sound of 'svaha', a wad of papers fell on Mr Ramashankar Acharya's fleshy thighs. Under the golden grip of his spectacles, his straight sharp nose began to quiver, as did the round red nostrils of Ram's fat flat nose.

## Outcry

As he climbed down the stairs from the seventh to the ground floor, he felt he was carrying the weight of the entire building on his broad yet slender shoulders. Not that long ago, he had walked up confident that his landlord, universally addressed as 'Seth', would hear his plea, and grant him a month's reprieve to pay his rent. It hurt his pride to beg for charity but he faced reality knowing he had to hold out his palm, recount his woes, and reveal his wounds. He had abandoned his self-esteem on the footpath before entering the big door of the concrete building because dignity is the one trait that can stand in the way of begging.

He had walked into the large room where Seth collected rent and joined his hands in salutation before standing to one side. Seth sat ensconced in an armchair, and as he looked up, several furrows appeared on his tilak-adorned brow. He opened a fat notebook with a hairy hand, and with his bulbous eyes, reviewed the accounts for the two buildings he owned. His coarse voice filled the room, 'Keshav Lal. Kholi Number 5. Two month's rent. Have you brought it?'

Keshav Lal opened his heart out and revealed all his old and more recent wounds, confident that Seth would understand his predicament but Sethji did not want to hear a word. There was mayhem in Keshav Lal's heart. He had delved deep into the past and dug out old wounds, which had healed, simply to gain Seth's sympathy. As yesterday's injuries became a part of today's pain, Keshav Lal was astonished by the hurt that filled his heart.

Overwhelmed by Seth's response, his mind turned to random thoughts about his dank house—the dim lamp, the tatty patched-up clothes hanging from hooks hammered into a wall or clinging to his filthy body. Invariably, in times of adversity, Keshav Lal turned to Andata and Bhagwan, who resided in some unknown place, supposedly protecting their worshippers. Confronted with Seth's absolute power to change 'this' to 'that' with a stroke of his pen created hitherto unknown chaos in his brain—and faith in Bhagwan or Andata did not cohere.

When the furious Seth hurled two hefty profanities at him, Keshav Lal felt hot melted iron flow through his ears and into his heart. Nothing could calm the anger that raged inside him like a stampede caused by some mischief at a political rally. All he had wanted was to share his old wounds with Seth but Seth's profanities entered Keshav Lal's head, where they collided against each other and caused an unfamiliar and unbearable pain. The scalding tears that welled up in his eyes seemed to emit smoke, and the world around him began to look hazy. Keshav Lal wanted to vomit and expel all the profanities he had ingested back on Seth's wrinkled face but recalled that he had dumped his dignity on the footpath—for what it was worth—the dignity of a man who sold salted peanuts at Apollo Bandar.

Keshav Lal thought of the cloth bag full of peanuts hanging from a hook in the ceiling of his house and getting drenched in the rain. He imagined the peanuts were dancing and wanted to laugh at the spectacle but the sour taste left by Seth's profanities stuck sickeningly in his throat. His inability to spit out the obscenities sharpened the pain, and his tears retreated to a corner of his heart where other sorrows had gathered.

Keshav Lal recalled the shower of garbage that had rained on him when Seth hurled a second profanity at him, fatter than Seth's fat neck full of blubber. In an involuntary gesture, Keshav Lal raised a hand to protect his face but not before the filth emitted by Seth was smeared all over him. By the time he reached the ground floor, Keshav Lal felt he was carrying the weight of the seven storeys of this concrete building on his shoulders, and he had accepted that in such situations, nothing coheres.

Seth had hurled not one, but two profanities at him, and Keshav Lal spat them out on the pavement like paan spittle, but the aftertaste remained, and obscenities continued to buzz like poisonous wasps in his ears. He did not know how to describe the dissonance that Seth's abuse had stirred in his heart and mind. Unable to think coherently, Keshav Lal wondered how to douse the fire in his being and continued to walk. He was about to eject his pain as vomit when a man walked past him, taking long strides. Keshav Lal wanted to stop the man and say to him, 'Bhaiya, I'm a ne'er do well', but when he saw the man's expression, the electric pole by which he was standing seemed more amenable to human sympathy. Keshav Lal swallowed gulp by rancid gulp the bile he was about to throw up.

He observed the orderly rectangular paving stones on the footpath. Never had Keshav Lal found them so unyielding; their rigidity touched his being. Keshav Lal had not ventured too far from Seth's concrete building when he lost his grip on himself. Yet, he continued to walk. He bumped into a girl and felt like a man who drops inadvertently the fruit gathered in the hem of his tunic. Keshav Lal thought he was falling apart because his arms began to flail involuntarily. He tried to collect himself. He slowed down his pace, but now, with his mind moving faster than his legs, he felt disjointed, as though the entire lower half of his body was trailing behind while his mind raced ahead. He stopped in his tracks several times to allow his mind and body to unite.

Keshav Lal walked along a footpath with a long line of traffic to his right, where cars tooted away, and horse carriages, trams, trucks, and lorries all imposed their weight on the road's black chest. There was loud noise all around him but his burning ears could not hear a thing. He bumped into a lame dog. The dog yelped, 'Chaaoon!' Perhaps, its leg was hurt. Keshav Lal stepped aside, and he felt Seth had hurled another profanity at him. He found himself entangled in Seth's words, rather like a rag caught in a gnarled bush. The more Keshav Lal tried to disentangle himself, the more he bruised his soul.

He was not worried about the khari sing getting soaked in the rain. In his thirty years, which made up Parmatma knows how many days, Keshav Lal had never slept on an empty stomach; nor had he roamed the streets naked. His only complaint was to do with the choices he had to make throughout his life: to feed his family or pay the hakim with a goatee for medicines? To spend two annas every evening on local alcohol, or save to pay the hideous bald Seth rent for his one-room kholi?

The logic of houses and rents always baffled Keshav Lal, but he knew that every month for the past five years when he left ten rupees in Seth or his agent's palm he felt they had snatched his money from him. Now, for the first time, he was two months in arrears. Did this give Seth the right to hurl profanities at him? This question troubled Keshav Lal more than the twenty rupees he knew he had to pay tomorrow, if not today. If he had not incurred a debt of twenty rupees, the profanities would not have left Seth's cesspit of a mouth. Seth was a wealthy man who owned two buildings and collected rent from one-hundred-and twenty-five rooms, but his tenants were not his slaves.

Keshav Lal thought, 'I understand Seth wants his rent, and I have paid him on time for the past five years, and as soon as I have the money, I shall pay him the arrears. The previous monsoon rain poured down on our heads; I did not hurl profanities at Seth although I can come up with far worse expletives than him. How many times did I plead with him, "Please, sir, have the broken balustrade fixed?" Yet, he paid no attention, and my darling daughter had a treacherous fall, and now her right arm is useless forever. Forget profanities, I could have cursed Seth, but the thought never crossed my mind. And for not paying two months' rent, I deserve to have such abuse hurled at me? It didn't even cross my mind that every evening at Apollo Bandar, Seth's children scrounge packets of peanuts off me.'

Keshav Lal reflected on the turn of events that had reduced him to such poverty. He knew that the bald Seth thought he could hurl two obscenities at him because he was poverty-stricken. Yet, Keshav Lal was not to blame for his lowly status. He had never dreamt of riches and lived his life quite contentedly, but two months ago, when his wife fell ill unexpectedly during her pregnancy, the expense of her treatment left nothing for the rent. How could Keshav Lal not spend money on her treatment? Was he not the father of the child? It was just a question of two months' rent.

Keshav Lal's loved all his children, including the one about to arrive. He asked himself if he would steal for his children and concluded that he was willing to sacrifice his life to recover what was his by right but would never allow himself to be labelled a thief. When Seth swore at him, Keshav Lal could have stepped forward, wrung his neck, and run away. He could have cleaned out the safe and run with all the green and blue wads of paper money, which had only ever figured in his life as images of Lajwanti or emblems of good fortune.

Keshav Lal recalled that last year, when a customer swore at him simply because four peanuts out of a two-paise batch were bitter. He had planted such a whack on the man's neck that people sitting on a bench at a distance could hear it. Yet, Seth had hurled two profanities at him, and he had remained silent. He was known as Keshav Lal, the seller of khari sing, the man who did not let a fly sit on his nose, and Seth had the nerve to hurl a second profanity at him—and he had remained silent like a lifeless statue.

Keshav Lal wanted to understand what had turned him into an inert figurine. The two profanities had come out like two fat rats, not out of their holes but from Seth's mouth, covered in his saliva. And Keshav Lal had remained silent because he had dumped his dignity on the footpath outside the seven-storeyed building. Why did he detach himself from his self-respect? A thought crossed his mind: perhaps, Seth had directed his profanities at someone else. But Keshav Lal did not need much time for reflection, he knew his heart did not ache so much for no reason. The two profanities were meant for him.

As Keshav Lal felt the two profanities melt and sink into every part of his body and soul, a car shone its headlights on him. The more he tried not to think about the obscenities, the more he could feel them bruising his soul, and this irked him. He swore under his breath at several passers-by, 'Who do they think they are, walking as though it is their grandfather's reign?' If this were Keshav Lal's reign, he would have taught that Seth such a lesson. How casually he had hurled two profanities at Keshav Lal from his cushioned armchair and disposed of him as though he had caught, killed, and flung aside two bedbugs! Honestly, if this were his reign, he would make Seth stand in the middle of a square, collect a large crowd of onlookers, and plant such a whack on Seth's bald pate that the fatso would squeal with pain, and Keshav Lal would turn to the crowd and say, 'Mock him! Mock him to your heart's content!' And Keshav Lal's unstoppable laughter would cause a stitch in his stomach. But why didn't he want to laugh now? When Seth hurled the profanities, why didn't he whack Seth's bald pate? After all, it was not Seth's reign. What was the obstacle?

Keshav Lal stopped in his tracks, and his mind paused for a

few moments. He thought, 'Well now let me settle this problem once and for all. Why don't I go running to Seth, twist his neck in one swift move, and put his severed head on top of the safe with a door that opens like a crocodile's mouth?' Yet, Keshav Lal remained transfixed to the ground like the nearby electric pole. Why didn't he turn towards Seth's house? Didn't he have the courage? He did not have the courage—how sad that his blood ran cold.

The profanities had bludgeoned his heart and soul. During the last Hindu–Muslim riots, when a Hindu thought him a Muslim and beat the living daylights out of him with sticks, he had not felt as much pain as he did now. Another car shone its headlights on Keshav Lal, the seller of khari sing, who liked to brag to his friends that he had never fallen ill in his life, but who had now picked up an ailment caused by two profanities and was walking around like a terminally ill patient.

He wanted to stick his hand inside his heart, pull out the two stones that refused to dissolve, and aim them at the head of any passer-by. Why didn't someone step forward to rid him of this pain? Didn't he deserve compassion? Perhaps, nobody knew of his predicament because his heart was not an open book. Please God, if anyone were to find out about the degrading incident, it would be enough for Keshav Lal of khari sing fame to die of shame. It was no small matter to hear profanities hurled at you and remain silent. He had lost face, and his name was mud. He had lost everything. He understood what it means to be a sweeper, who is considered lowborn and treated worse than a dog because he cleaned filth. Naturally, he would have profanities hurled at him. Keshav Lal wanted the profanities to leave him in peace, and to block out the events of the day.

Yet again, he asked himself, how dare anyone swear at him? Would he not chew up that person alive? But he answered himself, 'Forget it, my friend! It's all very well for you to protest and ask these questions, but you put up with Seth's profanities as though they were sweet music.'

'Ah, well then,' thought Keshav Lal, 'if it were sweet music and delicious nectar, I must be going mad. All these people walking around with such abandon, I think I will smash their heads. In Bhagwan's name, I don't have the strength to bear this. I think any minute like the mad dog that I am, I shall start biting passers-by and they will lock me up in a lunatic asylum, where I will bang my head against a wall and die. I will die. It's true, I will die, and my Radha will become a widow and my children, orphans. All this will happen because I heard two profanities from Seth and remained silent like a spineless weakling. Parmatma, crush my legs under a motor car. Chop off my hands. Why don't I die? The cacophony in my head will end. Forgive me, Lord, is there any respite from this pain? Should I tear my garments apart and dance naked in the street? Or stick my head under this passing tram? Or start crying out, "What should I do?"'

To rid the burden from his heart, Keshav Lal thought he should walk to the centre of the bazaar and stop the traffic and spew whatever comes into his mouth. Or simply remain where he was and shout, 'Help me...help me!' A fire engine drove past with its siren blaring, and it disappeared around the corner. Keshav Lal wanted to call out, 'Stop...extinguish my fire...save me!' He increased his pace and felt asphyxiated. Perhaps, if he walked faster, he would explode. He began to walk faster, and his mind became a ring of fire, and all his old and new thoughts wound themselves around it like a garland in flames—two months' rent, how he had entered the concrete building, Seth's coarse voice and his bald pate, a loaded profanity and then another, and his silence. A volley of gunshots emerged from the ring of fire, and Keshav Lal could feel his chest turn into a sieve riddled with bullet holes.

He increased his pace, and the ring of fire spun at such speed that it became a giant ball of flame rolling along the footpath. Keshav Lal started to run behind it, but suddenly from a swarm of thoughts, a new thought yelled out, 'Why are you running? What are you running away from, you coward?' Keshav Lal slowed down. He felt some power had stalled him. Indeed, he was a coward. Instead of running away, he ought to seek revenge. Revenge—he felt a salty taste on his tongue and a tremor run through his body. And blood—he saw the earth and sky turn red. Keshav Lal felt strong enough to draw blood from a stone. His eyes were bloodshot. He clenched his fists and with firm determined footsteps darted forward like an arrow through the crowd. He whizzed past electric lamp posts, shops, and bazaars. Keshav Lal did not lift his eyes even to look at the sparkling cinema auditorium.

He converted every atom in his body into an explosive that he would detonate at the right time, and winding his way through different bazaars, Keshav Lal arrived at Apollo Bandar. The rows of cars parked near the Gateway of India looked like vultures sitting around a corpse with their wings interlocked. He turned to look at the red neon lights that proclaimed the name of a majestic hotel as its reflection shimmered on the rippling water of the endless dark ocean.

Keshav Lal of khari sing fame stood beneath the hoarding with the neon lights in the dark shadow of the majestic hotel. With his feet firmly planted on the ground, he looked up at the brightly lit rooms all aglow. A sound emanated from his throat, and it came out of his mouth like molten lava in an earth-shattering war cry as he roared, 'Haat tere ki...off with you!' He expected the concrete building of the majestic hotel to collapse and crumble at his feet. Startled, the pigeons about to fall asleep in the eaves began to flap their wings. A passer-by who heard Keshav Lal's war cry put his arm around his terrified wife, and whispered, 'He's mad.'

## Taqi the Calligrapher

When Wali Mohammad, the head calligrapher, first brought Taqi to my office, the latter did not impress me in the least. Several ignorant and headstrong calligraphers from Delhi and Lucknow had singed my heart. There was one who liked to stick a 'pesh', the 'oo' sound, here and there at will—thus, he turned 'maut', death, into 'moot', excrement, and 'saut', second wife, into 'soot', yarn. I tried my utmost to make him grasp the difference, but he was a proud sahib-e-zubaan, a master and gatekeeper of the language. When I pulled him up on the matter of a 'pesh', he stroked his beard to claim his right over the Urdu language and informed me that that he had committed the entire Qur'an to memory, 'I am a sahib-e-zubaan and a hafiz-i-Qur'an. You can't tick me off on the subject of vowels.' I did not quibble further but sent him packing.

A calligrapher from Delhi replaced the gatekeeper of Urdu. He was fine but for his obsession with improvements—improvements that made my blood boil. One day, when I upbraided him, he mumbled something in a typical Delhi accent and handed in his resignation. There was a calligrapher from Rampur with a beautiful hand but he omitted lines, even whole paragraphs. When I asked him to rewrite a page, he said, 'Sahib, such hard work is beyond me.' This Rampuri calligrapher did not stick around for long either.

Mohammad Taqi did not impress me; his circles were not well-formed; his hand was not firm, and I am a stickler for a firm hand. He was young; there was an air of distraction about him; he could not keep still. During a conversation, he kept moving one arm back and forth like a pendulum. His complexion was fair, and the faint hair on his upper lip looked as though he had drawn a moustache with light brown ink. I hired him as a temp but he proved so decent and diligent that he created a permanent place for himself.

I had a cordial and informal relationship with Wali Mohammad, who often chatted with me to clarify his ideas on sexuality. Taqi heard our exchanges in silence but his earlobes turned red when we turned to carnal relations between a man and a woman. Wali Mohammad was married, and he enjoyed teasing Taqi in a typically unexpurgated Punjabi fashion. From time to time, he turned to me and said, 'Manto Sahib, this boy will lose his manhood; tell him to get married. You should see him after he returns from a movie, he tosses and turns all night long.'

Taqi always gave a standard response, 'Manto Sahib, he's lying.'

Whenever Wali Mohammad teased him, little beads of sweat appeared on the tip of Taqi's nose, and he blushed. Wali Mohammad's pointed black moustache quivered, 'And Manto Sahib, it's a lie that he ogles at the Jewish girls in his chawl and sketches their bare legs.'

'I'm…I'm learning how to draw.'

Wali Mohammad took a further dig at him, 'Learn to draw faces. Which drawing master has told you to draw bare legs?'

Often, I noticed that Mohammad Taqi was close to tears, and would ask Wali Mohammad to stop pestering him. And Wali Mohammad would respond, 'Manto Sahib, I've told his father and I'm telling you, get this boy married off, or else he'll lose his manhood.'

Mohammad Taqi's father was an elderly bearded gentleman, who ran a small ghee shop in Bhendi Bazaar in partnership with Wali Mohammad. He offered his prayers five times a day, and his prostrations had left a permanent dark blue mark on his forehead as a stamp of piety, and he fasted during the holy month of Ramzan. He adored Mohammad Taqi, and informed me during our first meeting, 'Taqi was two years old when his mother died. She was a very virtuous lady. May God shower His blessings on her. Believe me, Manto Sahib, after she died, friends and relatives pressed me to remarry, but I thought I might neglect Taqi and never entertained the idea again. By the grace and blessings of Allah, the sinner that I am, I have been vindicated. May Khuda guide him and keep him on the right path in life.'

The steadfast Mohammad Taqi chirruped in high praise of his father's sacrifice, 'Very few fathers would pay such a high price. Abba was young, and he had a comfortable lifestyle. Had Abbaji wished he could have found an excellent wife in no time, but he remained single for my sake. He brought me up with so much love and affection and never let me feel the absence of a mother.'

Wali Mohammad too was full of praise for Taqi's father but he did moan about Maulana's eccentricities. 'Manto Sahib, he is a wonderful man, trustworthy in business, and he loves Taqi. But his love—how do I find words to express myself—his love exceeds the limits of propriety. I mean, he loves Taqi like an obsessed lover loves his beloved.'

In search of clarity, I asked Mohammad Wali, 'What do you mean?'

Wali primed the tips of his moustache and said, 'I can't explain the meaning-sheaning. Please try to understand.'

I smiled and said, 'Bhai, if you attempt to explain, I'll try to understand.'

Wali Mohammad picked up a cloth to wipe the pen with which he was writing the headlines, and said, 'Maulana is an eccentric old man, and I'm not sure why. Taqi says his love was not always so obsessive. I mean, for the past few years, he has devised a complex system of surveillance to keep an eye on his beloved son. Manto Sahib, did I use the word "complex" correctly?'

'Yes, you did, but what is this system of surveillance?'

'The usual...why did you come home late last night? What were you up to in Safed Gali? What was that Jewish woman saying to you? Why do you watch so many films? What did you do with the four annas you earned from your calligraphy last week? What were you and Wali Mohammad talking about sitting by Byculla Bridge? I hope he's not leading you astray and advising you to get married.'

I asked Wali Mohammad, 'What does he mean by leading astray?'

'I don't know, but Maulana thinks that Taqi's friends are leading him astray by advising him to get married. Now, I don't think I am leading him astray, and often say to him, "My darling, get married or else you will lose your manhood." And I swear by God, Manto Sahib, the boy needs a wife badly.'

Four or five years passed, and the light brown hair of Mohammad Taqi's moustache turned dark. Now he shaved every day and parted his hair on the right at an obtuse angle. Whenever there was a discussion on sexual matters in the office, he held his pen between his teeth and paid attention. When we talked of sexual encounters between men and women, his earlobes did not turn red. I thought it highly likely that Mohammad Taqi needed a wife.

One day, when nobody else was in the office and Mohammad Taqi was sitting on a takht, leaning against a wall, and completing the back page, I fixed my gaze on him and asked, 'Taqi, why don't you get married?'

The question came out of the blue and Taqi was startled, 'I beg your pardon?'

'I think you should get married.'

Taqi tucked his pen behind his ear and responded bashfully, 'I've spoken to Abba.'

'What did he say?'

Taqi wanted to give a full account but all he could bring himself to say was, 'Sir, it's like this...it's nothing...Abba says, "What's the hurry?"'

'What do you think?'

'Whatever he thinks...'

His response stalled the conversation and Taqi completed the last page of the newspaper and left.

A few days later, Wali Mohammad said to me in Taqi's presence, 'Manto Sahib, what a big lafraa! Just missed a proper dheen pataas between Mohammad Taqi and his father!'

Wali Mohammad spoke Urdu, but to make his conversation more vibrant, often added a few words of Punjabi and Bombay Urdu. Taqi heard him but remained silent. Wali Mohammad looked down at his quivering pointed moustache before he adjusted the angle of his gaze and fixed it on Taqi. He said to me, 'The lad needs a wife and has tried to present his case to his father, who refuses to acknowledge this need. With Maulana, it's always in through one ear and out from the other...did I make correct use of the metaphor?'

Taqi turned to me, 'Manto Sahib, ask him to shut up.'

Wali Mohammad said, 'Tell him to shut up in his father's presence. If Maulana is withholding his permission for Taqi's marriage, Taqi should be okay with it; after all, his father knows what's good and bad for him.'

Taqi had asked Maulana to arrange his marriage with a girl from a suitable family. The request opened floodgates of scorn that Maulana poured on Taqi's friends, 'Your friends have infected the very foundations of your upbringing,' he said, before he added, 'when I was your age, I didn't even know there was an animal called marriage!'

Taqi responded cautiously, 'But you were married off at fourteen.'

Maulana barked at him, 'What do you know!'

Taqi fell silent. He was a soft-spoken and obedient boy.

After several informal and candid conversations with Taqi, I concluded that he most certainly needed a wife. One day, he turned to me as he blushed crimson and said, 'I am not sure why, but my thoughts are wayward these days. Wali Mohammad is married, and when he goes out with his wife, I'm not sure what happens to my heart. Once you had talked about a lack of self-confidence. I think soon this feeling will overpower me but I'm not sure what I should do. Abba simply doesn't agree. Whenever I broach the subject, he gets furious, as though marriage is a sin. Manto Sahib, what does his experience have to do with me? He got married, and it was God's will that his wife died. He made a huge sacrifice by not getting married for my sake but he wants me to remain a bachelor for the rest of my life.'

I asked, 'Why?'

Taqi responded, 'I don't know, Manto Sahib, but he is not willing to hear a word on the subject of my marriage. I have huge respect for him, but Manto Sahib, yesterday during a conversation I did something very cheeky.'

'What did you do?'

Taqi voice was full of remorse, 'I am tired of begging and pleading. Yesterday, when he told me that he was not willing to hear a word about my marriage, I told him, "Fine then, I shall get myself married."'

'And what did he say to that?' I asked.

'"Get out of the house this very minute!" And so, last night I slept here in the office.'

That evening, I spoke to Wali Mohammed and sent for Maulana. After a few emotional words, he embraced Taqi and turned on his tears before turning to blackmail as his tactic, 'I didn't know that this boy, for whose sake I remained single for so many years, would confront me with such insolence. I reared him like a mother; ate simple food but fed him parathas I kneaded in pure ghee with my own hands.'

I cut him short and said, 'Maulana, when has he denied your favours? Your sacrifices are inscribed on his heart and mind. You have done so much for him. Why can't you arrange his marriage?

All parents wish to see their offspring blossom and grow. You will have a daughter-in-law in your house, and there'll be children. Won't you be delighted when they call you Dadajan? I think Taqi is under the misapprehension that you're against the idea of his marriage.'

Maulana was at a loss for words. He dabbed his eyes with a handkerchief before he found his voice, 'But there should be a suitable match.'

Wali Mohammed said, 'All that is needed is for you to say, "Yes" and everything will fall into place. In other words, all that is needed is your stamp of approval.'

Maulana was on edge and asked, 'But what's the hurry?'

Now, I adopted the tone of an elder and said, 'There should be no delay in the performance of a good deed. Forget others. Find a good match of your choice. Mashallah, everyone in the community knows you, and if not here in Bombay, why not in our own Punjab... it's not as if it is in another world!'

Maulana shook his head but managed a non-committal, 'Yes...yes.'

I put my hand on Taqi's shoulder, 'There you are, Taqi, the decision is finalized. Now, don't pester Maulana like a spoilt child. I'll make sure I help him in this matter.' I turned to Maulana, 'There are a few families here. I shall speak to my wife, and she can look at some girls.'

Taqi said, almost inaudible, 'Thank you so much.'

⁓

Several months passed but the matter of Taqi's marriage did not progress. During this time, Wali Mohammad continued to torment him and his father. As a result, Maulana came to me one afternoon and said, 'In the third alley off Sangli Street, there is a family, you might know them, they are from UP...'

I responded with alacrity, 'I do know them...tell me.'

'What sort of people are they?' asked Maulana.

'Very decent.'

'The elder brother's eldest daughter, I'm told is quite nice.'

'I shall send the proposal.'

Maulana sounded nervous, 'Not in such a hurry...we must see what the girl looks like.'

'I shall find out through my wife.'

My wife approved of the girl, whose looks were acceptable. Besides, she had passed her Entrance and was most agreeable. I conveyed all these qualities to Maulana. He met the girl's father, and they discussed her dowry and haq mahr, a two-part settlement of maintenance that a Muslim woman is entitled to from her husband, notwithstanding divorce. These preliminary steps were agreed upon amicably. Taqi was delighted, but three months passed, and matters stood still. Finally, we learnt that the girl's family refused to have further discussions because they despaired of Taqi's father fussing over petty issues such as, 'How many outfits will she get in her dowry? How many utensils?' And his demands that on no account should she watch films—and she should observe purdah. And the final warning that if the girl did anything against his wishes, the punishment would be divorce.

When I spoke to Taqi about these unfair demands, he stood by his father and said, 'No, Manto Sahib, the girl's family aren't okay. Abba says they want me under her thumb.'

I said, 'If that's the case, then forget it. If not here, then look elsewhere.'

Taqi said, 'We are trying.'

Maulana instigated discussions with another family through a local acquaintance and settled matters. They had to fix a date for the nikah. The girl's family liked Taqi, but after they met Maulana a few times, matters fell through again, and they fixed the girl's marriage elsewhere. This time too, Taqi stood by his father and said to me, 'These people were very greedy, Manto Sahib, they found a wealthy boy and broke their word. Abba maintained from the very outset that these people were not honest brokers but I pushed him to fix matters.'

After some time, they instigated a third match, but this too resulted in nought. When discussions began for the fourth time, Taqi said to me, 'Manto Sahib, these people wish to meet you.'

'With pleasure,' I said.

I met the men of the family. They were decent folk, and they had a few brief exchanges with Maulana. I praised Taqi, and we finalized the marriage, but within a few days, matters went awry.

Someone told the girl's elder brother that he overheard Maulana tell a friend that if the girl did not follow his diktat, he would arrange a second marriage for Taqi. The brother came to see me. I sent for Maulana, who stroked his beard and said, 'What's wrong with what I said? I don't wish to bring into my house a daughter-in-law who will not follow my instructions. I'm getting Taqi married so I can be comfortable.'

I responded to this weird remark, 'Of course you should be comfortable, but I don't understand your philosophy. It seems to me that the relationship between a husband and wife is beyond your comprehension.'

My comment angered Maulana, and he responded, 'I've been a husband, Manto Sahib. Our thinking is not the same on these matters, and I'm sorry to say that working with you, my son's thinking has also changed.' He turned to Taqi and added, 'Do you hear me? I don't wish to bring into my house a girl who will not serve you and me.'

The conversation continued for a while. Finally, I turned to Taqi, 'Look here, I don't think your revered father wants to see you married. And that is why he puts a spanner in the works each time this matter comes up for discussion.'

Maulana remained silent and continued to stroke his beard. Taqi turned to me, 'Why? Why doesn't he want me to get married?'

'Because he is demented.' The words slipped out of my mouth and Maulana began to fume. He frothed at the mouth and spewed bellicose nonsense. I turned to Taqi, 'Take Maulana to a mental hospital and remember my words, that unless and until his mind is cured, he will not get you married under any circumstances. The sacrifice he has made for you is the cause of his mental illness.'

Maulana took Taqi by the hand and left, chanting vituperative comments against me. Wali Mohammad, who was sitting near me, heard everything. After Maulana and Taqi's departure, he fixed the angle of his gaze, scrutinized his moustache and said, 'Poor lad, his manhood is doomed. But, Manto Sahib, what you said was worth its weight in gold. Was the use of the metaphor apt?'

'Yes, very apt, but I'm afraid I did not use appropriate words to describe Maulana's condition.'

'He's a very odd man, Manto Sahib,' said Wali Mohammad. He

yanked a wayward hair from his moustache before he asked me in a sombre tone, 'Manto Sahib, what did you mean when you said that the cause of Maulana's mental illness is the sacrifice he made for Taqi? What you said is certainly worth its weight in gold! But my mind hasn't quite grasped it properly.'

I clarified the matter, 'A fleeting emotion impelled Maulana to announce his intention to remain a bachelor after his wife's death. In time, that emotion died and with it, the pain of his wife's death. He had to contend with two deaths—of his emotion and his wife. I tell you, Wali Mohammad, I pity this man. He constructed an emotional wall between himself and a woman, and it remains standing after twenty-two years. He cannot bear to see his young son with a young woman right under his eyes!'

Taqi did not come to work the following day. He sent an invoice for his calligraphy with Wali Mohammad, and I settled it. He was very distraught about my conduct with his father. I told Wali Mohammad that I was not in the least bit upset. Taqi should know that his father had an illness of the mind and soul, and I was sad that he had left work. Wali Mohammad asked Taqi to return but he did not, neither did he find employment in another office. He joined his father and sat in his shop, selling ghee. But pressed by Wali Mohammad, he took up some calligraphy and worked on it from the shop.

I had to go to Delhi for some work. When I returned to Bombay after three or four months, Wali Mohammad, who was there to greet me at the platform, informed me that Taqi had got well and properly married just a week earlier. I did not believe him but Wali Mohammad swore on the Qur'an, 'I am not lying, Manto Sahib. I have kept the dried dates from the nikah. They are an elixir for anyone who can't get married.'

I sent for Taqi but he did not come to see me. After almost a month and a half, Wali Mohammad arrived at the crack of dawn, and his moustache quivered as he said, 'Taqi has gone away with his wife.'

'Where?'

'I don't know,' he said, switching the angle of his gaze to look at his pointed moustache, 'Can't figure out anything, Manto Sahib. Can't figure out the basis of the disagreement. Maulana is silent.'

Maulana remained silent for ages, as did his son. Wali Mohammad and his mates looked for Taqi all over Bombay unsuccessfully. After several months, I received a letter from Taqi via Wali Mohammad. He had written:

> For some time now, I have wanted to write to you to explain the entire matter but haven't had the courage. Please, do not to share this letter with anyone. I took offence at what you said about my father because I did not understand the real problem, but whatever you had to say about my father turned out to be true. After I got married, I discovered that my father has a sick mind. Perhaps, at some point, he was all right, but after my marriage, he became mentally ill and did his utmost to keep me away from my wife. The awkward situations he engineered to forge a gulf between us could only have been the work of a madman. I put up with his behaviour for a long time. I feel ashamed recounting all the episodes, but one day, my wife was in the bath, and he started to peep at her through the door. What more can I write? I don't know what happened to his mind. May God forgive him. I am leading a happy life here in Delhi....

I was reading this letter when Wali Mohammad arrived, carrying another letter from Taqi, which he handed to me, saying, 'Taqi has written this from Delhi to his father...just a few words.'

'What does he say?' I asked.

'Read for yourself,' said Wali Mohammad.

I read the following words:

> Respected Father, I am well here. You made it possible for me to have a family. I wish that you too should have a family.

Wali Mohammad looked away and said, 'Manto Sahib, the boy has matured.' He smiled and continued, 'And Maulana has tied up matters for himself somewhere.'

'Where?'

Wali Mohammad's moustache quivered, 'She's a ghee seller! All five fingers in ghee and his head in the pot! Correct use of the metaphor, Manto Sahib?' He guffawed, referring to the Urdu aphorism signifying a bountiful existence. I laughed.

## Humiliation

Worn out by the day's grind, she lay down on her bed and fell asleep. The municipality's overseer for cleaning, whom she knew as Seth, had just gone home drunk out of his mind after a heavy bout of drinking brandy, and the local brew mixed with water after they ran out of soda. He wanted to spend the night with her and squeeze her body till her bones creaked but thought it better to head home because he was worried about his lawfully wedded wife, who loved him a lot. The overseer had paid her silver coins drenched in his saliva for her body's labour, and she stuffed them in her tight choli where they jingled in unison with the irregular beats of her heart and the heaving of her bosom. The alcohol had set her body on fire. She felt the heat of her burning breasts melt the coins and the silver flow into her bloodstream and turned to lie face down on the large teak bed. As she stretched her bare arms, they trembled like the frame of a kite from which the paper had peeled away; the crumpled flesh of her right underarm looked like the blue skin of a plucked chicken.

It was a tiny room stuffed with countless objects. Under the bed, a mangy itchy dog lay with its head resting on a pair of decomposed old leather sandals; its coat had worn away in several places, which from a distance made it look like a crumpled old doormat. A niche in the wall, full of clutter that had collected over time, included various items of make-up—lipsticks, rouge, face powder, and other sundries such as combs and hairpins for her chignon.

In a cage hanging from a hook in the ceiling, a parrot was fast asleep with its beak concealed in its feathers. Mosquitoes and flies hovered around the acrid pieces of stale raw guavas and tart tangerine peels that littered the floor of this prison. Near the bed, a wicker chair stood with oil marks left by all the heads that had rested against it. To the left of the chair, on a teapoy, sat a portable His Master's Voice gramophone with a tattered black cloth cover, and its used rusty needles lay strewn all over the floor. On the wall directly above the teapoy hung four frames with photographs of four different men. Slightly removed from these pictures, towards the left near the door, was a lively image of Ganeshji adorned with dry and fresh flowers. Perhaps, she had peeled off a brand label from a bale of cloth and framed it. Next to Ganeshji, on a small greasy wooden shelf, was a cup of oil next to an unlit lamp, its wick upright like a tilak on a forehead. Discarded pieces of old wick and ashes mingled with the other litter on the floor.

Every morning, when she performed bohni to seek a blessing for the first financial transaction of her day, she stretched her arm out to make sure the money touched Ganeshji's image before she touched it to her forehead and tucked it away in her choli. Her voluptuous bosom guarded the money she kept in her choli, but when Madhav was due on leave from Poona, she hid her earnings in a small hole she had dug under one of the legs of her bed. Ram Lal the pimp taught Saugandhi this trick when he heard that Madhav turned up regularly and made demands on Saugandhi. He asked her, 'Since when has this saala become your lover? I have never seen such a bizarre relationship between a lover and his beloved. Saala doesn't spend a paisa from his pocket, enjoys himself with you, and has the cheek to scrounge off you! I've been in the business for seven years and know how men exploit vulnerable girls like you.'

Ram Lal was a broker who worked across Bombay with a hundred and twenty girls, who ranged from ten to a hundred rupees. He told Saugandhi, 'Saali, don't squander your capital like this. He will take the clothes off your back, your mother's lover! Dig a small hole under this bed and bury all your money there. When he turns up, tell him, "I swear on your life, Madhav, I haven't seen a paisa since morning. Please ask the chap downstairs to get me a cup of tea and an Aflatoon biscuit. I am dying of hunger." Understood? Times are difficult, my darling. Saali Congress has banned alcohol and put a damper on the market. It's a challenge to find something to drink. When I see an empty bottle with the dregs from the night before or smell booze, I want to stick my face in your bosom and shout with joy.'

Of all the features of her body, Saugandhi loved her bosom the most. Once, Jumna had advised her, 'Keep these round watermelons secure. If you wear a bra, they will remain firm.'

Saugandhi had laughed, 'Jumna, you think everyone is like you. People rip off your flesh for ten rupees and leave, and you think this happens to everyone. Let someone touch me in an iffy butty place! Ah yes, let me tell you about yesterday. At two o'clock last night, Ram Lal brought a Punjabi and fixed a rate of thirty rupees for the night. When it was time to sleep, I turned off the light. Arrey, he was so scared, I swear by your head, all his bluster went bust. He was terrified. I said, "Why the delay? Hurry, it's almost three o'clock, soon it will be dawn."' '"Roshni," he pleaded, "Roshni, please."

'"Roshni?" I asked, "What's that?"

'He shouted, "Light! light!"

'"What do you mean by light, light?"

'"I mean switch on the light! Switch on the light!" he squealed, choking. I couldn't suppress my laughter, and continued, "My friend, I shan't switch on the light!" I pinched his fleshy thigh. He sat up, terrified, and switched on the light. Promptly, I covered myself with a sheet and said, "Don't you feel ashamed of yourself? You horrible man!" He approached the bed. I leapt up and switched off the light. He was so agitated, I swear upon you, it was a night full of fun, a play between darkness and light. As soon as he heard the rumble of the tram, he put on his pant-shant and fled. Saala! He must have won the thirty rupees gambling because he just gave it for free. Jumna, you are too stuck in your ways. I know many tricks to sort these chaps out.'

Saugandhi had several tricks up her sleeve, which she loved to share with her friends. She advised and cautioned them, 'If a man is a decent sort but is not a great conversationalist, be naughty with him; talk to him endlessly, tease him, tickle him, and play with him. If he has a beard, comb it with your fingers and pluck out a few hairs from it. If he has a potbelly, pat it, and play with it—even if you don't give him a chance to do what he wants, he will leave satisfied. Men who are the silent type are unsafe; given a chance they will break your bones.'

Saugandhi was not as crafty as she wanted people to think; she was an extremely emotional girl, and all her artistry vanished after she gave birth to a baby. The stretch marks on her tummy looked as though her itchy scratchy mangy dog had etched them with his paws because when a bitch passed by and ignored him, the mutt scraped similar marks into the ground with his paws to conceal his humiliation.

Although Saugandhi did not grasp the point of the union between a man and a woman, she melted the moment someone touched her and spoke a few gentle words, and every part of her body wanted to be pummelled and crushed until she fell into an exhausted sleep. She thought, how blissful and pleasurable is the blank stupor and the slumber after every muscle is lax! For a moment, you exist, and then you don't, and between this state of existence and non-existence you hang in the air from somewhere very high, with nothing but air all around you—and then what bliss to lose your breath and choke on this air!

As a little girl, when Saugandhi played hide-and-seek, she climbed into her mother's wooden trunk and closed the lid. She recalled the thrill when the fear of suffocating to death combined with the desire of not being discovered. Saugandhi wanted to spend her entire life locked up in a trunk surrounded by people going around in circles looking for her. For the past six years, her life had been like a game of hide-and-seek. Occasionally, she found someone, and someone found her, and this was how she passed her life. Saugandhi was happy because she had to be. Every night, some man lay beside her on her teak bed, and she had a rich store of tricks to please men. She had made up her mind not to meet any depraved demands and knew how to remain calm.

Often when swept away by emotions, Saugandhi was left feeling unfulfilled. Every night, an old or new acquaintance told her, 'Saugandhi, I love you.' She knew it was a lie, yet Saugandhi melted and felt showered with love. She wanted to melt love—that lovely word—and rub it all over her body so it could seep into her pores. At times, she wanted to become a part of it and enter love like she had entered the trunk and closed its lid. At times, when the desire to love overpowered her, she wanted to draw the man beside her close to her bosom, pat him gently, sing softly, and lull him to sleep.

The capacity to love was so overpowering in Saugandhi that

she could love every man who came to her, and she knew how to sustain the emotion. She was consistent in her love for the four men whose photographs hung on the wall in front of her. In her heart, she knew she was a good woman, and failed to understand why this goodness was not there in these men. One day, looking at herself in the mirror, she cried out involuntarily, 'Saugandhi, *time* has not treated you well.' By 'time', she meant every strand of her life entwined in the days and nights of the past five years.

Although these years did not yield the happiness she desired, she wished her days to continue in this manner. She had no desire for palaces and did not crave money. She had very few customers; ten rupees was her standard charge, from which Ram Lal the pimp deducted two-and-a-half. She earned at least seven-and-a-half rupees every day, and this was enough for her solitary self. When Madhav descended upon her from Poona, as Ram Lal said, she always gave him an offering of ten to fifteen rupees, simply because Saugandhi had developed that kind of feelings for him.

Ram Lal was right: there was something about Madhav that Saugandhi liked. Now, why hide it, we might as well talk about it. When Saugandhi first met Madhav, he asked her, 'Don't you feel ashamed of selling yourself? Do you know what you are selling? Why have I come to you? Chhee chhee—for ten rupees! And as you say, two-and-a-half are for the pimp, which leaves seven-and-a-half, isn't that right, seven-and-a-half? And now for seven-and-a-half rupees, you promise me something that you cannot sell; and I have come to buy something I cannot buy. I want a woman but do you want a man this very minute? Any woman will satisfy me but do you fancy me? What relationship do you and I have? None—just these ten rupees from which the pimp will deduct two-and-a-half and the rest you will fritter away here or there. Your heart desires something, and my heart wants something else. Why don't we settle for something where you need me, and I need you? I am a havaldar in Poona; I'll visit you once a month for three or four days. Leave this racket, and I'll pay your expenses. What is the rent for this shack?'

Madhav said a lot more. Such was the force of his words that for some time, Saugandhi began to think herself as a havaldarni. After he chatted her up, Madhav tidied the clutter and rearranged her room. Without asking her, he ripped off and threw away all the nude images Saugandhi had hung by her bedside, grunting, 'Look here, Saugandhi, I'll not allow you to keep such photographs here. And look at this pitcher of water, look how filthy it is; and these rags, and this dough—what an awful smell. Clear up all these things and throw them out! And look, how you have ruined your hair!'

After they talked about all manner of things for three hours, Saugandhi and Madhav melded into one another. Saugandhi felt she had known the havaldar for years. Nobody had ever noticed the smelly rags, or the dirty pitcher and the nude images. Nobody had allowed her to feel that she had a room she could treat as her own. Men came in, and they left without even noticing the filthiness of her bed. Nobody had ever said to Saugandhi, 'Look here, why is your nose so red today? What if you catch a cold? Wait, I'll get some medicine for you.'

Madhav was terrific; everything about him was pure gold. What home truths he told Saugandhi; she felt she needed Madhav, and the two of them developed a relationship. Madhav came from Poona once a month, and before he left, he always said, 'Look here, Saugandhi, if you start this racket again, you and I will split up. If I get to know that you kept a man in your room, even for one night, I'll drag you by your hair and throw you out. I'll send you this month's expenses by money order the moment I reach Poona. Remind me, what's the rent for this shack?'

Madhav never sent a paisa from Poona and Saugandhi did not stop her racket. Both knew the truth. Saugandhi never asked Madhav, 'Why do you go on in this manner? You've never sent me a paisa.'

Madhav never asked Saugandhi, 'Where do you get your money from, when I don't give you a paisa?'

Both were dissemblers but Saugandhi was happy. Those who cannot afford real gold are happy with plated gold.

Saugandhi was alone and dog-tired, and so she fell asleep. The harsh glare of the naked light bulb she had forgotten to switch off fell on her closed eyes but she was in deep sleep. There was a knock on the door, but the sound did not penetrate Saugandhi's ears. When it became louder, Saugandhi sat up, startled. Who could it be at two o'clock at night? She had mixed her drinks, and the particles of fish stuck in the gaps between her teeth left a stale residue in her mouth. She wiped the foul-smelling substance with the corner of her dhoti before she rubbed her eyes and looked under her bed. She was reassured to see her dog asleep with his face resting on her decomposed leather chappals. The parrot, too, was fast asleep with his head tucked under the feathers on his chest.

There was another loud knock on the door. Saugandhi had a splitting headache but got out of bed and took a cup of water from the clay pitcher, rinsed her mouth, filled another cup, and gulped it down. She opened the door slightly and, 'Is that you, Ram Lal?

An infuriated Ram Lal snarled, 'What happened to you? Snakebite? Were you unconscious? I have been standing outside, knocking on the door since one o'clock!' He had been knocking on the door for the past hour, 'Nobody with you?' he asked.

'No,' said Saugandhi.

Ram Lal raised his voice, 'Why didn't you open the door? Seriously, you are the limit. What sleep you are blessed with! What great business I'll do if I have to test my brain for two hours for every girl! Why are you staring at my face? Hurry, take off your dhoti, put on that floral sari and some powder-showder and come with me. I have a seth waiting for you in a car outside. Come on now; double-speed quick, quick!'

Saugandhi sank into the armchair; Ram Lal looked at himself in the mirror and picked up a comb. Saugandhi stretched an arm out towards the teapoy to pick up a bottle of make-up, and opened it, 'Ram Lal,' she implored, 'I don't feel very well today.'

Ram Lal put the comb back and turned around, 'Then you should have said so in the first instance,' he barked.

As she applied make-up on her forehead and around her ears, Saugandhi cleared Ram Lal's misunderstanding, 'It's not what you think, Ram Lal. It is just that I'm feeling a bit low. I've had too much to drink.'

Suddenly, Ram Lal felt thirsty, 'If there's a little left, let me fix the taste in my mouth!'

Saugandhi put the make-up back on the teapoy and said, 'If I had any left, why would I have this wretched headache? Listen, Ram Lal, the chap sitting out in the car, why don't you bring him here?'

A riled Ram Lal retorted, 'He can't come inside! He's a real *genterman* sort of chap! He was nervous about parking his car in your alley. Put on your clothes-shlothes and come to the corner of the alley and all will be well.'

It was a seven-and-a-half-rupee deal. Saugandhi would never have accepted it with such an acute headache, but she desperately needed the cash. The woman from Madras, in the kholi next door, lost her husband in a car crash and had to go to back home with her daughter but did not have the train fare. Saugandhi had reassured her, 'Don't worry, behen, my man is coming from Poona tomorrow. I'll get some money from him and make sure you get home.'

Madhav was coming from Poona but Saugandhi knew she had to find the money, and she rushed to change her clothes. Within five minutes, she had taken off her dhoti, put on the floral sari, applied powder, rouge, lipstick, and was ready. She drank a cup of cold water from the clay pitcher and set off with Ram Lal.

It was the dead of night, and the narrow alley slightly wider than most in a small-town bazaar was silent. There was a blackout because of the war, and the gas lamps were covered with paper and dimmed. In this faint light, a black car parked at the end of the alley cast a dark shadow. Saugandhi thought her headache had infected the atmosphere; laden with a stench of brandy and local rum, the air felt bitter. Ram Lal stepped forward and said something to the man inside the car.

Saugandhi approached the car, Ram Lal stepped to one side and said, 'Here you are, sir, she's here. She is a great lass. She hasn't been in the trade for long.' He turned to Saugandhi and said, 'Saugandhi, come here. Sethji is calling you.'

Saugandhi stepped forward and stood by the car window, twisting one corner of her sari pallu around her finger. The seth struck his matchstick and lit his biri close to Saugandhi's face. The light made her squeeze her sleepy eyes. As the brightness of the matchstick faded, she heard the seth press a button and say, 'Oonh'; the car's engine began to rattle, and it drove off into the distance.

Saugandhi had not collected her thoughts before the car drove off. The sudden light from the matchstick had filled her eyes, and she was unable to see the seth's face. After all, what had happened?

What was the meaning of the 'Oonh' ringing in her ears?

'What? What?' She heard Ram Lal the pimp's baffled voice before he continued, '...he did not like you. Well then, my dear, I am off. Wasted two hours for nothing.'

Saugandhi had an irrepressible desire to wave her legs, her hands, and her arms. 'Where was that car? Where was the seth? So, "Oonh" meant he did not like me! His...' A profanity erupted in her stomach but stopped as it reached the tip of her tongue. She did not understand at whom or at what to direct her anger. The car had gone, its red taillights faded before her in the darkness of the bazaar. The red lights and the 'Oonh' descended into Saugandhi's heart. She wanted to say, 'Arrey, Seth, stop your car just for a minute.' But that seth, damn him, had disappeared into the night.

Saugandhi stood in the desolate bazaar, the floral sari she wore on special occasions rustled gently in the breeze that usually rose at this time of night. How Saugandhi despised the sari and its silky sound; she wanted to rip it to shreds because its rustle continued to say, 'Oonh! Oonh!' When she recalled how she had applied make-up, powdered her cheeks, and put on her lipstick to look attractive, she felt humiliated and broke into a sweat.

What thoughts did Saugandhi summon to purge herself of her humiliation? 'I didn't paint myself to please that fatso! It is my routine! Not just mine, it is everyone's routine. But what was she doing in the middle of the night with Ram Lal the pimp, in this bazaar? From where did the car arrive in her alley? Who was the seth who lit the matchstick? Such questions buzzed in Saugandhi's head, and everywhere she looked, she saw the red lights of the car swirling around. All she could hear was the rattle of the car's engine in the breeze. The make-up on her forehead began to melt and mix with her sweat; she felt it enter her pores. Did her forehead belong to someone else?

Saugandhi wanted to concentrate on her headache and stifle her emotions but the rush of sentiments had made her forget her pain. She wanted every part of her body to ache. She wanted her head, her legs, her stomach, and her arms to hurt so much that she could forget the world and only think of her pain. These thoughts caused another change within her. Was it a pain that she felt? Her heart contracted, and then it expanded. What was it? To hell with it! It was that same 'Oonh' expanding and contracting in her heart.

Saugandhi was about to trace her steps home when she stopped to think. 'Ram Lal Dalal thought the seth did not like my face but he didn't mention my face. He said, "Seth didn't like you!" He did not merely dislike my face, but even if he didn't, so what! Often, I don't like men's faces. That chap who came on the night of Amavasya, what a repulsive face he had! Wasn't I repelled when he was about to sleep with me? Wasn't I about to throw up? Still, Saugandhi, you did not shun him. Did the seth sitting in his car see his face before he spat an "Oonh!" on your face? What exactly did he mean by his "Oonh"? "Arrey, Ram Lal, where did you find this lizard? You were praising this girl to the skies, this woman for ten rupees—a mule would do better!"'

Saugandhi could feel furious tremors run through her body from her big toe to her head. Her emotions veered between anger at herself and at Ram Lal, who had the nerve to disturb her sleep at two o'clock in the middle of the night. She absolved herself and the pimp and indicted the seth. The moment she thought of him, her entire body and her eyes and ears itched to run into him somewhere. She wanted everything that happened a few minutes ago to repeat itself just once more, so she could move slowly towards the car and wait for an arm to pop out of the window and light a matchstick to see her face. At the sound of 'Oonh', she would pounce on him and scratch his face with her claws like a wild cat, digging her sharp long fashionable fingernails into his face. She would drag him out of the car by his hair and pummel him with punches until she was so exhausted that she would weep.

Saugandhi thought of weeping simply because three or four rather large, furious, and defeated tears had welled up in her eyes. Immediately, she began to question her eyes, 'Why are you crying? What's happened to you that you've started dripping?' Her questions continued to swim in her tears, and Saugandhi stood staring through them into the void into which the seth's car had driven off. 'Flutter, flutter, flutter!' What was this sound? Startled, Saugandhi looked around but did not see anything. Was it the car's engine? Arrey, it was her heart that was aflutter. It always kept a steady beat but now it reminded her of a worn-out gramophone needle stuck in the groove of an old record, repeating, 'I spent the night counting stars...stars, stars, stars...stars...'

Saugandhi looked at the sky bejewelled with stars, and said, 'How lovely!' She wanted to divert her attention but when she uttered the word 'lovely', a thought entered her heart, 'The stars are lovely, but how hideous are you. Have you forgotten how he scorned your face?' Saugandhi was not ugly. One by one, all the images she had confronted in her mirror during the past five years lined up before her mind's eye. Undoubtedly, she no longer had the bloom or colour she had five years ago, when free of all cares and woes she lived with her parents. She was not ugly; she was like any average woman men notice. In her opinion, she possessed all the qualities any man thinks necessary in a woman with whom he wishes to spend a couple of nights. She was young, and she had a shapely figure. Occasionally, when she caught sight of her thighs when bathing, she appreciated their rounded firmness.

She was good-natured and was disturbed when she felt she had not satisfied a man. Saugandhi was amiable and kind-hearted. When she lived in Gol Petha, a young boy had come to her during Christmas. The following morning, when he went to the other room to take his coat off the hook, he was most distraught. Saugandhi's servant had swiped the poor lad's wallet. He had come from Hyderabad to Bombay to spend his holidays, and now had no money for his return fare. Saugandhi had taken pity on him and returned his ten rupees.

'What is so bad about me?' Saugandhi asked the dimmed gas lamp, the rectangular paving stones, and the rubble and gravel of the broken road. She looked at all these things before she looked up at the sky bending down towards her. Saugandhi did not find an answer, although it was inside her. She knew she was not bad but a good person, but she wanted someone else to praise her, someone just this moment to put a hand on her shoulder and say, 'Saugandhi, who says you're ugly? Whoever calls you ugly is ugly.' No, not even so much, all she needed was for someone to say, 'Saugandhi, you're very nice!'

Saugandhi was reflecting on why she wanted someone to praise her. Never had she felt the need for praise with such intensity. Why was she looking expectantly at lifeless things today, as though she wished to impress them with her goodness? Why was every particle of her being wanting to turn into a mother? Why did she wish to envelop everything on earth into her lap? Why did she want to wrap herself around the lamp post and rest her flushed cheeks against it to absorb the coldness of its steel?

For a moment, Saugandhi felt that in the quiet night, the dimmed gas lamp, the steel lamp post, and the rectangular flagstones of the footpath looked at her with compassion. She felt the sky and the twinkling stars had formed a thick grey chadar with countless holes to envelop and protect her because they understood her pain. Saugandhi felt that she, too, understood the twinkling of the stars. What was the chaos inside her? Why did she feel like the weather just before it rains? She wanted to know how to will every pore in her body to open so the lava inside her could flow out.

Saugandhi was almost at the corner of her alley near a postbox when a sharp gust of wind struck her, and her steps faltered. Involuntarily, her gaze turned to the direction where the car had driven off but she could not see anything. How she longed for that car to return but then she thought, 'Why the hell should I care if it doesn't return? Why should I lose sleep over it? Why don't I go home and lie down and sleep? What is to be gained by these questions except an unnecessary headache? Come on, Saugandhi, go home, drink a cup of cold water, rub some balm on your temples, and go to sleep. You will get *first-class* sleep, and all will be well. To hell with the seth and his car!' These thoughts lightened Saugandhi's burden, and she felt as though she had just stepped out after a bath in a fresh pond. Her body felt light just as it did after puja; but again, Saugandhi's steps felt heavy. She felt weighed down by everything she had experienced. A man had humiliated her. He had summoned her to the bazaar in the middle of the night and rejected her with an 'Oonh'. She could feel the pressure of hard thumbs around her ribcage, as though someone was inspecting her like she were a goat or a lamb to see if there was enough meat and not just a bundle of down. 'That seth…I hope Parmatma…!'

Saugandhi wanted to curse the seth but asked herself what would come of her wishing him ill. What fun if he were here and she could write curses all over his body, or she could swear at him to his face and call him a name that would make him restless for the rest of his life. She would rip her clothes apart and stand naked before him and say, 'Isn't this what you came to get? Here, take it. You don't have to pay for it. But whatever I am and what is inside me, forget you, even your father cannot buy for all the money in the world!'

New ideas on how to settle scores with the seth came into Saugandhi's mind. If only she could encounter him once again, but when she realized the impossibility of her seeing him again, Saugandhi hurled a small expletive at him, just a tiny oath that would sit on his nose like a fly glued to it forever! With these unsettling thoughts, Saugandhi climbed up to her kholi on the second floor, and taking the key out of her choli, she tried to unlock the door, but it was unlocked. Saugandhi pushed the door, which squeaked as it yawned open. Saugandhi walked in, and Madhav's laugh appeared beneath his moustache. He shut the door, and turned to Saugandhi, 'Finally, you took my advice and went downstairs—a morning walk is good for your health. If you do this every day, all your weariness will disappear, as will the pain in your back that you complain of every other day. Did you go to Victoria Gardens? No?'

Saugandhi gave no response, and Madhav did not express the need for one. When Madhav said something, it was not because he wanted to have a conversation with Saugandhi; he talked simply for the sake of talking. Madhav sat down on the wicker chair, the back of which had a fresh large nasty stain left by his greasy head. He crossed his legs and began to twirl his moustache. Saugandhi sat on her bed and said, 'Actually, I was waiting for you today.'

Taken aback, Madhav asked, 'Waiting? How did you know I was coming today?'

Saugandhi's pursed lips turned into a saccharine smile, 'I saw you in my dream last night but when I woke up, there was no one around; I just felt like going out for a stroll. And...'

A happy Madhav chirped, 'And I arrived! I tell you, great people do great things. Someone was right when he said, "Hearts speak to hearts!" When did you have this dream?'

'About four o'clock,' responded Saugandhi.

Madhav got up from the chair, and slunk close to Saugandhi, 'And

I saw you in a dream exactly at four o'clock! You were wearing a floral sari. Arrey, wearing exactly this sari you were standing next to me. What were you holding in your hands? Yes, you were holding a bag full of money, and you put the bag on my lap, and said, "Madhav, don't worry. Here, take this bag. Arrey, isn't my money your money?" Saugandhi, I swear upon your life, I woke up immediately, bought a ticket, and headed here. I am so worried. A case came up out of the blue! Now, if I had twenty rupees, I'd grease the inspector's palm and sort it out. You aren't tired, are you? Why don't you lie down? Should I massage your feet? You're not used to walking. You must be worn out. Here, turn your feet towards me and lie down.'

Saugandhi lay down on her side. She formed a pillow with both her arms and rested her head on her hands and looked at Madhav. She asked him in an atypical tone, 'Madhav, who is this character who has filed a case against you? If there's a danger of jail-shail, tell me. Forget twenty, thirty.... At such times, even if you hand the police fifty to a hundred, the gain is ours. You know the saying, "Save your life and gain a hundred million!" You can stop now. I'm not so tired, forget the massage and tell me all. My heart's racing at the thought of the case. When are you heading back?'

Madhav could smell the alcohol on Saugandhi's breath and thought this an excellent opportunity to try his luck, 'I have to go back by the afternoon train. I must give between fifty to a hundred to the sub-inspector by the evening. There is no need to give too much. I think fifty will do.'

'Fifty?'

Saugandhi remained calm. She stood up and proceeded slowly towards the four photographs hanging on the wall. The third from the left was Madhav's. He was sitting on a chair, a curtain with a large floral print served as the backdrop; his hands were on his thighs, and in one, he was holding a flower. Two fat books rested on a teapoy nearby. Everything in the photograph was crying out, 'I am being photographed! I am being photographed!' as Madhav looked uncomfortably at the camera with his eyes wide open.

Saugandhi burst into a ripple of laughter so sharp that Madhav felt needles had pierced his body. He walked up to Saugandhi, and asked, 'Whose photograph made you laugh so much?'

Saugandhi pointed to the first photograph on the left, which was of the municipality's overseer for cleaning. 'His…the *munshipulty's* overseer's…look at his fat face. He used to say, "A rani fell in love with me!" Oonh! That face and such airs!' Saugandhi yanked the frame from the wall with such force that some plaster came away with it. An amazed Madhav looked on as Saugandhi flung the frame out of the window. There was a sound of shattering glass as it fell to the ground from the second floor. Saugandhi said, 'When sweeper rani comes to clear the rubbish, she will take my raja with her!'

Once again, Saugandhi burst into a laugh that sounded like someone sharpening a knife on glass. Madhav struggled to produce an uneasy smile. Saugandhi pulled out the second frame and flung it out of the window, saying, 'What is this saala doing here? No man with such a hideous face can stay here. Why, Madhav?'

Yet again, Madhav managed a gawky smile and a fake laugh, 'Hee, hee, hee!'

With one hand Saugandhi pulled off the image of the turbaned man and with the other, she removed the frame that held Madhav's photo. Madhav shrank into himself as though he feared her hand was heading for him. Saugandhi laughed out loud, and in a split second, the frame was in her hand along with the nail. 'Oonh!' she said, as she flung both photographs out of the window. As the frames fell to the ground, the sound of shattering glass reached their ears. Madhav felt something inside him had cracked; he struggled to speak but managed to say, 'Well done! I didn't like this photo either.'

Saugandhi walked up to Madhav purposefully, 'You didn't like this photo! I ask you, is there anything in you for somebody to like? Your pakora-like nose, your hairy forehead, your swollen nostrils, your twisted ears, the stench of your mouth, the grime on your body—and you did not like your photo! Oonh! Why would you like it? It hides your defects.'

Madhav tried to move away from her, and finally, with his back to the wall, he found enough strength to say, 'Look, Saugandhi, I think you've started your business again. Now, I'm telling you for the last time…'

Saugandhi mimicked Madhav, '"If you start your business again, things will end between us. If you keep somebody at your place again, I will drag you by your hair and throw you out! Yes, what is the rent for this kholi?"'

Madhav felt his head go into a spin. Saugandhi continued, 'Well, let me tell you, the rent for this kholi is fifteen rupees, and my rent is ten rupees. And as you know, the pimp takes two-and-a-half rupees, and that leaves seven-and-a-half rupees. Doesn't that leave seven-and-a-half rupees? And for seven-and-a-half rupees, I promised to give you something I did not have to give, and you came to take something you could not take. What bond do you and I have? None. It was just the ten rupees that connected the two of us. You needed me, and I needed you. First, it was just ten rupees that connected us, today it is fifty. You know it and so do I. What's this mess you've made of your hair?' Saugandhi flicked aside Madhav's cap.

Madhav found this intolerable and shouted angrily, 'Saugandhi!'

Saugandhi pulled the handkerchief out from Madhav's breast pocket and threw it on the floor, 'This rag, uff...what an awful stench. Pick it up and throw it out!'

Madhav shouted, 'Saugandhi!'

Saugandhi responded in a biting tone, 'Saugandhi's ass, why have you come here? Does your mother live here that she will give you fifty rupees? Or are you some great handsome stud with whom I have fallen in love? You vile dog! You try to boss me around! Am I your mistress? You beggar, who the hell do you think you are! Who are you? A thief or a robber! Why have you come to my house at this hour? Should I call the police? I don't know if there is a case in Poona or not but I'll file a case against you here!'

Madhav shrivelled up. All he could bring himself to say in a very subdued tone was, 'Saugandhi, what's happened to you?'

'Your mother's head! Who are you to ask me such questions? Get lost—or else!'

Saugandhi's itchy scratchy mangy dog was asleep with his head resting on decomposed leather chappals. When he heard her raise her voice, he woke up agitated, looked at Madhav, and began to bark. When she heard the dog bark, Saugandhi laughed uproariously. Madhav was terrified, and as he leaned forward to pick up his cap, Saugandhi roared, 'Don't you dare! Leave it there, and just get lost! I'll send it to you by *money order*.' She began to laugh and sank into the wicker chair.

Her itchy scratchy mangy dog continued to bark and barked Madhav out of the room. After seeing Madhav off down the stairs, the dog returned, shook its mangy tail, sat down at Saugandhi's feet, and fluttered its ears.

Saugandhi saw a terrifying void all around her, a void she had never experienced before. She felt everything around her was empty like a once packed train standing in a metal shed after offloading all its passengers. The sudden emptiness at the core of Saugandhi's being was unbearably painful; she tried hard to fill her mind with countless thoughts, but it was like a sieve—here she filled it and there it was, empty. Saugandhi sat on the wicker chair for what seemed like an age. She racked her brain but could not come up with a remedy to console her aching heart. She lifted her mangy dog in her arms and lay down on her teak bed and fell asleep with it by her side.

## Mozelle

Trilochan was looking at the night sky for the first time in four years, and that, too, in a state of panic. He had come up to the roof terrace of Advani Chambers at around three o'clock because he needed time to clarify his thoughts in the open air. Under the cloudless sky in the darkness of the night, the city lights shimmered like countless stars and the tall buildings looked like giant trees with glow-worms shining on them. Trilochan relished the sea breeze and thought it a pity that he had remained cooped up in his flat for so many years. Invariably, he woke up in the mornings feeling dull after spending the night under the stale mechanical air of an electric fan.

Trilochan was on edge, but after some time on the terrace, his spirit felt calm and his thoughts gained clarity. Kirpal Kaur and her parents lived in a stronghold of Muslims zealots. Trilochan wanted to bring them over to his place because he had heard several accounts of killing and arson in their mohalla; the authorities had imposed a curfew, and nobody knew for how many hours—possibly forty-eight. Trilochan was trying to figure out what he could do. News from Punjab continued to pour in with details of atrocities perpetrated by Sikhs on Muslims. In a Bombay neighbourhood packed with bloodthirsty Muslim gangs, any Muslim could drag Kirpal Kaur to the well of death.

Kirpal lived with her blind mother and crippled father. She had a brother, Niranjan, who lived in Deolali completing work on a contract he had signed quite recently. Trilochan, who read the papers every day and kept abreast of the latest news, was furious because he had briefed Niranjan about the speed and intensity of the riots, 'Niranjan, forget about your contract for the time being. These are precarious times. If your family must remain in Bombay, move them to my place. I know I have limited space, but in troubled times people manage somehow or the other.'

Niranjan did not agree. He heard Trilochan's long lecture and smiled under his thick moustache, 'Yaar, you're worried for no rhyme or reason. I've seen several such riots here. This is not Amritsar or Lahore—this is Bombay! Bombay! You've only been here for four years. I've lived here for twelve—more than a decade!'

Perhaps, Niranjan thought Bombay was the impenetrable fortress of fairy tales or the kind of city that no misfortune can touch, where a riot can be waved aside by a magic wand. As he stood in the cool breeze, it became clear to Trilochan that Bombay was not safe at all, and he prepared himself to read news of the murders of Kirpal Kaur and her parents in the morning papers. He was not as concerned about Kirpal Kaur's paralysed father and her blind mother as he was about her—it would be fine by him if they died and she escaped. If someone killed her brother in Deolali, for Trilochan, that too would be fine. Niranjan was not a small obstacle but a massive boulder in Trilochan's path, and this was why in his conversations with Kirpal Kaur, he referred to her brother as 'Boulder Singh'.

Trilochan was enjoying the cool languid breeze, even as several fears haunted his mind. Kirpal Kaur had entered his life quite recently. Although the sister of the hefty Boulder Singh, she was petite with a slightly bashful air and a hint of a rather attractive swing in her walk. Kirpal had spent many winters and summers of her childhood in a village but did not have the full-bodied masculine strength often found in Sikh village girls who toil hard all day long. She had a creamy fair complexion with chiselled features so refined that they looked unfinished. Her body shone like mercerized cloth, but he thought her tiny breasts could do with a few extra dollops of cream in her diet.

Trilochan and Kirpal Kaur were from the same village, but even though he returned to his village countless times, he had never even heard the name of a girl called Kirpal Kaur. Perhaps it was because during his short stays, he spent most of his time planning the quickest way back to the city. After finishing primary school, Trilochan left for high school in the city, followed by college, and became a city lad. Ten years stood between the terrace of Advani Chambers and Trilochan's college campus. The intervening decade of his life was packed with extraordinary episodes in Burma, Singapore, Hong Kong, and finally, Bombay, for the past four years.

It was the first time in four years that Trilochan was experiencing what it was like to stand under a cloudless Bombay sky, feeling the sea breeze in the darkness of the night with the shimmering city lights. As he thought of Kirpal Kaur, his mind drifted to Mozelle, the Jewish girl who lived in Advani Chambers. There was a time when Trilochan was stuck knee-deep in love with her. In the thirty-five years of his life, he had never experienced such love. He had quite literally bumped into Mozelle the day he moved into a flat on the second floor of Advani Chambers, courtesy a Christian friend.

Mozelle's flat was opposite Trilochan's, with a very narrow corridor in between. One day, he was entering his flat when she stepped out of hers, and he stopped at the sound of her wooden clogs. Mozelle gazed at an astonished Trilochan through a veil of her unruly hair and laughed. She looked terrifyingly loopy. Her cropped brown hair was dishevelled, very dishevelled. Although her lips were not so thick, her dried dark burgundy lipstick looked as though congealed blood had cracked in several places. She was wearing a long baggy kaftan, and through its open collar, Trilochan could see almost three-fourths of her large breasts. Mozelle's arms looked as though tiny clippings of hair had fallen on them during a trim at the hairdresser's.

Hurriedly, Trilochan fished his keys out of his pocket and was unlocking his door when one of Mozelle's clogs slipped on the greasy cement floor, and she fell on him. Her long kaftan climbed up, and Trilochan found himself caught between her two rather strong bare legs. He tried to stand up, but to his bewilderment, Trilochan found himself trapped by Mozelle in her entirety—he felt a bit like soap spread across her entire body. A breathless Trilochan apologized using the most appropriate words he could find. Mozelle adjusted her kaftan and smiled, 'These clogs are kundum!' She tucked her big and adjoining toes into the errant clog and stomped out of the corridor. Trilochan thought it would be a challenge to befriend her, but in next to no time, Mozelle became quite unrestrained in his company. Still, if he tried to proceed further than her arms and lips, she ticked him off in a manner that made his passion retreat into his beard and moustache.

Trilochan had never fallen in love. In Lahore, Burma, and

Singapore, he had bought girls for a fixed time. It had never crossed his mind that the minute he arrived in Bombay, he would fall knee-deep in love with a headstrong Jewish girl, who treated him with singular insouciance. When he invited Mozelle out, she dolled up and promptly agreed to go to the cinema. No sooner did they take their seats than she began to look around, and if she spotted an acquaintance, she had no qualms in waving to the other chap and going off to sit next to him, without saying a word to Trilochan. On occasions when Trilochan took her out to dine out in a fine restaurant and ordered rare delicacies for her, if Mozelle happened to see an old friend, she left a half-finished morsel on her plate and took off to sit with the other man, leaving an incensed Trilochan to himself.

At times, Mozelle disappeared from Bombay with her old friends while Trilochan fumed and simmered for days. Often, she refused to see him even when she was in Bombay, deploying a string of excuses, including headaches, or an upset tummy. Trilochan knew that Mozelle's stomach was made of steel. When they met after one of her disappearing acts, she would say, 'You are a Sikh. These delicate matters are beyond you.'

A furious Trilochan would ask, 'What delicate matters? About your old lovers?'

In response, Mozelle rested her hands on her full rounded buttocks, spreading her strong legs apart, 'Why do you taunt me about them? Yes, they are my lovers, and I like them. If you feel jealous, then feel jealous!'

Trilochan asked with great sympathy, 'Then how will you and I get along?'

Mozelle laughed out loud, 'You are a Sikh! *Idiot*, who asked you to get along with me? If it's a question of getting along, find a Sikhni in your land and marry her. This is how things will be with me.'

Trilochan melted.

Mozelle became Trilochan's weakness, and he desired her company at any cost. Often, on her account, he put up with indignities and humiliation in the presence of nondescript Christian boys. Then again, a prisoner of his heart, he decided to put up with her insults. The usual response to humiliation is revenge, but not in Trilochan's case. He shut the metaphorical eyes and ears of his heart and mind. He liked Mozelle. Trilochan did not merely like Mozelle, as he often said to his friends, he was stuck knee-deep in love with her. And now there was no other option but to give in and allow whatever remained of his being to sink in the quicksand of his love for Mozelle and end the story.

Trilochan continued to suffer for two years but he remained steadfast. One day, when Mozelle was on a high, he enveloped her in his arms and asked, 'Mozelle, don't you love me?'

Mozelle pulled away from his embrace and sat herself down on a chair. She examined the hem of her skirt and lifted her large Jewish eyes, batted her thick eyelashes, and said, 'I cannot love a Sikh.'

Trilochan felt someone had put red hot embers in his long hair under his turban. His entire body was aflame, 'Mozelle, you always mock me. You are not only mocking me but also my love.'

Mozelle stood up, tossed her luxuriant cropped hair, and said, 'Get a shave and leave your hair open, I bet many young men will wink at you. You are beautiful.'

Trilochan felt his tresses go up in proverbial flames. He stepped forward, pulled Mozelle close, and pressed his moustachioed lips on her burgundy lips.

'Phoonh! Phoonh!' cried Mozelle, wriggling out of his hold. She took a small mirror out of her vanity case to examine the scratches on her thick lipstick and said, 'I swear by God, you don't put your beard and moustache to proper use. Your hair is so fine I could brush my navy-blue skirt with it. All we need is a bit of petrol.'

Trilochan's anger reached such heights that it ran cold, and he sank back quietly into the sofa. Mozelle joined him and began to unwind his beard. She pulled out the pins one by one and held them between her teeth.

Trilochan was gorgeous. Before he sprouted a beard and moustache and roamed around his village with his long hair hanging loose, people frequently mistook him for a beautiful adolescent girl. He knew better than most that the bushy mass of his beard concealed his perfect features, but he was a sensitive and dutiful son with profound respect for his religion. Besides, he did not wish to disassociate himself from the practices that were outward symbols and professions of his faith. He asked Mozelle, 'What are you doing?'

She answered with the pins clenched between her teeth, 'Your hair is very soft. I was wrong to think it can clean my navy-blue skirt. Triloch, give it to me. I'll have it plaited and made into a first-class handbag for myself.'

Trilochan turned towards Mozelle and said in a very grave tone, 'To this day, I have never poked fun at your religion. Why do you do this? It's not good to play with someone's religious feelings. I would never put up with this, but I do, because I love you immeasurably. Don't you know this?'

Mozelle began to play with Trilochan's beard, 'I know.'

'Then?'

Trilochan folded his beard deftly and removed the pins from Mozelle's teeth. 'You know my love is not some nonsensical fancy. I want to marry you.'

'I know.'

Mozelle tossed her hair ever so slightly and stood up. She began to study the paintings hanging on the wall, and said, 'I have almost decided to marry you.'

Trilochan jumped up, 'Truly?'

Mozelle's thick burgundy lips parted in a wide smile revealing her perfect white teeth, 'Yes!'

With his beard half wound up, Trilochan squeezed Mozelle to his chest, 'When? When?'

Mozelle moved away, 'When you have your hair chopped off.'

Trilochan was in 'a give it all one's got' mood, and without thinking, he said, 'I'll have it chopped off tomorrow.'

Mozelle broke into a tap dance number, 'You're talking nonsense, Triloch. You don't have the guts.'

Mozelle's words wiped off any lingering thoughts about religion from Trilochan's heart and mind, and he said, 'You wait and see.'

'I shall,' said Mozelle. She stepped forward hurriedly, kissed Trilochan's moustache, and walked off muttering, 'Phoonh! Phoonh!'

It is pointless to discuss the pain Trilochan experienced and the thoughts that went through his mind all night long, but the following morning in Fort, he sat with his eyes shut tight and had his tresses chopped and his beard shaved off. When the ordeal was over, he opened his eyes and sat for a long time looking at his face in the mirror—a face the loveliest girls in Bombay would be happy simply to gaze at for hours.

Trilochan quickened his pace as he walked up and down on the terrace because he felt the same inexplicable chill he had felt the morning when he left the hairdresser's salon. He looked down and focussed on the rows of parked taxis and water taps because he did not want the rest of that episode to enter his mind, but it did. After he had his hair cut, Trilochan could not bring himself to leave his flat. The next morning, he sent his servant with a note for Mozelle, saying that he was unwell, and she should pop around for a bit. Mozelle arrived in no time. When she saw Trilochan, she almost turned around to leave the room, but squealed, 'My darling Triloch!' Wrapping herself around him, she turned his face burgundy with her kisses. Mozelle caressed Trilochan's soft clean face; she ran her fingers through his English haircut, shouting catchphrases in Arabic. She made such a racket that her nose began to flow, and as she became aware of it, she lifted the hem of her skirt to wipe it. A bashful Trilochan pulled her skirt down and said, 'You should wear something underneath.'

His comment did not affect Mozelle in the slightest, who smiled with her stale cracked lipstick-stained lips, and all she said was, 'That irritates me to no end, and this works for me.'

Trilochan recalled the first day he bumped into Mozelle, and how they had got so peculiarly entangled with each other. He drew Mozelle close and said, 'We'll get married tomorrow.'

'Certainly!' Mozelle rubbed the back of her hand on Trilochan's soft chin. They planned a civil marriage, which required them to give the court a notice of ten to fifteen days, and decided to get married in Poona since it was nearby and both of them had several friends there. They arranged to leave the following afternoon.

Mozelle worked in Fort as a salesgirl; she asked Trilochan to meet her at a taxi stand near her workplace. He arrived at the appointed time. Trilochan waited for an hour and a half, but Mozelle never turned up. He heard she had gone off to Deolali for an unspecified period with an old friend, who had just bought a new car. What Trilochan endured is a long saga—to cut it short, he toughened his heart and forgot Mozelle.

Trilochan met Kirpal Kaur and began to love her. Before long, he came to think of Mozelle as a nasty hard-hearted girl, who hopped from one place to another like a sparrow. He was relieved he had not married her. Yet, from time to time, Mozelle's memory caused a twinge in his heart.

Mozelle did not care for anybody's feelings; yet, Trilochan liked her. Often, he found himself thinking of her. What was she doing in Deolali for so long? Was she with the same man who bought a new car, or had she left him and gone off with someone else? Although he understood Mozelle's disposition, it irked him to think of her with someone else. Trilochan had spent not hundreds, but thousands of rupees on Mozelle to please her, although, in this respect, she was not hard to please and content with inexpensive objects. Once Trilochan decided to buy Mozelle a pair of gold earrings that she liked, but in the same shop, she lost her heart to a pair of small flashy inexpensive earrings, begged Trilochan to buy those for her, and forgot about the gold earrings.

Trilochan failed to understand Mozelle. Of what clay was she made? She permitted him to kiss her for hours. She allowed him to spread like soap all over her body but did not let him proceed an inch beyond this. She loved to tease him and say, 'You are a Sikh. I hate you!'

Trilochan knew Mozelle did not hate him, because if that were the case, forget two years—she would not have spent a minute with him. She did not have an iota of forbearance. Mozelle took a clear view of matters, just as in the case of not wearing knickers because they irritated her. How many times had Trilochan tried to convince her to wear knickers? He invoked shame and modesty but Mozelle refused to wear knickers.

Trilochan's lectures on modesty and shame irritated Mozelle. 'This shame-vame is a load of rubbish. If you care about it, close your eyes. Tell me, is there any dress in which a person is not naked, and which your gaze cannot penetrate? Don't talk such rubbish with me. You are a Sikh, and I know that under your trousers you wear *silly underwear*, like a pair of shorts. It is part of your religion, like your beard and your hair. You should be ashamed of yourself—you are so old, and yet you fail to understand that you cannot keep religion in a pair of shorts!'

At first, Trilochan would lose his temper at such comments, but upon reflection, he did think perhaps, Mozelle's remarks were not entirely misplaced. After he cut his long hair and his beard, he did wonder why he had carried so much meaningless weight for so long.

Trilochan paused by the water tank, cursed Mozelle, and banished her from his thoughts. Kirpal Kaur, the chaste girl with whom he had fallen in love, was in danger. Her flat was in a neighbourhood full of Muslim zealots, where two or three incidents had taken place. Now, the area was under curfew for the next forty-eight hours. Muslims living in her building could erase all signs of Kirpal Kaur and her parents with utmost ease. Lost in his thoughts, Trilochan sat down by the massive pipes of the water tank. His hair had grown quite long, and he was sure it would grow back to the required length within a year. His beard had grown back quite fast, but he did not want it any longer. There was an expert barber in Fort who trimmed it with such finesse that it looked uncut.

Trilochan ran his fingers through his long soft hair and was thinking of going back to his flat when he heard the unmistakable sound of wooden clogs. He wondered who that could be. Several Jewish women lived in Advani Chambers, and all of them wore clogs at home. As the sound drew closer, he saw Mozelle near the other tank. She was wearing the same familiar kaftan typically worn by Jewish women, and she stretched her arms out with such strength that Trilochan felt they would crack the surrounding air. He stood up, thinking, 'Where has she descended from, and what is she doing here on the terrace at this time of night?'

Mozelle stretched her arms out again, and now Trilochan felt his bones crack. His heart quickened, and he coughed aloud. Mozelle turned around and saw him. Her response was impenetrable. She shuffled up to him in her clogs, inspected his beard, and asked, 'You've become a Sikh again, Triloch?'

Trilochan's beard began to prickle him. Mozelle stepped forward to rub the back of her hand across his chin, and said, 'Now this brush is good enough to clean my navy-blue skirt but I've left it behind in Deolali.'

Trilochan remained silent. Mozelle pinched his arm, 'Why don't you say something, Sardar Sahib?'

Trilochan had no wish to repeat his past folly. In the mottled darkness before dawn, he looked carefully at Mozelle. Not much had changed about her, except that she looked run down compared to those earlier days. Trilochan asked her, 'Have you been ill?'

'No,' said Mozelle, as she tossed her short hair imperceptibly.

'You look run down.'

'I'm on a diet.' Mozelle sat down on the massive pipe, tapped her clogs on the floor, and said, 'It seems you are becoming a Sikh, once again.'

Trilochan responded with a degree of obduracy, 'Yes.'

'Congratulations!' Mozelle took off one clog and began to tap it on the pipe, 'Started loving any other girl?'

Trilochan responded softly, 'Yes!'

'Congratulations! Is she somebody from this building?'

'No.'

'Bad show!' Mozelle stood up and added, 'You should always look after your neighbours.'

Trilochan remained silent and stroked his beard with all five fingers. Mozelle continued, 'Why…has this girl advised you to grow your hair?'

'No,' Trilochan responded in a sharp tone. He felt the same discomfort he felt when disentangling the hair of his beard with a comb. Mozelle smiled, and her lips with the dried burgundy lipstick reminded Trilochan of pieces of stale buffalo meat chopped from a chunk with a thick vein, like the ones he had seen hanging in the jhatka butcher's shop in his village. She laughed, 'Shave off this beard and make me swear on anyone—I'll marry you today.'

Trilochan wanted to tell her that he was in love with a decent and chaste girl, who was a virgin, and he was going to marry her. He wanted to add that in complete contrast, Mozelle was obscene, ugly, unfaithful, and uncaring, but he was not an unkind man, and he said, 'Mozelle, I have decided to marry a simple girl from my village. She is religious, and that is why I have decided to grow my hair.'

Not given to reflection, Mozelle thought for a while as she swung one of her clogs in a semi-circular motion around the index finger of her right hand, and asked Trilochan, 'If she is religious, why would she accept you? Doesn't she know that once you had your hair chopped off?'

'She doesn't know. I started growing my beard after you left for Deolali, merely as revenge, and I met Kirpal Kaur much later. The way I tie my turban perhaps, one person in a hundred can figure out that I cut my hair, and this too I shall rectify soon.'

Trilochan began to comb his soft long hair with his fingers. Mozelle lifted her long kaftan and began to scratch her hefty white thigh, 'That's very good...but wretched mosquitoes are here as well. Look how badly they have bitten me!'

Trilochan turned to look in the opposite direction. Mozelle licked her finger and applied saliva to the spot where a mosquito had bitten her. She let down her kaftan and stood up straight, 'When are you getting married?'

'I don't know,' said Trilochan, looking very anxious.

Mozelle remained silent for a few moments, but she sensed his anxiety and asked in a serious tone, 'Triloch, what are you thinking?'

Trilochan felt he needed sympathy, and even though it was Mozelle, he recounted his entire dilemma. Mozelle laughed, 'You are an *idiot* of the first order. Go and bring her. What's the difficulty?'

'Difficulty! Mozelle, you can't appreciate the delicacy of this situation—or any situation. You are a hot-headed girl, and this is the reason our relationship couldn't last. It is something I will regret all my life.'

Mozelle banged her clog on the water pipe, 'Regret be *damned*! *Silly idiot*! Just think—you must rescue what's-her-name from that neighbourhood! And here you are, weeping over our relationship. Our relationship could never have lasted. You are a *silly* man and a coward. I want a fearless man but forget these matters. Come, let's get your Kaur!' She grabbed Trilochan's arm.

Worried, Trilochan asked her, 'From where?'

'From wherever she is. I know every single brick of that neighbourhood. Come on, come with me.'

'But listen...there's a curfew!'

'Not for Mozelle! Come along now.'

Mozelle dragged Trilochan by his arm and took him to the door of the stairs. She was about to go down when she paused and looked at Trilochan's beard.

Trilochan asked, 'What's the matter?'

Mozelle said, 'Your beard...but it's fine...it's not too long...if you go bareheaded nobody will think you are a Sikh.'

'Bareheaded!' said Trilochan, 'I shall not go bareheaded!'

'Why?' Mozelle asked, looking innocent.

Trilochan fixed a stray strand of hair, 'You don't understand, it is not appropriate for me to go there without a turban.'

'Why isn't it appropriate?'

'Why don't you understand, she has never seen me without my turban. She thinks I have long hair. I don't want her to know my secret.'

Mozelle stamped one clog clad foot hard on the threshold, 'You are an *idiot* of the first order! Silly ass, it's a question of her life—what's her name, this Kaur you love?'

Trilochan tried to explain to her, 'Mozelle, she is a very religious girl. If she sees me bareheaded, she'll begin to hate me.'

Mozelle was exasperated, 'Ach, *damn* your love! Tell me, are all Sikhs as stupid as you? Her life is in danger, and you insist on wearing your turban, and perhaps, also your underwear that looks like shorts.'

Trilochan said, 'I wear it at all times.'

'You do very well, but now think about this neighbourhood where mian bhais live next to mian bhais and more mian bhais, and many are big dadas and pirs. Go there with your turban and they'll slaughter you on the spot.'

Trilochan gave a brief reply, 'I don't care. If I go there with you, I go with my turban. I can't endanger my love!'

Mozelle was so exasperated that her bosom began to heave, 'You ass, how will your love exist when your, what's the slut's name, when she won't be there...or her family? You are a Sikh, and I swear by God, a real *idiot* of a Sikh!'

Trilochan was furious, 'Don't talk rot!'

Mozelle laughed out loud. She put her arms, covered with light down, around Trilochan's neck, swaying gently as she said, '*Darling*, as you wish. Go put on your pagri; I'll wait for you in the bazaar.'

She was about to go down the stairs when Trilochan asked her, 'Aren't you going to get dressed?'

Mozelle shook her head and said, 'No. This kaftan will work fine.' She clickety-clacked down the stairs, and Trilochan could hear her wooden clogs until she reached the ground floor.

Trilochan pushed his long hair back and pulled it together before going down to his flat. He took no time to change his clothes. He picked up an already tied turban and fitted it on his head, locked the front door of his flat, and went downstairs where Mozelle was waiting for him. She was standing on the footpath with her strong legs wide apart, smoking a cigarette like a man. As Trilochan walked up to her, she exhaled a ring of smoke in his face merely to tease him, and he barked at her, 'You're so crude.'

Mozelle smiled, 'You haven't said anything new. Several people have called me crude.'

She looked at Trilochan and said, 'You've tied this turban well. It does look as though you have long hair.'

In the deserted bazaar, even the wind crept at a stealthy pace, as though it feared the curfew. The light from the dimmed streetlamps looked sickly. Usually, trams were running by this time, and people were rushing about, but the bazaar looked as though not a soul had passed or would ever pass by. Mozelle walked ahead with the loud clickety-clack of her clogs on the pavement breaking the silence. Trilochan cursed Mozelle in his heart for not exchanging her beastly clogs for something more appropriate just this once. He wanted to ask her to take off her clogs and walk barefoot, but he knew she would not pay the slightest attention and decided to remain silent.

Trilochan was terrified. If a leaf rustled, his heart stopped, but Mozelle continued to walk along. Fearless, blowing her cigarette smoke, she looked as though she was out for a stroll without a care in the world. They reached a crossroad, where a policeman roared at them, 'Hey, where are you going?'

Trilochan shrank, but Mozelle walked up to the policeman, and tossing her hair ever so slightly, she said, 'Oh you…you didn't recognize me, Mozelle?' She pointed to an alley and said, 'There, next door, my sister lives there. She is unwell. I'm taking the doctor to see her.'

As the policeman tried to recognize her, God alone knows from where Mozelle produced a packet of cigarettes. She took one out and offered it to him, 'Here, have a cigarette.'

The policemen took the cigarette. Mozelle took the lit cigarette out of her mouth and said to him, 'Here, have a light!'

The policeman took a puff of his cigarette. Mozelle winked at him with her right eye and at Trilochan with her left before she clickety-clacked towards the alley that led to Kirpal Kaur's neighbourhood.

Trilochan was silent. He felt Mozelle derived a peculiar thrill in defying the curfew; he knew she liked to play with danger. He recalled the times they went to Juhu Beach, and how she loved to swim far out into the sea to ride on the crest of the highest waves. He watched, terrified she might drown, but she returned to the shore without the slightest concern for her body bruised by the brine. Mozelle walked on ahead. A terrified Trilochan followed behind, on the lookout for someone who might attack him with a knife. Mozelle stopped. When Trilochan walked up to her, she said in an almost edifying tone, 'Trilochan dear, it's not good to look so scared. If you're scared, then something is bound to happen. I've experienced this.'

Trilochan remained silent. They crossed the central street and reached a lane leading to the neighbourhood where Kirpal Kaur lived. At a distance, they could see a Marwari's shop being looted in an atmosphere of complete calm. Mozelle assessed the matter for a moment and said to Trilochan, 'Not a problem. Come along.'

They resumed walking, but almost out of nowhere a man heading in their direction with a massive platter on his head bumped into Trilochan. The platter fell. The man looked at Trilochan, convinced he was confronting a Sikh, and stuck his hand into the belt of his shalwar. Mozelle approached him, swaying, and pretending she was blind drunk, she nudged the man hard in his ribcage and slurred, 'Hey, you want to kill your brother. I want to make marriage with him.'

She turned to Trilochan, 'Karim, pick up the platter and put it back on his head.'

The man took his hand away from his belt, gave Mozelle a lecherous look, and nudged her breasts, 'Have a blast, saali, have a

blast!' He picked up his platter and was gone.

Trilochan mumbled, 'The bastard! What boorish behaviour!'

Mozelle brushed her bosom and said, 'Nothing boorish about it. Everything goes. Come along now.'

Mozelle quickened her pace and Trilochan joined her. They walked through the narrow lane and arrived in the neighbourhood where Kirpal Kaur lived. Mozelle asked, 'Now, which alley do we take?'

Trilochan whispered very softly, 'The third…the building at the left corner!'

Mozelle headed in that direction. It was a densely populated area, but there was deathly silence all around—not a cry of a baby to be heard. As they approached the alley, they could see something amiss—a man ran out of a block of flats on the right and entered another on the left. Three men came out from this block and stood on the pavement; they looked around and rushed into the building opposite them. Mozelle figured something was afoot and signalled Trilochan to move into the dark, and she said very softly, 'Trilochan dear, take this turban off!'

'Never,' he replied firmly. 'I won't, come what may.'

She was infuriated, 'It's up to you. Can't you see what is happening before your eyes?'

What their eyes witnessed was chilling. Two men emerged from the building on the left. Mozelle saw something thick dripping out of the gunny sacks slung over their shoulders; she shuddered from head to toe and began to bite her lips, a clear sign that she was thinking. When both men reached the far end of the alley and disappeared, she said to Trilochan, 'Look, I'll run into the flats on the left, you come after me, very fast, as though you're chasing me. Understood? But all this must happen very, very fast.'

Without waiting for Trilochan's response, Mozelle ran fast towards the block of flats, her clogs clickety-clacking. Trilochan ran after her. In a few moments, they were inside the building. As they reached the stairs, Trilochan was out of breath, but Mozelle was not. She asked Trilochan, 'Which floor?'

Trilochan licked his dry lips, 'Second!'

'Come on,' she said and began to climb the stairs, her clogs going clickety-clack.

Trilochan followed her up the steps; he saw large stains of blood and his blood dried up. They reached the second floor and walked some distance along the corridor before Trilochan tapped gently on a door while Mozelle kept a watch on the stairs. Trilochan knocked yet again. He leaned his face against the door and called out, 'Mehnga Singhji, Mehnga Singhji!'

A weak voice from inside asked, 'Who?'

'Trilochan!'

The door opened softly. Trilochan waved to Mozelle who dashed towards him, and they went inside. Mozelle saw a terrified petite slim girl standing beside her. Mozelle studied the girl's sharp features and perfectly lovely nose, dripping because of a cold, and drew the girl to her ample rounded bosom, lifted the hem of her baggy loose kaftan, and wiped the girl's nose. Trilochan turned crimson. Mozelle turned to Kirpal Kaur and said tenderly, 'Don't be frightened, Trilochan has come for you.'

Kirpal Kaur looked at Trilochan with terrified eyes and moved away from Mozelle. Trilochan said to her, 'Tell Sardar Sahib to get ready quickly and, also your Mataji, but hurry.'

Just then there were sounds, and they could hear someone scream and shout on the top floor; it was the sound of a struggle. A suppressed scream escaped Kirpal Kaur's throat, 'They've caught her!'

'Who?'

Kirpal Kaur was about to respond, but Mozelle grabbed her by her arm, pulled her into a corner and said, 'Good if they have caught her. You take off these clothes!'

Before Kirpal Kaur had time to think, Mozelle pulled off her shirt and threw it aside; a petrified Kirpal Kaur covered her naked body with her arms. Trilochan looked away. Mozelle took off her loose kaftan and slipped it on Kirpal, and standing stark naked, she hurriedly undid the drawstring of Kirpal Kaur's shalwar, and as she pulled it down, she said to Trilochan, 'Go. Take her—but wait.' She untied Kirpal's hair and said, 'Go...hurry...get out.'

Trilochan turned to Kirpal Kaur and said, 'Come,' but he stopped and looked at Mozelle who was standing naked as the day she was born, with just her clogs on her feet. The soft down on her arms was standing on edge because of the cold.

'Why don't you go?' Mozelle's tone was prickly.

Trilochan said softly, 'Her mother and father are also here.'

'To hell with them...you take her.'

'And you?'

'I shall make my way.'

The men from the top floor had reached their door and were beating it down. Kirpal Kaur's blind mother and crippled father lay groaning in the other room. Mozelle came up with an idea. She tossed her hair ever so slightly and said to Trilochan, 'Listen, I think we have only one way out. I'll open the door...'

'Door!' Kirpal's Kaur's shriek was suppressed in her dry throat.

Mozelle continued talking to Trilochan, 'I'll open the door and run out, you run after me. I'll climb up the stairs, you follow me. These people who are beating down the door will forget everything and run after us.'

Trilochan asked, 'Then?'

Mozelle said, 'Your what's-her-name...will seize the opportunity and run. Nobody will trouble her in this dress.'

Trilochan explained everything to Kirpal Kaur.

Mozelle shrieked and opened the door. She fell upon the stunned men outside, stood up, and made for the stairs. As Trilochan ran after her, the men made way for him. Mozelle was climbing the stairs blindly, and now the men rushed after them. Mozelle's clogs slipped at the top of the staircase, and she stumbled and rolled down the concrete steps, colliding against the iron handrails. Trilochan rushed down and saw her lying on the concrete floor of the landing. He leaned forward and saw blood flowing from her nose; her mouth was bleeding, and blood was oozing out of her ears. The men who had come to break down the door gathered around her. Nobody asked what happened. Everyone stood silent, looking at Mozelle's grazed and naked white body. Trilochan shook her arm and called out, 'Mozelle...Mozelle.'

Mozelle opened her bloodshot large Jewish eyes, and she smiled. Trilochan took off his turban, unfurled it, and covered her naked body. Mozelle smiled and winked at Trilochan. As she tried to speak, small bubbles of blood came out of her mouth, 'Go. Is my underwear there nor not? I mean...'

Trilochan understood what she meant but did not want to move away from her. Mozelle growled, 'Truly, you are a Sikh. Go and look...'

Trilochan stood up and went towards Kirpal Kaur's flat. With hazy eyes, Mozelle looked at the men standing around her and said, 'He is a mian bhai but is a godfather type...I call him a Sikh.' Trilochan returned, and with a gesture of his eyes, he told her that Kirpal Kaur had gone. As Mozelle heaved a sigh of relief, blood gushed out of her mouth, and she said, 'Oh. Damn it...' She wiped her face with her arm covered with soft down, looked at Trilochan, and added, 'All right darling, *bye-bye*.'

Trilochan wanted to say something but his words were stuck in his throat. Mozelle removed his turban from her body. 'Take this away; this religion of yours,' she said, and her lifeless arm fell on her firm breasts.

## *Barren*

I first met him precisely two years ago at Apollo Bandar. It was evening, and the last rays of the sun had disappeared behind distant waves of the ocean. I left the first bench to a man who was getting a champi, a head massage in Bombay speak, and sat down on the second, opposite the Gateway of India. I gazed at the ocean stretching out as far as the eye could see, where the sea and the sky merged into one, and watched the waves rising sluggishly as a vast muddy carpet pulled from here to there.

Along the coastline, colourful reflections of night lights began to shimmer on the water. The unfurled sails and masts of several boats bobbed gently by a nearby wall, and the sound of splashing waves mingled with the chatter of spectators enjoying the vista. An occasional car horn reminded me of someone muttering 'Hunh' while listening to an engaging story. There are few things more pleasurable than smoking a cigarette in such a setting, so I took out a packet from my pocket, but could not find my matchbox, and was about to put the cigarettes away when someone said, 'Do have a light.'

I turned around and saw a young man standing behind my bench. Generally, Bombayites have sallow complexions, but his face was frighteningly yellow. I thanked him, 'Very kind of you.'

He responded by offering me a matchbox. I thanked him again, 'Have a seat.'

'Please, have a light. I must go now.'

It was clear from the young man's voice that he was in no hurry. You may well ask how I could gauge this from his tone but this is the feeling I had at the time. So, I repeated myself, 'Do have a seat. What's the hurry?' I offered him a cigarette and added, 'Please...'

He scrutinized the packet and responded, 'Thank you but I stick to my brand.'

Believe it or not, I could swear he was making this up, and yet again, it was his voice that gave him away. Instantly, I developed an interest in him.

I decided I must get this young man to smoke a cigarette with me. He wanted to sit with me but did not think it appropriate to smoke my cigarette. The conflict between a 'yes' to accept my offer and a 'no' to turn it down was evident from his tone. Even his body seemed to be in limbo between a state of being and not being. As I have said earlier, his face was very wan, and his eyes and facial features seemed blurred like a portrait someone had painted and washed away.

I tried to size him up. His lips seemed to protrude for a bit, but again they seemed to dissolve into a blur—and so it was with all his features. His eyes were the colour of muddy water, and his eyelashes jagged. His hair was black but it was the black of a piece of burnt paper. Upon close inspection, it was possible to decipher his nose, but from a distance, it seemed non-existent. As I have said earlier, his features were blurred. He was of average height, neither short nor tall, but when he allowed his backbone to dangle there was a perceptible drop in his height; similarly, when he pulled himself upright, he appeared too tall for his body.

Although in a sorry state, his clothes were not dirty. His coat sleeves had frayed with constant wear and tear, and tiny pieces of loose thread stuck out at the edges. His open-collared shirt could withstand possibly one more wash, and as was apparent from his attire, he was trying hard to stand tall with dignity. I was trying to size him up and sensed a restless current run through his body, as though he wanted to hide from my gaze. I stood up, lit a cigarette, and simultaneously offered him one as I lit a match, 'Do have one.' Something about my manner must have made him forget his reservations. He took a cigarette, stuck it in his mouth, lit it, and began to smoke. But instantly, he realized his mistake and took the cigarette out of his mouth, produced a mock cough, and said, 'Cavenders doesn't suit me. The tobacco is too strong, and it irritates my throat.'

'What brand do you like?' I asked.

He stammered and responded, 'I...actually I hardly smoke, Dr Arwalkar has forbidden me, but I smoke 555 because the tobacco is not very strong.'

The doctor whose name he dropped so casually into the conversation is famous in Bombay and charges a ten-rupee consultation fees. You must know that 555, the brand he mentioned, is expensive. He told two lies in one breath; I found this difficult to stomach but remained silent. My heart itched to unmask him—to reveal his deception, to embarrass and compel him to apologize to me. When I scrutinized him, I did not see the rush of red that invariably colours the face of a person who is telling a lie. There was a sincerity in his lies; when he lied, his moral compass did not waver in the slightest. Well, let us forget this angle of the story because if I go into the finer points, the narrative will run to countless pages.

After some polite conversation, I managed to break the ice and turned to the poignant vista of the sea. Since I am a conjurer of fiction, I recounted a few tales about the sea and the spectators who come and go by Apollo Bandar. After he had smoked six cigarettes, he asked my name. When I told him, he stood up and said, 'Sir, you are Mr... I've read several of your short stories. I had no idea—I am so happy to meet you. By God, I am so happy!'

I wanted to thank him, but he started talking to me about my work, and I did not detect any irritation in his throat as he added, 'Yes, just recently I read one of your stories. I have forgotten the name—but in it, you presented a young girl who is in love with a man who betrays her. The storyteller is also in love with the girl. When he learns of her tragedy, he goes to meet her and says, "You should live and gain strength from the memory of the few moments of joy experienced in loving him." I can't recall the exact words, but tell me, is this possible? Are you that man? Forgive my curiosity, but did you meet her on the rooftop? Did you leave her devastated in the somnolent moonlight to go down and sleep in your room?' He paused before he added, 'I shouldn't ask you these questions. After all, who wants to reveal the secrets of his heart?'

I responded, 'I'd tell you, but somehow asking and telling all in the first meeting doesn't seem appropriate. What do you think?'

The warmth in his tone turned cold, and he continued very softly, 'Forgive me, you're right, but who knows if we'll meet again.'

'Absolutely,' I continued, 'Bombay is a large city, but we can meet not once but several times. I am a useless man. I mean, I am a short-story writer. You will find me here every evening, that is, unless I'm unwell. You will find me here, every day, as part of my attempt to fall in love with one of the many girls who come here for their walks. Love is not such a bad thing!'

'Love…love…' he was unable to continue and wilted into silence. I had mentioned love in jest but the evening was so enchanting that had I fallen in love with some woman I would not have regretted it. A subconscious desire to fall in love is no surprise when night and day merge and countless electric lights begin to flicker, and at times a chill in the air adds to the aura of romance. I have no idea which short story he was referring to since I do not recall all my short stories. I tend to forget the romantic ones. I have met very few women in my life; hence the stories I have written about them lack warmth, and I do not reflect on them. I have interacted with women from a specific milieu and have written a few stories about them, but those are not romantic. Undoubtedly, he was referring to a second-rate romance I wrote to satisfy some personal need.

When the young man mentioned love and fell silent, I thought I ought to say something more about love. I held forth, 'Our ancestors have written several types of love stories, but whether love is born in Multan or Siberia, in winter or summer, in the hearts of the rich or the poor, it remains love. At times, babies are born after great pain—similarly, at times, love is born out of great hardship. Just like a woman can have a miscarriage, you can have a miscarriage in love. But at times, some people can be barren in matters of love. Like a woman who cannot give birth to a child because of some defect in her body, they cannot fall in love because of a spiritual flaw.' I was holding forth without looking at him; when I turned towards him and found him lost in his thoughts as he stared into the void beyond the ocean, I fell silent. He gave a start at the sound of a loud car horn and said meaninglessly, 'Yes, you are right!'

I wanted to say, 'Forget it! What have I just said?'

I thought it best to remain silent and to give him time to shed the burden he was carrying in his mind. He was deep in thought, but after a while, he said, 'You're right, but let's forget this matter.'

I was taken with my monologue and wanted an audience, so I started again, 'As I was saying, some men are barren in matters of love. I mean, they have a desire to love but can never fulfil it. I think the reasons are to do with some spiritual limitations within them. What do you think?'

He looked as though he had seen a ghost. The sudden change in him alarmed me, and I asked, 'Is everything all right? Are you feeling ill?'

'No...not at all...' but his restlessness increased, and he added, 'I have no illness-shillness. What makes you think I'm ill?'

I responded, 'Anyone looking at you now will think you ill. You look frightfully pale. I think you should go home. Come, I'll walk you home.'

'No. I can go on my own. I am not ill. Occasionally, I get a slight pain in my heart. Perhaps it's that, but I'll be fine soon. Do continue with what you were saying.'

I remained silent for a while; he looked in no fit condition to pay attention to what I was saying, but when he insisted, I started, 'I was asking your opinion about the people who are barren when it comes to love. I'm afraid I can't understand the feelings of such people, but then I think of a barren woman who grovels before God, praying for a baby son or daughter. When she gets nothing from this quarter, she turns to amulets and superstitions, rubs herself with ashes from cremation grounds, spends countless nights chanting mantras prescribed by sadhus, makes pledges, and gives alms. I think a man unable to fall in love must be like a barren woman. Such people deserve our sympathy.'

His eyes welled up with tears, and swallowing his saliva, he stood up and turned away from me, 'Oh, it's late. I have some important work. How much time we've spent simply talking!'

I stood up. The young man turned around and grasped my hand. Without looking at me, he said, 'I must beg your leave,' and walked off.

I met him for the second time, yet again at Apollo Bandar. I am not an enthusiastic walker, but those days, an evening walk had become a habit. A month later, my interest in Apollo Bandar vanished when a poet from Agra wrote me a long letter, merely to say how blessed I was to be in Bombay where I could catch sight of all the fairies who gathered at Apollo Bandar every evening. Now, I feel queasy when someone mentions Apollo Bandar.

Night had fallen; there was no sign of daylight. The October heat had not subsided but there was a breeze. There were rows of parked cars, and countless people were out for a walk. The benches on the seafront were occupied but I found one facing the road. On the bench next to mine, two chatterboxes were gabbling away since who knows when. One was a Gujarati and the other a Parsi; both spoke Gujarati but with different accents and intonations. The Parsi alternated between two pitches, one high and the other rather low. At one point, both started talking fast, their exchange sounding like a verbal duel between a parrot and a mynah. Irritated by their unending loud and banal conversation, I got up for a stroll and was about to turn towards the Taj Mahal Hotel when I saw him walking towards me. I could not call out to draw his attention since I did not know his name, but when he saw me, he seemed pleased, and his gaze rested.

There was no vacant bench, so I said to him, 'I'm seeing you after such a long time! Come, let us go to that restaurant. There's no place here for us to sit.'

After some polite exchanges, he decided to accompany me. We walked a few yards and found ourselves sitting on large cane chairs in a restaurant. I ordered tea and extended my cigarette tin towards him. By sheer coincidence, just that morning, I had paid ten rupees for a consultation with Dr Arwalkar, who had asked me to give up smoking or at least switch to a good brand, such as 555, and on his advice, I had purchased a tin. The young man studied the tin before he lifted his eyes to look at me; he was about to say something but decided to remain silent. I laughed out loud, 'You mustn't think that I've started smoking this brand because you said so. It's a coincidence that I had to see Dr Arwalkar today; I've been getting chest pains for some days now, and he told me, "You can smoke but very few cigarettes..."'

I saw he did not buy my story. Promptly, I took out Dr Arwalkar's prescription, and kept it on the table, before continuing, 'I cannot decipher his handwriting but it seems that Dr Sahib has included the entire vitamin family.'

The prescription had Dr Arwalkar's name embossed in black, and below his address, it had the date on it. The young man looked at it stealthily, and the anxiety on his face vanished as he asked with a smile, 'Why is it that writers often have a vitamin deficiency?'

I responded, 'Because they don't get enough to eat, and they work hard with minuscule returns.' Tea arrived, and the conversation turned to other matters.

There was a gap of about two-and-a-half months between our first and second encounter. The young man's complexion looked more jaundiced, and he had dark circles around his eyes. His soul seemed in perpetual agony. Several times, he stopped mid-stream in a conversation, and an involuntary sigh escaped him. If he attempted a laugh, there was no sign of life on his lips. I noticed his condition and asked him quite unexpectedly, 'Why are you sad?'

'Sad…sad…' he said with a vacant smile like the one that appears on the lips of someone who knows he is about to die and wants to show that he is not scared of death.

'I'm not sad. Perhaps, you are in a sad mood.' He drank the contents of his teacup in one big gulp and stood up, 'Well, I must take your leave. I have some important work.'

I forgot to ask his name but concluded he was mentally and spiritually troubled. Sorrow had permeated every fibre of his being; it coursed through his veins, and he did not wish to share his grief. He was trying to live two lives—one that was real and another that he tried to conjure, and both lives were failures.

I bumped into him for the third time, yet again at Apollo Bandar, and this time I took him home. We walked in silence, but after we reached my flat, we talked about all manner of things. After he entered my room, he remained immersed in sorrow but tried to come across as garrulous and full of vitality, which he was not. I felt a wave of sympathy for him. During our conversation, his eyes fell on the photograph of a girl in a metal frame on my desk. He walked towards it and asked, 'May I look at this photograph?'

I said, 'With pleasure…'

He cast a quick look at the photograph and sat down on a chair. 'She's a beautiful girl. I think she is your…'

Before he could finish what he wanted to say, I said, 'No. Some time ago, the thought of loving her had entered my heart; you could say that a hint of love stirred in my heart, but sadly, she didn't know of it. She was married off. This photograph is a memory of my first love, which died before it was born.'

'This is a memory of your first love... After this, you must have had many love affairs,' he moistened his dry lips with his tongue, 'I mean you must have had several such incomplete and complete romances in your life.'

I was about to say, 'Oh no! Like you, yours truly is also fallow in matters of love.' I'm not sure why I lied for no reason, 'Yes, such things happen all the time. The book of your life too must be full of such episodes.'

He fell silent, as though he had plunged into the depths of an ocean. He remained quiet for some time and looked tormented by his thoughts. Saddened by his silence, I said, 'I say, sir, lost in your thoughts?'

He gave a start, 'I... Oh nothing, I was just thinking of something.'

I asked, 'Did you recall some story from the past, or an encounter—a lost dream, an old wound that hurts?'

'Wounds, old wounds? Not wounds, just one, deep, very persistent wound. I don't want any more wounds. One is enough.'

He stood up as he spoke and attempted to pace up and down in my tiny room crammed with chairs, a desk, a bed, and so much else. He stopped by the desk and looked thoughtfully at the photograph.

'There is a strong resemblance between her and her, but her face didn't have this vivacity. Her eyes were large—eyes that see but also understand.' He drew in a deep sigh and sat down on a chair. 'Death is a matter beyond understanding, especially when it arrives at a young age. I believe there is a force other than God that is envious, and that is why God does not wish to see anyone happy—but forget this story.'

I said to him, 'No, no, do go on, if you wish. To tell you the truth, I thought you have never loved.'

'How could you think I have never loved? Just a moment ago you were saying that the book of my life must be full of such episodes.' He looked at me with questioning eyes, 'If I have never loved why do I have this pain in my heart? If I have never loved how did this sickness attach itself to my life? Why am I always sad? Why am I oblivious of myself? Why am I melting away like wax day by day?' All the questions were addressed to me, but he seemed to be talking to himself.

I responded, 'I lied when I said that there must be many such episodes in your life but you also lied when you said, "I am not sad, and I have no sickness." It is a challenge to know the secrets of somebody's heart. There can be several other reasons for your sorrow, but unless you tell me, I will never know. Undoubtedly, you are becoming weaker by the day. Indeed, you have suffered anguish and grief, and I have nothing but sympathy for you.'

'Sympathy...' his eyes welled up with tears. 'I don't need sympathy because sympathy will not bring her back. It cannot bring back from the obscurity of death and return to me the woman I love. I am sure you have never loved because its setback has left no blemish on you. Look at me. You will find nothing in me that does not have the imprint of my love. What you see is the wreckage of my body. Why should I tell you my story when you do not have the capacity to understand it? If someone tells you that his mother just died, it cannot have the same effect on your heart as it does in the heart of the bereaved offspring. The story of my love will seem quite commonplace to you or someone else, yet nobody can feel how it affected me because I was the one who loved and accepted what happened.' He fell silent. His throat was parched, and he kept trying to swallow his saliva.

'Did she betray you?' I asked, 'Or was it something else?'

'Betray! She was incapable of betrayal. For God's sake, do not use the word betray; she was an angel, not a woman. Confound the death that enveloped her in its wings and carried her away because it could bear not to see us happy. Ah, you have crushed my heart. Hear me out, and I'll tell you some part of the story of my ill-fated life.'

He continued, 'When we first met, she was a girl from a rich family, and I a young man who lost his forefathers' wealth in the pursuit of pleasure. Without a penny to my name, I moved from my hometown to Lucknow. I owned a car, and the only skill I had was that I knew how to drive. I decided to make this a career. The first job I found was at Deputy Sahib's house. She was his only child.' As he finished speaking, he drifted into his thoughts and became silent. I too remained quiet. After a while, he gave a start and asked, 'What was I saying?'

'You were employed at Deputy Sahib's house.'

'Yes, she was the same Deputy Sahib's only child. Every morning I took Zehra to school at nine o'clock. She observed purdah, but for how long can someone hide from a driver? I managed to see her on the second day. She was not merely beautiful; she had a distinct air of poise and elegance, and her straight middle parting added dignity to her bearing. I am left speechless when asked to describe her loveliness and candour.'

Yet, he continued to recount his Zehra's qualities and made many unsuccessful attempts at conjuring an image of her. It seemed too many thoughts had taken hold of his mind. Sorrow permeated his being, and his words came out as sighs, but he recounted his story in an unhurried manner.

And his story was that he fell immeasurably in love with Zehra, and every day he spent hours in working out ways to catch a glimpse of her. He reflected on his feelings and understood the chasm between them. Desolate, he faced the hopelessness of a driver falling in love with his master's daughter. Yet, one day, he dared to write a few lines to Zehra and slipped the note between the pages of her book. I recall those lines, 'Zehra, I know I am your servant. Your father pays me thirty rupees a month, but I love you. I don't know what I should or shouldn't do.'

The following day when he went to drop her at school, his unsteady hands lost his grip on the steering wheel several times. Thank God there was no accident. He spent the whole day in an agitated frame of mind. That evening when driving back from school, Zehra asked him to stop the car, and spoke to him in a solemn tone, 'Look, Naeem, never ever do anything like this again. I have not mentioned your letter to Abbaji, but if you do something like this again, I'll have to complain about you. Understand? Come on now, start the car.'

After this conversation, he thought he should leave Deputy Sahib's employment and erase his love for Zehra from his heart, but he was unsuccessful on both counts. A month passed. One day, yet again, he acted with courage, wrote another letter, and secreted it in Zehra's book. He awaited his fate, convinced that the following day he would be dismissed from his employment, but this did not happen. That evening, on the way back from school, Zehra spoke to him. Once again, she asked him to desist from such unacceptable behaviour, and added, 'If you don't care about your self-respect, at least have some regard for mine.' Yet again, she spoke with great dignity and composure and dashed all his hopes. He vowed to leave his job and Lucknow forever.

At the end of the month, two nights before he was to leave Deputy Sahib's house, Naeem sat in his quarters in the dim light of a kerosene lamp and wrote a letter of farewell to Zehra. And again, I recall the letter, 'Zehra, I have tried hard to follow your diktat but have no control over my heart. This is my last letter to you. Tomorrow evening I shall leave Lucknow, and you will have no reason to complain to your father. Your silence will seal my fate. Don't think that distance will stop me from loving you. Wherever I am, my heart will be yours, always. I shall never forget the days I drove the car so gently because I did not want you to feel the bumps on the road. What else could I have done for you?' He found an opportunity and kept the letter in her book.

In the morning, on her way to school, Zehra said nothing to him. That evening too, when returning home, she remained silent. Hopeless, Naeem went into his quarters, packed his few belongings, and kept them aside. In the dim light of the lantern, he sat on his charpai thinking of the vast gulf between him and Zehra. Naeem was distraught; he understood that as a lowly servant, he had no right to love his master's daughter. Although, at times, he thought it was no fault of his if he loved her because his love was not a lie. He was embroiled in these thoughts when around midnight there was a knock on the door. His heart skipped a beat but then he thought it must be the gardener; perhaps, someone in his house had taken ill, and he wanted help.

When he opened the door, Naeem found Zehra standing in front of him, and was dumbfounded. A few moments passed in silence. Finally, Zehra's lips parted, and in a trembling voice, she said, 'Naeem, I have come to you. Tell me what you want, but before I enter your quarters, I must ask you a few questions.'

Naeem remained silent. Zehra asked him, 'Do you love me?'

He felt somebody had struck him, 'Zehra, why are you asking me a question the response to which will insult my love for you. I want to ask you, don't I love you?'

Zehra did not respond. She remained silent for a while, and asked her second question, 'Will you cherish me as much without my riches? My father has a fair bit of wealth but I don't have a paisa to my name. Whatever is called mine is not mine; it belongs to him.'

Naeem was a very emotional man, and this question injured his dignity. He said to Zehra in a voice full of pathos, 'Zehra, for God's sake, don't ask me questions the answers to which are so commonplace that you will find them in every third-rate romantic novel.'

Zehra entered his quarters. She sat down on his charpai and said, 'I am yours and will always remain yours.' Zehra remained true to her word.

They left Lucknow and came to Delhi where they got married and started living in a small house. Deputy Sahib discovered their whereabouts and arrived at their door. Naeem was not at home because he had found a job. Zehra's father called her names and told her she had rubbed his good name in the dust. He wanted Zehra to leave Naeem and forget what had happened. He was willing to pay Naeem two or three thousand rupees. Deputy Sahib returned on his own. Zehra was unwilling to leave Naeem, and she told her father, 'Abbaji, I am very content with Naeem. You cannot find a better husband for me. We ask nothing from you, if you can give us your blessings, we'll be grateful.'

Deputy Sahib was furious when he heard this and threatened to have Naeem arrested but Zehra responded with great composure, 'Abbaji, this is not Naeem's fault. The truth is that both of us are blameless. We love each other. He is my husband, and this is not a crime. I am not a minor.'

Deputy Sahib was an intelligent man and understood that without his daughter's consent, he could not bring charges against Naeem. He departed, leaving Zehra forever.

Deputy Sahib tried to put pressure on Naeem, and through various individuals, tempted him with money, but remained unsuccessful. Naeem's income was tiny. Brought up in luxury, Zehra had to wear coarse cloth, cook, and do all the housework, but she was happy in the new world in which she found herself. At every step, she discovered exceptional facets of Naeem's love for her. She was most content; Naeem too was happy. One day, it was the will of God, Zehra got an acute pain in her chest. Before Naeem could do anything, she left this world and Naeem in darkness forever.

The young man cherished every moment as he related his story haltingly. It took him nearly four hours to recount the tale of the love of his life. His face was not wan but flushed, as though there was a rush of blood to it, and I saw a ceaseless flow of tears from his eyes; his throat seemed parched.

He stood up immediately, as though he was in a hurry and said, 'I've made a mistake by telling you my love story. I made a big mistake. Zehra's name should have remained confined to my lips. But...' his voice trembled, 'I am alive, and she...she...' Unable to speak, he squeezed my hand and left the room.

I never met Naeem again. I looked unsuccessfully for him several times at Apollo Bandar. After six or seven months, I received this letter, and here I quote it verbatim:

_____ Sahib,

You will recall that I recounted my love story to you at your flat. It was mere fiction—a fabricated story. There was no Zehra, and there is no Naeem. I exist, but I am not the Naeem who loved Zehra. You told me that some people are barren when it comes to love. I, too, am one such unfortunate person, who spent his entire life trying to lose his heart to somebody. I conjured Zehra's love for Naeem to soothe my heart. And, Zehra's death? I cannot figure out why I killed her; it is likely that too is coloured by the darkness of my life.

I do not know whether you think my story false or true. But let me tell you something rather odd, the creator of the story thinks it real. I felt I loved Zehra, and she died. It will startle you to learn that with time, the reality of this story intensified. Zehra's voice and her laughter began to ring in my ears. I could feel the warmth of her breath as the story came to life, and this is how I dug my grave. Zehra is no longer a fiction. She is dead, and that is why I too must die. You will receive this letter after my death. Goodbye. I do not know where, but I know I will meet Zehra somewhere.

I have written this brief letter to you because you are a writer of fiction. If you write a short story of my account, you will earn seven or eight rupees. You told me you are paid between seven to ten rupees for a story. This is my gift to you. Well, goodbye.

Your acquaintance,
Naeem.

Naeem created a Zehra and died. I created his story for myself and am alive, which is unwarranted on my part.

## My Sahib

'It was 1937, and the Muslim League was active in all its glory. I too was robust and in the early stages of adulthood, a time when a perpetually restless heart longs to achieve something for no reason. Ready to take on any power that confronted me, I wrestled with imaginary invincible foes. I was at a stage in life when a brave heart longs to accomplish a feat—not necessarily an extraordinary act, but one that draws people's attention. After this brief prologue, let me turn to the time when Ghalib was young, so to speak. I am not sure if Ghalib ever took part in any political movement in his youth, but yours truly was a hot-blooded worker of the Muslim League. I had little else to do in those days and was a dedicated member of the Ghaziabad Corps, a formation made up of many other young men like me.

'It was around this time that Muhammad Ali Jinnah graced Delhi with his presence, and there was a spectacular rally in his honour. The Ghaziabad Corps did everything possible to make it a memorable feat. The leader of our contingent was Anwar Qureishi Sahib, a very sturdy young man, famous as the Poet of Pakistan these days. An anthem written by him was on the lips of all the young men of our corps. I do not know if we remained true to its mood and tempo. After all:

A plea has no rhythm
A cry no fixed pitch.

'The historic rally in the historic city of Delhi began at the historic Jama Masjid, from where it wound its way, spreading its powerful slogans through Chandni Chowk, Lal Kuan, Hauz Qazi, and Chawri Bazaar to its destination at the office of the Muslim League. It was during this historic procession that Muhammad Ali Jinnah Sahib was proclaimed the Quaid-e-Azam by a consensus with no force of law behind it. He made his passage through the city in a carriage drawn by six horses. Every worker and member of the Muslim League joined the rally with a multitude of cars, motorcycles, bicycles, and camels—the impeccable logistics delighted the Quaid-e-Azam, a person naturally inclined towards discipline.

'At various points during the procession, I caught several glimpses of the Quaid-e-Azam. I was not quite sure of my first reaction, but upon reflection, all I can say is that goodwill has no colour. At the time, you could have pointed at any person and told me, "This is your Quaid-e-Azam," and I would have given him a place of honour in my heart. Admittedly, I felt a dent in my self-confidence. My Quaid-e-Azam—so, so lean, and so frail! But as Ghalib once said:

It is God's will my love visits my house
I gaze at my love and look at my house.

'It was God's will and generous of my beloved to visit my house, but by God when I compared his frail body with my hardy physique, I wished that either I shrink or he expands. I prayed to God to protect his delicate frame from the evil eye. Everyone knew his enemies had inflicted many wounds on him.

'It so happened that the larva of art dormant in my mind for some time slowly took a turn. Drawn to drama since childhood, I thought if I get to Bombay, I might get an opportunity to test my talent. I am not sure how to square my desire to serve the nation and its people with an obsession for acting. Ah well, a human being is a combination of many peculiar traits.

'When I arrived in Bombay, the Imperial Film Company was at its peak, and it was tough to get a foot in through the door. Still, I managed to wriggle my way in as an extra and worked for eight annas a day nurturing dreams that one day I, too, shall rise to stardom in the firmament of films. By the grace of Allah, I have the gift of the gab, and although not eloquent, I am not incoherent. Urdu is my mother tongue, and it came to my rescue in Bombay. My proficiency in Urdu did not stand out in Delhi, but the film stars at the Imperial Film Company were enamoured by the language, although they did not know the first thing about it. I was asked to write daily logs of their activities, which I had to read back to them. Whenever they received a letter in Urdu, I was called upon to interpret its meaning and write an appropriate response. Yet, this unpaid job as their munshi and letter writer did not yield any tangible reward. I was an extra and remained an extra.

'It was at the Imperial Film Company that I struck up a friendship with Budhan, Ardeshir Irani's most favoured chauffeur. He proved his true worth as a friend by teaching me how to drive during his free hours. Budhan feared the consequences of his seth learning of his misconduct and restricted the time for my lessons. Consequently, I did not master the art of driving a motor car. To master the art of driving is a tall claim, you could say that Budhan taught me how to drive Ardeshir Irani's Buick on a road as straight as an aleph. My knowledge about the spare parts and technology of a car was zero.

'The acting bug that brought me to Bombay had infected my head, but the permanent resident of my heart was the Muslim League and its soul, the Quaid-e-Azam Muhammad Ali Jinnah. It did not matter whether I was at the Imperial Film Company, at the Play House in Bhendi Bazaar or Mohammad Ali Road. When talk came up of the Congress and its attitude towards Muslims, everyone knew I was a diehard supporter of the Muslim League.

'Those were the days when a Hindu did not want to kill a person for merely mentioning the Quaid-e-Azam's name. Demand for the creation of Pakistan was not commonplace at the time. When people at the Imperial Film Company heard me praise the Quaid-e-Azam, they thought he was also some film hero that I worshipped. One morning, D. Billimoria, the top film hero of the day, handed me a copy of the *Times of India*, and said, "Here, my dear, your Jinnah Sahib."

'I thought Billimoria was referring to a photograph and took the newspaper from him. I turned its pages, but could not find the image, and turned to Billimoria, "Why, dear fellow, where's the photograph?"

'Billimoria's John Gilbert-style pencil moustache stretched across his upper lip as he smiled, "No photo-voto, it's his advertisement."

'"Advertisement? What advertisement?" I asked.

'Billimoria took the newspaper, pointed to a long column, and said, "Mr Jinnah needs a car mechanic who will oversee the entire work of his garage."

'I looked at the place where Billimoria had put his finger, and said, "Oh," in a manner that seemed to indicate that I had read the entire advertisement in a single glance. The truth of the matter is that my knowledge of English was as extensive as Billimoria's knowledge of Urdu.

'As I said earlier, my driving skills were limited to driving on a road as straight as an aleph. Knock me down if I knew the first thing about the mechanism of a car, or why an engine starts when you press the self. If somebody had asked me these questions, I would have said it's a simple rule of motor cars and human intelligence has nothing to do with it. You will find it astonishing that I asked Billimoria for the address and details of Jinnah Sahib's house and noted them down. I had made up my mind to make my way there the following morning, not with any intention to seek employment. I did not entertain any hopes in that quarter; I simply wished to see the Quaid-e-Azam at close quarters in his residence.

'Taking my good intentions along as a diploma, I arrived at the Quaid-e-Azam's grand house on Mount Pleasant Road on Malabar Hill. At the gate, I saw a Pathan chowkidar kitted out in a white shalwar made of several bales of cloth and a grand silken turban on his head. It warmed my heart to see him. When I calculated his girth, it satisfied me to no end because the difference was merely around half an inch in comparison to mine!

'Several hopefuls had arrived before me, all with their credentials tucked under their arms. I joined them. Forget credentials; I did not even have an ordinary driving licence. My heart was beating solely at the thought that soon I was going to have an audience with the Quaid-e-Azam. I was thinking about my heartbeat when the Quaid-e-Azam appeared on the porch, accompanied by his tall and slim sister, of whom I had seen several photographs in newspapers and magazines. And ever so slightly away from them stood Matloob Sahib, his respectful secretary. I stood to attention with all the hopefuls but shrank to one side. Jinnah Sahib adjusted his monocle and scrutinized all the applicants. When his gaze turned towards me, I shrank a little further. Immediately, his penetrating voice rose slowly, and all I heard was, "You…"

'I knew enough English to understand that he meant "tum" in Urdu, but who was the "You" he had addressed? I thought it was the person standing next to me, and I nudged him and said, "Say something. He is addressing you."

'My companion asked hesitantly, "Sahib, me?"

'The Quaid-e-Azam's voice rose again, "No. You."

'He pointed his thin but firm iron finger at me. My entire body prickled, "Sir...sir, I?"

'"Yes!"

'I felt a couple of .303 bullets pierce my heart and throat. The throat that never failed to raise slogans in support of the Quaid-e-Azam went dry, unable to utter a word. When he took off his monocle and said, "All right..." I thought, perhaps, he heard me and had figured out my dilemma and said "All right", to protect me from the painful outcome of my folly.

'He turned around and said something to his fit and handsome secretary, after which he stepped inside with his sister. I gathered my thoughts and emotions and was about to leave when Matloob Sahib walked up to me and said, "Sahib has asked you to present yourself on duty at ten o'clock tomorrow morning."

'I could not bring myself to ask Matloob Sahib the million-dollar question, "Why has Sahib summoned me?" Nor did I find it in me to tell him that I was unworthy of the summons; I was not qualified for the post the Quaid-e-Azam had advertised. He, too, went inside the house, and I returned home. The following morning, once again, I presented myself at the august door, and the fit, handsome, and elegant secretary stepped out into the veranda to give me the astonishing news that Sahib had selected me. He told me to take charge of the garage immediately. I wanted to reveal the secret of my incompetence. I wished to say quite plainly that His Eminence the Quaid-e-Azam was mistaken about my abilities. I wanted to say, "I came along for mere amusement. Why are you placing the weight of the garage on the shoulders of this unqualified man?" I am not sure why I remained silent, but as a result, abracadabra, I was made the boss of the garage, and Matloob Sahib handed the keys over to me. There were four cars of different makes, and all I knew was how to drive Seth Ardeshir Irani's Buick—and that too on a road as straight as an aleph.

'There were several twists and turns on the road to Malabar

Hill, and I did not have to only drive myself around Bombay to God knows how many vital assignments, but the Leader whose life was tied to the future of countless Muslims. The first thought that came to mind was to leave the keys etc., and beat a retreat—collect my luggage, get a ticket, and head to Delhi, but I thought this most inappropriate. I reckoned I should tell Jinnah Sahib the unexpurgated truth and apologize like a decent human being before I headed back to where I belonged. You must believe me when I tell you that I didn't get an opportunity to do this for six months.'

'How come?' I asked.

Mohammad Hanif Azad replied, 'Please hear me out. The following day an order was issued for Azad to bring the car. I decided that the moment Sahib appeared I would greet him with a salaam, hand over the keys of the garage to him, and fall at his feet. These intentions did not materialize because when he appeared on the porch, his presence was so powerful that this useless man became tongue-tied. Moreover, Miss Fatima Jinnah was with him. I mean, to fall at someone's feet in the presence of a woman, Manto Sahib, just felt a bit...'

Azad's large eyes were bloodshot with shame. I smiled to comfort him and asked, 'Well, then what happened?'

'Well, Manto Sahib, what happened was that I had to start the car. I took Allah's name, and somehow or the other, managed to steer it out of the driveway with great precision. As I drove down Malabar Hill and reached the turning of the traffic light—you understand the one I'm referring to—the signal was red.'

I shook my head in the affirmative.

'Well, Sahib, at the traffic light, I encountered a problem. Ustad Budhan had taught me how to apply the brake, but in a state of nervous confusion, I applied the brake in such an amateur fashion that the car jolted to a halt. The Quaid-e-Azam's cigar fell out of his hand; and as she put her foot forward to steady herself, Fatima Jinnah Sahiba began to swear at me. The blood froze in my body, my hands began to tremble, and my brain went into a spin. The Quaid-e-Azam picked up his cigar and said something in English, which meant, "Take us back." I followed his orders. He asked for another car and another driver and went wherever he had to go.

After this episode, I had the opportunity to serve him for the next six months.'

I smiled and asked, 'You continued to serve him in the same manner?'

Azad smiled back, 'Yes, but you could say that Sahib gave me no opportunity to repeat my mistake. There were other drivers. They, too, wore the same uniform and at night Matloob Sahib told us which driver and what car was on duty the following morning. Nobody could question Sahib about anything because everything he said had a purpose. Although I was in such proximity to him, I could not figure out why he had appointed me as the quaid of his garage, and subsequently cast me aside like a useless spare part.'

I said to Azad, 'Perhaps, he forgot all about you.'

A hearty laugh erupted from Azad's throat, 'No, my dear, Sahib did not forget. He never forgot. He knew full well that for the past six months, Azad the freeloader is sitting idle in the garage. And Manto Sahib, when Azad freeloads it's no ordinary freeloading—look at the size and weight of this body!'

I looked at Azad. Who knows the size and weight of his body in 1937–1938? A decade later in Karachi, I found a reasonably stolid hunk of a man. You must know him as an actor; before Partition, he worked in Bombay films. These days, in Lahore with his fellow actors, he is trying to ensure the downfall of the local film industry.

Before I met Azad in Bombay, I had heard from a friend that the Quaid-e-Azam Muhammad Ali Jinnah had employed a dark-complexioned, large-eyed, broad-built actor as a driver. From that day onwards, I kept an eye out for him, and whenever I met him, I touched upon the subject of his master and filed his stories in my memory bank. Yesterday, I went to meet him with this in my mind, and he recounted several incidents I was familiar with, but plenty of new and exciting facets of the Quaid-e-Azam's life came to light.

One aspect of the Quaid-e-Azam's personality left a deep imprint on Azad's mind. He thought that just as Allama Iqbal preferred everything tall and lofty, his master the Quaid-e-Azam favoured all things robust and sturdy. Mohammad Hanif Azad reminded me that the Quaid-e-Azam's secretary, Matloob, was a well-built and handsome man. All his drivers were embodiments of perfect health, and the household staff was appointed with similar considerations in mind. What were the possible psychological reasons for this? The late Mr Jinnah, who was physically frail but had a strong personality, did not like anything insubstantial and decrepit around him. Come to think of it, the frailty of his body added strength to his unbending impressive demeanour and comportment. How he walked and strolled, stood up or sat down, ate and drank, spoke and thought—in short, all his actions revealed his strength.

Usually, a person pays meticulous attention to the style and appearance of anything dear to him, and the Quaid-e-Azam was fastidious when it came to the apparel of every member of his household. The Pathan chowkidar had instructions to wear his national dress on duty. Although Azad was not a Punjabi, at times he, too, was required to wear a turban, a particularly noteworthy headgear because it adds several attractive inches to the wearer's height, and this pleased his master. The latter usually awarded him a token gratuity when he saw him thus attired.

Mohammad Hanif Azad informed me that the Quaid-e-Azam had a simple diet, 'He ate so little that at times I wondered how he survived. If I were kept on that diet, without a doubt, within a day, my fat would begin to melt. Every day, the kitchen staff ritually slaughtered four or five poussins, and the broth of one was served to Sahib in a small cup. Large quantities of fruit were bought every day, but all went into the stomachs of the household staff.' Azad continued, 'Every night, Sahib placed a tick against items of food and drink on a list and handed me a hundred-rupee note for expenses for the following day.'

I asked Azad, 'Every day, a hundred rupees?'

'Yes, a full hundred, and the Quaid-e-Azam never asked for an account. At times, the daily balance was thirty, at others forty, and occasionally, even sixty and seventy, and this was divided among the staff. Sahib understood we creamed off a lot of money but never mentioned it, though Miss Jinnah was very sharp and often furious. She called us thieves who claimed a rupee for something worth one anna. At such moments, Sahib would say to his sister, "It is all right, it is all right," and the matter ended. Sahib's response made us deaf to his sister's rants because we thought what belonged to him was ours.

'Once, the matter did not end after Sahib said, "It is all right," and Mohtrama Miss Jinnah fired the cooks—not just one cook but both cooks because the Quaid-e-Azam kept not one but two cooks in his kitchen. One, who excelled in Hindustani cuisines and another, an expert in European cuisines. Usually, the Hindustani chef sat idle, his turn came up all too rarely after months of sitting around when he was asked to prepare a Hindustani menu, but the Quaid-e-Azam did not enjoy this food.'

Azad told me, 'Sahib did not comment when Miss Jinnah fired both cooks. He did not interfere in his sister's domain. For several days, he ate both meals at the Taj Mahal Hotel, and during this time all of us made merry. We took a car from the garage to head out in search of new cooks and roamed the city for hours and returned home to announce our failure to find a suitable person. Finally, on Miss Jinnah's advice, Sahib asked the old cooks to return.

'Often, a person with a small appetite is either squeamish at the sight of others stuffing themselves or delighted. The Quaid-e-Azam was from the second tribe. His pleasure at feeding others was heartfelt, and this was why he gave us a hundred rupees every day and forgot about the accounts; this does not mean he was wasteful.'

Mohammad Hanif Azad related another curious episode.

'It was 1937. One evening I was driving him along Worli Sea Face in his white Packard. The waves were tapping lightly against the shore, and there was a pleasant chill in the air. Sahib was in an excellent mood. I thought this an opportune moment and touched upon the subject of Eid, the meaning of which was obvious. In the rear-view mirror, I could see from the thin smile across Sahib's lips that he had caught on immediately. He removed the inseparable cigar from his mouth and said in his broken Hindustani, "Oh well, well, you've become an ek dum Muslim, now try and become a little Hindu."'

I learnt from Azad that four days before the drive along Worli Sea Face, the Quaid-e-Azam had confirmed him a Muslim, so to speak, by giving him two one-hundred-rupee notes for Eid; and that was the reason for his advice to Azad to become a little Hindu. It seems the Quaid-e-Azam's words had little effect on Azad because that same Eid, to claim his status as a Muslim, he went to see the film producer Sayyid Mustafa Jillani. That is where I first met him and got some information to write this essay.

Everyone knows that the record of the Quaid-e-Azam's personal life at home is hidden and will remain unknown. As far as I can see, the personal and political were so entangled in his life that their contours are lost. There was a wife, separated from him for some time. There was a daughter who had married a Parsi against his wishes. We can only say, from what we have learnt from external sources, that the Quaid-e-Azam was distraught. Mohammad Hanif Azad told me, 'Sahib was deeply saddened by this. It was his wish that she marry a Muslim, albeit from any race. His daughter presented the argument that when Sahib had full freedom to choose his life's partner, why didn't he grant her the same freedom?'

It was common knowledge that the Quaid-e-Azam had married the daughter of a very grand Bombay Parsi. Very few people know that the Parsis were very unhappy with this match. They wished and endeavoured to seek revenge from Jinnah Sahib. Those suspicious about everything concluded that the Quaid-e-Azam's daughter's marriage to a Parsi was the result of an organized Parsi conspiracy. When I mentioned this to Azad, he said, 'God alone knows, but I do know that in Sahib's life, after his wife's death, this was the second big tragedy. He was deeply affected when his daughter married a Parsi. His face was so expressive that the most ordinary incident left an imprint that others could see; the light furrow on his brow deepened into a frightening mark of sorrow. Only the deceased can tell us what his heart and mind endured because of this event. For more than a fortnight, he remained secluded and did not meet anyone; smoked many cigars and walked hundreds of miles as he paced up and down in his room.

'When he made an appearance after fifteen consecutive days of mental and spiritual distraction, no signs of the tragedy were visible on his face. His neck, which had developed a slight tilt because of the burden of sorrow, now was erect as always. But don't take these outward manifestations as signs that he had forgotten the tragedy.'

When Azad mentioned this tragedy in the Quaid-e-Azam's life in another conversation, I asked him, 'How did you find out that he did not forget this tragedy?'

Azad replied, 'What can remain hidden from the household staff? From time to time, he ordered the staff to bring out and open a large cabin trunk full of clothes that belonged to his late wife, and his disobedient daughter from the days when she was a toddler. Sahib had the clothes taken out and looked at them in stony silence, his sorrow apparent in the deep furrows that spread like a web across his slim spotless face.'

According to Azad's account, the Quaid-e-Azam paced up and down in his private chamber in a thoughtful mood. In the silence of the night, he strolled for hours in measured steps on the hard, spotless wooden floor, his black and white or brown and white shoes producing a curious tapping rhythm in an even tempo like a clock that marks time. The Quaid-e-Azam loved his shoes because they walked at his behest.

I learned from Azad that the Quaid-e-Azam had three sisters, 'Fatima Jinnah, Rehmat Jinnah, and I do not recall the name of the third. I believe she lived in Dongri. Rehmat Jinnah lived in Chowpatty Corner near Chinoy Motor Works. Her husband was employed somewhere on a meagre salary. Every month, Sahib gave me a sealed envelope with some paper currency. At times, I had to deliver parcels; I think they contained some clothes. From time to time, Miss Fatima Jinnah and Sahib visited Rehmat Jinnah. The sister who lived in Dongri was also married. All I know about her was that she was comfortably off and did not require any assistance.'

Azad told me, 'There was a brother, whom Sahib helped regularly, but did not permit inside his house.'

I had seen the Quaid-e-Azam's brother one evening at the Savoy Bar in Bombay, and his face resembled the Quaid-e-Azam's—the same features, the same style of brushing his hair back, and almost the same strands of grey hair. He was ordering half a peg of rum. I asked someone and discovered that he was Mr Muhammad Ali Jinnah's brother, Ahmed Ali. I observed him for some time, sipping a peg of rum in a grand leisurely style. He settled the less than one-rupee tab as though he was paying out a substantial sum. From his manner, you would think he was sitting at the Taj Mahal Hotel and not in one of Bombay's lowly bars. A friend told me that sometime before the historic meeting between Gandhi and Jinnah, there was an important convention of Muslims in Bombay. When the Quaid-e-Azam was on stage, delivering his speech in his singular style, my friend spotted Mr Jinnah's brother, Ahmed Ali, standing in a far corner; sporting a monocle, he looked as though he was chewing his brother's words under his teeth.

Azad informed me, 'Among indoor games, the Quaid-e-Azam was only interested in billiards. I had permission to go into the billiards room because I, too, had a little interest in the game. Occasionally, when Sahib wished to indulge in the game, he ordered the billiards room to be opened. As it happened, all the rooms were cleaned and dusted every day, but if Sahib expressed a desire to visit a room, the staff made sure that everything was spotless and in its proper place before he entered the room.

'Often, Mohtrama Fatima Jinnah was with him, and Sahib chose one from among the twelve balls presented to him and started play. Sahib lit his cigar and pressed it between his lips while assessing the exact position of the ball he was about to strike. After the Quaid-e-Azam fixed his aim, he took several minutes to consider the situation from one angle and then from another. Sahib weighed the cue by moving his slim fingers along it like a musician feels the bow of his sarangi, and muttered sotto voce. If a more appropriate angle came to mind, Sahib curbed his move and struck the cue against the ball after a full evaluation. Invariably, the outcome proved spot on, and he turned to his sister with a smile and a victorious gleam in his eyes. In the game of politics, too, the Quaid-e-Azam was equally cautious and did not take impulsive decisions. He brought his cue into play when certain that his move would be advantageous. Before he struck, he observed every aspect and selected his firearm in response to the opponents' logistics. He was an exceptional marksman.'

According to Azad, the Quaid-e-Azam was allergic to random socializing and pointless chit-chat.

'He only spoke with a specific purpose, and there too, he exercised economy, and listened very carefully. Very few people were allowed into his private sitting room, sparsely furnished with one sofa and a small vintage table with an ashtray into which Sahib flicked the ash from his cigars. Next to the sofa stood two cabinets that held his papers, filed securely, and two Holy Qur'ans presented to him by his admirers.

'Generally, Sahib spent most of his time in this private room in which there was no desk. The papers he was perusing were scattered on one half of the sofa, and if he had to dictate a letter or a statement, he summoned Matloob or the stenographer. The person summoned remained standing in the doorway, from where he listened to Sahib's orders and left walking backwards. His accent was firm. I am not familiar with the temperament of the English language, but it seemed to me that he stressed syllables not usually stressed by Indian speakers of English.'

From Azad's statements, it seems that the unconscious and subconscious effects of the Quaid-e-Azam's physical weakness made him appear harsh. His physique was fragile but he gave the impression of a man who could confront a cyclone. Some people believe that he lived for as long as he did because of the strength he derived from the knowledge that his body was weak.

According to Mohammad Hanif Azad's account, the late Bahadur Yar Jung was among the Quaid-e-Azam's most cherished friends. It was only with him that he interacted informally. Whenever he stayed in the house, the two men discussed national and political matters with affable sincerity, and for some time, the Quaid-e-Azam set aside his imperious traits.

'This is the sole person with whom I have seen Sahib interact as a friend. You'd think the two of them were childhood buddies. When they talked to each other, often we heard loud and carefree laughter through the heavy closed doors. Apart from Bahadur Yar Jung, other frequent visitors included Muslim League leaders such as Raja Mahmudabad, I. I. Chundrigar, Maulana Zahid Hussain, Nawabzada Liaquat Ali Khan, Nawab Ismail, and Ali Imam Sahib. Still, Sahib always met them with official detachment—where was that informality reserved for Bahadur Yar Jang!'

I asked Azad, 'Nawabzada Liaquat Ali Khan must have been a frequent visitor.'

Azad replied, 'Yes. Sahib treated him as his most brilliant pupil. And Khan Sahib too listened to him and followed his instructions with deference and diligence. When summoned, occasionally he would ask,

"Tell me, Azad, how is Sahib's mood today?" And I would inform him of Sahib's disposition.' When something was amiss, the entire bricks and mortar of the house became aware of it.

'The Quaid-e-Azam was very particular about the character and conduct of his household staff. He loathed an unwashed body, and equally, could not stand a soiled heart. He was very fond of Matloob but was distressed to hear of his affair with a Razakar girl. He did not put up with such irritants for long; he summoned Matloob and removed him from his employment. Still, after his dismissal, the Quaid-e-Azam continued to treat him as he would a friend.'

Azad told me that once after a night out, he returned to the house at two o'clock in the morning.

'Those were the days when I felt a strange thrill in bringing to the boil the young blood that coursed through my veins. I thought Sahib did not have a clue of my late nights, but somehow, he found out. The following day he summoned me, and I was told in English, that I was ruining my character. And then in broken Urdu, Sahib said, "Well, now I'll make your marriage." Four months later, when in Delhi for a convention, he gave instructions to fix my marriage. It was my good fortune that through Sahib's good offices, I was betrothed into a Sayyid family, although I am a Shaikh. The girl's family accepted me for no other reason than that I was the Quaid-e-Azam's servant.'

I turned to Azad and asked him quite arbitrarily, 'Did you ever hear the Quaid-e-Azam utter the words "I am sorry"?'

Azad shook his strong fat neck in negation, 'No. Never', and he smiled, 'If on the off chance the words, "I am sorry" had come out of his mouth, he would have had them erased from the dictionary.'

I think this sentence sums up the Quaid-e-Azam Muhammad Ali Jinnah's entire personality.

Mohammad Hanif is alive in Pakistan—a gift to him from the Quaid-e-Azam—a country struggling to survive on the map of the world under the leadership of the Quaid-e-Azam's able pupil Liaquat Ali Khan. In this free (azad) land, I found Azad sitting on a rickety charpai in front of a paan shop near the entrance to Punjab Art

Pictures. He did not even have money to buy a paan. Yet, with his hands raised in prayer, he awaits the good times when he will get his salary on time. He is willing to follow the Quaid-e-Azam's suggestion to become a little Hindu, given the opportunity to do so.

When I asked Azad some further questions about the Quaid-e-Azam's life, he looked troubled. I tried to dispel his anxieties and began to talk about this and that. He heaved a huge sigh, 'Sahib has gone to the other world; how I wish I were with him on his final journey—in his white Packard, with my hands on its steering wheel. I would have driven him with care to his destination. I know his discerning disposition did not care for bumpy rides. I have heard, and Allah Almighty knows if this is true or false, that when his plane landed at the aerodrome in Karachi, the engine of the ambulance that drove him from there to the Government House broke down en route. How downcast my Sahib must have felt at the time!'

Azad's eyes brimmed over.

## Mummy

She was an elderly lady of medium height, and her name was Mrs Stella Jackson, but everyone called her Mummy. Her husband, Jackson, died in the Great War, and Stella was receiving his pension for almost ten years now. I haven't a clue how she got to Poona or for how long she had lived there. Frankly, I made no effort to uncover her antecedents because on meeting her, a person lost interest in everything other than her enigmatic personality. To say that Mummy was connected to every bit of Poona might seem an exaggeration. Still, Poona is the Poona of my recollections—and for me, every memory summons the outlandish Mummy, and I first met her in Poona.

I am a sluggish individual, but my heart always longs to travel. If you were to hear me talk, you would think that I am about to embark post-haste on a mission to conquer Kanchenjunga or some peak in the Himalaya with a similar name. While this feat is a remote possibility, if I were to capture a mountain, it is more likely that I would merge with its summit forever. God alone knows how many years I had spent in Bombay. And in almost a decade in the city, although I always intended to do so, I never visited Victoria Gardens or the museum.

I decided to travel to Poona on a whim after a pointless disagreement with the proprietors of the film company where I worked. I thought a trip to Poona would help assuage my anger. Perhaps, the idea was triggered by the twin facts that Poona was not too far and a few friends lived there. My wife and I were heading to Prabhat Nagar, where an old film associate of mine lived, but it was after we hired a rattletrap of a tonga that we discovered our destination was quite far. Far worse than any tonga I'd seen in Aligarh: it was the type in which passengers sit in perpetual fear of being thrown off because when the horse lunges forward towards the north, they are facing south sitting on narrow sloping seats in an open carriage.

I had come to Poona to cleanse my heart of anger and was in no real hurry to get to Prabhat Nagar, but with an inherent mistrust of anything that moves at a slow pace, I became fidgety. Our progress through several dusty bazaars was in prolonged slow motion. So I consulted my sensible wife about the best course of action under the circumstances. She said, 'The sun is blazing hot. Besides, the few other tongas I have seen are much the same. If we give up this one, we shall have to walk, which obviously will be far worse than the ride.'

I thought it unwise to disagree with her—the sun was blazing hot.

The horse had covered about a furlong when an equally ramshackle tonga drove past us; I was giving it a cursory look when someone shouted, 'Oye, Manto's horse!'

I gave a start when I saw Chadda and a jaded white woman huddled close to each other. My first reaction was one of dismay as I wondered what on earth had happened to Chadda's sense of aesthetics. Why was he hanging out with an old hag who was behaving like a filly? It was a challenge to figure out the woman's age, but her wrinkles were peering out through layers of powder and paint.

Chadda was an old friend with whom I had a warm and candid relationship. I had not met him for ages but I am sure that in response to 'Oye, Manto's horse!' I must have responded with a similar greeting. But after I saw his female companion, my enthusiasm scrunched up like her wrinkles.

Nonetheless, I asked my tongawallah to stop, and Chadda asked his tongawallah to stop. As he jumped off the tonga, he addressed the woman in English, 'Mummy, just a minute,' and stretched out his arm to offer me his hand as he bellowed, 'You...what are you doing here?' Chadda directed his outstretched arm to shake, with great warmth, my rather formal wife's hand, as he added with an air of familiarity, 'Bhabijan, what a miracle. Finally, you managed to drag this Gul Muhammad here.'

I asked him, 'Where are you off to?'

Chadda bellowed, 'I have some work, but you must head straight...' He turned to our tongawallah and continued, 'Look here, take Sahib straight to my house. And don't charge any fare-share.'

Now, Chadda turned to me in a manner that viewed the matter

as settled. 'Off you go! You'll find a servant there, and you can sort out the rest.'

He leapt back into his tonga and sat next to the old white woman whom he had called 'Mummy'. I felt enormous relief.

Chadda's tonga drove off. I did not need to say anything to our tongawallah. After three or four furlongs, he stopped by a dak bungalow-like structure and alighted, saying, 'Sahib, let's go...'

'Where?' I asked.

'This is Chadda Sahib's house,' he responded.

'Oh?' I gave my wife an enquiring look. We'd been married for five years, and I could tell from her expression that she was not in favour of Chadda Sahib's house. If truth be told, she did not like the idea of our trip to Poona because she knew I would find drinking buddies and use my Bombay problems as an excuse to drink night and day. I climbed out of the tonga and lifted our small attaché case before I turned to her and said, 'Let's go.'

She figured she had little choice in the matter and accompanied me without a word of protest.

The bungalow was a simple structure in an abysmal state of disrepair. With its lime and gypsum plaster peeling off in several places, it looked like temporary accommodation built and abandoned by the military. All the doors were wide open and we entered Chadda's house. The disarray was what you would expect of a careless bachelor, a film hero employed by a company that paid his salary after three months, and that, too, in instalments. I knew any wife would suffocate in these shabby surroundings but thought it best to await Chadda's return. He could accompany us to Prabhat Nagar, where my old colleague from the movies lived with his wife and children, and where my wife would spend a few days without feeling like a lamb led to the sacrifice.

Chadda's servant was not around, but when he returned, he turned out to be a peculiar couldn't-care-less type of chap. He walked in and took not the slightest notice of our presence. We were strangers, but he walked past without acknowledging our presence as though we were permanent fixtures in the house. I thought he was some minor actor living with Chadda. When I asked him about the servant, I discovered that His Eminence was Chadda Sahib's cherished servant.

My wife and I were thirsty and asked him for some water. He began his search for a glass, and after what felt like an age, he pulled out a chipped mug from the bottom of a cupboard and muttered, 'Sahib sent for a dozen glasses last night. Wonder where they've disappeared...'

I pointed to the wreck of a mug in his hand and asked, 'Are you off to get oil?'

'To get oil' is a unique Bombay metaphor, and though my wife did not know what it meant, she laughed out loud. The servant looked baffled, 'No, sir, I was looking for glasses.'

My wife told him to forget the water, and he put the chipped mug back under the cupboard with exceptional care as though the entire household would fall apart if he were to keep it elsewhere. He fled the room, looking convinced that we were going to bite him.

I sat down on a bed which I thought was Chadda's. At some distance from it stood two armchairs, and my wife sank into one, restlessly shifting her weight from one side to the other. We sat in silence for several hours, and finally, Chadda arrived. He was on his own and showed no awareness of the fact that we were his guests, and as such, it was incumbent on him to be attentive. He walked into the room and addressed me, 'So, here you are, *old boy*! Come on, let's go to the studio for a bit. If you're with me, I might get an advance this evening...'

But that very moment, he remembered my wife and stopped midstream and began to laugh, 'Bhabijan, you haven't turned him into a maulvi!' He laughed some more, 'Down with maulvis! Stand up, Manto! Bhabijan will be fine here. We'll be back in a flash!'

My wife, who was already a smouldering ember, turned into proverbial ashes. I set off with Chadda hoping that she would fume for a bit and fall asleep—and that is what she did. The studio was nearby. In the frenetic buzz of everyday activity, Chadda managed to badger Mehtaji into giving him two hundred rupees. We returned after about fifteen minutes and did not think it proper to disturb my wife, who was fast asleep ensconced in an armchair.

We retired to another room that looked more like a junkyard, where every object was noticeably damaged and coated with dust. Still, everything, including the layers of dust, formed a perfect whole, integral to the bohemian character of the room. Chadda located his servant and handed him a hundred-rupee note with directions, 'Prince of Cathay, bring two bottles of third-class rum...I mean XXX rum and half a dozen glasses.'

I discovered that his servant was not merely the Prince of Cathay but became the prince of whichever country's name came to the tip of Chadda's tongue. Now, the Prince of Cathay, he took off, crackling a hundred rupees between his fingers.

Slouching on a bed with broken springs, Chadda smacked his lips at the thought of XXX and said, 'Then...*after all*, you made your way here,' but suddenly he remembered my wife and became anxious. 'Yaar, what's to become of Bhabi?'

Chadda, who did not have a wife, revered other men's wives and such was his reverence that he remained a bachelor. He explained, 'Low self-esteem has deprived me of this blessing for so long. Whenever the subject of marriage comes up, I agree like a shot but then it strikes me that I am unworthy of a wife and consign the entire matter to cold storage.'

The rum arrived in no time and the glasses too. Chadda had asked for six, but the Prince of Cathay brought three. Unquestionably, three broke en route, but Chadda did not seem to care, instead he thanked God the bottles were intact and rushed to open one. As he poured the rum into the unwashed uninitiated glasses, he said, 'To celebrate your visit to Poona!' We took hearty long swigs and emptied our glasses. Before we started the second round, Chadda went to the other room to check on my wife. His heart warmed to her, and he said, 'Let me make a bit of noise, and she'll wake up. But first, let me get some tea.' He sipped some rum and called the 'Prince of Jamaica', who arrived immediately. Chadda instructed him, 'Look here, ask Mummy to send *first-class* tea. Pronto!' The Prince of Jamaica went off. Chadda emptied his glass and poured another substantial peg, 'I shan't drink too much. The first four pegs always make me emotional, and I must go with you to Prabhat Nagar to drop Bhabi.'

After half an hour, tea arrived in a service of fine bone china arranged in genteel style. Chadda lifted the tea cosy to sniff the aroma and expressed his delight, '*Mummy is a jewel*!' But then, his wrath descended on the Prince of Ethiopia, and he made such a racket that my ears began to ring. When done with his tirade, he lifted the tray, turned to me, and said, 'Let's go wake up Bhabi!'

My wife was awake. Chadda put the tray down on the teetering teapoy with utmost care and said, 'At your service, Begum Sahib!'

My wife did not care for his jest, but when she saw the immaculate tea service, she accepted his offer and drank two cups and found them most agreeable. She looked at both of us and said in a meaningful tone, 'You must have drunk your tea by now!'

I did not respond, but Chadda declared in all honesty, 'Yes, we've erred, but we are sure you will forgive us.'

When my wife smiled, he gurgled and continued, 'The two of us are swine of the finest breed; for us, everything that is haram is halal. Come, let's take you to the mosque.'

My wife did not care for Chadda's joke. She loathed Chadda. You could say that she disliked all my friends but found Chadda particularly irksome because, at times, he crossed the limits of informality. Chadda did not give such matters a thought, and considered etiquette a pointless indoor game, more meaningless than ludo. He scrutinized my wife's roasted expression with his bright eyes and called his servant, 'Prince of Kebabistan, get a tonga of the Rolls-Royce kind!'

The Prince of Kebabistan took off, as did Chadda.

After Chadda left and we had some time to ourselves, I tried to explain to my wife that there was no need for her to feel and look like a grilled kebab. Occasionally in life, people must confront unforeseen situations, and the best way to deal with them is to let them pass. Of course, as always, she did not accept my Confucian advice and continued to mutter. Soon, the Prince of Kebabistan arrived with the Rolls-Royce tonga, and we set off for Prabhat Nagar.

It was just as well that my old colleague from the movies was not at home, but his wife was, and Chadda handed my wife over to her, saying, 'Like two peas in a pod, the two wives no doubt will have fun together.' He turned to me and said, 'Come on, Manto, let's find your friend in the studio.'

Chadda was an expert at creating confusion of the kind that did not give the opposition time to think about what was afoot. He caught hold of my arm and dragged me out, leaving my wife to her thoughts. Once back in the tonga, he turned to me, 'Ah well, now what's the programme?' and burst out laughing as he added 'Mummy...great Mummy!'

I was about to ask which Tutankhamun was the ancestor of the Poona Mummy when Chadda launched into such an endless stream of pointless conversation that my questions died a natural death. The tonga returned to Saeeda Cottage, the house that looked like a dak bungalow. I thought it got its name because everyone living in Saeeda Cottage had problems and were indebted to Chadda—and Saeed means good fortune. I discovered this was not the case.

Although at first, Saeeda Cottage looked uninhabited, several people lived there. They worked for the same film company that paid their salaries every three months and that too in several instalments. When I met all the inhabitants of Saeeda Cottage, I discovered that other than the actors, every one of them was an assistant director. Someone was an assistant director, and someone else was his assistant's assistant, although by their attire and demeanour, all could pass off as heroes. Among them, some assistant's assistants were saving money, hoping to lay the foundation of their own film company. Although it was an era of controls, none of the inhabitants of Saeeda Cottage had ration cards; they bought whatever they could on the black market and at what they thought was a reasonable price. All of them were keen cinemagoers, and during the racing season, they liked to place bets. Out of season, they speculated. Rarely did they win but they lost something every day.

The density of population at Saeeda Cottage meant there was a shortage of space. Even the garage was used as a dwelling for the family of a woman called Shireen, whose husband was not an assistant—perhaps, to break the monotony—he worked for the same film company but as a driver. I had no idea when he left the garage or when he returned because I never saw this good man around. Shireen had produced a little boy, cosseted by all the inhabitants of Saeeda Cottage whenever they had a free moment. Shireen, who spent most of her time in the garage, was perfectly acceptable in the looks department.

The less rundown part of the cottage was with Chadda and his two companions, who were actors, but not heroes. One was Saeed, whose screen name was Ranjit Kumar, and from time to time, Chadda liked to remind everyone, 'Saeeda Cottage is famous by this bastard's name; otherwise, its name was Kabeda Cottage, or Cottage of the Troubled.' Saeed was a handsome man of few words. Occasionally, Chadda referred to him as 'The Tortoise' because he was rather slow at whatever he did. I do not know the other actor's name because everyone called him Gharib Nawaz, or Benefactor of the Poor. He belonged to an ordinary Hyderabadi family and had come to Poona to fulfil his dream to act. The studio had fixed his salary at two-hundred-and-fifty rupees a month, but all he had received in almost a year was an advance of two-hundred-and-fifty rupees—and that too because Chadda had to pay back a loan to a bloodthirsty Pathan. Gharib Nawaz enjoyed writing screenplays in a high literary style and occasionally composed an acceptable couplet. Every inhabitant of Saeeda Cottage owed him money.

And there were two brothers, Shakeel and Aqeel, both assistants to some assistant director, who were trying hard to make a name. The three seniors—Chadda, Saeed, and Gharib Nawaz—looked after Shireen but at no time did the trio visit the garage together. There was no fixed time for these men to call on her, but whenever the three men were sitting together in the large room, one walked out to the garage to discuss household matters with Shireen, while the other two remained engrossed in whatever they were doing. The assistants ran Shireen's errands—they did her groceries, delivered her laundry, and lulled her boy when he wailed. Nobody in Saeeda Cottage looked deprived, all seemed quite content. Undeniably, their lifestyle was extraordinary.

As we entered the gate of the cottage, Gharib Nawaz was stepping out, and Chadda pulled out some paper money from his pocket and handed it to him without counting. 'We need four bottles of Scotch. Please make up the difference. If there's any change, I want it back.'

A thoughtful smile descended on Gharib Nawaz's dark Hyderabadi lips. Chadda chuckled as he looked at me but addressed Gharib Nawaz, 'You don't have time for a proper introduction,' he looked at me and added, 'He's been drinking rum; let's get Scotch for the evening. You better go now.'

Gharib Nawaz went off, and we walked in.

Chadda yawned as he picked up the more than half-empty bottle of rum and held it up to the light to gauge the quantity and called his servant, 'Prince of Qamazistan!' When the Prince did not show up, Chadda poured a double peg into his glass and told me, 'The wretch has had too much to drink!' After he finished his drink, he added with distinct anxiety, 'Yaar, I'm sure you've brought Bhabi here for a good reason, but I swear upon God, my heart feels heavy thinking about her.' To reassure himself, he continued, 'But I don't think she'll get bored there.'

'Yes,' I said, as I poured myself some rum that tasted like rancid gur, and added, 'besides when she's there, she can't carry out her plans to murder me forthwith.'

The junk room where we were sitting had two windows that looked out onto a large empty maidan from where we heard somebody shouting for Chadda at the top of his voice. Startled, I looked out through the iron bars of the windows and discovered it was the music director Venkat Atre. It was impossible to figure out Atre's pedigree. Was he Mongol, Black, Aryan, or some other-worldly creature? Occasionally, when you are about to reach a conclusion, some feature of his face becomes more prominent than others, and you have to revise your opinion.

Nonetheless, Venkat Atre was a Maratha, but instead of Shivaji's straight sharp nose, his was astonishingly gnarled and flat. According to him, this is what enabled him to sing on a singularly nasal pitch. When Venkat Atre saw me, he hollered, 'Manto! Manto Seth!'

Chadda yelled back even louder, 'To hell with Seth, come on in.'

In next to no time, Venkat Atre was with us; he laughed as he pulled a bottle of rum out of his pocket and kept it on the table. Venkat Atre spoke a curious mix of Bombay Hindi, with a disregard for grammar and a Marathi 'chhe' and 'la' added to the end of several verbs. He said, 'Saala, I gonechhe there to Mummy, and she tell your friend visitla. I saychhe to self, who your friend? Saala, I not know it saala Manto!'

Chadda planted a whack on Venkat Atre's pumpkin-like head and said, 'Be quiet now, saala…good you've brought some rum.'

Venkat Atre rubbed his head, picked up my empty glass and fixed himself a peg, 'Manto, this saala Chadda, the moment we metchhe, he said, "I think drinkla this evening...""

Chadda planted another whack on his head, 'Oye, be quiet. As if you're capable of thinking!'

'I no thinkingchhe then from where this batli?' he asked, pointing to the bottle, 'your father givela?' Venkat Atre finished his peg of rum in one swig. Chadda ignored his question and asked, 'Now tell me, what did Mummy say? Did she say anything? When will Mozelle return? And, what about that platinum blonde!'

Venkat Atre wanted to say something in response, but Chadda grabbed my arm and started, 'Manto, I swear upon God, what a specimen! We used to hear about platinum blondes, but yesterday, I saw one for the first time. Her hair is like fine strings of silver! *Great*! Manto, God is *great*! Long live Mummy!' He cast a venomous look at Venkat Atre and snarled at him, 'Venkat Atre, was your father deaf? Why don't you raise a toast? Long live Mummy!'

Together Chadda and Venkat Atre raised a toast, chanting, 'Long live Mummy!' several times.

Chadda did not wait for Venkat Atre's response and continued, 'Forget it, yaar, I've become emotional. I thought the beloved's tresses are black, usually compared with dark rainclouds, but something else is happening here.'

He turned to me, 'Manto, nothing makes sense; her hair is like silver filaments. You can't even call it the colour of silver. I'm not sure of the colour of platinum; I've never seen it. But hers is a strange colour...if you mix steel and silver.'

Venkat Atre finished his second peg and added, 'And you can mixchhe some XXX rum with it.'

Chadda directed a stout expletive at him, 'Don't talk rot!' and continued with an almost tragic air, 'yaar, I've become emotional. Yes, that colour, I swear by God, it's indescribable. You've seen the backs of pomfret fish—what are those things called? No...more like the tiny scales on snakeskin. You've seen those tiny arrow-shaped scales called khapra? Yes, khapra—her hair is the colour of khapra. I first heard this word from an Urdu speaking Hindustora. What a horrible name for something so beautiful! In Punjabi, we call them chaanay—the word has a sparkle to it, the same sparkle as this girl's hair. By God, it sways like a young snake.'

He stood up rather abruptly and said, 'To hell with baby snakes! I've become emotional.'

Venkat Atre asked in all innocence, 'What's that?'

Chadda responded, 'Sentimental! What would you understand, Balaji Baji Rao and Nana Phadnavis's offspring!'

Venkat Atre fixed another peg and turned to me, 'This saala Chadda he thinkchhe I not understand English. I matri-clate, saala, my father loved me. He…'

An infuriated Chadda cut him short, 'And he made you into a Tansen. He twisted your nose so you could produce nasal notes. He taught you how to sing dhrupad in early childhood. As an infant, when you cried for milk, it was in raga Mian ki Tori, and when you wanted to urinate, it was Adana. Your first words were in raga Patdeep, and your father was a great ustad. Born in the same era as Baiju Bawra, he would have put that legendary maestro to shame. And today, you put him to shame; that is why your name is Earless the Peerless!'

Chadda turned to me, 'Manto, whenever this saala drinks, he starts praising his father. If his father loved him, it was no great favour to me. And if he saw to it that he passed his matriculation, it doesn't mean I should tear up my BA degree and throw it away!'

Venkat Atre tried to stop Chadda's tirade, but Chadda intercepted him, 'Be quiet! I've told you I'm feeling sentimental. Yes, that colour, like a pomfret fish—no, like the tiny khapra on a snake, quite the same colour. God alone knows what raga Mummy played on her pipe to bring this Nagin lady out!'

A thoughtful Venkat Atre said, 'Get harmonium, and I'll playchhe!'

Chadda began to laugh, 'Oi sit quietly, you *Choc-late* of a *Matri-cu-late*!' He poured the dregs of rum into his glass and turned to me, 'Manto, if Chadda doesn't hook the platinum blonde, he will retreat to a Himalayan peak.' And with this declaration, he finished the contents of his glass.

Venkat Atre opened the bottle he had brought, 'Manto, this number one changli!'

I said, 'We'll see.'

Chadda chimed, 'Tonight… Tonight I am throwing a party. How wonderful that you arrived, and all because of you Shri Mehtaji gave me an advance. Tonight, tonight...' Chadda began to sing in a tuneless voice: 'Tonight, don't play that sad air...'

Poor Venkat Atre was about to cry in protest when Gharib Nawaz and Ranjit Kumar walked in, each carrying two bottles of Scotch. I knew Ranjit Kumar quite well, but since I was not on informal terms with him, we indulged in small talk of the 'When did you get here?' 'Just today' variety. We clinked our glasses and began to drink.

An overwrought Chadda continued to mention the platinum blonde in every sentence. Ranjit Kumar downed a fourth of the second bottle of rum, and Gharib Nawaz drank three pegs of Scotch. These men could not hold their drink, but I had my wits about me, since I am a heavy drinker. It was clear from their conversation that the four men fancied the new girl Mummy had produced.

This peerless item called Phyllis worked in some hairdressing salon in Poona. She was not more than fourteen or fifteen years old, and hung around with a boy who was probably a transvestite. Gharib Nawaz was so hot on her that he wanted to sell his share of his inheritance in Hyderabad and stake it on her. Chadda held one trump in his hand—his good looks. Venkat Atre believed that the fairy would yield to him after hearing his harmonium, and Ranjit Kumar considered a direct amorous assault the most effective way forward. I figured that the woman I had seen with Chadda in the tonga could hand over Phyllis to whoever she chose, and all these men understood this as well.

Chadda cut short the conversation about Phyllis to look at his watch and said to me, 'To hell with this girl. Let's go, yaar. Bhabi will be a kebab by now. What if I become soppy over there? Ah well, you'll handle me.' He poured the last few drops from his glass down his throat and called his servant, 'Prince of Egypt, the country of mummies!'

The Prince of Egypt, the country of mummies, arrived rubbing his eyes, and Chadda sprinkled some rum on his face before asking him to 'bring two tongas that look like Egyptian chariots'.

Our chariots arrived, and the five of us set off for Prabhat Nagar.

Haresh, my old colleague from the movies, was at home, and in one look Chadda conveyed the entire situation to him, which proved very handy. My wife looked content. Haresh and his wife were great hosts. An expert in feminine psychology, Haresh kept my wife engaged in amusing banter and even invited her to visit the studio to watch his shoot. She asked, 'Are they filming a song?'

Haresh answered, 'No, that's scheduled for tomorrow. I think you should visit tomorrow.'

Bored with accompanying visitors to film shoots, Haresh's wife turned to my wife and said, 'Yes, tomorrow's better. Today, she must be tired after her journey.'

All of us breathed a sigh of relief, and Haresh continued with his banter. Finally, he said to me, 'Come on, yaar, you better come with me.' He looked at my companions and continued, 'You can't take them; Seth Sahib wants to hear your story.'

I looked at my wife and said to Haresh, 'You better get her permission.'

My gullible wife said to Haresh, 'When we were leaving Bombay, I told him to bring his document case, but he said there was no need for it. Now, how will he narrate the story?'

Haresh responded, 'He will ad lib.' He looked at me as if to say hurry and say yes.

With a straight face, I added, 'Yes, I could do that.'

Chadda gave the final touch to this drama, 'Ah well then, we'd better leave.' Everyone exchanged greetings, and we left. We found the tongas parked outside Prabhat Nagar, and Chadda let out a loud cheer, 'Long live Raja Harishchandra!'

Haresh had to meet some girlfriend, but the rest of us left for Mummy's house. Built in the same architectural style as Saeeda Cottage, it was a spotlessly clean and stylish testament to Mummy's housekeeping skills. The furniture was ordinary, yet everything looked attractive. Before we set off from Prabhat Nagar, I had imagined Mummy's establishment to be some bordello, but nothing in this house had a hint of anything sordid. On the contrary, it looked as decent as the homes of most middle-class Christians.

In stark contrast with Mummy, her house seemed young. When she entered the room, I thought everything around her looked young; although from a past era, it had remained frozen in time. It was just that Mummy had raced ahead and grown old. I observed the layers of garish make-up on her face, and I am not sure why, but I wished with all my heart to see her robust and young, like the atmosphere around her.

Chadda presented me briefly before introducing her to me with equal economy, '*This is Mummy. The great Mummy*!'

Mummy smiled. She looked at me and said to Chadda, 'You sent for tea in your usual slapdash manner. I'm not sure if it met with his approval or not.' She turned to me and said, 'Mr Manto, I'm very embarrassed. It's all because of your friend Chadda, my irredeemable son!'

I deployed my best manners and choicest vocabulary to thank her and praise the tea. Mummy asked me to desist from empty praise and turned to Chadda, 'Dinner is ready. I took the liberty because I did not want you to descend upon me at the last minute.'

Chadda hugged her, '*You're a jewel, Mummy*! We'll have dinner right away!'

Taken aback, Mummy remonstrated, 'What! No, never!'

Chadda informed her, 'We dropped Mrs Manto off at Prabhat Nagar.'

Mummy cried out, 'God curse you, why did you do that?'

Chadda chortled, 'Because we are throwing a party tonight.'

'I cancelled it the moment I saw Mrs Manto,' Mummy lit her cigarette.

Chadda's heart sank, 'God curse you now. We hatched the entire plan for a party.' Deflated, he fell into a chair, 'There you are, all my dreams...shattered. The platinum blonde and her hair the colour of tiny scales on snakeskin...' He leapt up, and holding Mummy by both her arms, said, 'You cancelled it...but you cancelled it in your heart. Here I'll mark it on your heart.' And after making a substantial imaginary cross over Mummy's heart, he shouted, 'Hurray!'

Although Mummy had informed everyone concerned that she had cancelled the party, it was clear that she wanted to please Chadda. She gave him a warm, affectionate pat on his cheek and said, 'Don't you worry, I'll just organize everything.' And off she went.

Chadda let out another hurray and turned to Venkat Atre. 'General Venkat Atre, get all the bottles from the headquarters.'

Venkat Atre saluted Chadda and took off to follow orders. Saeeda

Cottage was around the corner, and he was back within ten minutes with bottles of alcohol and Chadda's servant, whom Chadda greeted, 'Come along, my Prince of the Caucusas! That young lass with hair the colour of snakeskin will be here soon. You too can try your luck.'

Ranjit Kumar and Gharib Nawaz disapproved of Chadda's open invitation and complained to me of his boorish behaviour. But, as usual, Chadda continued his babble, and they continued to sit in their corner, sipping rum and sharing each other's discontentment.

I continued to reflect on Mummy and thought Gharib Nawaz, Ranjit Kumar, and Chadda looked like toddlers waiting expectantly for their mother to return from town with some toys. Chadda looked secure in the knowledge that as his mother's favourite, he would get the best toy. Gharib Nawaz and Ranjit Kumar understood each other's pain, and a sense of camaraderie developed between them.

When I first saw Mummy in the tonga with Chadda, the aesthete in me was hurt, but sitting in her house, I regretted my nauseating thoughts about their relationship. I continued to wonder why Mummy wore such loud make-up, which was an insult to her wrinkles and the maternal feelings she had in her heart for Chadda, Gharib Nawaz, and Venkat Atre—and God knows how many others. I asked Chadda, 'Tell me, yaar, why does your Mummy wear such garish make-up?'

'Because the world likes garish things,' was his pat answer, 'there are very few idiots like you and me who appreciate subtle tones. Most people like to see youth masquerade as childhood and the gloss of youth on old age. We think we are artists, but we are fools. Let me relate an interesting episode about a Baisakhi mela in your Amritsar. Some Jats were passing through the bazaar in Ram Bagh, where all the harlots live. Among them was a virile young man brought up on pure milk and butter, whose brand-new shoes were dangling from a lathi held across one shoulder. He looked up at a balcony on the top floor of a house and spotted a dark-skinned harlot smeared in garish make-up, her unattractive long hair oiled and plastered across her forehead. He turned to his companion and said in Punjabi, "Oi, Lehna sweetheart, look, look…remember…we and the buffaloes in our village…"'

God alone knows the last word of Chadda's sentence because he allowed it to evaporate into thin air as he chuckled. He poured some rum into my glass before continuing, 'For this Jat, that hideous witch was like a fairy from the Caucasus Mountains because she reminded him of his village and the buffaloes that to him were no less than beautiful belles. We are imbeciles of the second league because nothing in the world is in the premier league. Everything is either in the second or third league. But Phyllis is in a league by herself—that snakeskin...'

Venkat Atre picked up his glass and emptied its contents on Chadda's head, 'Snakeskin! Snakeskin, you're off your rockerschhe!'

Chadda licked the drops of rum dripping from his forehead and said to Venkat Atre, 'Well then, now that my head has cooled down, you can tell us how much your father saala loved you.'

Venkat Atre addressed me in a solemn tone, '*By Godschhe*, he love me a lot. I only fifteenschhe when he arrangela my marriageschhe.'

Chadda laughed out loud, 'The saala turned you into a cartoon. I pray Bhagwan will give him Kesar Mal's harmonium in paradise, which he can play while he looks around for a beautiful houri for you.'

Venkat Atre became very serious, 'Manto, I no liela, my wife is at once beautifulschhe. In our family...'

Chadda interrupted him, 'To hell with your family! Talk about Phyllis. Nobody can be more beautiful than her,' he asserted. He turned to look at Ranjit Kumar and Gharib Nawaz sitting in a corner exchanging views on Phyllis's good looks and warned them, 'Makers of the Gunpowder Plot, take heed! Not one of your conspiracies will succeed. The field will remain open for Chadda! Why Prince of Wales?'

The Prince of Wales was eyeing the fast-disappearing rum. Chadda chortled and poured out half a glass for him. Ranjit Kumar and Gharib Nawaz exchanged notes on Phyllis with abandon, but they did not reveal their plans to win her.

Darkness was about to fall, and someone switched on the electric lights in the drawing room. Chadda was chatting with me to catch up on the latest gossip from the Bombay film world when we heard Mummy's voice from the veranda, speaking rather fast. Chadda gave a loud cheer and dashed off. Ranjit Kumar and Gharib Nawaz exchanged meaningful glances before they turned to look at the door. Mummy walked in chatting away with four or five Anglo–

Indian girls of varying heights, physiques, and features—Polly, Dolly, Kitty, Elma, and Thelma—and a young man, probably a transvestite, whom Chadda later addressed as Sassi. Phyllis, the platinum blonde was the last one to make an entry, and that too with Chadda, who had one arm around her tiny waist. I took note of Ranjit Kumar and Gharib Nawaz's reactions. They did not care for this display of one-upmanship on Chadda's part.

The moment the girls entered the room, there was a right din in the air. Suddenly, so much English rained upon us that Venkat Atre must have failed his matriculation examination several times, but he could not have cared less and continued to prattle incessantly. When he saw that nobody paid attention to what he was saying, he went to sit in a corner with Elma's elder sister, Thelma, and began to interrogate her about how many new mnemonic sequences of Hindustani dance she had learnt. He proceeded to teach her new moves, converting 'dha ni na kat' and 'ta thai thai,' into 'one, two, three' and so on. And Chadda continued to regale the girls with the choicest lewd English limericks from a repertoire of thousands he had committed to memory.

Mummy sent for soda and gazak. Ranjit Kumar sat and stared fixedly at Phyllis, inhaling deep puffs from his cigarette, and Gharib Nawaz repeated his offer that if Mummy was short of funds, she should take some cash from him. They opened another Scotch, and the first round started. When asked to join in, Phyllis flicked her platinum blonde hair imperceptibly and declined, saying she did not drink whisky. Everyone insisted, but she did not relent. When Chadda expressed his disappointment, Mummy fixed a light drink and turned to Phyllis with warmth as she touched the glass to her lips and said, 'Be a brave girl and drink it up.'

Phyllis could not refuse, and a cheerful Chadda recited twenty-five more limericks.

Everyone was having fun, and I observed how, in search of freedom from the mundane, a sense of abandon could compel a person to throw caution to the wind. Mummy was a picture of contentment as she mingled with the young girls and joined in their laughter at Chadda's lewd limericks. Visible through layers of her lurid make-up, her wrinkles looked happy.

I asked myself, why do people disapprove of recklessness? Although unpleasant to my eyes, what I found most agreeable was the hidden impulse of warmth behind this manifestation of reckless abandon. For instance, take Polly standing in a corner and telling Ranjit Kumar how cleverly she managed to transform two useless pieces of cloth by having them stitched into a stylish new frock at a bargain price. And Ranjit Kumar promising to have two new dresses made for her, although he had no hope of his film company paying the required money in one instalment.

Dolly was trying to extract a loan from poor Gharib Nawaz, reassuring him that she would repay him the moment she got her salary. Gharib Nawaz knew she would not return his money—she never did, but he continued to have faith in her. Thelma knew that it was a pointless waste of her own and Venkat Atre's time, yet she was trying to learn complicated mnemonics of the Tandav dance. Venkat Atre knew Thelma's feet could not perform these complicated moves, but he appreciated the humility with which she concentrated on her lesson. Elma and Kitty were enjoying their drink and discussing some Anouilh, who had wreaked vengeance for God alone knows what reason and gave them a wrong tip for a race. And Chadda was dunking Phyllis's snakeskin-like platinum blonde hair into his molten gold Scotch and sucking it. Phyllis's friend Sassi took a comb out of his pocket and fixed his hair from time to time. Mummy flitted around, talking to this one and that one, seeing to everything—which included a ready supply of soda and getting shards of broken glass swept off the floor. She was like a cat that looked fast asleep but had an eye on everything and knew the exact whereabouts and antics of her five kittens. Was any colour or feature of this riveting tableau out of place? Even Mummy's loud make-up seemed integral to the picture. As Ghalib said:

Imprisoned in life and trapped in sorrow
Why be released from sorrow before death?

Indeed, why shouldn't a human being indulge in a few moments of self-deception? Mummy's heart, filled with maternal love, was a font of goodwill for all the people around her. But, perhaps, she did not have the physical strength to be a mother to the world, so she had chosen a few individuals on whom to shower her love and compassion.

Chadda had given Phyllis a stiff peg of whisky, not on the quiet but in full view of everyone in the room. Mummy had no idea because she was in the kitchen frying potato chips, as French fries are known in India. Phyllis was tipsy and in a mild ecstasy. It was past midnight. Venkat Atre had taught Thelma several mnemonic sequences and had moved on to tell her how much his father saala loved him, made his marriage in his childhood with his 'so beautifulschh wife'. Gharib Nawaz had given Dolly a loan and forgotten about it. Ranjit Kumar had taken Polly out somewhere. Elma and Kitty had exhausted themselves talking about the whole world and needed some rest. Mummy and Phyllis's transvestite friend were sitting around a teapoy, and a pacified Chadda was sitting with Phyllis by his side after she had tasted the ecstasy of alcohol for the first time. The pride of winning her was apparent in his eyes, and Mummy was not oblivious to this.

Not much later, Sassi stretched himself out on the sofa and fell asleep, combing his hair. Gharib Nawaz and Dolly disappeared. Elma and Kitty took their leave, and saying goodbye to Mummy, they departed as they continued to chat about some Margaret. Venkat Atre praised his wife's beauty for the last time and looked at Phyllis with longing before he took Thelma's arm and ushered her out to the maidan to show her the moon.

I think I missed what happened, but a heated exchange broke out between Mummy and Chadda. Phyllis made a gentle attempt to intercede between the two. Chadda wanted to take Phyllis to Saeeda Cottage, and Mummy objected. Chadda threw a tantrum in his slurred drunken speech. Mummy tried hard to reason with him, 'Chadda, my son, why don't you understand? She is young, very young.' The tremulous appeal in her voice invoked a dire warning. Loath to heed her caution, Chadda continued to repeat words to the effect, 'Mummy, you're mad! You, old hag! You pimp! Phyllis is mine! Ask her!'

Mummy heard Chadda's abuse in complete silence. He was obsessed with the idea of attaining Phyllis. I looked at the pubescent Phyllis's gorgeous face; it reminded me of a raindrop surrounded by silvery clouds. For the first time, it struck me that she was a child—barely fifteen. Chadda grabbed her arm and squeezed her close to his chest, in the style of a film hero. Mummy cried out in protest, 'Chadda, leave her...for God's sake...leave her!'

When Chadda refused to release Phyllis from his expansive embrace, Mummy planted a tight slap across his face, and shouted, 'Get out! Get out!'

A stunned Chadda pushed Phyllis away. He gave Mummy a ferocious look and stormed out. I got up to take my leave and followed Chadda.

When I reached Saeeda Cottage, I saw Chadda lying face down with his shoes, shirt, and trousers on. I crept into the other room and fell asleep on the large table. The following morning, I woke up late. According to the clock, it was ten. Chadda had woken up early and gone somewhere. Where? Nobody knew. As I was coming out from the bathroom, I heard his voice deep in conversation with someone near the garage and stopped in my tracks. I heard him say, 'She is an incomparable woman. I swear by God, she is an incomparable woman. Pray that when you reach her age, you will be as great as her.' I detected a peculiar bitterness in his tone and am not sure if it was directed at himself or at the person to whom he addressed his comment.

I waited inside for Chadda for half an hour, but when he did not show up, I did not think it appropriate to hang around and left for Prabhat Nagar. My wife's mood was equable. I thought we had reached the end of our visit to Poona and asked Haresh's wife to excuse us. Ever gracious, she asked us to stay on for a few more days. That morning, when leaving Saeeda Cottage, I told myself that the previous night's episode was enough to keep my mind occupied for some time.

On our journey back to Bombay, I discussed Mummy with my wife and related the entire incident to her. She thought Mummy had clashed with Chadda because Phyllis was Mummy's relative, or the older woman was saving her for a better punter. I remained silent and did not agree or disagree with her. After several days, I received a letter from Chadda in which he made a perfunctory reference to that night's incident, but indicted himself, 'That night, I turned into an animal. May I be cursed!'

Three months later, I had to go to Poona on some urgent business and headed directly to Saeeda Cottage. Chadda was not around, but I bumped into Gharib Nawaz, who was giving Shireen's little boy a peck on the head, on his way out of the garage. He greeted me with great warmth. After some time, Ranjit Kumar strolled in at his usual tortoise pace and sat down. I learnt that after the night of the party, Chadda did not visit Mummy, and she did not visit Saeeda Cottage. The following day, Phyllis, who had run away from home with her transvestite friend, was sent packing to her parents. Ranjit Kumar had convinced himself that if Phyllis had stayed on in Poona for a few more days, he would have succeeded in flying off with her. Gharib Nawaz, who had no such illusions, was merely sad that she had left.

I discovered that Chadda was poorly, and for the past few days, was running a high temperature. He had not consulted a doctor and spent his waking hours roaming around aimlessly. As Gharib Nawaz was recounting all the details to me, Ranjit Kumar walked off, and through the window with iron bars, I saw him head towards the garage. I was about to interrogate Gharib Nawaz about Shireen when Venkat Atre walked into the room, looking anxious. Venkat informed us that he was out with Chadda but had decided to bring him home because he was running a high fever, and Chadda had fainted in the tonga. Gharib Nawaz and I ran out. The tongawallah was supporting a comatose Chadda. Together, we carried him to his room and lay him down on his bed. I put my hand on his forehead. He was running a high temperature—no less than a hundred-and-six degrees, and I said to Gharib Nawaz, 'We must call the doctor at once.' He asked Venkat Atre, who muttered, 'Just be back...' and rushed off.

Venkat Atre returned with Mummy. She was breathless. She took one look at Chadda and shrieked, 'What has happened to my son?'

When Venkat Atre informed her that Chadda had been unwell for several days, Mummy responded in a woeful yet angry tone, 'What sort of people are you? Why didn't you inform me?' She issued various instructions. One of us had to rub Chadda's feet, the other had to fetch some ice, and the third person had to fan him. Mummy looked perilously frail as she observed Chadda, but with true grit, she went off to call the doctor.

I'm not sure who informed Ranjit Kumar in the garage, but shortly after Mummy's departure, he arrived looking very worried. In response to his queries, Venkat Atre told him how Chadda had fainted, but when he heard that Mummy had gone to fetch a doctor, Ranjit Kumar looked somewhat reassured. I saw that the three men were more at ease now that Mummy had assumed the burden of responsibility for Chadda's health. We followed her instructions, rubbed his feet, and applied a cold compress to his forehead. By the time Mummy returned with the doctor, Chadda had regained consciousness. The doctor took some time to examine him, and it was apparent from his expression that Chadda's life was in danger.

After the examination, the doctor signalled Mummy, and the two of them left the room. I looked out of the window with the iron bars and saw the jute curtain on the garage door move. Not much later, Mummy returned. She addressed Gharib Nawaz, Ranjit Kumar, and Venkat Atre in turn and told them not to worry. By now, Chadda had opened his eyes and could hear everything. He seemed perplexed and gave Mummy an astonished look. After a few moments, when he figured out why Mummy was there, he held her hand and said, '*Mummy, you are great*!'

Mummy sat near Chadda on his bed. Generous and compassionate, she stroked his searing forehead, smiled, and all she said was, 'My son, my poor son.'

Chadda's eyes brimmed with tears, and he said, 'No. Your son is a *scoundrel* of the first order. Get your late husband's pistol and put a bullet through his chest!'

Mummy gave Chadda a light affectionate pat on his cheek and said, 'Don't talk nonsense!'

She jumped up like a spritely efficient nurse and addressed us, 'Boys, Chadda is not well, and I have to take him to hospital. Understood?'

Everyone understood. Immediately, Gharib Nawaz arranged for a taxi, and we lifted Chadda into it. He protested, 'What is the calamity? Why am I being admitted to a hospital?' Mummy insisted. She told Chadda that although it was nothing serious, he would be more comfortable and better looked after in the hospital. Chadda was very wilful, but he did not have the psychological or physical strength to argue with Mummy.

When we were on our own, Mummy told me Chadda's illness was dangerous, 'It's the plague.'

Her remark left me stupefied. Mummy, too, was anxious, but she was hopeful that this challenging time would pass and very soon Chadda will be well. His treatment continued in a private hospital. Although the doctors treated Chadda with great attention, a few complications arose. His skin began to tear in several places, and his temperature kept rising. Finally, the doctors advised us to take him to Bombay, but Mummy disagreed. She had Chadda discharged from the hospital and moved him to her house.

I could not stay in Poona much longer, but after I reached Bombay, I telephoned several times to enquire about Chadda's health. I did not think that he would recover from the plague but learned that gradually his condition was beginning to stabilize. I had to go to Lahore for a court case; when I returned after a fortnight, my wife handed me a letter from Chadda, in which he wrote, 'The great and saintly Mummy has rescued her prodigal son from the jaws of death.'

Unusually overcome, I mentioned Chadda's letter to my wife, who was very touched, but all she said was, 'Usually, such women are very considerate.'

I wrote several letters to Chadda but did not get a response. I learnt that Mummy had taken him for a change of air to a friend's house in Lonavla, where a bored Chadda barely managed to stay for a month. The day he returned to Poona, I happened to be there. The plague had left Chadda very weak; yet, his spirit had not waned. He talked about his illness as someone would of a minor bicycle accident. Now that he was hale and hearty, he thought a conversation about his illness was a complete waste of time. There were a few minor changes in Saeeda Cottage during Chadda's time in hospital and his convalescence in Lonavla. The Brothers 'L', I mean Aqeel and Shakeel, had moved elsewhere because they did not find the atmosphere in Saeeda Cottage conducive to setting up their film company.

A Bengali music director called Sen took over Aqeel and Shakeel's room, which he shared with a young man called Ram Singh, who had fled Lahore and contacted Chadda at Mummy's behest. Chadda consulted Ranjit Kumar and Gharib Nawaz if they should accommodate the young man in Saeeda Cottage. Since there was space in Sen's room, Ram Singh set up home there. Everyone at Saeeda Cottage took advantage of this decent and genial young man, who was constantly asked to run errands.

The film company had selected Ranjit Kumar as the hero for its new venture and promised him that if his film did well, he would get a chance to direct a movie. Chadda had managed to get a lump sum payment of one-and-a-half thousand rupees from a backlog of two years' salary. He told Ranjit, 'My love, if you wish to get paid you better get the plague. I think it's far more lucrative than becoming a hero or a director.'

Gharib Nawaz had just returned from Hyderabad, and Saeeda Cottage had a prosperous air. I noticed several rather lovely upmarket sets of shalwar–qameez on the clothesline outside the garage, and Shireen's toddler had new toys.

I was in Poona for fifteen days. My old colleague from the movies was busy trying to fall in love with the new heroine. She was from Punjab, and he was terrified of the consequences if the Punjaban's strapping hulk of a husband with a large moustache were to discover their dalliance. Chadda reassured Haresh, 'Don't worry about that saala! Any Punjabi actress with a wrestler for a husband is bound to fall in love with someone else. Just pay me a hundred rupees per word and learn some *heavyweight* expletives. They should come in handy at difficult times.'

Haresh memorized six in the exact Punjabi diction and accent, at the rate of one bottle of whisky per oath, but had no opportunity to rehearse them since he did not encounter any obstacle in the arena of love.

At Mummy's house, the usual gatherings continued. Polly, Dolly, Kitty, Elma, Thelma, and so on were all there. As usual, Venkat Atre was teaching Thelma the basic one, two, three of Kathakali and the 'dha, ni, na, kit' of Tandav dance. And she was trying her best to learn. Gharib Nawaz was giving loans whenever his pocket permitted. Ranjit Kumar, who now had a chance to act as a hero in the company's new film, was going on regular outings with one of the girls to get some much-needed fresh air. And the same laughter rang out in response to Chadda's lewd limericks—but the one on the colour of whose hair Chadda had spent so much time searching for an appropriate simile was not there. And Chadda's eyes were not looking for her at these assemblies. Occasionally, when his gaze collided with Mummy's, he lowered his eyes, I felt he regretted his madness that night—such regret that to recall it caused him pain. At times, after his fourth peg, involuntarily a sentence escaped his lips, 'Chadda, you are a damned brute!'

If Mummy heard him, she concealed her words in a quiet smile, as if to say, 'Don't talk rot!'

When Venkat Atre sang hymns to his father and his wife, Chadda continued to joke with him and cut him short with a sharp verbal rap. Hearing Chadda's reprimand, poor Venkat Atre mentally folded up his matriculation certificate and tucked it away in his pocket. Mummy was the same Mummy—Polly's mummy, Dolly's mummy, Ranjit Kumar's mummy. She was busy with the same warm enthusiasm as before, sending for bottles of soda, gazak, and all the paraphernalia to make her gatherings a success. The make-up on her face was the same, and her clothes were as flashy as ever. Her wrinkles continued to peep out from the layers of powder and paint on her face, but now I thought them venerable. I knew that the shadow of those venerable wrinkles smeared in garish colours had protected Chadda's body and turned it into such an impenetrable fortress that the plague mites retreated and fled.

When everyone attacked Venkat Atre for mentioning his beautiful wife, it was Mummy who came to his rescue. When Thelma fell prey to a Marwari kathakar in her pursuit of Hindustani dance and discovered she had contracted a vile disease, Mummy gave her a right telling-off and wanted to cut off all ties with her. Mummy wanted to consign her to perdition, but when she saw tears in Thelma's eyes, her heart melted; she related the entire matter to her sons and petitioned them to pay for Thelma's treatment. When Kitty won a five-hundred-rupee prize for solving a puzzle, Mummy weighed on her to give half the sum to Gharib Nawaz who was hard up at the time. She advised Kitty, 'Give it to him, now. You can continue borrowing from him later.'

And during my fortnight in Poona, Mummy asked several times

about my *missus*. She was concerned and wanted to know why we did not have another child even though four years had elapsed since the death of our first child. Mummy was not on informal terms with Ranjit Kumar. It seemed she did not like his flashy personality, and I had heard her express such sentiments a couple of times. She loathed Sen, the music director, and if Chadda took him along to her place, she would say, 'Don't bring such a low-down character here.'

When Chadda asked her to give reasons for her dislike of Sen, she responded in a grave tone, 'I find this man a fake. He doesn't look right to me.'

Chadda laughed.

I returned to Bombay, taking with me the warmth of Mummy's house, and gatherings that exuded excess, intoxication, and sensuality with nothing concealed—protuberant like a pregnant woman's belly, giving the onlooker much to reflect upon even though everything was predictable. Yet, the morning after my return from Poona, I read in the papers that the music director Sen had been murdered in Saeeda Cottage. The name of his killer was Ram Singh, who was fourteen or fifteen years old. Immediately, I telephoned Poona but got no reply.

A week later, Chadda's letter arrived with details of the episode. In the dead of night, when everyone was fast asleep, someone fell on Chadda's bed, and he woke up with a start. When he switched on the light, he saw Sen drenched in blood. Before Chadda could gather his senses, Ram Singh walked through the door with a knife in one hand. Ranjit Kumar and Gharib Nawaz arrived at the scene, and restrained Ram Singh. They snatched the knife from his hand, and lay Sen down on Chadda's bed. In no time, all of Saeeda Cottage was awake. Before Chadda could ask him about his wounds, Sen took his last gasp of breath. Ram Singh asked Chadda, 'Bhapaji, is he dead?' Ranjit Kumar and Gharib Nawaz trembled as they held on to Ram Singh, but when Chadda answered in the affirmative, Ram Singh turned to Gharib Nawaz and said, 'Please let go. I will not run away.'

Chadda could not figure out what to do and immediately sent his servant to fetch Mummy. When Mummy arrived, everyone was relieved because they knew she would handle matters. She asked Ranjit Kumar and Gharib Nawaz to release Ram Singh. After some time, they took him to the police station, where he filed his statement. For some time, Chadda and the others remained preoccupied with the filing of the police report, the investigation, and the court hearing. Mummy did a lot of the running around. Chadda thought that Ram Singh would be acquitted, and he was—at least in the lower courts. His evidence was the same as his first statement to the police. Mummy had advised him, 'Don't fear, son. Tell the truth about whatever happened.'

Ram Singh followed Mummy's advice. He related how Sen ensnared him with an offer to make him a successful playback singer. Ram Singh was fond of singing, and Sen, an excellent singer. Trapped in a circle of deceit, Ram Singh cursed himself but fulfilled Sen's sexual desires. In time, a disgusted Ram Singh warned the composer that if forced to continue their relationship, he would kill him. Eventually, this is what happened the night he killed Sen. Ram Singh's explanation to Mummy constituted his evidence in court, where Mummy was present. She looked steadfastly at Ram Singh, and her eyes told him, 'Remain calm and speak the truth because the truth always triumphs. There is no doubt you have blood on your hands, but it's of something unclean—depraved—and an unnatural bargain.'

Ram Singh related the entire episode with simplicity and innocence. His account moved the magistrate, who acquitted him. Chadda had written, 'In an age of lies, this was truth's astonishing victory. And the laurel rests on my old Mummy's head.'

Chadda invited me to the party organized by all the residents of Saeeda Cottage to celebrate Ram Singh's acquittal but I could not attend because of a prior commitment. The Brothers 'L', Shakeel and Aqeel, had returned to Saeeda Cottage. The atmosphere in the world at large was not conducive to the setting up of their film company, and they joined their old film company as assistants to some assistant. They had a few hundred rupees left from the capital they had collected for laying the foundations of their film company. Chadda advised them to contribute all this money to make Ram Singh's celebrations a success, and added, 'I shall drink four pegs and pray that He sets up your film company instantly.'

Ten days after the party to celebrate Ram Singh's acquittal, I visited

Poona for some urgent work and heard all the details. According to Chadda's account of the party, Venkat Atre did not launch into praise of his father or mention his beautiful wife. Gharib Nawaz gave a two-hundred-rupee loan for Kitty's immediate needs and told Ranjit Kumar, 'Don't pull the wool over these poor girls' eyes. Maybe your intentions are honourable, but when it comes to taking, your intentions are not so pure. You should give them something in return.'

Chadda told me, 'I was very avuncular towards Ram Singh and advised everyone to encourage him to return home. The following day, Gharib Nawaz organized his ticket. Shireen cooked and packed a tiffin for his journey, and everyone went to the station to see him off. Ram Singh continued to wave for as long as it took the train to pull out of the station.'

I detected no change in Saeeda Cottage. It seemed like the kind of place that never changes even after thousands of itinerants have passed through it. You could call it a place that fills its void on its own. The day I arrived, Shireen had given birth to another son. Venkat Atre turned up with a box of Glaxo milk powder, which was almost impossible to get in those days. Somehow, he managed to procure two tins for his baby and brought one over for Shireen's new arrival. Chadda stuffed the last two laddus into Venkat Atre's mouth and said, 'You've brought this tin of Glaxo! What a feat! But under no circumstances mention your saala father or your saali wife!'

Venkat Atre replied in all innocence, 'Saale, I not drunkla at the moment. It's booze that speakla…but by God, my wife very *handsome*!'

Chadda's laughter was so uproarious that Venkat Atre did not get an opportunity to add another word.

After their exchange with Venkat Atre, Chadda, Gharib Nawaz, and Ranjit Kumar turned to me to discuss the story I was writing for a film producer whom I had met through an old colleague from the movies. Our discussion shifted to choosing a name for Shireen's baby: of the thousands proposed, Chadda did not like any. Finally, I suggested that since the new arrival's place of birth was Saeeda Cottage, the boy was Masood, the fortunate or lucky one. Chadda did not like it but accepted it temporarily. During our conversation, I noticed that Chadda, Gharib Nawaz, and Ranjit Kumar seemed a bit off colour, and put it down to the autumnal weather that can make a person feel tired for no apparent reason. Possibly, Shireen's new baby was also affected by this mood, but I was unable to confirm this suspicion. Was it the tragedy of Sen's murder? I had a strong feeling all of them were sad. They laughed but I detected an underlying dissonance.

I was busy writing my story in Prabhat Nagar at the house of my old colleague from the movies, and this preoccupation continued for seven days and nights. From time to time, I asked myself why Chadda had not interrupted my work. Venkat Atre was also missing. I was not so close to Ranjit Kumar to expect him to barge in on me. Perhaps, Gharib Nawaz had gone off to Hyderabad. My old friend was conducting a love affair with the new heroine. I must add, all the action took place in her house, right under the nose and moustache of her wrestler husband. I was writing my screenplay and had reached an exciting turn when Chadda entered the room like an unanticipated devil, and asked, 'Have you received any money for this rubbish?'

'Yes. I took the second thousand the day before yesterday.'

'Where is that thousand?' Chadda asked and stepped towards my jacket.

'In my pocket.'

Chadda put his hand in my pocket, took out four hundred-rupee notes and said to me, 'Come to Mummy's place this evening. There is a party.'

I was about to ask him about the party but he took off. Again, I noticed the sadness I had observed in him a few days earlier. I detected the same underlying dissonance, but when I tried to think about Chadda's mood, I found my mind embroiled in a thrilling turn in the screenplay.

At about five-thirty that evening, after chatting about my wife with my friend's wife, I left Prabhat Nagar and arrived at Saeeda Cottage around seven o'clock. I saw wet nappies hanging out to dry on the clothesline outside the garage. The 'L' Brothers were playing with Shireen's older boy near the tap, and the jute curtain on the garage door was pulled back. Shireen was preoccupied talking to them about Mummy, and they stopped when they saw me. When I enquired after Chadda, Aqeel told me he was at Mummy's. I arrived at Mummy's, where a right din greeted me. Everyone was dancing—Gharib Nawaz with Polly, Ranjit Kumar with Kitty, and Thelma and Elma with Venkat Atre who was reciting Kathakali mnemonics to Thelma. Chadda was twirling around with Mummy in his arms. Everyone was in high spirits, and there was a buzz about the place. As I walked into the room, Chadda's cheer and an explosion of local desi and semi-foreign voices filled the air and reverberated for some time. Mummy greeted me with a warmth tinged with informality. She took my hand and said, '*Kiss Mummy, dear*!' But instead, she kissed me on the cheek and dragged me to the crowd of dancers. Chadda yelled out at once, 'Stop it...now it's time to booze!' Then he called his servant, 'Prince of Scotland, bring a new bottle of whisky!'

The Prince of Scotland brought a new bottle of whisky. He was drunk to his eyeballs and was about to open the bottle when it slipped from his hands, fell on the floor, and broke into smithereens. Mummy was about to tell him off but Chadda restrained her, 'Mummy, let it be. What difference will one broken bottle make when there are so many broken hearts around?'

A pall seemed to descend on the party but immediately Chadda's laughter brushed aside the momentary sadness in his tone. A new bottle arrived, and he poured a grand peg into every glass. Chadda began an unstructured speech. 'Ladies and gentlemen,' he said, 'May all of you go to hell. Manto is with us today, and he claims to be a great short-story writer who descends into the nuanced depths of human psychology. I say all this is rubbish! Those who descend into wells... descend into wells...' he looked here and there and continued, 'pity, there is no Hindustora here. There is a Hyderabadi who pronounces "qaaf" as "khaaf". Even if your first meeting with him was ten years ago, he will remember the meeting and say, "I met you the day before yesterday." To hell with the Nizam of Hyderabad who has a zillion tonnes of gold, crores worth of jewels, but no Mummy, yes, those who descend into wells, what did I say...? In Punjabi, we call them "tobay"—those who dive into wells—they understand human psychology considerably better than Manto. That is why I say...'

Everyone began to cheer, 'Zindabad!'

Chadda shouted, 'All this is a conspiracy. Manto's conspiracy, otherwise I signalled you like Herr Hitler and all of you should have raised a slogan, "Down with…" Down with all of you. But first—first I…' Chadda was overcome. 'I…who that night…the girl with hair the colour of snakeskin. I upset my mummy for that girl. I who think myself a Don Juan of God knows where but…no…it was not a difficult matter to get her. I swear on my manhood, in one kiss I could have sucked the virginity from that platinum blonde—with just one kiss from my thick lips, but it was an inappropriate act… she was underage—so tender, so weak and her…'

He looked at me with questioning eyes, 'Tell me, yaar, in Urdu, Persian, Arabic what would you call "*character*"? Ladies and gentlemen, she was so young and weak and her character so unformed that had she participated in that sin on that night, either she would have regretted it for the rest of her life, or she would have forgotten it altogether. The memory of those few moments of pleasure would not have taught her how to live, but the sin would have lived with me forever. It was good Mummy stopped me there and then. Now I shall finish my nonsense. I wanted to make a long speech, but since I am at a loss for words, I shall have another peg.'

Chadda had another peg. Everyone was silent during his speech and remained silent after it. Who knew what Mummy was thinking? Under layers of powder and paint, her wrinkles too looked as though they were deep in thought. Chadda seemed hollow after his speech. He roamed around the room as though he was looking for a corner where he could lose something. I asked him, 'What's the matter, Chadda?'

He laughed and said, 'Nothing…the problem is that today the whisky is not kicking the hell out of the buttocks of my mind.'

His laughter was hollow.

Venkat Atre asked Thelma to shift to make room and invited me to sit next to him. After we talked about this and that, he began to praise his father, who was a very learned man and a gifted harmonium player who left his audience speechless. Then he turned to admire his wife's beauty and told me how his father had chosen this girl for him and married him off while he was still a child. When the subject of the Bengali music director Sen came up, he said, 'Mr Manto, he was a fake man. He claimed he was a disciple of Khan

Sahib Abdul Karim Khan! Lies all lies—he was the disciple of some pimp in Bengal.'

As the clock struck two, Chadda stopped his jitterbug with Kitty and pushed her away. He whacked Venkat Atre's pumpkin-like head and said, 'Stop your nonsense. Get up and sing something, and don't you dare sing a classical raga!'

Venkat Atre began to sing. He did not have a good voice, and his throat could not produce the delicate embellishments required of a good singer, but he sang wholeheartedly. One after the other, he performed two or three film songs in the raga Malkauns, and the atmosphere became quite melancholic. Mummy and Chadda looked at each other, then turned their gaze in another direction. Gharib Nawaz's eyes brimmed over with sad tears. Chadda gave another loud laugh and said, 'People from Hyderabad have very weak tear ducts that leak with or without reason.'

Gharib Nawaz wiped away his tears and began to dance with Elma. Venkat Atre put a record on the turntable and placed the needle on it. A tired old tune began to play. Chadda lifted Mummy in his arms and began to leap around, making an awful racket. His throat was sore, and he sounded like a mirasi, a man from a group of hereditary music professionals, known for singing themselves hoarse at marriages and other life cycle events.

It was four o'clock in the morning before this screaming, shouting, and leaping around came to an end. Suddenly, Mummy became silent. She turned to Chadda and said, 'That's it now. Finish!'

Chadda put a bottle to his mouth, downed its contents, and threw it aside before he turned to me and said, 'Come Manto, let's go!'

I wanted to take my leave of Mummy but Chadda dragged me away, 'There will be no goodbyes tonight!'

As the two of us stepped out, we could hear Venkat Atre weep. I said, 'Wait. Let's check on him.'

Chadda pushed me forward, 'This saala has no control over his tear ducts.'

Saeeda Cottage was around the corner from Mummy's house, and Chadda did not utter a word on the way. Before we went to bed, I tried to ask him about the rather peculiar party we had just attended. But he said, 'I am very sleepy,' and lay down on his bed.

In the morning, I woke up and went to the bathroom. When I came out, I saw Gharib Nawaz standing and weeping near the jute curtain. When he saw me, he wiped his tears and moved away. I walked up to ask what had upset him, and he said, 'Mummy has gone!'

'Where?'

'I don't know,' said Gharib Nawaz and he took to the road.

Chadda was lying on his bed, looking as though he had not slept a wink. When I asked him about Mummy, he smiled and said, 'She's gone. She had to leave Poona by the morning train.'

'But why?' I asked.

Chadda's tone was bitter. 'The government did not like her ways, did not like the way she looked. In its eyes, the gatherings in her house were objectionable. The police called her "mother" but wanted to use her as a pimp. For some time now, a case against her was under investigation. Finally, the government accepted the findings of the police enquiry, and she was banished or declared tari par from the city—exiled from her city. If she was a harlot or a pimp, and her presence was unbearable for society, they should have finished her off. Why dump Poona's filth somewhere else?'

Chadda gave another loud laugh, and remained silent for a while before he continued in a voice full of emotion, 'I am sorry Manto, but with her filth, something very chaste has left the city—something that wiped away a depraved emotion from my heart and mind. I should not be sad. She has gone away from Poona, but I am sure wherever she goes, she will make her home, and there will be young men like me with depraved emotions in their hearts. I hand them over to my mummy's care. Long live Mummy! Let us look for Gharib Nawaz. These Hyderabadi's have weak tear ducts that tend to leak quite easily.'

I turned towards Chadda. The tears floating in his eyes looked like human cadavers.

## Mahmooda

Mustaqeem first saw Mahmooda at his wedding, just after his nikah and before the arsi mushaf, a ritual in which the bride and groom see each other for the first time. He was about to lower himself down to the floor to sit under a canopy, opposite his bride, when he caught sight of Mahmooda's extraordinarily large eyes. Dazzled by their exceptional beauty, he could not focus on his bride's face in the mirror. Consequently, he was at a loss for words when the ritual came to an end, and several young girls began to tease him, and asked him to comment on his bride. He managed to sneak several looks at Mahmooda even as a cluster of females chirped around him, cracking customary jokes at his expense. She continued to sit by the window with her chin resting on her knees. Her clothes were ordinary; she had a fair and lovely complexion, and her black hair reminded him of the smooth ink used for writing on a wooden takhti. A centre parting added to the beauty of her classic good looks. Mustaqeem reckoned she was short, and this was confirmed when she stood up. Her dupatta slipped from her head and fell to the floor, and as she bent down to retrieve it, he noticed that her bosom was firm and voluptuous, her nose sharp, her forehead broad, her mouth small, and of course her eyes—the first thing anyone noticed about her.

Mustaqeem brought his bride home, and a couple of months passed. Although content with Kulsoom, his beautiful and efficient wife, he could not get Mahmooda's eyes out of his heart and mind. He did not even know her name. One day, in a light-hearted mood, he asked Kulsoom, 'Who was that girl at our wedding, sitting by the window during our arsi mushaf?'

Kulsoom responded, 'How would I know. There were so many girls there at the time. Who knows which one you are referring to?'

Mustaqeem said, 'The one with the really big, big eyes.'

'Ah, you mean Mahmooda. Yes, her eyes are rather large, but

they don't look bad. She's from a humble family. Very quiet and decent...she just got married yesterday.'

Startled, Mustaqeem asked, 'She got married yesterday?'

'Yes. That's where I went. Didn't I tell you I gave her a ring?'

'Yes. Yes, now I remember, but I didn't know that the friend whose wedding you were going to was the girl with the big, big eyes. Whom has she married?'

Kulsoom folded a paan into a conical gilauri, which she handed to her husband, and said, 'Someone from her wider community. Her husband works in a railway workshop and earns a hundred-and-fifty rupees a month. I hear he's a very decent man.'

Mustaqeem tucked the gilauri under his cheek, 'Ah well, good for the girl. As you were saying, he's decent.'

Kulsoom was surprised at her husband's interest in Mahmooda, and unable to contain herself, she asked, 'Quite astonishing that you remember her after seeing her just that once.'

Mustaqeem responded, 'Her eyes are a bit like that...the type a person can't forget. Am I wrong?'

Kulsoom, who was making another paan, paused and turned to her husband, 'I don't find anything attractive in her eyes, but then how would I know how men look at her?'

Mustaqeem thought it best not pursue the matter further. He smiled in response to his wife's comment and went to his room.

It was a Sunday, and as always, Mustaqeem was going to a matinee with Kulsoom, but talk of Mahmooda made him restless. He stretched himself out on an armchair and from a nearby teapoy picked up a book he had read several times and opened it on the first page, but the words went gobbledygook and turned into Mahmooda's eyes. Mustaqeem thought, 'Perhaps, Kulsoom is right; there's nothing particularly attractive about Mahmooda's eyes. Perhaps, nobody else finds them beautiful. Why am I the only one who finds them appealing? I just saw those eyes for a fleeting moment. Why have they overpowered my heart and mind?'

Mustaqeem began to reflect upon Mahmooda's marriage. 'So, she is married. Well, that is good, but my friend, why the slight twinge in your heart? Did you want her to remain unmarried all her life? You had no plans of marrying her and haven't given her a second thought, then why the jealousy? Why do you want to see her now? Even if you see her, what will you do?' Mustaqeem had no answers to his questions.

Now Mahmooda was married, and while Mustaqeem was turning the pages of his book, she was probably sitting as a coy bride in her marital home. She was a decent girl and her husband a decent man—an employee in the railway's workshop earning a hundred-and-fifty rupees a month. Mustaqeem should have been pleased but was agitated by the twinge in his heart.

Finally, Mustaqeem realized the pointlessness of it all and pushed all thoughts of Mahmooda from his mind. Two years passed, and he had no news of her, nor did he try to find out. Mustaqeem lived in Mahim, and he knew that Mahmooda lived with her husband in a small street in Dongri. Although there was a fair distance between Mahim and Dongri, had he wished, Mustaqeem could have seen Mahmooda. One day, it was Kulsoom who brought up her name, 'That Mahmooda of yours, with the big big eyes, her fate has turned out rather rotten!'

Mustaqeem asked with great concern, 'Why? What's happened?'

Making a gilauri, Kulsoom said, 'Her husband has become a total maulvi.'

'So, what's wrong with that?'

'At least listen to what I have to say. Imagine a husband who talks about nothing but religion and spouts nonsense all the time. He spends his time chanting sacred verses and goes into meditative seclusion, and forces Mahmooda to do the same. He keeps the company of faqirs for hours and is oblivious to both home and the world. I hear he has grown a beard and roams around with a tasbih in his hand. Now he absents himself from work for days, and she, poor thing, sits grieving at home. There is no food in the house, and she goes without eating for days. When she complains to him, he says, "Allah the Great and Bountiful loves abstinence."' Kulsoom said everything in one breath.

Mustaqeem took some betel nut out of her small paandaan and asked, 'He hasn't lost his mind, has he?'

Kulsoom said, 'This is what Mahmooda thinks, but she is not sure. He roams around wearing large beads around his neck and sometimes even wears a long white robe.'

Mustaqeem took the gilauri and retreated to his room, where he stretched himself out on his armchair and began to think of Mahmooda. 'What is she going through? A husband like that is the bane of any wife's existence. The poor thing is in a real mess. I think the germs of madness must have been there in her husband from the outset. The question is, what is Mahmooda going to do? She has no relatives here. A few came from Lahore to get her married off, but they returned.' Kulsoom had told him that her parents died when Mahmooda was a child, and her chacha married her off. He continued to worry about her. 'Perhaps, she has well-wishers in Dongri. No. If she did, why would she go without food? Why doesn't Kulsoom bring her here? Have you gone mad, Mustaqeem? Come to your senses!' Once again, Mustaqeem tried to divert his thoughts because thinking of Mahmooda generated endless anxiety.

Several months passed, and one day Kulsoom told Mustaqeem that Mahmooda's husband, whose name was Jameel, was at the point of insanity. 'What do you mean?' Mustaqeem asked.

Kulsoom said, 'I mean, now he doesn't sleep at night and remains standing in one place for hours. Poor Mahmooda weeps incessantly. Yesterday, I went to see her. Poor thing, she'd been starving for several days. So I gave her twenty rupees because that's all I had at the time.'

Mustaqeem said, 'You did the right thing. Until her husband recovers, keep giving her something from time to time, so the poor thing doesn't have to starve.'

Kulsoom hesitated before she added, 'Actually, the real problem is something else.'

'What do you mean?'

'Mahmooda thinks Jameel is enacting a farce; he is not mad-shad in the least. The problem is...'

'What?'

'He is of no use to a woman. So he goes to faqirs and sanyasis to fix that problem and uses their amulets and potions.'

Mustaqeem said, 'This is more tragic than madness. Imagine, Mahmooda's marital life is a void.'

Mustaqeem retired to his room to reflect on Mahmooda's

predicament. 'What would life be like for a woman whose husband is a total zero? How many desires must she have buried in her heart? How full of despair must the poor girl be when confronted by the void around her? How often must she think of the blessings of motherhood? What will she do now? What if she commits suicide? For two years, she did not share this secret with anyone. May God have mercy on her.'

Several weeks passed. Mustaqeem and Kulsoom went to Panchgani for an extended vacation and returned to Bombay after two-and-a-half months. A month later, Kulsoom gave birth to a son. Caught up with her new responsibilities, Kulsoom did not visit Mahmooda. Then, one day, a friend came to congratulate her, and during their conversation, she asked Kulsoom, 'Have you heard...about Mahmooda, the one with the big big eyes?'

Kulsoom nodded her head, 'Yes, yes, she lives in Dongri.'

Her friend added on a poignant note, 'Her husband's indifference has forced the poor thing into bad ways.'

Kulsoom asked her with concern, 'What bad ways?'

'Strange men come and go from her house.'

'That's a lie!'

Kulsoom's heart began to race as her friend continued, 'No, Kulsoom, I am not lying. The day before yesterday, I went to see her. I was about to knock at her door when a young man, who looked like a Memon, stepped out and hurried down the stairs. I didn't think it proper to meet her and came home.'

'This is terrible news. May God protect her from the path of sin! The Memon could be her husband's friend.'

Kulsoom's friend smiled, 'Friends don't open the door and flee like thieves.'

When Kulsoom related this information to her husband, Mustaqeem was beside himself with grief. He had never wept in his life, but when Kulsoom told him that Mahmooda had taken to a path of sin, his eyes welled up. He decided that Mahmooda should live with them and said to his wife, 'This is terrifying. Bring Mahmooda here.'

Kulsoom responded very dryly, 'I can't keep her in my house.'

'Why?' asked an astonished Mustaqeem.

'That's what I think,' said Kulsoom, in a tone laden with poisonous sarcasm, 'Why should Mahmooda live in my house? Because you like her eyes?'

Mustaqeem was furious, but he swallowed his anger. It was pointless to argue with Kulsoom. There was only one way out: he should push Kulsoom out and bring Mahmooda home, but he could not even contemplate such a step. Mustaqeem's intentions were entirely honourable. He had never desired Mahmooda. He was obsessed with her eyes but could not articulate what he felt.

Mahmooda had set foot upon the path of sin but had only taken a few steps. It was possible to rescue her from an abyss of ruin. Mustaqeem had never offered his prayers, never observed a fast, and never given charity. God was giving him a perfect opportunity to drag Mahmooda away from the path of sin, get her a divorce, and get her married off elsewhere, but he could not perform this righteous act because he could not stand up to his wife. Mustaqeem's conscience continued to trouble him for some time. He tried to convince his wife on a few occasions, but that proved to be a pointless exercise. Mustaqeem thought if nothing else, surely Kulsoom could go and check on Mahmooda, but he was disappointed. His wife did not mention Mahmooda's name again.

There was nothing more to be done, and Mustaqeem decided to remain silent on the subject. About ten years passed. One day, he stepped out of his house for a stroll, and on the footpath outside the kholi on the ground floor of the butcher's building, he thought he caught a glimpse of Mahmooda's eyes. He walked past her, but he turned back to confirm his suspicion. It was Mahmooda. The same big big eyes. She was busy chatting to an old Jewish woman who lived in the kholi, and everyone in Mahim knew of her as a procuress of young girls for debauched men. She had two daughters, whom she put to work. Mustaqeem shuddered when he saw Mahmooda's face smeared with lurid make-up. He did not have the heart to look upon this unfortunate tableau for too long and walked away.

Mustaqeem did not feel the need to mention this incident to Kulsoom. In his mind, Mahmooda had transformed into a full-fledged peddler of promiscuity. Whenever he imagined her face smeared in obscene make-up, his eyes welled up with tears, and his conscience chastized him, 'Mustaqeem, you are the cause of all this. What would you have lost if you had put up with a few days of your wife's anger? At the most, she would have ranted and gone to her parents for some time, but you would have saved Mahmooda's life from the filth she is stuck in now. Were your intentions not honourable? If you had remained truthful, Kulsoom would have come around. But instead, your conduct was callous, and you have sinned.'

Mustaqeem could do precious little to make amends. Too much had transpired, and there was nothing left to rescue. Now, any attempt to save Mahmooda would be equivalent to giving oxygen to a patient in the throes of death. Shortly after Mustaqeem saw Mahmooda outside the kholi on the pavement near his house, communal riots engulfed Bombay, and Partition devastated the country. People were leaving Hindustan and going to Pakistan in droves. Kulsoom pressurized Mustaqeem to leave Bombay. He booked their tickets on the first available flight, and husband, wife, and children arrived in Karachi, where he started a small business.

Within two-and-a-half years, Mustaqeem's business did so well that he gave up the idea of getting a job. One evening, after closing his shop, he set off on an aimless stroll and arrived in Saddar Bazaar. Craving a paan, he looked around and about twenty or thirty steps away, he spotted a paan shop with a crowd gathered around it. Mustaqeem walked towards it. Horrified, he stared at the shadow of Mahmooda's eyes. The wrinkled face was unmistakably hers, smeared with the same lurid make-up he had seen years ago. She sat there, making paans, and laughing at the lewd jokes she was sharing with her customers. Mustaqeem shuddered. He was about to flee when Mahmooda called him, 'Hey, Mr Bridegroom! Let us feed you a *fust-class paan*! We were at your wedding!'

Mustaqeem turned to stone.

## My Marriage

Somewhere, I have written about three significant accidents in my life. The first was my birth, of which I know nothing; the second was my marriage; and the third was my becoming a short-story writer. Since the third is ongoing, it would be premature to say anything about it. However, to satisfy the curiosity of people who wish to peep into my life, I shall recount the tale of my marriage, not exactly as it happened because discretion demands that I skirt around specific issues.

First, let me present the background to this accident. I do not recall the year, but twelve or thirteen years ago, I was diagnosed with consumption and thrown out of Aligarh University. I took some money from my sister and went to convalesce in Batote, a village between Jammu and Kashmir, where I spent three months. When I returned home to Amritsar, I learnt that my sister's son had died. She had been married off to someone who lived in Bombay. She spent a few days in Amritsar with Bibijan, our mother, and returned to her marital home.

I think it is worth adding that I had lost the protection of a father at a young age. After my sister's marriage, my good-hearted and guileless mother handed over all our worldly belongings to my brother-in-law, and this left Bibijan and me at the mercy of others. My two older brothers gave us forty rupees a month. I returned to Amritsar with a troubled heart and mind and wanted to perish or commit suicide. If I were stronger willed, undoubtedly, I would have killed myself. Such was my state of mind when Mr Nazir, the owner of the weekly *Mussavir*, wrote to me from Bombay and invited me to take over the editorship of his journal.

I packed bag and baggage and set off for Bombay. It did not cross my mind that I was leaving Bibijan all by herself in Amritsar. Mr Nazir hired me as his servant at forty rupees a month. I slept in his office, and for this, he deducted two rupees from my monthly salary. Still, Mr Nazir got me fixed up as a munshi, a dialogue writer, at the Imperial Film Company, at forty rupees a month, and cut my pay by half. So he paid me twenty rupees a month, from which he deducted two rupees for my use of his office as a residence.

When I arrived in Bombay, the Imperial Film Company had scaled the heights of fame and was now in decline. Its intrepid owner, Seth Ardeshir Irani, was doing his utmost to stabilize his company's fortunes. Obviously, employees did not get their salaries on time. Seth Ardeshir had earned fame and fortune as the producer of *Alam Ara*, the first Indian talkie. He desired similar recognition as the producer of the first technicolour film and committed a fatal error: he imported new colour processing equipment from abroad. When the weight of colour landed on Imperial's shoulders, its already shaky finances began to wobble further. Yet, somehow work continued, and we were paid something by way of an advance, with the balance credited to our accounts.

Seth Ardeshir handed over the direction of the technicolour film to Mr Moti B. Gidwani, an educated man who happened to like me, and asked me to write the story, which I wrote and he liked, but there was an obstacle. How was he going to convince Seth Ardeshir that the screenwriter of the first technicolour Indian film was an ordinary, unknown munshi? Gidwani gave the matter much thought and concluded that to secure a sound financial deal, we needed the name of a well-known personality. There was no such person in my immediate circle. When I cast my mind about, my thoughts turned far away to Professor Ziauddin, who was teaching Persian at Santiniketan, Tagore's university, and was well-disposed towards me. I wrote to him, and he became complicit in our *fraud*. His name appeared in the credits for the screenplay. *Kisan Kanya* flopped at the box office, and the company's finances deteriorated further.

In the meantime, Mr Nazir pulled some strings, and I got a job in Film City for hundred rupees a month. Kardar Sahib had arrived in Bombay from Calcutta, and Film City finalized a deal with him; he invited stories and liked one of mine. Work started on the film, but Fate had other things in store. Seth Ardeshir Irani discovered I was working at Film City. Although he no longer retained his former stature, he continued to exercise considerable influence and power over all film-makers of his generation. He gave such an earful to the owners of Film City that they sent me and my story packing back to Imperial Film Company. Now, however, instead of forty, I was earning eighty rupees. Although the company promised me an additional sum for my story, I never received that payment. Hafizji, of Rattan Bai fame, was chosen to direct this movie.

After starting work at Film City, I gave up my accommodation in the *Mussavir* office and rented a kholi at nine rupees a month in a squalid chawl, where bedbugs rained down from the ceiling. It was at this time that Bibijan moved to Bombay to live with her daughter. I had a fraught relationship with my brother-in-law, may God bless him—he was a bad character. Since I did not refrain from denouncing him, he forbade my entry into his house and my sister from meeting me.

Bibijan dropped by to visit me. When she saw my fleapit, she wept and lamented how the wheel of time had reduced to penury her son raised in comfort. My mother could not bear the idea that I worked through the night by the light of a kerosene lamp and ate every meal in a hotel. All the time Bibijan spent with me in my kholi, she continued to weep, and this was both mentally and spiritually punishing for me. I live in the present, and think it a bit pointless to dwell on the past and fret about the future. What has happened has happened and what will be will be. When done with her weeping, Bibijan turned to me and asked in all seriousness, 'Saadat, why don't you earn more?'

I replied, 'Bibijan, what will I do by earning more? Whatever I earn is enough for me.'

She taunted me, 'No. The fact of the matter is that you cannot earn more. If you were better educated, it would be a different matter.'

She was right but I never enjoyed being educated.

After I failed my Entrance three times, I had joined college, where my truancy had ratcheted, and I failed my FA examination twice. Finally, when I got into Aligarh, I was misdiagnosed with consumption and expelled. Bibijan was adamant that I confront these unpalatable realities, while I tried to make light of her words, saying, 'Bibijan, whatever I earn is enough for my needs. If I had a wife in the house, then see how much I could earn. Earning an income is no big deal.

A person without higher education can amass a lot of money.'

Bibijan came up with an unexpected response, and asked, 'Will you get married?'

I responded as though getting married was no big deal, 'Yes, why not!'

'Well then, come to Mahim this Sunday. Wait on the footpath, and I'll come downstairs when I see you.'

She placed her hand on my head to bless me and said, 'We'll arrange your marriage, inshallah, but look here, you better get a haircut before Sunday.'

I did not get a haircut, but on Saturday night I polished my canvas shoes, and on Sunday morning I was standing on the footpath outside Aninglitov Mansions wearing a pair of white trousers, freshly laundered at a premium rate. Bibijan was waiting for me on the balcony of a flat on the third floor. When she saw me, she came downstairs and asked me to accompany her. We walked about twenty to twenty-five yards and arrived at a building called Jaffar House.

My mother knocked on the door of a flat on the second floor, and a maid answered. We stepped in. Mother was ushered to the zenana, and a fair-complexioned elderly gentleman greeted me with gracious conviviality. He made me comfortable in the mardana, or the men's section, and promptly ceased to stand on ceremony, and we chatted mainly about how we spent our time. He was a government servant who worked on a small salary as a fingerprint expert for the police department. Although the father of several offspring, he had a taste for horse racing and flush, the card game. A regular with crossword puzzles, he had never won a prize.

I told the gentleman all about myself, including the fact that I worked for a film company where I did not get a salary but occasionally was paid something in the way of an advance to keep me alive. I was surprised he did not mind my indulging in a beer every evening, even under my straitened circumstances. He paid great attention to everything I had to say, and by the time I rose to take my leave, Malik Hassan Sahib had perused every page of the book of my life.

When we left Jaffar House, my mother told me, 'These people have come from Africa, where they knew your brothers.'

By this time, my half-brothers had been working as barristers in East Africa for over a decade. Bibijan continued, 'They have a daughter they wish to marry off. They have had several proposals but did not like any. The point is they want a Kashmiri family. I've spoken to them about you and have not hidden anything.'

Mother had filled them in on whatever I might have missed out. When I reflected upon the turn of events, I reckoned I did not possess a single trait that could persuade a family to give their daughter to me. I didn't think they would but I did wonder, 'What if they accept the proposal. Will I have to get married and earn a lot of money?'

Malik Sahib invited me to lunch the following Sunday. I turned up as promised, and they fussed over me. Lunch was a delicious fare of chicken, koftas, saag saalan, and a coriander and mint chutney with dried pomegranate seeds. I swear the garam masala and blistering chillies made me break into a sweat, although gradually my palate became accustomed to the flavours. Within a couple of Sundays, I formed a very cordial relationship with the family. Still, when my mother informed me that they had accepted my proposal, the shock sent my head into a dizzying spin. I thought all this talk about marriage was in jest. I could not believe that anyone in their right minds would give me their daughter's hand in marriage. I possessed nothing worthwhile. I was Entrance pass, and that, too, in the third division. As an employee, I received an advance rather than a salary. I knew that decent folk did not like to associate with people involved in film-making and journalism. I had to pull many strings just to rent my hovel after the landlord discovered I worked for a film company.

I was not in the least bit prepared to hear that my mother had fixed the match. I said nothing to Bibijan but all I could think of was how to get out of the muddle. I racked my brain and concluded that thinking about the mess was pointless—what will be will be—and I should launch my ship in the sea of matrimony. I had taken the decision but the question that plagued me was, 'How was I to get the money for the nikah ceremony?' Here, Bibijan fixed the date of my marriage, and there, the company stopped paying me an advance.

Several times I thought of running away from Bombay but an unknown power trussed my feet. There was just one solution—to see Seth Ardeshir and ask him for some money for my nikah. If the company paid me the almost one-and-a-half thousand rupees that it owed me, the cloud of worry would lift, and I could have a feast! I met Ardeshir Sahib, who was not disposed to wasting time listening to my woes but found himself cornered, and finally, he said, 'Look, you know the company is in trouble. If things were better, we would have organized your wedding.'

It is true that when the company was doing well, Ardeshir Irani was generous to his employees. He was distraught because he had to tighten his purse strings with somebody who had come to him for help. Think of my disappointment, but as I turned around to leave, he said, 'All I can do is purchase some basic items. Go, get Hafizji.'

When I returned with Hafizji, Seth Ardeshir gave him the address of two shops and said, 'Take Munshi Manto with you and get him whatever he wants.'

I set off with Hafizji in Seth Ardeshir's car to a cloth merchant's, from where we bought two saris on the seth's personal account. Our second stop was at a jeweller's, from where a man accompanied me to the girl's house because I wanted her to choose her jewellery. The jeweller's assistant and I reached Jaffar House, where he showed some ornaments to the girl's mother, whom I called Khalajan. All she chose was a diamond ring, tiny pearl earrings, a pendant, and two gold bangles of a tola each. I pressed Khalajan to select some more jewellery but she did not wish to burden me. I regret I did not tell her that we should not let this extraordinarily rare opportunity slip by. The company owed me one-and-a-half thousand rupees. Sadly, I recovered merely four to five hundred rupees from these transactions, and the company went bust immediately after my nikah.

After my engagement, Nazir Sahib raised my salary to forty rupees. It was some consolation that the rounds of beer in the evening would continue. The nikah proved quite disadvantageous for me—the money owed to me by the Imperial had vanished, and to compound that hurt, I had injured my knee. I had no young friend or close associate in Bombay—just my sister. With a ban on my entry into her house, I had to make all the arrangements for my nikah—inform a few people, buy dried dates and cardamoms, get a haircut, and take a bus to the battlefront.

I was returning from Shah Jahan Hotel after inviting its owner

Sayyid Fazal Shah to the nikah ceremony, when I slipped so treacherously on the stone floor that I fainted. I have fainted just three times in my life. First, after inviting the late Sayyid Fazal Shah to my nikah, the second time on Bibijan's sudden death, and again, when my son left this world. Falling and fainting did not bode well. The injury was severe, and when I regained consciousness, I had to hobble down the stairs because my leg refused to walk. Somehow, I managed to reach the market shuddering in pain, bought the dried dates and cardamom seeds, and headed to Mahim, where I limped up the stairs of Jaffar House and made it to the nikah ceremony, for which fifteen or twenty people had gathered. I sat down among them and leaned against a bolster.

Unable to bend my injured leg, I stretched it out, knowing it was bad form. When Qazi Murkhay (what a strange name) told me to sit with my legs tucked under my knees, I had to abide by his orders. I hardened my heart, gulped, and tried to forget my pain. When the nikah was over, and the marriage contract signed, I breathed a sigh of relief, gulped, and straightened my leg, and received the blessings of elders and good wishes from all who had assembled. I limped my way home, where I lit the kerosene lamp and stretched myself out on my charpai infested with bedbugs.

I had to ask myself if I had just had my nikah, and although I had an injured knee and dried dates and cardamom seeds in my pocket to remind me, I could not believe that such an earth-shattering event had occurred in my life. I was nearly married, with just one step missing—my wife was not with me in my nine-rupees-a-month hovel. According to the law, I could have asked her to join me whenever I wished, but where did I have the courage? How would I feed her? From the Irani hotel across the road, and that, too, on credit! Where would I keep her? The kholi did not even have space for an extra chair. Wives bathe. I lived in a two-storeyed tenement with forty kholis, and for the many people living in these forty rooms, there were just two bathrooms—with doors, but nobody knew when the latches went missing.

One day, I had to start my new life as a husband to a girl; I had no such experience or the least idea of what it meant to be a wife or a husband. Two or three girls had entered my life but they were maidservants with whom my encounters were like two blind wayfarers who collide, relieve themselves of the shock, and move on. I felt I could become anything but never become a husband.

Time moved on, and after much running around, I got a job at a hundred rupees a month with a film company called Saroj Movietone, which was waiting for my luckless arrival. Less than two months after I joined, the company went bankrupt. Now, did I need more proof that my nikah had proved inauspicious for me? Nevertheless, the bright spark owner of the now-deceased Saroj Movietone, the late Nanubhai Desai, made some dodgy deal and trapped a wealthy Marwari financier, changed Saroj Movietone's name, and established a new company called Hindustan Cinetone. I wrote another screenplay, called *Keechar* (Slush). This film was not even half-finished when the Marwari seth speculated on the silver market and lost all his wealth, including his grand spanking white motor car. I linked this event to my nikah and was waiting for this new company to go bankrupt as well, but again, using some nefarious means, Nanubhai Desai borrowed money from here and there and finished the film. It was released with a most inappropriate name, *Apni Nagariya* (Our Land), but was successful.

Nearly ten months after my nikah, I found myself in a rather delicate situation. One evening, Ashiq, an extremely foolish and uneducated friend, who was an ignorant sucker but an expert in the art of dancing, decided to cheer me up. He plied me with beer, helped himself to a little as well, and took me in a friend's car to visit a girl he claimed was his student. When he knocked on the door, a female voice asked, 'Who is it?'

Ashiq responded, 'Ashiq,' which means, lover.

A fat expletive rang out, 'Ashiq's...!'

A furious Ashiq broke into the house. I followed him in and saw him thrash a servant. Let me cut the story short—the following day, when Ashiq was arrested, he told the police that there was another man with him, and I was detained.

In no time, my in-laws in Mahim heard about this misadventure. I was not quite sure how to face them. I put myself in the position of my lawfully wedded wife and imagined her in tears, thinking, 'It is not even possible for me to get rid of this scoundrel I have married.'

I decided I should speak to Khalajan about the shameful episode. Nonetheless, when I expressed my concerns to her, she said, 'You're mad to have such concerns. We're sure you're blameless.'

Although relieved by Khalajan's response, I continued to believe that the nikah had brought me nothing but bad luck. The company's finances were reeling, and again, we were getting an advance payment instead of a salary. The fees for my story were due by right but I saw no likelihood of getting it.

Almost one year after the nikah, my in-laws were fed up of waiting, and at their insistence, Bibijan fixed a date for the rukhsati, a ritual when the bride's family send her off from her childhood home (maika) to her marital home (susral). Worried that my inability to run a household would turn a decent girl's life into hell through no fault of hers, I was in no hurry. I wished with all my heart for matters to not head to a rukhsati, which for me was no less than the Day of Judgement.

Now, the weekly *Mussavir* was doing very well. Its office had moved to a more pleasant area, and Mr Nazir and I now lived in this office. There was a telephone, and Mr Nazir had a tiny car which he drove around the city to procure advertisements. Every Sunday, I went to Mahim and occasionally, through the cracks in the door, I caught glimpses of my wife. I returned home after dinner, cursing myself and asking why I had played the game of marriage when I knew I would be lousy at it.

With just ten days left for the rukhsati, I jolted into action and rented a flat at thirty-five rupees a month near the office—in fact, in the same building. I earned forty from Mr Nazir and asked him to pay the rent every month. I had to feed my wife and myself on an assured income of five rupees a month. I cleaned the flat thoroughly, wiped its dirty wooden floor and doors with caustic soda, and locked it up. I gained an audience with Nanubhai Desai, and nursing a fantasy of goodwill, I asked about my salary and the fees for my story. But Seth Sahib asserted he could not give me a single paisa. Livid at his blunt response, I swore at him and was physically thrown out of the company's premises.

Immediately, I telephoned Baburao Patel, editor of *FilmIndia*, and recounted the entire episode to him; and added that if Nanubhai does not settle my account, I would go on a hunger strike. Familiar with my hit movie, a vexed Baburao immediately telephoned Nanubhai and told him that if Manto goes on hunger strike, the entire press would stand by him and therefore, the seth must arrive at a compromise immediately. Baburao and Nanubhai did not reach an agreement over the telephone, but when they met in the latter's office, they summoned me. Nanubhai and I apologized to each other. Finally, we decided that because of the company's sorry state, I should agree to half the amount owed to me and was given a post-dated cheque for nine hundred rupees.

After a few days, when I telephoned Nanubhai Desai to remind him that the due date was approaching and I was going to cash the cheque, he asked me to meet him before going to the bank. When I met Nanubhai, he asked me in a rather pathetic voice if I would accept five hundred rupees in cash. I agreed immediately, although the proper amount owed to me for my honest hard work was eighteen hundred rupees, from which we had subtracted nine hundred in our agreement, and now he was offering me five. With just four days to the rukhsati, my hand was forced, and I had to take prompt action. I took the company's car, which had just enough petrol to reach the petrol pump, where I paid for the gasoline and asked the driver to take me straight to the market. I had five hundred rupees, and I used it to buy saris and other sundries for my bride. When I reached home, my pocket was almost empty, as was the flat—without even a broken chair.

I had an elder in town, Hakim Muhammad Abu Talib Ashk Azimabadi, a very refined gentleman. When he heard that I was bringing my bride home to an empty flat, he took me to a furniture shop, where the owner knew him well. On easy instalments, I bought goods from him that included two spring beds with steel frames, a cupboard for crockery, a second-hand dressing table, a desk, and a chair for me, and so on.

When the consignment of goods arrived in my flat, I was disheartened because the furniture disappeared in the two massive rooms. I purchased two wicker moorhas and put them in a corner, but like the rest of the furniture, they disappeared as well. I filled up the rooms with whatever I could find from here and there, and inspected the flat, in an attempt to delude myself that now it looked fully furnished.

Finally, the Day of Judgement arrived. Bibijan had moved in with me, and I had told her that I was going to arrange everything for the barat, the bridegroom's procession to the bride's house. Mr Nazir had sent invitations to several people, most of whom were filmwallahs, and my barat, therefore, was a filmi barat. The guests included Mian Kardar; Director Ganguly; E. Billimoria and D. Billimoria, famous actors of the time; Noor Muhammad Charlie; Mirza Ashraf; Baburao Patel; and Padma Devi, the heroine of the first technicolour film. When Baburao Patel heard that Manto's mother was on her own, he sent Padma Devi to our place to help Bibijan look after the guests. I managed to hire some chairs and order bottles of Vimto from the nearby Irani hotel but remained anxious, wondering how I was going to run my household.

I had just entered my office when my sister telephoned from Mahim and asked, 'Tell me, how are you?'

I repeated Agha Hashr's famous phrase, 'The lion is in an iron cage', and added, 'I am facing a strange dilemma. I am preparing for my barat but have only four-and-a-half annas in my pocket. Four annas will buy me a packet of cigarettes and a matchbox for two paisas—and then the story's over.'

The poor soul could not help me, and even though her husband had not permitted her to attend the rukhsati or see her brother as a bridegroom, she said to me, 'Saadat, I'd give my life for you. Stop your car for a bit in front of my flat. I want to see you.'

She became very emotional, and I tried to keep our conversation brief, after which I went to the neighbouring salon, got a haircut, and bathed in the hammam—all on credit. By the evening, I had smoked an entire packet of cigarettes. And now all I had was a matchbox in my pocket—and that was half-empty.

I changed my clothes and put on the suit given by my in-laws and fixed my necktie. My hair was of an acceptable length; when I looked at myself in the mirror and was confronted by a cartoon, I laughed a lot. After the guests joining the barat had assembled, someone turned on the festive lights. Padma Devi and my mother attended graciously to the guests before a cavalcade of ten to fifteen cars headed towards

Mahim. I was in Nanubhai Desai's car, bareheaded and without a sehra, the traditional veil of flowers that covers the bridegroom's face. When we reached Jaffar House, I asked the driver to drive on a little further where I could see my sister standing on the footpath. I got out and walked up to her, and with her eyes brimming with tears, she stroked my head lovingly, congratulated me, and offered a prayer for my future happiness. I hurried back to the car and asked the driver to reverse.

As I walked in, I saw Raffique Ghaznavi, Director Nanda, and Agha Khalish Kashmiri engrossed in banter. Khalajan had made excellent arrangements for a splendid feast upstairs on an open terrace. The food, in keeping with Kashmiri tradition, was as delicious to eat as it was a sight to behold. Everyone ate to their hearts' content, and after dinner, the guests began to chat. Agha Khalish Sahib recited a humorous poem, extempore. When the festivities were over, I was summoned downstairs and delivered to the bride. Now, everything feels like a dream. I cannot recall the jumble of thoughts in my mind when my bride was with me. I caught her hand, and in a shaky voice, said, 'Come on, then.'

We walked down the stairs, and Billimoria offered his car. Bibijan made the bride sit in the back seat, and sat next to her, before she asked me to sit. This meant that Bibijan was sitting with a Qur'an wrapped in a velvet cover on her lap, between my bride and me. My bride's neck was laden with garlands of flowers. When the car started, my mother began to recite a verse from the Qur'an under her breath. By now, I was less agitated and wanted to tease my bride, but what with mother sitting between us reciting the Holy Qur'an, all desire froze instantly.

I cannot recall how long it took us to complete the journey. Suddenly, we were home, in a building constructed in the old style, with more wood and less brick, and commonly held to be one of the grand hotels of Bombay at one time, won in a bet from a friend by His Highness Sir Agha Khan. Mother went up to the flat with the bride. I was thanking my friends when Mirza Ashraf arrived with a truck carrying the bride's dowry. As the dining table, chairs, a sprung bed, teapoys, a sofa set, trunks, and so on were offloaded, Mirza Ashraf and the truck driver began a longish argument over the fare. With Mirza Ashraf acting the clown, finally they settled matters, carried everything to the flat, and arranged all the items here and there temporarily. Before he left, Mirza Ashraf whispered in my ear 'Look here, young man, don't make us lose face!'

I was exhausted; besides, my throat was parched and did not respond to Mirza's jest. The following morning, one-fourth of my body had transformed into a husband, and this had a calming effect on me. I drifted into my imagination and could see stretched across the balcony a clothesline with swaddles and nappies hanging from it.

## Recite the Creed

'La ilaha ilallah Muhammad a'rasul Allah. There is no God, but Allah and Muhammad is His Prophet. You are a Muslim, believe me, whatever I say will be the truth. This incident has nothing to do with Pakistan. I am willing to give my life for the Quaid-e-Azam Muhammad Ali Jinnah but I speak the truth when I say that this incident has nothing to do with Pakistan. Do not rush me. I understand that in these days of utter chaos, nobody has time, but for God's sake, pay attention to everything I have to say. I killed Tuka Ram, and you are right when you say I slit his stomach with a sharp knife. But I did not kill him because he was a Hindu. You may well ask, "If this was not your reason for killing him, why did you kill him?"

'Well now, let me tell you the entire story.

'Let us recite the creed, La ilaha ilallah Muhammad a'rasul Allah. Which heathen could guess that I'd get stuck in this mess? I killed three Hindus in the previous Hindu–Muslim riots but believe me that killing was something else and this killing is something entirely different. Well, now do pay attention to what happened that day and try to understand why I killed Tuka Ram. Well, sir, what are your thoughts on women? I think our elders were right when they said, "God protect you from her antics." If I escape the gallows, I tell you, I swear, I'll stay on the straight and narrow and never go near a woman again. But, sahib, women are not the only culprits, saale men are no less! They see a woman and their flesh goes weak, and Inspector Sahib, this was the condition I was in after I saw Rukma.

'Now, somebody should ask me: my good man, you are employed at a salary of a mere thirty rupees a month, how can you afford to pander to love? Why didn't you just collect the rent and buzz off! Nonetheless, disaster struck one day when I went to collect the rent for tenement number sixteen. I knocked on the door, and Rukma Bai answered it. As it happens, I had seen Rukma Bai several times, but that day the wretch had oiled her body and wrapped a flimsy dhoti around it. I don't know what happened to me, but I wanted to tear off her dhoti and give her a vigorous massage. That's it, sir, from that day onwards I was helpless. I gave my heart and mind to Rukma. What a woman! Her body was hard as stone. When I massaged her, I ended up panting like a dog. But there was no satisfying her, she continued to mutter under her breath, "A little longer…"

'She was married, yes sir, married. Khan the chowkidar had told me she has a lover. Listen to the whole story, lover-shover and all will make an appearance. Yes, well sir, the devil take me, that day I was obsessed with love! She, too, figured this out and from time to time enticed me with a sidelong glance and a smile. With God as my witness, I tell you, when she smiled a tremor of fear ran through my body. At first, I thought it was that special feeling you get when your love is near you, but later I discovered—well, let me recount the story from the beginning.

'I've told you that Rukma Bai had caught my eye. I spent day and night thinking about how to hook her but her wretch of a husband was always around their kholi, busy making wooden toys. There was no way I could get a chance. One day, I spotted her husband in the bazaar. God bless you, what was his name? Yes, Girdhari… I saw Girdhari carrying his wooden toys tied up in a sheet and headed for tenement number sixteen. My heartbeat quickened as I knocked on the door, and it opened. Rukma Bai stood there, and she stared at me. I swear upon God, my soul shuddered. I should have fled from there, but she beckoned me in with a smile.

'After I stepped into her kholi, she locked the door and said, "Sit down!" I sat down. She sidled up to me and said, "Look, I know what you want, but as long as Girdhari is alive, I cannot fulfil your wish."

'I stood up ready to leave, but to find her so near me, my blood warmed up, and my temples began to throb. Again, the wretch had rubbed oil on her body and wrapped the same flimsy dhoti around it. I held her by her arms and squeezed her. Uff, how hard were the muscles of her arms! I can't find words to describe the kind of woman she was. Ah, well, please listen to the story. My blood turned hotter, and I pressed her closer and said, "Girdhari can go to hell.

You have to be mine."

'Rukma pushed me away and said, "Watch it, you'll have oil smeared all over."

'I said, "Let me," and again, I squeezed her to my chest.

'You must believe me. If you had rained lashes on my body and peeled the skin off my back, I would not have pushed Rukma Bai away. The wretch kissed me in a manner that simply shut me up. I sat where she asked me to and relaxed. I knew what was on her mind. Saala Girdhari is out, so no need to be frightened. After a while, unable to contain my desire, I said to her, "Rukma, we'll never get such an opportunity again."

'She stroked my head ever so tenderly and smiled, "We'll get a better opportunity. First, tell me, will you do what I ask?"

'Sir, I was obsessed by the devil and said with heightened passion, "I am willing to slaughter fifteen men for you."

'She smiled, "I believe you."

'I swear upon God, once again, my soul shuddered, but I thought perhaps this was because of my heightened passion. Well, I sat there a little longer talking to her of love as I ate bhajias she had cooked, and stepped out quietly. Although that business didn't take place, sir, I told myself such business doesn't take place on the first day. If not now, then later.

'Ten days passed. On the eleventh day at two o'clock at night, yes it was two, when I felt someone trying to wake me up inaudibly. I sleep downstairs—you know the space near the stairs. I opened my eyes and saw Rukma, "Arrey, Rukma Bai!" My heart began to race, and I whispered, "What is it?"

'She hissed softly, "Come with me."

'Barefoot, I took off with her. I didn't have another thought in my head, and the moment I stepped into her kholi, I squeezed her to my chest. She whispered, "Just wait," and switched on the light. My eyes were dazzled, but as soon as I could focus, right in front of me, I saw a man asleep on a rush mat, his face covered by a cloth. I signalled and asked, "What's this?"

'Rukma said, "Sit down," and like an idiot, I sat down. She walked up to me, caressed my face, and said something. Stupefied, I froze. If you had cut me, you'd have drawn no blood from my body. Do you know what Rukma Bai said to me? La ilaha ilallah Muhammad a'rasul Allah, I have never seen such a woman in my entire life. The wretch smiled at me and said, "I have killed Girdhari."

'You must believe me. Rukma killed a hale and hearty man with her hands. What a woman, sahib! Whenever I think of that night, I swear by God, my hair stands on end. That cruel creature showed me the sturdy woven cable of electric wires with which she strangled Girdhari. She used a plank of wood and gave the cable such a twist that the poor chap's tongue and eyes popped out. She said, "I did the work within the snap of a finger."

'When she lifted the cloth and showed me Girdhari's face, I felt my bones turn to ice. What a woman! With the corpse in front of us, she pulled me down beside her. I swear by the Qur'an, I thought I had become impotent for the rest of my life, but, sir, when her burning body touched mine, and she made love to me in such an unexpected manner, God knows my entire body came alight. I shall never forget that night for as long as I live. A corpse lay in front of us, but oblivious to it, our bodies entwined around each other.

'At dawn, Rukma and I cut Girdhari's corpse into three pieces. It was not too much trouble because his implements were around. There was much banging, but her neighbours must have thought that Girdhari was making toys. You may well ask, "God's creature, why did you participate in such a heinous act? Why didn't you file a report with the police?"

'Sahib, my submission is that in one night, the wretch made me her slave. If she had asked me, perhaps, I would have killed those fifteen men. Do you recall what I had said to her in a passion?

'Now the problem was how to dispose of the corpse. After all, Rukma was a woman. I told her, "Love of my life, don't you worry, for the time being, we'll lock the pieces in a trunk, and at nightfall, I'll carry it away."

'Now, sahib, as God willed, that night, there was mayhem with rioting and killing in five or six areas, and the government imposed a thirty-six-hour curfew. I vowed to myself, Abdul Karim, come what may, you must get rid of the corpse today. Accordingly, I woke up at two o'clock and carried the trunk downstairs. God have mercy on me—it weighed a ton. I walked on, terrified I might encounter a yellow turban, and get arrested for breaking the curfew, but sahib, who can harm the person God protects! I walked through several bazaars with no sign of life and saw a small mosque near a deserted market. I opened the trunk, took out the chopped-up pieces of Girdhari's corpse, dumped them in the forecourt, and headed back to Rukma.

'I am willing to sacrifice my life for His omniscience. The next morning, I heard that Hindus had burnt that mosque. I think Girdhari must have turned to ashes with the mosque because there was no mention of a corpse in the newspapers. Now, sir, as they say, there were no obstacles in our way. I told Rukma to spread the news in the tenement that Girdhari was away for work. I told her I would come between two and two-thirty every night, and we'd have a blast. She said, "No, Abdul, not so soon. We should not meet for the next fifteen to twenty days." What she said made sense, and I kept quiet.

'Seventeen days passed, and several times Girdhari appeared to me in my nightmares. To reassure myself, I said out loud, "Saale, you're dead and gone, what harm can you do me now!" On the eighteenth day, sahib, I was sleeping as usual by the stairs on a charpai when Rukma arrived around midnight or one o'clock and took me upstairs. She lay down naked on a rush mat and said to me, "Abdul, my body aches…just give me a massage."

'Promptly, I took some oil and began to massage her, but after half an hour I was out of breath, and even though beads of my sweat were dripping on her body, she did not say, "Abdul stop, you must be tired."

'Eventually, I had to say, "Hey, Rukma…finito now!"

'She smiled. My God, what a smile! After I caught my breath, I sat down on the rush mat. She got up, switched off the light, and lay down beside me. I was so exhausted that I was oblivious to everything around me and lay my hand on Rukma's chest and fell asleep. I'm not sure what time it was but I woke up startled. There was something hard digging into my neck. Immediately, I thought of the wire cable, but before I could free myself, Rukma was sitting on my chest. She gave one or two such hard twists to the cable that I could hear my neck creak. I wanted to shout, but my voice remained in my stomach. And after this, I fainted.

'I think it must have been around four o'clock that gradually I began to regain consciousness. I had the most acute pain in my neck. I lay straight and inert for a while but slowly I began to unwind the cable. Suddenly, I heard sounds and held my breath. The room was pitch dark. I tried to open my eyes wider and wider but could not see a thing. I thought I was hearing two men wrestle, and heard Rukma gasp as she said, "Tuka Ram, switch on the light!"

'Terrified, Tuka Ram said, "No, Rukma, no!"

'Rukma said, "You're a sissy! How will you carve him into three pieces and take him away in the morning?"

'My body turned cold. I was not conscious of Tuka Ram's response, or what Rukma said in turn. Suddenly there was light, and I sat up, scrunching my eyes. Tuka Ram let out a scream before he opened the door and fled. Tuka Ram was no stranger to me; he visited our tenement regularly to sell mangoes. I have no idea how Rukma had ensnared him.

'Rukma rushed to shut the door and bolted it. Sahib, how can I describe my condition? My eyes were open. I could see, I could hear, but did not have the strength to move. Rukma stared at me; she could not believe her eyes. She had killed me, but there I was, sitting alive in front of her. She was about to pounce on me when there was a knock on the door, and we heard several male voices. Rukma dragged me by my arm and pushed me into a cupboard before she opened the door. The men were her neighbours, and they asked Rukma, "Is everything all right? We heard a shriek."

'Rukma responded, "All's well. I walk in my sleep. I opened the door and stepped out and bumped into the wall. I was so terrified that I shrieked." Reassured, the neighbours left. Rukma shut the door and bolted it.

'Now I was worried. The thought that this ruthless woman was not going to spare my life gave me immeasurable combative strength. I resolved to chop Rukma into bits and stepped out of the cupboard. She was leaning out of the open window and peering at something. I lunged forward, lifted her from her buttocks, and pushed her over and out. All this happened before you could snap your fingers. I heard what sounded like a thud and walked out of the kholi. The whole night I lay on my bed, nursing my injured neck, rubbing oil on it; you can see the marks. I thought nobody would suspect my involvement because Rukma had told her neighbours that she was a sleepwalker. When people discovered her body on the other side of the tenement, they would think she walked out of the window and fell to her death.

'Finally, it was morning. I tied a handkerchief around my neck to conceal the wounds. The clock struck nine and then noon, but there was no talk of Rukma's corpse. I had pushed her out into a narrow alley between two buildings; it has doors on both sides to stop people from entering to urinate and defecate. Mounds of rubbish have accumulated in the alley because inhabitants of both buildings throw their garbage out from their windows. Early every morning, the municipal sweeper opens the doors to clear the trash, and she would see Rukma's corpse and raise the alarm. I wanted people to discover this matter sooner rather than later and wondered what was up.

'At two o'clock, I mustered the courage to open one of the gates to the alley. There was no corpse, and the sweeper had cleared the trash. How very strange! Where was Rukma? I swear on the Qur'an, I will not be as surprised to escape the gallows, as I was at Rukma's disappearance. I had pushed her down from the third floor to the stony ground. How did she survive? And the question remains, who took away her corpse? Makes no sense, but, sir, for all you know, the witch is alive. In the tenement, people believe that some Muslim either abducted or killed her. May God Almighty bless the man who killed her, but if he has abducted her, you know what that poor fellow's end will be. God help him, sir.

'Now, sir, please hear what happened to Tuka Ram. I bumped into him precisely twenty days after the Rukma episode, and the chap began to interrogate me, "Tell me, where is Rukma?"

'I said, "I have no idea."

'He said, "No. You do."

'I replied, "I swear on the Holy Qur'an I have no idea."

'He said, "You are lying. You've killed her and I'm going to file a police report. First, you killed Girdhari and then Rukma."

'He went off, but, sir, I broke into a sweat. I couldn't figure anything out for some time, but finally, I came up with a solution—to get rid of him. Think about it, what other option did I have? And, sir, secretly I sharpened a knife and set out to find Tuka Ram.

'At six o'clock that evening, quite by chance, I saw him at the corner of the street by the urinal. He had left a basket of mausumis by the door and gone in to urinate. I followed him. He was undoing his dhoti when I called out, "Tuka Ram!"

'He turned around to look at me. I had a knife in my hand and thrust it into his stomach. As Tuka Ram's entrails oozed out, he held them with both hands, folded up, and fell to the ground. I should have fled the scene—but look at my foolishness. Unsure, I sat down to check his pulse to confirm he was dead. I have heard that there is a pulse near the thumb or on the other side, and it took me some time to find it. A constable walked in, unbuttoning his trousers, and I was arrested. That's it, sir, the entire story. I recite the creed, La ilaha ilallah Muhammad a'rasul Allah, if I have told a grain of lie.'

## *Acknowledgements*

I owe my first encounter with Manto's writing to the feminist Urdu poet Zehra Nigah, beloved friend and mentor. I was thirteen when, in a conversation with Zehra Bi, I mentioned a girl at school who refused to wear knickers. She responded in a matter-of-fact manner, 'Some girls find knickers irksome. There is a story by Manto called "Mozelle"...' and she recounted it. I was stunned and hooked. Brought up in a milieu that buzzed with the love of Urdu poetry and literature, I had heard Manto's name but never read his work, or anything remotely like 'Mozelle'.

My mother, Qamar Sultana Begum (1930–2008) was surprised to hear that I had never read Manto. She had introduced me to Manto's friend Ismat Chughtai, her favourite writer of Urdu fiction, and conjured her *Naqush Manto Number,* which sadly, disappeared when, without consulting me, a family member in Pakistan decided to donate the books given to me, mainly by my father, to a library that never materialized.

It was not easy to find Manto's work, and I did not understand why I got such strange looks when I asked for his books in bookstores in Rawalpindi. Here, I recall countless hours listening to Asma and Ayesha Apa read Urdu novels in their refined and beautifully modulated voices, which enhanced my love for the language. Now, I must mention my dear friend, Asma Jahangir (1952–2018), the brilliant lawyer and fearless fighter for human rights in Pakistan and across the world, who brought the Sang-e-Meel collection to my attention in the 1990s. On her frequent visits to London, often Asma stayed with us. A thoughtful friend, she was a Santa Claus for all seasons, bearing gifts that never ceased to surprise and please. The most memorable included a large carton with countless towels in an assortment of bright colours. Seeing my flabbergasted look, she declared with her mischievous smile, 'Since your flat is like Paddington Station and T. J. (her husband) manufactures towels, this made perfect sense to me. Put all those white ones away for yourself and use these for the hordes!' Another time, she ferried a rather sophisticated pedestal fan with remote control, because, she asserted, 'England is extremely backward when it comes to gadgets, and it is a myth that it does not have a summer.'

From time to time, Asma's favours included volumes of Manto's stories or essays—as and when they came into print, courtesy Sang-e-Meel Publications, Lahore. As she said, 'I know you will read and enjoy them'. Indeed, I have enjoyed Asma's volumes for decades and have used them for my translations. When I started this project, I wanted to surprise her with the dedication, but Asma disappeared forever. In a tribute, Amartya Sen called her, 'the angel of humanity'—and angels do not die. So, wherever she is, I dedicate this volume as intended: to Asma and knowing she would approve, for our children and grandchildren. I am grateful to the late Niaz Ahmed Sahib of Sang-e-Meel for collecting and making available so readily Manto's work to readers of Urdu, several decades after I began looking for Manto, usually unsuccessfully, in bookstores and libraries.

There are many people I must thank for bringing the first volume of this initiative to its conclusion. At Aleph Book Company, I begin with David Davidar for asking me to translate Manto's short stories; and both David and Aienla Ozukum for their patience as I took longer and longer to finish the first volume. In the immediate Manto family, without the intervention of historian and friend, Ayesha Jalal, this project could not have taken off. Ayesha answered my phone call while busy shopping in Liberty Market, Lahore. The question of sorting out rights was a must, and she put me in touch, immediately, with Nuchi (Nusrat Manto), her sister-in-law, Saadat and Safia's youngest daughter.

Through almost half a decade, Nuchi has been a patient, generous, and candid interlocutor, who has discussed her parents' lives and provided sharp insights into her father's work. This project brought back into my life Nuzhat Manto, my long-lost old friend from our days at Kinnaird College, Lahore; Nuzi too shared thoughts and memories of her parents with me. For Zakia Khala, Begum Zakia Hamid Jalal, I could see it was emotionally fraught to discuss her sister Safia and Bhai Saadat, her brother-in-law and her husband Hamid Jalal's cherished maternal uncle. Yet, she did; often to reveal the visceral dilemmas the family had to confront simply because they

loved both Saadat and Safia.

I must acknowledge my readers, who helped and spurred me to polish my work and hope they continue to comment on remaining warts. Riaz Mohammad Khan, the first person to read many of the translations in this book, made countless suggestions—of which I incorporated all. Besides, I so enjoyed his insights and remarks on the stories. In Delhi, Prem Mamun's and Usha Mami's enjoyment of the first draft of my translations encouraged me to carry on. In Cambridge, Shruti Kapila was there through bright and dark times; that she heard me read my work in progress meant I could carry on; Sunil Purushotham remained a warm and witty interlocutor. In London, the discerning Javed Majeed was always there for discussions on Manto. And Hugo, Lulu, and Izzy just made life so much more fun.

My debt to the late Professor Sir C. A. Bayly is immense because without his encouragement this project would not have started. Special thanks are due to my childhood friend Shahla Rafi, who enhanced my understanding of Manto's life and work by sharing her research and views. Finally, a mention of those who made it impossible for me to sign off the project: Vikram, who raised the bar; Mariam, who read, copy-edited, and returned various drafts and cheered me up as I worked long hours; Nasho, for her valuable critical interventions, and Nuscie, who commented, made suggestions, laughed, and cried as I read the stories out to her.

I must mention several conversations, over the years, with Khalid Bhai, Professor Khalid Aziz, who gently urged me to complete my work, and introduced me to *Dozakhnama*, after a discussion on Manto's affinity with Ghalib. And here, I must remember endless long arguments on Manto with the one and only Dharamsay Bhai, who generously sent me a copy of *Dozakhnama*. If I have not managed to convince him that Manto's essays on film personalities are not entirely fictitious, I hope this book will dispel at least some of his doubts.

None of this work would have been possible without the unqualified support of my biological and adopted family and friends, spread mainly across Bangladesh, India, Pakistan, the UK, the US, and the hereafter: Aubhro, Adolfo, Ahaana, Allo, Amo, Ammu, Aradhana, Arun Bhaiya, Appoo, Ashu, Amanda, Bachchu R. B. L., Bapsi, Baubles, Bratto, Cathy, Chocs, Clare R., Claire A.,

Dani, Dipro, Doodle, Duncan, Dush, Ehsan, Elizabeth, Fauzi, Frances B., Frances M., Haitch, Husain—chak-e-gireban, Java Mama, Javed Bhai, Jeremy, Jeelo Bhai, Jimmy, Joe, Junaid, Kairu, Kartik, Kirni, Leo, Mani, Marina, Micro, Mustafa, Munno, Myra, Nado, Nahas, Nandini, Nephlet, Nilanjana, Cousin Nina, Omar N. F. B., Pablo, several paternal first cousins, Phuppo, 'Q' se Qouzins, Radhika, Rasho Bi, Rukho, Rupa, Comrade S., Sabiha, Sara S., S. B. Apa, Shabana, Shahla, Shruti, Tammy, Teenmateen, TJ, Tunu Mama, Vasvi, Vinod, Vivek, Vinu Bhaiya, Zalla, and Zehra Bi. Absent friends who continue to shape my life: Abba and Amma for all their love, and several addictions: reading, music, theatre, and the cinema, and such happy times; Abi Mama, Bare Abba, Bare Mama, Bari Ammi, Uncle Bharatram, Chacha, Aunty Husna, Ismail, Majid Cha, Mami, Manju Bhabi, Cousin Nazi, Nauman Mama, Aunty Naz, Panna Bhabi, Pat R., Shaukat Chachi, Tari Massi, and Baba Zain-ul Abedin.

It is with great sadness and regret that I must add six people to the coterie of absent friends. My childhood friend, artist and chartered accountant, the inimitable Shahid Jalal, married to Nuchi Manto, whose appreciation of my work meant so much to me. Shahid left without warning on 18 August 2020 in Lahore. Nina (Shaheen Choudhury), a cherished friend through life, was snatched away by Covid-19 on 29 April 2021 in Dhaka. Nina read almost everything I wrote and made me read parts of this work to an invited audience in Dhaka in February 2020. I await the opportunity to upbraid her for her sudden departure. Premnath Seth and Leila Seth, Prem Mamun and Leila Khala whose warmth and love continues to sustain me.

Rupa Exi
20000546
3/11/2022